1.25

The Alba ... ...

The Alan Titchmarsh Collection

Also by Alan Titchmarsh

Only Dad

The Alan Titchmarsh Collection

Mr MacGregor
The Last Lighthouse Keeper
Animal Instincts

SIMON &
SCHUSTER

LONDON • SYDNEY • NEW YORK • TOKYO • SINGAPORE • TORONTO

This Alan Titchmarsh Collection edition first published in Great Britain by
Simon & Schuster UK Ltd, 2002
A Viacom Company

Mr MacGregor first published in Great Britain by Simon and Schuster UK Ltd, 1998
A Viacom Company

The Last Lighthouse Keeper first published in Great Britain by
Simon and Schuster UK Ltd, 1999
A Viacom Company

Animal Instincts first published in Great Britain by Simon and Schuster UK Ltd, 2000
A Viacom Company

1 3 5 7 9 10 8 6 4 2

Simon & Schuster UK Ltd
Africa House
64-78 Kingsway
London WC2B 6AH

www.simonsays.co.uk

Simon & Schuster Australia
Sydney

A CIP catalogue record for this book is available from the
British Library.

ISBN 0-7432-3889-3

Typeset in Goudy by SX Composing DTP, Rayleigh, Essex
Printed and bound in Great Britain by
The Bath Press, Bath

Mr. MacGregor

Acknowledgements

A number of people have gone beyond the call of duty in helping *Mr MacGregor* see the light of day. My grateful thanks go to Luigi Bonomi, Chris Beith, Jilly Cooper, Rosamunde Pilcher, Jo Frank, Clare Ledingham, Hazel Orme, William Spooner, Steve Alais and Dr Phil Cunliffe who have, in order, enthused, directed, inspired, encouraged, contracted, edited, copy-edited and advised me financially, legally and medically. Without any of them I simply could not have managed. Neither could I have coped without the help of the woman I love.

For Kats

Chapter 1

"Counting out: ten, nine, eight, seven . . ." The voice in Rob MacGregor's earpiece seeped into the back of his mind while his lips continued to deliver words unrelated to those he was hearing. The bright lights of the television studio shone on him from above and three large grey cameras stared at him – one on a wide angle, another on a mid-shot and the third on close-ups of the lily bulbs he was planting in a terracotta pot on the bench in front of him.

Over his shoulder were mock-ups of a potting-shed interior, a pastoral backdrop of an English country garden and a pale blue cyclorama of a summer's afternoon, although it was February. Beneath his welly-booted feet the wooden shed floor was laid over plastic grass.

"And when they've been potted up like that, water them in and stand them outside by the house wall . . ."

"Six, five, run VT," came the count in his ear.

". . . so that they're protected from the worst of the winter weather. It's as easy as that."

"Four, three, two, one . . . and cue the trail . . ."

Computer graphics whirled brilliant pictures of verdant lawns, bright flowers, lawn-mowers and garden views on to the monitor suspended from the lighting gallery above him as Rob went into the voice-over: "Next week I'll be showing you how to make a new lawn from turf, finding this year's best new seed varieties, looking for the kindest cut of all when it comes to lawn-mowers, and paying a visit to Pencarrick in Cornwall, a place where spring always comes early."

"Just loike Mr MacGregor," said a rustic voice off-screen. For a moment Rob froze, then turned to see the portly man with sandy-coloured hair advancing towards him. Bertie Lightfoot was wearing yellow corduroy trousers, a green waistcoat over a check shirt, and a scarlet handkerchief around his neck. The ruddiness of his cheeks was due more to Max Factor than Jack Frost. He smiled deviously at Rob, then sweetly at the camera, his gold filling (third on the right in the top set) twinkling in the bright light.

"Goodbye, all, and just remember that what goes in must come up," said Bertie, in his Somerset burr, looking at Rob then touching his forelock and winking at the viewers.

"Er, yes, until next week," said Rob, and then, recovering himself and smiling at the camera, "From Bertie and me, goodbye."

The upbeat signature tune for *Mr MacGregor's Garden* started, while the animated cartoon credits of Rob pushing a wheelbarrow appeared on the monitor, names flashing up in time with the music until the cartoon gardener closed the garden gate behind him and the producer's name came to rest on the watering-can.

"Thank you, studio." The voice of the floor manager cut through the final bars of the music and he wove among the cameras towards Rob before he had a chance to say anything to his portly co-presenter. "Thanks, Rob. See you again next week. Oh, and I'll bring you my fern. It's got brown fronds."

"Don't bring it in," said Rob, casting a nervous glance towards Bertie. "Just water it, and stand it on a tray of damp gravel so that it has a moist atmosphere around it – it's dry air that's burning it up. Your central heating's probably on full blast."

"Oh, I never thought of that. Simple when you know, isn't it?"

"Oh, yes, dear, a piece of cake . . . when you know," said Bertie. His Somerset burr had been replaced by camp, flattened Yorkshire vowels and a sour expression had taken the place of the smile that, moments ago, had creased his ruddy cheeks. He grunted, cast a sideways look at Rob, then turned on his heel and minced off into the shadows towards the distant yapping of a small dog.

Rob sighed distractedly, wiped his hands clean of compost and walked off in the opposite direction. Once through the hefty double doors of the studio, he went into Makeup, grabbed a handful of baby wipes from the plastic drum in front of the brightly lit mirror, smiled at the girl doing her best to pacify a neurotic newsreader, whose bald patch was taking more than the usual amount of black pancake to make it invisible, then wandered along the corridor to find his producer.

It was a strange environment for a lad who had begun his working life as a gardener in the Yorkshire Dales, but one in which Rob had always felt comfortable – at least, until Bertie had started being a problem. His first call to the studio had come out of the blue one summer three years ago. Greenfly had invaded gardens in their millions, blown over the North Sea and the English Channel by warm winds from Europe. Painters in coastal resorts had found thousands of fat little bodies stuck to their non-drip gloss. The newsroom of Northcountry Television, like those all over Britain, was peopled by eagle-eyed hacks who knew a quirky story when they saw one and they needed an 'expert' to tell gardeners what to do. Their resident gardening man, Bertie Lightfoot, was then on holiday in Tenerife, so an alternative had to be found at short notice. One of the news editors came across Rob's column in his local paper and put in a call, expecting some horny-handed old son of the soil to turn up. Instead, a man in his early twenties had put his head round the newsroom door, a man whose looks and build would have been perfectly at home modelling rugged outdoor wear in a Racing Green catalogue.

When he'd turned up at the studio, Rob's mind was whirling with information and excitement and he was fighting the desire to be sick.

"Don't panic," he'd said to himself. "You know the answers, it's your job. Just be bright and pleasant and try not to speak too fast."

The producer of the early-evening news programme had been very encouraging. "Don't worry," he'd said to Rob. "Be yourself and try to relax. The interviewer will ask all the right questions. He's handled people far more nervous than you are. Enjoy yourself!"

He'd felt as though he was on the threshold of something new that day. He wondered what his dad would make of it. He was anxious not to let him down. If he did a bad job it would reflect on Jock MacGregor and on the nursery where a father had taught his son all he knew about plants and gardening. He didn't want that. He knew his mum would think he was wonderful whatever he did, but if the old man grunted that he'd not done too badly then he'd be well pleased.

Jock had worried about a son learning his trade at the hands of his father. He needn't have done. Rob had the sense and the patience to make allowances for his dad, and for old Harry Hotchkiss who'd helped Jock since before Rob had been born.

Rob's five-year apprenticeship of boiler-stoking, pot-washing, cutting-taking and shrub-growing with his father was boosted by day-release classes at the tech in Bradford – a place as foreign to Rob as if it had been on the other side of the world, but by the time he came to the end of his indentures he was itching to get away. He left for York, for a year's full-time training at the county agricultural college, and then to the Royal Botanic Garden, Edinburgh, for three years, which made his Scottish father almost burst with pride.

Rob did well. He'd grown into a good-looking lad with a passion for gardening and an infectious enthusiasm for passing on his skills. Now a six-footer, he had green eyes and a mop of untameable curly brown hair that framed a face which, more often than not, sported a crooked grin. And Edinburgh had opened his eyes. There was the entertainment and culture provided by the Festival, and the entertainment and culture provided by the women. Leaving at the end of the three-year diploma course had been a bit of a wrench, for one girl in particular.

He'd come back to the nursery for a few months but was soon restless. Gardening and selling plants were no longer enough for him: he really wanted to pass on his passion.

He rang up the local paper, the *Nesfield Gazette*, and spoke to the editor – a young raven-haired beauty, Katherine Page. She called him in, looked him up and down, asked him a few tricky questions then took him on, first as a columnist and then as a boyfriend. She was sparky and opinionated, and gave Rob a good run for his money both professionally and personally. His column caught on quickly: he had a flair for turning out copy that came to life on the page.

Which was exactly what had caught the eye of the man in the newsroom at Northcountry Television. His first appearance, when he waxed lyrical about greenfly, had gone down well. He could remember that first moment of live television even now: the countdown on the hushed studio floor; the red light and the wave of the floor manager's arm that indicated they were on air; the thrill, the dryness in the mouth, the fluttering in the stomach and the strange sensation that the sensible words coming out of his mouth didn't belong to him. It was all over before it had begun and they were patting him on the back and saying, "You must come back, you must do more."

He'd left the studio light-headed, and come home with his feet barely touching the ground. He *wanted* to do more. This was what he had been born to – communicating his passion for gardening to a huge audience. Then he watched the video recording his parents had made and for the rest of the week he didn't want to think about television again. What a let-down. His voice sounded strangled. Why hadn't he known what to do with his hands? Why had he kept looking at the wrong camera?

But they did ask him back. Would he stand by if Bertie couldn't make it? There were several occasions when Bertie couldn't make it – due to gippy tummy, said Bertie (due to Johnnie Walker, said the newsroom).

Slowly but surely his camera technique improved, he gained confidence and began to present his own pieces. 'I don't think you need me any more,' said the interviewer, good-naturedly. By now he knew what to do with his hands: if he carried something they looked natural. He knew that the camera to look at was the one with the red light, and if ever you wanted to change cameras, look down or look away first and then come back to the new camera whose light would already be on. Simple when you knew how. He could even carry on talking when the voice of the production assistant was counting down the minutes and the seconds in his ear, though for the first few times he felt his eyes glazing over as he listened to her too intently. It was, he decided, a matter of practice and aptitude. If you had both, the technique would become secondary and you could concentrate on your style and the content of the programme.

Some time later Rob was given a short programme of his own, regional at first. It captured people's imagination, and just a year later it was expanded to half an hour and screened live right across the country – most other gardening programmes were recorded. Their viewers, so used to staid, sober television gardening, or Bertie's phoney Mummerset, had shown their approval by making *Mr MacGregor's Garden* one of the most popular programmes on the network, and almost before he knew it – if, indeed, he ever believed it – Rob MacGregor was a star, especially with the female viewers who found his drop-dead good looks and slightly off-hand charm irresistible.

His friends had teased him mercilessly and Katherine had refused to take his new status seriously and persisted in making him push the trolley whenever they shopped together in the supermarket. When people asked for his autograph, she would stand behind them while he signed, making faces at him over their shoulders.

Rob wouldn't have known how to be starstruck. He'd dealt with customers in the nursery since he was a boy, and this was just the same. Be nice, smile and answer questions. There was nothing insincere about his manner: he was open and at ease in company. It was only when female fans flattered him too much about his looks and his flower-bedside manner, or asked if they could see if his fingers were really green, that he coloured and fumbled for words. One woman who bumped into him at the nursery even went so far as to try to roll up the leg of his jeans, saying, "Ooh, Mr MacGregor, you've got the sexiest legs on the box." Katherine had had silent hysterics behind a very large hanging basket.

Rubbing off the last of his makeup with the baby wipe, Rob pushed open the wood-veneered door to the office at the end of the corridor and walked in. There were around twenty desks in this open-plan area, and he threaded his way between them. At each sat a man or a woman, gazing at a computer screen, and, more often than not, remonstrating with some caller on the phone. His own producer, Steve Taylor, was no exception.

Fresh out of the studio gallery, glasses on the end of his nose, lank black hair pushed back and the sleeves of his white shirt rolled back, he waved at Rob and raised his eyebrows as he continued his conversation. "Yes, I understand that but, you see, he gets so many requests like this . . . I know, I know . . . Yes, you're right, it *is* a good cause. I will put it to him. But if you could just send him a note." A flailing arm motioned Rob to sit on a tubular steel chair next to the desk. "Yes, that would be lovely. Thank you. Yes. OK. Goodbye." He dropped the receiver into its cradle and slumped back into his chair. "Aaah! Why did they put her through to me? I hope your ears are burning."

"Why?" asked Rob.

"I'm getting fed up of acting as your secretary. When are you going to get one?"

"When you give me one."

"Steady! The budget for your programme's large enough already."

"What? I did all that stuff at Pencarrick last week as a single camera shoot, and now I'm doing winter programmes on a studio set that looks as though it's been designed by Walt Disney."

"Oh, God, prima-donna temperament already and you've only been on telly for a couple of years."

"No, not really. It's just . . . Well . . ." He sighed a long sigh, looked out of the window at the dark February sky, then back at Steve "It's Bertie."

"Tell me about it." Steve leaned back in his chair, pulled off his glasses and rubbed his eyes. "'What goes in must come up'? I ask you."

When Rob had been given his own programme Bertie Lightfoot's nose had been put well out of joint. *Mr MacGregor's Garden* had replaced *Bertie's Beds and Borders*, and Bertie, yet again, had seen his career on the skids. Once a variety artiste – 'Bertie Lightfoot, a song, a dance and a merry quip' – Bertie had found his work on the boards diminishing and decided he needed to branch out to survive. His hobby had always been gardening, and his garden, in Myddleton-in-Wharfedale where he lived with his partner Terry and two King Charles Cavalier spaniels, was regularly open to the public and had given him something of a reputation as a green-fingered thespian.

He'd written occasional articles for glossy magazines, and eventually been given his own television programme, for which he had adopted a stage accent more suited to Shakespearean mechanicals or rustics in Restoration comedy than to a twentieth-century gardener.

"Makes the advice sound more authentic, dear," he'd said to Rob, off camera on their first meeting.

Eventually Bertie's television programme had been considered past its sell-by date, and his bulbous nose too purple to cover up with concealing cream. The up-and-coming Rob MacGregor had been earmarked as a suitable replacement.

At first, Bertie had decided that he'd go quietly, with just the odd tart retort aimed in the direction of the young up-and-coming star. It had all been made easier in that his usurper was a friendly sort with no overblown ego, and Steve had suggested that the old stager should have a small slot in *Mr MacGregor's Garden* each week as a kind of sop.

Rob had foreseen no difficulties with this, and for a time the two had rubbed along fine. But lately Bertie had been getting just a touch more venomous towards his successor, and Rob had felt uncomfortable. The once-witty asides were now verging on animosity, which was not lost on Steve Taylor.

"Look, I'm sorry, old son. I know it's a problem – I can see it is. The trouble is, he's got friends upstairs."

"I can believe it," said Rob.

"Now, don't be unkind."

"Oh, but come on, Steve. I hate making a fuss about this. It's not that I haven't got a sense of humour, it's just that it's getting so embarrassing."

"Leave it with me. I'll see what I can do."

"I don't know what the solution is," said Rob. "I don't want to see the old bugger pensioned off. It'd break his heart, even if it is pickled. Perhaps I'd better try and sort it out for myself. Look, don't say anything. I'll have a word with him."

"You know, sometimes I think you really are a star," said Steve, with a relieved smile. "I'll see if I can't get you a bit of help with your secretarial work. Perhaps Lottie could take you on. Only part-time, mind. She's got her work cut out with me, so don't get excited about it."

"Thanks, Steve. You're a star yourself. Anyway, I'd better dash. I'm off to see a lady about a garden."

"Oh-ho-ho."

"No, she's old enough to be my mother." A shadow crossed Rob's face and his words hung in the air.

"Well, just watch out. I've seen how these old biddies look at you."

Rob recovered himself. "Oh, not you as well! Why does everybody seem to think that every single woman over the age of thirty is about to pounce on me?"

"It's not just the single ones."

"Thank you! Even Katherine's got this bee in her bonnet that I'm easy prey for vultures."

"And are you?"

"I think I'd better go. This conversation's getting far too personal." He laughed.

"Cheers, then – and good luck with the old son of the soil."

"I'll need it!" Rob lobbed the now salmon-coloured wipe into Steve's waste-bin, went back through the desks towards the door and, as he pushed it open, almost bowled over a devastating blonde. "Sorry!" he stammered.

"Don't be," replied Lisa Drake, giving him a look of amused admiration. She and Rob had never met before, although they were two of Northcountry Television's most popular figures. Rob was regarded as the rustic hunk, but as the station's main newsreader,

Lisa's reputation was anything but that of a blonde bimbo. Politicians took this girl seriously.

"I'm in a bit of a rush I'm afraid."

"Evidently." Perfectly enunciated by glossed lips, set off by the wide smile of even teeth. The two-piece navy blue suit, with a white silk blouse beneath it, was the ultimate in soft-edged power dressing.

Rob took her in at a glance. Rather too long a glance.

She tucked the script she was carrying under her arm and offered her hand. "I'm Lisa Drake." She looked him straight in the eye. The handshake was firm and sure. "You're Rob MacGregor, aren't you? I can't think why we haven't bumped into each other before."

"Nor me. Funny, really."

"Your programme's going really well. You must be pleased?" She leaned on the door frame, legs crossed, sizing him up.

Rob felt as though he were about to be given the sort of grilling that Lisa normally reserved for cabinet ministers. "Er, yes, very pleased. Lucky really."

"Oh, I don't think it's luck. You're very good. You must be. I've never watched a gardening programme before in my life but I try to catch yours. It's fun."

Rob looked at the floor, then became aware that Lisa might think he was looking at her legs, which were certainly worth looking at, so he lifted his eyes again, in time to see her flash a final smile, glance at her watch and say, "I must dash. I've a bulletin in a couple of minutes. Great to meet you, I'll see you again some time."

And she was gone. Only a whiff of Chanel remained.

The bonfire crackled and a plume of amber sparks spiralled upwards into the lowering February sky as Jock MacGregor, his flat cap protecting his watering eyes from the heat, hurled another young tree into the centre of the blaze. Through the shimmering haze above the flames he saw the youth retreating towards the nursery gate, his khaki lunch-bag slung over his shoulder and a young pot-grown tree in each hand.

"Oi!"

The lad stopped dead in his tracks and looked around sheepishly, the whites of his eyes almost luminous against his black skin.

"Where do you think you're going?"

"Home," said the lad.

"Not with those you're not," said the old man. "They're for the bonfire."

"Aw, go on. If they're going to be burned I might as well take 'em 'ome." He stood near the old wrought-iron gate, embarrassed at being caught out.

"And where will you say they came from?"

"From work."

"Oh, yes? And what will folk think of this nursery then? If the lad who works here takes home shapeless trees with half their branches missing, what kind of advert is that for a business?" Jock beckoned the lad over. "Do you really want two trees?"

"No, not really. One'd be enough. It's for the old lady's garden – you know, the one I do of a weekend."

The old man looked at the youth. His tightly curled hair was close-clipped into a spiral pattern above his wide, honest face, and three rings were spaced around his left ear. Not the way apprentice gardeners had looked in Jock MacGregor's day. Then they had worn green baize aprons, clogs and corduroy trousers, rather than the baggy jeans, gaping trainers and sloppy sweaters that oozed out from beneath Wayne Dibley's slogan-painted donkey-jacket.

"Get yourself over there." The old man pointed to the standing ground where container-grown maples and birches, rowans and limes stood in neat rows, their vigorous young trunks strapped to stout horizontal wires to stop them blowing over in the wind. "If you want a tree for your old lady take a decent one."

He shuffled back to the bonfire, poked it with his long-handled fork and sent another fountain of sparks dancing upwards into the darkening sky.

"Thanks," said the lad, his eyes widening. "Can I have a birch? They've got dead cool bark. She'll be chuffed wi' that."

The faintest glimmer of a smile came to the old man's lips, then he was serious again. "Just remember," he said, "it takes years to build up a reputation and seconds to destroy it. Folk come here for quality plants and I don't like them to be disappointed at what we turn out."

"Sorry. I didn't mean to –"

Jock MacGregor cut him short. "Go on. Get off home. I'll see you in the morning."

The old man watched him go, a spring in his step and a tree in his hand, whistling some God-awful tune. He looked up at the sky, now a

14

dark blue-grey, and then back at the dying fire. He prodded again at the bright embers that lit his craggy old face with an orange glow. A sad face. The face of a man once happy with his lot but which now reflected a hollowness inside.

Wayne Dibley, for all his unruly appearance, was, Jock thought, a good lad. Jock had thought he was joking when he had arrived there a fortnight ago, looking like a refugee in his ill-fitting clothes. But something about his persistence had told the old man that he might be worth taking on. Harry Hotchkiss was approaching eighty and his muscle power was worth next to nothing. Jock could do with a couple of strong arms about the place, provided they didn't cost too much.

"I don't mind 'ard work," the youth had said.

"I should 'ope you don't," said Harry. "There's plenty of it 'ere."

The irony of Harry's response was not lost on Jock, an early riser who unlocked the nursery gates to let himself in at seven thirty every morning. Harry, with good luck and a following wind, could usually drag himself in by a quarter to nine, and would then sit in an old armchair in the corner of the dusty potting shed, downing sugary dark-brown tea from a stained pint pot. He had a smoker's cough that could rattle the roof tiles, and spent a good half-hour every morning ensconced in the toilet with a Capstan Full Strength hanging off his lower lip and a copy of the *Sun* on his lap. Jock made sure that he was watering in the greenhouses while Harry's routine was in full swing. Yes, he could do with some fresh company as well as fresh muscle power. It might help to take him out of himself.

Jock perched on the side of the wooden cart that held the trees he considered too inferior for his customers. The lad had thought him barmy for not selling them. Maybe he was. But his own training had left him with a carefulness that he recognized as truly Scots. How far away it all seemed now. Like another world. Another life.

Young Murgatroyd MacGregor – he'd been happy to let folk call him Jock – had left school in Perth at fourteen and gone straight into service like his parents before him. He'd never shone at school – for him the three Rs meant rambling, rabbiting and ratting – but give him a plant in a pot or let him loose in a garden and he felt instantly at home. He'd tried to work out why and had decided that quite simply you were born with an affinity to nature; it was not something you could acquire.

Looking at the nursery now, even in the dim twilight, Jock could see why he and Madge had known that this was their rightful place. It was a picturesque spot: the beer-coloured river flowed by at the bottom of a steep grassy bank. When Jock and Madge had come to view it on that warm May day it had been swathed in cow parsley and red campion. It was only a couple of acres, but lapped by the river on one side, and with the moorland rising above the small town of Nesfield behind it, it had seemed like a patch of paradise to the young couple.

On the opposite bank of the river, crossed by a small, hump-backed stone footbridge, was the nursery cottage, a simple affair of local sandstone with a purple slate roof and small sash windows. It was surrounded by its own garden and enclosed by a drystone wall. Over the wall leaned a green sign with gold lettering, though when Jock and Madge had come here its message had been faded and peeling: "Wharfeside Nursery. Prop: F. Armitage", it had said, with an arrow pointing across the river.

Fred Armitage, the bespectacled old Yorkshire nurseryman had quietly impressed on Jock the need to keep down weeds and produce good-quality stock, and asked if it would be possible for his "lad", Harry, to remain with the business. Harry had been in his thirties then, and willing to work, if a little slow. Gradually Jock turned round the flagging nursery and built up the business, with Harry doing the labouring, and Madge keeping the books and looking after the boy.

All things considered, he couldn't have wished for a better son. And now they called him a star. One newspaper had even dubbed him 'The King of Spades'.

Jock couldn't have been happier. And then it had happened. For a month or two Madge had not been feeling herself. Just dizzy spells, she had said, no point in seeing the doctor. Until Jock returned home from the nursery one night and found her on the kitchen floor. There had been no time to take it in; no chance to help her. She had waved him goodbye from the doorstep in the morning when he'd walked over the bridge to the nursery, and when he returned that evening she was lying dead by the kitchen table. A brain haemorrhage, the doctor had said. Instant and painless. But not for Jock. The loss was agonizing, bewildering. What was the point in going on?

He watched the embers of the bonfire turn from bright orange to dull red, and felt a tear trickle down his stubbly chin. It was six months since Madge had died and the fire had gone out in his heart. He turned towards the wrought-iron gate, walked through it, secured the padlock, pocketed the key and crossed the bridge for home.

Chapter 2

The slightly foxed pale green Ford Fiesta was tucked into a corner of the studio car park, salt from the winter roads caked on its sills. Rob unlocked the door and slid into the driver's seat through the narrow gap between it and the charcoal grey BMW. Lisa Drake's car went perfectly with her image. A rust-spotted Fiesta wasn't exactly a bird-puller but it had belonged to his mother and Rob had been reluctant to sell it straight away. As long as it remained, so did the memories of her driving him around. Her woolly hat remained in the glove compartment, not through sentimentality but because Rob felt happier to leave it there. To remove it would be to clear his mother from his life and he wasn't ready to do that. He doubted that he ever would be.

He turned the key in the ignition. The engine coughed reluctantly into action and a little orange light illuminated the dashboard. Nearly out of petrol. Still, there was enough to allow a detour on the way home to visit the one remaining older woman in his life. It was a fortnight since he'd last dropped by. She might think he'd forgotten her.

He'd known Lady Helena Sampson since he was sixteen, when lack of funds had necessitated an evening job. He thought of her now as he drove away from the studios in the city, up the dale towards his home town. The depressing dark grey of the tower blocks and the sooted deep red brickwork of Victorian Leeds eventually gave way to rolling green fields crisscrossed by drystone walls and speckled with black-faced sheep. The twilight deepened and the plum-purple moors disappeared into the mist above the river valley as he turned up the moorland road towards Helena's house. There were few women whose company he enjoyed more, and few people in whose company he felt so at ease. He swung the Fiesta over the cattle grid between the hefty stone gateposts and it growled up the gravel drive to Tarn House, its exhaust making even more of a din than usual.

As he got out of the car the lantern in the porch came on, and Helena, a tall, good-looking, grey-haired woman in a heather-coloured tweed skirt, grey polo-necked jumper and pearls came out to meet him. He pecked her on both cheeks and walked indoors.

"You know, I remember when it was only one," she said, as they walked through the print-lined hallway into the handsome Victorian drawing room.

"One what?"

"One cheek that got a peck."

"I remember when it was no cheek at all, and just, 'Will that be all, ma'am?'"

"I don't believe you've ever said that in however many years it is that I've known you." She laughed.

"It's this television lark, you see," said Rob. "Two cheeks get kissed all the time."

"Quite right, too," replied Helena. "As long as both parties know and there isn't that embarrassing mis-hit when you go for the second. Anyway, it's nice to see you. How have you been?" She motioned him to sit on the plump, chintz-covered sofa, planting herself on the padded arm of an overstuffed chair by the fire.

"Well enough," said Rob. "Apart from a little local difficulty with a short fat man called Bertie."

"Oh, yes. Vera's been telling me. Your Mr Lightfoot's been getting a bit shirty with you, hasn't he?"

"You could say that. And folk are beginning to notice."

"I see. Are you rattled by it?"

"Well, not so much rattled as uncomfortable. It's such a pain. It won't be long before people start tuning in just for the end of the programme so that they can see us at each other's throats."

"So what will you do about it?"

"I don't know. I've told my producer I'll handle it myself so he's off the hook, but I don't know where to begin."

Helena got up, went to the door of the drawing room and called to her housekeeper.

"Scotch?"

"After the day I've had I'll have a large one."

"And I'll join you."

As she poured two large Glenlivets from the decanter on a side table into two cut-glass tumblers a plump, pink-overalled figure put her head round the door.

"What was it, ma'am? It's nearly six o'clock. I'm just about to go." And then, much louder and bursting with enthusiasm, "Oh 'ello, Mr Rob, 'ow are you? It's lovely to see you," and without waiting for an invitation Mrs Ipplepen waddled across the room to where Rob stood on the Chinese rug in front of the log fire. She put both arms around him and reached up and planted a moist kiss on his cheek. Just one. Rob felt the prickle of her whiskers. In spite of her advanced years, Vera Ipplepen had something of a crush on the youth she'd watched grow up from apprentice gardener to TV star. She was old enough to be his granny (and frequently told him so) but thoroughly enjoyed basking in his reflected glory. "I was watching today. Old Fatty's getting a bit above 'imself, in't he?"

"Vera!" admonished Helena. "Don't be rude!"

"We-e-ell," said Vera, her pink nylon overall straining at its buttons, "my Cyril says that when it comes to gard'nin' he dun't know what he's talking about, that Bertie Lightfoot. The last time we saw him was at City Varieties in Leeds when he were with Robb Axminster."

"I think it was Robb Wilton," said Helena, trying hard to stop her mouth going up at the corners.

"'E was still better at that than 'e is at gardening, whatever 'is name was," answered Vera.

She was not the kind of daily you'd have expected to find looking after Helena Sampson. Where her mistress was tall and elegant, Vera Ipplepen was short and dumpy. Helena's grey hair had the sheen of silver and was sleek and elegantly coiffed; Mrs Ipplepen's grey locks had been tightly curled and rinsed with lavender blue at Sharon's near the station, and her lips were courtesy of Clara Bow, usually a shade of pink that came nowhere near matching her overall. Dame Edna Everage would have killed for her spectacles.

She might have had a mouth that, on occasion, said more than it should, but her heart was twenty-four carat and she would have defended Helena with her life, and with her Cyril's too.

"How's Cyril?" asked Rob, casting a glance at Helena, who shot him a withering look. Mrs Ipplepen could offer a graphic account of the precise workings of her husband's large intestine at the drop of a rubber glove. Rob knew this, and had only risked asking because Cyril's tea had to be on the table in front of him at six thirty every evening and there was no way Vera would stay more than a few minutes. The spuds would have to go on soon.

"We-e-ll. 'Is arm's still playin' 'im up."

"Why's that?"

"Daft blighter went an' broke it. Fell over carryin't coal up from't cellar."

"Oh, I bet that's cramped his style."

"It's stopped 'im fillin' in 'is pools coupon. It were 'is right 'and. That's 'is writin' 'and. I've told 'im 'e'll 'ave to learn to use the other one and be amphibious, then it won't matter."

"Ambidextrous, you mean?"

"Yes, and that as well if 'e wants me to keep lookin' after 'im. I told 'im one bottle of Mackeson's enough for a man of 'is age. But will 'e listen? N-o-o-o. Anyway, I'll 'ave to go. Time to get the spuds on. I'll see you tomorrow, ma'am."

"All right, Vera. Take care going home, it's a bit frosty."

"I will. Nice to see you, Mr Rob. And don't let old Fatty get the better of you." She looked at Rob and gave him the sort of smile schoolgirls give to boys they fancy. "Ta-ra," and she sashayed out of the room in her pale blue mules to the whistle of nylon on corsetry.

Rob's and Helena's eyes met and they dissolved into silent laughter.

"Cheers!"

"Cheers! Here's to Cyril's arm," said Rob.

"And Fatty's sense of proportion," replied Helena, raising her glass and taking the first sip of the day. "So to go back to my earlier question, how have you been?"

"OK, apart from dear old Bertie. Except that I'm a bit worried about Dad. He soldiers on, tough as old boots, but he has these quiet spells. Kind of in a trance. I know what he's thinking about but I don't seem to be able to say anything."

"Has it ever occurred to you that he might not want you to say anything?" asked Helena.

"But I feel I should be able to help."

"You can help. And you do help – just by being there. But there are times when someone in that situation needs to be on their own and in their own mind. It has to be gone through."

"But when will he come out of it?"

Helena turned her eyes towards the fire. "Oh, there are those who say it takes a year to get over all the anniversaries. And when Jumbo died I found there was a lot of truth in that. But it doesn't end there. There's a whole new life to build from scratch. It's like being reborn as somebody else and not knowing who they are. Not knowing any of the rules. It takes longer than you'd imagine. And just when you think you're recovering you find yourself driving home and suddenly thinking, Oh, I must tell him about such and such, and it stops you in your tracks. It's like Snakes and Ladders – you think you're climbing out of the mire and in a moment you slide back down to square one. You start to climb up again sooner as the years go by. But it's never quite the same. Ever. It's different. But bearable. Eventually. And then you feel guilty for being able to cope." She looked wistfully at the blazing logs. "Don't rush him. Six months isn't long."

"I know. I suppose the problem is mine as much as his. It would help *me* to think that I was helping *him* get over it, so I suppose there's a bit of selfishness in there somewhere."

"Don't blame yourself for that. Keep doing well and that will take his mind off things. He's very proud of you, you know. And so am I."

Rob turned his gaze from the fire to meet the eyes of his patron. The Glenlivet was helping him to unwind. "Well, you helped me to get there. Gave me the confidence."

"Nonsense. You're your own man. I just watched you grow."

"Keep watching."

"Oh, I will. Along with half the nation's women, I should think."

"Don't you start. I've already had a dig in the ribs from my producer and a close encounter of the newsroom kind, and that's quite enough for one day."

"A close encounter of what?"

"I bumped into Lisa Drake on the way out of the studio. Never met her before. And I did tonight."

"Oh. She's that rather sharp newsreader, isn't she? Bit of a reputation. What did you make of her?"

"Well, for the first time ever I knew what a hare must feel like when a fox looks it straight in the eye. A mixture of terror and the thrill of the impending chase."

"So you think there'll be a chase, do you?"

"Oh, I don't think so."

"I should hope not. Katherine positively dotes on you."

"Not so's you'd notice."

"Nonsense. She cares as much about you as I do and she's had even more of a hand in your career. It was Katherine who gave you your break into journalism, I'll have you remember."

"Yes, and I'm very grateful."

"Sorry, I didn't mean . . . well . . . you know."

"I know," said Rob. "A tricky patch, that's all. It'll be fine."

Helena took another sip from her glass.

"Oh, it's just that we seem to have been getting off on the wrong foot a lot lately. Silly things. Arguing more than we used to. She's been working hard on some story or other and I've been away filming. I really look forward to our time together and then when we actually manage to be home at the same time . . ."

"It's hard when you both have demanding careers. You end up being tired in tandem at the end of the day. Or one of you is raring to go and the other is whacked. I know. I've been there."

"Well, with any luck we'll get it together this weekend. All we need is for the rest of the world to go away for a while and give us some time to ourselves."

He drained his glass and looked at the clock. "Time I went. I don't want the old feller to start brooding. I told him I'd cook his supper tonight and if I don't get back soon he'll be sitting in front of an empty grate and I'll have a job to snap him out of it."

"Thank you for coming," she said, passing her empty glass from one hand to another. "It's good to see you."

"And you." He kissed her on both cheeks, then she walked him to the door and waved the pale green Fiesta goodbye.

Rob parked the car by the nursery fence and walked over the bridge towards Jock's cottage, pulling his duffel-coat around him to keep out the cold. The house was in darkness except for a dim light at the downstairs window to the right of the front door. Rob stopped on the brow of the bridge, leaned on the stone balustrade and gazed at the silhouette of the cottage, surrounded by a trim garden stuffed with all Jock's favourite plants.

It was in this small garden, as much as in the nursery, that Rob's passion for plants had been nurtured by his father, and it had given both of them pleasure to watch rare shrubs grow slowly, year after year, the ground below them carpeted with trilliums and wood anemones, snakeshead fritillaries and hardy cyclamen.

There was little sign of all these riches on this crisp February evening, as the dark water sped under the bridge, making glooping noises as it eddied in the shallows. The moon was almost full, and Rob looked up at the black velvet sky, studded with stars, and across at the slumbering moors, under which the lights of the town winked. Then he heaved a sigh, headed towards the cottage and opened the wicket gate that led into the garden. He walked the flagged path to the bottle-green front door and knocked three times before pressing down on the old sneck.

The door opened into an old kitchen with a stone-flagged floor. The ancient black range still stood against one wall, though there was no sign of a fire. The only light came from a small lamp standing on the kitchen table, at which Jock sat, his flat cap pushed to the back of his head, revealing a few damp strands of grey hair.

"Dad?"

"Aye?"

"Are you OK?"

"Huh!" The old man almost laughed.

Rob was uneasy. "What is it?"

"The last straw, that's what it is," said Jock, pushing a letter across the table towards his son. Rob picked up the envelope and looked at the address. It was neatly typed. He pulled out the crisp white letter, unfolded it and looked at the green letterhead: "Gro-land Garden Centres". Rob knew instantly why his father looked so low. The letter confirmed what he had suspected:

Dear Jock

For some time now I have, as you know, been wanting to expand my business with a view to extending the leisure side of my marketing.

We have talked in the past about the possibility of my acquiring Wharfeside Nursery, and I know that so far you have not looked favourably upon my offers. However, bearing in mind the events of the last few months, and the current economic climate, it occurs to me that the situation may have changed and I am writing to enquire if you are now disposed to sell. We are, as you know, highly thought of in the horticultural retail trade locally, and feel sure that any reservations you have about selling up will be more than compensated for by the fact that your nursery will become part of a respected chain.

I would appreciate your reaction as soon as possible, so that we can start talking in more detail. In an ideal world I would like, if possible, to get things up and running this spring, rather than having to wait until the autumn.

Please reply at your earliest convenience.

Yours sincerely,

Dennis Wragg.

"Oh, God," said Rob. "That man only opens his mouth to change feet. What the hell's he thinking about at a time like this?"

"Money, that's what he's thinking about. That's all he's ever thought about. Your mother always said that Dennis Wragg had a one-track mind and that the track was papered with ten-pound notes."

"Well, this time he's gone too far. I'm off up the road to see him."

"Nay, son. Leave him be. I'll be damned if Dennis Wragg is going to see me off. There's no way your mother would have put up with that. I may be nigh on retirement age but I'm not giving up yet. What the hell else would I do?"

Rob looked at his father. Jock turned to meet his eyes. "This is a battle I'll have to fight on my own now, but maybe it'll give me something to think about, eh?" The corners of Jock's mouth flickered into a smile. "I've not been much in the way of company lately, have I?"

Rob lowered his eyes.

"No, I know," Jock went on. "It's tough. But then it's tough for you, too. I lost a wife, but you lost a mother and I shouldn't forget that."

The two men, one standing the other seated, neither moved nor spoke for what seemed like an age. Both were clinging tight to their emotions, neither wanting to let the other down. The old station clock on the wall ticked loudly and Rob felt his heart pounding in his chest.

"Come on," said Jock. "You promised me supper. It's time a fire was lit in that range. This kitchen is as cold as – well, it could be warmer."

*

25

That evening Rob saw a glimmer of the old spirit beginning to return to his father, an indication that the old man had not given up.

By the time he reached Katherine's flat in the centre of town he was worn out. It was nine thirty when he parked the car in the cobbled yard at the side of Wellington Heights, a large Victorian building with a baker's, a 'Country Pine' shop and a florist's on the ground floor. He let himself in through the heavy glass-panelled side door and walked up the ornately banistered steps to the top floor, four storeys up. He rang the bell of Flat 5 and waited. From inside, he could hear the honeyed tones of James Taylor on the sound system, then a voice asked, "Who is it?"

"It's me!"

The door opened to reveal Katherine, her jet black shoulder-length hair gleaming in the lamplight. At the sight of him her dark brown eyes widened in welcome, and she smiled, revealing shining white teeth. "Where's your key?"

"I picked up the wrong bunch this morning."

"Dummy." She tugged him inside, and shut the door, then stood with her hands on her hips and looked quizzically at him.

"Where've you *been?*"

"Seeing Helena and seeing Dad."

"No time for me?"

"Loads of time for you." He looked at her wistfully.

She threw her arms round him, pulling herself up to plant her lips on his. "What took you so long?" she asked, eyes closed and the side of her face resting on his coat.

He stroked her hair with one hand, his other arm around her shoulders. "Oh, I hadn't seen Helena for a couple of weeks, then I cooked Dad supper and then I came on here."

"So you've eaten?" There was a note of disappointment in her voice as her dark eyes looked up at him.

"Yes. But I'll have some cheese."

She turned from the tiny hall and went into the living room. Rob took off his coat and hung it on a peg by the front door, then crept up behind her and dropped a soft kiss on the nape of her neck.

"How's Jock?"

"If you'd asked me that question a couple of hours ago I'd have said that he was exactly as he was yesterday, and the day before that. Lost in a world he doesn't know. But now . . . Well, I think the mist might be beginning to clear from his eyes."

"Why?" asked Katherine, looking up from the CD player, whose volume she had lowered to a level that allowed more intimate conversation.

"Dennis Wragg has written to him again asking him if, 'bearing in mind the events of the last few months', he wants to sell."

Katherine spun round, her eyes flashing. "The bastard!"

"I couldn't agree with you more."

"It's obvious that he thinks Jock's defences are down and that he'll just give in and sell out."

"Dead right."

The fiery side of Katherine that leaped to the defence of what she considered to be a just cause drove her on. "His wife's even worse than he is – grasping woman. You know what they call her?"

"What?" enquired Rob.

"The Wragg Bag. She's a social-climbing cow with the dress sense of a colour-blind Tiller girl. I mean, aren't you furious?"

"I was. I'd every intention of going round to Dennis Wragg's nasty little bungalow and planting something very firm on the end of his crooked little nose."

"So what stopped you?" She was square on to him now, looking up demandingly into his face.

"The fact that for the first time since Mum died I saw a spark of fire in the old man's eyes. Maybe a fight is just what he needs to bring him back to life again."

She looked questioningly at him.

"I don't remember Dad ever looking at me like that before. We had supper together and he didn't talk about Mum, he talked about the nursery and how things were doing – the dogwood stems were especially bright this year, and how folk kept saying so."

Katherine watched his face change, as it always did when he talked about plants. She'd been irritated by him lately. He never seemed to be there when she was, barely had time to listen to her news, but when he spoke like this, with a faraway look in his eyes, she knew why she loved him and why she wanted so much to be a part of his life.

"Dad sold some Oriental hellebores to a woman who'd travelled here from the other side of Leeds because she'd heard that he had a good collection – yellows and pinks as well as the usual white and purple – and she'd gone away happy and promised to tell her friends. It was somehow as if the plants are dependent on him now and he shouldn't let them down. Almost like his children. Does that sound daft?"

"Oh, it would have done once," she said softly. "Before I knew you and your father and what plants could mean to people."

Rob grimaced. "Oh, God, I'm beginning to sound like an anorak. 'Plants are more interesting than people.' Wait a minute while I talk to my aspidistra."

Katherine uttered a peal of laughter. "No. You're just a passionate man, and there's nothing wrong with that. Not unless you suddenly start getting interested in diesel engines or removal lorries. Then I'll start getting worried."

"There are only two things I'm passionate about and one of them isn't Eddie Stobart," said Rob.

"Well, I'm relieved to hear it. Any clues as to what the second thing might be, assuming that the first thing has roots, leaves and flowers?"

"I'm looking at it."

"Well, about time, too," said Katherine, reaching for his hand. "I thought you'd never get round to me. I haven't seen my friend in ages." There was a twinkle in her eye as she pulled him towards the kitchen. "Red Leicester or Double Gloucester?"

"Oh, I'll have none of that foreign muck. Just give me a bit of Wensleydale and a couple of digestives and I'll do anything you like."

"Anything?" Her crooked grin almost matched his.

"Anything."

Chapter 3

When Rob woke the following morning the pillow next to his was empty. He tried focusing his eyes, but the brilliant sunlight streaming in from the tall sash windows made it difficult to see anything clearly except the blurred lines of a distant wooden wardrobe, the sweep of long oatmeal-coloured curtains, and two brass bedknobs.

As his vision began to clear, his nostrils flared in response to the aroma of newly baked bread and fresh coffee. The fragrance of warm loaves drifted up through the crack of the open window from the baker's below, but the coffee was being made in the kitchen. The large stripped-pine door with its crystal knob opened slowly to reveal Katherine with a tray in her hands and a newspaper between her teeth.

Rob looked at her as he raised his shoulders clear of the duvet and stretched out his arms to relieve her of the tray. She wore nothing except a sloppy white T-shirt, and her hair had been swept back and held in place with a watercolour brush pushed through its glossy black knot. Her face was fresh scrubbed, her lips bright pink. She planted a kiss on his cheek and sat on the end of the bed, opening the *Nesfield Gazette* and scrutinizing the front page.

"Yes!" She punched the air with her fist and let fall one half of the paper. "That'll get them going."

"What will?" said Rob, rubbing his eyes and reaching for the coffee jug.

"Today's headline."

"Have you been stirring it again, then?" he asked, raising an eyebrow.

"Well, it's a good job somebody has," she retorted. "Otherwise heaven knows what would be happening to this place we call home."

Rob squinted at the headline: "HOW GREEN IS OUR VALLEY?"

"What is it now?"

"Whitaker's cotton mills. They wanted to be allowed to set up a new plant five miles up the Wharfe from here on those water-meadows that used to be farmland."

"I thought they were *still* farmland?" said Rob, taking a sip of Katherine's decaffeinated but welcome brew.

"Well, technically they are, but they've been owned for years by Whitaker's and now they want to stop letting them to old Tom Hardisty and his herd of pedigree Friesians and make use of them."

"Oh, I see. And our editor in her 'Green Pages' is giving them what for, is she?"

"Too right I am."

"The words 'hobby' and 'horse' come to mind," said Rob teasingly. "What's the big problem?"

"The big problem is that a part of the dale which has always been regarded as a beauty spot will be swamped with buildings and plant and chimneys. The traffic levels will be unacceptable, the roads will be clogged and before we know where we are we'll look like Bradford."

"Oh, I see. We're being a nimby."

"We are not being a nimby!" she snapped back.

"Excuse me for a moment," said Rob. "There is no way that the local council will allow the setting up of a monstrosity that will change the face of the dale, and this plant will provide jobs that are badly needed locally."

"Just whose side are you on?" asked Katherine, kneeling over him on the bed and looking menacingly into his eyes.

Rob carried on, "What's more, people need clothes unless they're to go round stark naked. But you, because of your and your paper's stance on conservation will oppose it as a matter of course."

"You bet we will."

"Well, you can't simply oppose every kind of industrial development that comes along or the countryside will grind to a halt."

"I don't believe what I'm hearing!" she cried, shocked at his reaction.

"Poppet!"

"Don't call me Poppet!"

"You can't object to every single plan to build anything other than a farm shop."

"That's not fair. We haven't stood in the way of every development in this dale. What we have done is open people's eyes to the dangers of some of them. There would have been a bypass carved through here if we hadn't taken a stance on that, and now it's this. The green belt is not nearly so sacred as it was – and money talks."

She was warming to her subject now. "This development will not only ruin the landscape but it will also affect the river."

"Yes," responded Rob, "and the National Rivers Authority comes down like a ton of bricks on anyone who pollutes their water."

"I know they do, but by then it might be too late. Whitaker's have already been fined twice for polluting other Yorkshire rivers, and there are other things to take into account as well."

"Such as what?"

"Such as the temperature of the water returned to the river afterwards. What people don't realize is the delicacy of the balance in a river. Any tampering with the temperature and its depth and speed affects the fish, the insects, the growth of aquatic plants."

"And that, ladies and gentlemen, is the case for the prosecution," said Rob.

"Don't you take this seriously?" she asked.

"I take it very seriously. I just wanted to see if you really had done your homework or if this was a knee-jerk reaction."

"Thank *you*," she said indignantly.

"All right, I'm sorry. I just wanted to sort out in my mind why you're taking the angle you are taking."

"And do you understand now?"

"Perfectly."

"And do you agree?"

"I'm not sure. I'll think about it."

"Sometimes," muttered Katherine, "I wonder why I stick with you."

"You stick with me," said Rob, "because I'm the only person who'll listen to you shrieking about your causes."

Before he had time to draw breath, the pillow beside him had been snatched up and brought down on his head, sending a coffee cup skittering across the scrubbed wooden floor.

"Now look what you've done." Rob watched a rivulet of decaffeinated coffee seeping through a crack in the boards.

"Damn!" exclaimed Katherine, springing up from the bed and darting for the kitchen. She returned with a bowl and a J-cloth, wisps of dark hair framing her face as she knelt to mop up the coffee which had stained the boards a darker shade of brown. "Damn!"

"If it's not one kind of pollution it's another!" said Rob, realizing his mistake as soon as the words had left his mouth. "I'm sorry. I didn't mean it. I'm as concerned about the environment as you are – you know that – but as far as gardening is concerned I try to strike a balance."

"Well, I wish you'd balanced your coffee cup better. People will think I've got an incontinent cat with an addiction to gravy."

"Sorry," said Rob.

"My fault," she admitted, smiling at him gently. "But you do see why I get so worked up, don't you?"

"Yes, of course I do. It's just that sometimes it's difficult for me to be quite as green as you are. I try, but it's difficult."

"Only because you have to hobnob with unfriendly things like chemical companies."

"They're a large part of the horticultural industry. I can't pretend they don't exist." Rob groaned. "Anyway, enough of all this, it's Saturday. What are we going to do?"

"Didn't I tell you?" Katherine got up off the floor and sat on the edge of the bed. "I have to go to Yeadon Airport to meet the boss."

"On a *Saturday?*"

"He's dropping in on his private jet from Glasgow before he goes on to Plymouth. He wants to talk about circulation."

"So do I," said Rob. "Or the lack of it in my foot. Can you move?"

She eased herself to one side and Rob leaned forward and kissed her.

"So I have to amuse myself today, then, do I?"

"And tonight, I'm afraid. I have to have dinner with the boss and his wife before they fly off to sunny Devon."

"Couldn't they make it lunch?" asked Rob.

"Oh, no. Her ladyship has to visit Lord and Lady Myddleton for lunch, so I have to be on call for dinner."

"Can't I come?"

"'Fraid not. The boss likes to think he has my undivided attention."

"Bloody-minded, I call it. And a pain. Fancy asking you out to dinner on a Saturday night and expecting you to pretend you live the life of a nun."

"Well, over the past few weeks I might just as well have been in a convent, bearing in mind the number of times I've seen you," said Katherine.

"I've been away filming!" he said defensively.

"Oh, I know where you've been. The thing is, you haven't been *here*, and I didn't know whether or not you'd be here tonight, not that I could have done much about it."

Rob looked crestfallen.

"I have my own life to lead, Rob, and just occasionally I wonder if you remember that. Rob?" She lifted his chin with a forefinger and looked into his eyes. "I'll be here tomorrow and we can go off up the dale for the day. The forecast's good. We can have lunch at the Devonshire Arms in Grassington and I'll give you my undivided attention. Yes?" She looked at him as a mother would look at her small child: kindly and lovingly with the hint of tears in her eyes.

Rob raised his eyes to meet hers. "Yes, OK. I'll go and get some sandpaper and sort out your floor. It's time you put some sealer on it to stop it being stained every time you throw coffee over me."

He got up and went towards the bathroom. She watched him go, lowering her eyes from his tousled brown head, to his broad, freckled shoulders, trim waist, tight bottom and shapely legs.

"Oh, Mr MacGregor," she whispered, "I do love you."

While Rob MacGregor was brooding over the absent Katherine, Guy D'Arcy was letting himself into his town-house in Fulham. It was an early-morning return after a long night out.

Of the modern breed of gardening broadcasters Rob MacGregor and Guy D'Arcy were the two rising stars. They had replaced the old breed of television gardener with a brand of youthful enthusiasm that would once have been thought gimmicky, but which now appealed not only to householders under the age of forty but also to ladies of a certain age who enjoyed the glamour that was now coupled with their compost.

The new wave of television gardeners might have swept away many of the techniques of their predecessors, but one tradition they continued was the subterranean rivalry that has existed among sons of the soil since Adam turned the first sod in the Garden of Eden.

Where Rob was the earthy offspring of working-class parents, Guy D'Arcy was a scion of the aristocracy. And he looked it. His jaw had a patrician cut, his thick blond hair was trimmed so that he could throw it back with a flick of his head, and he wore his clothes with that casual yet studied elegance that comes of breeding.

Rob had first met Guy at the Chelsea Flower Show a couple of years previously. He'd recognized him from the gossip-column pictures but, then, only a hermit would have failed to recognize Guy D'Arcy – the man who was seen with a duke's daughter on his arm one week, a wealthy socialite the next, a mixed assortment of A-list celebrities and even a European princess.

Guy had fallen out with his father and been asked to leave the family estate agency in the Cotswolds. He had decided that gardening was just the thing for him and set about redesigning the gardens of his well-to-do friends.

His notoriety had provided him with a few contacts in journalism, so it wasn't long before he had written a book or two and acquired a fat fee from the *Sunday Herald* for a weekly column, "Guy's Garden". A year or so later he landed his own programme on a rival television network and Rob had noticed that Guy D'Arcy now treated him rather differently than he had before. A cursory nod was all he could expect from the man who, a year or two previously, had been all over him.

Guy D'Arcy tried to push open the royal blue front door of his Victorian villa. "Oh, bugger!" He leaned on it with his shoulder, then stooped to free it from whatever was preventing it from swinging open smoothly. A pile of post like a large molehill spilled over the doormat. Padded envelopes, long white envelopes, pale blue envelopes, pink, crinkle-cut envelopes, manila envelopes – enough to open a small branch of W. H. Smith, thought Guy, scooping up the mound and carrying it across to the hall table. Every envelope was painstakingly readdressed from the newspaper office or the television studio. Why couldn't they simply lob them all into one hefty envelope and post that instead? he wondered. Stupid.

Two hundred letters a week was not Guy's idea of fun. He wanted the fame but could cheerfully have done without the by-products, and especially the postbag, which, every week, included putrefying apples, crisp foliage and assorted items of rotting vegetable matter. There were reams of Queen's Velvet, Basildon Bond and scraps of paper torn from shorthand notebooks that carried queries about flowerless African violets and leafless weeping figs. Why was it that only the clinically insane and the terminally dyslexic chose to write to him?

The mail slithered in a miniature Niagara from the hall table on to the Afghan rug below and Guy kicked shut the door and walked to the kitchen. The answering-machine winked at him from a pine dresser. Nine messages. A chap had only to be away for a day and the world and his wife were breaking his door down by dusk.

He pressed the 'play' button and went over to the kitchen cupboard, took down a tube of Alka-Selzer, filled a tumbler with water, dropped in two tablets and slammed his hand over the top of the glass. The sound of the effervescence was not improving the state of his head, which throbbed.

"Beeeeep. Hello, Guy, it's Sophie. You muttered something about supper tonight. Is it still on or am I being stood up again? Give me a call. Please?"

"Oh! Bugger." He'd forgotten.

He put two slices of bread into the toaster.

"Beeeeep. This is Chelsea Roofing Contractors," said an East London accent, with more than a hint of the cowboy about it. "We're returning your call abaht your roof what wants fixin'. We'll call back liter."

Guy chuckled to himself, and then frowned when he remembered why it had been necessary to make the call in the first place. His house, though pleasingly proportioned and in a desirable street, had a roof that was the Welsh slate equivalent of a string vest. Two pictures and an Indian rug had been the price of the last downpour. He gulped down the fizzy medication in the glass, grimacing at the bitter taste.

"Beeeeep" . . . There were several messages related to his programme, an enquiry as to the whereabouts of his column for the *Herald* and then a message that made him pause as he was jamming two slices of bread into the toaster.

"Mr D'Arcy," exclaimed a somewhat inebriated man's voice with flat Yorkshire vowels and the merest hint of sibilance, "it is a truth universally acknowledged that a single man in possession of a television programme must be in want of some information. I wonder if I might have a word with you?"

Good God! thought Guy. What the hell does he want?

"I'm sorry to bother you on this fine evening when you're probably getting ready to go out on the toot, but there are a few things I'd like to talk over that might be to your advantage. Cheerie-bye."

"That was your last message," said the unfeeling female voice of the answering-machine, as it clicked and whirred back to the beginning.

Guy caught the toast as it flipped up. He spread it with butter and a thick coating of Gentlemen's Relish before flopping down in a wheel-back chair at the side of the Aga and wondering what on earth a sozzled Bertie Lightfoot could have been warbling on about.

The brass doorknob clinked as Jock entered the old white-painted greenhouse at Wharfeside Nursery. He looked down at it and grunted. The ferrule needed a new screw. He went out, closed the door behind him and walked across to the potting-shed.

All his life he had been like this. Madge had teased him about it, but Jock had always said that if a job didn't get done the moment it needed doing it wouldn't get done at all. He pulled out a hefty green drawer from beneath the potting-bench and rummaged about until he found an old screwdriver. The screws were in an ancient tobacco tin. He took two – one to lose and one to use – and went back to the greenhouse, past the neat rows of tethered trees and pot-grown shrubs sparkling with ice on what was turning into a bright February morning. Frost patterned the glass on the old cold frame outside the greenhouse and Jock stood for a moment taking in the view.

He hardly heard the river nowadays for its comforting sound had been with him, day and night, for the better part of his life. This morning, below the frosted banks, the amber water glittered as it flowed past. A blackbird sang loudly from a naked sycamore, whose silver-grey trunk leaned out over the water. The moors that rose up as a backdrop to the scene seemed sprinkled with icing sugar.

Jock breathed in deeply and the cold air stung his nostrils. For the first time in months he felt glad to be alive. It was a novel sensation. He looked round at the trim nursery. To many folk it was a dead time of year, nothing moved, nothing grew, few things were in flower, but Jock saw the promise of things to come in the primroses, snowdrops and hellebores, and the wintersweet, which decorated the old brick wall alongside the lean-to greenhouse with its waxy pale yellow bells, which, when you looked up into them, showed themselves to be stained with blood.

He was not, as a rule, given to flights of fancy, but he remembered a poem that Madge used to quote on days like this at this time of year:

Gardener, if you listen, listen well:
Plant for your winter pleasure, when the months
Dishearten; plant to find a fragile note
Touched from the brittle violin of frost.

He loved the last line in particular.

"Morning, Dad!" Jock snapped out of his reverie at the sound of his son's greeting and turned to see Rob walking up the nursery path towards the greenhouse.

"Morning, son! All right?"

"Fine. And yourself?"

"Well, you know, I'm all right."

Rob smiled at him, relieved at his relatively light-hearted response. The blackbird darted from the sycamore branch, shrieking its alarm call and burying itself in the bushes. "Thought I'd just call in to see how you were – after last night and all. What are you up to?"

"Fixing the door. A screw loose. Good as new now, though. And there's no need to worry about me. I'm fine."

"No Harry? No – whatsisname . . . Wayne?"

"It's Saturday. Harry'll be in the Legion by lunch-time and Wayne's doing his gardening job. He'll be here by eleven. I've told him I probably won't be rushed off my feet this morning so he's planting a tree for his old lady. Mind you, he'll have a job getting through this frost."

"Yes, it's a hard one, isn't it?"

"So what are you doing with yourself?" enquired Jock of the son who didn't usually spend his Saturdays at his father's nursery.

"Oh, I said I'd varnish Katherine's floor for her."

"On a day like this?" Jock raised his eyes to the sky, which was now a clear forget-me-not blue.

"Yes, shame, isn't it? I just thought I'd call in and see what you'd got planned."

"Oh, the usual. A spot of watering in the greenhouses, a bit of leaf-picking, and I thought I'd spend the next couple of hours sowing a few tender perennials in the propagator, if too many folk don't come and distract me."

There was a twinkle in his eye as he said it, but Rob knew that his father was happiest in his own company, and that of his plants. Not that his customers would ever guess.

"You know, there are times, Dad, when I think you'd rather you didn't have any customers."

"Oh, I don't know. One of them's just sent me some rose-bushes. Or, rather, his widow has."

"What do you mean?"

"Old Professor Wilberforce from over the moor. Keen rosarian. Dabbled a bit in breeding. You remember him – he worked at that research station the other side of Leeds – gave you a fiver once for rooting some rose cuttings for him. Good at the science but not so hot at the practical gardening."

"Nice chap," Rob remarked. "Roman nose and bald dome of a head."

"That's the one. His missus came round here yesterday with these bushes in a sack, pruned to within an inch of their lives and said that the Professor would have liked me to have them. I think she just wanted an excuse for a natter. I suppose I'd better try to break the ground and heel them in."

Jock's nursery was something of a rarity in an age of massive garden centres with five-acre car parks and lines of school-leavers at the check-outs. The takings went first into his dark blue apron pocket, then into an old wooden drawer. He ran the nursery more or less single-handed (you couldn't really count Harry now as part of any labour force, and Wayne was a newcomer) but somehow he eked out a living by selling unusual plants as well as his bread-and-butter lines. The customers who came here were assured of sound advice and well-grown plants that were not overpriced. Jock had little time for Dennis Wragg's Crystal Palace half a mile away where the girls on the tills knew as much about plants, he said, as he knew about the top ten, and where the rule of sales seemed to be that if you slapped something into a larger pot you could add a nought to the price.

"Cup of coffee?" Rob asked.

Jock glanced at his watch. "Aye, there's just time before I open the gate to the masses. Come on then, look sharp!" He turned and walked towards the potting-shed, his son following.

Over coffee and a digestive biscuit or two, they chewed the fat about this and that – the state of the nursery, the promise shown by young Wayne.

"You like him, don't you?" said Rob.

"I suppose I do. It takes a bit of determination to drag yourself out

38

of the kind of place he's grown up in and come and ask for a job. I bet his mates take the mickey out of him."

"Oh, I know what it feels like. I remember when I decided to do it myself," said Rob, gazing at the mound of compost on the wooden bench then out through the cobwebby windows. "I took some stick from the lads at school. Whenever any of them walked past the nursery I used to head for the greenhouse so they couldn't see me."

"I know," said Jock.

"You noticed?"

"I was beginning to wonder what you were growing in there until I rumbled you. I felt a bit sorry for you, really."

"Oh, I got over it," said Rob. "Once they realized that there was a career to be had in gardening and that I wasn't destined to spend the rest of my life weeding they accepted it. But I did have to call it horticulture and not gardening, to give myself a bit of respectability."

"And look at you now," said Jock.

"Yes, look at me," said Rob, draining his cup. "I'd better be off or that floor won't get varnished."

"How's Katherine?" asked Jock.

"OK. She's meeting her boss today. No time for a gardener's boy. High-powered discussions and all that. I'll see her tomorrow when she's back down to earth."

Jock detected a faint note of discontent in Rob's voice but chose to ignore it. "Well, remember me to her."

"I will." He turned for the door. "See you soon."

From the potting-shed doorway Jock watched his son go down the path to the old wrought-iron gate where he flipped the 'Closed' sign to 'Open' on the green notice-board, waved, turned and was gone. Jock walked back to the bench, pulled out the drawer and dropped the spare brass screw into the tobacco tin. He gathered up a fistful of seed packets and headed, once more, for the greenhouse.

It was six o'clock by the time Rob made it back to his own place. He had never moved in with Katherine, they had both felt it important to hang on to their independence. He lived at End Cottage – the last dwelling that qualified as being in Nesfield, up at the top end of the valley. It had cost him next to nothing a couple of years ago, but then it had been little more than a shell, unlived-in for ten years or more.

He never imagined that he'd be able either to find or afford a house by the river, so when the dilapidated two-up and two-down had come on the market he was first on the phone and there with his deposit before the yuppie estate agent could say negative equity. Rob had spent all his spare time doing the place up. He'd always been good with his hands and enjoyed turning this one-time farmhand's cottage into a home.

He'd converted the outside privy into a bathroom, and done up the rest of the house to make the most of what little space there was. A tiny conservatory, more of a porch, really, was tacked on to the back and when the sun streamed in through the sash windows the place came alive. Rob loved it, which was another reason for not moving into Katherine's flat.

Outside, there was an old stone path and the riverbank. He had only a tiny garden, bounded by a low stone wall and surrounded by field, and though, at first, this had seemed a disadvantage, Rob had grown used to having the riverbank instead of a herbaceous border. It was scarcely less colourful: in spring it erupted first with orange coltsfoot and the weird pink drumheads of butterbur, then came cow parsley and red campion and bright yellow buttercups. The garden itself was just big enough to allow him to keep his hand in and try new plants. It was all he could want.

Rob let himself in by the door that went straight into the kitchen and dumped his car keys on the table alongside the *Daily Post*. He flipped through it to check his column. He'd been poached from the *Nesfield Gazette* a year ago now. He'd worried at first that Katherine would be miffed at his departure. Instead, she'd been genuinely delighted for him, making the move from a local to a national paper. "Don't be stupid!" she'd said. "It's what every hack wants."

"But I'm not a hack!" he'd replied.

"Oh, yes, you are, a horticultural hack. The subject may be rustic and rural but you're a hack just the same."

She'd taken him out to dinner that night, and he'd always thought she must have been more disappointed than she let on.

Page forty-two. They always put gardening fairly near the back, and there was no guaranteeing that your copy would not be cut to bits. If advertisements came in it had to be reduced. If there was a big story, it would be squeezed. This week it had survived almost intact. A large piece on winter-flowering shrubs, a smaller panel on a garden famous for its snowdrops, and a list of topical tips. It was a difficult time of year. Three weeks of snowfall and the gardening public would forget their plants to slump in front of the TV. You couldn't blame them, but it did exercise a gardening writer's ingenuity.

Rob folded up the paper and went to put the kettle on. Then the phone rang. He picked it up.

"Hello, is that Rob MacGregor?"

"Yes."

"Hi! This is Lisa Drake."

For a moment Rob couldn't think what to say. He felt himself flush.

"Er . . . hello! How – how are you?" He managed to get the words out without too much of a stammer.

"I'm fine. I just wondered if you fancied a drink tonight. It seems stupid that we both work for the same TV station and that we've only just met. I thought it was about time we put things right. Are you free?"

All manner of thoughts flew across Rob's mind: Lisa Drake's reputation; how she got hold of his number; the fact that what she said was absolutely right – it was ridiculous that they had only just met; the fact that he found her more than slightly attractive; and the fact that she undoubtedly fancied him. Then there was his loyalty to Katherine, and the fact that Katherine was out all evening, but most of all there was the fact that Lisa Drake had caught him off his guard.

"Yes, I'm free and I'd love to come for a drink."

"Great. Look, why don't we make it supper? There's a new restaurant opened in Myddleton and I've been promised a free meal on the strength of a news item I did. Why don't I ring them and book a table for two and you could pick me up at eightish? It should be fun."

There was little Rob could say except, "Fine."

She gave him the address – a flat in a smart Edwardian block in Harrogate – and said, "Ciao," before she put the phone down.

"Ciao," muttered Rob under his breath, as he replaced the receiver. He felt strangely unnerved as he unscrewed the cap from the whisky bottle, poured himself a tot and threw it back in one. "Ciao," he repeated as he walked, trance-like, upstairs to his bedroom.

He took more than his usual care in getting ready over the next hour and a half. Bathing, shaving, deciding what to wear. This is ridiculous! he thought, as he towelled dry his hair and tried to make up his mind whether he should go for navy-blue trousers or chinos. He chose the chinos, a pair of Timberland shoes, and a white T-shirt underneath a blue linen shirt. He looked at his watch – a quarter to eight. "Oh, shit!" He grabbed his wallet, car keys and duffel-coat, glanced in the mirror as he left and locked the door of End Cottage behind him.

She'd been waiting on the pavement stamping her feet to keep warm when he'd drawn up outside the grand Edwardian pile. She said she'd thought she'd better come down and keep a look-out just in case he couldn't find it. He'd confessed that he wasn't too familiar with Harrogate, except for the Valley Gardens, the green common known as The Stray, and Betty's Café, where his mother had taken him for toasted teacakes when he was a child.

She didn't seem to mind having been kept waiting, and Rob felt his stomach lurch as she got into the car beside him, and he took in the waft of Chanel as she pecked him on the cheek. Don't blush, don't blush, he thought. With his colouring it had always been a problem.

The conversation in the car was polite – studio and weather-orientated – and she'd broken off every now and again to offer directions he didn't need – the restaurant was in the next village to Nesfield – but which he was too polite to mention.

She was wearing dark brown trousers and a coffee-coloured jacket with a figure-hugging Lycra top under it. Her blonde hair shone and her skin seemed to be a soft shade of peach.

When they arrived at the restaurant they were seated at a table in the far corner where they had a good view of everyone else, and where everyone else had a good view of them. The restaurant had clearly become popular quickly: there was hardly a table spare. The white damask-covered tables were barely visible among the bodies. The branded ends of wine cases decorated the bare brick walls and candles flickered from bottles on the tables and black iron sconces on the walls. Rafters was really an old Victorian conservatory, sandwiched between high Victorian houses, that had once been a flower shop.

"I thought it was particularly appropriate that I came here with you," she said.

Rob said that he remembered what it had been like when it was still a flower shop. "In those days it smelled of mimosa and Longiflorum lilies, and great galvanized buckets were dotted around this damp stone floor and stuffed with cherry blossom and forsythia. I remember the scent of the freesias that I used to come and buy for my mum and she said how nice it was to have flowers that hadn't been grown at home. It made them more special."

"It's all a bit different now," said Lisa, looking around.

"Yes. I don't suppose they sell nicotine shreds any more."

"Nicotine what?"

"Shreds. Bits of shredded cardboard soaked in nicotine. We'd set fire to little piles of them in the greenhouses and the fumes would kill off greenfly and whitefly. We used to buy them in tins and we had to sign a poison book before we were allowed to take them away. The bar over there was once the shop counter with a wooden till that pinged when it was opened."

"You're a great story-teller, you know," she said, gazing at him across the table with her head resting on her hands.

He looked across at her and felt himself colouring again. "Oh, I don't know, it's just memories," he said, taking a sip of wine.

"Yes, but they're lovely memories. Tell me more about this place – the way it was before."

They dined on ciabatta and sun-dried tomatoes, sea bass and fresh vegetables, and drank a bottle of Chablis that Lisa said she particularly liked. She dropped questions into the conversation, about Rob's childhood, why he had followed his father into gardening, and as he answered she appeared to hang on his every word. Rob was enjoying himself. His audience was attractive and he was flattered by her rapt attention. Lisa continued to play him gently, like a speckled trout on the end of a line. She was, after all, a professional.

The waiter cleared away their sorbet glasses and asked if they wanted coffee. Before Rob had time to say anything Lisa had already shaken her head and dismissed the young man.

"I thought we could go back to my place for coffee. OK?"

"Fine. Lovely." He felt so stupid. What else could he say? The waiter brought Rob's coat, indicated that there was nothing to pay, said he hoped that they'd enjoyed their meal and that they'd come back again.

As they walked towards the door, just a few tables away Rob caught sight of the back of a familiar head. Its hair was dark and held back with an ebony skewer. Seated across the table from it was a tall, handsome man with a tanned complexion and a grey pin-striped suit. The fork, raised in one brown hand, stabbed the air. The other brown hand was clamped on that of his dining companion and his eyes gazed deeply into hers. He was holding forth in a loud voice about the importance of circulation, and he was not a doctor.

Chapter 4

"Are you all right?" asked Lisa, as they got to the car.

"Yes, fine," said Rob, fumbling to get the key in the passenger door. He let her in, shut the door and walked round the car, breathing deeply.

She leaned over and pulled the inside handle to let him in. "You look as though you've seen a ghost," she said.

"Do I?" Rob slid into the driving seat and tried to pull himself together. A dozen thoughts ran through his head. Had Katherine seen him? Why was her boss young and handsome rather than old and fat, the way she had described him? She *had* described him like that, hadn't she? Rob had certainly pictured him pasty and plump, not tanned and trim. And where was his wife? Katherine had said she was dining with her boss and his wife. Had she lied to him? Was there more to this relationship than just business? His mind reeled.

"Do you want me to drive?" asked Lisa.

"Sorry?" Rob's mind was elsewhere.

"Do you want me to drive?"

"No . . . No, I'm fine, sorry. Just felt a bit strange. All right now. Home?"

"If you're sure."

"Yes. Yes, I'm sure. A cup of coffee would be great." Rob started up the car, shot a reassuring smile across at her, then leaned over and deliberately kissed her cheek. She smiled back at him and settled down for the short journey to Harrogate.

The atmosphere in Rafters was getting smokier by the minute and

Katherine's eyes were beginning to water. She sipped at the still mineral water the waiter had just poured over a mountain of ice and a slice of lemon in the thick-bottomed glass, and surreptitiously sniffed at the sleeve of her jacket. It stank of tobacco. Charles Wormald, her boss, was half-way down the fat cigar he had ordered with his brandy, and more than half-way up her arm with his sun-tanned hand.

His wife, he said, had not felt too well after her visit to Lord and Lady Myddleton and had gone back to their hotel for a lie-down.

It had not come as a surprise to Katherine. The evening had degenerated into the usual run of sexist innuendo for which Charlie Wormald was well known among the women he employed. "Wormy" had no time for male editors in his thriving stable of regional papers. He liked sparky women who would look good across the dinner table from him on occasions like this, but experience had taught him that the women who had the backbone to produce the best newspapers would seldom allow him even a glimpse of their vertebrae. So it was with Katherine.

She found the dinner ritual tedious, but although she was an idealist she had an equally strong streak of realism. If being nice to Wormy two or three times a year over the dinner table was all it took to keep him happy, then who was she to throw in the napkin?

As he rattled on about her talents and the great job she was doing with the *Nesfield Gazette*, she smiled absent-mindedly, looked out of the window into the dark night and wondered what Rob would be doing now.

The journey back to Harrogate had been silent but highly charged. Lisa could hardly take her eyes off the broad-shouldered man next to her. They wandered from the dark brown curls at the back of his neck and the muscles pulsating in his cheek, to his strong legs and the gentle-looking, fine-boned hands that gripped the wheel of the little car.

Rob agonized over Katherine's apparent lack of loyalty and Lisa's evident sensuality.

Lisa Drake's apartment block was everything that Katherine's Victorian flat above the baker's was not. It had a wide pavement outside, beside which Lisa suggested Rob leave his car. As he was locking the door, distractedly, he saw her looking at the rust-spotted Fiesta with a gentle smile.

"Go on, say it. It's not what you'd have expected."

"Well, no. I don't suppose it is," she replied.

"What *would* you have expected then?"

"Oh, a Range Rover, or a Discovery at the very least."

"Oh, please!" said Rob. "Credit me with some taste. It would be a battered Land Rover or nothing, not one of those posey Harrogate-housewife jobs."

"Yes, you're not pretentious. That's what's so nice about you."

Rob was losing count of the number of times she'd made him blush.

"Come here, Mr MacGregor. My turn now." She planted a soft kiss on his cheek, put her arm through his and walked him towards the glistening plate-glass doors of Richmond House. As they mounted the final polished marble step, she produced a swipe card from her pocket and deftly passed it through the steel jaws mounted on the wall. They entered a large marble-floored atrium, dotted with weeping figs and modern art. The soft peach walls were lit with brass up-lighters and a uniformed security man sat behind a light oak counter, listening to a radio with the volume set low.

He stood up as they walked in. "Good evening, Miss Drake, sir." He nodded at Rob and recognition flashed across his face as they walked over to the open lift. The doors closed behind them and Lisa pressed the top button, marked 4.

"Go on, say it," she said, turning towards him and smiling again.

"Say what?" he asked.

"That it's all a bit grand."

"Well, it is. But this is exactly what I would have expected."

"Yes, but it's also secure and it's private. George down there is the soul of discretion, and he and his mates have eyes like hawks. I don't have to live in fear of burglars or stalkers – well, not as much as I would if I lived anywhere else."

Rob's mind swam. Why was he here? What would Katherine think? But her mind was clearly on other things. She should have been out with him, not the tanned tycoon. And he was here with Lisa Drake who was . . . well . . . gorgeous. And fascinating. Lame word. But she was. And she had asked him back for coffee. He liked her. She listened. She liked him. The lift stopped and the doors slid open. They walked out on to a wide landing with cream carpet, more peach walls and brass up-lighters, and Lisa fished a bunch of keys out of her handbag, slipping the largest into the brass lock on the door opposite.

As they walked into her apartment the faint scent of Chanel that Rob had noticed earlier seemed stronger. She dropped the keys on a small glass-topped table inside the door, where they landed with a clank, and flipped a couple of switches. Several table lamps came on and Rob saw in front of him a stylish but sparsely furnished apartment in pale primrose yellow with two blue sofas facing each other across a low oak table. A massive oak chest was pushed against one wall and a folding screen stood in a corner. There was a carved mirror over the chest and three or four enormous black-and-white photographs on the other walls – views of mountains and rivers and towering trees.

"Coffee? Or a proper drink?" asked Lisa, slipping off her jacket, dropping it on to the sofa and walking towards him.

"Um. What are you having?" asked Rob.

"Oh, I don't know that I feel like anything . . . to drink," she said, looking up at him. Suddenly she seemed so still, so quiet and so much smaller than she had before. Rob's heart beat faster and, with unanswered questions echoing inside his head, he found his arms around her and his lips on hers. She was so soft, so sweet, so tender.

She drew away from him a little, and looking all the while into his eyes, she took his hand and led him towards another door, to one side of the folding screen. Opening it with one hand, she softly pulled him into the shadowy bedroom.

Without saying a word, she picked up a box of matches and lit half a dozen candles set in brass candlesticks on top of the chest of drawers. Then she came back to his arms and raised her lips once more to his, at the same time undoing the buttons on his pale blue shirt.

His hands stroked her shoulders and her arms, then slid the Lycra top down to her waist, revealing her perfectly formed breasts. By the time they had slipped naked under the duvet and wound around one another like the ivy embroidered on its cover, his doubts and worries had slipped away and he was lost in the warm and fragrant passion of Lisa Drake.

It was midnight by the time Katherine had extricated herself from the clutches of Charlie Wormald. She could still feel his clumsy kiss and smell the fetid mixture of Havana cigars and Issey Miyake aftershave that would take ages to evaporate from her jacket.

She drove back to Wellington Heights determined to shower away the unwanted aromas of the evening and to dump her clothes into a bin liner until they could be cleaned on Monday.

Her hair fresh washed and her face scrubbed clean of any trace of the lingering aftershave, she pulled the fluffy white towel around her and looked at the clock, which said that it was a quarter to one. It was late. Never mind. She would ring him and wake him. Her varnished floor shone like a conker and she wanted to tell him how pleased she was and to thank him for the bar stepping-stone patches he had left for her to get into bed. She dialled his number. It rang for ages but he didn't answer.

Chapter 5

Sunday morning in Bertie Lightfoot's cottage at Myddleton-in-Wharfedale was always the same: while Bertie walked the King Charles's, Alhambra and Palladium (or Ally and Pally for short), Terry would prepare breakfast of devilled kidneys and kedgeree. Bertie was the gardener; Terry was the cook. Well, chef, really. Terry Bean ran a little restaurant in the town based on traditional English cooking of the Michael Smith school. Plates were presented on brass chargers, glass was Old English, napkins were double damask, pies came with paper frills and, as Bertie would say of Terry's efforts when it came to poultry and game, "Every orifice is stuffed."

The two had met when Terry became Bertie's dresser in variety at Stockport. They'd lived together for nearly twenty years now, and seemed to complement one another perfectly in the garden and the kitchen: when Bertie grew it, Terry cooked it. Their dinner parties were the talk of the village, and no one had any problem in reconciling Bertie's on-screen image with the off-screen reality.

Bertie's everyday attire bore little resemblance to his 'costume'. He favoured pastel-coloured cashmere sweaters, pale slacks and soft Italian shoes, but always with a silk handkerchief around his neck – a nod in the direction of his rustic on-screen trademark, the red spotted kerchief. Outdoors, on the edge of the moor with Ally and Pally yapping at his heels, he wore a tweed trilby and a long sheepskin coat, and on this particular Sunday morning he had worked up quite a sweat in the wintry sun, trying to drag Pally backwards out of a rabbit hole and preventing Ally from feasting on sheep muck.

Finally he hauled them back down the moorland lane, only to have

Pally start to gnaw her lead and Ally decide that she would prefer to travel on her bottom, just as the vicar's wife came round the corner from church. "Morning, Mrs Cunnington!" said Bertie, raising his hat and pulling the two dogs along with difficulty. "Lovely day for a walk." The woman crossed the lane, her face now set in a rictus grin.

"It's worming tablets for you, my girl." Mrs Cunnington darted a glance over her shoulder to check that he was no longer addressing her.

Bertie opened his garden gate and walked down the gravel path to the front door of the long low stone cottage. Just as he was wiping his boots on the scraper by the stone-roofed porch, the door opened and Terry, in a crisp, white shirt, canary yellow V-necked sweater and William Morris floral apron, opened the door.

"You're back. It's just as well – the kidneys have been to the devil and back and there's Pride and Prejudice on the phone for you."

"Who?" asked Bertie.

"D'Arcy. Says you rang him yesterday. You didn't tell me." Terry looked a bit peeved, his toupee a touch lopsided.

"You were in bed with one of your heads," said Bertie, slipping the two dogs off their leads. They bolted between Terry's legs, knocking him momentarily off-balance but straightening his toupee.

"That's better," said Bertie, tapping him fondly on the head with the palm of his hand. "I can't be doing with rugs that aren't straight." At the same time he used his toe to square up the doormat that the dogs had sent skidding across the parquet. He smiled sweetly at Terry and went into the tiny study by the front door. There, among the black-and-white photographs of past theatrical triumphs, he picked up the phone.

"Mr D'Arcy?"

Guy had not had a good Saturday evening. His features editor had played hell with him for being late with his copy and seemed hardly impressed with Guy's witty title for the piece on choosing the best varieties of witch hazel. "Which Hazel?" was, he said, hardly Booker Prize material. And he'd had to take a different sort of witch out to supper.

Sophie, the Sloane Ranger who had left the message on his answering-machine, was as horsy as Harvey Smith and not all that different in appearance. She had a pair of thighs, thought Guy, each of which could feed a Third World country for a week. But he needed to get on the right side of her father, who wanted his garden in Gloucestershire completely redesigning. It was Guy or royal favourite Edward Siggs-Baddeley, already rumoured to be lined up for redevelopments at one of the palaces, and Guy viewed the prospect of a commission on that scale with a watering mouth. He'd stop at nothing short of an engagement to clinch this deal.

He'd managed to drop her off at her Hampstead home by half past eleven and get home to Fulham for what he considered was a well-earned rest. In the morning he woke bright-eyed and raring for a little sport. He would ring Bertie Lightfoot and find out just what was to his advantage.

"Bertie, you old soak, how are you?"

It was not a response guaranteed to get on the right side of Bertie, who was beginning to be irritated that folk were remarking on his predilection for bottles from north of the border.

"Guy D'Arcy, you are a wicked boy and you don't deserve any friends."

"I haven't got any," quipped Guy. "What's all this about information that could be to my advantage?"

"Oh, wouldn't you just like to know?" replied the Yorkshire voice.

"Well, yes, I would rather. Come on, Bertie, dish the dirt."

"I just happened to be having a drink the other day with Sir Freddie Roper who, as you might know, is chairman of the board of a well-known chemical company."

"Oh, yes, shooting pal of Pa's," said Guy.

"Oh, I thought he'd be a bit down-market for your father, being a working-class boy made good," rejoined Bertie, tartly.

"Now don't be unkind, Bertie. I'm a working-class boy myself nowadays. What were you talking to Freddie about?"

"Does the name BLITZ mean anything to you?"

"No, I don't think so. Other than the war and some old musical by Lionel Bart. Should it?"

"It soon will. Sir Freddie's company are promoting it as what they call 'a revolutionary new product'. It's some special pesticide, guaranteed to kill off loads of bad things and leave loads of good things unharmed."

"Oh, you mean ghastly to greenfly and lovely to ladybirds?" teased Guy.

"Something like that, except that it also bumps off whitefly, scale insects and all sorts of creepy crawlies that other pesticides don't."

"But you *can* kill whitefly and scale insects with other pesticides," said Guy, dredging up the knowledge he'd acquired from reading the right magazines.

"Yes; but they come back after a week or two. BLITZ is supposed to finish them off for the whole season."

"Sounds lethal," said Guy.

"Ah, but that's the thing. It isn't. It's as near to being organic as you can get – kind to hands, bees, butterflies and flowers, just lousy to lice."

"And why are you telling me all this?" There was a note of distrust in Guy's voice.

"Because Sir Freddie told me that they'll be looking for someone to spearhead their advertising campaign. Someone well known with a bit of gardening street cred."

"And you thought of me?"

"To tell you the truth, I thought of Rob MacGregor. You might be well known, Mr D'Arcy, but your street cred isn't quite up to his. But, then again, I thought you might appreciate it more than he would."

"And why not you, Bertie?" asked Guy, well aware of Bertie's growing antipathy towards his young usurper.

"Don't be daft," said Bertie. "I might be old but I've not lost me marbles. I know I went to school with old Freddie Roper but I'm not the sort of image they want. They want a macho male who's young and thrusting. I might thrust every now and again, but the years aren't on my side. And neither is Terry at the moment," he added, as an afterthought.

"Sorry?"

Terry walked past the study door, carrying a silver salver with a domed lid, from under which a wisp of steam gently seeped, redolent of devilled kidneys. He looked sideways, and rather sourly, at Bertie then mouthed "BREAKFAST", in large, silent letters.

"Just a witty aside. You wouldn't understand."

"So what am I supposed to do with this knowledge?" asked Guy.

"Use it to your advantage," said Bertie. "Just make sure you're in the right place at the right time. There's a press conference next week to do the usual yearly PR bit for Amalgamated Agricultural Chemicals."

"Yes, I know. Deadly boring those dos. I never go to them."

"Well, if you've any sense you'll go to this one, and you'll pay attention, too, unless you want someone else to carry off the glittering prize. With careful negotiation you could be talking about a six-figure sum here – TV advertising and all."

Guy whistled. "Right," he said, suddenly serious, the cogs in his brain almost audible. "I'll be there."

"Just don't forget that when that one great scorer comes, in the shape of your accountant, it was old Bertie who put you right."

"Oh, I won't forget. Love to the old Bean, and I'll see you at the AAC do. In the meantime, take care of yourself," said Guy absently.

"Oh, I will," said Bertie. "Ta-ta." He put the handset back in the cradle and set off towards the aroma of the offal.

The fragrance that drifted into Rob's sensibilities on this Sunday morning was of a gentler nature. He came round slowly, conscious of soft, warm skin next to his and a delicate perfume that brought back in detail the events of the night before. He drifted on this heavenly cloud for a while before other thoughts trickled into his mind.

Lisa Drake's warm breath wafted across his chest where her head lay, her tousled fair hair falling across her face. His arm rested across her naked shoulders and his eyes gradually took in the green and white canopy, the collection of guttered candles on the painted chest of drawers and the shafts of silvery light that darted beneath the linen blind at the window.

She felt warm and perfectly comfortable. So did he, at first, but then his conscience pricked and hollow feelings of guilt and discomfort made him turn to one side.

She stirred, murmured softly and put her arms around him, drawing herself up close behind him.

"Hello," she whispered sleepily, running her finger up his spine and twisting the hair at the back of his head around it.

"Morning," he replied, his eyes focused in the middle distance.

"Coffee?" she asked.

"Mmm," he said.

"Black or white?"

"Sorry?"

"Your coffee. Black or white?"

"Oh, black, please." He came to and turned to see her slipping out of the ivy-covered bed. Her body was even more perfect unclothed, honey-coloured all over, finely toned and slender. She moved noiselessly across the room and took down a cream silk robe from the back of the door, fastening it around her in one circular movement.

She came back to the bed and bent forward to kiss his lips. Again his nostrils caught the warmth and fragrance that made his stomach flutter. Again he couldn't quite believe where he was. His eyes darted down the front of her loosely fastened robe and something inside him stirred again.

She turned and was gone, leaving him alone with his thoughts. Why had he come here? Because he'd felt let down by Katherine. Was that all? Or was he trying to prove to Katherine that he didn't need her? And had Lisa really fallen for him or was she just out to amuse herself? It hadn't seemed that way last night. What did he feel about her? Where was Katherine now?

He buzzed alternately with anger, pain, profound pleasure, confusion, lust – but, above all, guilt.

His soul-searching was interrupted by the door opening and the return of Lisa with a tray loaded with coffee and warm croissants.

She slid it on to the side of the bed, untied the robe and let it fall to the floor before she slipped under the duvet and nestled alongside him.

"How soon do you have to go?" she asked.

"Soon," he said, remembering Katherine's promise of a day out in the Dales and lunch at their favourite pub. "I have some writing to do," he lied, hearing his words echo hollowly in the room.

"Well, don't go just yet." She kissed his shoulders and neck, then his mouth, and ran her hand down his body until she found what she was looking for. She stroked him softly until once more he gave himself to her, then lay peacefully in her arms.

Eventually he slid out of bed, scooped up the crumpled heap of his clothes and made his way to the bathroom. He washed, dressed and returned to the bedroom, unshaven, to kiss her goodbye.

"Don't be gone too long," murmured Lisa, as he drew away from her. "We must do this again."

He smiled as brave a smile as he could manage, took a sip of the now cold coffee, and backed towards the bedroom door.

From the window she watched as he left the luxurious apartment block that had, for an evening, ensnared him in gossamer.

Chapter 6

By the time Rob reached End Cottage it had begun to rain. The skies were leaden grey; rivulets of muddy water ran from the side of the road and down the riverbank. The dull purple moors were almost invisible, shrouded in a veil of thick, wet mist, and the tall, naked branches of the riverside alders and willows flailed about the cottage, tossed by an increasingly brutal wind. The weather matched his mood. His feelings of the night before had refined themselves now. The elation seemed far away, only the confusion and guilt remained. And Katherine. What could he say to Katherine? And what would Katherine say to him?

He did not have to wait long to find out. As he slid the key into the lock of the green front door he heard the phone ringing. He glanced at the kitchen clock. It was a quarter to ten.

"Hello?"

"It's me."

"Hi, how are you?" he asked, trying to sound natural.

"I'm fine. How are you?"

"Fine." He felt the heat rising within his cheeks. The last time he had blushed it had been out of embarrassment; now it was generated by fear.

"Where've you been?" asked Katherine's voice, with a hint of hurt behind irritation.

"Oh, just out for a paper." A lame reply – he hoped it would be good enough.

"But last night? I rang you when I got back. I know it was late but you didn't answer. It rang and rang and rang. Were you asleep?"

"Must have been," muttered Rob. His blood was reaching what felt like boiling point. His forehead had broken out in a sweat. He struggled to take off his jacket and also to change the subject. "How's the floor?"

Katherine softened. In the mixture of worry and annoyance at his apparent absence she had forgotten about it. "It's lovely. And thank you for the note."

"The note? Oh . . ." He remembered with a little relief. He'd left it propped up against the tin of varnish with a clean paintbrush: "Please paint over the stepping stones in the morning when you get out of bed, working backwards towards the door. Then your floor will sparkle like your eyes. Love you, R x.'

He began to cool down. At least he knew now that she hadn't seen him at the restaurant. Hadn't seen him leave with Lisa Drake.

"And how about you?" he asked, chancing his arm. "How was your evening?"

"Oh, pretty deadly," she said. "My boss was as charming as ever. A real chauvinistic pain in the arse."

"And his wife?" he went on, trying hard to sound casual. "How was she?" He waited with a mixture of pain and pleasure for the expected lie.

"She didn't come. She was ill. At least, that's what he said. Though I don't believe him for one minute."

A sense of rising panic gripped him. Now he felt a chill breeze sweep across his skin.

There was only one question left to ask. "What does your boss look like? I've always had this image of him being fat and pink."

"Charlie Wormald? Oh, no. Tanned and trim. A martyr to his bullworker and a real ladykiller, he thinks. But his aftershave is too strong, his technique is far too obvious and he's about as sexy as a pot-bellied pig. It took me an hour just to get the smell of him out of my hair."

There was silence at the other end of the phone. Had a Dulux colour chart been to hand, Rob would have noticed that his face was 'white with a hint of lemon'.

"Are you all right?" she asked. She was the second person to ask him that in the space of twelve hours. He was far from "all right". He was all wrong. Entirely wrong. Katherine had done exactly what she had said she would do. She was as honest as the day was long. He, in a fit of misplaced jealousy, had blown it. And she didn't suspect a thing. It should have come as a relief that she didn't know. Instead, it made his guilt harder to bear.

"Anyway, why are you so interested in Charlie Wormald all of a sudden? You've never bothered about him before."

He floundered. "Oh, just curious. I had this mental picture of him being old and fat and unattractive and . . ." His words petered out. He wished that the earth would swallow him up. It didn't.

"So when are you coming round?" she asked.

"Er . . . I'm not sure." Confusion verging on panic. He needed time to sort himself out.

"What do you mean?"

"Well, the weather's so foul it's going to be miserable up the Dales. There'll be no chance of sitting outside at Grassington in this." Clutching at straws. "Have you seen the rain? It's coming down like stair-rods. I thought I'd knuckle down and get some writing done. Do you mind?"

A long pause. "No – no, fine. If you want to write then you write." She sounded angry, but he could hear bewilderment, disappointment too. Bad weather had never put them off before. They'd often sat in the car while the rain lashed down, eating doorstep cheese and tomato sandwiches and watching sodden sheep turn their backs to the rain-laden moorland wind as the windows steamed up.

Normally Katherine would have bullied him into it, but a note in his voice told her not to. She knew that something was wrong and yet for the first time she didn't want to ask what it was.

"Give me a ring later," she said, trying to sound as if she didn't mind.

"OK." There was an uncomfortable pause. "Er . . . sorry," he said.

"And me," she said softly.

She put the phone down and curled her legs up underneath her in the large armchair. As she gazed at her shining floor, the tears began to roll down her cheeks.

Jock MacGregor had been at Wharfeside Nursery since half past seven, even though it was Sunday. He didn't open on a Sunday: his Calvinistic Scottish upbringing would never allow him to consider Sunday trading, but plants needed watering and nurturing every day of the week, and while he could not allow himself to make money directly on the Lord's Day he had no compunction about tending his charges.

Through the potting-shed window, over the steam rising from his mug of tea, he could see storm-tossed branches and hear the wind whistling even louder. Twigs were snapping off and being hurled down among the plants below.

He took his coat from a hook at the back of the door, pulled it on and walked out, hanging on to his cap. Dense grey clouds, heavy with rain, lumbered across the sky as Jock walked nearer to the river. No longer were its waters clear amber, instead they were rich brown gravy, laced with sticks and soggy leaves and whipping up into a cream froth where they hit the rocks and boulders at the edges of the bank.

"Now, you just stay where you are," said Jock under his breath to the waters. He knew how quickly they could rise, given enough rain and the wind in the right direction. There had been a couple of occasions over the last thirty-odd years when the nursery had come perilously close to being flooded, but the water had always gone down before the banks had been breached. Old Fred Armitage had said that the nursery had been awash only once and that was back in the 1920s. Jock had been careful to ask about this: his love of the picturesque had not totally overcome his common sense.

Now he looked at the violently swirling waters with unease, and then up at the sky to confirm his suspicions that more rain was to come. He pulled his coat about him and headed back to the shed. As he did so he heard the tooting of a car horn in the lane outside the nursery. He leaned over the old stone wall in time to see a brand new wine-red Jaguar splashing its way towards the gate. It drew to a halt, its wipers still beating time to the music he could hear from inside, the door opened and a slight, stooping man with a short grey raincoat got out. He had a shiny pate with a few wisps of black hair snaking over its surface. Almost bent double, he slammed the door shut and scuttled towards the gate.

Dennis Wragg resembled nothing more than a red-faced tortoise with beady eyes and a hooked nose. His manner, though, was more hearty than that of your average testudo.

"Now then, Jock," he bellowed as he executed an informal minuet in trying to dodge the puddles that would wreak havoc with his soft, shiny shoes.

"Shall we go in?" He nodded in the direction of the potting-shed.

"I don't open on a Sunday, Dennis," said Jock. "Unlike you."

Had Dennis Wragg really been a tortoise, he would have pulled his head inside his shell by now, but as he wasn't he tried, ineffectually, to pull his head inside his collar to shelter from the rain. Jock watched the water trickle down his skull dragging the strands of hair with it.

"I thought we might have a natter," offered Dennis, half closing his eyes to keep out the rain.

"Well, you thought wrong, I'm afraid," countered Jock, standing solid as a rock inside the nursery gate while the other man hopped from one foot to the other outside.

"Did you get my letter?" he asked.

"I did," said Jock, "and there's no need for a reply. You know what my answer is."

"Come on, Jock," snapped Dennis, as a rivulet of water ran down the back of his neck and under the collar of his pale yellow shirt. "Be realistic. How long can you afford to stay here? Take my offer. It'll give you a good retirement."

"I've no intention of retiring, Dennis. This is what I do. I like doing it and I don't want to see a plantsman's nursery turned into a small branch of your empire with padded sun-loungers in the greenhouse and concrete gnomes in the potting-shed."

"Oh, the buildings won't be here. We'd redevelop the entire site. It'd be modern and tasteful, it wouldn't look like your nursery at all," said Dennis, hoping that this information would make Jock feel better about selling up. Not surprisingly, it had quite the reverse effect.

"Dennis, I'm getting wet, you're getting wetter, and there is no way that I'm selling up. Now, I'd be grateful if you'd go back down the road and listen to your cash registers ring and let me get on. I don't want to be rude, but you're forcing my hand. I want to hear no more about your offer."

The horn of the Jaguar gave an irritated 'parp-parp' and Jock could faintly make out the image of a woman in the passenger seat. The blonde meringue of hair that was Gladys Wragg was getting impatient. Dennis looked over his shoulder and gestured that he wouldn't be long, then turned back to Jock for one final tirade. "You're mad. You can't manage this place on your own. You should pack it in while you've still got your health. And that won't last long. There's no future in this kind of business. People want a day out when they go to buy something for the garden. They want a tea shop and a kiddies' playground. They want to be able to buy everything from jam and honey to garden furniture and barbecues. Plants are just a tiny part of this business, MacGregor, and you're better off buying them in bulk from a specialist supplier. The money's to be made on all the other things."

Jock had heard more than enough. He pulled his cap down over his eyes to keep out the rain. "It might come as a surprise to you, Dennis, to know that in my life money is not the most important thing. It might sound old-fashioned, and I know you think I'm as doomed as the dodo, but you should know that I do what I do for love. I love my plants. They don't let me down, they don't argue and they don't answer back. I earn just enough money out of growing them to make a living, and the pleasure I get from sharing my love of them is something that you could no more understand than fly. You're a lucky man, Dennis. You're a successful businessman who's made a lot of money. Whether or not you're a happy man I don't know and, to be perfectly frank, I don't really care. But I *am* happy here, Dennis. I've made a small success out of this patch of land, thanks to my wife and a grand lad who's done all right for himself, and I'm not giving it up for a lump of money that will sit in the bank and earn interest, because there's absolutely no interest in it for me. Have you got that?"

Dennis Wragg looked Jock straight in the eye, a drip of water on the end of his hooked nose and another on his curled upper lip. As he drew breath, the horn of the Jaguar sounded once more. He turned towards the car and waved, then turned back to Jock. He was too late. The old Scot was now half-way down the path to the potting-shed.

Dennis cursed under his breath as the insistent tone of the horn resumed. "I'm coming, I'm coming!" he shouted angrily into the wind, and picked his way through the puddles and back to the car to face his wife. She would doubtless be less than pleased at her husband's failure to land this particular catch on the riverbank, and she would not relish the prospect of pools of water on her nice cream leather upholstery.

Chapter 7

The news studio of Northcountry Television was compact and purpose-built, situated right next door to the hangar-like studio that was used for drama and the winter editions of *Mr MacGregor's Garden*. With a wide blue screen behind her and a massive monitor to her right, Lisa Drake sat in one of two padded chairs behind the curving crimson counter that was the newsdesk. Her freshly cut bobbed blonde hair just reached the top of the cream polo-necked sweater that rose above her deep green jacket, and the soft-toned face that had so captivated Rob the night before was now enhanced with a crisp makeup that meant business.

The Sunday early-evening news was two minutes from transmission, and a blue light shone over the heavy door in the blackened corner opposite her. In two minutes' time it would change to red. Three large grey cameras pointed at the desk; two were locked-off remote cameras that produced the standard mid-shot, which made every newsreader look as though they were born without legs. The man behind the other camera, rather strangely, seemed to have legs but no body. At least, that's how it appeared from where Lisa was sitting. Once on air a cameraman's face was a rare sight; usually all she could see were his arms adjusting shot size and focus, and his legs spread wide for balance and comfort.

She checked her watch, leafed through the pastel-coloured script in front of her, and pushed the top of her Mont Blanc ballpoint pen in and out nervously. Where was he?

There was a commotion over in the dark corner by the door and a loud apology as a huge man ambled out of the darkness towards the newsdesk, a disorganized script in his hands and a pen clenched between his teeth. He hauled on the second sleeve of his light grey suit jacket, aided by a nylon-coated makeup girl, who dabbed at the rivulets of perspiration on his forehead. A man from the sound department scuttled behind him, slipped the transmitter into his back pocket, then dashed round to fix the tiny microphone at the other end of the wire to his lurid tie, all as Frank continued to make a bee-line for the seat next to Lisa.

"Darring, shorry I'm rate," he mumbled through the pen, then took it out to make himself clearer. "Bloody subs. When will they find someone who has the remotest grasp of syntax? I said to one of them this morning, 'Where's your grammar?' and he said, 'At home with my grandad.' I ask you!"

Frank Burbage flapped his arms to get rid of both the makeup girl and the soundman as though he were shooing away flies. He had been anchoring *Northcountry News* since the station had been granted the franchise umpteen years ago. A huge Yorkshireman with grey hair that looked like steel wool, he had the stature, the booming voice and the right accent for this neck of the woods, and it was not put on.

He had come to Northcountry Television on the understanding that as well as being anchorman of their news programmes he could also cover Leeds United matches every Saturday in the season. Frank could bore for Britain when it came to football, but he was also a force to be reckoned with in the newsroom. Not that he cared much now for the goings-on in the broader political scene. It was a case of "been there, done that, read the script" as far as he was concerned. But he still had a mind as sharp as a rapier when he chose to unsheath it. Most of the time he didn't. Except when Lisa kept him on his toes and tried to poach some of his more choice interviewees. Then he would shake off the torpor borne of boredom and Tetley's bitter and do something about it.

Most of the time they rubbed along pretty well as a pair. It wasn't long after Lisa joined the station that Frank had realized she was no airhead. He'd tried to butt in on one of her interviews during her first week on the desk and been classily put in his place with one waspish line. He'd not done it again. Instead they'd forged a relationship based on mutual tolerance and professional envy, as is the custom with all newsreaders. These characteristics evinced themselves in wrangling for the opening and closing words of the bulletin, the seat to camera left, which indicated seniority, and being the first named in the credits, regardless of alphabetical order. Frank Burbage clearly beat Lisa Drake by a margin of two in the alphabet stakes, but nowadays they tended to take it in turns for the main story or interview and for opening and closing the programme.

"Why the hell they need two of us for a Sunday bulletin beats me," he grumbled. It was a remark that could be taken in one of two ways: either he didn't need Lisa to be there muscling in on his act, or he'd rather be in the bar while she got on with it. In fairness, it was probably the latter.

"Fifteen seconds, studio," the floor manager's voice rang out.

"Good weekend, love?" enquired Frank, shuffling his papers into some semblance of order.

"Not bad."

"Get yourself laid?"

His robust familiarity was, as usual, like water off a duck's back. "Yes, thank you. And you?"

"Only laid out legless last night after United lost to some God-awful team from over the Pennines. Three bloody nil. It'll be Millwall next. It's time I started doing the snooker. At least Steve Davis has more balls."

"Even if he doesn't know what to do with them," added Lisa, smiling, as the stirring signature tune of the lunch-time news boomed out its clarion call.

Frank took a deep breath: "In today's news, Helmingdale's biggest woollen mill goes up in flames, local farmers complain about the Government's attitude to beef, and the chief executive of Yorkshire Water warns of possible flooding as the weather worsens."

The picture illustrating all three stories faded and Frank Burbage came into vision on television screens throughout the region.

"Good afternoon . . ." The first story was his, and Lisa watched him read the autocue with polished professionalism. Funny how people thought it was easy. "Oh, all he does is read the autocue," they'd say, but there was a technique to it, just as there was with any other skill. Get the camera too close and the viewers can see your eyeballs moving from side to side. Lift your chin too high and you appear to be talking down to the viewer. Stare too intently at the words rolling up in the lens and you look like a frightened rabbit. Get the camera too far away and you can't see the words. Find the right distance and move your head occasionally without getting 'the nods' and nobody would guess you were reading, provided that the emphasis on the words was natural and your technique polished.

Lisa's mind wandered idly as she watched Frank drawing in the Yorkshire viewers with his avuncular style. The second story – the one about local cattle – would be hers, and then they'd alternate until the end of the five-minute bulletin.

Frank was right: it was pointless having the two of them here for this cough-and-a-spit of news. There were seldom any interviews to conduct on a Sunday; it was nearly always a straightforward read. Boring, really. Her mind drifted back to the previous night, and the man who, in a few days' time, would be back in the cavernous studio next to the one in which she now found herself. She suspected the worst – that he'd wished their meeting had never happened.

Something roused her from her thoughts. It was a silence. Only a fractional one, but long enough to shake her wide awake: Frank had finished his item on the mill fire and it was time for the beef. She caught his eye as she launched into her own autocue script; his mouth was turned up at the corners and he was grinning. For the first time since he had begun working with her he had seen Lisa Drake caught off her guard. Perhaps she had feet of clay, after all.

As far as Rob's feelings were concerned, Lisa's assessment of the situation was only partially accurate. He did wish that the whole thing had never happened, that it had not presented him with such a crisis of conscience, and yet he could not pretend that he was not enormously attracted to Lisa. All through Sunday morning he swung between wretched guilt and high exhilaration, the screen of the word-processor staring blankly at him as he tried to pen something that would pass for a column in the *Daily Post* the following Saturday. By early afternoon a few uninspired sentences were all he had produced. He couldn't bear to be cooped up in End Cottage any longer.

He pulled on an ancient Barbour, a pair of tough fell boots, and walked out of the door and along the riverbank, eyeing the churning waters. He crossed the river by an old plank footbridge and struck out across the winter meadows, upwards towards the moor on a narrow, winding track, carpeted with silver sand. Soon the sheep-cropped tufts of grass at the side of the path were replaced by a thick rug of heather and the coppery fronds of dead bracken. As his boots bruised and crushed the plants that spilled in front of him, the true aroma of the moors reached his nostrils. It was a rich, earthy scent, a combination of sodden peat and the fruitily fragrant sap of heather and crowberry. The rain flattened his curly brown hair to his head, and ran off his chin and the end of his nose, washing his face as it poured over his skin and dripped from his fingertips.

He stopped for breath every now and again, gazing down into the valley that was obscured by thick mist, reinforced with the rain that moved sideways in great swathes. He gulped in the fresh, watery air, and still his head refused to clear. On he walked, eventually stumbling upon a vast black rock. A huge lump of millstone grit, it looked familiar, along with the wind-ravaged pine tree that arched over it. He remembered it now. Moving forward to the edge he found the spot he had discovered as a child. Part of the rock had fallen away, centuries ago most likely, and created a flat area a few feet below the upper surface. It was hardly visible from above, but as an exploring child he had found that it offered a fine view of the valley below and invisibility from parents walking above. He scrambled down to the ledge. Thanks to the overhang it was barely dampened by the rain that was driving away from it and out across the valley. Carefully he lowered himself into the hole, only just large enough for a grown man, and sat, panting for breath. He looked at his watch. He had been walking for three hours. Soon the light would fade, but not for an hour or two yet. He could sit for a while, and think, or try to stop thinking, or do anything that would rid his head of the miasma that seemed to have overtaken his mind.

He thought of Katherine and the hurt in her voice when he had made excuses not to go up the Dales. They could be sitting in the car now, eating and drinking and watching the water tumbling in milky veins down the sides of the fells of Upper Wharfedale. He thought of Lisa and the tenderness and sensuality of Saturday night. He thought of Katherine's encouragement at the start of his career, of her caring, her patience, her quick temper and her vital spark.

What if Katherine found out? The cold hand of panic gripped at his stomach and he felt momentarily sick. What if they lost everything they had because of one night of passion brought on by misplaced jealousy?

Occasionally the sun would shine weakly through a faint break in the clouds, allowing him a clear glimpse of a patch of the valley. In the same way he could momentarily see clearly what he knew was the only way forward. Lisa had been a flash in the pan, nothing more. He had been flattered by the attentions of someone so attractive, so highly rated. Katherine was a good friend, a good companion and a good lover, too. And he loved her, perhaps more deeply than he had realized of late. Maybe they had known each other too long; taken each other too much for granted. Familiarity had made them both careless. He must somehow retrieve what he had briefly lost. As the wind slackened a little he began to understand why the events of Saturday night had had such an effect on him. It was hardly surprising that he had tumbled into bed with the delicious Lisa: she had offered him a safety valve. But now he felt wretched on two counts. He would make it up to Katherine. Somehow. Without her knowing it had ever happened. But what about Lisa?

The light started to fade. He heaved himself out of the hole, stiff and damp from sitting too long, and picked up the track that led downwards into the valley towards another familiar landmark – Tarn House.

Helena had been surprised to see him. "Bless you! How nice of you to come on a Sunday. Of all the days of the week to be on your own I always think that Sunday is the worst." Then, recovering herself, "Where on earth have you been? You look like a drowned rat!"

She eased Rob's saturated Barbour from his back, "You do have to reproof these things from time to time, you know," and hung it by the Aga to dry, along with the sweater that smelled of wet sheep. Then she made tea, and they sat in her kitchen, eating shortbread, sipping Earl Grey and talking about this and that.

"There've been flood warnings on the television, you know."

"Mmm?" He hardly seemed to register.

"It's Katherine, isn't it? What's the matter?"

Rob was cagy at first. Opening up never came naturally to him. It was only lately, since his mother's death and his father's low spirits, that he had begun to share some of his thoughts with Helena. She never pried, simply listened and only offered advice where it was asked for. Rob didn't know how much he wanted to reveal; didn't know whether he wanted to reveal anything at all. Why should he tell anyone what was going on in his mind? It was up to him to sort it out himself. But the events of the last few months had lowered his defences. He ended up giving Helena the bare bones of the case without mentioning any names and without going into graphic detail.

"And now you don't know what to do?"

"Oh, yes, I know what I have to do."

"But it must be difficult."

"Yep." He gazed out of the window, preoccupied.

"The grand passion versus the comfortable, caring love?"

He hesitated slightly and inclined his head. "Yes. You've no idea what it's like.'

"Oh, I think I have."

Rob turned his head towards her.

"It happened to Jumbo and me," she said softly. Now it was Helena who looked away. "It was a long time ago. When we were in our forties. I thought it was the end of everything."

"And it wasn't?"

"No. Things changed. But it wasn't the end. Far from it. You can't turn off love like a tap. But I always remember one thing that Jumbo said to me." She faced him now. "He said that a man with two houses loses his mind, and a man with two women loses his soul."

Chapter 8

Now it was Rob's turn to find his telephone call unanswered. It was seven o'clock on Monday evening when he rang Katherine, only to find her answering-machine switched on. There were more than a couple of beeps at the end of her recorded message so he knew he wasn't the first person to ring that evening. He wondered who had left the other messages, then stopped himself from travelling down that unfruitful track. Jealousy had caused him enough problems over the last few days. It was probably her mother. Bunty Page had to speak to her daughter daily or she didn't feel she was on top of the scandal in the dale. He didn't leave a message. When he had put the phone down, he flipped on the television with the remote control and walked into the kitchen to get a beer from the fridge.

It was the end of the weather forecast. ". . . so there we are, dull in the south and west, but strong winds in the north with heavy rain. A very good evening to you." The weatherman smiled and winked, and Rob switched off the set.

He flipped off the cap with a bottle opener and put the ice-cold Beck's to his lips. Strange weather to be having an ice-cold beer, he thought, until the bubbles hit the back of his throat and he knew it was exactly what he wanted after a wearying day. He had, at last, crafted something reasonable for the *Daily Post*, although it had taken him the best part of four hours, thanks to a phone that wouldn't stop ringing. He'd settled on a piece about coping with cats in the garden – recommending his readers to use mothballs or lengths of hosepipe that looked like snakes to myopic feline eyes – had sung the praises of a garden famed for its daffodils and narcissi, given a plug to the *Plant*

Finder directory in the hope that it might help reduce the size of his postbag, and jotted down yet another list of gardening tips for the week ahead. God, February was a bloody awful month to get excited about. He hoped there would be enough to fill the half-page he seemed to be getting at this time of year, and punched the buttons on his word-processor that sent it scooting off through a modem directly on to the paper's computer in London.

He had hoped for a call from Katherine, but it hadn't come. Instead he had heard from Steve Taylor about this week's programme in general, and Bertie's contribution in particular, which was to be about sprouting seed potatoes. Rob could hear Bertie's voice in his ear now and prepared himself for the *double-entendre* that was bound to hit the airwaves when it came to the word 'chitting'.

There'd been a call from some PR woman to check that he was going to the Amalgamated Agricultural Chemicals press briefing at the Dorchester on Wednesday, which he thought was odd since he'd already confirmed that he was, and a call from his agent to say she had some exciting news and that as he was coming up to London on Wednesday could he pop in and see her.

Rob had been with Liz Cooper for a year now. He'd always hated negotiating his own fees but had been terrified of being dictated to by some harridan from London who knew nothing about him or about gardening. And yet there was always the feeing that you were working in the dark when you did your own haggling. Nobody else in the television-gardening business ever breathed a word about what they were paid, in case they should be seen as coining it or, worse still, earning far less than everybody else. The fiscal pecking order was a closely guarded secret. Guy D'Arcy, with his aristocratic bare-faced cheek, had tried to tease out of Rob the details of his fees when they had lunched together, but Rob had stonewalled him and muttered something about everybody doing their own thing. He was damned if he was going to tell Guy D'Arcy how much he earned.

Liz had been recommended to him by the weatherman at Northcountry Television, Archie Salt, who was more famed for his bright waistcoats than his accurate predictions. In spite of Archie's relatively regional appeal, Liz had managed to get him quite decent fees in the after-dinner speaking line, secure him a longer contract at Northcountry Television, and had persuaded one clothing company to produce a range of all-weather garments marketed as 'Salt of the

Earth'. Rob and Liz had hit it off from the first and he had never regretted signing up with her.

After a couple more swigs of beer, he sifted through the post that had arrived by courier in a large, fat, manila envelope from Lottie Pym. Steve had been true to his word and first thing on Monday morning the bustling, deep-voiced Lottie had endeavoured to make some sense of the fruit and vegetable post that had winged its way to the studios addressed to Mr MacGregor. Alas, she could not help him at all with the stuff that came through from the *Daily Post*.

Rob sighed over a couple of wizened apples that fell out of a cardboard box with a spidery note requesting to know their variety. He remembered one of his college lecturers who could identify any variety of plum simply by looking at its stone. A lovely old chap he was, passionate about fruit. Well, you'd have to be to go to those lengths. Rob took his beer with him to the window and looked out through the rain-lashed panes. He shuddered and lowered the blind to cut out the sight of the hurtling rain and at least some of the sound of the wind. Then the phone rang.

Jock had finished his tea and had not been able to settle down to anything that evening. He couldn't concentrate on his book, his mind wandered when he tried to do the crossword in the paper, and with the wind howling around the cottage he felt a need to check that everything was all right in the nursery. He had to cling to the parapet as he crossed the bridge, so strong was the wind, and the sound of water thundering under the old stone arches was deafening.

He unlocked the nursery gate and let himself in. The young trees tethered to the strong horizontal wires were straining to be free like young colts tugging at their reins. Evergreen shrubs shook and rattled in the wind and the branches of the sycamores by the river were hurling themselves around at an alarming rate. Fallen leaves fled across the ground, chased this way and that by the icy blast, which would occasionally whip them up into the sky before letting them fall in a cascade of damp confetti. Jock made for the greenhouses. Their fragile panes would be the first to go, and as soon as one pane of glass popped the wind would get in and wreak havoc. Jock examined them as best he could from the outside, not wanting to open the doors for fear that the wind would take them out of his hands. As yet all seemed to be well. He struggled across to the potting-shed, almost bent double to butt his way through the gale.

He'd left some seedlings and trays on the potting-bench, half-way through a spot of pricking out. He might as well carry on for half an hour. The light above the bench would be bright enough to let him see what he was doing. He needed to do something.

He'd been working for barely ten minutes when he began to feel cold. His body was chilled and his feet were frozen. He looked down and saw the floor of the shed was awash. Brown water was seeping in under the door. He dropped a pan of seedlings, swore and made for the telephone in the cubby-hole. His hand shaking, he dialled Rob's number.

Rob would have been there faster had not Tom Hardisty been herding his Friesians down the riverside lane, away from the meadows where, half an hour later, they would have been cut off. End Cottage was higher up the riverbank than the nursery and, hopefully, might escape. He parked a few yards up the lane for safety, and then ran for all he was worth towards the gate and down the path to the potting-shed, cursing himself for not thinking of his father and the nursery when he heard the weather forecast earlier.

Jock was standing outside the potting-shed, his cap pulled down over his eyes, but not far enough to prevent Rob seeing the look of fear. His long black oilskin ran with water and his sodden boots were submerged in the eddying water of the river that was now creeping across the nursery.

"What shall we do?" shouted Rob, trying to make himself heard above the wind.

"We'll have to try and stop the water coming over the bank behind the shed. I've been heaving some sacks of compost over there but I'm just about done in," bellowed Jock, using up what little breath he had left.

"Mr MacGregor!" shouted a voice through the wind. The two men turned round to see Wayne running down the path, his open donkey jacket flapping in the gale. "I was on my way to youth club. I wanted to see if everything was all right. What's 'appened?"

"The river's breached its bank," said Jock. "We need to try and shore it up. Help Rob bring some of those sacks of compost over here. We'll have to use them like sandbags."

Rob cast his eye across at the river. By the light of the old street lamp at the corner of the bridge he could see a wide, heavy torrent of water gliding weightily by. It argued noisily with the bridge before tumbling over the rougher riverbed below and erupting into an angry cream spume. Just behind the potting-shed it was seeping into the nursery. The sacks of compost laid on top of the bank were containing it for now, but Rob did not hold out much hope for their continued success.

Furiously, by the light of the lamp, Rob and Wayne ferried the heavy sacks across to the low stone wall that capped the grassy embankment and piled them on top. Jock did his best to help, but the strain was beginning to tell and his face looked white and drawn. When the supply of compost ran out, he brought an armful of hessian sacks from the still swimming potting-shed.

"What are those for?" asked Rob, straightening up, his hair matted with sweat and rain.

"There's no compost left. We'll have to start bagging up sand."

Jock's voice cracked and his eyes darted around the nursery. Rob could see him checking up on his plants like the mother of a large family counting her children.

"OK. Give them here."

"The sand's underneath the old lean-to by the shed."

"I know, Dad, I haven't forgotten." And then, anxious that he might have sounded too sharp, "Don't worry."

"Wayne!" Rob called him over from the corner of the nursery where he had been searching in vain for more sacks of compost. The lad looked up, his face a mixture of fear and fatigue. "Over here!"

Wayne came running, his oversized black wellingtons splashing in the large puddles of water that lay on the path, the rain glistening like mercury in his tight curly hair.

"Grab a shovel from the shed and meet me in the lean-to. We need to fill these bags with sand."

"Right." Wayne hovered for a moment, as if unable to believe what was really happening, then turned on his heel and ran off. In seconds he was back and followed Rob into the darkness of the lean-to. "I can't really see what I'm doing," he said.

"Over here," shouted Rob. "Follow my voice. Your eyes will get used to the dark in a minute."

Rob held the sacks while Wayne shovelled sand into them, his aim improving as his eyes got used to the darkness. All the while the wind rattled at the corrugated iron roofing like some malevolent percussionist, until they were half deafened by the din.

A dozen sacks filled, Wayne put down the shovel and the two of them took each sack between them, carrying it like a dead body and trying not to let the sand spill out of the open end, and struggled towards the river. The damp sand weighed far more than the compost they'd been heaving around before. As they approached, the noise of the river was unnerving, like some grumbling, threatening giant lumbering by.

After a couple of journeys, Rob shouted, "We need to do it faster! Let's try carrying one each," though in his heart he knew it would really slow them down. He staggered towards the riverbank with a third sandbag, his knees buckling beneath him, and heaved it into place on top of the long snake of plastic compost sacks. But the weight of water behind was making the whole construction unstable. As he turned to go for another sack, Rob heard a dull thud and whooshing sound. He spun round to see a tumbling Niagara of water coming straight for him.

"Get out of the way, Dad!" he shouted. Then he turned back to face the water, but lost his footing on the greasy mud. As he slipped sideways the gush of brown water knocked his feet from under him and bowled him along like a rubber ball. A three-foot section of compost sacks had collapsed. The water poured through in a narrow torrent with all the force of the river behind it. He put out his arms and grabbed at a tree trunk, pulling himself upright and spitting out filthy water. It was almost up to his waist and racing past him into the nursery, scooping up flower-pots and tubs and ripping newly planted shrubs from the now viscous earth.

On it swept, like an army of brown rats, slithering its way around cold frames and kerbstone and picking up the wheelbarrow as though it were a small boat being tossed on a foaming sea.

Wayne was retreating up the path, pulling at Jock's arm. Rob waded up the path towards them, watching the water swirl and gush past him along one side of the nursery. When it reached the wall at the other end it would start to back up and fill the enclosure, drowning the plants and undermining the greenhouses.

Jock, Rob and Wayne looked on helplessly for a few minutes as the light from the lamp glistened on an ever-increasing lake. A dull-coloured broth swirled over the ground, scooping up the dark earth and mixing it into an all-enveloping organic soup. The lights in the potting-shed went out, fused by the incoming water.

Rob looked up at the sky. The clouds were beginning to clear and the moon highlighted their deep blue-greyness as it leered between their fringes.

"What's that sound?" asked Wayne.

Rob listened. The rattling had stopped. Now there was only the deep bass roar of the water.

"It's the river. The wind's dropped." The noise was so loud, Rob could almost feel the vibrations in his chest.

He looked at his father. Jock stood, trance-like.

Rob racked his brains for inspiration. The sacks. They could move the sacks of sand and compost. Although the water covered more ground now, it was shallower and they should be able to wade further up the nursery with some of them to stop the water spreading to the fractionally higher ground. If they had the energy.

"Are you still OK?" Rob asked Wayne.

"Yeah. Fine." Wayne had little breath to spare but seemed willing.

"Could you help me get some of those sacks in a line across the nursery? That way we might be able to save the greenhouses."

"Course," replied Wayne, the vital spark returning to his eye.

Half wading, half running, the two scooped around in the slowly swirling water near the riverbank, delving into it as far as they dared to retrieve those bags that had not burst or been swept downriver by the raging torrent. Their legs sank into the mire, sometimes knee-deep, which hampered their progress and made balancing difficult. Slowly at first, and then more speedily, they built a low wall half-way up the nursery like some fall-back position in a pitched battle. After half an hour they had achieved a knee-high barrier, which was now only a few yards from the advancing water.

By the time they had finished they were panting and bent double. All they could do now was hope and pray as nature took its course. Rob turned to Wayne and his silent father. "There's nothing we can do here now. Come on." It was only then that the thought struck. What had happened to Jock's cottage? He hardly wanted to look. He strode swiftly ahead of the others and climbed over the bridge. The wind had dropped completely now, but the water below raged on.

The cottage sat calm and still, in a garden that held not a trace of water. The ground on the opposite bank was clearly a fraction higher than the nursery, and yet the threat was still there.

Rob turned to his father. "The cottage is fine, but you're not staying there tonight. Come with me." Jock said not a word, but followed his son to his car.

Helena Sampson had taken in the silent Jock with no fuss, just as Rob had known she would. Then he drove straight back to the nursery and met up with Wayne, who had been able to do nothing except lean on the wall and watch the water's progress. "It seems to be slowing down. I've watched it for 'alf an hour and it's coming up much slower now. You see that row of young trees over there? It's been just below their lowest branches for ten minutes now and it doesn't seem to be getting any higher. Maybe it's because the wind's dropped."

Rob cast an eye over the nursery and tried to estimate the extent of the coverage. Water had submerged about half of the ground but was being held back by the line of sandbags and compost, which now looked like the Kariba dam. The greenhouses sat like great white swans on the edge of a lake but the potting-shed was probably about three feet deep in water. The branches of young trees sprouted like reeds from the water, but the upper reaches of the nursery, where container-grown plants were spaced out on the standing ground, was untouched. Thank God for that, thought Rob. At least he'll still have something to sell, although it occurred to him then that his father might never want to sell anything again.

"Come on," he said to Wayne, nudging his arm, "let's have another look at the cottage." They crossed the bridge once more and went through the front gate. The squat stone dwelling crouched peacefully in its plant-filled garden. All was well. At least it had the protection of a stout wall, should the river rise higher. Only the wicket gate provided a weak point of entry. "Do you think we could find a few more of those bags of compost and fill the gateway with them?"

"Course," replied Wayne, already loping up the hump of the bridge. Rob watched him set off. His dad was right. What a find.

They waded once more into the muddy waters of the nursery, kicking to find what they were looking for.

"I didn't think TV stars did jobs like this," said Wayne ingenuously, as he passed Rob with a sodden sack on his shoulder.

"I'm just a gardener, really," replied Rob, puffing under the weight of his saturated load.

Slowly they hauled the last half-dozen sacks over the bridge and dumped them in the gateway of the cottage, before leaning on the wall to gasp in the chill night air, their chests heaving. Sweat poured from them, their legs were weak and shaking, but the gateway was, hopefully, impassable to water. Only now did Rob feel the deep cold of the evening and realize that he was soaked to the skin.

"I think you'd better go home and get dry," he said to Wayne. "There's nothing we can do now until the morning."

Wayne nodded. He had no energy left to speak, just raised his hand and turned to cross the bridge in the direction of home.

"And, Wayne . . ." shouted Rob, summoning up all his remaining strength. The lad turned round. "Thanks. *You're* the star."

A flash of white teeth, another wave, a shrug, and Wayne had disappeared into the darkness, leaving Rob alone and at the beginning of what he suspected would be an uphill struggle with his shattered father.

Slowly he stood upright, his head spinning and his lungs feeling as though someone had plunged a red-hot poker into them. He dragged himself towards the bridge, searching for his car keys in his saturated pocket. As he began to climb he saw, at its crest, the silhouette of a small figure, clad in black and muffled against the cold. For a long time the two of them stood still and stared at each other while the river thundered beneath their feet.

"I thought you might need help," Katherine said. He looked hard at her, then walked slowly towards her and wrapped her in his arms, resting his head on her shoulder. His body shook and she held him tighter than she had ever held him before.

"Hey," she said soothingly, stroking his sodden, stinking clothes, "come on. Let's get you into something warm."

He straightened his stiffening back. "What made you come?" he asked, softly.

She put her arm around his waist and led him over the bridge. "Because," she said. "Just because."

Chapter 9

Katherine didn't say much that night. She didn't need to. She undressed him and took him to her bed, cradling him in her arms until he slept.

When he woke in the morning the bed was empty and there was no sign of her. He forced his naked, aching body out from under the covers and made his way to the kitchen where the clock on the wall said ten to ten. No wonder she'd gone. He stretched his arms over his head and arched his back to relieve the stiffness in his muscles. Then he saw the note propped up against the toaster. 'Love K x' was all it said. No message, no indication of a return time, just 'Love K x'.

Rob shaved and showered with the stuff he always kept in a sponge bag in her bathroom, and slipped on clean underwear, a pair of old jeans and a sweatshirt that lived in her wardrobe. He found a pair of her socks and pushed his feet into the damp wellies that sat by the radiator in her kitchen, before leaving the flat for Helena's.

Half-way there he changed his mind. It would be better to go to the nursery first and size up the damage, see if the cottage had escaped the flood waters.

He parked in the same spot that he had used the night before, pulled an old waterproof out of the back of the Fiesta and walked down the lane. It was one of those classic 'calm after the storm' mornings. The sky was clear, washed a bright borage blue by the rain of the day before, and the blackbird with the strong survival instinct sang from the still branches of the riverside sycamore.

Rob reached the nursery gate and found it unlocked. He shouldn't have been surprised. How could he have expected his father to have waited this long before coming to see the state of the place? He looked further along the lane and caught a glimpse of Helena's car, then turned to take in a full view of the nursery. Amazingly the water had gone down. Now there were just a few large pools on the more heavily compacted areas of ground – the paths and lower areas of hard standing. The greenhouses, thank God, had survived without one broken pane, but the scene of devastation in the lower half of the nursery was heartbreaking. Everywhere was coated in a thick layer of silt, into which were mixed broken twigs, fallen leaves and litter. The once-neat rows of plants were submerged under a confection of mud and rotting vegetation.

The door of the potting-shed was open and Rob could hear voices from within as he walked down the path. He stuck his head round the door and saw Helena, Jock, Harry and Wayne standing inside in a semi-circle, each holding a plastic cup of coffee that had been dispensed from a large flask that stood on the bench where a tray of seedlings remained from the previous night's pricking out. The water had stopped about three inches below the level of the bench.

"Good morning." He greeted them with a note of enquiry in his voice.

"Good morning," they chorused, though, to be strictly accurate, Harry just coughed his usual bronchial greeting.

"Well," he said, "what a night." He looked across at Wayne, who stared at his trainers. "How are you feeling, Dad?"

"I've been better." Jock drew in breath slowly. "But I suppose it could have been worse. At least the greenhouses are still standing, and it didn't reach the cottage. It would have swamped both, except that somebody had the sense to block its path with sandbags."

"Well, you've got a crack labour force, haven't you?" said Rob, glancing at Wayne, who now raised his eyes from his mud-spattered footwear and grinned at him.

"God, it's bloody 'orrible out there," offered Harry, dragging on his fag but at least having the presence of mind to blow out the smoke in the opposite direction to Helena.

"Thanks for looking after him," said Rob.

"Oh, it was no problem at all. It was a pleasure. I'm only sorry it was in such rotten circumstances," she replied. "It is a bit of a mess, isn't it?" she said, walking out of the potting-shed. The others followed and, once again, took in the scene of devastation that lay before them.

"Dad," asked Rob, "are you insured?"

Jock shook his head. "The premiums were too high, being near the river. I know it's against my nature but with old Armitage saying that it hadn't happened very often I thought it was a risk I had to take."

"Have you any idea how much you've lost?" asked Helena, with real concern in her voice.

"All the shrubs and perennials down there are goners," Jock nodded in the direction of the lower part of the nursery next to the river, "though some of those over the other side we might save."

"How much were they worth?"

"Oh, a few hundred." Jock turned to Wayne and Rob. "But we were lucky. It's not the end of the world, thanks to you two. It's just the time it will take to clean up that's the problem. With the start of the season looming we're just going to have to knuckle down and crack on. Yes. We were lucky," he muttered again, pushing the toe of his boot through the thick film of mud that lay on the path.

Harry grunted, depressed by the amount of slave labour that loomed large on the horizon.

"So what do we do now?" asked Rob. Before anyone could answer they heard the wrought-iron gate clang against its catch. They turned and saw a small black-clad figure in woollen tights and a short skirt with a black woollen jacket. She was walking down the nursery path and picking her way between the puddles and the mud.

"Hello," said Katherine, tentatively. "Would you mind if I came in?" And then, without pausing for an answer, "I'm so sorry about the flood, Mr MacGregor, but do you think I might be able to write a piece for the paper? Or would you rather I came back later? Is it a bit too soon?"

"No, it's fine, lassie," said Jock. "I've just been saying that it could have been worse. I've still got a house."

Katherine looked at Rob to check that he didn't mind her intruding. Rob raised his eyebrows, surprised at his father's equability. Katherine pulled her shorthand pad and pencil from the pocket of her jacket and pushed a stray wisp of hair behind her ear. It shone in the sunlight, and Rob noticed that her face was shining, too, her cheeks flushed pink from the walk down the lane.

"You're sure you don't mind?"

"No, you carry on."

"I'll just need a few facts first about how long you've been here and that sort of thing . . ." Rob watched Katherine go to work. He'd never seen her operating professionally before. She was firm but, thankfully, sensitive. Rob had got used to newspaper reporters over the last couple of years: as a breed they were accomplished at feigning an interest in the basic facts as they cunningly picked their way towards the intimate or prying question that had been their aim all along. Katherine had a rare sincerity about her, and she cared passionately about justice and about people's well-being, especially in the dale, her home; their last argument had proved that. He found himself spellbound as he watched her win Jock's confidence. Even though his father knew Katherine quite well, here was a different kind of relationship in the making – that of inquisitor and respondent. She asked about Jock's background, about his passion for plants and about how long he thought it would take to get the nursery back in shape. And then she asked about the son who had become a famous television gardener. It seemed odd to hear Katherine asking questions about him. He wondered what she would say in her piece. She'd never had to write about him before, had never wanted to mix business with – well . . . love.

Her questioning completed, she turned to Rob. "Can I say that you helped save the nursery and the house?"

"Well, er, Wayne and I did what we could to . . . er . . ."

Katherine looked across at Wayne, whose head was bowed.

"What's your surname, Wayne?"

"Dibley." Wayne fidgeted and made circles on the ground with his welly.

Rob stepped in. "You can say that if it hadn't been for Wayne the nursery would probably not have survived. He stacked sandbags until he could barely walk and he's a star."

Wayne blushed, and grinned sheepishly, then loped off down the nursery to start the clear-up operation. Harry, too, shuffled off, coughing.

"All right, you two, enough of this," said Jock. "Do you want a cup of coffee before we start shovelling mud?" As Helena poured Rob and Katherine some of the steaming brew, they all heard cars coming down the lane rather faster than normal, splashing through the deep puddles that dotted its surface. The first was a Renault Espace with Northcountry Television emblazoned on its side, and the second was a charcoal grey BMW with a blonde at the wheel.

During the next few moments of Rob's life he contemplated many things: the proximity of Katherine, the state of his wellingtons, the colour of the sky and suicide, though not necessarily in that order.

Two men climbed out of the Espace and proceeded to heave camera equipment through its side door. Lisa Drake slid out of the charcoal grey BMW in a long camel coat and shiny brown boots. She pushed open the gate of the nursery and trod a path that was quite clearly about to lead to an interesting situation.

As far as Rob could see, several alternatives were open to him: he could pretend to faint; he could run away; he could sneak into the potting-shed lavatory and lock the door; or he could call upon all the experience he had accrued at the local amateur dramatic society and bluff his way out. If he tried the first he might hurt himself, if he tried the second they'd think he'd flipped, and the third scenario was out of the question since Harry had beaten him to it.

"Good morning," shouted Lisa from the top of the path. Jock, Helena, Rob and Katherine stared at her. Drawing her expensive coat around her she tiptoed gingerly down the path between the silt-swamped beds and came towards them. Rob thought his heart was going to burst through his chest. He was convinced that his face must be the colour of pickled beetroot and that, any second now, his head would probably explode.

Thankfully, Jock was the first person Lisa addressed in the bright but brusque manner that had become her trademark. "Mr MacGregor, Lisa Drake, Northcountry Television." She reached out a well-tailored arm that ended in a brown leather glove and shook his hand. "Terribly sorry about the flood. Do you think we could take some shots of the nursery and have a brief interview?" She flashed Jock a devastating smile. He opened his mouth to reply, but before he could say anything she'd turned to address the two men walking down the path behind her. "Martin, set up over there on a wide shot and I'll walk up the path towards you for the intro. This is *so* kind of you, Mr MacGregor. I realize it must be a bit of a morning. We'll do our best to get it over with in no time. Morning, Rob. How are you?" She felled him with another smile and walked towards her two-man crew, who were setting up the camera as bidden.

Her style was breathtaking. Rob glanced at Katherine, whose mouth was partially open and whose eyebrows, had they not been attached to her skin, would otherwise have been hovering somewhere above her head. Jock looked as though he had been run over by a velvet-covered steamroller, and Helena's brow was knitted as though she were trying to solve a particularly tricky crossword puzzle. Rob himself was in shock.

After a moment's consultation with the cameraman Lisa returned to the stunned group. "Where shall we do the interview? In the potting-shed?" She stuck her head round the door. "No, perhaps not. Bit of a smell in there. Must be the river water." She turned away and walked down the path. "Would you mind if we got the piece to camera out of the way first, Mr MacGregor?"

Jock, unsure of whether or not he wanted his nursery shown on television in its current state, was about to ask her a question, but she breezed past him and set herself up in front of the cameraman, who adjusted his shot size, and the soundman who, earphones in place, was twiddling a row of dials and holding a furry sausage on a pole in front of her as if he were trying to tempt a donkey to eat a large, hairy carrot.

Rob looked again at Katherine. She seemed mesmerized. She had seen some smooth operators in her time, but none with quite as much bottle and charisma as Lisa Drake. He wished he was anywhere but there. Perhaps if he kept quiet and still nobody would notice him. Lisa was ready to perform.

Another smile at her small audience and then, "Quiet, please!" It wasn't necessary. The rest of the assembled company was speechless.

"After last night's floods, the worst in forty years according to the locals, the residents of Wharfedale are piecing together their lives and assessing the damage that the flood waters have left behind. Farmland has been drowned, and gardens swamped. Thousands of pounds' worth of destruction has been caused by the Wharfe in full spate." As she talked earnestly to the camera she walked forward in her elegant coat, casting a leather-gloved hand sideways as she went, her shiny boots ploughing through the soft black sludge. "Most houses in the community escaped unscathed, but among the few low-lying properties that were damaged is the delightful riverside nursery of Jock MacGregor, father of television's 'Mr Gardening', Rob MacGregor. Just how will he and his nursery recover from the dramatic deluge which has left this scene of devastation in its wake? And cut. OK for you, Martin?" The cameraman nodded his approval. "Right, let's do the interview."

By now Jock was powerless to stop her. Helena and Katherine were hypnotized, and Rob was one step nearer to heart failure. Lisa carefully positioned Jock on the path, with the flood-damaged potting-shed and a few of the largest pools of water visible over his shoulder. "Do those pools of water read, Martin?"

The cameraman screwed up his face. "Well, they're OK."

"Yes, it's a shame there isn't more water here, really. Still, never mind." She turned back to Jock and massaged him with another smile. "Running?" she enquired of the cameraman.

Martin nodded and said, "Speed." The soundman, without lifting his eyes from his dials, nodded too. "OK. Mr MacGregor, what was your reaction to the flood?"

Jock endeavoured to convey his feelings, though he felt like a rabbit being sized up by a fox. "Will you be able to open again or will this mean the end for Wharfeside Nursery?"

At least she got the name right, thought Rob. But he didn't like her line of questioning.

"Whose fault do you think it is that the banks of the Wharfe were breached by the flood waters?"

Jock was beginning to find his feet. "You can't blame anyone for a flood. It's part of nature. I work with nature every day and I understand that sometimes it can be cruel."

"You don't think that the Yorkshire water authority is at fault because of its tampering with water levels in the river?"

"I'm afraid that's out of my province. You'd have to ask them what they feel about that," said Jock.

"Meanwhile, there's talk of you being taken over by a local chain of garden centres. Will they still want to buy you out now that they know the nursery is subject to flooding?"

The question came as a hammer blow. There was an audible intake of breath from Katherine, and Helena muttered, "Good God."

"This nursery has never been for sale," Jock replied evenly, "so the flood makes little difference to the situation. We'll tidy up and then get on with our work. And now, young lady, if you don't mind, we have rather a lot of clearing up to do." Jock raised his cap to Lisa and indicated that the interview was over.

"Thank you, Mr MacGregor. That was very kind of you. I'm so sorry I had to ask those questions but I'm afraid that's my job." And then, turning to her cameraman, "Martin, is the first half of that last answer usable?" The cameraman gave a thumbs-up.

She turned to Rob. He watched her eyeing him. He could see in front of him the devastatingly attractive woman whose bed he had shared just three nights before and he could also see a hard-nosed reporter stalking her quarry. The scent of Chanel caught his nostrils for the first time that morning and he felt the fluttering in his stomach.

Lisa said directly, and for all to hear, "Can I ask you how you feel? This is where you grew up, isn't it?"

Rob nodded, as yet unable to find words.

"Just a snatch about what it means to you, how it will affect your father and . . ." she waved her arm around her, taking in the assembled company, "and how it will change your life." On this line she darted a flicker of a smile in Katherine's direction, and a broad one back at him.

She knows, thought Rob. She bloody well knows. What would she do now? Nothing. She wouldn't do anything. She'd just make him sweat.

"Er, can we do it quickly? As Dad said, there's a lot to do."

"Yes, of course. Sorry. I don't want to make this any more uncomfortable for you than it is already. Ready, Martin?"

Martin grunted in assent.

"Rob MacGregor, you grew up here on your father's nursery. It must be sad to see it looking like this?"

"Yes, very sad, but we'll cope. It won't be long before the nursery is back to normal."

"It must be a terrible blow to your father, coming as it does in a year that has held more than its fair share of tragedy for him, with the loss of his wife?"

Rob felt his colour rising. "Yes, it's been a hard time, but thankfully we've had lots of support from our friends," he looked at Helena and Katherine, "and we're pulling through." He fought to control himself, aware that she would not give up until she had what she wanted. He'd have done better to have declined the interview, but what would she have done then, with Katherine only a few yards away?

"And the takeover bid by Gro-land Garden Centres. Has it never been on the cards? Your father is, after all, not a young man."

"No, he's not young, and he's had a hell of a year. But my father has never ceased to surprise me." Jock was standing just outside the potting-shed, looking grimly at the muddy earth. He raised his eyes as Rob talked, and glanced across at him.

85

Rob continued, looking Lisa straight in the eye, "You see, what I think you have to grasp is that gardeners are not normal people. They don't give in easily because ever since they learned how to grow things they've coped with the failures as well as the successes. They rise to a challenge. My father taught me most of what I know about gardening, and the one thing he taught me more than any other is that you don't fight nature, you work with her. She doesn't let you down in the same way that people let you down. She's never disloyal, but she is sometimes fickle." Lisa backed off an inch.

Rob carried on, fixing her with a burning stare. "She's flexed her muscles a bit, but now, with any luck, she'll start to be a bit kinder." And then, more gently, "Wharfeside Nursery will soon be back in business, selling the sort of well-grown plants that only a good nurseryman like my father can produce."

Lisa stood still, looking at him. There was a long pause. "Rob MacGregor, thank you very much."

"My pleasure," said Rob, holding her eye. "And now I'm afraid we'll have to get on."

"Yes, of course. I'll get out of your hair." She turned to the rest of them. "Thank you, Mr MacGregor," she said to Jock, "and good luck. I'm sure everything will soon be back to normal." She nodded at Helena, then shot a glance at Katherine.

"Goodbye, Katherine. It seems you've beaten me to it. Today, anyway." She walked swiftly down the path, got into her BMW and splashed away down the lane, leaving her camera crew to pick up the pieces.

Chapter 10

The 7.38 pulled out of Leeds City station on time, with Rob slumped in a forward-facing seat in a non-smoking first-class carriage. Ordinarily he felt a pricking of conscience if he travelled first class, his canny father having instilled in him a keen sense of economy, but today he felt in need of as much privacy as he could get. First-class passengers might be more reticent about asking gardening questions than those in second class, and the events of the previous few days had left him longing for the peace and quiet of his own company. The train journey to the AAC press briefing in London would offer him that – for the next two hours and seven minutes anyway.

Big junkets like this never appealed to him, and neither did London, but he felt a duty to keep his finger on the pulse, even though the rest of the day always seemed to be wasted and the same old characters would crawl out of the horticultural woodwork, happy to enjoy a free buffet and drinks at the Dorchester.

The flood had given him yet another reason for abandoning the trip, but Jock had insisted that his "little local difficulties" should not get in the way of Rob's work.

He flipped through the *Daily Post*, not his favourite paper but he felt obliged to scan it daily, and kept the *Daily Telegraph* and its crossword for later in the journey. There was also the added treat of a cooked breakfast to look forward to in the dining car.

There had been barely time for a cup of coffee before he'd left End Cottage. In the excitement and confusion of the flood the day before he had almost forgotten about his own home. As Lisa had swept away in her BMW, and Helena had left, making him promise to come and see her soon, he had tried to follow a few minutes later in the Fiesta, with the excuse that he hadn't seen his cottage since the flood, before the questions from Katherine became embarrassing. He almost got away with it.

"Do you want me to come?" Katherine had asked, but he'd assured her that he would be OK on his own.

"Some lady," she had said, looking down the road where the puddles were still settling after the disturbance from Lisa's radials.

"I didn't know you knew her," said Rob, nervously.

"I don't," replied Katherine.

"But she called you by your Christian name," he countered.

"Well, we sometimes see each other across a crowded room at press briefings or, like today, when there's a story that we're both after, but I wouldn't say I knew her, and I've never seen her operate before. That came as a bit of a surprise. Talk about sharp."

"Well, you're not so dull yourself," Rob pointed out.

"Yes, but wading in like that as though she were Jeremy Paxman on *Newsnight* when she's interviewing a local nurseryman who's had his livelihood threatened by a flood. Bloody insensitive, I call it. Anyway, I thought you were great." She smiled at him, a proud, proprietorial smile, and rubbed her hand up and down his back. "You put her in her place rather well, I thought. Showed her what you're made of." Then her brow knitted a little. "How well do *you* know her? Do you ever bump into her at the studios?"

Rob tried to look casual, and hoped he succeeded. "Oh, now and again. Our studios are next door to one another." He paused. "But I couldn't honestly say I know her." He looked down the lane. "No. I hardly know her at all." That much, at least, appeared to be true. And then, changing the subject, he said, "Something puzzles me."

"Mmm?"

"Why all this interest in Dad's little nursery, first from Dennis Wragg, then the television newsroom, and you here reporting on it?"

"Why it's interesting to Dennis Wragg I've no idea. He obviously has something up his sleeve. Or did have. I don't know how he'll feel after the flood. But as far as the newspaper and the television go, I'm afraid you're being a bit naïve."

"What do you mean?" He looked down at her.

"Rob, you're probably the most famous gardener on British TV and when the nursery where you grew up and which is still run by your dad gets flooded it's news. People want to know."

Rob blushed. Would he ever learn to cope with, or even remember, his fame? Katherine hoped not, she said. She rather liked him the way he was. If only he liked himself the way he was. Having to lie to Katherine was not something he wanted to become a habit. He hugged her, promised to ring her later and kissed her goodbye.

His car splashed down the lane to End Cottage and his heart beat faster as he approached, wondering what kind of scene would meet his eyes. The lane was sprinkled with twigs, leaves and other debris that the river had left behind, but the tidemark came to just below his doorstep. Someone had been watching over him. He looked skyward and mouthed a silent 'Thank you', at whoever was up there.

He had checked that all was well, grabbed a larger pair of socks – those he had borrowed from Katherine had bobbles on the back that dug into his heels in his wellies – then went back to the nursery to help with the clean-up operation.

Only when it was becoming dark had they stopped shovelling the silt and barrowing it back into the river, to carry on its journey down the dale. Paths were hosed clean, greenhouse walls and floors scrubbed down and the nursery was returning to some semblance of order under the direction of Jock, the muscle power of Rob and Wayne and the grumbling of Harry.

"Never remember it like this when old Armitage was 'ere," said Harry, who was using his yard broom as a leaning post and occasionally poking it in the direction of the malodorous mulch that adorned the path.

"Old Armitage was lucky," said Jock.

Rob had watched his father during the day for any tell-tale signs that he was slipping back into introspection. But the disaster seemed to have strengthened his resolve. Some folk needed sympathy to get out of their depression, thought Rob, others needed a challenge. His father clearly fell into the last category.

Wakefield. Ten to eight. The train sped on. It would soon be time for breakfast. His appetite was sharpening. He'd spent last night at home in his own bed, needing to change into smarter clothes for the briefing, and not wanting to wake Katherine when he got up at six. He left End Cottage at a quarter to seven and drove to Leeds, leaving the Fiesta in the station car park before boarding the train.

An announcement came over the loudspeaker system: breakfast was ready. Rob grabbed the *Telegraph* and walked down the train, the aroma of bacon and eggs becoming stronger. He planted himself in a seat half-way down the dining car and examined the menu, though he knew already that it was the complete works or nothing.

Five across: 'Effeminate gathering of boy scouts (4)'. He was just starting on the crossword when the voice he knew so well asked a steward if breakfast was being served. He might have guessed that his journey was not destined to be a relaxing one. Bertie Lightfoot was travelling to London, too.

He had swaggered into the dining car looking to left and right to see if anyone recognized him. He was difficult to miss in the outfit he had chosen for this particular trip to the big city. His baggy corduroy trousers were corn-coloured and his brogues shone with Cherry Blossom oxblood polish. Beneath the brown tweed jacket, with its leather elbow patches, he wore a check shirt, maroon tie and primrose yellow V-necked sweater. Nobody raised an eyebrow, however, as he made his regal progress.

Interesting, Rob thought, that when Bertie was out for the day on official business he adopted his official accent and not the flat, rather fey northern tones he used at home. At least this thought helped him with his crossword. Four across: 'Effeminate gathering of boy scouts' – CAMP.

He buried his head in the paper, hoping that Bertie might choose a seat further up the dining car. One down: 'French bread in English gullet induces irritation (4, 2, 3, 4)'.

Bertie spotted him and lapsed into his native tongue, *sotto voce*, as he bent down level with Rob's paper-hidden face. "Oh, Mr MacGregor. Going up to London to see the Queen?"

Rob looked up and tried to feign surprise. "Oh, hello, Bertie. You too?"

"I thought you hated these dos," said Bertie, settling himself in the seat opposite Rob without waiting for an invitation.

"I'm not mad on them, but you know what it's like, you have to keep in touch with new developments," replied Rob, determined to be pleasant. He filled in the answer to one down: PAIN IN THE NECK.

Bertie kept to his northern tones, several decibels lower than his fortissimo Mummerset burr. "Oh, it'll be full of those boring old farts as usual. Just tell me why most gardening experts are such dreary old sods. Except for the ones that think they're Brad Pitt in wellies."

Rob raised his eyes, but Bertie was now scanning the menu. "You having the lot?"

"Mmm," answered Rob. Eight across: 'Celebrity queen becomes snake (5)'.

"No devilled kidneys today," moaned Bertie. "Why is it that all the chefs on British Rail were trained at the Lucretia Borgia school of cookery?"

Rob put down the crossword. If he was going to keep his word and take Bertie to task about his asides, this was as good a time as any. "Bertie."

"Mmm?" He looked up from his menu.

"What's the problem?" asked Rob, trying to put it as gently as he could.

"What do you mean?"

"Your problem. I know it's a pain for you, this programme. I mean, having to share it, after you having your own programme. But we've got to sort this out."

"I don't know what you're talking about."

"These asides at the end of the programme. Folk are beginning to notice."

"I should hope they are. Just little rays of sunshine designed to bring light relief to an otherwise dreary landscape."

"They were at first. Don't you think they're getting a bit . . . well . . . strong?"

"Oh, for God's sake. You've been on telly for half an hour and you think you know the lot." Bertie's cheeks coloured until they almost matched his nose. "I've been doing this gardening lark since you were in your pram and you come along with your college education thinking you can wipe me off the face of the earth. Well, you can't, you little shit."

Rob sat back in his seat, stunned at the outburst. But Bertie was in full spate now. "Just because someone upstairs thinks you're the new face of gardening you think you can walk your little welly-booted feet all over me." He was raising his voice now, stage accent forgotten. "But I'll tell you this, young Mr MacGregor. I'll see you off. Oh, yes. You might think you're God's gift to your lady viewers in your tight jeans and your rugby shirt, but just remember that the higher up the gardening tree you go, the bigger the drop when you fall."

He was leaning across the table, pushing his face closer to Rob's now, and almost spitting. "You can't have it all your own way. There are others just as good as you and who are hot on your tail, even if you *have* caught the eye of a certain lady newsreader." At which he flung down the menu and stomped off to the bar at the end of the dining car where Rob heard him order, in his Yorkshire accent, a large malt whisky.

It was a few moments before the dining-car steward could drag Rob from his troubled trance and take his breakfast order. Suddenly his appetite had gone. "Coffee, please. Black. And a slice of toast."

"It'll have to be the full Continental breakfast, sir."

"Fine. That's fine." He stared absently at the steward, who retreated with his order.

He looked out of the window at the industrial landscape of South Yorkshire as Bertie's words echoed in his ears, ". . . even if you have caught the eye of a certain lady newsreader."

His eyes drifted down to the crossword again. Eight across: 'Celebrity queen becomes snake (5)'. He filled in the letters slowly: VIPER.

Chapter 11

The large reception room at the Dorchester was already teeming with people, mainly men in sports jackets or suits, mainly middle-aged. Underneath the glittering crystal chandeliers, waiters glided among the guests, plying them with drinks. Rob stopped at the check-in table near the door and was given his lapel badge by a pretty girl who made a great fuss of pinning it to his jacket.

This was the moment he hated most, when, just inside the door, you had to hover and spot a familiar face and head for it as quickly as you could before you were buttonholed either by someone you knew you didn't want to talk to, or by a company executive who had a legitimate excuse to cut off your exit and extol the virtues of his latest range of products. God, how he hated these dos.

From where he stood he could see Bertie holding court conspiratorially in a corner with Guy D'Arcy and a couple of regional hacks. He wondered what they were talking about. He also wondered again just what Bertie knew about Lisa Drake, but convinced himself that it was nothing more than malicious speculation. Lisa wasn't the only person at Northcountry Television who gave him the eye – it was something he was learning to live with. But why should Bertie pick on her?

He tried to banish all these thoughts from his mind as he turned to enter the mêlée, but his arm caught someone standing directly behind him. In the fraction of a second it takes fizzy mineral water to leave an upturned glass Rob felt liquid soaking through his shirt for the second time in less than twenty-four hours.

"Oh, God, I'm so sorry."

Rob looked up from brushing the water off his clothes to see a bright-faced girl with open features and freckles, her fair hair tied neatly into a French plait that reached her shoulders. She had the clearest cornflower blue eyes he'd ever seen and wore a checked jacket over a cream top and dark brown trousers.

"No. Don't worry, it was my fault. I should have looked where I was going. And it's only water, not red wine. I'll dry out in a minute." He grinned at her and took a glass of orange juice from a passing tray, along with another glass of mineral water.

"You'd better have this – there's nothing much left in yours now." Then he thought he'd better introduce himself. "Rob MacGregor from Northcountry Television."

"I think I know that already. In fact, you're the only person here that I do know – by sight I mean."

Rob smiled. "It's good to meet you . . ." he glanced down at the badge on her lapel ". . . Rebecca."

"Rebecca Fleming. My friends call me Bex. I write for the *Worcester Star* and I do a bit of TV in Birmingham. I don't normally come to these things. Well, to tell you the truth, I'm not normally invited. This is my first biggie." She looked around the room, uneasily. "They're a bit daunting, aren't they? A bit grand."

"To be honest I can't stand them. The trouble is, you feel you've got to come or it looks as though you don't care," admitted Rob.

"Anyway it's good to meet you," she said. "I like your stuff."

"I'm very flattered."

"Well, we needed someone of our generation to give gardening a decent image. It's been dusty for too long."

"So how did *you* get into this lark?" Rob asked.

"Oh, the usual way." They were interrupted by a waiter carrying a tray of glasses that held champagne and Buck's Fizz. Bex shook her head. "Champagne at this time in the morning and I'll be asleep by lunch-time," she said. "In answer to your question, I got into this lark when I started work on my dad's nursery in Somerset."

"That's funny. I did the same only in Yorkshire," said Rob. "What then?"

"Oh, the usual thing – college, then Kew Gardens."

"Well, I really shouldn't be speaking to you," said Rob.

"Why?"

"Edinburgh man."

She laughed, an easy relaxed laugh, and he noticed that, as she did, two deep dimples appeared in her cheeks. "Oh, well, in gatherings like this we botanic-garden lot had better stick together," she said cheerfully.

"Are you still working for your father?"

"No, I manage a local garden centre now apart from the bits of writing and local telly."

"Do you enjoy it?" he asked.

"Oh, it's fun, but I could do with a bit of a change in the day job."

"You've never thought of doing the writing and the telly full-time?" asked Rob.

"Never had enough of it to earn a living," said Bex. "I'd love to if I could. Maybe one day."

Rob liked her. She was easy company, light-hearted and with no apparent hang-ups.

"Well, most of this lot manage to do it," he said, looking around the room. "How ambitious are you?"

"Oh, I'm keen to do what I want to do, but I'm not driven. I think that's my problem. I love the work, I love the plants, but I've no career plan."

"Don't apologize," said Rob. "There's enough naked ambition in this room to make up for your lack of it. But you really should think about it. Someone like you, I mean someone as good-looking as you, could make a killing in this business. Sorry. Was that a bit offensive?"

"My turn to be flattered," she said, with a giggle. "Are you ambitious, then?" she added, looking up at him.

"I suppose I am." He paused. "But I can't be doing with all the backbiting that goes on. I've been lucky so far. I love my job and I'm doing exactly what I want to do, but I couldn't say I was ruthlessly single-minded. I'm still too crazy about plants to be bothered with meeting the right people and being in the right place at the right time. Stupid, really, isn't it?"

"Level-headed I call it," replied Bex. "Anyway, who are all these people?"

"You don't know any of them?" he asked.

"Well, I see Guy D'Arcy's over there. A real womanizer."

Rob raised his eyebrows.

"All right, so I'm being offensive now, but he does rather fancy himself, doesn't he?"

"You might say that but I couldn't possibly comment." Rob's mouth stretched in its crooked grin. "So who else *don't* you recognize?"

"Well, I've seen Bertie Lightfoot before, but I'm not a fan. When you've grown up with a father who had a real Somerset accent Bertie Lightfoot's rolling Rs are a bit hard to take. And, anyway, he keeps having digs at you on screen and I don't like that."

"You've noticed."

"Hard not to. Does he have a bit of a problem with you?"

"Yes, I think he does, but I'm blowed if I know why."

"I'd have thought it was pretty obvious, really. You've taken his programme from under his nose. I suppose you've put it out of joint."

"Yes, but he was OK at the beginning. It's only lately that he's been a bit sharp."

"Seen the writing on the wall, I suppose."

"Do you know that little group, over there in the corner?"

Bex craned her neck to see. "Mmm . . . nope. Not at all."

"They're the radio lot. The stars of *Up the Garden Path*, or, as it's come to be known lately, *Gardeners' Ego Time*."

She laughed. "Why?"

"Well, if you think Bertie Lightfoot has a bit of a problem with me, then you've clearly never heard about what goes on in *Up the Garden Path*. They stick together at dos like this but they all hate one another. There's the fellow with the white hair for a start."

"The one with the bristly moustache?"

"That's him. Conrad Mecklenburg. One-time biochemist with an ego the size of a nuclear reactor. Cultivates the image of a mad scientist. His father was a Moravian prince so he expects every man to bow to him and every woman to . . . Well, you can guess. He can't stand the fellow on his left, Sid Garside, vegetable grower from Blackpool. Famous for his parsnips. His recipe for liquid manure is a closely guarded secret."

She chortled. "You're not serious."

"Deadly. You see the woman next to Sid?"

She nodded.

"Wendy Wooster. The only woman Conrad wouldn't make a pass at. He's very unkind about her. Refers to her as Miss Menopause. No one's ever seen her legs. Greenhouse expert at that difficult time of life."

"Oh dear," said Bex.

"Who else?" he asked himself, scanning the room. "Ah, well, there's the fellow over there with the headband in the linen suit and canvas shoes – Dave Philimore, the organic king. You've heard of him?"

"Only that he pees on his compost heap every night."

"And morning, even when there's a nip in the air. Wendy Wooster has a crush on him. Dying to get him into her conservatory. She's having trouble with her melons and thinks he's the only man who can sort her out."

Bex gave him a withering look. "Do you think he'd like to try?" She turned in the direction of Dave Philimore. "No, probably not. Anyway, if he's the organic king why is he here at a chemical bash?"

"Well, they're supposed to be launching some new product that's as good as organic so I expect they want his approval. Bet you anything he won't give it. No one's won him over yet."

"Who are the ladies over there?" She pointed to a small group of grey-haired women in tweeds and pearls.

"They're referred to as the Trust Fund. All very big in the National Trust – upmarket bunch."

"Aren't you a fan of the National Trust, then?" asked Bex.

"I'm the biggest fan they've got. I think they do a great job, but they've still got a bit of an image problem because they always seem to be represented by county types. You know the sort, Colonel and Mrs Satin-Buttocks."

"So who are those three?"

"Felicity Fortescue runs Dickers, the garden in Devon that's had all the publicity lately – mainly because it's just reopened after restoration, but partly because the head gardener ran off with the female landscape architect to set up a nursery on the Isle of Skye. Felicity is a bit yock-yock, but she can root anything."

"And the short dumpy one?"

"Emma Coalport. Writes the sort of books middle-class ladies adore. Something of an expert on colour. A Vita Sackville-West disciple. Knew her, too. In the biblical sense, some say. Has breath that could fell a Gladiator. Why am I telling you all this? I sound worse than Nigel Dempster."

"I'm beginning to think you *are* Nigel Dempster. And I thought you were such a nice man!"

"You mustn't believe all you read. I'm dreadful, really. If you breathe a word about any of this I'll be shot."

"Who by?"

"My girlfriend, for a start. She edits the local paper and she's taught me to be very careful about what I say and to whom I say it."

"Well, you're safe with me. It's been great fun. Do you think we ought to go through? They seem to be moving into the room next door."

"Come on, then," said Rob, and walked with his new-found friend into the large room that led off the reception area. Here they would be regaled with the latest exciting developments of Amalgamated Agricultural Chemicals. He could hardly wait.

Guy, Bertie and the coterie that had surrounded them sat on the front row of padded and gilded seats in the elegant room, whose great swags of turquoise velvet curtains had been drawn to keep out the weak winter sun. Spotlights illuminated five men and a scarlet-suited middle-aged woman seated behind the long table at the far end, whose pure white damask cloth was dotted with bottles of Buxton spring mineral water. An ironic touch, thought Rob, bearing in mind the company's less than sparkling track record when it came to river pollution.

He and Bex slid in at the back of the room at the end of a row, but in spite of their surreptitious entry Rob noticed that the largest of the five men had looked over in his direction and nodded at him. Rob had not met Sir Freddie Roper before, but he acknowledged him with a weak smile.

Guy looked over his shoulder to identify the recipient of Sir Freddie's greeting, saw that it had been Rob and, without any change of expression, turned his eyes once more to the front, running his hand through his thick fair hair to pull it back, temporarily, from his high forehead.

The chandeliers above them dimmed, allowing the spotlights to highlight the five grey suits, and Sir Freddie, as chairman of the proceedings, and of the company, rose to speak. The lady in red looked at him admiringly.

"Ladies and gentlemen, welcome to the Dorchester Hotel. It's my pleasure, as chairman of AAC, to pave the way for the announcement of what I'm sure you will find to be an exciting and quite unique breakthrough in the world of plant protection . . ." Rob sighed and glanced sideways at Bex, who looked back at him and raised her eyebrows.

Sir Freddie, his index fingers now pushed into the pockets of his ample pin-striped waistcoat like a farmer boasting about his prize pig, warmed to his subject and continued in a northern accent that had had the corners knocked off it in the interests of deputy lord-lieutenantship (West Yorkshire). Every now and again, he let himself down by falling over a vowel. Here, thought Rob, was the big-business equivalent of Helena Sampson's Mrs Ipplepen. Woe betide Sir Freddie if he had to say the word 'pluck' or 'duck', or ask a neighbour for a cup of sugar. Bearing in mind the subject of today's speech, the first two words were unlikely to feature, and the latter request had probably never been uttered since Sir Freddie had made his fortune with the abattoir he had founded back in the fifties. Rob brought his eyes down from the gilt and stuccoed ceiling and back to the man.

"For many years now AAC has been at the cutting edge of pesticide manufacture. In fact, I think I can say that our name stands out in the chemical business . . ."

"You can say that again," whispered Rob, softly in the direction of Bex's ear. She grinned and put her finger to her lips.

"Our scientists have been deeply conscious of the public's concern with the environment, and we at AAC have endeavoured to match that concern with our own painstaking research into more ecologically friendly products."

Sir Freddie's round, rosy face beamed a touch too smugly in the direction of the Trust Fund, but this was a man who enjoyed an audience and whose inability to embarrass himself was matched only by his ability to cause unease in others. The three ladies exchanged self-conscious glances. Bex looked at the floor. Rob looked again at the ceiling, and then remembered that he ought to try to look politely interested even if he was becoming slightly irritated.

Sir Freddie, his platitudinous preliminaries finished, proceeded to hand over "to one of our boffins – the lads who have been beavering away in the backroom" to explain the "exciting and quite unique breakthrough".

A thin, pale-faced man with a pale tweed suit and a pale grey moustache lurched nervously to his feet, coughed and riffled through the papers in front of him. "Er, thank you, Sir Freddie," he muttered, staring through his wire-rimmed spectacles to left and right across the room, as though he were a child looking for a lost parent. "The world of plant protection is complex and ever changing." He shifted his weight from one foot to another. "To stay at the forefront in such a volatile business it is necessary for research to be continuous and on-going." A dry cough. "New products need to be developed to cater for the ever more sophisticated needs of a growing market, not only on a commercial scale but also within the domestic scene. It is in this particular area that our latest product will make its mark."

Rob noticed that the man hardly looked up from his notes, such was his discomfort.

"For many years now we have been searching for a product that will satisfy three basic criteria – a broad spectrum of control over pests and diseases, and an environmentally friendly approach to those insects that are beneficial to the gardener. Added to this, it is important, from the gardener's point of view, that control is long-lasting. This new product fulfils all three of these requirements. It will kill a broad range of pests – from aphids and whitefly, to red spider mite, mealy bug and scale insects – as well as fungal and bacterial diseases. It will then keep them all under control for an entire season, while leaving beneficial insects, such as ladybirds and bees, unharmed."

There was an audible murmur about the room. Rob looked quizzically at Bex. "Sounds interesting," he whispered.

"I didn't think it was possible," she replied. "Not for years yet, anyway."

The edgy scientist proceeded to regale his audience with the chemical components of the new product, in terms vague enough to put other companies off the scent, and gave details of the comprehensive tests that had been carried out to prove its efficacy.

"This new product will be available to gardeners this spring. In May, in fact. It will transform pest and disease control as we know it, rendering obsolete a whole armoury of pesticides and fungicides. From this spring onwards the gardener will need only one product to make sure that his flowers, fruits and vegetables remain pest- and disease-free throughout the year. Thank you." He sat down, relieved, and wiped his now glistening forehead with an off-white handkerchief.

The room hummed with the muttered asides of the assembled company. Guy cast a conspiratorial sideways look at Bertie, while the *Up the Garden Path* team swapped anxious glances, aware that half their questions about pest problems were going to evaporate in the face of the new product.

Sir Freddie Roper rose to his feet. "Yes, ladies and gentlemen, I can understand your excitement. Such developments occur only rarely in the field of plant protection and it is understandable that you should be so enthusiastic about our new product. As you can imagine, we're pretty excited about it ourselves –"

"Can I ask a question?"

Sir Freddie was cut off in mid-flood. "I'm sorry?" His eyes scanned the room and lighted, eventually, on David Philimore, the organic king.

"Yes, Mr Philimore?"

"This new product."

"Yes?"

"Is it organic?"

"Well, it's been tested thoroughly and been found to be perfectly safe and reliable and, as you've heard, it's –"

"Yes, but is it organic?"

"Not exactly, but then, as we've explained –"

"Bloody typical. Another cop-out. Spraying your noxious crap around as though there's no tomorrow. You'll realize one day that the only way forward is with nature. I can't believe you lot can carry on being so irresponsible."

He leaped to his feet, stormed to the back of the room and out of the door. Wendy Wooster looked wistfully in his direction, not sure whether to follow. She thought better of it, stayed put, crossed her legs and bit her lip.

Sir Freddie, endeavouring to pour oil on the troubled waters, carried on. "Well, well, Mr Philimore will put his point, won't he?"

(At this point Bertie turned to Guy and whispered in his ear, "Stupid little sod. Does it every year just to make sure he gets the coverage in his paper. I wouldn't mind but he'll be driving back to Essex in his V12 Jaguar with bugger all thought for the environment.")

Rob said, "Oh, Lord," and buried his head in his hands. Bex looked bewildered. "Don't take any notice," he said. "He only does it to attract attention," then smirked to let her know that they were all used to Philimore's outbursts, even if Sir Freddie did not quite know how to deal with them.

Sir Freddie motored on with his speech, endeavouring to make up for the hesitancy of the scientist. "Such a product needs to be brought to the attention of the public in a manner befitting its importance. To give you details of the specially planned campaign, here is our PR adviser Simon Clay." He sat down, happy, for once, to let someone else step into the spotlight.

A thirty-something arty type in green-framed frog-like glasses with a nattily cut navy-blue suit and lemon waistcoat got up – the exact opposite of the pale-suited boffin who was now examining the contents of his handkerchief.

"Hi. Well, folks, it promises to be the development of the century for gardeners. One spray that will take care of their garden for a whole season. Handily packed, easy to apply and competitively priced, it makes for peace of mind in every gardening family. No more epidemics while the family are away on holiday. No more ruined crops. Goodbye, greenfly, so-long, scale insects, *auf wiedersehen*, aphids, and bye-bye, blackspot."

Rob winced and Bex giggled quietly. The lady in red shot Simon Clay a withering look.

"With your help," he continued, "by the start of this year's growing season every British gardener will be clamouring to get their hands on this panacea for plants. As you can imagine, the launch for this new product will be high-profile. We plan a combined TV, radio and national press campaign that will leave no one in any doubt that our new product is the one thing they can't be without. But what to call it? We thought long and hard about this, and came to the conclusion that there was really only one name that could be applied to a product that promises long-term control of all these garden problems."

The advertising man turned to the shrouded pyramid behind him and placed his hand on the corner of the green fabric that, as yet, hid the logo of the new product. As he spoke he grasped the corner and pulled away the concealing folds to reveal the name in all its glory, emblazoned on a mountain of red and green cartons. "Ladies and gentlemen, we proudly present the answer to a gardener's prayer – BLITZ."

The mixture of oohs and ahs that greeted his announcement was more muted than that provided by the audience of a TV quiz show who have just been told about tonight's star prize, but as everyone overcame their professional restraint, the gentle clapping that followed quickly built into a crescendo of applause – for most people, that is. The Trust Fund ladies were restrained, while Wendy Wooster sat guiltily silent, and the *Up the Garden Path* team were stern-faced, yet clapping robustly.

For the third time, Sir Freddie heaved his body to its feet and indicated that a buffet lunch and drinks would be served in the adjacent room where the company executives would be pleased to answer any questions informally. A press release would be available to everyone before they left.

Chairs rumbled backwards and the horticultural hacks spoke excitedly as they made their way towards the longed-for refreshments.

Rob drew breath to speak to Bex but was prevented from saying anything because a large hand slapped down on his shoulder. He turned round to identify its owner and came nose to bibulous nose with Sir Freddie.

"Mr MacGregor. Do you mind if we have a word?"

"No, not at all," responded Rob. And then, to Bex, "I'll see you in a minute. OK?"

"OK," she said, and turned to join the exiting masses.

Half an hour later Rob had still not appeared from the adjacent room and Bex, who had devoured enough canapés to assure the puff-pastry industry of a healthy future, decided she would slip out of the hotel and home to reality.

She squeezed past Bertie Lightfoot who, glass in hand, was swaying perilously from side to side and holding forth on the benefits of facelifts for men, and noticed that Guy D'Arcy had now distanced himself from his erstwhile companion and was chatting up another executive. He seemed to be working his way through them. She saw that his eyes kept raking the room for a person he evidently could not see. He smiled vaguely in her direction as a reflex reaction but his mind was clearly on business, not pleasure.

Bex remembered she still had a few questions she wanted to ask about this revolutionary new product. She couldn't leave yet. She looked around for the back-room boffin. There were half a dozen grey-suited men full of bonhomie who were singing the praises of BLITZ to anyone who would listen, but the scientist seemed to have left early. Shame. Clearly not a people person. She retrieved her Barbour from the cloakroom and glanced around once more, in the hope now of saying goodbye to her new-found acquaintance. He was nowhere to be seen.

She walked down the Dorchester's steps and caught a cab to Euston.

Chapter 12

Soft amber light flooded from the lower windows of End Cottage as Rob parked his car alongside the old stone wall by the riverbank and walked through the rickety front gate. He was glad. The thought of spending the rest of the evening on his own with the events of the day milling around in his head did not appeal. His spirits rose as he clicked open the ancient iron sneck and breathed in the aroma of warm bread and eastern spices.

"Hi!" he called, poking his head round the door.

"Hi!" she replied, and came towards him, smiling, with flour on her nose.

He wiped it off with his finger, licked it, said, "Mmmmm!" and took her in his arms, pressing his face into her soft, warm, fragrant neck. "I missed you," he mumbled.

"And I missed you, too," she said, her upturned face, eyes closed, wearing an ecstatic smile.

They squeezed one another, forgetting their recent troubles, and then he stepped back to look at her – shiny dark hair pulled back from her face, cheeks flushed from the heat of the kitchen, and her body encased in a black woollen sweater and white jeans. Her neat bare feet sported scarlet nail polish that made him smile.

"What is it?" she asked.

"Just looking at your cherries," he said.

"What's the matter with them?"

"Nothing at all, they're very pretty."

"Well, I did them especially for you."

"I'm glad. Is there anything to drink?"

"That's it, then, is it? Loving bit over, thank you very much, now where's my supper?" She turned away in mock disgust and walked towards the dresser.

"Oh, I'll make it up to you later – I've got stuff to tell you. What a day. You wouldn't believe it."

"Try me," she replied, returning with a bottle of Fleurie and a corkscrew, and pushing both into his outstretched hands.

Without taking off his coat he attacked the cork, pulled it out with a squeak and a plop, and poured two large glasses of the deep ruby wine. Giving one to Katherine and raising his own in the air, he said, "Here's to . . . whatever."

"Us," she said. He clinked her glass with his own before they both took a sip. They sighed in unison.

"Mmm," said Katherine. "I needed that. What took you so long? And what do you mean by 'What a day'?"

Rob put down his glass, slipped off his coat and jacket and pulled off his tie. "Where do I start?"

"Well," said Katherine, "let's follow Julie Andrews's recommendation. At the very beginning."

They sat at the scrubbed-pine table with a cluster of candles in the centre as Rob unfolded the events of the day, including his encounter with Bertie on the train and his acquaintanceship with Bex Fleming.

"Pretty?" asked Katherine.

"Very," replied Rob.

"Watch it!" she warned.

Rob laughed a touch too loudly and assured Katherine that a Torvill and Dean relationship was all that this friendship promised.

He recounted the events of the press briefing, told her who had been there, described the amazing claims being made for the new product, and then paused.

"Is that it?" she asked.

"Not quite. I was just about to push off when Sir Freddie Roper and a couple of his cronies collared me and took me into a room next door."

"What for?"

"They want me to front the advertising campaign for BLITZ."

"What?" Katherine's eyes widened in disbelief, then narrowed as her face hardened. "You said no, of course."

"I said very little. Except that I'd think about it."

"You said you'd think about it? Putting yourself in the pocket of a chemical company whose environmental record is second only to Attila the Hun?" The vibration of the table when she got up almost registered on the Richter scale and her pink cheeks turned carmine.

"Steady. I just wanted to talk to you about it before I did anything."

"Well, you knew what I'd say." She crossed to the stove and stirred a saucepan.

"Yes, I did. But I wanted you to be *able* to say it before I did anything."

She turned to face him, with a wooden spoon in her hand, looking chastened. "Sorry. I'm sorry." Then she became inquisitive. "But what will you do?"

"I'll run everything over in my mind, including the amount of money it would have made me, and then I'll . . . gracefully decline."

"Are you sure?" she asked.

"No. Not at all." He took another sip of the warm red wine and let it run over his tongue.

"Why?"

He swallowed. "It's a real quandary. Point number one: I am being offered a ludicrous sum of money by a chemical company who have done enough damage to the environment already. Answer: Turn them down flat."

"And point number two?" Katherine looked up from her stirring.

"My dad's nursery has just been flooded and he has lost more than he can afford. Answer: Accept the offer. Point number three: If I took the job, how can I be an impartial TV gardener and recommend whatever I want to recommend if I'm in the pocket of some commercial company? Even if they are paying me a mint."

"How much?" she asked gently, walking back to the table and sitting next to him.

"Well, Liz reckons we'd be talking about a six-figure sum."

"No!" She pushed back her chair, which scraped on the stone-flagged floor.

"'Fraid so. I nipped in to see her after the meeting. With TV and newspaper adverts she reckoned it would come to about a quarter of a million." Rob took another reflective sip.

"Holy shit." Katherine looked stunned and stared into the middle distance, then she looked back again at Rob. "Does Liz think you should do it?"

"Oh, you know Liz."

"No, I don't."

"Well, you can guess her reaction. Very excited. 'Darling, sit down and listen. We're talking about a lot of money. Think very carefully before you turn it down.' But she did see my point when it came to keeping my nose clean. If I took it on, before I knew where I was I'd be advertising double-glazing and doing voice-overs for washing powder. What would happen to my gardening street cred?"

"But a quarter of a million . . ." Her voice trailed off.

"Just a minute Miss Green Pages, are you saying I should do it?"

She got up from her chair, walked round behind him, put her arms round his neck and bent down to whisper in his ear. "I'm saying, Mr MacGregor, that I think you're an absolute star for turning it down. I'm very proud of you. I know that sometimes when I go off at the deep end and don't give you a chance to get a word in edgewise you must think that I claim to have a monopoly on principles. Well, I don't. You're just about to turn down a quarter of a million quid, and if that's not a case of putting your money where your mouth is I don't know what is. I know I rattle on about my principles, but I've never been put to the test and I've never had to make that choice. You're a mega-star. And I'm sorry."

She kissed him gently on the top of his head and he leaned back towards her and smiled. "You're very kind, but I haven't yet put their money where my mouth is."

"Well, talking of mouths, what would you say to some curried prawns?" she asked.

"Hello, curried prawns," he said.

"You silly boy," she said, giggling.

Then he pulled her head down and kissed her softly on the lips.

It was midnight before they went to bed. She slid under the duvet next to him and listened to the sound of the river through the open window. Lying naked, enfolded in his arms and with her head on his chest, she felt warm and secure and wondered why they did not spend every night like this.

"Oh, there was something else," he murmured, stroking the sleek black strands of her hair which fell over her pale shoulders.

"Mmm? What's that?" she whispered.

"Liz had some more news."

"What sort of news?" Her eyes were closed, her arms wrapped round him, and she was beginning to drift off.

"They want me to present this year's Chelsea Flower Show programme."

She squeezed him and tried, vainly, to open her eyes. "There you are, you see. I told you you were a star."

He looked down at her, and noticed the contented smile spread right across her face. He could just hear her whispered words: "Who needs a quarter of a million when you've got all those lovely flowers?" And then she sighed and slid into a deep sleep.

Guy D'Arcy had not had a very good day. No one had come up and spoken to him at the Dorchester – at least, no one of any importance – and Rob MacGregor looked as though he was going to carry off the glittering prize. Added to which, Guy was stuck in a lumpy bed with Miss Pony Club 1975, in the hope of keeping his head above water and landing the contract to do her father's garden.

He would have to think of some way to make them see that *he* was the right man for the job. The only man for the job. But how? His present situation was hardly conducive to him coming up with a brilliant idea.

He looked across the pillow at her, snoring. Hair the colour of marmalade and the face of a Welsh cob. God! What a sight. He heaved her weighty leg off his body, eased the leather riding crop from her now relaxed hand and dropped it to the floor before he fell asleep.

Chapter 13

"Make those letters neat, now. I want to be able to read it when you've finished." Wayne Dibley was kneeling in front of the potting-shed door painting on it a black horizontal line and the date to mark the level of the flood water. Jock passed by with a watering-can on his way to the greenhouses.

The black line was half-way up the door, and there were other reminders all around of the river's recent misbehaviour. Mud, Wayne had discovered, was not easy to deal with. When it was wet it ran with the unpredictability of quicksilver, and when it began to dry it stuck like the proverbial shit to a blanket. The trick was to catch it with your shovel when it was half-way between the two extremes.

He stood up and admired his brushwork. Not bad. Even Jock wouldn't grumble at his printing now – pretty readable and every letter the same size.

"There's another R in February," said a voice over his shoulder. Wayne looked round to identify his critic and discovered a small man in a grey mac with crinkly grey hair and a briefcase under his arm.

Wayne turned back to the lettering. "Oh, bugger!" and then, "Sorry! I've been ages at that."

"Well, you can probably just squeeze it in between your B and your U if you don't put too big a top on it," said the man, sympathetically. "Is Jock around?"

"Yeah, he's in the far greenhouse," said Wayne, now preoccupied with his calligraphy and dipping his brush carefully into the can of black gloss paint that had an impressive row of runny drips around its rim.

"I'll go and find him, then. You must be Wayne."

Wayne looked up from his kneeling position. "Yeah, that's right."

"I'm Stan Halfpenny, Jock's accountant."

"Oh. Great name for an accountant," said Wayne, his face at last breaking into a grin.

"And it's not the first time I've been told that," said Stan, moving off in the direction of the greenhouses. "See you later."

Wayne took up his brush once more and, tongue poking out from between his teeth, he crafted his final letter.

Jock was tapping the clay pots of some cinerarias with a wooden cotton reel fastened to the end of a piece of bamboo when Stan opened the door of the old greenhouse and walked down the flagstone path. "What are you doing? Testing them for dry rot?" he asked.

"No. I'm seeing if they're dry."

"With a hammer?"

"Tricky blighters. Keep them too dry and the leaves start to curl and crisp. Keep them too wet and they'll wilt and die. This way, when the compost is damp enough you hear a dull thud, and when it's dry the pot rings – like this." He rapped the cotton-reel mallet against a pot that sported a green dome of leaves covered in a rash of blue and white daisy flowers. It rang out as though it were made of bone china.

"Clear as a bell," said Jock, and he pushed the narrow spout of the watering can up under the rosette of downy leaves and tipped out the water.

"I thought you didn't go in for things as common as house plants?" remarked Stan.

"I don't. I just like to grow a few cinerarias because they're tricky. I like to prove to myself that I've still got the knack."

Stan saw his opening. "Yes, well, you've definitely got the knack of growing plants. It's the other knacks of the business that I'm worried about."

Jock looked up from his watering. "What do you mean?"

"I've just been doing the books."

"I know you have. What's the problem?"

"The problem, old chap," said Stan, knitting the bushy grey eyebrows that matched his hair and his mac, "is that you have what people in this day and age call a cash-flow problem."

"I don't owe anybody anything," snapped Jock, defensively. "You know I always pay my bills the day they come in."

"Yes, you do – in spite of the fact that I've suggested, time and again, that you wait thirty days before settling any account."

"Madge always paid on the nail and I've continued to do the same. Is that why I've got a problem?"

"Not exactly. The main cause of it is that not much seems to have been coming in lately. Your bank accounts are in the black but they're on the low side and you don't seem to have much put by. When Madge was doing your books it was easy to see just what was happening. Your incomings and outgoings were set in columns, but all I get from you is this." He clicked open the brass clasp on his fat leather briefcase and pulled out a battered buff envelope stuffed with receipts. "It doesn't seem to add up."

Jock put down his watering-can and the mallet. "Well, Madge had the time to do all the book-keeping. I don't. But I give you all the receipts."

"Yes, but judging by what's left at the end of every month you must have more outgoings than I can see from the bills. I know you have to pay young Wayne's wages now, but they're not excessive. It seems to me that your takings have been drastically lower this year than they have previously."

"Stan, are you suggesting I'm on the fiddle?"

"My dear chap, that's the last thing I'd suggest. If I had to choose between you and George Washington in the honesty stakes he'd come a poor second. It's just that I'm a bit baffled as to why your funds are so low."

"It's the middle of winter. Trade's always slack in February. You'll have to bear with me. Things will look up," said Jock, picking up his mallet and tapping at his cinerarias once more.

Stan watched the old man at his work, a cloth cap on his head and a faded denim apron covering his old brown cardigan and baggy corduroy trousers. His feet were encased in an ancient pair of black leather boots. He was fond of Jock. They'd never socialized over the years, but his occasional visits to the nursery had resulted in an easy-going relationship, which seemed, now, to be under some strain. Stan smoothed his soft clean hand over his hair. "I was speaking to Dennis Wragg yesterday."

Jock cleared his throat warningly then carried on with his mallet, refusing to look up at the mention of a name that, in his mind, ranked on a par with Himmler or Dr Crippen.

Stan braved the iciness of the atmosphere, fishing for clues. "He still wants to buy you out, in spite of the flood."

"Does he now?" muttered Jock, tapping even more ferociously.

"He says that once in sixty years is not very frequent for a river to burst its banks, and a protective wall would be easy to build."

Jock didn't answer, but bent down and dunked the watering-can into a large tank of rainwater beneath the bench. It gurgled and glugged as the cool, clear water filled to its galvanized brim. Jock hauled it out, with some difficulty, and resumed his task as though he were alone.

Stan refused to be beaten and sought an olive branch. "I know you can't stand him, but he might be offering you a way out of this situation."

"Yes, and on what terms?" retorted Jock, still not meeting the eye of his questioner.

"Well, I know he'll expect a reduction in price due to the flood damage but it would get you out of a tricky spot."

"No, thanks." Jock's reply was brief. Dennis Wragg's reaction to the flood was as insensitive as he had expected – and Jock's response was exactly what Stan had expected. He knew that he'd taken this conversation as far as he could.

"Well, I'll be off, then. I'll leave you to your tapping."

Jock set his jaw and carried on with his work.

Stan walked back down the path of the old Victorian greenhouse, admiring the cinerarias on the gravel-covered benches to left and right and wondering how a man who was so good at the difficult job of growing plants could be so hopeless at understanding the simple workings of a profit-and-loss account. He paused at the door of the white-painted greenhouse, wrapped his fingers around the shiny brass knob and turned back with the intention of bidding his client, and friend, farewell. But the right words failed him.

Jock heard the door close, put down his watering-can and mallet, and looked through the condensation on the glass to see his accountant walking back up the nursery path.

Katherine had left End Cottage at half past eight, having shared a shower with Rob and torn herself away for her editorial meeting at nine. Rob had wolfed down a bowl of cereal and worked out the contents of the following day's programme before ringing up Steve Taylor to confirm the running order. He'd had an hour in his garden – enough to get it sorted at this time of year – another hour and a half at his word-processor, tapping out his weekly piece for the paper, and then decided to nip over and see the old man.

Stan Halfpenny greeted him at the gate of the nursery. "Hello, Rob. Nice day for a change."

"Hello, Stan. Great, isn't it? Good to see a bit of blue sky after all that rain."

"Yes. Blue sky. Lovely," said Stan, raising his eyes absent-mindedly to the heavens. "Lovely."

Rob saw the accountant's distracted look and felt the need to probe further. "What's the problem?"

Like father, like son, thought the accountant. He'd faced that question twice in ten minutes. He hesitated, unsure what to say.

"You would tell me if everything wasn't OK, wouldn't you?" asked Rob.

"What do you mean?"

"Stan, you've been Dad's accountant longer than I've been his son."

"I know." Stan reflected as he looked around at the familiar nursery. He'd been coming here since the days of one old greenhouse and a potting-shed in the days when S. W. Halfpenny FCA had just had the windows of his new office in town painted with gilded initials.

"I know you pride yourself on your confidentiality, but I am the old man's son and if something was bothering you you would tell me, wouldn't you?"

Stan looked him in the eye. "If something was bothering me I wouldn't know whether to tell you or not."

"If it meant the difference between Dad sinking or swimming, then I think you probably should."

Stan rested his briefcase on the wall and gave Rob a succinct, if circumspectly vague, indication of the state of his father's accounts, before apologetically picking up his case and walking back to his car.

Rob looked after the small, grey-macked figure as it trudged up the lane, then he turned through the gate and walked down the mud-spattered path to the potting-shed, where Wayne was blowing hard at the paint on the door.

"Oh, very neat," said Rob. "Won't it dry?"

"I just don't want it to drip or Mr MacGregor will give me a right earful," Wayne confessed.

Mr MacGregor probably has his mind on other things right now, thought Rob.

"Well, at least you've spelt February correctly," he offered encouragingly, eyeing Wayne's artistry. Wayne looked suitably smug. "Crikey, the mud's still a bit whiffy."

"Er, I don't think it's all down to the mud," said Wayne, tilting his head in the direction of the small room next door to the potting-shed.

They looked at each other and muttered, in unison, "Harry." Then laughed.

"Where's Dad?" asked Rob.

"He's in the far greenhouse," said Wayne.

"I gather he's just had a visitor."

"Yeah," answered Wayne. "He didn't stay long, though. Only here for a few minutes."

"So I gather. I'll go and see how the old man is."

Rob walked across the nursery in the direction of the greenhouses, looking to left and right at the gradually improving scene. Most of the clearing up had been down to Wayne, he reckoned. Harry might have shaken a broom at the mud now and again but he would have been unlikely to have made much of an impact on the devastation. But perhaps this devastation was only a taste of things to come.

He looked down towards the river, friendly and docile now, though the flotsam of dried grass and leaves in the branches of the trees showed how high the water had been. A pied wagtail hopped from stone to stone at the water's edge, its tail flicking up and down as it foraged for food.

He opened the door of the greenhouse. His father was at the far end, restaging the cinerarias.

"Every plant has a front and a back," offered Rob.

"I'm glad you haven't forgotten," said his father, without looking up.

"Some things you never forget. How are you doing?"

"I'm fine."

Jock still didn't meet his eye.

"I've just bumped into Stan Halfpenny," said Rob, as casually as he could.

"Nice for you."

Rob was surprised at the ice in his father's reply.

Jock went on, "And what did he have to say? Has he told you about the state of the business?"

"He didn't want to, but I think he understood why I needed to know."

"So he told you what he advised me, did he? That's it's time I sold out to Dennis Wragg and got this old liability off my back. Told you I haven't got a cash-flow, or whatever it is. Mentioned that the books aren't done like your mother used to do them."

Rob felt a churning in the pit of his stomach. Just as he thought his father had turned the corner another blow had been landed on him and he was beginning to buckle.

"This is my business. It's always been my business – mine and your mother's."

The old man's voice broke. A cineraria slipped from his hands on to the flagged path, its pot smashing into a hundred shards of terracotta and its perfect dome of velvety green leaves crumpling under the weight of the damp compost.

"Damn!" Jock turned away and held on to the edge of the staging, then pushed his cap to the back of his head before removing it and wiping his eyes with his forearm.

"I'm sorry, Dad. Dad?" Rob walked slowly towards his father. "I just wanted to help." Jock's shoulders heaved and he stuffed his hand silently into his pocket for a large white handkerchief, which he shook out then used to blow his nose loudly. Rob stood next to him, waiting, his hand on the old man's shoulder.

"Oh dear," murmured Jock, trying to hold back an old man's tears. "Oh dear, oh dear. What a mess. What a bloody mess." He blew his nose again, then gazed out through the glass of the greenhouse at the nursery beyond, stuffing the lump of damp linen back into his pocket. "I've got so wound up in this place that I can't see the light sometimes."

"What's happened?" asked Rob.

Jock fought to pull himself together, aware of the panic that might be rising in his son. "Oh, don't worry. It's nothing dishonest. I've just been less than careful, which is not something you'd ever expect a Scot to admit."

"What do you mean?" asked Rob, gently.

Jock wiped his eyes with the back of his gnarled hand, then turned to look at his son. "It's Harry."

"What do you mean?"

"Oh, he's been having problems."

Rob's mind went blank. "What sort of problems?"

"He's been living with his sister for years now. She's even older than he is. Their house is rented. A fairly modest amount. Or rather it was. The lease came up for renewal and the landlord decided to increase the rent. He wanted to bring it in line with the rest of his property. A small fortune. Harry knew he couldn't afford to pay it so he told his sister they would have to move. The old lady went doolally. She kept waking up at nights and started rambling, went off her food."

Jock rubbed his hand across his stubbly chin to wipe it dry and Rob heard the rasp of his grey whiskers. "The doctor warned Harry that she couldn't take this kind of upheaval at her age. Some folk in their eighties are adaptable and some aren't, he said. Harry's sister fell into the last group. Harry came and asked me about it. He didn't know what to do. I told him not to worry and said that I'd pay the increased rent but he wouldn't hear of it. Even Harry has his pride."

"So what happened?"

"I went round to see the landlord. Explained what effect it was having on the old lady."

"And what did he say?"

"Not much. Tough as old boots. Heartless bugger. Said it wasn't his problem. Didn't seem to care if they ended up on the streets. As far as he was concerned the house was part of his income and he wasn't a charity. Life was tough, he said. If they paid the new rent they could stay, if they didn't, they'd have to leave. Simple as that."

"I think I know the rest," said Rob. "You pay their extra rent without Harry knowing, don't you?"

"It was the only way round it. The only way that Harry could save face and his sister could live out the rest of her days in peace. She's eighty-six, for God's sake. Eighty-six! I told Harry that the landlord had said that the two of them could have another five years at the same rent and then he'd think again. Harry seemed happy with that. I just put the money aside from the takings in my apron pocket. It doesn't leave me much at the end of the week but I can manage. I keep all my receipts and everything's declared."

"Except the rent?"

"Except the rent."

"Oh, Dad," said Rob. "What am I going to do with you? You're so kind." His eyes filled. "And I wouldn't have anybody else for a dad."

"Now don't start that," said Jock, clearing his throat. "We've had enough emotion over the last few weeks to last us a lifetime. Let's just try and get on with things and hope we come out the other side OK. It's been a long, hard winter but spring's coming and trade will quicken up. The money will start coming in soon. It's nothing to worry about. I'll go and put the kettle on." And with that he walked out of the greenhouse towards the smell of new paint.

Rob bent down to pick up the shattered cineraria. The plant was beyond recovery; its stem had snapped clean in two and its pot seemed to have shattered into a quarter of a million pieces. At least a quarter of a million.

Chapter 14

Rob wound down the Fiesta's windows to allow the fresh morning air to whistle through his hair. With any luck it might help to clear his head. He'd said nothing to his father about the offer he would now find it hard to refuse, knowing what the old man's reaction would be. But if things were as bad as Stan Halfpenny had suggested, it wouldn't be long before some kind of action had to be taken. Jock couldn't fund Harry and his sister indefinitely, and Rob couldn't stand by and watch his father bleed himself dry.

He took the moorland road. The damp tarmac glistened in the morning sun and black-faced sheep with matted grey wool nibbled at the fine grass on the roadside, baaing bleakly as he passed. Hunks of millstone grit, their surfaces blackened by centuries of smoke from the town below, towered over the purple-grey of the moor and a lone grouse scuttered up from the heather with a coarse 'go-back, go-back' and flew across the top of the thick mattress of crisp, coppery bracken.

He pulled up in a gravelly lay-by that commanded a fine view of the valley and got out to stretch his legs. The nip in the morning air almost took his breath away. Up here, amid the heather and the bracken, the troubles of the dale below seemed far away; they always did. He found it reassuring, and wondered if city folk ever had this opportunity to put their lives into perspective, to enjoy that feeling of being small and insignificant. Did they ever feel the need to?

From his lofty perch, the houses below seemed like specks of grit, and the mighty river was just a slender ribbon of silver grey, snaking its way between them.

Sweeping woodland, naked except for the deep green of Scots pine,

118

furnished the slopes of the valley and beyond the far bend of the river lay Wharfeside Nursery, the glass of its small greenhouses twinkling like fragments of crystal in the early-morning sun. Further up he could just make out the black dot that was End Cottage and below him, larger due to its proximity, was Tarn House, whose sweeping lawns, banks of rhododendrons and curving hedge of lustrous laurel still showed signs of his activity with spade, fork and hoe.

He looked at his watch. Eleven o'clock. Coffee time at Tarn House. He thought better of it. Helena had listened to him enough of late. As his father had said, "We've had enough emotion over the last few weeks to last us a lifetime." But Sir Freddie would want an answer, and he would want it soon.

"When you're dry you can have a Bonio, but until then you lie in your basket and don't interrupt while Daddy's thinking." Bertie stopped towelling Pally's muddied feet and plopped her with her sister in the blanket-lined basket under the mahogany writing table in his red-walled, theatrically festooned study.

Gilt-framed photographs of George Robey and Bud Flanagan watched him disappear as he walked through the red-plush curtain, held back with a fat golden tassel, and took the towel into the kitchen. He dropped it in a wicker linen basket then washed his hands at the sink, using his soap-on-a-rope in the shape of a carrot. He looked out at the February garden for inspiration. "Dear God!" he said to himself. "I wish I were a fairy with a magic wand. Well, I wish I had a magic wand. Snowdrops, a few clumps, winter-flowering irises without flowers, a witch hazel, a mahonia and what else? Winter jasmine on its last legs. Oh, well, I suppose I can cobble something together out of that little nosegay."

He made himself a coffee and noticed that, as usual, Terry had methodically laid out on the worktop all the cooking utensils he would need to prepare their supper when he returned from the restaurant that evening. Just for once it irritated him. He moved a few of the things around. Put a knife back in a drawer. He didn't really know why: he just felt a need to interfere. Then he walked back down the Indian-rugged hall to his study and took down a fat book from the middle shelf. *Exotic Water Gardens*, it said, in gilt letters on the spine. Bertie laid it on his desk and opened the cover. Then he turned to page forty-three, took out the little bottle of whisky that nestled in a cut-out compartment and poured a generous tot into his mug. Ally and Pally looked up, showing the whites of their eyes. Bertie noticed. "Just Daddy's medicine. No need to look so disapproving." He took a gulp of the enriched coffee, said, "That's better," and put back *Exotic Water Gardens*, complete with its secret. He took down another volume: *The Year In Your Garden*. It was a pity that the section for February was so thin; it wouldn't help him much with his column for the *Sunday Sphere*. Still, tired old tarts couldn't be choosers. As he thumbed through the half-dozen pages looking for inspiration the phone rang.

"Honeysuckle Cottage," Bertie answered, his rustic tones in operational mode.

"Bet you haven't got any in flower, though," replied the voice at the other end.

"Mr D'Arcy." Bertie dropped his Mummerset burr and carried on, "I bet *you* haven't got any in flower either at this time of year."

"Never heard of winter-flowering honeysuckle, Bertie? Call yourself a gardener? Try saying *Lonicera fragrantissima*."

"Don't be so cheeky. What can I be a-doing for you?" asked Bertie.

"Very little, judging by yesterday's fiasco."

"Yes, that was a turn-up for the books, wasn't it?" said Bertie, nonplussed.

"What went wrong? I thought you reckoned Freddie Roper was going to be all over me?"

"Oh, no, I didn't. I just said that what he was looking for was a young, thrusting type and that you should make yourself available. It seems as though he must have found another available thruster."

"Has he asked Rob MacGregor to front the campaign, then?"

"I wouldn't know, though judging by the time they spent closeted together I wouldn't be at all surprised. I'll try and find out tomorrow. It's programme day and Mr Smarty-pants'll be in the studio most of the time. I'll get it out of him."

"Well, I shall be deeply pissed off if it's him and not me."

"You're not worried about sullying your reputation by advertising, then?"

"Can't afford principles, Bertie. Too expensive. And with that amount of money in my pocket I wouldn't have to worry about them."

"I see." Bertie smiled to himself.

"There must be some way I can get in there."

"Well, you haven't got much time. You know how fast these advertising types move."

"Yes. Faster than greased lightning. Want everything done yesterday." Guy sounded a touch impatient, as if he wanted to move on to more important things. "By the way, Bertie, who was that woman sitting at the top table at the press do?"

"Which woman?"

"Well, there was only one. Plump piece. Hair like a Barbie doll. Sitting next to that PR bloke, Clay, or whatever his name is. The woman in the red suit."

"Oh, her," said Bertie, sniffily. "She's Simon Clay's boss. Head of PR. Rather a bolshie bird. Claudia Bell. Right old bag. Can't think why they keep her on. Puts everybody's back up. I think she must have something going with Freddie."

"Married, is she?"

"Divorced. Several times. Why are you asking?"

"Oh, just curious."

"And is that what you're ringing about?" asked Bertie, getting impatient.

"Not really. It's just that I did have one piece of good news yesterday," said Guy.

"Oh, yes?" asked Bertie, his ears pricking up.

"They've asked me to present the Chelsea Flower Show programme this year. Not bad, eh? Bit of prestige at last. That should make Mr MacGregor look to his laurels."

"Ooh, I'll say," said Bertie, with a touch too much relish. "Am I allowed to drop it into the conversation tomorrow?"

"Not likely. I want the pleasure of telling him myself."

"You're really not a fan, are you?" mused Bertie.

"Not much, no."

"Why not? Why's he put your back up? I mean, he's pinched my programme from me, but what's he ever done to you?"

"Got in the way, Bertie. Smug bastard. He can't be for real, he's too good to be true. And, anyway, he's too much of a son of the soil for my liking. Just find him a pain in the arse, frankly. The ladies seem to quite like him, though. Speak to you soon. Pip-pip." And Guy rang off.

"That's all it is," said Bertie softly, replacing the receiver in its cradle and looking under the table at the two King Charles spaniels.

"Just two pretty boys as jealous as hell of each other. Well, we wouldn't know anything about that, girls, would we?"

Mrs Ipplepen was the reason why Rob found himself sitting at the kitchen table at Tarn House drinking coffee. He'd intended to go straight back home and finish his piece for the *Daily Post* but she'd spotted him driving along the road, as she was on her way to make Lady Sampson's lunch, and flagged him down. How was he? How was his father? Wouldn't he come in and have a quick coffee? Lady Sampson would love to see him. He felt relieved that he had been bullied into it.

Helena was, indeed, pleased to see him. Fresh from the hairdresser, her hair an immaculately coiffed silver grey, she looked bright-eyed and almost young in well-tailored black trousers and a roll-necked sweater of charcoal grey.

They talked of the nursery's recovery and of Wayne's gilt-edged worth, and Helena asked after Harry and how he had taken the shock of it all. Rob had been about to get round to the subject of Harry when Mrs Ipplepen, a symphony in turquoise nylon, rustled her way into the kitchen bearing a quiche from the freezer.

"Vera," said Helena, "do you think there's enough for two?" And then, to Rob, "You'll stay for lunch? Or are you in a hurry?"

Before he had time to answer Mrs Ipplepen was in like a shot, "Ooh, yes, Mr Rob. It's a very big kweesh. It'd be a shame to de-thaw it just for one. An' I've got some running beans and some of Cyril's taters from the allotment."

"Well, if you're sure it's no bother?"

"No bother at all," said Helena, a relieved look on her face. "Lovely. A glass of sherry?"

"Well, I have to go back and write my Saturday piece," he offered feebly.

"A small one, then. Bound to make it flow better. I'll get it, Vera, you carry on with the quiche," and she left the two of them in the kitchen.

"I'm glad you came in, Mr Rob," said Mrs Ipplepen, speaking conspiratorially and looking over her shoulder to check that the coast was clear. "I thought she needed a bit of company. It would 'ave been Sir's birthday today."

"Oh, heavens, yes," said Rob. "I'd forgotten. Is she OK?"

"She's fine, really," replied Mrs Ipplepen. "Just a bit intraflective, if you know what I mean."

"I know," said Rob, smiling gently.

Helena came back with a sherry bottle and three glasses. "A new bottle. Jumbo's favourite. Rather appropriate today," she said brightly.

Rob crossed the kitchen to intercept her. "Here, let me," and he took the bottle from her, pulled his budding knife from his jeans pocket and began to cut away the plastic seal.

"Ah, that's what I like to see," said Helena, "a real gardener who always carries his knife in his pocket. Very impressive."

"Yes, but it's not as sharp as it should be. When I worked on Dad's nursery I could sharpen it every day on his whetstone. Now I have to do it when I call in, and when I remember, and I forgot this morning."

"Oh, so you've been in this morning?"

"Yes."

"Ooh, I bet it's a right mess," said Mrs Ipplepen, looking up from the bowl of beans she was topping and tailing by the sink.

"Glass of sherry for you, Vera?"

"Oh, no, thank you, your ladyship. If I have a drop while I'm topping and bottoming these beans I'll lose a finger."

Rob pulled out the cork and poured two glasses of the tawny liquid.

Helena raised her glass, Rob raised his, and they both said, "Cheers," quietly. Nothing more. Mrs Ipplepen busied herself with her beans.

"Vera's got some news, haven't you, Vera?"

"Ooh, 'aven't I just."

"What's that, Mrs Ipplepen?" said Rob, trying to stop his mouth from turning up at the corners.

"It's my Tiffany, Mr Rob. She's expectant."

"Oh, well done, Mrs Ipplepen. I *am* pleased for you."

"Well, it was nothing to do with me, though I did offer 'er plenty of encouragement. Eight years it's been, but that 'usband of 'ers finally got his finger out at last."

"Er, yes," said Rob, not knowing quite where to look. Helena averted her eyes, for fear of meeting his.

"Yes, you can just see the bump," Mrs Ipplepen went on.

"It must make you feel very proud," offered Rob.

"Ooh, yes. Every time I look at 'er I feel quite nocturnal."

"Vera, it was the other bit of news I was thinking of," said Helena, speaking louder than normal to drown the laughter in her voice.

"Other news?" asked Mrs Ipplepen.

"About Mrs Wragg."

"Oh, *her*," said Mrs Ipplepen, disapprovingly.

"Mrs Wragg? Gladys Wragg?" asked Rob.

"Yes, Old Glad-rags," confirmed Mrs Ipplepen, warming to her subject. "Bumped into 'er at the 'airdresser's – you know, Sharon's by the station," she said, patting her cerulean curls into shape. Rob noticed that both hair and overall had changed from shades of pink to shades of blue, but that the two were still a million miles from matching. The spectacles remained pink.

"She was cookin' under the drier and goin' on about 'er Dennis and 'is plans for expansion. Said that the nursery down by the river was their next priority and that now that it 'ad been flooded they felt as though it were an act of mercy to take it off old Mr MacGregor's 'ands."

"Did she, now?" said Rob.

"Yes. Well, I told 'er to keep 'er nose out of other people's business an' that we didn't want another big garden centre in the dale. One was quite enough."

"Good for you, Mrs Ipplepen," said Rob, raising his glass to her.

"I thought it'd stop there," she continued, "but then when she came out from under 'er drier she came over to see me under mine and gave me a right earful. No class, that woman. Flaunts 'erself around as though she's aristocratic, begging your ladyship's pardon." She nodded in the direction of her employer and flashed her a Clara Bow smile. Orange lips. "Any'ow, she starts goin' on about 'er Dennis and about 'ow 'e was a fillinfropisist for bein' considerate an' all that. Said that the land was 'ardly big enough to be worth 'is botherin' with but that 'e felt sorry for Mr MacGregor an' wanted to 'elp 'im out."

"Cheeky blighter," said Rob, and then, turning to Helena, "You see, that's what I've always found difficult to understand."

"What's that?"

"Dad's nursery is tiny. Two acres at the outside. It's not nearly big enough for Dennis Wragg to be interested in. There's no access, except for a country lane, and there's certainly no room for a car park. There's nothing I know of that would conceivably make the plot in any way desirable to an investor. Added to which it's just been flooded."

"And still he wants to buy."

"What is it about this small patch of riverside that makes Dennis Wragg so keen to have it? I just can't understand it." Rob's brow was furrowed and his sherry glass nearly empty.

"Another one?"

"No, thanks."

"Do you suppose there's some sinister reason, then?" she asked, helping herself to another half glass.

"Like what? Buried treasure?"

"I don't know. What an exciting thought! But it could be something like that."

Rob laughed.

"Oh, I know it sounds silly, but there has to be a reason why this dreadful man is determined to get his hands on Jock's nursery, and if it isn't for the obvious reasons then it has to be for hidden ones. So what are they?"

"Blowed if I know," said Rob, draining his glass.

"Maybe I'll make some enquiries," said Helena, with a sparkle in her eyes. "Jumbo had plenty of good contacts in all the right places and it's a shame to let them go to waste. Perhaps I'll be able to find out something. Anything. Anyway, I'll try. It's quite exciting, really."

"I'm glad you think so," said Rob, puzzled.

"Come on, then," said Helena, putting down her glass. "You've just time for a quick garden tour before lunch." And then, under her breath as they walked out into the hall, "We'll have to make it a quick one or those beans will be cooked to death. As far as Vera's concerned *al dente* is some kind of American gangster. Ha-ha. That was rather good, wasn't it?"

"Don't call us," said Rob, chuckling, "and we probably won't call you."

It was eleven thirty before Rob tramped his way up the stairs to bed at End Cottage. He looked at the clock by his bed and sighed. Half-ten was his normal turn-in time on the day before a programme, but since he'd been waylaid by Mrs Ipplepen he'd spent the rest of the day trying to catch up with himself and failing. By the time he'd brooded about his father, rung the studios and ordered the props he needed for *Mr MacGregor's Garden*, brooded some more, put away a poached egg on beans on toast, spoken to Katherine on the phone (being careful not to say anything about Jock) and completed his piece for the *Daily Post*, the day had all but gone.

He could have killed a large Scotch but thought better of it. Dumping his clothes in a heap in the corner of the bedroom and stretching his whole body so that his hands almost touched the ceiling, he walked to the bathroom to get ready for bed and found himself wishing he could slide under the duvet with Katherine again tonight. She was working late. She wouldn't want to disturb him when she came in and would sleep at Wellington Heights. But how warm she had been, and soft, and fragrant. As he lay alone in the centre of the double bed, hovering between sleep and consciousness, another figure came into his mind and his body stirred. He did his best to banish the fluttering in his stomach before finally falling into a deep sleep.

He failed to hear the telephone ring at ten to twelve, and it wasn't until early the following morning that he listened with rising panic to the single message on his answering-machine: "Hi, it's Lisa. Just to say . . . I'm missing you. And your body. That's all. Lots of love. See you soon. Ciao."

There was no message from Katherine. But then, she hadn't wanted to wake him when she got home from a frustrating day at the office at half past midnight.

Chapter 15

"Close those barn doors a bit on number twenty-four, Jeff" came the shouted instruction across the studio floor. Jeff, a tall, lanky, acne-covered lad wielding a long aluminium pole, poked and prodded at the floodlight high above him, clouting the two metal doors that acted like blinkers on either side of it until the fat man with the glasses and the light meter seemed satisfied.

Ten o'clock in the morning. The cavernous drama studio at Northcountry Television echoed to the sounds of carpentry and shouted instructions as the set for *Mr MacGregor's Garden* began to grow out of nothing. The green plastic lawn was rolled out and secured in place with stage weights. A noisy dumper truck ferried in mountains of compost to act as flower-beds and give rise to yet another fusillade of sarcastic letters asking Rob if he got his soil from Fortnum and Mason.

A potting-shed interior – or three sides of it – was being erected in one corner, and a white-raftered greenhouse, without any glass, was already complete in another, its slatted staging waiting for the primulas, the alpines and the pots of spring bulbs that would make up one of Rob's items this week.

Hefty stage-hands in grey overalls lumbered in, cradling in their Popeye arms huge rhododendrons and spotted laurels, the background shrubs that would be 'planted' in front of the trellis fence that marked the perimeter of Mr MacGregor's studio garden. Behind it curved a cyclorama of pale blue sky which, within half an hour, thanks to Jeff's ministrations with the pole, would be free of shadows.

Four grey cameras skulked silently on their own in the centre of the floor, each pointing at a rectangular board covered in a black, white and grey pattern. They crouched there, hunched and still, like four old men in the public library intent on reading the newspaper for free. It was something referred to in reverential tones as 'line-up'. In two years Rob had never properly fathomed what it meant.

A pony-tailed props girl busied herself at the back of the rustic-toned shed, hanging up old sieves and stacking flower-pots of warm terracotta on the shelves. A skein of raffia dangled from a hook on the back of the potting-shed door, and the battered brown potting-bench, carried in by two panting men with rivulets of sweat running down their foreheads, was positioned to one side.

Another commotion and shouts of, 'Watch those lights,' heralded the arrival of a fifteen-foot evergreen tree that would be positioned somewhere between greenhouse and potting-shed to give the garden a feeling of 'real lived-in permanence', according to Edgar Prout, the set designer. He bobbed between the bushes in his faded denim smock, looking angst-ridden, and danced, like a mayfly, among the mayhem that would become, he hoped, in the fullness of time – well, in the next half-hour actually – a delightful English country garden in the Rosemary Verey mould, even if most English country gardens were, at this time of year, drowning under a deluge of drizzle, and Rosemary Verey probably was enjoying warmer climes.

It mattered not to Edgar. He sucked at his forefinger, nervously ran his fingers through his thinning hair and pointed here to direct the planting of a spiky holly, there to indicate the position of a diaphanously draped concrete nymph, all the time wearing a pre-occupied look as though he were searching for something he couldn't find. It was probably perfection.

Rob pushed open the heavy swing door from the outer corridor and walked into the studio. He liked this time of day, the feeling of anticipation, the nerves gripping the stomach. The only other time he had felt a sensation remotely like it had been when Helena had taken him to concerts: when the orchestra began to tune their instruments from the oboist's A it made the hairs on the back of his neck stand on end. It was the same now.

He stood quietly for a few moments just inside the door, looking up at the bright lights that shone down from the blackness of the studio flies to cast their brilliance on the blossoming rural scene below. He half smiled, half winced at the phoniness of it all, and heard his

128

producer Steve Taylor's voice in his head: "It's only to get a bit of colour into the programme in winter. You'll be outside again in a couple of weeks, back in the muck where you belong."

A trim youth with a shaven head perforated by one earring came towards him. "Hi, Rob. Are they in your dressing room?"

"Yes. It's the blue and green rugby shirt and the 501's. OK?"

"Fine. Do they need pressing?"

"No. I think they're OK, thanks. As long as you're happy with the colour."

"Sounds fine to me. Nothing there to strobe and we're not using CSO so you won't disappear!" The youth from Wardrobe gave Rob a friendly pat on the shoulder and disappeared into the shadows, having satisfied himself that the costume requirements were as disappointingly minimal as usual. Shame they weren't doing *Martin Chuzzlewit*.

Rob was aware now of what he could and could not wear on the programme. Small checks tended to flicker and flash in front of the camera so he stayed clear of them. If Steve Taylor wanted to do something clever – make a plant appear and disappear, or stand Rob in front of a scene that didn't really exist in the studio – he would use CSO, Colour Separation Overlay. Rob would stand in front of a plain blue background which, thanks to electronic wizardry upstairs, could be turned into any chosen background on the screen. The only problem was that if any part of Rob's clothing were blue that, too, would soak up the scene.

He moved towards the frenzied activity to check that his props had arrived and that everything was being placed where he would need it, and as he did so Steve crossed the studio floor with a beaming smile. "Hi, sunshine. You OK?" he asked.

"You're very chirpy this morning," said Rob.

"You'd be chirpy if you'd just had two days on News and been released into the pastoral beauty of an English garden," he said, making a sweeping gesture in the direction of the horticultural panorama unfolding before him.

"Yes," said Rob, sardonically, and then, "Everything OK with the stuff I asked for?"

"Yep. No probs," said Steve, his lank black hair falling in front of one of his eyes. He began to roll up the sleeves of his pale blue shirt and slackened the knot in the floral tie at his neck. "Like it?" he enquired.

Rob looked closely at Steve's tie and shook his head. "Botanically inaccurate. Single roses don't have six petals. They have five."

"Smug sod! I thought it was just the job. It cost me thirty quid!"

Rob laughed. "Well, you've been done, but it's nice to know you care."

"I do! I tell you, a few days in the newsroom among those back-biting buggers and you realize that there's more bullshit on the second floor than there is in your compost heap."

"Oops, sorry." A cameraman wheeling his equipment across the studio floor missed Steve by a fraction of an inch, and a rigger whipped the cable from around him.

"Right," said Steve, recovering his balance. "Let's give 'em hell today, shall we? What have we got?"

He cast his eyes down at the bright yellow script handed to him by the floor assistant. Each programme's content was agreed in advance, but the basic blocking – deciding on the positions of cameras and presenters – was finalized on the morning with a kind of good-natured horse-trading. Steve, as producer/director, would have his own idea of how the programme would look, and Rob would know how he could make each item work best for himself. The morning involved compromise on both sides. Usually it passed without acrimony, unless Bertie started playing the prima donna.

They had come to the part of the programme that involved the son of the soil. They were standing in the potting-shed where a sack of seed potatoes had materialized on the potting-bench, but where Bertie had not materialized to go with them.

"Anyone seen Bertie?" asked Steve. There were a few mutterings from cameramen but no positive identification.

"No sign yet," said the robust girl in Doc Martens, who was the floor assistant.

"The old bugger's probably slept in," said Steve, looking at his watch. He caught the eye of a young body-building type in his early twenties, with close-cropped hair, black T-shirt, black jeans and sandy-coloured Caterpillar boots. Looking between him and his watch he said, "Twenty minutes OK for you, Rory?"

"Yeah, fine, Steve, fine." Rory Watson turned to address the floor. "Coffee break, then, chaps. Back here ready to block in twenty minutes, please. Not half an hour, twenty minutes."

There was a good-natured 'Oooooh' from the cameramen and floor crew and Rory turned a delicate pink, before shrugging and walking off the floor.

"It's his first show as floor manager," confided Steve. "AFM until yesterday, but I think he's ready for it. Reliable as the smile on your face," he said, in the direction of Rob, who was gazing transfixed across the studio floor.

"I said, reliable as the smile on your face," repeated Steve, pointedly, and Rob came partially down to earth. He had noticed a female face peering in through the tiny window in the studio floor. She waved to him, and smiled. His mouth had gone dry and his stomach had executed a back flip. Lisa Drake disappeared from view and Rob tried to concentrate on what Steve was saying.

"Coffee, I think. Yes?"

"Mmm? What? Oh, yes, coffee." Rob flashed a bright but nervous smile at him and they walked across the studio floor in the opposite direction to the door that had reminded him of another door in his life which was, as yet, not quite closed.

"Where the hell is he?" Steve Taylor's voice boomed across the studio floor. *Mr MacGregor's Garden* was broadcast live at 7 p.m. It was now 6 p.m. and there was still no sign of Bertie. Calls had been made during the morning to his house; there was no reply. In the afternoon a taxi from a Bradford company had been sent round to his cottage to pick him up. He wasn't there. All obvious avenues had been explored and Bertie was nowhere to be found.

"Right, sod it." Steve Taylor turned to Rob, who was standing in the middle of the studio lawn, surrounded by banks of rhododendrons and a selection of mowers. "Let's think this thing through. You start off with the welcome and the menu from under the tree, right?"

"Right," agreed Rob, clamping his thumbnail between his teeth and concentrating hard.

"We come out of the graphics to find you here on the lawn and you launch into Bloomer of the Week which is that rhododendron behind you. Then you walk forward and go into the piece on selecting a mower. Right?"

"Yep," confirmed Rob. "And then we go into the snowdrop VT from Pencarrick."

"We come out of that and find you in the greenhouse for your flowery bit and then you link into the VT piece about what's on this weekend."

"Fine."

"Now, during that VT you'll have to move while you're doing the voice-over and end up over there in the potting-shed to do Bertie's bit on seed potatoes. Do you know what he was going to do?"

"Not exactly but it's no problem; I can go through all the usual things with the props that Bertie's ordered – you know, how to choose your variety, what makes a good seed potato, how many you'll need for a ten-foot row, and then show folk how to sprout them. He's ordered egg boxes so they'll be fine for standing them in. How long do you want on that?"

"Three and a half minutes. OK?"

"Yes, just get the PA to give me really clear counts in my ear and I should be able to pace it. Do you want to block it now?"

"Good idea." Steve turned from Rob to address the assembled company. "Cameras, we'll block the spud bit in the shed – the bit that should have been Bertie's – with Rob, and we'll have to go without the old sod, even if he does turn up. It's too late to rehearse him now."

They walked towards the potting shed, and as the cameras waltzed across the smooth studio floor in front of the green plastic lawn, Steve went through the rest of the programme with Rob. "There's the final VT which is your choice of this year's best seed varieties with music and voice-over, and then we come out for your final piece on turfing over there by the shrubbery. Then it's into next week's trail and goodbye. The PA will give you a hard count but you can't skip anything on the VT, so if you need to shorten your ending I suggest you do it once we've come out of the pictures. Have you got about thirty seconds worth of words you can keep for the end so that we can chop them if we need to?"

"I'll think of something. It shouldn't be a problem."

"Right. OK cameras let's get this last bit sorted; we're on air in half-an-hour. God! And I thought the newsroom was hair-raising. Are you OK?"

Rob nodded.

"It's a hell of a lot to carry on your own. They'll probably be bored rigid with you by the end of the half hour so keep it perky. Only joking, you'll be great. I'll kill the bastard for this. Anyway let's crack it and give the lads a ten-minute break before we go on air. I'm off to the gallery. Good luck."

And he was gone. Rob fiddled about on the potting bench with his potatoes, egg boxes and assorted props and muttered to himself as he laid them out in order, going over it rapidly in his head so that the props led him through the story.

"Ready to rehearse, Rob?" asked Rory, a look of mild panic on his face.

"Yes; ready when you are."

"Quiet, studio!" yelled Rory, as though he were trying to quell a riot. And then, more quietly: "When you're ready, Rob."

Rob picked up out of the imaginary voice-over for the 'what's ons' and launched into his piece on potatoes. The count from the PA was loud and clear in his ear but there was a lot to cram in and he came out fifteen seconds too long. "You'll need to chop it by fifteen," said Steve, a touch tartly in his ear.

"OK. I'll have it sorted by the time we do it," Rob responded. "I'll drop a couple of the varieties.'

He knew by now that when a piece had to be shortened there was no point in trying to go faster and cram everything in. The piece would look rushed and sound gabbled. Something nearly always had to be cut out.

It was now half past six and the atmosphere in the studio was noticeably tense.

Rory was listening intently to his earpiece and muttering replies to the voice he was hearing in the walkie-talkie on his chest. "Right, studio, a fifteen-minute break, please. No more. We're up against it tonight so can you please make sure you're back in here in fifteen minutes. Thank you."

He turned to Rob. "Makeup, Rob, please."

"On my way," said Rob, wiping his hands together to rub off the earth that had clung to the potatoes.

He pushed open the door into Makeup and sat down in the chair next to Lisa Drake.

Only her head was sticking out above a pale blue nylon cape, which was more Mrs Ipplepen than Miss Drake, and her eyes were closed as the makeup artist applied eye-liner to her upper lids. But she had heard him come in and knew he was there without opening her eyes. "I hear you've a bit of a panic on," she said quietly.

"Yes. No Bertie."

"Will you be able to cope?" The voice sounded genuinely concerned.

"I think so. I'm just wondering what's happened to him. I hope he's all right. Not gone under a bus or anything. What are you doing in here? I thought News had its own makeup room upstairs?"

"We do, but it's being renovated so they're sending us down here to share yours. I hope you don't mind?"

"Don't be silly." Rob's eyes, too, were closed now as Josie Peart, the makeup girl, sponged tawny-biscuit foundation on his face. It suddenly struck him that it was like being in bed with her again – both of them lying back with their eyes closed and communicating naturally, relaxedly, easily. He felt the fluttering again in his stomach but took comfort in that he could put it down to nerves rather than the proximity of Lisa Drake. At least, that was what he told himself. He didn't believe it.

He heard the rustle of the nylon gown as she got out of the chair, but saw nothing – his eyes were still closed. Josie continued dabbing. Lisa picked up a comb and ran it through her hair, checked her lip gloss in the mirror and brushed specks of dust from her deep green jacket and skirt.

"Must dash. I've a recording in two minutes. Good luck." He didn't see her, but the peck on his cheek burned like fire, and the fragrance of her skin made his heart leap.

The door closed with a heavy clunk, Josie finished powdering his eyelids and Rob opened his eyes to discover a small envelope with his name written on it on the worktop in front of him, and a pink flush on Josie's cheeks.

"Ten minutes, Rob." Rory's head bobbed around the makeup room door.

"Fine. I'll be there in a minute." Rob checked his appearance in the mirror.

"Batteries, Rob," said another voice, and a lumbering untidily dressed middle-aged man with a beard came into the room with a small screwdriver in his hand and a couple of batteries.

"Oh, God!" said Rob. "Why do you guys always leave it until the last minute? I've just tucked my shirt in."

"It's all right, I can do it without taking your shirt out." The soundman walked behind Rob and pulled, with some effort, the small metal transmitter from his back jeans pocket. He prised off a small panel, flipped out the old battery with his screwdriver and pushed in a new one. He clicked the panel back into place, tucked the transmitter into Rob's pocket and checked that the short black aerial was dangling free.

Then he came round to face Rob and spoke into his chest. "This is Rob's mike, one-two-three, one-two-three. OK?" A voice in the soundman's ear told him that it was, indeed, OK, and he bumbled out of the makeup room with muttered apologies, scattering old batteries and Cellophane wrappings as he went.

"I wouldn't mind," Rob confided to Josie, "but they have bloody hours to change your batteries and they choose to do it about five minutes before you go on air."

"Perhaps it's because they've been in a bit of a rush tonight," she offered, as unflappable as ever.

"Yes, I suppose so. Anyway. Done now. Better get out there."

"Good luck, I'm sure you'll manage." Josie was already tipping a plastic bagful of soiled makeup sponges into a sink to soak. She'd seen it all before, and they usually did.

Rob patted his microphone to make sure it was comfortable, fluffed up the front of his hair, checked his flies, said, "Thanks, Josie," and pushed open the heavy door into the studio, sliding the small envelope into his empty back pocket.

Chapter 16

"Quiet, studio!" Rory's command was uncompromisingly authoritative, even if it was his first live programme as floor manager.

"Very impressive," said a growling voice behind him, and Rory jumped as he noticed Frank Burbage, sleeves rolled up, tie slackened at the neck, script in hand, surveying the sylvan scene. "Mind if I watch?" asked Frank, in a stage whisper.

"No, not at all."

"Bugger all else to do," mumbled Frank. "Madam's recording her bit so I can't crack on for half an hour. Thought I might kill a bit of time in the garden. Sure he won't mind?" Frank nodded at Rob on the other side of the studio floor.

Rory, torn between the etiquette of informing Rob that he had a professional onlooker, and the desire not to break his concentration that such an interruption would cause, shook his head and motioned Frank to join the other hangers-on who stood silently in a dimly lit corner, then crossed the floor towards his presenter.

Mr MacGregor's garden positively shimmered under the lights. Candy-floss clouds sauntered nonchalantly across the azure sky, and the damp earth below released its sweet fragrance into the warm air of the studio.

The set designer's hopes had been realized: the once bare concrete floor of this cavernous aircraft hangar of a studio had blossomed under Edgar's influence into an English garden – banks of gloriously verdant shrubs luxuriated under the majestic tree that now looked as though it had been growing there for years. A few coppery fallen leaves were strewn here, terracotta flower-pots slithered on to the earth there, and a white-painted bench on which Rosemary Verey would have been proud to recline was enveloped by the sparkling emerald leaves of laurel. The whole confection was embellished by potfuls of brilliant flowers in the white-raftered greenhouse. The dusty, russet-toned potting-shed, hung with the impedimenta of a century of horticulture, looked venerable enough to have been used by Adam.

On the Regency-striped lawn in the middle of this televisual Eden stood Rob MacGregor in navy blue and bottle green rugby shirt, blue jeans and black wellington boots, his hair shining under the lights like amber, and his clear complexion pretty well composed, bearing in mind the events of the day. A phalanx of lustrous lawn-mowers cut an arc to his left, his green eyes shone, and the once ordinary if good-looking guy seemed to take on an extra dimension, infused with a new power that switched itself on only moments before the programme began.

There was no falseness about his demeanour, just an enhancement of his natural characteristics. It was, as one prominent television executive had remarked, "as if someone had turned up the knobs marked 'colour', 'contrast' and 'brilliance'". Some called it charisma. Others called it star quality. Whatever it was, Rob MacGregor had it, rather fittingly for a gardener, in spades.

"Good luck, Rob," Rory whispered in his ear, and gave his arm a squeeze.

"And you," said Rob. Their eyes met for a moment, their smiles flickered and then Rory took the reins. His words quelled the final studio mutterings: "Counting to titles in five, four, three . . ." The 'two' and the 'one' were counted out silently with a show of fingers, and on 'zero' Rory gave a downward wave of his arm as the signature tune engulfed the studio.

As it approached its coda, Rory's voice broke in once more, "Coming to you in five, four, three," again the fingers, and then, as the graphics sequence mixed through to a wide but steadily tightening shot of Rob in the centre of his floral paradise, Rory's eyebrows were raised, his hand was lowered, and Rob kicked off the programme with a cheery "Hi!"

A fly watching these goings-on from high up on the wall would have been impressed by what he saw. The man in the rugby shirt and the four grey objects around him seemed to be engaged in some kind of courtship ritual. They appeared to dance with one another. First the rugby-shirted figure would pay attention to one of his suitors, and then to another. You could always tell which one had attracted him at any given time, for a little red light would show that he had won its undivided attention. As he moved across the floor from one place to another the grey objects would follow him like sheep, and every now and again, pictures unrelated to anything going on in the studio would come up on a large screen and they would all relax for a while and the little red lights would go out. People would talk during these sequences, until silenced by the man with the clipboard who kept counting backwards. Then the little red lights would come on again and the courtship would be resumed.

The opening had gone smoothly. Frank Burbage was impressed at the way Rob had worked neatly through the lawn-mowers and linked in and out of the first film on snowdrops. The greenhouse piece on winter flowers had passed off well, with only one messy close-up thanks to a careless cameraman bumping his equipment into the front of the staging.

Rob was now moving across the studio, speaking the words he could see on the autocue of the retreating camera. These made up the voice-over to the short film of this week's 'what's on' sequence. Rory, walking backwards to one side of the camera so that he was still in Rob's eye-line, counted him silently out of the commentary using his fingers, and the voice of the production assistant counted him out through the earpiece in his left ear so that there could be no doubt as to when he was back in vision for the sequence on potatoes in the potting-shed.

It was at this moment that he heard a voice in his other ear which momentarily threw him. The doors at the corner of the studio burst open just before the 'what's on' film came to an end and the little man they had given up for lost almost fell in. His hair, normally so neat, was tumbling over his left eye, his clothes were in disarray and his nose was the colour of beetroot. His voice, though the words were indistinct, was loud. Bertie Lightfoot was not a happy man. He was also rolling drunk.

After a brief silence, perhaps half a second, but in Rob's mind half a lifetime, Rob began the introduction to the seed-potato sequence.

Bertie, recognizing that the programme had reached his spot, was having none of it. He toppled towards the set with every intention of reclaiming his potting-shed. Half-way across the studio floor, he tore off his coat and let it fall to the ground. Five seconds later his body followed it as Frank Burbage executed the quietest rugby tackle ever seen outside a Trappist monastery. As Bertie hit the deck, Frank's hand hit Bertie's mouth, preventing the expletives, for which he was already drawing breath, from reaching the ears of the nation.

Up in the gallery Steve, who had glimpsed the fracas on a fortunately untransmitted wide shot, said, "Shit!" The production assistant, who had been nudged by Steve's flailing arm, dropped her stopwatch and also said, "Shit!" Then, regaining her composure, she grabbed her spare timepiece and said into Rob's ear, "Three minutes left on this item."

Rob tried hard not to look to where Frank was now sitting on top of Bertie, who was beginning to sob through Frank's smothering hand. Rory looked from one scene of activity to the other, aware of his responsibility in both areas. But Frank seemed in control of the fallen body so he stuck with the one that was still vertical. Rob motored on, trying to look relaxed and trying, also, to make sense of the words coming out of his mouth.

Bertie's face was turning the colour of his nose. Two riggers had now stepped in to relieve Frank of the hysterical heap, from which strangled cries were emerging. Rob raised his voice a little as the burly men tried to manhandle Bertie from the studio floor. It seemed as though they were having some success – supporting him under each arm as though he had lost the use of his legs, which he almost had – when Bertie finally shook his head free. He looked back at Rob and half shouted, half sobbed, "It's not fair. It's not bloody fair. I didn't do anything wrong. I bloody loved him." And then he was gone, and his voice was no more than an echo.

For a split second the studio was enveloped in an almost sepulchral quiet, but Rob battled on, did his best to brighten the tone and see the programme through to its end. He could not remember laying the turf, though at the end of the programme he could see a small lawn, so he guessed he must have done it. His pay-off seemed, to his own ears, to have a hollow ring, and as he reached his final words in time with the tense production assistant's count, the relief in his voice was almost tangible. He had never been so glad to say goodbye in his life.

The final notes of the play-out music hung in the air for a few moments until Rory said, with more than slight relief, "Thank you, studio." A brief pause and then a booming "Well done, lad!" from Frank Burbage was followed by a cacophony of raised voices as everyone, from cameramen to floor assistants, riggers to sound crew, swapped reactions to what they had just seen.

Steve burst through the studio doors, his floral tie streaming behind him like the tail of a kite, raced over to Rob and threw his arms round him. "Are you OK?" he asked, as he straightened up.

"I think so," replied Rob, dazed. "What happened?"

Just what had happened became clear over the next half-hour in the makeup room. Bertie had been carried there and dumped in a high makeup chair, where he sat looking as crestfallen as a child at the dentist's.

Rob and Steve stood in front of him as he sobbed uncontrollably, his nose running and his eyes streaming. His anger had gone now; all that remained was misery and exhaustion. Josie pushed a mug of black coffee into his hand, which he occasionally sipped, as he regaled them bit by bit, with the events of the last twenty-four hours.

For several months now, relations between Bertie and Terry, his companion of more than twenty years, had become progressively more strained. Terry, worried about Bertie's drinking habits, which had waxed at the same rate that his career had begun to wane, had tried to persuade him to ease off the bottle. Bertie had told him to mind his own business, so Terry had turned for solace to the young chef at his restaurant. What had begun as a friendship had developed into love. Last night Terry had not come home. This morning he had rung to tell Bertie that it was all over. He would be collecting his things at the weekend.

Bertie sat in the makeup chair in an untidy heap, the picture of a broken man, with tears and saliva running down his face and his eyes as rheumy as those of a bloodhound. Steve and Rob listened attentively as he recounted his sorry tale in fits and starts between wiping his eyes and sniffing. Over the past few weeks he'd driven Rob to despair; now Rob felt only sympathy for the pitiful man in front of him.

"What do you want to do?" asked Steve, gently.

"Just go home," said Bertie, quietly. "Just go home." He blew his nose on an already soggy red spotted handkerchief and tried to pull himself together. "I'm sorry I've let you down and caused all this trouble. I think perhaps I'd better give the programme a miss for a bit. Sort myself out."

"Whatever you think," said Steve. "We'll do whatever you want."

"I think that would be best," said Bertie, as he eased himself out of the chair. He looked at the floor and said, almost to himself, "I really loved him, you know. Really loved him. Stupid old fool." And then he looked up at Rob. "I'm sorry I messed it up for you. Bit of a day, though. Just blame it all on a tired old queen."

"Don't be daft," said Rob. He watched as the normally dapper Bertie pulled on his now bedraggled mac and tottered, unsteadily, towards the door.

He heaved it open with some effort and then turned back for a moment. "Well, you've got the programme now, so good luck. I hope it goes well, I really do. Just a shame about the Chelsea Flower Show." He wiped his nose on his sleeve. "I gather they've given that to Mr D'Arcy. Ta-ta." His valediction delivered, the door swung closed and he was gone.

Rob gazed after him, puzzled and saddened in equal measure.

"Well, that's that, then," said Steve, scratching his head. "I'd better get Lottie to book him a cab home or he'll probably start walking."

"The poor old sod," said Rob, reflectively. "I wonder what he meant about Chelsea?"

Steve looked up from dialling a number on the phone in the corner of the makeup room. "Yes, the poor old sod. But it does leave us in a bit of a spot, old son. With the best will in the world I can't really see you doing this entire series of programmes on your own. We'll have to find you a co-star. Any ideas?"

Chapter 17

Katherine sat on the end of her bed at Wellington Heights with her legs crossed underneath her. Wrapped in a fluffy white towelling robe, she listened, wide-eyed, as Rob, standing naked in front of her, towelled dry his mop of curls and recounted the events of the evening.

"Wow!" gave way to "Oh, God!" as the sorry tale of Bertie's fall from grace was related.

"It sounds as though Frank Burbage was a bit heavy-handed," she observed.

"I guess it was a spur-of-the-moment thing."

"I thought football was his speciality, not rugby."

"It seems he's quite keen on both. Mind you, I think he knocked the wind out of himself as much as Bertie."

"Have the papers got hold of it?"

"Thankfully, no. Apparently Bertie was far enough off-mike for his words to be indistinct. It just sounded like some kind of technical gaffe."

"You did well to keep going," she said, looping a stray strand of jet black hair around the watercolour brush that held the rest of it in a knot at the back of her head.

"Oh, I felt a bit stupid and useless, really. There's old Bertie falling to pieces in front of me and all I do is carry on regardless and let other people do the mopping up."

"Well, there wasn't a lot else you could do. It would have been far worse if you'd just stood there gawping."

"I guess so." He let the towel drop and sat beside her on the bed.

"So what will happen to Bertie?"

"Steve reckons he needs a rest. I feel really sorry for him. He really

142

loved that guy he lived with, you know. He looked completely empty, drained. As if his world had ended. He looked a bit like Dad." Rob gazed reflectively into the middle distance, as if seeing Bertie's breakdown all over again.

"Poor old man," said Katherine softly. "I hope someone keeps an eye on him."

"Me too. You know, he did say one strange thing."

"Mmm?"

"He said that Guy D'Arcy was presenting the Chelsea Flower Show programme."

"I thought it was you."

"Well, it is."

"Odd," she said. There was a momentary lull in the conversation. "Anyway, in the meantime what's going to happen on your programme?" she asked brightly.

"Steve asked me if I had any ideas."

"And have you?"

"Well, not really. I guess he would be happy if I could get some tasty babe to front it with me."

"Clean out of tasty babes, then, are you?" she asked, running her hand up his naked arm. "I know what you could do. You could get Guy D'Arcy to make a guest appearance each week and they could rename the programme *Me Oh My It's Rob and Guy*."

"You little swine! Just wait till I sort you out." He pushed her back on the bed and dug his fingers into each side of her waist.

She shrieked at him, "Don't you dare touch me there or I'll scream," and then began to giggle loudly as he continued. "Stop it, stop it!"

He slipped the belt of her towelling robe undone, and the shrieks became murmurs of pleasure as he stroked the curve of her hip, enfolded her in his arms and kissed her. "You smell wonderful," he whispered into her ear.

"Mmm. Not as wonderful as you." She ran her hand down his back towards his firm bottom, then slid from the bed and stood in front of him. He rolled over on the white duvet and gazed up at her through a fringe of damp brown curls.

"You look lovely in your eye-liner," she said softly, slipping the robe off her smooth white shoulders and letting it fall to the floor.

He gazed at her. "Could you ever see yourself making love to a man who wore makeup?"

"Only one particular man." She pulled the paintbrush from the back of her head and shook out the knot of shining black hair, which fell half across her face. Then she walked towards him, conscious that he was drinking in her every move.

"I love your body." He sighed.

"And I love yours."

She trailed her index finger slowly from his heel up to his shoulder as she walked beside the bed, then lifted up the duvet and slid in. "It's cold out there. Don't you want to come in?"

"Oh, yes, please." He sprang up and all she saw was a flash of freckled flesh and taut muscle before she felt him nuzzling up to her under the crisp, white linen. He pulled her so close that she felt she might almost be a part of him, and as he wrapped his body around hers it seemed as though they could never again be prised apart. She hoped it might be true.

The glint of early-morning sun through muslin and the smell of bread reminded Rob that he was waking up in Katherine's bed. She was still beside him, lying with the side of her face against his shoulder and her arm across his chest. He listened to her relaxed, regular breathing and smiled contentedly at the thought of their gentle lovemaking after the traumas that had gone before. Maybe now they could get their act together again and rediscover the closeness they had enjoyed before the pressures of their jobs had pulled them apart. Stupid, really. At moments like this he knew they were soulmates; it was only the mechanics of their daily lives that had got in the way of their relationship. Absence, he had discovered, made the heart grow fonder . . . of somebody else. It was time they made more of an effort to be together. He pulled a wisp of her shining hair from her warm, pink cheek.

It was only now that he remembered he had not yet told her about Jock's financial problems. He would wait a while before he did. It was ages since they'd had a relaxing weekend together, and he didn't want to spoil it. As Steve Taylor had once remarked, "A trouble shared is a trouble dragged out till bedtime."

She stirred and sighed, then, her eyes straining to open, asked what time it was. Rob glanced sideways at the clock on the bedside table. "A quarter to nine."

"Mmm. Coffee time," she murmured. "Are you going to make it or shall I?" still with her eyes tight shut.

He grinned and stroked her hair. "I'll make it, you stay there." He slipped out of the bed and picked up the towelling robe that lay where she had dropped it on the floor. He put it on, even though it barely came half-way down his thigh, and ambled towards the kitchen, rubbing his hands through his tousled hair and stretching.

He noticed his shirt and jeans tossed over the back of a chair, and saw something square and white on the floor below them. Still trying to focus, he bent down to pick it up. It was a small envelope with his name written on it in stylish fountain-pen script. He slid it into the pocket of the towelling robe and went into the kitchen.

He filled the coffee-maker with water, plugged it in and reached for a couple of mugs from the hooks over the worktop. As he did so, two arms slid around his waist from behind and he realized that Katherine had slipped from the bed as soon as he had left it, pulled on his old shirt and wandered blearily into the kitchen.

"I was getting cold," she murmured, stifling a yawn and nuzzling him between the shoulder-blades. As she did so, she slid her hands down into the pockets of the towelling robe to hold him closer.

"What's this?" She pulled her right hand from the pocket. In it was the small white envelope.

Fear leaped like a tiger into Rob's stomach. "It's nothing. Just a card. Give it here." He spun round and tried to snatch the envelope from her.

She grinned and danced backwards over the floor, holding it out of his reach. "Not so fast, Mr MacGregor. What is it?"

"It's nothing. Just a card from a fan. Give it to me."

"Oh, goody. I wonder what it says." She tore open the envelope and took out the small card, which bore an illustration of a man with a beard and glasses planting out cabbages, watched by a small rabbit in a blue coat. Rob's heart was pounding. Time stood still. The coffee-maker seemed to be dripping in slow motion.

Katherine opened the card and read out loud the message inside:

Dear Mr MacGregor,
Thank you for the most wonderful time.
　　Perhaps next time we can meet in your garden rather than mine.
　　With love,
　　Lisa.

The butterflies in Rob's stomach turned into vultures.

Katherine's face paled. She let the card drop to the floor.

"I'm sorry." His words hung lamely on the air.

"Sorry?" She looked at him quizzically, not knowing what to say. Then, almost to herself, she murmured, "Lisa Drake."

Rob blurted out, "I didn't know what it said. She gave it to me last night, before the show. I didn't even think about it."

"No. Obviously." She sounded stunned, but quite calm. Rob looked at her, standing on her own in the middle of the kitchen floor, tiny inside his baggy shirt. She folded her arms and looked at him. "How long has this been going on?"

"It hasn't. I mean, it was just once."

"Just once?" Katherine's face hardened and the colour started to come back to her cheeks. Her eyes did not leave his. "When?"

"The night you went out with Charlie Wormald."

"Oh, please! We're not talking about a fit of jealousy because of Charlie Wormald, are we? Please tell me we're not!"

Rob floundered and felt himself awash with a sickening mixture of shame and agony. "I didn't know – I mean – I thought . . . When I saw you in the restaurant with him and he was all over you . . ."

"You saw us in the restaurant? You saw us . . . *in the restaurant!* You mean you followed us there? What is this?" Her face was red now, and her voice raised.

"No, I didn't follow you deliberately. Lisa and I dined there, too, we were over in a corner. I worried that you might see us but –"

"I bet you did – 'Lisa and I . . .'" She half turned and put her hand to her forehead. "I don't believe I'm hearing this. Tell me I'm dreaming." She turned back to him, incredulously, half laughing as the words tumbled out. "You dined with Lisa Drake in the same restaurant as me and then you took her home and –"

"No. I didn't take her home."

"Oh?"

"We went back to her place."

"Oh. Well, I suppose I should be grateful for that."

"I was confused. You'd said that you were going out with your boss and his wife. I was fed up. I'd been looking forward to a weekend on our own. We've hardly had one lately. Then Lisa rang and asked me out for a drink. What could I say?"

"How about no?"

"OK, so I said yes because I was pissed off at the thought of you preferring to go out with your boss than me. But then when I saw you two sitting together and him all over you, I thought –"

"You thought I was having an affair with Charlie Wormald?" Tears were now hot on the heels of her anger and she began to shake. "Charlie bloody Wormald. You stupid, stupid man. There's only one man I care for and that's you – Well, it was." The tears rolled down her cheeks and she swept them impatiently aside with the sleeve of his shirt.

"You bastard!" She almost spat the words at him through the tears. "How could you? I suppose you slept with her?"

Rob could not bear to look at her. He turned away and put both his hands in the pockets of the robe, gazing at the floor. "Yes." Never in his life had he felt so wretched or such a cheat.

"Oh, God! And are you seeing her again?"

"No."

"And am I supposed to believe that?"

"I can't expect you to believe anything, I suppose."

"Dead right you can't."

"I'm sorry." Rob looked at her. "I'm so sorry. I feel so ashamed. I didn't mean to let you down."

He crossed to her and put his arms out to hold her. She stepped back. "No. Please don't. Please."

She sidestepped him and walked quickly to the bedroom.

"I'm sorry," he said, as she disappeared around the corner.

He walked slowly after her, not sure what to expect. She met him at the bedroom door, her eyes red-rimmed and her nose running. In her arms was a pile of his clothes. She pushed them towards him. "Just go. Please."

He opened his mouth to speak.

"Just go." She turned away and closed the bedroom door quietly behind her.

Rob could hardly believe it had happened. One minute they were lying in bed next to one another, as close as it was possible to be, and the next he was standing outside her front door on a chilly pavement watching busy shoppers coming out of the baker's with loaves of bread wrapped in white paper bags.

He felt a mixture of helplessness and anger, frustration and stupidity – stupidity that had resulted in him losing the one woman he really cared about. Why was it so easy to see that now, when it had been confusing before? As a chill breeze blew across the pavement he felt deep sadness at his folly.

He pulled his jacket around him and walked around the corner to his car, uncertain of quite where he was going.

Chapter 18

When Guy D'Arcy lifted his head from his pillow that bright Saturday morning he remembered he was alone. Normally he would look upon such solitude as failure, but this morning immense relief surged over him. He had discovered from a brief phone call the previous evening that he had lost the contract to design Sophie's father's stately acres in the heart of the British countryside. Losing it had been, indeed, a blow, but losing Sophie was not. He had had no compunction in giving her the riding boot as soon as he knew that her father's preferences lay in the direction of Edward Siggs-Baddeley. It did not come as too much of a surprise. Sophie's father had always been an ardent royalist.

She had wailed inconsolably when he packed her off, mascara coursing down her plump cheeks, Prada bag slung over her arm, but he felt thankful that he would no longer have to wake up next to a girl he considered marginally less attractive than Red Rum.

He hobbled over to the window, recovering from a partially celebratory, partially consoling hangover, and hauled back the curtains to gaze at the morning.

"The middle of February, D'Arcy, and where are you? Time for a stock-take, old boy," he said aloud, pulled on his bathrobe and headed downstairs to the kitchen. He lifted the left-hand lid of the Aga, filled the kettle and slapped it on the middle of the hob.

Pulling back the kitchen curtains, he gazed on the frosty scene before him – a small garden, fenced with willow hurdles that seemed strangely out of place in Fulham. They protected the plot from the prying eyes of its neighbours, but in spite of the garden's tasteful appointments – a small rostrum of timber decking, a pale ochre Cretan pithoi and a path of old bricks – little seemed to flourish in the grey, silty earth.

He turned his back on the bitter scene and sat at the kitchen table while the kettle sighed on the hotplate. "What have we got at the ripe old age of twenty-nine? No girlfriend. No roof, except one that's auditioning as a colander, and no money to pay for its repair, thanks to too many expensive meals with too many expensive women. The *Sunday Herald* is getting tetchy and may give you the old heave-ho sooner rather than later, but at least you have the Chelsea Flower Show to look forward to, and that might be a bit of useful street cred as far as the paper's concerned.

"Freddie Roper, whom God preserve, preferably in aspic, would seem to have passed over you in favour of the northern oik when it comes to impressing his customers with your charms, but who knows? Maybe fate will smile upon you soon." He picked up a business card from his AAC press pack and stared at it: Amalgamated Agricultural Chemicals, Claudia Bell, Public Relations, with a telephone number. He smiled to himself.

His musings were interrupted by the kettle, and he poured its contents into a large cafetière. He collected another pile of post from the doormat, along with *The Times* (he might write for the *Herald* on a Sunday but that didn't mean he had to read it on the other six days of the week), sauntered back to the kitchen table and poured himself a large mug of coffee.

He dumped the post on a chair, then opened the paper and turned first to the obituaries. None of his father's contemporaries appeared there today, only an octogenarian circus acrobat, who had perfected the forward double somersault on a slack wire, and a Master of Foxhounds who had ridden to hounds until, at ninety-four, arthritis had confined her to one of those all-terrain vehicles. In this she had apparently made herself a nuisance to one and all by regularly following the hunt until she ended up in a ditch, calling for help through yards of bombazine, top-hat and veil. Guy smiled at the thought of the indomitable old biddy. Rather like Granny, he thought.

The weather forecast offered more of the same – crisp and bright – and the arts pages seemed to be full of plays by Strindberg in Islington. A sod of a day for anything remotely amusing. And then on page four (he had started at the back of the paper as he always did) he saw a small item at the foot of column three: 'By Our Media Correspondent', was the byline, and the brief piece was headed 'FRESH FRONT FOR FLOWER SHOW'.

Guy read on:

> The highlight of the gardener's year, the Chelsea Flower Show, will this year have a new look on television screens. Presented for the last fifteen years by an assortment of current-affairs presenters, the show is now to be fronted by two of the small screen's most popular gardening gurus, Rob MacGregor and Guy D'Arcy.
>
> A spokesman for Unicorn Television, the independent production company responsible for the Chelsea Flower Show coverage, said: "Rob and Guy are phenomenally popular with viewers and we hope the combination of the two will bring the world's best flower show to a wider audience."
>
> Chelsea Flower Show runs from 19 to 22 May.

"Bloody hell!" exclaimed Guy, hurling the paper on to the kitchen table, and knocking over a bowl of sugar. "Oh, buggeration!" And then the phone rang.

"Yes?"

"It's me . . . Bertie," said a rather weak voice at the other end.

"Why didn't you tell me about MacGregor, you old sod?"

"What about him?"

"He's presenting the Chelsea Flower Show programme."

"I thought you were," replied Bertie.

"According to *The Times* we're doing it together, which the bastards never told me when they asked me to do it."

"So are you going to decline?"

"I've a good mind to. Bloody MacGregor. Gets everywhere. But no, I'll give him a good run for his money. It's about time the show had a bit of class."

"Mmm," said Bertie.

Guy detected the absence of Bertie's usual bounce and asked if anything was the matter.

"Just a bit down. I've decided to go for a little holiday. Take it easy for a while."

"But what about the programme? Are you leaving MacGregor to his own devices?"

"Oh, I think he'll cope. They'll probably find somebody else to make a guest appearance. I don't really care."

Guy recognized that this was not the usual Bertie by a long chalk. "What's happened? What's wrong, old love?"

Bertie told him of Terry's departure, but said nothing of his embarrassing performance at the studio.

"Oh, God, I'm sorry," said Guy, "really sorry."

"Me too," muttered Bertie. "So if I'm not around for a while you'll know why."

"You take it easy, you old bugger. I'll speak to you when you get back. Oh, by the way, I don't suppose you know Claudia Bell's home number, do you?"

"No, I'm afraid I don't. Sorry."

"Not to worry . . . it's just that it being Saturday . . ."

"Sorry?"

"Never mind. You take care of yourself. Goodbye."

"Goodbye." Bertie put the phone down.

"Bugger," muttered Guy under his breath.

Chapter 19

The shrill clarion of the copper alarm clock heralded Rob's reluctant entry into Monday morning. The weekend had passed for him in a sullen blur. He'd wandered around End Cottage in a kind of low-key trance, uncertain of time, and dabbled outdoors in the damp earth around his plants as the river ran relentlessly by. From time to time he stretched upright from the spade and looked towards the moor, but he lacked the energy to scale the heather-covered peaks where, as before, he might have been able to rise above his troubles and see them with a clearer eye.

He slammed a hand on the clock to silence it, and tried to divine, from the chink of light sneaking between the bedroom curtains, just what kind of day it was. The curtains gave little away and he slid his aching, naked body out from beneath the covers, idly tugged back the curtains and gazed out on a pale, watery sky.

It struck him that whatever his mood, and whatever happened to him, his one overriding interest each day was the state of the weather. Pathetic, really, but understandable. He'd spent so many years of his life being governed by the sun and rain that the habit of looking up at the sky and listening to every available weather forecast was not something he could shake off.

He wondered what Katherine was doing now, and wished, whatever it was, that she were doing it with him. He wished so much he could speak to her, but fear of upsetting her more, and shame at his fall from grace, kept him from the phone. The depth of this emptiness was something he'd never felt before. Sadness, yes, and frustration. But never this bottomless hole.

He sighed a deep, sorry-for-himself sigh and hauled on yesterday's clothes. What was it she had said to him on their last evening together? "Clean out of tasty babes, then, are you?" They had been talking about a new co-presenter. Never had he been cleaner out of tasty babes. Bar one, of course. Perhaps he should give her a ring. The more he thought about it, the more sense it made. Why hadn't it occurred to him before? The perfect co-presenter for *Mr MacGregor's Garden* was Bex Fleming.

Jock MacGregor had been at work an hour by the time his son surfaced. He, too, was not feeling very chipper, but he knew that after a while among his plants his mood would improve.

He carried a tray of Victorian gold-laced polyanthus plants into the potting-shed, having fetched them from the cold frame attached to the greenhouse, and picked his way through the last of the flood-borne mud that Wayne and Harry were still attempting to clear. By the end of the week the place would be ship-shape again. Jock was relieved – he had begun to find the disorder wearing.

Placing the plants on the old stone bench, he took down a dozen four-inch clay flower-pots from the wooden rack at the back of the shed. A mound of compost, like a miniature Everest, was piled in the centre of the cold, hard bench and he took up a handful and rubbed it between his fingers, grunting appreciatively. Then he sniffed it, enjoying the cool, organic aroma that reached his nostrils. Satisfied that the hand-mixed concoction of loam, leaf-mould and sharp grit would suit the plants in question he began to prise the young clumps from their seed tray and pot them up.

It was a satisfying job, sullied only by the faint noisome smell that emanated from Wayne and Harry's handiwork. He watched them working together – Wayne like an eager young pup, scooping up the mud at the rate of three shovelfuls to Harry's one. He smiled to himself and looked beyond them to the beds, now freshly forked over and newly lined out with plants. In spite of the flood they looked as full of promise as they always did at this time of year. The window was fringed with the white blossom of Japanese quince, and by the path he could see the amethyst spears of *Crocus tomasinianus*, planted thirty years ago as a handful of dry bulbs. Even the flood waters had not managed to dislodge them, and now they had grown into a long ribbon of blooms which, if the sun came out later in the day, would turn into pale purple stars. Jock took the trouble to pot up a few dozen of them each autumn, knowing that, come late winter, they would sell on sight to anyone with an eye for quiet beauty and an easily grown plant.

He glanced at the clock. Almost nine. He'd better open the gates. Wayne had left Harry to his shovelling and was down in the far corner of the nursery getting together an order of hardy perennials and shrubs that would be collected later that day. Jock took the bunch of keys from his pocket and strolled down the path.

A gentle breeze ruffled the leaves of a row of mixed evergreens down the side of the gravel walk, and he noticed, at the end of the row, the three rose-bushes that had been given to him by the late Professor's wife. Wayne had retrieved them from the flood waters and planted them in the first available patch of ground. They were beginning to break into bud; their crimson shoots defying the chilly late February air. He smiled again. Spring couldn't be far away.

At the gate he pushed the stubby key into the padlock, turned it, released the chain and noticed a Land Rover Discovery coming down the lane. It drew to a halt, and Jock recognized Lady Helena Sampson. She locked the car and walked down the lane towards him.

"Good morning, Mr MacGregor."

"Good morning, Lady Sampson, how are you?"

"I'm well, thank you, and you?"

The preliminaries over, Jock opened the gate and invited her into the nursery, curious to know of the reason for her early-morning visit but too full of Scots circumspection to ask.

She did not keep him waiting long. "I hope you don't mind me calling so early but I have to go out later this morning and wanted to leave Makepiece something to plant."

Makepiece was the old gardener who had replaced Rob. His specialities were salvias and grumbling, but Helena tried, each year, to ensure that he also planted things that she wanted.

"Have you any hellebores?"

"We've only a few left," Jock told her, "but you're welcome to have a look."

He walked her to the cold frame adjacent to the greenhouse and pointed to a couple of dozen plants at one end, their stout stems topped by a range of flowers that varied in colour from white and pale yellow to pink and deep crimson.

"Oh, aren't they lovely?" she exclaimed, with genuine pleasure.

"Aye, they're not bad. It's taken years of selection to get such a good colour range and I'm quite happy with them now. They'll do."

As Jock helped Helena to pick out half a dozen plants that suited her, she asked him about the early years at the nursery, and about Fred Armitage who had owned the place before him. She talked fondly of Rob, and Jock felt that ripple of pride at his son's achievements as she sang his praises. "I'm sorry to hear that Mr Wragg seems determined to continue being a nuisance."

"Aye, a nuisance he is," replied Jock. "He's like a dog with a bone. I don't know how we'll shake him off. Or why he wants the place. I just can't fathom it."

"I was just wondering," said Helena, "did you know that Mrs Wragg was an Armitage before she married?"

"I'm sorry?" Jock looked puzzled.

"Gladys Wragg. Her maiden name was Armitage. She was Fred Armitage's niece – the man who owned Wharfeside Nursery before you did."

"Was she now?" said Jock, his brow knitted and his thoughts scattered to the wind. "D'you think they want the nursery for sentimental reasons, then?"

"Oh, it doesn't strike me that Mr and Mrs Wragg have enough sentiment between them to write a birthday card, from what I've heard from Mrs Ipplepen. I just thought that it was a strange coincidence."

"Very strange." Jock rubbed his whiskery chin thoughtfully. "His niece, you say?"

"Yes, she was Fred Armitage's brother's girl."

"I wasn't aware that he had a brother."

"Well, apparently he did. Not at all like Fred, I'm told. Black sheep of the family. I think he went to prison for a while. Bit of a wide boy. Mrs Ipplepen says Fred never spoke about him. Wouldn't even admit to having a brother. Sad, really."

"Well, well." Jock was lost in his thoughts, trying to work out the significance of what he had just learned when Helena brought him down to earth.

"Well, I must be going. Can I pay for these, Mr MacGregor?" She looked at the labels, swiftly totted up the prices and placed several notes in Jock's hand saying, "I think that's right."

Jock touched his cap, pushed the notes into his apron pocket without looking at them and walked towards the potting shed with Helena to find a box for her plants. But all the time he was thinking about Fred Armitage and his brother.

Rob had thought of ringing Katherine every ten minutes from the moment he had left her flat, but her words – "Just go" – kept echoing in his ears, and he lacked the courage to phone and put matters right in case they went even more wrong.

He'd thought round and round it, determined to come up with some way of making her understand how bad he felt, how much he wanted her, but knew in his heart that it was too soon, that Katherine's wounds would be too raw, as were his own.

He flopped in the spoke-backed chair by the table in the small back room he used as a study, and looked out over the top of the word-processor at the river and the moors beyond, seeking inspiration.

He scanned the list of things to do that he'd jotted down on a primrose-yellow Post-it pad:

–Ring Sir F. – Yes to advert.

He would have to say yes, even if it meant that Katherine would be even angrier with him for abandoning his principles. He could no longer risk his father having to close down the nursery. It would break Jock's heart. Just like Rob had broken Katherine's heart. At least this way he could help one of the people he loved. He should have been pleased at the prospect of such a lucrative deal. He wasn't. He cast his eye further down the list:

–*Daily Post* piece.

–Ring Bex Fleming.

–Sort prog ideas.

–Mail.

As his hand reached for the phone, it rang.

"Hello?"

"Can I speak to Rob MacGregor, please?"

"Speaking."

"Hello, Mr MacGregor, it's Simon Clay's secretary here from Amalgamated Agricultural Chemicals. Mr Clay would like a word. Will you hold for a moment, please?"

"Yes, of course." A sharp click and then a small but fully orchestrated chunk of Vivaldi's Four Seasons – Spring – before Simon

Clay, the arty PR man of AAC who had been so full of himself at the press briefing, came on the line with a distinctly apologetic tone. "Rob? Simon, hi! I'm sorry to bother you . . ."

Rob was about to apologize for not having got back to the company sooner with his affirmative reply, but Simon Clay pressed on.

"Look, I'm dreadfully sorry but there's been a bit of a cock-up at this end as far as the BLITZ thing is concerned."

"Sorry?"

"Well, it's just that it's usual for the advertising and PR department to sort out the personnel for advertising campaigns, but it seems in this instance that the chairman wanted to involve himself as well. I gather Sir Freddie asked you about fronting the new campaign?"

"Yes. He did."

"Well, look, this is dreadfully embarrassing, but I'm afraid the PR department had actually decided to go in a different direction. I do hope you won't mind, and I can only apologize for the inconvenience we've caused you but . . . I'm afraid we won't be able to use you. So sorry. I do hope you understand."

"Yes, fine. No problem. These things happen. Do I need to ring Sir Freddie?"

"No. No need. I'll explain and say that I've spoken to you. OK?"

"Yes. Fine. Er . . . fine."

"By the way, very pleased to hear that you and Guy D'Arcy will be presenting the Chelsea Flower Show programme this year."

"I'm sorry?" Rob was puzzled.

"Yes, saw it in the paper. I think it will be a really great combination. Anyway, must dash. Cheerie-bye then." And he was gone.

Rob replaced the receiver, calmly and thoughtfully. Two bombshells in one phone call. He felt he should have been hugely disappointed at the loss of the advertising campaign and the subsequent windfall. But he wasn't. He was relieved. The money would have been useful, particularly as far as his father was concerned, but how could he ever have squared it with him? Or with himself. Or with Katherine. He'd like to talk to her about it now. And about Guy D'Arcy. Why hadn't his agent mentioned that he was to co-present? Liz Cooper was up-front about such things, as a rule. Maybe they hadn't told her in case he declined. Not that he would have done. It might add a bit of sparkle to the proceedings.

He took a sharp pencil and crossed 'Ring Sir F. Yes.' off the list. How the hell was he going to help his father now?

He skipped the next instruction to write his *Daily Post* piece and came to 'Ring Bex Fleming'. The image of the fresh-faced girl swam into his mind and made him feel marginally better. Only one snag here: he didn't have her number. He dialled the Birmingham television company. The call was answered by a telephonist, who recognized his voice and said that OK, she would give him Bex's home number and the number of the garden centre where she worked, "Although I shouldn't really, but as it's you, Mr MacGregor, I'm sure it will be all right," followed by a girlish giggle from the fifty-something voice.

He dialled her home number first. No reply, just an answering-machine saying, in that bright voice he remembered, "Hi, this is Bex. I'm not in, but please leave a message after the tone and I'll get back to you when I can. Thanks for calling." He decided that before he did he'd try her at work.

The phone at the garden centre was picked up by a clueless youth who said, vaguely, that Bex was around somewhere. When Rob asked if he could locate her, the youth reluctantly agreed to try. The phone was laid down and Rob listened for what seemed an age to general garden-centre noise, magnified by the evidently cavernous selling area where punters were probably milling around buying artificial flowers, jam purporting to be made in country cottages and expensive watering-cans. He was glad his dad just sold plants.

"Hello?" The voice broke his train of thought.

"Hello? Bex?"

"Yes?"

"It's Rob MacGregor."

"Hi! How are you?"

"I'm fine. Look, I'm sorry to bother you at work but I wondered if you fancied coming on the show?"

"What?"

"Well, it's a long story but I need a new co-presenter."

"Me?"

"Well, why not?"

"But you don't know what I'm like. I might be useless."

"I don't think so.'

"Well . . . when?"

"Er . . . how about this Friday?"

"*This Friday?*"

"Yes. Do you think you could?"

"Well, yes – if I can arrange it with my boss I'd love to . . . but why?"

"Oh, I'll fill you in on the details later but basically Bertie can't do it any more. My producer asked me if I had any ideas so I thought of you. He'll have the final say, of course, but I just thought I'd sound you out and see if you fancied it."

"Well, I do. I'd love to. But what do you want me to do?"

"Oh, we'll work all that out later. As long as you can do it, that's great."

"Shall I wait to hear from you, then?"

"I'll get Steve Taylor to give you a call, if that's OK. He's the producer. He really ought to sort it out, not me. I'm just glad you're keen and I hope your boss doesn't mind."

"He's usually OK about it – sees it as a way of promoting the business. Just one thing."

"Yes?"

"How did you find my number?"

"I got it from an extremely helpful telephonist at your studios."

"Well, you were lucky. Normally it's easier to get eggs out of a cockerel than it is to get phone numbers out of Brenda. But I'm glad she recognized your voice."

"Yes, me too. Well, I'll see you later, then, I hope. And thanks. I'm really pleased."

"Me, too. Speak to you later. 'Bye." Before Rob hung up he heard her whisper softly to herself, "Oh, *yippee!*"

Chapter 20

"You were brilliant, simply brilliant!" Steve Taylor bestowed a large kiss on Bex's left cheek. Her soft, peachy makeup failed to disguise the rosy glow that suffused her face, and the warm hum from the technicians around the studio floor left her in no doubt that she had done all right. She looked over to where Rob was standing behind the potting-bench at the far corner of the set and blushed again when she saw the warm smile that greeted her.

He ambled over and put an arm around her shoulder, looked her in the face, grinned and gave her a hug.

"Wow!" he said, quite softly. "You were terrific. Really cool."

"Thank you. Are you sure?"

"Is *he* sure? Never mind him – *I'm* sure and that's what matters." Steve, black hair flopping over his horn-rimmed glasses, turned to speak to Bex once more, having thanked his minions. "Are you ready for this on a weekly basis, then?"

"Me?" Bex couldn't believe her ears.

"Yes, you," he answered. "I knew that one day I'd see a bit of UST in this programme and now I've found it I'm not going to let it go."

"UST?" enquired Rob.

"I'll tell you later," said Steve, already retreating. "Look, I've got a news bulletin to sort out but I'll be in touch with you both in the next couple of days. Bex, can you come up with an item for next week? It's our last studio day and after that we'll be on location now that the weather looks like getting better. Don't agree to do anything else on TV for the foreseeable future. OK?" The door swung to and he was gone.

"OK," muttered Bex. "Well. There we are, then." She looked up at Rob. "He seemed quite happy with that, didn't he?"

"Yes. Especially the UST, whatever that is."

"You mean you really don't know?"

"No."

"You clearly don't read enough teeny girls' magazines."

"And you do?"

"Well, I did once."

"So what does it stand for?"

"Unresolved Sexual Tension."

Rob was disconcerted. "Ah. I see."

"It's all right. We just have to make sure it stays unresolved."

There was a pause. Rob looked at Bex, and then she burst out laughing.

Katherine tapped the top of her pencil impatiently on her desk and gazed at the ceiling of her office at the *Nesfield Gazette*, the telephone clamped to her ear. The late-afternoon sun glinted in through the tall bay window of the Victorian building, past the gilded old-fashioned lettering whose shadow printed the newspaper's title across her desk. On her notepad she saw: 'Est. 1843'. At the other end of the line her boss Charlie Wormald, Est. 1943, was in full flow.

"Fine. Yes, Charlie, I will. Fine. No. Yes . . . yes, I will. Goodbye." She dropped the handset back into the cradle and muttered under her breath, "God, that man." And then her eyes glazed over. She thought of another man. The one who, in spite of her efforts, was occupying her mind every moment of every hour of every day. Anger mixed with pain and love in equal measure until she found herself running round in emotional circles.

It had been like this since she'd asked him to go, almost a week ago now. Her anger kept her cool to start with, but it subsided regularly and she found herself wallowing in the fact that she missed him. Missed his clothes on the floor. Missed his toothbrush in the mug. Missed his touch. Missed the smell of him. She had never liked to feel dependent on any man but in the case of Rob MacGregor she had failed. Damn him! She'd thought he was different from the rest. He was no different at all. Just as responsive to flattery as any of them. At the centre of her life now was a big black hole, and she felt empty. She pulled a large handkerchief out of the sleeve of her black jumper and blew her nose on it. It smelt of him and she bit her lip.

There was a light tap on the glass of her door and Nancy Farrer, the well-preserved secretary who manned the phone in the lobby next to Katherine's office, turned the knob and put her head tentatively round the door.

"Lady Sampson's here to see you, Katherine."

Katherine wiped her eyes quickly. "Fine. Tell her to come in." Surprised at this sudden interruption, she stuffed the handkerchief back up her sleeve and got up from her chair, smoothing down the black corduroy mini-skirt over her black tights.

Muted thanks could be heard outside the door, and then Helena, smartly turned out in a well-tailored tweed jacket, cream turtle-neck jumper and dark brown trousers, her hair pinned back with a tortoiseshell comb, came into Katherine's office and greeted her warmly. "Katherine, how are you?" She shook her hand and Katherine motioned her to sit down.

"Oh, no, I won't if you don't mind. I'm dashing off up the dale for supper with one of Jumbo's old partners," she glanced at the large man's watch on her wrist, "and I mustn't be late. It's just that I wanted to ask you something."

Katherine found herself wondering if Helena knew about her and Rob. Perhaps Rob had told her. She decided that from her manner he had not. She would say nothing.

"It's about Dennis Wragg – you know, the man wanting to buy up Jock MacGregor's nursery?"

Katherine nodded and gave a brief sniff.

"I know this sounds dreadful of me but I thought I'd try to look into the background of it all. I don't want to do a Miss Marple or anything but I just have some kind of feeling that there might be an ulterior motive."

"I think you're right there," Katherine agreed.

"I wondered, does your newspaper have any kind of indexed archive?"

"We do have back numbers – why?"

"Well, I want to try to find out a bit more about the Armitages. Fred Armitage, who used to own the nursery before Jock did, had a brother who was a bit of a bad 'un, according to my daily, Mrs Ipplepen. Gladys Wragg happens to be his daughter."

Katherine's journalistic instincts went into overdrive. "Really?"

She came round to the front of her desk and perched on the corner.

"It seems to me to be a bit of a mystery. Why is Dennis Wragg so keen on such a small piece of land which has no real value to him except that it once belonged to his wife's family? I wondered if the paper might offer any clues."

Katherine reached over the desk for her notepad. "When was this black-sheep-of-a-brother last heard of?"

"Somewhere about the nineteen forties, I think."

"And his name?"

"Reggie. Reggie Armitage. Younger brother of Fred. Nearly went to prison, apparently. Don't know why. Am I being a frightful old busybody and wasting your time?"

"Not at all. I'm as curious as you. Leave it with me and I'll see what I can come up with. Nancy loves raking through the old copies of the paper in the back room. They go right back to . . ." she glanced at the shadow, which had now moved to the corner of her desk ". . . 1843." It faded before her eyes as a cloud obscured the weak, setting sun.

Helena watched Katherine lose herself in her thoughts, thanked her and took her leave. The purple-grey evening enveloped her in a gentle sadness as she headed off up the dale for supper.

Guy had never seen so much flesh, except on a Sumo wrestler. Great folds of it enveloped him, pure white and oozing, so that he could hardly move. He forced his head back on the pillow of the ornate, lace-encrusted bed, and tried to breathe in air that was not laden with Estée Lauder Youth Dew.

"I know exactly what you're thinking, you know," said the voice of his companion.

I bet you don't, thought Guy, who was imagining what it would be like to be a baker suffocating in dough.

"You're a calculating little bastard and I know exactly why you're here and exactly when you'll give me the old heave-ho."

"So why don't you throw me out?" Guy heaved his naked body as upright as was possible thanks to the constraints of the too, too solid flesh beside him. He'd thought that Sophie's thighs were hefty but they were put in the shade by the monstrous limbs he gazed upon now, which made the Michelin man look anorexic.

Claudia Bell was fifty-something and well preserved facially, but her figure in the red suit at the press conference had clearly owed a good deal to the art of Rigby and Peller, the Queen's corsetiers.

"I don't throw you out, you dreadful little boy, because you're fun. Wicked, but fun. And you're better in bed than anyone I've ever known." She giggled girlishly and then added, with a rueful note, "I only hope I don't lose my job."

"Now why would you do that?" asked Guy, forcing himself to stroke a relatively inoffensive stretch of flesh on her forearm.

"Because Freddie is a jealous man and likes to think I'm his and his alone."

"And aren't you?"

"Not now, you vile boy. Not after last Saturday. And certainly not after tonight. Come here and let me smother you!" Guy gasped for breath as, once more, a tidal wave of quivering carnality threatened to engulf him.

He screwed up his eyes as Claudia clenched him in a leg- and armlock that squeezed out of him every last drop of breath. It was agony, as he gulped at the perfumed air through the lacquered blonde locks, but it had been worth it. This temporary discomfort was a small price to pay for the glittering prize. BLITZ was his, thanks to Claudia, and Rob MacGregor was history.

Rob had wanted to ask Bex out for supper, to celebrate her success, but she'd said she had to be at work early the following morning and must catch her train. She was sorry, but she really couldn't stay. They agreed to speak soon and parted at the studio doors.

As he walked across the darkening car park towards the battered Fiesta, he was conscious of footsteps behind him. He turned, expecting to see Bex again, but found himself looking into the eyes of Lisa Drake. For a moment he stood quite still, surprised by her sudden proximity and aware that his mouth was open and that no words were coming out.

"Hi," she said, smiling.

"Hi."

"Did you get my card?"

"Card. Yes. Card. Thank you. Yes, I did." He was speaking as if programmed by computer and heard words coming out of his mouth that seemed nothing to do with him.

"So when are we going to do it again?"

She quite took his breath away, standing there in her well-tailored bottle green suit, the hem of her skirt a full hand-span above her shapely knees. And those legs that seemed to go on for ever. And her wide eyes. And the scent of Chanel. Already he felt the customary churning of his stomach that occurred whenever she came close. His mind ran through the alternative replies, all in a split second. Should he say 'tonight', or 'tomorrow night' or 'never'? Should he treat Katherine as a thing of the past? Was she a thing of the past? Should life move on? His mouth and some distant part of his brain took over as he heard himself say, "Lisa, I'm sorry, but I don't think we can do it again. I had a wonderful time, and I think you're great, but it's just that I'm already in a relationship that I don't want to give up."

She smiled a disbelieving sort of smile. "What?" She almost laughed, looking at him as though he were teasing her.

"We can't do it again."

"You're not serious, are you?"

"'Fraid so." He said it softly and with feeling, hardly knowing where to look.

Her face registered the incredulity of one not used to being contradicted. "You're prepared to throw away terrific sex just for old-fashioned loyalty?"

"Yes."

"But why? I thought you felt the same as I did. I thought this was something special." She smiled an encouraging smile. A smile that a black-widow spider probably smiles at a fly. She was not going to give in easily.

"It is. It was. I just can't go on leading a double life." It hurt him to say so. Even now, the evening they had spent together was replaying through his mind. The ecstasy and the complete losing of himself in her, and now the knowledge that she had felt the same. He had never experienced sexual attraction on this level before. Probably never would again. The combined feelings of danger and passion were a heady brew. He could hardly bear to look at her. When he did look up, the first signs of anger were beginning to spread across her face.

"Well, this is a first," she murmured. She half laughed and looked away. "Right. Well, I'm sorry I got it wrong. I only hope she realizes what she's got." She looked back at him, trying to hold his eye, but Rob could only gaze at the ground.

She carried on, "OK. Have it your own way. I'll let you get on with your life. And if you don't mind, I'll get on with mine." She raised a hand and quickly stroked it down his arm. "Goodbye."

She paused, about to say something else, then thought better of it. Turning away smartly, she pressed a button on her key-ring to open the door of the charcoal-grey BMW, slid in and roared out of the studio gates, her rear tyres kicking up chippings like the hooves of a galloping horse. In a few seconds, the throaty growl of her 325i was lost among the general hum of traffic.

"Fuck," he said slowly, under his breath. "Oh, fuck." And as he pushed the key into the lock of his car he noticed that his hand was shaking.

Chapter 21

"Gone? What do you mean she's gone?" Frank Burbage's voice boomed across the desk at Steve Taylor at a decibel level that was uncomfortable at any time of the week, but especially so at ten o'clock on a Monday morning. "Gone to her bloody hairdresser or gone for good?"

"Gone for good, I'm afraid."

"But she can't just bloody well up and leave. Who the fuck's going to do all her bulletins?"

Lottie Pym raised her eyebrows as she passed on her way to the photocopier with a P45.

Steve endeavoured to placate him. "We'll appoint a replacement as soon as possible. Some time this week, I hope. Tomorrow we'll get a stand-in, but for today you'll just have to do the bulletins yourself."

"Fucking hell!"

Lottie Pym raised her eyebrows again on the way back to her desk. She was used to the language but not the volume.

"But she seemed fine on Friday. Positively buoyant," said Frank Burbage, with a note of bewilderment in his voice. "What the hell's happened since then?"

"She was made an offer she couldn't refuse, apparently."

"What sort of offer?"

"The only offer that Lisa would consider unrefusable. An offer to work on the network bulletins in London."

"Bugger me!"

"And me for that matter. It's not going to be easy to find a replacement."

"But had anyone any inkling that she wanted out? And, anyway, hasn't she got a contract to keep her here?"

"'No' to the first and 'yes' to the second, but the powers-that-be felt that the month left on her existing contract wasn't worth making a fuss about. The boss reckoned that it would reflect badly on the station if we tried to hold on to her and we'd come out of it better if one of our newsreaders was seen to be doing well on the network."

"But how come none of us had any idea?" asked Frank, settling himself into a chair opposite Steve Taylor and leaning forward on his desk. He rested his large chin on his hands and began his interrogation. The initial anger was gradually being replaced by curiosity and an appetite for gossip.

"None of us had any idea because I don't think Lisa had any idea herself. I know she had itchy feet – what young regional newsreader with any intelligence doesn't? – but I didn't realize that her departure would be quite as sudden. But then, to be fair to Lisa, I don't think she did either. I think it came like a bolt out from the blue and she was given twenty-four hours to make the decision."

Frank Burbage pushed his ruddy face nearer to Steve Taylor's pasty one. "Who by?"

"The Beeb."

"Oh. Well, that's it, then. Look out Jill Dando and Anna Ford, Lisa Drake is about to leave you standing."

He slouched back in his chair. "I wouldn't mind but she never even whispered anything to me. Three bloody years and she never breathed a word. Taught her all she knows and what thanks do I get?"

It was Steve's turn to raise his eyebrows.

"Oh, all right, so she was bloody good, but you've got to let me have my moan. Is she coming back for anything?"

"No. Wardrobe are sending her clothes direct to Telly Centre. Lottie's cleared her desk for her and boxed up her stuff – that's going off today by carrier. I am a bit surprised. I thought she might want to say goodbye but she said she'd rather not."

"You've spoken to her, then?"

"Yes, she rang me last night, about elevenish. Said it had all happened suddenly on Friday night. She'd been invited to London on Saturday morning, met the head of News who said he wanted an answer by Sunday morning and could she start on Monday. Said she'd rather just slip out quietly. Didn't want a fuss. Sounded a bit upset, actually, rather than elated. Odd, really."

"Bunch of bastards. They don't hang around, do they? Not like it was in my day. Gentlemanly, it was then. 'Come to my club and have lunch, old boy, and we'll make you an offer you can think about.'"

"Mmm." Steve took off his glasses and rubbed his eyes, replaced them and looked back at Frank, who was now launching into a reflection of his own halcyon days at the BBC.

Frank had never made the top flight of newsreaders, but had been sufficiently close to let a note of wistfulness creep into his voice. "You know, in those days they had career plans for you. I remember talking to a senior executive who said, 'This year we'll keep you in Industry, then next year we'll give you a stint as junior Court Correspondent' – you know, descriptions of Princess Margaret's dresses on visits to the poor in Nigeria – 'and then we'll give you a diplomatic stint in Paris or New York and when you've gained your street cred there' – except that in those days they didn't call it 'street cred', they called it 'experience' – 'we'll bring you into the studio as anchor.' Had it all mapped out for me, they did."

"So what happened?"

"Buggers changed their minds. Took on Martyn Lewis instead. Left me in Industry with a Saturday football match to keep me sweet. I never got so much of a sniff at Princess Margaret's skirts, let alone Nigeria. So I buggered off up here."

"Very much after the fashion of Lisa buggering off down there."

"Except that I did have the good grace to work out my contract."

"Well, there we are." Steve adjusted his body to indicate to Frank that this conversation had better come to an end as he had a lot to sort out. Frank took the hint without offence and pushed back his chair.

"You going to say anything to the viewers?" he asked, as he retreated towards his own desk by the window.

"Not sure yet. They'll know soon enough. We're putting out a statement to the press today about how delighted we are that Lisa has done so well – that sort of thing. We might not need to mention it on air."

"You'll have all the little old ladies writing in. And the dirty old men. They'll miss their early evening bit of fluff," said Frank, mockingly, as he pushed on his gold half-moon spectacles and began sifting through the sheets of paper on his desk. He picked up a scrap torn from a spiral-bound shorthand pad and read out loud: 'Dear Mr Burbage, Could you please ask Lisa Drake if she could send me a signed photograph for my bedroom. I am a big fan of hers and it would give me great pleasure to see her in front of me when I wake up.'"

He grunted, tore the sheet of paper into tiny pieces and dropped them like confetti into the round grey litter bin by his desk. "Well, you'll have to tune into the Beeb now, you little pervert."

The news spread round Northcountry Television faster than a flu epidemic. The talk in the canteen and in Makeup, in the car park and the loos was of nothing else. The station had lost its pin-up. Who would replace Lisa Drake? Junior female reporters began to smarten up their appearance. By Tuesday lunch-time Next and Principles had reputedly sold out of tailored two-piece suits.

Rob had heard about it on Monday afternoon during his conversation with Steve about Friday's programme. The news left him stunned. As stunned as Frank Burbage, but for different reasons. Should he tell Katherine? She would probably know by now, anyway, and it was not a piece of news that he felt comfortable breaking to her. He would leave it a while.

Several times during the last week he had dialled half her number. Once he completed the sequence and the phone began to ring at the other end but he lost his nerve and hung up. As long as he didn't speak to her there was still hope that she would take him back. He was too frightened of ringing her and discovering that she wanted nothing to do with him. But he could not keep on like this for much longer. That much he knew.

He needed a day out. A day away from the dale. He looked at the papers on his desk at End Cottage, among them a calendar of Royal Horticultural Society shows. The Early Spring Show at Westminster opened the following day. He hated London, but he would go. Just to get away. Then he remembered that London was where Lisa had gone, but he told himself that London was a big place and that there was no chance of them encountering one another and, anyway, if he were presenting this year's television coverage of the Chelsea Flower Show he ought to put in an appearance at one of the smaller shows. His reasoning ended there, which is why, on a sunny Tuesday morning, he found himself standing in one corner of the Royal Horticultural

Society's lofty hall in Westminster rather than on the banks of a clear Yorkshire river.

The words 'cat' and 'cream' came into Rob's mind. A few yards away, between the stands of flowers and trees that proved spring really had arrived, he could see the figure of Guy D'Arcy, lording it over the ladies of the Trust Fund.

In navy blazer, grey trousers, sky blue shirt and pale yellow tie, Guy, with his easy aristocratic charm, was the sort of chap with whom Felicity Fortescue, the doyenne of Dickers in Devon, and the dumpy, tweed-trousered Emma Coalport – the Sackville-West disciple – felt comfortable.

"It's good news that you're doin' Chelsea," said Felicity, perforating the parquet with the spike of her battered shooting stick. "Time the programme had a bit of quality about it. Not that I ever watch the box meself."

"No. Never have time," snapped Emma Coalport, her beady eyes raking the stands of early herbaceous perennials. With any luck there would be some that she might be able to snaffle at low prices if she were to squash against some poor nurseryman with her cottage loaf of a figure and beat him into submission with her halitosis.

Rob smiled to himself and walked towards a long, low table covered in dark green hessian where a young nurseryman from Scotland had arranged a miniature landscape of rare Petiolarid primulas of the kind that folk south of the border could only dream of growing. He bent down to look at them closely, their leaves dusted with white flour and their blooms a soft azure blue. How his father would love them. He should have brought him, but then, Jock would never take time off from the nursery at this time of year.

He stood up and looked at the layout of the hall. For all the fact that he hated London, he did like coming to the monthly Westminster flower shows once or twice a year. What gave him a buzz was the smell of leaf and flower and rich earth that hit your nostrils as you left the exhaust fumes of the London traffic outside. The flashing of the press pass and the clicking through the turnstiles took him into a towering grey hall with high windows and a dark wooden floor that seemed as large as a football pitch. All over it, like small gardens, stood the raised wooden-sided stands draped in dark green cloth, each replete with flowers, fruit and vegetables of the highest quality, and all manned by some of the country's finest nurserymen.

At the top of the wide flight of steps at one end of the hall was a sort of loggia equipped with rows of chairs where old ladies would park their weary bodies, knees apart, showing off to all below the salmon sheen of their directoire knickers. Rob tried to avert his eyes, not always successfully.

He always took a notebook with him, and found it hard to resist coming home without a couple of RHS-crested carrier bags holding new treasures to try in his own garden or to give to Jock. He was just convincing himself that he could not grow the Scottish primulas in his riverbank garden when he recognized the voice at his elbow.

"Rob, how *are* you?"

He looked up from the miniature Caledonian landscape and found Guy D'Arcy beaming at him and offering his signet-ringed hand. Rob shook it firmly and smiled.

"I gather we're going to be working together again," said Guy, positively oozing bonhomie.

"Yes, so I hear." Rob did his best to keep an even tenor in his voice.

"Should be fun."

"Yes. Great fun." Rob tried to sound keen.

"I've been thinking about the programme quite a lot, and I think we should be really careful to make it a class act, don't you?"

"Sorry?" Rob was unsure that he had heard correctly.

"Bring a bit of class to the whole thing. I mean, Chelsea is a part of the Season, isn't it? Along with Ascot and Wimbledon. You know the sort of thing."

"Er . . . yes."

"It seems to me that we need to emphasize that. It would be very easy to let the programme slide into a sort of matey gardening show, but I think that would be a mistake, don't you?"

"Well, I'm not sure I quite see –"

"You have a great touch, I know, but I think this show probably calls for a different sort of style. I hope you don't mind me mentioning it?"

Rob found himself unable to answer, taken aback at Guy's brass neck.

"Oh, and have you heard about . . ." Guy looked over his shoulder to left and right in too theatrical a way for it to be kind. Satisfied that they were not being overheard, he continued *sotto voce*, "Have you heard about BLITZ?"

"Well, yes, I was at the press conference."

"I know. But no. I mean, have you heard about the advertising campaign?"

"No." Rob thought it best to admit nothing.

"Oh. I thought you might have done. Confidentially, of course . . ."

"Of course."

"They've asked me to front it. Rather good news, isn't it? They seemed to think I had the right kind of image for such a product. You know – a bit classy and go-ahead, I suppose. Not for me to say, but it's rather good to inspire such confidence, isn't it?"

"Very. Er . . . good luck with it," Rob said, pleasantly.

Before he had time to say any more, Guy brought their conversation to an end. His arrow having struck home, he had no further need to stay in the company of this populist man of the soil.

He was about to turn on his heel when he was almost bowled over by a little old lady in a grey mac, laden down with carrier bags, out of the top of which poked leaves and flowers in amazing diversity. She ignored Guy and turned her kind but myopic gaze on Rob. "Ooh, hello! Goodness! It's Mr MacGregor, isn't it?" she asked, with a genuine thrill in her voice. "Well, I never. I've been coming here for years and I've never bumped into you before. Great fan of yours, I am. I'm a member of the RHS, you know. I know a lot of folk think it's snobby but I like the plants and I like the nurserymen." She beamed at him from under her transparent rain hood, her wire-rimmed glasses framing pale blue rheumy eyes. "Well, I just can't believe it." She smiled at him and seemed to be examining him, like a keen butterfly collector taking pleasure in spotting a rare species. "Wait till I tell my sister. She thinks you're wonderful, too. It's so good to see a really young gardener who knows his stuff and who gets his hands dirty. I've been following your advice ever since you started and I've learned all sorts. Look. Would you mind? Just a minute . . ."

She thrust her overflowing carrier bags – all eight of them – into Guy's hands and delved into a large brown handbag for a battered envelope of photographs. "Here we are. This is my garden. We live in Cambridge, me and my sister, and this is what we had when we started."

The old lady went painstakingly through the two dozen photographs that illustrated the progress of her garden in Proustian detail, while Rob listened attentively and Guy, horrorstruck but unable to extricate himself gracefully, stood by holding her bags.

"Oh, now, look, I'm holding you up. I'm sorry to go on about it. Daft old lady that I am. But, you see, you've helped Esmé and me so much with our little garden that it's nice to say thank you in person, so to speak. I'll let you get on. And good luck."

She turned to Guy and took back her carrier bags. "Thanks ever so much. It's just that we're great fans of his, see. Sorry to interrupt your conversation. Goodbye." And then, to Rob only, "Lovely to meet you."

She bustled off into the crowd saying, "Goodness me," to herself, leaving Rob trying hard to suppress a smile, and Guy, for one rare occasion in his life, totally speechless.

Chapter 22

Two more weeks elapsed before Rob plucked up enough courage to dial Katherine's number, and even then he felt nervous. Supposing she refused to answer? Supposing the answering-machine was switched on: should he leave a message? What if she answered and then put the phone down on him? Having gone through a seemingly inexhaustible list of pessimistic permutations he eventually found his index finger punching out her number on the phone in his kitchen at seven o'clock one evening.

He heard the engaged tone at the other end and replaced the receiver. She was in. Either that or somebody else was leaving a message.

He poured himself a glass of red wine – Fleurie, they'd always drunk it together. He took a sip, and another, waited a few minutes, then dialled her number again.

It rang at the other end. Apprehension oozed from every pore. Then a small voice answered, "Hello?"

"Hello," he said, softly.

There was a pause. Then, "Hi. How are you?" Non-committal.

"OK. How are you?"

"Oh, you know."

"Yeh. Guess so." There was a longer pause. Then he said what he really wanted to say. "I miss you."

"I miss you, too." She sounded measured, unemotional.

"I'm sorry about everything," he half muttered, half blurted. "I'm sorry I cocked it up."

"Me too." There was more of a hardness in the voice now.

He was uncertain whether this was a motion of censure or simple agreement. "I just wanted you to know that I've explained to – the other person – that there's no chance of anything happening. That's all."

"Oh?"

"And I'd love to see you some time."

"I see."

"If that's all right."

"I'm not sure. Look, I'm sorry but I'm still hurting. I wanted us to be together because we *wanted* to be together, not because we thought we *ought* to be together or because it had become a habit."

"I know."

"What are you doing?"

She asked the question matter-of-factly, but Rob thought he detected a softer note in her voice. "Having a glass of wine."

"What sort?"

"Guess."

She paused for a moment. "Fleurie."

"Yes."

She paused again. He could hear her breathing. Then, hesitantly, she said, "Our wine."

"Yes. I only wish you were drinking it with me."

"Look, I'd better go."

"Do you have to?"

"I think so, yes. Thanks for ringing me."

"I'll speak to you soon, then?"

"Why?"

The question took the wind out of his sails. "Because I love you."

Silence, and then softly, "Do you?"

"Yes."

The pause seemed to last for ever. "I must go. Mamma's coming round. You take care. 'Bye."

"'Bye."

And she was gone. He held the receiver to his ear a little longer to make sure she had rung off, and then, aware of the loneliness of the moment, when one caller puts the handset down and the other still holds it to their ear, he replaced it smartly in the cradle and took another sip of wine. Somehow it didn't taste like it used to.

Chapter 23

God, it felt good to be outside. Good to feel the sun making you squint. Good to be rid of the studio and making programmes in real gardens. Rob looked across to where Bex Fleming was standing among a sheet of daffodils, talking to the camera as though it were an old friend. He watched her from his perch on top of a flight of stone steps at the side of the Old Manor House in Nidderdale from where *Mr MacGregor's Garden* would be broadcast this week.

Behind the house the hills rose towards the soft blue sky and were now flushed with fresh green as the buds began to break. Rooks cawed in a clump of poplars alongside the tumbling beck that argued with the rounded boulders in its path. Now the scent in his nostrils was of pollen and unfurling leaves, not of baby wipes and Max Factor.

Location filming meant that the programme would no longer be live but recorded. Despite his love of the adrenaline that only came with live broadcasts, the change was something of a relief in the wake of Bertie's outburst.

He watched Bex pick her way among the nodding blooms, talking to the camera as she did so. She would stoop now and again to caress a flower, and pause occasionally to make some point more forcefully.

He watched quietly, and at a distance, admiring her skill and her rare ease with the camera. He had forgotten about his own technique, it was now so much a part of him, but he had seen enough people pass through the studios as guest presenters to know that her combination of horticultural knowledge, ease with the camera and a pleasant personality was unusual. Couple them with blonde good looks and the mixture was irresistible.

And yet he watched Bex going through her paces with a brotherly rather than a lecherous eye. It surprised him a little. She was stunning to look at, had a personality that he found hugely attractive, and yet right now he felt that nothing intimate would come of their friendship. Odd. But thank God for that.

"And cut." Steve's voice sliced through the spring morning. "I think that's lunch."

He walked over to where Rob sat on the old stone steps. "All right, sunshine?"

Rob smiled at the spring in his step and the colour that was beginning to appear in his normally sallow cheeks. "I'm surprised you can cope with it," he said.

"What?"

"The air. I'd have thought it would have been much too strong for you, an indoor type."

Steve pushed his horn-rimmed glasses back up his nose and inhaled deeply, smiling beatifically as he did so. "You know, I think I could get into this gardening lark. Wonderful life. No worries, leisurely pace, meeting other delightful men of the soil. It's a recipe for a ripe old age, I reckon, rather than being stuffed into a newsroom with all those jaundiced journos."

"You coming out here for good, then?" Rob asked.

"I wish," replied Steve, his smile disappearing like the sun behind a cloud. "I wish."

"That's a definite maybe-not, then?"

"That's a definite no, I'm afraid."

"Shame," said Rob.

"It's all down to Miss Drake, I'm afraid."

Rob was conscious of the flush rising in his own cheeks now and did his best to arrest its development. "Oh? Why's that?" He rose from the step, brushed down the seat of his jeans with his hands and looked out across the valley.

"We need a replacement before the week's out, so I've auditions to organize for the next couple of days and then I'll be studio-bound getting the new girl into the swing of things."

"Well, you'll enjoy that."

"Yes. But it'll be a bit of a slog, and the prospect of all those babes making eyes at me and offering me their beds in return for a job will be a real strain."

"Oh, I bet," said Rob, turning round to look at him and see just how straight he had been able to keep his face.

"It's true. The sexual appetites of female newsreaders are known to be voracious.'

"Really?" Rob turned his back on his producer once more.

"You mean you hadn't noticed?" Steve queried.

Before Rob had time to reply, or even to turn round, Bex interrupted.

"Did somebody say lunch?" she asked, flashing a smile at the two men.

"Yes." Steve pointed in the direction of an old stone barn. "The lady of the house has knocked up some home-made soup and rolls. Help yourself. We'll be over in a minute, I just want a word with Rob."

Bex smiled again, said, 'OK,' and sauntered off.

"That sounds ominous," said Rob.

"No, not really. It's just that we've been looking at the way you two have been getting on on screen."

"Mmm?" Rob raised his eyebrows.

"You and Bex."

"And?"

"You must have noticed how well it's been working? And the ratings have been going through the roof."

"I know." Rob wondered what was coming.

"It's not that we want to reduce your content in the programme, but just that we think it would be a good idea if Bex had fractionally more to do, rather than just a single item. The programme would still be called *Mr MacGregor's Garden* and you would still have all the links and the lion's share of the work, but Bex's presence would be rather larger than Bertie's. What do you think?"

Rob was not sure how he felt. Disappointment was the first emotion to flood through him. Then he paused, remembered what he had been thinking about Bex only moments previously, and realized that there was only one reaction he could voice without being either vain or hypocritical. "I think it's a great idea. She's great. We get on well. It's fine. I'll just put my enormous jealousy on the back-burner."

Steve smiled. "Good man. We're not pensioning you off, you know, just making you even more sexy by pairing you with a fanciable co-presenter." He watched Bex walking into the barn below them, her corn-coloured hair glinting in the spring sunlight. He shook himself out of his temporary reverie. "Anyway, think what Lisa Drake did for Frank Burbage's reputation. Everyone thought he was a tired old warhorse until she came along to liven things up. I'm not suggesting you have an affair with Bex or anything. Of course I'm not. Having nursed Frank and Lisa through theirs I've had quite enough of that sort of thing."

And he got up from the step and walked towards the barn for his lunch.

"Could we do that just once more, Guy darling?"

Two girls descended upon Guy D'Arcy, one with a powder puff, the other with a can of hairspray, as he stood beneath the mouth parts of a gigantic plastic greenfly wearing a white tuxedo with a red carnation in his buttonhole, a black tie, black trousers and patent-leather shoes.

Under the arc-lights of the massive studio he stood square on to camera, legs slightly apart, in classic James Bond stance, his left hand tucked into his right armpit, and his right hand grasping a weapon, which rested on his left cheek after the manner of the Ian Fleming hero. Admittedly, he looked slightly less macho than Sean Connery, Roger Moore or Pierce Brosnan, but that was probably because the Beretta normally used in this classic pose had been replaced by a hand-sprayer filled with pesticide.

Three more young women stood on the sidelines in the half-light, clucking about the jacket, the buttonhole and the state of Guy's eyeliner, while the hero of the piece continued to reduce to jelly any of them who came within breathing distance of him. He did look good. He felt good, too. And the prospect of not having a leaky roof any more, or even of moving upmarket from Fulham to Chelsea, cheered him no end. His thoughts never turned to Rob MacGregor. Not once. And even thoughts of Claudia Bell were, mercifully, receding into the depths of his memory. Lovely lady. Large lady. But very grateful.

"Just once more, darling, if we could," came the disembodied voice of the director over the studio PA. He would be happy to do it as many more times, darling, as the director of the commercial requested.

"Thank you, studio," said the voice, and the floor manager, a girl with short dark hair and a crisp white T-shirt that emphasized her figure, raised her eyebrows at Guy to check that he was happy before saying firmly, "And cue . . ."

Thunderous music in pseudo-Bond style boomed out from vast speakers at the edge of the studio floor. As it reached its crescendo in the short cadenza it paused. Guy looked into the camera at his most appealingly macho and said, "The name's BLITZ. Licensed to kill." Then he spun round on his heel and aimed the spray gun at the massive greenfly. It exploded in a coruscating shower of sparks and flashes, while brilliant spotlights beamed through white smoke to put our hero in dramatic silhouette.

"And cut. Lovely, lovely. I'm coming down."

And I'm coming up, thought Guy, conscious that over the past week his career had taken a much more promising turn.

It had been a spectacular shoot. A week on location with helicopters, filming dramatic aerial sequences in Italy where things looked greener at this time of year, followed by two days in the London studios for the dramatic dénouement. The theme of the piece was a James Bond chase in which the villains were not Spectre and Smersh, but greenfly, whitefly and scale insects. Our hero triumphed in the end, thanks to his trusty spray-gun filled with BLITZ, which put paid to the lot.

Two more girls came over to tend Guy; one offered him a chamois leather dampened with eau-de-Cologne to dab on his temples, another helped him out of the white tuxedo.

The director, a grossly overweight man with a pink shirt, yellow bow-tie and rosy cheeks, waddled out of the gloom and across the studio floor as the smoke began to clear to offer his congratulations. "Wonderful. Absolutely lovely. I'm very excited about it. Guy, you were just what we needed and I'm sure the campaign will be a huge success. Go home and put your feet up, you're a star."

Guy thanked him politely, shot his cuffs and left the studio floor with a bevy of attentive girls in his wake. He could get used to this, he thought. He could very easily get used to this.

Helena Sampson's day had not been nearly so fulfilling. She had spent several hours thumbing through back issues of the *Nesfield Gazette* in the dimly lit storeroom at the newspaper offices and come up with little. What she had discovered was the death notice of the wayward Armitage brother in the Hatches, Matches and Dispatches column during the December just gone – Katherine had remembered having seen it. Strange that he should only just have died. But it was the sole indicator of his passing and offered no clues as to the character of the man:

Armitage, Reginald Steadman, aged 77 years, on 23 December, in Devon, after a short illness. Husband of the late Susan Armitage and brother of the late Francis (Fred) Armitage. Beloved father of Gladys. Private funeral. No flowers.

Not the kind of announcement that would have made Miss Marple sigh one of her inscrutable sighs.

She asked Nancy, Katherine's secretary, if it would be possible to have a photocopy. The copy was taken and the large, dark green linen-bound volume of the *Nesfield Gazette*, July–December 1997, was returned to the grey metal shelves of the storeroom until some other curious researchers needed to delve within its covers.

Helena folded up the piece of paper, put it in her handbag and blinked as she left the gloom of the storeroom for the sunlit street.

Chapter 24

Rob was deeply pissed off. For several days after the revelation of Frank Burbage's affair with Lisa Drake, he had alternated between feeling angry and stupid, sorry for himself and annoyed at his folly. Where once he had felt the excitement of having a new lover, he now felt the sensation of crushed pride. Clearly he had been just another amusing conquest along the way. It irritated him that he was so affected by it. Saddened him that he had been so taken in.

He forced himself not to think of her, to concentrate, instead, on Katherine. Katherine, who'd seemed reluctant to talk when he'd rung her. So what was the point? He would wipe both of them from his mind, for a time at least, and concentrate on his work.

It wasn't easy. He messed about in the garden at End Cottage. He wrote his pieces for the paper and soldiered on with his weekly sortie into *Mr MacGregor's Garden*, happier now that it was being recorded in the great outdoors and with someone whose company he enjoyed. He picked up the *Daily Post* one day and discovered, on page seven, an article about Bex Fleming. They'd given her a make-over, to prove that this girl with the T-shirt and jeans who wielded a spade with Mr MacGregor on Friday nights could look surprisingly glamorous when she let down her hair, put on some makeup and showed off the legs that were normally encased in denim and wellies. They were not bad legs at all, thought Rob, gazing at the full-length photograph and trying hard not to feel like yesterday's man.

He folded up the paper and sighed. He didn't enjoy these gnawing feelings of jealousy and rejection. From riding the crest of a wave just a couple of months ago, he now found himself in the Slough of

Despond. The programme was doing better than ever; he and Bex had been offered a two-year contract, which he had been pleased to accept. But Jock's financial problems had not gone away and neither had Dennis Wragg. What *had* gone away was the imminent possibility of having enough money to sort things out. What had also gone away was love.

Guy D'Arcy could not have felt better as he sauntered around his garden in Fulham spraying the promising young shoots of roses and shrubs with his trial sample of BLITZ. Young greenfly were already beginning to show on the fresh green growth, and Guy hummed the Bond-like music to himself as he sprayed here and there, using his spray-gun like a pistol and providing his own bullet-like sound-effects. "Pow . . . pow-pow!" He checked over his shoulder now and again to make sure that the neighbours were not watching him, then went indoors to wash his hands.

It was funny, he thought, how when one thing went well, everything seemed to go well. It was almost the end of April. BLITZ would be launched in a couple of weeks' time and the *Sunday Herald* had been happy to promote the fact that their gardening correspondent was about to launch something that would change the face of gardening for ever. Then there would be the Chelsea Flower Show programme to look forward to. He'd probably take a holiday after that. And he knew just the person to go with him.

Since the heavy-hocked Sophie had cantered out of his life, and he'd given Claudia the old heave-ho, he'd been happy to resort once more to the little black notebook from Smythson in Bond Street – the one labelled 'Blondes, Brunettes, Redheads'.

He'd needed to go no further than the first page of the section labelled 'Brunettes' – thoughts of Claudia's blonde, lacquered hair still sent a shiver down his spine, and the merest whiff of Elnette or Youth Dew was enough to make him break out in a cold sweat. He needed someone young and fresh, and nearer to featherweight than his conquests of late.

He had a 'yes' to his first phone call the night after Claudia bustled back to Sir Freddie. The new girl in his life was Serena Clayton-Hinde – legs up to her aristocratic armpits, sleek black hair that flicked up above her shoulders, the impeccable voice and manners that came straight from South Kensington and a sex drive that came straight from *Farmer and Stockbreeder*. Serena's appetite between the sheets, Guy discovered, was on a par with his young nephew's appetite for chocolate Hob-Nobs.

Serena had class and good looks in abundance, but no money to speak of (Daddy had been a Name at Lloyd's). Still, now that Guy's fortunes had changed, and the cheque was already in the bank, that didn't seem to matter. She knew all the people he knew, looked great on his arm and made no excessive demands on him, except when she was on her back. It was time, he thought, to start looking for some kind of permanent relationship, and Serena had all the makings of a suitable spouse.

Guy smiled to himself as he dialled the number. The phone rang just three times at the other end.

"Hello?"

"Serena? It's Guy."

"Sweetie, how are you?"

"I'm fine. Look, I was wondering if you fancied dinner tonight."

"Mmm. I'd love that."

Guy adored the husky aristocratic tones. He smoothed down the short hair at the back of his neck with the hand that wasn't holding the phone. "Shall I pick you up at around seven thirty? Then we could have a drink in Covent Garden before we go somewhere round there to eat?"

"Great. And what about afterwards?"

Good God! thought Guy. She's thinking about it already. "We'll come back to my place. You'd better bring whatever you need. OK?"

"Lovely, Guy. Lovely. See you later, then. I'll go and get myself ready for you. By-eee," and she chuckled, half to herself and half to him, as she put down the phone.

Guy shook his head. Serena's conversation wouldn't keep Stephen Hawking entranced for long, but for the brief history of time into which the evening would soon pass she would do very nicely. He whistled the Bond theme again as he climbed the stairs.

Helena Sampson never whistled. But she did hum to herself as she walked out of the front door of Tarn House, depositing her front-door keys safely in her handbag. They nestled alongside an envelope she had received that morning from Katherine Page.

*

186

Wharfeside Nursery on a spring morning, thought Wayne Dibley, was the best place on earth. He sat on a large, moss-encrusted boulder down by the river, eating a freshly baked pie that Harry had brought back from the local pork butcher. He threw back his head to drink the warm liquor through the hole in the top of the shiny crust, then crunched through the crisp pastry into the succulent meat inside.

It was lunch-time, and Wayne liked to leave Jock and Harry to their desultory old-men's conversation in the potting-shed and sneak down to the water's edge. Here he could have time to himself, to watch the minnows darting from pool to pool in small shoals, and speckled trout nosing upstream in the deeper water. If he sat quite still, a white-breasted dipper would sometimes appear and probe around in the rapidly running water that tumbled over pebbles at the edge of the stream.

Something caught his eye. A flash of blue-green. He sat still, his half-eaten pie in his hand, watching a hole in the sandy bank opposite. Moments later, a kingfisher skimmed low over the water then up on to the overhanging branch of an alder.

This, thought Wayne, was real living. He munched slowly on the remains of his pie, watching the bird preen and ruffle its vivid feathers. He reached for the pint pot of warm, sweet tea at his elbow and, as he drained the cracked mug, he looked at his watch. Five to one. Better get going. Jock was a stickler for punctuality and the lunch-hour lasted an hour, not an hour and a minute. Wayne scrambled back up the bank with the empty pint pot in his hand. The kingfisher flew off, downstream.

Shading his eyes from the sunlight that flashed between the branches of the willows and alders that lined the bank, now speckled with the fresh, juvenile green of unfurling leaves, he ambled down the path, pushed open the nursery gate and strolled towards the greenhouses to check his watering.

After a few months of proving himself to Jock, the old man had finally conceded that Wayne could take charge of one of the ancient greenhouses and its plants, with the result that he had become so anxious to do the job properly that he checked his watering three times a day. A bit much, Harry called it, grumbling whenever Jock enquired as to the lad's whereabouts. Jock only smiled to himself, aware that Wayne was following in the steps of his own son, with his liking for moments of solitude. It was a rare tendency in a lad from

Wayne's part of the town, where youths tended to feel left out unless they were roaming around in a gang.

Wayne pushed open the door of 'his' greenhouse, plonked the empty pint pot on the staging and set about scrutinizing the pots and trays of plants that sat, cheek by jowl on the damp gravel. There was no sign of dryness in the compost of any of them, even when he pushed his finger in to check for moisture. Jock had been insistent on this point: you could not tell how dry a plant was merely by looking at the compost, you had to feel it with your fingers.

Wayne's greenhouse contained bedding plants – antirrhinums and nicotianas, he had learned to call them, instead of snapdragons and tobacco plants. And pelargoniums, masses of them, not to be confused with true geraniums, which he now knew were hardy garden plants.

He wandered to the end of the stone-flagged path that ran down the centre of the greenhouse and looked at some shrubs that he'd dug up and put into large pots a few weeks ago. Jock had been talking about how the Victorians used to force them into flower early by growing them in pots and bringing them into a cool greenhouse in January. Wayne had asked if he could try it and Jock, not wanting to dampen the lad's enthusiasm by pointing out that it was now late February, had said that he could have a go with three or four, provided they weren't his best plants.

Wayne had potted up a lilac, a deutzia, a viburnum and several of the old Professor's rose-bushes that had almost been washed away in the flood. The deutzia looked a bit sickly, but the others were doing well and flower buds were clearly in evidence. The lilac was showing colour, and fat, promising rosebuds indicated that in a few weeks' time, all being well, Wayne would have succeeded in the task of encouraging his rose-bushes to bloom in May.

Satisfied that all was well, he picked up his mug, closed the old greenhouse door behind him and headed for the potting-shed, dribbling an imaginary football in front of him and singing under his breath the words of the latest bit of rap that had come his way.

Harry was at the white porcelain sink in the corner of the potting-shed when Wayne opened the door, washing mugs in the cold stream of water that trickled out of the solitary brass tap. He looked round and held out his hand. "Give us it 'ere an' I'll rinse it."

Wayne handed over the mug and Jock, already at the potting-bench, turned round to the lad.

"Everything all right down there?"

"Oh, yes, fine. I thought there might be something dry, what with the sun and all, but everything was fine. I'll check it again later. I saw a kingfisher down by the river. Brilliant, it was."

"Not here often enough, though. I think the bad weather must have brought it in. It usually likes smaller streams, but that sandy bank must be to its liking."

"I couldn't see a nest."

"No, you wouldn't. It nests in a hole – like a rabbit. Probably got a brood of chicks already. It has two broods a year, you know – one in April and another in June. Keep your eyes open and you might see more of them, unless it decides to move off."

"Do you think it will?" Wayne asked, concern in his voice.

"Difficult to say. You can't predict what birds will do, least of all kingfishers. They're getting rarer, I'm sad to say, but I hope this one stays. I watch it from the kitchen window most mornings now. Lovely bird –" Jock broke off from his musings at the sound of a car coming down the lane. He poked his head out of the potting-shed door and saw Lady Sampson's Discovery pulling up by the wall outside the nursery gate.

She got out, locked the car door, pushed open the gate and walked purposefully down the path towards the potting-shed.

"Good morning!" she hailed Jock.

"Good morning to you," answered Jock, stepping out of the potting-shed and raising his cap. "How are you, Lady Sampson?"

"I am *very* well, thank you."

"Well, that's pretty definite," countered Jock.

"Do you have a few minutes to spare, Mr MacGregor? I've got something to tell you. Is there somewhere we can have a quiet chat?"

"Aye, if you like. Over there on yon bench. Will that do?" Jock's face now showed a mixture of emotions – curiosity, bemusement and not a little worry.

Helena looked towards the green-painted, slatted Victorian bench at the far end of the path where it had been placed so that visitors to the nursery could pause for a while and admire the view of the river and the dale beyond.

"That would be fine," she confirmed, and the two of them set off down the path.

"This sounds a bit serious," ventured Jock.

"It is, rather. I was going to talk to Rob about it before I spoke to you, but he's not in so I've come to you first. I hope you don't mind. It's to do with Dennis Wragg."

"Oh. I hope you're not going to try to persuade me to part with the nursery. Everyone else is and I'm afraid I'm digging in my heels," said Jock, trying hard to remain polite in the face of what appeared to be more interference.

"Not at all. I think it would be a great shame if you parted with the nursery. It's the last thing I want to see."

Jock felt relieved that at least one person appeared to see his point of view.

"So what's to do with Dennis Wragg?"

"You remember the day I came to see you and said I'd discovered that Gladys Wragg was the daughter of Fred Armitage's brother?"

"Yes. Bit of a shock that was."

"Well, I think you should prepare yourself for another shock. Sit down."

Jock lifted his checked tweed cap, smoothed down his grey hair and replaced it before parking himself on the green-painted bench.

"It seemed to me just too coincidental that Gladys Wragg was the daughter of Reggie Armitage who, in turn, was the brother of old Fred Armitage, the man you bought the nursery from. I thought this must have something to do with why the Wraggs wanted the nursery."

"Aye. I can see that," admitted Jock.

"Well, being an old woman with far too much time on her hands, I thought I'd try to get to the bottom of it. And I think I might have done."

Jock sat up and turned his head towards her. "You have?"

"Yes. I hope you don't mind. Oh, goodness, you *don't* mind, do you? I hope you don't think I was just interfering?"

"Lady Sampson, you know me well enough to know that I would tell you if you had overstepped the mark. You haven't, and I'm flattered that you've taken the time. Go on."

"Well, although Vera Ipplepen might be something of a gossip, her grasp of local knowledge is usually based, to some degree, on fact."

"Aye." Jock smiled.

"Well, according to Vera, Fred Armitage's brother was a bad 'un. All she said was that Reggie was the black sheep of the family. I didn't want to pursue it with her so I went off and did a bit of research. I wasn't really getting anywhere until Katherine stepped in. She discovered that not only was Reggie 'a bit of a bad 'un', but that he only just escaped going to prison for armed robbery."

"What?"

"Katherine plodded her way through back issues of the *Nesfield Gazette*. That girl has even more staying power than I have. It must have taken her ages."

Jock looked reflective. "Aye, she's a grand lassie."

"I managed to discover that Reggie Armitage had died recently, but Katherine found out that he had been accused of being involved in a jewel robbery in Leeds in nineteen thirty-nine."

"But he didn't go to prison?"

"No. The evidence was too slight. Reggie was accused of being the driver of a van that he and his supposed accomplice used to make a getaway. But the prosecution couldn't make it stick. The man who was reputedly his partner was sent down but Reggie got off scot-free."

"His accomplice didn't shop him, then?"

"No. You see, they never found the loot. The accomplice, who was the Mr Big of the piece, probably reckoned that if he shopped Reggie they'd both lose the proceeds, whereas if one went to prison and the other guarded the loot, at least the one who was put away would have something to look forward to when he came out."

"But he'd be away a long time for armed robbery."

"If they'd been able to pin him down for armed robbery, yes. But they couldn't. All they could get him for was being in possession of a firearm without a licence."

"So what did he get?"

"Six months."

"And he claimed his share of the loot when he got out?"

"No. He never came out. He died in prison of a heart-attack a week after he was sent down."

"So Reggie had all the loot and was a free man?"

"If he *was* a part of the robbery, yes, but he would have known that he would have to be careful. He knew the police would be watching him like a hawk, so even if he converted the loot into a lot of money he couldn't do anything ostentatious in case he was found out."

"But how do you know all this? It isn't the sort of thing they print in newspapers, is it?"

"Well, the facts of the case were published, with quite a degree of speculation about what really happened. The feeling was very much that Reggie and his partner had done it but got away with it due to lack of evidence. They didn't say so in as many words but the implication was there."

"If they did commit the robbery, how much did they get away with?"

"Just a minute." Helena opened her handbag and withdrew a buff envelope from which she pulled several photocopies of news clippings. "Here we are. The jeweller's in the Headrow was robbed of uncut stones worth eighty-five thousand pounds."

Jock whistled. "That was quite a sum of money then. It's quite a sum of money now. And did they never get the stuff back?"

"No. Even though the getaway van wasn't exactly speedy, they somehow managed to spirit the loot away."

"So what happened to it?"

"Who knows? It could have been tucked away in a safe deposit box somewhere. But then there is always the chance – and I know this sounds a bit far-fetched and straight from *Boy's Own Paper* – that it could have been hidden somewhere. And with Reggie being the brother of Fred Armitage . . . Well, there's always the chance that it could have been hidden in the nursery."

"Get away!" Jock looked baffled.

"Well, that would explain why Mr and Mrs Wragg want to get their hands on the place."

"But that's just too ridiculous." He looked at Helena, who raised her eyebrows.

Jock continued, partly incredulous and partly embarrassed at not believing her seemingly ludicrous conjecture, "You don't really think the loot is here, do you? I mean, wouldn't he have given it to a 'fence' or whatever they call them? Or wouldn't he have collected it before? The robbery was – what? Sixty years ago?"

"Almost, yes. But Reggie was a teenager and he wasn't a big-timer. His accomplice was the real villain, and he wasn't someone Reggie mixed with regularly, according to the newspaper reports. They reckoned Reggie was well out of his depth. It's possible that he wouldn't have known how to find a fence."

"So when did Reggie die?"

"Just a few months ago, down in Devon. He was seventy-seven. 'After a short illness', the death notice said."

"And you think that he told Gladys Wragg about it on his deathbed and she's out to reclaim her father's ill-gotten gains?"

"It's certainly possible."

"But I still can't see why he didn't reclaim the stuff earlier. Why on earth would he leave a load of jewels anywhere, then tell his daughter about them sixty years later? It just doesn't make sense."

"Oh, it could make very good sense. I've been a magistrate long enough to know that people do the strangest and most unpredictable things when they're under pressure. There must have been times when he was tempted to use the loot, but there would always have been the risk that if he were shown to be worth a lot of money the long arm of the law would have noticed and come down on him like a ton of bricks. On balance, life would be less of a strain without it. To use it might also have been more than his conscience could bear."

"So presumably Reggie thought that, sixty years on, folk would have forgotten about the raid and he could safely tell his daughter where the loot was?"

"I'm only guessing, but it's perfectly possible. People often see things more clearly when they're facing death." For a moment, Helena was lost in her thoughts, and Jock in his. The river ran slowly by beneath them.

Then Jock broke into the stillness. "So the Wraggs are not likely to give up just yet, then?"

"On the contrary, I should expect a fair degree of activity over the next few months, and quite a bit of urging you to sell."

"But why do they need to buy the place? If they're just looking for loot they could simply do the place over." Jock's face darkened.

"Well, as yet the Wraggs have shown no signs of being into robbery or violence. Oh, maybe my imagination is just too well developed. But we'll see. There has to be some reason why the Wraggs want your nursery and this reason strikes me, fantastic though it might seem, as perfectly plausible."

"So I need to keep my eyes open everywhere for the glint of diamonds?"

"Yes. Though I doubt that they'll be lying around in full view."

"No," mumbled Jock. "No, I suppose not."

Chapter 25

Rob ran himself a deep, hot bath, and tipped in half a packet of pine
Radox. After a morning chained to his word-processor he'd felt a
burning desire to get out into the fresh air and work off his pent-up
emotions. As a result he'd driven down to the nursery to offer his
father his services for the afternoon. Jock regaled him with Helena's
theory about why the Wraggs were so interested, and was not in the
slightest bit surprised when Rob made disbelieving noises. He really
did begin to wonder if she had flipped.

"Yes, I know it sounds far-fetched, but it is possible," his father
insisted.

"Possible but hardly probable."

"That's what I thought at first. But the more you think about it, the
more it makes sense."

Rob had become a little impatient with his father and had taken
himself off to his old greenhouse, only to discover that it was occupied
by Wayne. He should not have been surprised. He'd been gone for
several years now and could hardly expect his father to regard it as his
territory indefinitely. He smiled at the new occupant, exchanged
pleasantries, then walked to the potting-shed, took down a well-worn
spade from a hook and sauntered off towards the plot of vacant ground
by the river.

The young trees that had been growing in this patch of black,
crumbly earth had been sold during the winter, and Jock, Wayne and
Harry had not got round to digging it over. Rob knew that this was
where the wallflowers would be sown in May and set to, turning it over
with his spade and pulling out the odd patches of chickweed,

groundsel and annual meadow grass that had sprung up since the flood and hurling them into a barrow.

In just a few minutes he was into his rhythm, pushing the spade into the dark, yielding earth, lifting up a lump of soil, flicking it over and allowing it to fall back into the hole from which it had been removed.

This kind of exercise he found far more rewarding than anything on offer at the local gym. Spend an hour on a rowing machine or an exercise bike and what had you to show for it except a sodden T-shirt and a lack of breath? Here, as the sweat speckled his brow and ran down his cheeks, he could pause now and then to lean on his spade and look at the freshly cultivated soil appearing in front of him. He had always found it supremely satisfying, and every time he felt unsettled or agitated, a spot of digging would sort him out.

He stuck at it until the patch of ground was completely cultivated, free of weeds and even in its clod size. Then he trundled his barrow to the compost heap in the far corner of the nursery, cleaned off his spade with an oily rag and hung it up in the potting-shed before bidding his father farewell and heading for home.

Jock looked at the patch of newly turned earth and bit his lip. Father and son had exchanged few words since the conversation about Lady Sampson, but Jock felt a wave of emotion as he looked at the cultivated ground that bore the marks of his son's spade. He'd never met anyone who could turn over soil so evenly, but there it sat, the peak of each of its clods at exactly the same height, and all achieved so effortlessly, it seemed. He sniffed and shook his head, smiled and returned to the potting-shed, grateful.

Rob pulled off his damp rugby shirt and jeans, dumped his underwear and socks in the dirty linen basket and slid his aching body down beneath the fragrant suds with a sigh. He was out of practice, but the afternoon had been just what he had needed. He reached for the bottle of beer at the side of the bath and took a long swig before lying back and allowing the warm water to ease the stiffness of his muscles. "Oh, Katherine," he whispered, "where are you?"

Rob might have been facing the prospect of an evening alone, but Guy D'Arcy was not. He had taken his time in dressing for his evening out with Serena Clayton-Hinde, putting on the pale blue Turnbull and Asser shirt, the silver watering-can cufflinks, the understated soft lemon tie and the grey Ralph Lauren slacks and navy blue blazer.

He picked up Serena from her home in Chelsea and drove her first to a wine bar in Covent Garden then on to Le Caprice, where they dined at a corner table and enjoyed scallops and lobster and a modest amount of champagne before Serena hinted that she was ready for the rest of the evening's activities, and wasn't it time to go? Aware that he had put away more champagne than he should have done, Guy drove very steadily towards Fulham in his new black BMW and parked it a few doors down from his house, thanks to the extra cars that always seemed to be there nowadays due to partying neighbours. The sooner he moved to Chelsea the better.

Serena was giggling and pulled him in through the front door as soon as he had opened it and extracted his key. Guy was feeling in pretty good spirits himself and pinned her to the wall in the hallway, running his hands down the slender body, encased in a little black velvet number. Serena pushed her arms inside his jacket and pulled him towards her. "Oh, Guy, Guy," she sighed, pressing hot kisses on his lips, all the while darting her tongue into his mouth. Guy eased himself away from her, took her hand and led her upstairs, a lecherous grin on his face. Serena giggled again, "Where are you taking me, you naughty man?"

"I'm taking you exactly where you want to go," replied Guy, walking backwards up the stairs with practised skill.

"Mmm . . ." A wide and slightly drunken smile lit Serena's face as she kicked off her shoes and began to climb. The lack of footwear made her legs seem even longer in the short black dress. She teetered up the stairs, led by Guy's outstretched hand, while he used the other to take off his jacket and tie.

Once inside the bedroom, lit only by a small lamp on a tall mahogany chest of drawers, they faced one another and began to remove each other's clothes, grinning and kissing as they did so. Serena popped the buttons on Guy's shirt, slid it from his shoulders then set to work on his belt. Guy reached around her back and found the zip of her dress, easing it from her shapely white shoulders and running his middle finger down her long, smooth back.

Soon they stood in front of one another, naked.

"Mmm . . . just look at you," purred Serena, holding both his hands in hers and eyeing him up and down.

"And you," replied Guy, taking in the endless legs, the slim waist and the firm, if slightly small, breasts.

Slowly Serena pulled him towards the bed, flipped up the corner of the duvet, then fell back and pulled him on top of her. She was all animal now, her hands roaming everywhere over his body, her limbs thrashing around and twining round his waist, his chest and his neck. She planted moist, hot kisses all over his body, her once-neat black flicked-up hair ever more wild and unruly, falling over her face as she abandoned herself.

Beads of sweat began to appear on Guy's forehead as he became more entangled in the lissome limbs of this human boa constrictor. For fully fifteen minutes their mutual passion heightened, with groans, sighs and liquid noises.

Then Serena stopped. She pulled away from Guy and leaned up on her elbows, a troubled look in her eyes. "What's the matter?" she asked.

Guy was lying perfectly still, on his back. "I don't know." He tried to speak calmly.

"Does this happen often?" The concern in her voice matched the crestfallen expression on her face.

"It's never happened before in my life."

"Perhaps you need a bit more help." Serena's face broke into a mischievous smile. "Let me see what I can do." She reached down and began to stroke Guy between his legs. He groaned with ecstasy and arched backwards with pleasure as Serena's gentle and caressing touch made his heart thump in his chest.

"Come on, baby," she murmured, running her tongue over his firm stomach and gradually working her way down. Her smile faded as her lips reached the objective of her anatomical quest. She raised her head and looked Guy sympathetically in the eye. "What's the problem?"

"I really don't know."

They both lay there silently, looking up at the ceiling, the picture of disappointment. Every few seconds their heads would turn, as if to convince themselves that it really had happened, in the direction of that which hung pathetically down between Guy's legs. For the first time in his life, Guy D'Arcy had been unable to get it up. It was doubtful that he would ever get over the shock.

Chapter 26

The month of May dawned, if not as brightly as diamonds then at least as sparkling as the dew that garlanded every blade of grass. Katherine sniffed at the keen morning air as she walked down the road from her flat towards the offices of the *Nesfield Gazette* in the centre of town. Although she had left home early, Nancy had beaten her to it. The gilt-emblazoned door had been unlocked and the smell of fresh coffee greeted her as she pushed it open and walked into the paper's small reception area.

"Morning, Nancy."

"Morning, Katherine," came the voice from the kitchenette behind the old mahogany counter. "Lovely day."

"Yes, lovely," replied Katherine, sounding less than convinced, as she slipped off her jacket and hung it on a tall Victorian hat-stand. She peered out of the window through the back-to-front copperplate script that decorated it and looked upwards towards the moor: a lush green sheen was beginning to take the place of the russety brown and purple rug that had been its winter livery. She sighed. Would she ever get used to being without him? She sighed again. Enough. To work.

Nancy bustled in with a tray of coffee and rich-tea biscuits. "Would you like it in here or in your office?"

"Oh, in my office, please. I've a lot to do this morning. Any messages?"

"Only from Mr Wormald, saying he'll call at some point today."

"Now, there's a surprise," muttered Katherine, under her breath. "Everything else OK?"

"I think so. The two lads are out covering the stories you talked

198

about yesterday, and everything's fine with this week's issue down at the printers. Oh, and the member of the council planning committee called and said that ten o'clock this morning would be fine. Is that OK?"

"Yes, fine." Katherine looked at her watch. "A quarter to nine. I've time to sort out a few things here and then I'll nip over to the County Council offices"

"Ah. She said could she meet you somewhere else? She thought the Council offices might be a bit public."

Katherine immediately perked up. "Did she?"

"She did," replied Nancy, looking knowingly at Katherine. The two of them knew by now that meetings with councillors that were not held at the Council offices tended to yield more tasty titbits than those that were.

"She suggested the lay-by on the Myddleton road, just after the footbridge. Are you on to something, do you think?" Nancy knew when she could risk asking and when to leave well alone. On this occasion her curiosity had got the better of her.

"Rumours about a bypass again – and you know how excited people get about that."

"I certainly do," said Nancy, as she dispensed the steaming brew. "Oh, well, good luck."

"Thank you." Katherine took a mug of coffee and walked towards her little office at the side of the reception area with decidedly more spring in her step than she'd had on her arrival. Now it was not simply the smell of coffee in her nostrils but the smell of a story, too. Nancy watched her go. It was nice to see her sparkle for a moment or two. She hadn't sparkled much at all just lately. Nancy took a biscuit and dipped it in her coffee. She had just slipped the soggy half into her mouth when the phone rang.

"*Neshfield Gashette*," she spluttered.

"Nancy?"

Nancy managed to swallow the soggy morsel and clear her throat, putting one hand over the handset while she did so.

"Yes?"

"Nancy, could I speak to Katherine, please? It's Rob. Rob MacGregor."

"Rob! Hello, yes, of course. I'm sorry, I was half-way through a biscuit. Just a minute, I'll see if she's there."

Nancy pressed a couple of buttons on her phone and Katherine picked up the handset on her desk.

"Yes?"

"It's Rob for you," said Nancy. "Are you in?" She asked without any edge in her voice, years of training having taught her the knack of sounding detached.

"Yes. Yes, of course," though half of her wanted to say no to give herself time to think.

A couple of clicks and then: "Hello? Katherine?"

"Yes?"

"Hello, it's me."

"I know."

"Hi!" A pause while both of them got used, once more, to hearing each other's voice on the phone.

"I'm sorry to ring you at work. I tried you at home but you'd gone."

"Yes, I left early."

"It's just that I needed to speak to you. It's about Helena."

Katherine's heart sank a little. She'd hoped that perhaps he wanted to talk about other things. But he didn't seem to.

"Do you think I could come and see you at the office? It wouldn't take long."

Her heart beat a little faster. How could she say no? She had to be professional. "Yes – yes, of course you can." Why was she speaking to him as if he were just another person and not *the* person? "When would you like to come round?"

"How about this morning?"

"I can't do this morning. I've someone to see. But I could make it this afternoon."

"Fine. What time?"

"About three. Would that be OK?"

"Fine."

He paused and she listened. Then she said, "I'll see you this afternoon, then."

"Yes . . . 'bye."

"'Bye." She put down the phone and tried to concentrate on the work that lay on her desk. But she failed, and her eyes, again, rose upwards to the moors, though she didn't see them, only him.

A smart rap on her office door brought her down to earth. It was not Nancy's polite tap. The door opened and Charlie Wormald stepped into the room, beaming what he considered to be a lady-killer smile.

"Good morning, Miss P. How are you?"

"Charlie! I thought Nancy said you were phoning me later today?" She tried to hide her irritation, not entirely successfully.

"Well, I thought I'd call in person. Better that way." The sunlight beaming through the window glinted on the high forehead that had been browned by frequent visits to the sunbed.

"What do you mean?"

"Oh, just wondered if you fancied lunch?"

"No thanks, Charlie."

"Go on. Take an hour or two off – all work and no joy makes Kate a dull girl!" He moved around to her side of the desk and perched his nattily suited body rather too close to hers. "There's a lot to talk about and we haven't dined together for weeks. What do you say?" He reached out his hand to clamp it on hers but she was too fast for him, rising smartly from her seat and walking over to the window.

"Oh, come on, Charlie. You know it's a waste of time."

"Waste of time? What's a waste of time?"

"All this."

"All what?"

"Do you really want to know?"

Charlie Wormald looked at her as if he knew what was coming. "Can't think what you mean."

"I think you can. I've had enough of your games, Charlie. You're old enough to be my father and you're a married man. I'm not interested. I'm here to look after your paper, not your love-life."

Charlie looked surprised. "I see."

"I've got quite enough problems with my own love-life without getting mixed up in yours, so just back off and let me get on with my job."

Charlie was still perched on the edge of Katherine's desk. "Well, that's told me I suppose." Half of him didn't want to give in so easily. The other half reminded himself that sexual harassment cases were all too frequent nowadays, and spiky Miss Katherine Page was probably just the sort to rush into litigation.

"Don't look so worried, Charlie. I'll still run your paper for you. Just don't push me on any other counts, that's all."

"R-i-g-h-t. Well, I suppose lunch is out of the question, then?"

201

"For now, yes. You can take me out to lunch when you want to discuss business."

"Well, there is one bit of business I do want to discuss."

"What's that?" Katherine remained at a safe distance by the window, her arms folded.

"I've . . . er . . . had a few approaches about a new road. Something to do with a bypass. Know anything about it?"

"What sort of thing?" Katherine asked cautiously.

"Just this and that. Nothing definite. I just thought you ought to know that there are certain people who'd rather the paper kept a low profile on the subject. It might be a good idea not to stir anything up. Know what I mean?"

"I know exactly what you mean, Charlie, and the answer is no."

"What?"

"You promoted me to editor of this paper because you trusted my judgement. I seem to remember that you told me at the time I was the only person you couldn't imagine being corrupted by power, or was that just a chat-up line?" Charlie drew breath, but Katherine continued before he had a chance to speak. "If you want a yes-man in this job, or a yes-woman, you've employed the wrong person."

"Now, look here –"

"No, Charlie, you look here. I've already buggered up a relationship because you were over-friendly in a restaurant and someone got the wrong idea. That's something I've had to learn to live with. But I'm not prepared to bugger up my professional life as well. I'm having to learn to live with my first mistake, but there's no way I could live with myself if I started kow-towing to pressures from people who should know better. And that includes you."

"I see."

"Good. And now you probably want to give me the sack." She turned her back to Charlie and looked out of the window. She guessed she should have felt sick; instead, she felt strangely elated. If he sacked her now, she really wouldn't care. It had done her good to get things off her chest.

"No. I don't want to give you the sack. You're a bloody good editor. I've always admired your guts. That's half the problem, I suppose. I should have stuck to admiring them and not the rest of you."

Katherine suppressed a smile, relieved at Charlie's acceptance of her stance.

"Fine. Well, I'd better let you get on."

Katherine looked at her watch. "Yes. I've someone to see. I won't tell you what it's about. You might think it's rubbing salt in the wound."

A stiff, chilly breeze, not unusual for early May up in the dale, blew through the open window of Katherine's old Renault 5 as she waited in the lay-by as arranged. It was already ten past ten and there was no sign of the councillor. She wondered how long to wait before deciding that she had been stood up when a large, dark green Rover cruised in behind her. The door opened and Councillor Mrs Gosport heaved her portly, plum-coated body out and slammed the door. She crunched in her sensible black court shoes towards the passenger door of Katherine's Renault and tapped lightly on the glass. Katherine leaned over and pulled on the handle to release the lock and Councillor Mrs Gosport ('Call me Molly') compressed her bulky frame into the modest amount of available space.

Molly Gosport was classic county councillor material. A no-nonsense woman with a strong sense of community spirit, she was, nevertheless, not averse to using the local paper to further her own ends – strictly for the public good, of course. She pulled off her black leather gloves, laid them in her ample lap and thanked Katherine for coming. "I'm sorry to have suggested such a covert meeting but I thought the Council offices might just be a little too public."

"I see." Katherine slid her hand into the pocket of her jacket and pulled out her shorthand notebook.

"Yes, you'll need that," confirmed Molly Gosport. She unbuttoned her coat, which eased itself open with a sigh of relief from every seam, and warmed to her story. "You've heard about the bypass, I presume?"

"Well, it's been off and on for years, but there's not much activity at the moment, is there?"

"More than you'd think. The original plans were thrown out but there are new ones afoot, though it's not generally known yet. This sort of thing happens now and again, but this time I think there are some parties involved who are in it to feather their own nests and that's really not on." Molly Gosport's chins wobbled in unison, like the wattle of a prize turkey.

"So what's the story?" asked Katherine, her ballpoint pen poised over her pad.

Half an hour later Councillor Mrs Gosport extracted herself with not a little difficulty from the Renault 5 and wobbled back to her own car, leaving Katherine alone with two things – the scent of a hot story and the acrid tang of mothballs. In spite of the chilly air, she wound down her window for the journey back, marshalling her thoughts as she drove alongside the river towards the centre of town.

To see Rob sitting in front of her almost took Katherine's breath away, until she reminded herself why they were no longer together. She must stay cool and not give in to her feelings. She tried not to sound too hard. "So what is it?" She hoped she had avoided coming across as an impatient schoolmistress.

"It's Helena. She's read all the clippings you dug up for her about Reggie Armitage and has come up with a scenario that's worthy of Agatha Christie."

"Oh, God!"

Rob filled Katherine in on the elaborate chain of events that Lady Sampson had envisaged, all the time just grateful to be in Katherine's company, and hardly daring to hope that she felt the same. Katherine watched him, drinking in every movement of his body, every flicker of his features, at the same time registering the absurdity of the complex scenario. At the end of his explanation, having managed, in spite of her feelings, to keep pace with the story, Katherine admitted that she had no idea that Helena would have made so many assumptions. "Do you think it's really possible?"

"Well, I suppose so, but it's hardly likely, is it? The only thing it would do is make sense of why Dennis Wragg wants the nursery, and there's no other plausible reason as far as I can see."

"Until this morning I'd have agreed with you," said Katherine.

Rob looked at her keenly. "What do you mean?"

"I've just had a meeting with Councillor Mrs Gosport, and the reasons for Dennis Wragg's interest in Wharfside Nursery are suddenly crystal clear."

When Rob left the offices of the *Nesfield Gazette* at half past four his love for Katherine knew no bounds. The only trouble was, he was still without her.

Chapter 27

"You've probably just been working too hard." The Harley Street specialist washed his hands at the sink in the corner of his consulting room as Guy D'Arcy put on his shirt and tucked it into his trousers. "There's nothing obviously wrong. Your blood pressure's fine and so are your blood-sugar levels. I've checked your peripheral circulation and the neurological tests don't show anything. It's probably just a temporary thing. I should think it will pass. It happens to most men at some time."

None of which Guy found very comforting. His ability to pull anything was as important to him as his career, and the prospect of Serena spreading it abroad that, once between the sheets, he really wasn't up to it filled him with gloom.

He needed to take his mind off things. He walked from Harley Street all the way to Jermyn Street to buy himself a new shirt and tie for the Chelsea Flower Show. But even lunch at Fortnum's with an old school chum couldn't take his mind off his predicament. He kept putting his hand in his pocket to make sure that it was still there.

Frank Burbage was whistling "You're Gorgeous" to himself as he marked up the pages and shuffled around the rough draft of his script for the lunch-time news. He sat behind his desk, putting gold cufflinks into the starched cuffs of his boldly striped shirt and barking things at secretaries from time to time in between looking out of the window at the bright morning.

"Wonderful day," he hollered at Lottie Pym, as she passed his desk on her photocopying run. She looked at him and smiled nervously.

She always preferred it when Frank was grumpy – at least then you knew where you were with him. When he was cheerful you wondered when the next flare-up was due. She pressed the buttons on the photocopier and waited while the machine spewed out the scripts.

Frank may have had one eye on the weather, but the other eye was on the clock. It had taken Steve Taylor longer than he had hoped to find a replacement for Lisa. Frank had had to sit next to a motley crew of temporary substitutes, many of whom he considered to be as ugly as sin or as useless as a chocolate fire-guard. Some had gazed at the autocue, transfixed; others had dried up altogether. But at last Steve had succeeded in his quest and was due, this morning, to introduce his news-star-in-the-making to her workmates.

Why her identity had been kept such a closely guarded secret was a mystery to Frank, but Steve had said that the station didn't want any leaks before the official announcement and photocall due at noon today. Frank adjusted the knot in his brightly striped tie, looking in the hand mirror he always kept in his drawer, and hoped that the lavish amount of aftershave he'd dabbed on earlier in Makeup was lasting well.

He checked his teeth for spinach (unlikely as he'd not eaten it for breakfast) and ran a steel comb through his wiry grey hair, wincing as a handful came away between the teeth. He pulled out the departing filaments and dropped them from a dizzy height into his litter bin, looking wistfully after them as they disappeared from view among the old scripts and envelopes.

Frank mused on the possible identity of Lisa's replacement. There had been rumours abroad for a week or more. Some put their money on a BBC name being wooed over to this side – a sort of tit-for-tat arrangement or, as Frank preferred to put it, tit-for-tit. Others were convinced that the newcomer would be just that, an unknown plucked from journalistic obscurity and thrust into the limelight where she would either blossom or wilt and die.

Frank didn't give a bugger as long as she made him look good and wasn't averse to a bit of private tuition on the side. Or the back.

There was a brief commotion in the corridor on the other side of the pale, wood-grained door of the Northcountry Television newsroom. Frank Burbage slipped off the gold half-moon spectacles, which although they made him look distinguished also added to his years (his ex-wife had told him), and coughed to clear his throat. He stood up behind his desk, assuming that television persona of the wise but fanciable uncle his viewers had come to recognize, as Steve ushered into the room the tastiest bit of crumpet Frank had set eyes on since he'd interviewed Elle Macpherson nine months ago.

"Hello!" he whispered, under his breath. "Hello-ho-ho!"

Steve steered his new charge over to Frank, who thrust out his hand. "Hi! Frank Burbage." He took her right hand in his, covered it with his left and looked into her hazel eyes as if gazing into a crystal ball.

"Hi! I'm Jessica Swan." She firmly withdrew her hand.

"Really?" And then, half to Steve and half to his new potential partner behind the newsdesk, "Well, I reckon that swapping a Drake for a Swan can only be good news."

Jessica smiled a rather strained smile. "I hope so."

Steve butted in to smooth over the initial stickiness. "Jessica is from Suffolk. She's been working at Anglia for a while. But she can tell you herself. OK, folks, back to work." He shooed off the peering group of journalists and secretaries, who'd been hovering around Frank's desk, on the pretext of clearing some scripted item with him or asking him if he wanted a coffee, with the intention of getting closer to the station's new bit of glam.

He turned to Jessica. "I'll see you in my office in five minutes and then we'll go down for the photocall. OK?"

"Fine. Thanks." She smiled at Steve and watched him go.

"Sit down . . . please." Frank gestured to a chair alongside his desk and watched keenly as Jessica lowered herself into it and crossed her long legs, easing down the checked tweed skirt to cover at least half her shapely thigh. The neatly tailored matching jacket was open wide enough for Frank's all-invading eyes to notice that underneath her ribbed turtle-necked sweater was a perfect pair of breasts. Her hair was short and dark brown, perfectly framing almond-shaped hazel eyes, a dainty upturned nose and full, wide lips. He looked at her teeth, like a vet examining a filly, and gave her a clean bill of health. In short, she was a stunner.

"So . . . welcome to Northcountry Television," breathed Frank, leaning across his desk in his most avuncular and friendly style – and almost suffocating Jessica in a cloud of Listerine vapour.

"Thank you. It's great to be here." The voice was clear and confident with no trace of an accent, and although there wasn't a lot of warmth in it, thought Frank, at least she wasn't sounding quite as chilly as she had in her first greeting.

"Tell me where you've come from."

Jessica leaned back in her chair, looking round the office as she replied, not giving Frank the undivided attention he would have preferred. "Oh, you know, the usual channels. University, then local papers, then local TV. I thought it was time for a move so kept my ears open. When I heard this was up for grabs I got my boss to put in a word and . . ." having taken in the staffing, the seating arrangements and the colour of the walls, she finally brought her eyes back to Frank ". . . here I am."

"Which university?" asked Frank, now a little wary of Miss Cool-and-Confident.

"Cambridge. Newnham College."

"Ah, same as Joan Bakewell."

"Yes, and Germaine Greer."

"Mmm. Double first?"

"Yup. English."

"Good for you." Frank was wilting, but attempted one more sally. "So, as I say. Welcome. And if there's anything I can do," here he leaned forward again and put his hand on her arm, "don't hesitate to ask. I always think that the relationship between the newscasters – and I always use the term newscasters, not newsreaders, just in case those bloody hacks over there," he waved an arm in the direction of his scribbling minions, "get too full of themselves – I always think that our relationship is a vital part of the programme. The viewers like to see us getting on. Know what I mean?" He raised his eyebrows and smiled across at her.

"Yes," replied Jessica. "I know exactly what you mean, Frank." She leaned across the desk so that her face was barely a foot from his. Frank could smell her perfume and something stirred inside him. "And if you make one false move, Frank, I'll cut your balls off." With that she rose from the chair, smiled the most glittering smile at him, and walked off smartly towards Steve's office.

Frank sat back in his chair, looking for all the world like a schoolboy who had just been beaten at conkers.

Jock MacGregor's relationship with Harry Hotchkiss was not something to which he had ever given much conscious thought.

Harry had come as a fixture and fitting with the nursery, and the two men had always rubbed along fine. Jock felt responsible for Harry's welfare, as the episode over the rent increase proved, but the two men never socialized, and their conversation at work seldom achieved intellectual heights, Harry's main preoccupation being the British Legion, his cough and his bowels.

Although Jock's daily preoccupation was now the survival of his business, there was no way he could communicate any of his fears to Harry. He would have to live with them for as long as it took the business to get back on an even keel. He tried to rid his mind of depressing thoughts.

On this particular morning, as the two of them were in the potting-shed brewing up the PG Tips, Jock found himself wondering about Harry's relationship with his previous employer and, come to that, with his previous employer's brother. Wayne was down in his greenhouse, checking his watering again, and two customers who had come in to look for 'something unusual in the shrub line' were rummaging about among the viburnums at the bottom of the nursery. Jock, finding a window in Harry's bronchial and bowel activity, tentatively asked a question. "Old Fred Armitage . . ."

"Mmm . . . harrumph?" asked Harry.

"How long did you work for him before I came along?"

"Oh, let's think . . ." Harry gave a loud, rumbling cough that seemed to emanate from somewhere near his groin and then offered, "It would'a been about ten year. I started wi' 'im in nineteen forty."

"Did you ever meet his brother – Reggie?"

Harry paused with the grubby brown kettle hovering over the even grubbier teapot. He looked up at Jock, then down again, and carried on pouring the scalding water over the pile of brown leaves in the bottom of the pot.

"Aye. Just the once. He were a bad 'un. Mr Armitage'd 'ave nuthin' to do wi' 'im."

"So when did you meet him?" Jock carried on potting up young scented-leaf pelargoniums and trying to sound casual.

"Just after I came 'ere. Mr Armitage were raising 'is voice in't pottin'-shed, which weren't like 'im. I 'eard 'im across't nursery."

"Did you know why he didn't like him?"

Harry had another clearing of the tubes and fished out his packet of Capstan Full Strength. "'E were up to no good. 'E'd nearly been put away for summat and Mr Armitage were reet cross wi' 'im." Harry tapped the end of the cigarette on the packet and put it into his mouth, lighting it with a match from a packet of Vestas.

"Do you know what he'd done wrong?"

"Summat to do wi' a jewel robbery, though me mother din't reckon as 'e done it."

"Oh?"

"Nah. Said 'e were too thick. But then 'e only drove't get-away car."

"You think he did it, then?"

"Oh, 'e done it all right."

"But he didn't go to prison?"

"No." Harry drew heavily on his cigarette, filling what was left of his octogenarian lungs with the richly flavoured smoke. "'E goroff. Then 'e came 'ere to see if Mr Armitage would 'elp 'im out."

"And did he?"

"No. Told 'im to bugger off."

"So he went?"

"Not for a bit. I'd see 'im 'angin' round the gate of the cottage some nights when I went off 'ome. I think 'e were tryin' to squeeze some money out of Mr Armitage."

Jock paused before putting to him the sixty-four-thousand-dollar question. "So what do you think happened to the stuff that he stole?"

Harry exploded into a fit of coughing, a shower of grey ash tumbling from his cigarette and tears streaming from his reddened eyes. His body bent as double as his age would allow, and gradually worked its way upright again as the coughing spasms subsided.

"Oh, I know what happened to it."

Jock stopped his potting and quietly turned to face an exhausted-looking Harry, who was now pouring tea into two large mugs on the corner of the potting-bench.

"It were found a few weeks later."

"Who found it?"

Harry ladled four spoonfuls of sugar into his tea before handing Jock his own unsweetened mug.

"I did."

Jock nearly dropped his tea. "*What?*" He looked at Harry, who was now stirring the rich brown brew in his mug to try to dissolve the small sugar mountain that had just been added to it.

"Reggie Armitage 'ad been fiddlin' around 'ere for weeks after't robbery. I kept out of 'is way. Mr Armitage never talked to 'im an' I din't want to upset 'im. But I saw Reggie leavin't nursery one night when I were goin' past on me way to't Legion. When 'e saw me 'e chucked summat into't bushes by't river. In't mornin' I 'ad a look at wot 'e'd lobbed an' it were a builder's trowel. I couldn't work it out so I told Mr Armitage."

"And what did he say?"

"Not much. 'E didn't seem to think nuthin' of it."

Harry paused.

"So what did you do?"

"I looked around't nursery for a bit of new brickwork."

"And did you find any?"

Harry took a swig of his sweet, tan tea.

"Yup."

Jock's heart beat faster. This was beginning to sound like the last chapter of the book written by Lady Sampson. "Where?"

Harry gestured sideways with his head, "In yon," tilting his flat-capped head in the direction of the lavatory next door.

"In the toilet?"

"Yup." Harry took another fag from the packet and lit up.

"So what did you do?"

"I got an 'ammer an' chisel and knocked out the bricks."

"And what did you find?"

"A biscuit tin with a black bag inside it an' some bits of glass. I gave 'em to Mr Armitage an' mended t'wall. 'E'd no right doin' that to somebody else's property."

"But why have you never told me this before?" asked Jock, pushing his cap on to the back of his head and scratching his pale forehead in disbelief.

"Because you've never asked me," replied Harry. "An' it's not something I've ever told anyone else. It were private. 'Tween Mr Armitage an' me."

Jock sat down on a slatted chair in the corner of the potting-shed, the wind temporarily knocked out of his sails. "What do you think Mr Armitage did with the bits of glass?"

"'E told me 'e was goin' to give 'em to't police."

"Do you think he did?"

"I don't know. Only I know that they never took Reggie away, an' I'd 'ave thought they would've done if they'd 'ave found the stuff.

Funny, in't it?" He looked at Jock with an expression that was difficult to fathom.

"Yes, very funny." Jock sipped his tea. His legs, it seemed, had temporarily lost their ability to support his weight, which was a shame because right now he would have dearly loved a breath of fresh air.

Chapter 28

"Shine, Jesus, shine," hummed Mrs Ipplepen to herself, as she swiped over the worktops in the kitchen of Tarn House. "Fill the world, dah, dee-dee-dah-dum-dum . . ." She buffed up the chrome taps over the sink with her J-cloth, her squat frame swivelling from side to side and making whistling noises inside her nylon overall as she did so. She beamed like a Cheshire cat.

The front door slammed and her dumpling body lifted three inches from the floor. "Ooh! Who's there?" She spun round to look, her overall following a split second later.

"It's only me!"

"Ooh, ma'am, I was miles away, you made me jump!"

"Sorry, only it was rather difficult to shut the door quietly with my hands so full." Helena crossed to the pine table at the centre of the kitchen and dumped on it a wicker basket filled with food shopping.

Mrs Ipplepen gazed proprietorially at the freshly cleaned table. "Oh, and that reminds me, I'm almost out of polish." She crossed to the slate hung by the kitchen door to add to the catalogue of wants on her own shopping list for hygienic rather than gastronomic necessities. ANTIQUACKS, she wrote, on tiptoe. Spelling had never been Mrs Ipplepen's forte. She hummed as she chalked, and motes of white dust glinted in the shafts of sunlight slanting diagonally through the window.

"You sound cheerful."

"Oh, I am, ma'am," replied Mrs Ipplepen, lowering herself from the dizzying heights of her tiptoes and turning round to face her employer. "I can 'ardly retain myself. It's my Tiffany."

Helena slipped off her grey felt coat and laid it over the back of the chair. "Oh, goodness. Has she –?"

"Yes, ma'am. It came early, almost a month. They reckoned it was something to do with 'er being ultraviolated."

Helena, bewildered by her cleaner's meaning even after all these years, chose not to enquire as to the relevance of ultraviolation and instead rushed up to Mrs Ipplepen and threw her arms around her. They didn't quite meet. "Oh, Vera, I *am* pleased! But it seems like only yesterday that you told me she was expecting."

"Well, she'd left it six months before she told me an' Cyril. Didn't want to get our 'opes up in case anything went wrong."

"Very wise. And are mother and baby both doing well?"

"Yes, ma'am, except for a bit of trouble early on."

"Oh dear."

"The baby came out with its unbiblical cord wrapped around its neck. A bit blue in the face, but they soon put him right."

"It's a boy, then?"

"Yes, a bonny, bouncing boy," confirmed Mrs Ipplepen, pausing and wringing her J-cloth in her hands as the tears welled up in the beady little eyes that positively shone behind elaborate blue spectacles.

"Oh, how wonderful. And is Cyril pleased?"

"I'll say. 'E says that at long last 'e'll 'ave some reinforcements. Bein' surrounded by women for all these years."

"This calls for a celebration. I'll go and find a bottle of champagne in the cellar!"

"Oh, ma'am, I couldn't, it'll make me all tiddly."

"I think, just this once, Vera, that it really won't matter. And if you do get all tiddly I'll make sure you're driven all the way home."

Their conversation was interrupted by the ringing of the front doorbell and, once more, Mrs Ipplepen's body was elevated a few inches nearer to the ceiling.

"Ooh! Who could that be?"

"It's difficult to tell from here. You go and answer it, Vera. I'll get the bottle.'

Helena opened the door to the cellar and disappeared into the cool gloom, while Mrs Ipplepen bustled off towards the front door, where she found Rob MacGregor standing on the mat.

"Mr Rob, Mr Rob, you 'aven't 'eard!" and she flung her arms around him. Hers didn't meet either, but that was because they were short.

"Heard what?" asked Rob, laughing at her enthusiasm and excitement.

"It's my Tiffany. She's just 'ad a little boy."

"Wonderful, Mrs Ipplepen. Really wonderful!" Rob gave her a kiss on both cheeks, and she blushed like a schoolgirl.

"Oh, 'eck. You'll make me come over all unessential."

"When did it arrive, Mrs Ipplepen? I thought it wasn't due for ages yet."

"This morning. It was a month early. They had to introduce it because of complications."

"Who is it, Vera?" Helena came into the hall carrying the champagne. "Rob, hello! Perfect timing. You've heard the news?"

"Yes. It's wonderful. I'm really pleased for you, Mrs Ipplepen. And for Tiffany."

They walked through into the kitchen, Mrs Ipplepen bouncing along with all the excitement of a child on Christmas morning.

"Here you are, Rob. You can open this," said Helena. "A little celebration of – What's the baby's name, Vera?"

"Well, they can't decide at the moment. There's a few favourites but I don't like 'em all."

"So what are they?" asked Rob, removing the foil and unscrewing the wire around the champagne cork.

"Tiffany's keen on George and Henry, but I keep telling 'er to 'ave something unusual like Tarquin or Merlin. You know, make 'im stand out in a crowd."

"Ye-e-es." Helena and Rob were momentarily speechless, but the pop of the champagne cork broke the silence and the glasses were filled for the toast to Mrs Ipplepen's first grandchild.

"Here's to the new arrival," proposed Helena. "May he have a long and fruitful life."

"And here's to his grandmother," added Rob. "May she enjoy his company for many years."

"Ooooh!" said Mrs Ipplepen. "Cheers!" and sipped at her champagne, spluttering as the bubbles went up her nose.

Helena and Rob left her to her inebriated cleaning in the kitchen and walked through to the old conservatory at the back of the house, where the new season's leaves of an ancient peach tree provided shade from the bright spring sunshine.

"Bless her," said Helena. "She's so thrilled. I think I shall have to drive her home in an hour or so, if she isn't asleep!" She turned to Rob. "So how are you, this lovely spring morning?"

"Oh, I'm fine. Fine. I've just nipped in to pass on some information that you might find interesting – on the Dennis Wragg front."

Helena perked up for the second time that morning. "Oh, yes, what?"

"I think I owe you an apology."

"What on earth for?"

"I was a bit scathing about your dramatic reason for Dennis Wragg's interest in the nursery, and having spoken to Dad I don't think I should have been."

"What do you mean?"

Rob, having listened open-mouthed that morning as Jock recounted Harry's story, filled her in on the details.

"So, you see, you were right. The only trouble is that the treasure trove was discovered rather a long time ago."

"Oh dear." Helena's excitement at being proved right was replaced by disappointment at not having produced the real reason why the Wraggs were so keen to get their hands on the nursery.

"But supposing they don't know that the jewels were found? Supposing they think they're still there, simply because Reggie Armitage might have thought they were still there and told them so?"

"It's possible I suppose," admitted Rob. "But I think there's a more likely reason why Dennis Wragg wants the land. A reason that's rooted in the present, not the past."

"And what's that?" Helena lowered herself into a white Lloyd Loom chair underneath the overhanging boughs of the peach tree.

Rob explained about Katherine's meeting with Councillor Mrs Gosport and furnished her with the precise details of Dennis Wragg's involvement.

"It seems that the town's bypass was held in abeyance for a while. It's always been an on/off thing, anyway. But when it became a runner again, one or two people with their fingers in assorted pies saw it as a way of making some money. If they happened to own the land that would be compulsorily purchased for the building of the bypass, they would come into a tidy sum. The new route of the bypass is scheduled to go – guess where – right through Wharfeside Nursery. They were keeping the details of the route quiet for obvious reasons, including the fact that it would mean the acquisition and demolition of a couple of houses, too.

"Dennis Wragg has a friend on the planning committee who's clearly in line for a cut of the proceeds, and he tipped Dennis the wink, according to Molly Gosport – though she says that all this is quite off the record, for legal reasons – so he's after the land before the announcement is made."

"But this is dreadful," Helena exclaimed. "Does this mean that Jock will lose his land anyway?"

"Not now. Molly Gosport reckons that once the beans are spilled about the shenanigans that have been going on, there will be no way that the council will want to proceed. It's just too much of a hot potato, and they have enough on their hands already, what with by-elections coming up. She's convinced that the bypass idea will be dropped on the grounds of insufficient funding, and that Dennis Wragg will deny any knowledge of it."

"So what's Katherine going to do? What can she say?"

"Molly Gosport has told her the things she can say, and advised her on what would be libellous and what would be fair comment. She'll go into print on Friday."

"Well I never. What a story. It gets more and more amazing."

"You're telling me," agreed Rob, looking out across the garden at the rhododendrons, now in full bloom around the wide, curving lawn.

Helena watched him as he spoke. "That's not all, is it?"

"What do you mean?"

"Rob, I've known you for long enough to know when there's something wrong." She hesitated. "I saw Katherine the other day. She had the same faraway look in her eyes as you do."

"Did you say anything to her?"

"Of course not. It's not my place to interfere. But are you and Katherine . . .? Well, you know. Are you still having a bad patch?"

Rob looked up at the peach tree, bedecked with long green leaves and studded with small, green, downy peaches. He sighed. "'Fraid so."

"Can I ask you something?"

"Mmm?" He gazed, absently, at the young, ripening fruits.

"Is it the other girl?"

He came out of his reverie and turned to face Helena.

"Not any more. I was besotted for a bit but I managed to sort myself out. Realized I'd been stupid. I thought I'd got away with it and then

Katherine found out about it and – Oh, it's hell being involved with two women."

"Were you in love with her? The other girl, I mean."

"No. At first I thought I was. Infatuated, more like it. A 'grand passion' – even if it was a brief one. Completely out of my head. I didn't guess how much it would affect my relationship with Katherine. Funny, really."

"No. I don't think it's funny at all."

"Oh?"

"No. This might not seem to have anything to do with it, but when you have your first child, you love it so deeply that you can't imagine loving the second one anything like as much. Can't imagine having any love to spare. But when the second one arrives, you suddenly find yourself with an increased capacity for love. Your love is somehow multiplied by two, and then by three, or as many times as the number of children you have." Helena paused, remembering her years as a mother of young children. "But when you fall in love it's quite different. If you fall in love with a second person it doesn't work out the way it does with children."

Rob listened intently. "No?"

"No. Somehow it divides into two, and each half is less than the whole. You end up not being able to love either party fully." She turned and looked out of the peach-fringed window. "Children multiply your love. Lovers divide it."

It was a few moments before she heard the door close quietly behind her. She turned to see the remains of his champagne still fizzing in the glass.

Chapter 29

At first Rob did not recognize the burgundy-coloured Jaguar parked in the lane adjacent to Wharfeside Nursery. It simply crossed his mind that his father could do with a few more such well-heeled customers. Then he spotted the number plate: 2429 DW and his heart leaped. The car belonged to Dennis Wragg.

Rob pushed open the green wrought-iron gate and walked down the nursery path. Two old ladies were cooing over some perennials in an open-topped frame, and Wayne stood by them with a small, wire-framed truck in which they were depositing their selection of plants. Wayne looked distracted and, on seeing Rob, pointed to the bottom corner of the nursery where he could see his father in conversation with two men, one in a short cream raincoat, the other with a briefcase and a navy-blue mac.

He strode purposefully towards them and, from a couple of yards away, greeted them with a firm "Good morning."

Jock, who was facing Rob, looked up, and the other two men wheeled round. One of them was Dennis Wragg, his balding, Brylcreemed head shimmering in the sun; the other was Stan Halfpenny.

"Good morning," they replied, almost in unison, clearly wrong-footed.

"All right, Dad?" Rob enquired of his father.

"Fine, thanks, son. I was just explaining to these two gentlemen that I still have no intention of selling the nursery, but they don't seem to believe me."

"Really?" Rob was surprised, and a little unnerved, to see Stan Halfpenny. "Stan, why are you here?"

"I came with Mr Wragg, who is my client."

"But Dad is also your client, isn't he?"

Stan shuffled a little and developed a sudden fascination for the gravel path. He looked up to reply. "Yes, he is. So that makes my position especially difficult. I'm just trying to act in the best interests of *both* my clients."

"But one of them is rather more important than the other, I guess."

"Sorry?"

"One client is, I suppose, rather more profitable than the other."

"That has nothing to do with it."

Dennis Wragg, who had been silent thus far, drew himself up to his full five feet four inches and addressed himself to Rob. "Look, sonny, this is between your father and me. It's nothing to do with you."

Before Rob could reply, Jock interrupted, "It's every bit as much to do with him as it is with me. I hope I've a while to go yet, Dennis, but when I do go then Rob will inherit this nursery and it will be his to do with as he wants."

Rob was taken aback. From time to time, he had wondered about the future of the nursery, and about his own future in relation to it, but his father had never mentioned it and Rob had not wanted to ask for fear of seeming as though he were either muscling in or pushing his father out.

Jock looked directly at Rob, but spoke for the benefit of the other two men. "So, you see, he has as much of a say in its sale as I do."

Dennis was clearly irritated. "Well, then, if he has any sense he'll see that now is a very good time to sell. And if he knows his stuff as much as the nation thinks he does, he will know that there is no future for small nurseries like this one that can't offer the facilities the punters want in this day and age."

Stan Halfpenny continued to be hypnotized by the gravel as Dennis Wragg warmed to his subject and turned on the charm. "Look, Rob, I don't want to sound like some prophet of doom, but you know as well as I do that this nursery, run as it is, just isn't profitable, even if it is owned by the father of a gardener who is a household name. It's a dinosaur. All I want to do is turn it into something more suited to the twenty-first century and give your father a decent lump of money to see him comfortable for . . . well, you know . . . in his retirement."

"And you think so, too, do you, Stan?"

Stan Halfpenny looked up, his forehead glistening with perspiration. "I think it makes great economic sense, yes. But the decision is up to your father. And you," he added, as an afterthought. "I'm just here to advise."

"And would the route of the Nesfield bypass have any bearing on things?"

The two men reacted as though they had been threatened with the same fate as King Edward II, but swiftly regained their composure. Or, at least Dennis Wragg did. Stan Halfpenny looked even more nervous.

"What do you mean?" asked Dennis Wragg, half smiling and at his most innocent and oily.

"I think you know what I mean," suggested Rob. "My father hasn't heard yet, but I have."

Jock regarded his son questioningly, but he did not speak.

"I've discovered, from sources that I'm not prepared to reveal, that the Nesfield bypass is on the cards again, and that the proposed new route runs right through the nursery. As a result of which, whoever owns this land at the time will come into a tidy sum courtesy of a compulsory purchase order. And if that person were you, Mr Wragg, you would make far more money than you would have paid my father for the land in the first place."

He turned to Stan. "And I suppose your commission, Stan, would be quite considerable?"

Stan reacted quickly. "It's not like that."

"Shut up, Stan!" Dennis Wragg shot Stan Halfpenny a look that could have turned him to stone, had he been looking in his direction. As it was, he seemed intent on locating the nearest exit, which was clearly too far away.

Dennis Wragg advanced two paces towards Rob, as Jock looked on with his mouth half open. "You have no proof of this. This is malicious gossip, and it's the sort of thing that gets people into deep trouble. There are laws against slander, and I'm not one to stand by and be slandered. This could cost you a lot of money, young man. And a lot of embarrassment."

"I know it could. If it isn't true. But, then, if it is true it could cost *you* a lot of money, not that I think you're capable of being embarrassed. So, for everybody's sake, it would be better if you took my father at his word and stopped harassing him to sell. And I think that, in the interests of us all, it might make sense, Stan, if you were to stick with one client in this case, rather than two. Don't you?"

Stan Halfpenny struggled with his feelings, then admitted that it would probably be a good idea.

"I suggest you go now. If you do as we ask, I've no intention of talking about this to anyone else, and as far as I'm concerned this conversation has never taken place. All right, gentlemen? Goodbye. Tea, Dad?" And with that Rob headed for the potting-shed, smiling cheerily at the two old ladies, who nearly fell over their trolley as he breezed by. Jock nodded absent-mindedly at the two raincoated men and followed in the slipstream of his son, wondering if there would ever be an end to the surprises that life seemed to produce with the frequency of a top-class conjuror.

Once inside the potting-shed, and while Rob filled the kettle, Jock found enough wind to ask about the bypass.

"Don't worry. It won't happen now, Dad."

"What do you mean it won't happen? Why not?"

"Because Katherine is about to blow the gaff on the whole thing in the *Nesfield Gazette* at the end of the week. She was tipped off by a disgruntled councillor, who smelt a rat."

"You don't think she'll mention Dennis Wragg? He'll sue."

"No, I doubt that she'll mention him by name – she's got more sense than that. All she has to do is hint at corruption and intrigue in relation to the routing of the bypass. The paper's lawyers will go over what she's written with a fine-tooth comb to make sure there's nothing libellous in it, but it will be such a can of worms that, with the by-elections coming, it's a safe bet that the whole thing will be shelved indefinitely. That's the inside knowledge."

"Well, I'll be blowed." Jock sat on the slatted chair by the loam-filled bench, leaning forward with his hands on his knees as though he had just run a marathon.

Rob poured the contents of the boiling kettle into the pot. "Dad?"

"Mmm?" Jock looked exhausted.

"Did you mean what you said about the nursery?"

"What?" He looked up at his son.

"That it would be mine when . . . well, you know."

"Of course it will. What else did you think would happen?"

"Well . . . it's just that we've never talked about it."

"I didn't think we needed to. You see, I didn't want you to think that you had to take it on. Why should it become a millstone round your neck? It's up to you to do what you want once I've finished with it." He looked up and smiled at his son. "I'll let you know when I have. Now then, is that tea ready?"

Rob began to pour the strong brew into two mugs. "Just about."

"Well, it'll have to wait for a minute or two, I've a customer to see to." Having watched the large woman in the plum-coloured coat bustle down the nursery path, Jock pushed himself up from the chair and crossed to the door. "She's one of my regulars. Very keen on old-fashioned roses."

He left the potting-shed at a brisk pace, knowing that Councillor Mrs Gosport did not like to be kept waiting.

Devon, thought Rob, was his second favourite county after Yorkshire: it went up and down and it had a dramatically rugged coastline. He couldn't stand the flatness of Lincolnshire and the fens, where the lack of hills to look up to made him feel uneasy, but Devon was almost like home, if a tad warmer. He dumped his overnight bag on the kitchen floor of End Cottage, and stretched to flex the muscles that had stiffened on the long train journey back from Totnes. This week *Mr MacGregor's Garden* would be broadcast from a garden near Salcombe that had been awash with rhododendrons, dogwoods and other spring-flowering shrubs. The place had seemed like the Garden of Eden and had given Rob a welcome break from the intrigues of Nesfield.

He picked up the post that he had stepped over so carefully on his way in and dropped it on the kitchen table. The local paper, folded up, sat underneath the small mountain of envelopes. He eased it out and unfolded it.

"BYPASS BLUNDER" trumpeted the headline. Rob raised his eyebrows, read the article and whistled through his teeth at what Katherine had been able to get away with. She had named no names, but reported more than enough to set this particular hornets' nest buzzing loudly. The locals would not be happy with the implications suggested by an "informed source".

Rob wondered whether to call Katherine and congratulate her on her scoop when the phone rang.

It was Bex. "Hi! Did you get back OK?"

"Yeh, fine, thanks. How about you?"

"Fine. No probs. Great garden, wasn't it?"

"I'll say." He wondered why she had called. She didn't normally ring him. He didn't have to wait long to find out.

"I tried to speak to you after we'd finished but I couldn't find you. I just wondered if you were OK."

"Sorry?"

"You seemed a bit down. I just wondered if there was anything wrong?"

"No. Not really. Just a bit of woman trouble."

There was a pause at the other end of the line. "I'm a good listener, you know."

"Thanks. You're very kind. But it's time I did something about it instead of just hoping that it will sort itself out. A bit scared too, I suppose."

"Come on, then."

"Come on then, what?"

"Tell me all about it."

"I don't know that I want to tell you all about it. Why should I lumber you with my problems?"

"Because I'm a mate. And I'm probably the only half decent girl you know who isn't madly in love with you."

"Bloody cheek." Rob smiled, relieved at her candour. "Why not?"

"Because I don't fancy you, that's why, but I'm incredibly fond of you. So there you have it. I'm a pain, I know. But I might be able to help. Have you talked to anyone else about it?"

"Only an old friend of mine – someone old enough to be my mother."

"No one who's your age and who knows what it's like right now?"

"No. No one." Slowly at first, he began to fill Bex in on the details of his love-life, unsure at first why he was doing so, but then, as she listened quietly, saying, "Mmm," at intervals, he talked more freely. He did not identify Lisa, did not go into the most intimate details, but by the time he had finished Bex was in possession of most of the facts.

"So where are you now?" she asked, sympathetically.

"In limbo. I want to get back together with her. I'm desperate to, but I'm too frightened that she'll say no and God knows what I'll do if she does."

"Well, she's not going to come to you, you know."

"You don't think so?"

"I'm sure so. And she wouldn't be much of a woman if she did. I'm sorry to sound harsh, but if you want her back you'll have to prove to her that you want her enough."

"I suppose so. I'll go and see her as soon as I get back from Chelsea."

"Look, I feel for you, I really do, and I'll do anything I can to help, you know that. But for God's sake stop being such a wimp! Go and tell her. Let her see how much you care, how much you really want her back. It's the only way you're going to get together. It's knight-in-shining-armour time now."

"You're right." Rob sighed. "Thanks."

"Oh, don't thank me. I'm great at giving advice but not so good at taking it. I spend every night with this square-faced fella in the corner" – and she flipped on the television with the remote control. "My love-life at the moment is about as exciting as – Oh, God! *No!*"

"What?"

"Turn your telly on – quick – ITV."

Rob reached for the remote control on the corner of the pine dresser and zapped the television standing on a worktop by the sink. Up came an image of Guy D'Arcy in a white tuxedo, spray-gun at his side, riding in a fast sports car, pursued by a gigantic whitefly, which cruised above his head like a pallid Stealth bomber. Rob watched, wide-eyed, as the voice-over, supplied in part by Guy D'Arcy, with expletives by Bex Fleming, provided a running commentary.

"The name's BLITZ – licensed to kill," and a huge greenfly exploded in a shower of sparks.

"Did you see that?" she asked incredulously. "What a load of crap! How does he get away with it?"

"I don't know," answered Rob, truthfully. All jealousy he may have felt towards Guy D'Arcy had evaporated and been replaced by relief that he, himself, had not had to play cowboys and Indians with an assortment of insect predators.

"Have you see it before?" Bex asked.

"No, that's the first time."

"But weren't *you* going to do it?"

"I was, but they changed their minds. Thought they'd use somebody who was a bit more cool and suave, I suppose."

"Well you're well out of it. 'Licensed to kill', I ask you! What a hoot! Mind you, I'm surprised his TV programme let him do it. The man has no scruples at all."

"From what I've heard he has very large scruples."

"Thank you, Mr MacGregor. That's more like it."

"And, anyway, you know we're beating him hands down – thanks to your good looks, charm and impeccable horticultural pedigree."

"Watch it, MacGregor!"

"It's true! Anyway, I'm just glad it didn't turn out to be me, even if it does make Guy D'Arcy a rich man. Hey-ho!" He chuckled. "Mind you, I might have looked quite good in a dinner-jacket."

"Yes, but not as good as you look in jeans and a sweatshirt. Anyway, that's enough flattery for one evening. I'm off to have a bath. You doing anything?"

"No, I shouldn't think so. A bath sounds like a good idea."

"Well, take care. I'll see you next week. 'Bye."

He put the handset down and opened the fridge to grab a cold beer, at the same time reaching for the remote control to switch channels to BBC 1 for the news. The trumpet fanfare blasted through the old beams of End Cottage, but it was the face that came into view immediately afterwards that made Rob start and almost drop the bottle of Black Sheep Ale. It was Lisa Drake's.

If Lisa's appearance on the BBC evening news had come as a shock to Rob, then Jessica Swan's appearance on Northcountry Television's news had come as a pleasant surprise to people in Yorkshire. All bar one. Frank Burbage drove home that night in a state of shock. He had read the news with his new co-presenter, and was still being careful not to overstep the mark on a personal level. But it would not be long, he thought, before he could start to be more familiar. Already Jessica was becoming more relaxed in his company. So much so that after the programme she had suggested they go for a drink. Frank tried hard to control his excitement and anticipation, but he did not have to try hard for very long. As they sat down at a corner table in the Dog and Fox, a pub suggested by Jessica, the door opened and another customer came in, tall, good-looking and wearing a heavy coat.

"Frank," said Jessica, warmly, "there's someone I'd like you to meet."

"Who's that?" asked Frank.

Jessica beckoned over the customer who had just walked in. "This is my partner, Charlie Whitehead. Charlie's a doctor. We met in Suffolk and Charlie's just got a posting in the local infirmary. We're buying a house together up the dale."

Frank shook hands with Charlie in something of a daze. He thought he'd almost cracked it and now he knew he hadn't. What he also knew was that he'd never crack it. Charlie Whitehead was the prettiest female doctor he'd ever set eyes on.

Chapter 30

Saturday morning, 16 May, dawned with a diluted light that barely had the energy to squeeze its way between Rob's bedroom curtains. He swiped at the clanging alarm clock on the bedside table, then slid his naked body out from under the duvet and loped across the rough coir matting to the window. The curtains, pulled back, revealed a soft grey mist hanging like cows' breath over the water-meadows. Beyond them the sun, no brighter than a torch with a faded battery, was doing its best to burn off the vapour of the morning, and failing. Rob gazed on the pallid scene that seemed only to add to the draining sadness deep within him and sighed a long, soft sigh.

How tired he was of sighing. How tired of being tired. There were moments when his mind was occupied with other things and he could, for a while, forget Katherine. Well, not forget her, but at least put her from his mind. But then, when the writing finished or the programme was made, he looked ahead of himself at a pale emptiness that the early morning in front of him now seemed to personify. It was all so flat. So colourless. So hollow.

He stood for some minutes, mesmerized by the watery scene beneath his window, then shivered and hurried off to shower. At least for the next few days he would be fully occupied. The week of the Chelsea Flower Show loomed ahead. By nine o'clock he would be on a train speeding to London. There would be little time to mope. He had plenty to look forward to. Plenty to do. Just no one to share it with.

Katherine, wrapped up in a fluffy white towelling bathrobe, sipped her coffee in bed, the scent of freshly baked bread drifting upwards as it always did on a Saturday morning – as it always did every morning except Sundays – from the shop below. The previous day's paper had been a triumph for her. Charlie Wormald had told her so. She should have been pleased with herself. She *was* pleased with herself. Just low. And alone. And missing Rob. A watery May day stretched out in front of her. She reached for the television remote control that sat on the pine chest at the bottom of her bed. She pressed the 'on' button. Whatever her mood, she found it impossible to start the day without catching up on the overnight news. The fact that the morning bulletin was being delivered by Lisa Drake did nothing to dispel her gloom.

At half past ten Guy D'Arcy left Serena to the comfort of his bed. Only her tousled black hair was visible above the duvet as she lay spreadeagled beneath its warm, downy filling. The poor girl was exhausted, but last night had been especially frantic. Guy was back to his old self again. Serena had been well pleased with his performance, and he with hers. God, she had some energy. And thank God he had rediscovered his.

Wearing corn-coloured corduroy trousers and a navy-blue Guernsey, topped with matching Barbour, he slipped quietly out of the front door of the Fulham terrace house and pointed the automatic key at the black BMW nestling alongside the kerb a few doors away. The locks popped up, the hazard-warning lights blinked a morning welcome, Guy slid into the driver's seat and inhaled the rich aroma of leather upholstery.

He hardly noticed what a dull morning it was as he turned the key in the ignition. A few moments later the car purred away, and Guy purred almost as loudly as he and his motor cruised off in the direction of Chelsea. It would be the last journey they would make together, but at eleven o'clock on the morning of Saturday 16 May Guy D'Arcy didn't know that.

The traffic along the Chelsea Embankment was almost at a standstill, so Rob stepped out of the black cab and paid off the driver before walking the last few hundred yards to the Bullring entrance of the Royal Hospital. "Have a good week, guv!" shouted the taxi driver after him. "I'll be watching you!" Rob turned, smiled and waved as he lugged his overnight bag on to his shoulder and tried to remember which pocket contained the passes that would get him through the gates. This was a ritual he'd go through every morning between now and next Wednesday when filming would be finished.

He'd been to the Chelsea Flower Show several times, but never with so much anticipation – and never before the show's official opening day on Tuesday. Previously he had been a visitor. This year he was part of things. Through the railings he could see the vast marquee – said to be the largest in the world at three and a half acres – and behind the soaring off-white canvas, the roof of Wren's majestic hospital, the home of the scarlet-coated Chelsea pensioners.

Lorries jostled with one another at the main gate, ferrying their loads of plants and equipment on to the football pitches and tennis courts, lawns and shrubberies that for one week in every year became the most famous flower show in the world.

"Hello, Mr MacGregor!" A woman hailed him from across the road. He waved back. He remembered how his mother would always ask, "Who's that?" and then be embarrassed when her son confessed that he didn't know. He steeled himself for the week ahead, remembering that most people here would know exactly who he was, even if he didn't know them.

Gaudy banners advertising gardening magazines and newspapers were being strapped to the wrought-iron railings that curved inwards towards the entrance gates. The small roundabout outside them, encircled by slow-moving cars and trucks, was planted with bright bedding, and a motley assortment of people – each with their own part to play in this botanical extravaganza – came and went through the heavy iron gates. Rob found the appropriate pass, showed it to the peak-capped security man, who nodded him through, then began to take in the unready spectacle.

The tarmac drive that circumnavigated the grounds of the hospital was almost solid with vehicles, each displaying a sticker indicating to which stand it belonged. Some disgorged enormous steel trolleys packed with plants, which were wheeled into the marquee, others were being emptied of buckets of exotic flowers, stylish furniture or terracotta flower-pots. Many contained one person being shouted at by another person from behind, and occasionally a brief toot would indicate a blocked passage or an impatient dumper-truck driver – not so much road rage as road minor-irritation. But then this was the

Chelsea Flower Show on a Saturday afternoon, not Briggate in Leeds.

Rob picked his way through the horticultural mayhem along the narrow asphalt drive that ran parallel to the Embankment where, beneath the towering London plane trees, a dozen spectacular gardens lay side by side. All over them, welly-booted gardeners were pushing in plants here, stemming a flood there, and scrubbing paths of sandstone and slate. Three weeks ago this patch of paradise would have been just a grassy slope; now it was becoming a floral wonderland where banks of trees and shrubs, border perennials and rare foreign treasures seemed to have been growing for years. Everywhere the sound of water met the ear – tumbling over rocks, squirting from fountains, skimming over plate-glass weirs and bubbling through rills.

Rob watched it all and lost himself for a moment, remembering the poem by Robert Southey that his mother had recited to him when he was a child,

> 'How does the Water Come Down at Lodore?
> . . . shining and twining,
> And rattling and battling,
> And shaking and quaking,
> And pouring and roaring,
> And waving and raving,
> And tossing and crossing,
> And flowing and going,
> And running and stunning . . .'

and that was as much as he could remember. His parents had loved the Lake District. His father would love the Chelsea Flower Show, but Rob had never been able to persuade him to leave the nursery and come and take a look. The prospect of coming to London had never tempted Jock, who found Nesfield quite busy enough for his liking.

Rob walked by the lavish gardens bearing the sponsorship signs of perfume companies and upmarket magazines, past smaller plots, designed and built by working landscape architects, that owed less to the chic London fashion houses of their neighbours than to the painting-by-numbers movement. Between them the twenty-odd gardens catered for all tastes, with varying degrees of success. What they all had in common was a breathtaking standard of finish.

Rob found himself staring at a perfect miniature of an old kitchen garden – the peeling, white-painted conservatory invaded by its ancient vine and spilling old clay flower-pots on to the worn flagged path outdoors. A cold frame alongside the greenhouse had lost its battle to contain the rampant, adventurous shoots of cucumbers that were making a bid for freedom. In the rich, damp earth, rows of cabbages and peas mingled with gooseberry and redcurrant bushes, half a dozen old-fashioned bell jars sheltered a crop of early lettuces, and a white picket fence separated the old-world garden from the admiring present-day audience who stopped to take it all in.

"You should be standing in the middle of all this, you know!" boomed a voice from behind him. Rob turned round to see Sir Freddie Roper advancing on him.

"What do you mean?" he asked.

"Haven't you seen the sign?" asked Sir Freddie, perching his all-too-solid frame rather too trustingly on a shooting-stick in the last stages of metal fatigue.

Rob looked at the corner of the garden where, below a scarecrow made of a blue jacket and some dangling shoes, was the sign "'Mr McGregor's Garden', sponsored by Amalgamated Agricultural Chemicals".

"Ah! Different spelling. I think that's another Mr McGregor."

"That's the trouble," replied Sir Freddie. "That's the bloody trouble. You see now why I wanted you to front the campaign for BLITZ, but the bloody ad-men thought they knew better. Wanted to give the product a more modern image – hence the bloody James Bond stuff and young D'Arcy. I told 'em it would fit in far better with our Chelsea garden if they'd had you, but would they listen? No. Daft buggers."

"It's hard to see how it fits in with BLITZ," admitted Rob, looking at the garden, which quite clearly owed more to Beatrix Potter than Ian Fleming.

"It doesn't fit in at all. That's what's so daft about it." At this point a figure came barging through the milling throng of workers and tradesfolk who were surrounding the garden and made a bee-line for Sir Freddie.

"There you are!" Rob recognized Simon Clay, the bespectacled PR man for AAC who seemed less cool than Rob remembered. He looked agitated.

"What is it?" asked Sir Freddie Roper, glumly.

"I need a word. Now. Over in the hospitality suite."

"But I was just having a look round," grumbled Sir Freddie, relieving the shooting-stick of his weight.

Simon Clay could barely bring himself to offer Rob a greeting. He took Sir Freddie by the arm and led him off in the direction of the gents' which led, in turn, to the small hospitality village. Rob watched them go, then turned to look back at Mr McGregor's Garden. It was pretty, and convincing – but down to the last pea in the last pod completely phoney.

The sleek black BMW 325i turned off Royal Hospital Road and into Burton Court where, for the duration of the flower show, the grounds surrounding the cricket pitch and tennis courts of this salubrious square in SW3 had been turned into a car park. Guy locked up and crunched his way over the gravel path, crossing the road to the side entrance of the Royal Hospital and passing, as he did so, the small military cemetery and several glossy black cannon mounted as if to repel boarders. He shuddered. His father had once suggested that Guy follow in his footsteps as an officer in the Guards before joining the family estate-agency business.

The prospect had appalled Guy, whose preference for manoeuvres of a different kind had led him in other directions. Then came 'The Big Row' and neither career had been mentioned again. He walked past the scarlet post box set in the pillar of the black iron gates and said, 'Good morning', to the peak-capped soldier on duty. A couple of Chelsea Pensioners in their navy-blue day-wear, were slowly making their way, with sticks, towards the flower show at the bottom of their garden. Guy overtook them and nodded a greeting. They plodded on, oblivious.

He checked his watch. A quarter to twelve. He had fifteen minutes before he was due to meet his co-presenter and the production team in their Portakabin on the other side of the showground; just time for a walkabout to see who was there and what sort of grisly things some of the garden designers had perpetrated this year. The more of these that he could foist on to Rob MacGregor the better. He had every confidence that he could commandeer the better ones for himself. Gardens sponsored by Cartier and *Harper's & Queen* would do him nicely; some modest little 'family' gardens and displays of vegetables should be more Mr MacGregor's bag.

Fifty yards past the newly erected turnstiles at the top of Eastern Avenue he turned right, leaving behind him the presently vacant trade stands covered in security sheets of nylon netting (their exhibitors would turn up and stuff their stands to bursting point on Sunday and Monday). Ahead of him sprouted greenhouses and conservatories, from the humble to the luxurious. Guy peeped inside one octagonal summerhouse painted in *eau-de-Nil* and ivory, and discovered a confection of Colefax and Fowler, all deep-coloured chintz and mahogany, that would not have been out of place in the V and A – not so much a garden shed, more a garden château – and then looked upwards at the glazed tower of a conservatory-cum-pavilion, whose design had clearly been influenced more by Mad King Ludwig of Bavaria than Robinson's of Winchester. It was the kind of conservatory that should have been home to the Addams Family or Boris Karloff, but which would probably be purchased by a merchant banker or an Arab.

Guy mused on this. If he had been a merchant banker perhaps he would have got on better in the Royal Horticultural Society: so many of the council members seemed to be merchant bankers of one kind or another.

He looked again at his watch. Mustn't be late. A couple of minutes to twelve. He strode off down Mains Avenue to the Embankment side of the showground, returning the occasional greeting that came his way, though more of his acquaintances would be here on Monday afternoon during the exclusive Royal Preview, he reassured himself. Today the bodies milling around were mainly those of the workers, plus one or two freeloaders who knew somebody who knew somebody who was connected with the show.

"Guy, over here!" A tall man in a sheepskin jacket, his fair hair cropped as short as that of the shorn animal that had provided his clothing, waved a greeting as he walked over with outstretched hand.

"Tim Cherry, Unicorn Productions – I'm the executive producer of the programme."

"Hello!" Guy turned on the charm. "How nice to see you – and what an appropriately horticultural name." The two shook hands, Tim Cherry smiling good-naturedly but making no comment on Guy's observation simply because it must have been the twentieth time he had heard it that day.

"We're over here in the press tent – more room than in our

Portakabin. I thought I'd stick my head out and see if you were around. Thought you might have got lost. Not that you're late or anything . . ."

"I hope not."

"No, no. It's just that the sooner we all say hello, the sooner we can all go off and do our own thing." He walked with Guy towards the steps that led to the press tent at the end of the Rock Garden Bank. "Now, you know from the schedule we sent you there's no filming today, just a recce. Hopefully there will be enough stuff finished to let you see what takes your eye, then you can decide what you might like to cover." He ushered Guy up the steep flight of steps that led to the pavilion-like canvas structure which, over the next few days, would house the world's press. Today it was empty except for a couple of dozen folding chairs, Formica-topped tables littered with shortbread biscuits and coffee, and about a dozen men and women chatting away with pink running orders in their hands.

Guy noticed Rob MacGregor sitting talking to a girl with a nose-ring and a black T-shirt bearing the legend 'Iron Maiden'.

Tim brought the meeting to order. "OK, folks, we're all here now. This is Guy D'Arcy. Guy, I think you know Rob MacGregor, your co-presenter?" Guy nodded across the table at Rob and Rob responded with a "Hi, hello."

"I'll just run round the table so everyone knows everyone," and Tim proceeded to supply a mini-CV of the assorted men and women, boys and girls, who peopled the tent and who would be, in various capacities, responsible for getting the televised version of the Chelsea Flower Show on to the screen.

Guy and Rob both concentrated on trying to remember who was who, so that a runner would not be confused with a director and a production manager with a researcher. Rob thought it wouldn't do to ask a director if she could toddle off and find you a cup of tea; Guy made a mental note not to bother about anyone less than a director.

Each of the presenters was given a director with whom they would work individually, Tim being the all-seeing producer. Rob was put with Rosie Duff, a middle-aged old hand who knew her stuff and brooked no nonsense from prima-donna presenters. Her dumpy figure supported a broad face framed by a bob of dense, silver hair and she carried herself in a way that defied argument. For all her matter-of-factness she seemed sunny enough, and Rob was relieved to be with someone on whose experience he could rely.

Guy was assigned to Oliver Shakespeare – hooked nose, a shaved bald head, an earring in the left ear, black leather jacket, motorcycle trousers and long leather boots. Ollie raised his right hand as though being sworn in at the Old Bailey – it was his customary cool greeting. He was usually a producer on *Clobber*, the fashion programme, but like most freelancers he took on other work when *Clobber* was off air because he needed a steady income. Added to that, the fashion scene at Chelsea interested him, and he was sure he could give the programme a more upbeat feel with shots at wacky angles and sexy close-ups of lilies and the like.

"Well, now that you all know each other we'll go through the running order – not that it's set in stone. I've put it together how I think it might work, but I'm happy to do a bit of horse-trading. Guy and Rob, if you're not happy with the items I've given you please say so and we can sort things out amicably, I hope."

They glanced at one another. Rob was determined not to be the one who was difficult but, at the same time, did not want to be lumbered with items that might be at best weak or at worst naff. Guy wondered how he was going to saddle his rival with items that were exactly that. At the moment the running order was vague enough to allow each man to feel reasonably confident.

"What I don't want," explained Tim, "is a programme that's too arty-farty."

Ollie perked up. "What do you mean?"

"It's Unicorn's first shot at this programme. I know it was getting tired but I don't want to go off completely in the opposite direction and make it look like *Gardener's World* meets *Eurotrash*, OK?"

Ollie shrugged. "OK, boss."

"People want to see the flowers and they want to hear good advice from Rob and Guy, so trust your presenters and believe that what you're looking at is interesting enough without having to turn your camera on its side, OK?"

Ollie shrugged again.

Various people chipped in with questions about this and ideas about that until, at last, Rosie pushed back her chair, rose to her feet and said, "Right. I think we should get on and have a look round, don't you?"

Tim hummed in agreement and Ollie gave his Shakespearean salute to indicate his compliance. Guy looked at him with an expression that seemed to Rob a mixture of incredulity and distaste. Then he left the table with the little posse that had gathered around Ollie and which, clearly, constituted his team.

Rosie smiled at Rob and muttered quietly, "Should be fun, this!" before turning round and instructing her own little coterie – the girl in the Iron Maiden T-shirt, who was the production assistant, a youth with gold-rimmed spectacles called Colin, who was their runner or general dogsbody, and Penny, a petite, dark-haired researcher, who had an armful of notes and a navy-blue cardigan full of holes.

Together they walked down the steps of the press tent and along the Rock Garden Bank in search of inspiration. The two groups had barely separated when Simon Clay, AAC's PR man, came bustling along the pathway, narrowly missing a collision with a dumper-truck in which, in spite of his cast-iron confidence, he would undoubtedly have come off worst. He hurried up to Guy, grabbed his arm and spluttered, "We need you for a moment."

Guy, looking a touch embarrassed, turned to indicate Ollie. "I can't come now, we're just about to go round the show for the programme. Can I come over later?"

Simon Clay looked deeply stressed, pushed his frog-like glasses further up his nose and ran his fingers through his thick brown hair. "How much later?" he asked, anxiously, looking for a reply at both Ollie and Guy.

Guy looked at Ollie and Ollie looked at the black Rolex on his wrist and swung his head from side to side. "Ooh, a couple of hours. Say three o'clock to be safe."

"Oh, God!" Simon muttered under his breath. "Fine. OK. Three o'clock. We'll be in our hospitality tent – it's not finished yet but it's round the back, past the gents' loos. OK? Three o'clock. OK?"

"Fine." Guy watched him go, his mane of dark hair streaming out behind him. He looked extremely worried. And now Guy was worried, too.

Chapter 31

The sun had finally melted the early-morning gloom that had swamped the country from Penrith to Putney. By three o'clock it was a clear, still, sunny afternoon. Katherine had stirred herself from her morning torpor and pulled herself together. She had nipped downstairs to the bakery and bought herself a fresh wholemeal loaf. She could feel the warmth coming through the paper bag as she enfolded it in her arms, and back upstairs the two fat slices she cut from it tasted good, dipped in honey and washed down with fresh coffee.

She had showered, put up her hair in a mock-tortoiseshell clip and changed into a white Arran sweater and jeans, but when she found herself staring wanly at her conker-shiny floor she muttered, 'Damn,' pulled on a pair of dark brown suede boots and her woolly jacket, and took herself out for the day.

She shopped at first, but nothing seemed appealing. Either it was the wrong size or the wrong colour, too long or too short, or the fabric didn't feel right. So she walked down to the river, quickening her pace to force herself to breathe more vigorously and shake off her lethargy. Soon, the colour rose to her cheeks, the soft pink cheeks that Rob loved so much and which he had not seen for so long . . .

He thought about Katherine as he looked at the rosy-cheeked apples piled high on the National Farmers Union stand 250 miles from home. Thought about sharing one with her, along with a chunk of cheese. "Do you want to do something on this, then?" Rosie had asked him, breaking into his thoughts.

"Mmm?"

"Do you want to talk about the apples?"

"No, I don't think so. No, not really. Just looking." He smiled lightly, and walked on past the strawberries and some towering delphiniums, trying to bring his mind back to the matter in hand. But Katherine's face kept swimming into his head. How he wished she were here to share it with; to walk round together and point out her favourites.

The walkie-talkie strapped to Rosie's hip crackled into life. "Rosie? . . . Tim."

Rosie unclipped it from her belt, pressed the button on its side. "Tim? . . . Rosie."

"Rosie, we've got a bit of a problem. Can you get yourself over to the Portakabin. Bring Rob with you. The others can take half an hour for tea or whatever. As soon as you can, please."

"OK. Be with you in a couple of minutes."

Rosie looked at Rob, who returned her curious glance. "Sounds ominous," she observed.

Rob agreed. Tim's tone was more severe than it had been earlier in the day, and held an unexpected note of urgency.

"We're not late, are we?" he asked Rosie, looking at his watch.

"No, we're not," she confirmed, the two of them now walking through the Great Marquee as briskly as the clusters of unplaced plants and sacks of chipped bark would allow. "We're not due back for another half-hour. It's only four o'clock." They strode in silence towards the Portakabin and walked in to discover Ollie standing in a corner with his arms folded and Tim, sheepskin jacket discarded, sitting on a chair with his head in his hands.

"Hi?" said Rosie, half in greeting, half enquiring. "What's the problem?"

Tim looked up and folded his arms across his chest. "The problem is Mr D'Arcy."

"Being difficult, is he?" asked Rosie, as though she had suspected temper tantrums all along.

Rob wondered what had happened. All kinds of possible scenarios raced through his head in the few seconds that it took Tim to reply. Had Guy refused to work with him? Had Guy asked for a greater share of the programme? Had Guy made a pass at one of the girls?

"Guy's off the programme," said Tim, matter-of-factly.

"What? He's only been on it for a couple of hours," Rosie pointed out.

"Thank God. It would have been worse if this had happened half-way through the shoot – then we really would have been up shit creek without a paddle. As it is, we might just be able to stop this programme turning into a complete disaster. Rob, the girl you work with on *Mr MacGregor's Garden*, what's her name?"

"Bex Fleming."

"Is she free, do you think? Would she be able to co-present with you?"

"I don't know."

"Can she get a couple of days off? It'll mean her taking on board a hell of a lot of information very fast. We've lost one day, but with any luck she'll be able to pick it up quickly. We can brief her an item at a time – there's no other way of doing it. As far as her day job goes we should be through by Tuesday evening."

"I can give you her number and you can ring her and find out."

"Would you be happy to work with her?"

"Well, yes, of course. But why? What's happened?"

"A bloody disaster, that's what's happened. A bloody disaster. It's going to cost a lot of people a lot of money. But it's Guy D'Arcy I feel sorry for. Poor sod."

At three o'clock, as arranged, Guy D'Arcy had taken his leave of Ollie Shakespeare and made his way past the gents' toilet to the series of hospitality tents at the rear of the exhibitors' refreshment marquee. These canvas homes of the corporate beano would not be finished for a couple of days yet and were strewn with piles of white plastic chairs and small round tables.

Guy walked across a patch of grass enclosed by a white palisade fence at the front of the enclosure marked AAC and went into the small, taffeta-lined structure. In a few days from now, he thought, this would be the place where he would be able to hold court and sip champagne with his friends, courtesy of the manufacturers of BLITZ.

Inside the tent a handful of grey-suited men and one woman were sitting round a table engaged in low-volume but earnest conversation. As Guy entered they looked up and the conversation stopped. "Gentlemen," Guy said, breezily. Then he noticed their expressions and said again, "Gentlemen?" His eyes scanned the table. "And Claudia?" with less confidence and the merest hint of fear.

"Guy!" Simon did his best to sound normal, stood up and indicated that he should take a seat.

Sir Freddie Roper sat at the opposite end of the table, his face like thunder, but he didn't look up. His brow was furrowed, his lips pursed and his face the colour of the begonias Guy had noticed only half an hour earlier in the Great Marquee. Claudia Bell sat next to him, impassive.

Simon looked at Sir Freddie Roper and, when it became obvious that the chairman's silence was terminal, decided he'd better speak. All colour had gone from his cheeks. He looked as though he had just been sentenced to death and was about to make his last request. "I'm afraid we have a bit of a problem," he began, looking around him for support. It did not come. Claudia Bell gazed straight ahead. So he continued: "We have a bit of a problem with BLITZ."

"A problem?" asked Guy, disconcerted.

"Yes. Quite a big problem. We're going to have to withdraw it from the market."

"What?" Guy was baffled. "The campaign was OK, wasn't it? Didn't the adverts work?"

"Oh, yes. They worked very well. BLITZ has sold really well."

"So what's the problem?"

"The problem lies with our research department. I'm afraid the product didn't quite . . . well . . . It didn't quite . . . come up to scratch."

"It's a bloody failure!" Sir Freddie exploded, leaping to his feet, thumping the table and bouncing the grey suits into temporary animation. He was clearly unable to contain his anger any longer. "A failure that'll set the company back years. A company I've given the best years of my life to. A company in which I've sunk my reputation." He vented his spleen in the direction of all the grey suits sitting round the table, who now looked down as if in prayer.

Sir Freddie's eyes bulged and gobbets of saliva shot across the table like guided missiles as he continued his harangue. "Folly, bloody folly! I've banged on for years about the importance of research as well as marketing in this company. There are laws about what can and cannot be released. Laws! Not just recommendations but bloody *laws*. Laws designed to protect the public. They're even more strict nowadays than they were twenty years ago. The EU and all that. Why this didn't come to light earlier I just can't understand. What the fuck were you lot thinking about? Have you any idea what this is going to cost you? Cost the company? In reputation as well as money?"

The suits adopted a stillness more appropriate to Madame Tussaud's than the Chelsea Flower Show. Sir Freddie glowered at them. Claudia Bell picked a stray blonde hair from her sleeve.

Guy sat like a schoolboy hauled before the headmaster for a misdemeanour of which he was unaware. When, at last, Sir Freddie paused in his tirade and his colour had subsided to rich pink rather than deep crimson, Guy asked, tentatively, "Doesn't it work, then? BLITZ, I mean. Doesn't it kill the . . . baddies and not the goodies?" He sounded like a small child asking his father to explain the plot of the latest adventure film.

Sir Freddie, now spent of much of his energy, slumped back into his chair and took out a white handkerchief to mop his perspiring brow. "Oh, yes. It does all that. And bloody effectively, too."

"So what's the problem?" Guy dared to allow a flicker of a smile to cross his face.

Simon, seeing that Sir Freddie had expended more energy than perhaps was good for him, supplied the information Guy requested. "I'm afraid that BLITZ has a rather unfortunate side-effect."

"A side-effect? What sort of side-effect?" asked Guy, worry now etched clearly on his face.

"It's a side-effect that our research didn't reveal because it's not something that has happened with any of our chemicals before. Consequently, we were not looking for it. It's only since the product has been tested by our sister company in the States that this . . . er . . . unfortunate side-effect has come to light."

Guy looked bewildered.

"Go on, tell him," bellowed Sir Freddie.

"First of all the tests were carried out on rats."

"But rats don't use bloody insecticides, do they?" jeered Sir Freddie, in a voice heavy with sarcasm.

Simon continued, "Then it was discovered that when the chemical was used by gardeners some of them found that it gave rise to . . . similar problems."

"What sort of problems?"

Guy couldn't have been sure but he thought that he detected, on the face of Claudia Bell, the faintest glimmer of a smile.

"Well, it doesn't always happen, and it is only temporary – lasting a day or so after application. But, you see, BLITZ has been found, in certain men, to cause . . . impotence."

Chapter 32

Nobody seemed quite sure how Guy D'Arcy had left the show-ground, or where he had gone, but by the time the story hit the early-evening news he was 'unavailable for comment'.

Rob sat on the bed in the small hotel room off the King's Road, toying with a plate of pasta and watching the BBC bulletin. Had they no one else but Lisa Drake? he asked himself. He had turned on his television only a couple of times during the past week, but Lisa had flickered into view each time. It was as if she were getting her own back. His stomach tightened at the sight of her, and he would have turned off, had he not been anxious to see what was reported about BLITZ.

It was the lead item. "Chemical conglomerate AAC found themselves at the centre of a scandal today," intoned Lisa, "as their latest product had to be withdrawn from the market due to an unpleasant and unforeseen side-effect." Over Lisa's shoulder the commercial for BLITZ, with very low sound, was being screened to illustrate the point.

"BLITZ, the company's revolutionary new garden insecticide, was discovered, under certain conditions, to cause temporary impotence."

"Bloody hell!" Rob dropped his fork.

Lisa continued, oblivious to the interruption, "Sales of the product have been high due to a popular advertising campaign fronted by television gardener Guy D'Arcy who was, this evening, unavailable for comment at his London home. Gardeners who have bought the product are being advised to return it to the point of sale where they will be offered a full refund, and anyone who has used the product is advised to consult their doctor. The manufacturers say that there is no cause for alarm as the side-effect of the chemical, discovered in tests in the United States, is only temporary and no long-term damage is evident. Our science correspondent Richard Soames reports . . ."

There followed a brief but authoritative report from the stern-voiced Soames, who explained the nature of the chemical and its side-effects. A spokesman for AAC was grilled about BLITZ and did his best to salvage the company's reputation. The item finished with the exploding greenfly, and Lisa Drake moved on to the latest news about a single European currency.

Rob switched off the set and got up, putting the tray with the unfinished plate of pasta on the table by the wall. He flopped back on to the bed and reflected that it might have been he who had had to do the disappearing act and not Guy D'Arcy, except that he knew he would have stayed and faced the music. Someone had clearly been watching over him. If they had not, it would have meant the end of his gardening career and, worse, still, probably the end of his father's nursery. He turned his eyes heavenward, muttered, "Thank you," then came back down to earth and thought of Guy D'Arcy. Nobody deserved that kind of luck.

"What a way to go!" he said to himself. "Poor Guy." And he tried very hard not to smile.

Bex had been stunned, not only by the news but also by having been asked to co-present with Rob. Shock was followed by surprise and then worry as she questioned her own ability to step into Guy D'Arcy's hand-made shoes. She need not have worried. As Rob knew she would, she took to it like a duck to water and rose to the occasion. Rob had greeted her at the show on the Sunday morning with a hug and a kiss, and assurances that she would be fine.

Bex changed into a pair of smart brown trousers and a tailored cream jacket, and put up her hair in a French plait. When she came out of the makeup caravan Rob gasped. She looked stunning. She smiled at him and asked, "Will I do?"

Rob flashed her his crooked grin. "You'll do." He put his arm around her shoulder and gave her a squeeze.

"You look nice," she said perkily, looking at him in his dark blue jacket, grey trousers and crisp white shirt with a floral tie.

"A bit smart for me," he claimed, running his index finger around the inside of his collar.

"No. You clean up really well!" She smiled at him again, and the dimples came to her cheeks.

"Watch it, Miss Fleming! Are you ready, then?"

"No, but never mind."

"You'll be fine, come on. Tim said he'd meet us by the water garden on the corner of Main Avenue. And, if it's any consolation, I hate this bit, too. I'm always happier when I've got the first piece to camera under my belt. At least you feel then that you've made a start."

They walked together down the avenue lined with gardens, unaware of the heads that turned as they passed, and found the camera crew set up and ready to roll alongside an enchanting water garden. Birch trees decorated the top of the slope, and between them and mounds of spring-flowering shrubs, a silvery ribbon of water tumbled over rocks and down into a pool fringed by primulas and flag irises. An old rowing-boat was pulled up on a shingle bank, and a length of rope held it fast to a weather-worn post.

Rob and Bex were positioned leaning on an old five-barred gate to one side, and the soundman fiddled with their microphones as they swapped lines with one another.

Tim instructed the two cameras: "OK, this is the opening piece to camera. We thought we might as well do it first as the garden's ready, so is everyone happy?" The two cameramen nodded. The soundman twiddled a few knobs, held up a long, fluffy sausage of a microphone and, after a few more seconds, gave a thumbs-up.

"OK, chaps. Do you know what you're going to say?"

"We think so," confirmed Rob. "We'll give it a go anyway and see what you think."

"Do you want a rehearsal?" asked Tim.

"No. We'll rehearse on tape – if that's OK with you?" He turned to Bex.

"Fine." She smiled.

Rob looked down at her. "Good luck!" he whispered.

"And you, Mr MacGregor."

He bent and pecked her on the cheek.

"If you're ready then?" There was just a touch of sarcasm in Tim's voice.

Rob and Bex settled themselves comfortably by the five-barred gate. Rob straightened his tie and Bex picked a piece of fluff off his jacket.

"And cue . . ."

Chapter 33

At 4.45 p.m. on the fine afternoon of Monday 18 May, the maroon Rolls-Royce Phantom VI bearing a silver maquette of St George slaying the Dragon atop its gleaming radiator swept silently through the gates of the Royal Hospital, Chelsea, and drew to a graceful halt outside the Great Marquee. The sky was duck-egg blue and so was the suit worn by Her Majesty The Queen as she stepped out of the shiny limousine to be greeted by the Panama-hatted president of the Royal Horticultural Society. Sir Ormsby Proctor had the appearance of our man in Havana in his cream suit and striped Eton tie, and he removed his headgear with practised swiftness as the door of the car eased open. Sir Ormsby bowed, then shook hands with his monarch, from his lofty height, and the line-up of Royal Horticultural Society luminaries were presented, in turn, to their patron.

"Isn't she small?" whispered Bex in Rob's ear. They were standing only a few yards away, behind the row of officials, all filming having been suspended for the duration of the Queen's visit, except for vital royal footage.

"Yes. But what a smile. She should do it more often. Her face really lights up." They walked, side by side, into the Great Marquee, gossiping like two old women over a garden fence, Bex forgetting all about the horticulture and eyeing the Queen's *haute couture* while Rob filled in his colleague as to the identity of the other members of the Royal Family who had preceded her. It was a good year – the Kents and the Gloucesters, Princess Alexandra, the Princess Royal and Princess Margaret were all now ruminating among the roses.

"I didn't know Princess Margaret was keen on gardening,"

confessed Bex, as the Queen's sister ambled by in pink only a few yards away, with Emma Coalport of the Trust Fund in tow.

"Mad keen on rhododendrons, apparently," whispered Rob. "I hope she doesn't get too close to Emma Coalport. That halitosis will fell her if she does."

Bex stifled a giggle. "I like the hat!" Emma Coalport, a woman with about as much fashion sense as a Bactrian camel, was wearing on her head what at first glance seemed to be an inverted waste-paper basket, but which, on closer inspection, proved to be a hat woven from palm fronds and decorated with dried flowers. The Princess seemed not to have noticed.

Bex looked around at the growing numbers of people, among whom the members of the Royal Family were gliding, quite unconcerned.

"What happens at the Royal Gala this evening? Do we get to stay?"

"Yes. Tim says he has some passes and we have to be there in case they want to film us hobnobbing with royalty."

"Oh, well, I'm sure the Queen will want to talk to me about her begonias," quipped Bex. "Do you fancy a cup of tea? I'm gasping."

"Yes, I do. Especially as Princess Michael is about to be buttonholed by Conrad Mecklenburg and I don't think I want to be splashed by the saliva. Come on."

They walked through the marquee in the direction of the Embankment, past the newly completed stands of flowers. Soon they emerged from the fragrant confines of the canvas into the clear May afternoon, but just as they were about to cross Main Avenue and head for the seclusion of their Portakabin behind the RHS enquiries pavilion, a voice boomed, "'Allo Mr MacGregor," in the rounded, Mummerset tones. "'Ow be ye doin' on this foine day?"

Rob froze in his tracks, looked down at Bex with a horrified expression, and the two of them turned round together.

Standing in front of them, his skin browned by the sun and with a twinkle in his pale blue eyes, was Bertie Lightfoot.

"Bertie?" enquired Rob, as if to make sure of the identity of his interlocutor.

Bertie grinned and dropped his false rustic burr. "That's right, luv. Fresh as a daisy and right as ninepence. Thought we'd 'ave a little day out."

"But . . . where've you been? How are you?"

"Been away for a bit, luv. Got meself in a right old state." The flattened camp northern vowels were still there, but the venomous sting had gone out of them. There seemed to be no acid left in the Queen of Myddleton.

"You look really well," Rob said, as yet unsure of how to proceed with the man, who, on last meeting, had been a sorry mixture of hatred and despair. Now, here he stood, in a pale grey suit and crisp white shirt, wearing a blue tie embroidered with golden palm trees. He looked the picture of health, and the epitome of contentment, too.

"Went abroad for a bit. Majorca. Lovely place. They know how to treat you there. Know how to live. I've rented a little villa. Thought it was time I treated meself so I've decided to spend part of the year out there now. Go into retirement. I should just about be able to afford it and I've 'ad a good innings."

Rob stared blankly at him, baffled.

"Oh, I know it's difficult to believe, duckie, and I'm sorry I was a bit of an old cow towards the end. Acid old queen, wasn't I?" Seeing that Rob was finding difficulty in summoning up a reply Bertie's eyes lit on Bex, who was standing silently by his side. "Is this your new co-star?"

"Yes. Er, Bex Fleming, this is Bertie Lightfoot."

Bertie shook Bex's hand. "Pleased to meet you, luv. Just make sure you keep him in hand and you'll be fine," he instructed, with even more of a twinkle in his eye.

Rob, at last, managed to speak. "I'm glad you're happy, Bertie."

"Well, it's all down to 'im, really." Bertie tilted his head in the direction of the show gardens and at a tanned young man walking towards them. "I'd like you to meet my new partner, Paolo. Paolo, this is Rob MacGregor, the lad I've told you about, and this is Miss Fleming, his new co-star."

Rob and Bex were silenced by the sight of the devastatingly handsome Spanish youth in grey slacks, grey polo-necked sweater and navy blue blazer with brass buttons, who politely shook hands with them and bowed. Bex blushed, Rob gawped, and the two of them listened rapt as Bertie told them, very simply and rather touchingly, how much he was in love, and how he couldn't see what someone as young and handsome as Paolo saw in him. They were still standing quietly together a few minutes later when Bertie and Paolo walked away from them, admiring the planting of a garden that had a tropical theme. "We could do something like that," were the last of Bertie's words that fell on their ears.

*

The Queen did not ask Bex Fleming about her begonias, but the Royal Charity Gala was an evening to remember. Society ladies in outfits that were clearly D & G rather than C & A wandered with their smartly turned-out squires among the flowers, fruits and vegetables of the Chelsea Flower Show, sipping a seemingly endless supply of champagne and nibbling exotic-looking canapés. Rob and Bex had done their best to abstain, in spite of regular approaches from guests enquiring why they did not have a glass. Rob explained politely that they had work to do, though he knew full well of Tim's concern that if his presenters were seen sipping champagne, questions would be asked about the licence fee. Tickets for the gala cost a three-figure sum, and Tim's bosses – some of whom had paid for theirs – would probably not be amused to see their employees getting tipsy in front of them, gratis.

At 8 p.m., an end having been called to the filming, Rob made a move to go.

"Oh, what a shame," sighed Bex, as he slid his jacket and tie on to a hanger in the corner of the Portakabin, "having to go and leave all this."

"It's all right for you," Rob complained. "You're not on camera until half past seven, and you're staying with friends. I have to be ready to go at six with only a grumpy hotel porter to wake me up."

"You poor old thing!"

"Save your sympathy!" he scolded. "If the Queen wonders where I've gone, tell her I had to go to bed early to keep up with my young co-presenter." He kissed her, flung a woollen jacket over his shoulder and headed off in the direction of the King's Road.

At five thirty the next morning, on the banks of the River Wharfe at Nesfield, Jock MacGregor was crossing the old stone bridge that linked his house and the nursery, listening to the sounds of the dawn chorus and the river running beneath his booted feet, just as his son was listening to the early-morning traffic clearing its throat as he walked down the tarmac drive to the Hospital Road entrance of the Chelsea Flower Show.

For Jock, this was the best time of day at the best time of year. Every leaf on every tree was clean and unsullied by weather. The water of the river tumbled clear and sparkling over the rounded boulders that tried to throw it off course, and the damp air smelt pure and clean in the nostrils of this connoisseur of early mornings.

He wiped the dew from the brass padlock with his gnarled thumb and turned the key to open the old gate, wondering how many more mornings like this his enfeebled bank account would enable him to enjoy. He paused to look around the neat nursery that was his life. Rows of trees and shrubs strained at their support wires, brimful of energy and raring to be free. Serried ranks of perennials lined the path, and underneath a long swatch of close-weave netting the bedding plants were now set outdoors in their trays, protected from the late frosts that could so often be treacherous in this part of the dale.

He mused on his good fortune at finding Wayne, who had brought to the riverbank a degree of energy and muscle power that he and Harry were no longer able to command. The nursery had improved its appearance as a result. He nodded to himself, a satisfied nod.

The winter had been perilously quiet, but this was the busiest time of year and the nursery would soon be alive with small groups of customers intent on buying their bedding plants, a necessary bread-and-butter line as far as Jock the plantsman was concerned. With any luck, those who came for something run-of-the-mill would go away with a treasure or two as well, if Jock managed to open their eyes.

He pocketed the old key and walked towards the potting-shed to begin another day, hoping with all his heart that this would not be his last spring at Wharfeside Nursery.

Rob showed his pass to the solitary security man on duty at the gate and walked through the deserted showground to the film crew's Portakabin. Here he put on a clean shirt, gasping as the chill morning air crept over his naked torso, and then the jacket and tie he had been wearing for the previous day's shooting.

It was a crisp morning, laced with a faint haze of mist, courtesy of the adjacent River Thames – a broad, lazy, dark brown motorway of a river, so different from the shimmering Wharfe at home. Where the Wharfe shone coppery in the Yorkshire dawn, the Thames glowed a dull bronze in the early-morning London light.

He looked at his watch. A quarter to six. He was early. No one else had arrived yet. The gardeners and nurserymen, the growers and landscapers were still tucked up in bed: having worked from dawn till dusk for three weeks they needed all the sleep they could get. It would be another hour or two before they stirred.

Rob walked from the Portakabin along the Rock Garden Bank, pulling his jacket around him to keep warm and looking at the gardens, whose waterfalls and fountains were stilled by the overnight lack of power. A blackbird broadcast its wake-up call from the branch of a maple that, just a couple of weeks ago, had not been there. Now the blackbird considered it a resident.

He turned left towards the Great Marquee, found the entrance and discovered that it was laced up, exactly like the big old bell tent they had used at Scout Camp in his youth. He looked round for help. No one was there.

He examined the rope fastening more closely and discovered that it was simply threaded through brass eyelets to hold the flap in place. Slowly he unpicked it until around four feet of canvas flapped free and he was able to duck underneath it and into the marquee.

What he saw took his breath away. Slowly he walked forward into the three-and-a-half-acre garden that had appeared as if by magic overnight. Gone were the champagne-sipping socialites; gone was the Royal Family. Now he had the place to himself and not another soul gazed on it with him. He stood alone in a floral paradise, the blackbird silent, the air still.

The feeble morning sun shone through the opaque canvas and released, in spite of its weakness, the fragrances of a spring garden. Scents met his nostrils in rich profusion – the heady perfume of lilies and narcissi, the fresh, light tang of sweet peas, and the sweet, cloying aroma of pine bark and crushed grass.

He wandered, like a small child let loose in a toyshop, among this creation of hundreds of gardeners, who had toiled night and day to bring together their object of floral perfection. Towering over him were royal blue spires of delphiniums and pastel pyramids of honey-scented lupins. Begonias from Bristol, their flowers like dinner plates, grinned their red and orange faces at him, and exotic blooms from Barbados erupted like succulent lollipops from fountains of juicy foliage.

Proteas and other spiky flowers from South Africa kept company with gigantic mounds of seemingly freshly lacquered strawberries, and roses in beds and borders, vases and urns, tumbled in indecent quantity into the botanical tapestry on which he gazed.

He stood in the very centre of the marquee like Adam in the

Garden of Eden, and slowly turned around. Flowers met his eye whichever way he looked, and within a minute he could no longer see for tears. Here, in a corner of Britain's largest city, where smog and traffic normally reigned supreme, the best gardeners in the land had come together to show off their skills; gardeners like his father who had learned their craft over a lifetime and who shared it, each May, with an admiring and incredulous public. He felt a mixture of wonder and pride. Wonder at the impossible grandeur and size of it all, and pride that this was his job, these were his people, and this was what he had always wanted to do. He felt a burning desire to share it all. But Katherine was not there.

He took out his clean handkerchief, blew his nose, and went off in search of an early-morning cup of coffee.

Ollie Shakespeare, his glistening skull just visible over a long navy-blue greatcoat, had both hands wrapped round a polystyrene cup and was standing on the steps of the Portakabin. "There's a cup for you inside, if you want it, and a bacon roll."

"Great," said Rob. "Why are you here so early? I didn't think you and Bex were due to start until half past seven."

"Just been looking at the pieces I cut together last night." Ollie jerked his head in the direction of the video player in the corner of the Portakabin. "It's looking good. I think you'll be pleased. You and Bex work together really well."

"Thanks." Rob poured himself a cup of coffee and began to put himself on the other side of a bacon roll, the warm fat dripping down his chin. He staunched its flow quickly with a paper napkin, aware that if it got on to his jacket he'd be in deep trouble with Wardrobe.

"Come here," instructed Ollie, walking towards Rob with a fresh napkin and tucking it into his neck. "Better safe than sorry."

Rob grinned above the fresh white bib that now covered his jacket and asked, "Any news of Guy D'Arcy?"

"Not a word, except that everyone's fairly sure he's left the country."

Rob paused mid-chew. "How do they know?"

Ollie continued, warming to his subject, "Well, there's no sign of him at home and even his car was still parked in Burton Court until yesterday. The garage came to take it back. Really odd. He seems to have disappeared into thin air."

"Poor bugger."

"Yes, poor bugger," agreed Ollie. "He was a smug git, but it's a hell of a way to go. Did you see the news?"

"Yes. Has there been more?"

"Only about Guy. Saying he's disappeared without trace. I suppose he must be used to the publicity – I mean, all that stuff about him being a ladies' man, real gossip-column fodder. But I guess he thought all that had ended."

"Mmm," Rob mumbled, through a mouthful of bacon roll.

"The show was buzzing with it all yesterday. Folk going on about how daft the commercial was, but secretly dead jealous about the amount of money he must have made."

"I suppose that must be his only consolation," mused Rob. "I hope he got the money out of them before disaster struck."

"He insisted on it, apparently," said Ollie. "I heard him talking to one of those National Trust biddies on Saturday. She was giving him hell for mixing with trade but he said he'd needed the money and they'd paid him up front."

"I should think that went down well with the Trust Fund."

"Like a lead balloon. She told him he'd really let the side down. Guy just shrugged and said, 'I can't afford principles, darling.' I bet he wished he'd saved up a bit now."

Their ruminations were interrupted by Rosie Duff, muffled in a duffel-coat. "All right, my lovely?" she asked Rob.

"Fine, thanks. We were just musing on the fate of Mr D'Arcy."

"Ooooh. Now there's a story. Anyway, we haven't time for all that. Had your coffee? Good. Come on, then. The crew are there already. Off we go to the Big Top. It's time for the circus to hit town." She bowled off in the direction of the Great Marquee, with the bespectacled Colin and Penny of the perforated cardigan in tow. Rob plucked the napkin from his neck, wiped the bacon fat from his chin, waved a silent farewell to Ollie and tried to think what he was going to say about a display of cacti from Congleton.

By half past eight the Chelsea Flower Show had transformed itself from a tranquil, bucolic oasis into a bustling flower festival. Only thirty minutes after the turnstiles had opened, those people who could call themselves Members of the Royal Horticultural Society were allowed their special preview, which would last for two days, the general public being allowed in on Thursday and Friday.

Rosie had been wise enough to get her filming in the marquee finished by 8 a.m., knowing that the punters would make life more difficult as soon as they arrived. She was not wrong. Journeys across the Royal Hospital grounds that had taken two minutes on Sunday and Monday now took at least ten, thanks to the crowds. They were intent on seeing the exhibits, but also opportunist enough to stop Rob MacGregor in his tracks and let him know how much they liked his programme.

Rosie shepherded him from garden to garden, like a small but determined bouncer, amused at people's reaction to the man they felt they knew, even though they had never met him. She did her best to remain patient when they engaged him in conversation, and bit her lip when someone told him, "You're better-looking in real life than you are on telly."

More than one man had asked Rob, "Where's Bex, then?" and when they came together on a lavishly planted Mediterranean garden for the final pay-off, there was a cheer as Bex stepped over the swags of rope that separated the real world from that of horticultural make-believe.

"Where's Mr D'Arcy?" yelled a voice from the crowd. The brief, tense moment was short-lived.

Another voice shouted, "Nah, these two are better-looking," to a cheerful round of laughter.

"And they know their stuff," put in a little lady at the front.

Bex gave her a smile and then whispered to Rob under her breath, "Wow, it's like being in a zoo."

"Yes. But at least the natives are friendly. You OK?"

"Yeah. It's been great . . . and I've met this guy."

"What sort of guy?" asked Rob, thinking for a moment that Mr D'Arcy had returned.

"Grows begonias."

"Begonias!"

"Yes. Look, I know they're not exactly the height of fashion but he's great. He's got an earring, too, but he's really nice. Asked me out."

"You don't hang around, do you?" Rob was suddenly aware of his own loneliness.

"Excuse me." Ollie was fighting his way towards the garden with his camera crew. "Can we come through, please?"

The mass of bodies parted like the Red Sea, emphasizing Oliver Shakespeare's biblical appearance in a flowing greatcoat that was almost as voluminous as the robes of a prophet. Show catalogues were being waved by one or two people at the front of the crowd. "Autographs in a minute, ladies and gentlemen," instructed Rosie. "We've got to make them work for a living first."

Ollie and Rosie went into brief conference about the last shot and were joined by Tim. Rob and Bex turned their backs to the crowd and sorted out their words. Fifteen minutes later the filming of *The Chelsea Flower Shower Special* was finished and it was now up to Rosie, Oliver and Tim to turn the ragbag of disparate items into a cohesive whole that would please a gardening public unable to make the journey from their corner of the land to the riverbank of London SW3.

Rob zipped up the suit carrier and hung it on the hook at the back of the door of the Portakabin. He pulled on a white Arran sweater and sat down to tie the laces on his Caterpillar boots. That felt better. Better to be back in jeans and a sweater rather than a shirt and tie. He felt normal again.

A soft knock rattled the door. "Are you there?" It was Bex. She, too, had changed from her smart suit into jeans and a sweater. "I've come to say goodbye."

She stepped up into the Portakabin as Rob rose from the plastic chair in the corner. "And I've come to say thank you, too, for everything." She put her arms round him and gave him a hug, her head resting on his shoulder.

Rob heaved a sigh.

"What's up?" asked Bex, looking up at him.

"Oh, nothing. It's just nice to have a hug."

Bex paused and looked into his eyes. "You haven't gone and claimed her yet, have you?"

"No."

"Don't leave it too long."

"No."

They parted and Bex looked him in the eye. "She won't wait for ever." She rubbed her hand up and down his sleeve. "I've got some news for you. I've taken the plunge."

Rob looked alarmed. "Not –"

"No. Not the begonia man. That's just a bit of fun. I've handed in my notice. I'm going freelance. The *Sunday Herald* have asked me to take over Guy's column so I thought I'd bite the bullet and try to make my own way in the world. It's all thanks to you, really."

Rob smiled. "I'm glad. You're very talented."

"No." She gazed at him intently. "I've just been very lucky. Finding you." The smile that followed flickered a little. "Find her. Soon."

She walked to the door with her bag flung over her shoulder. She turned. "Silly man," she said.

And then she was gone.

Chapter 34

"I can't say I'm sorry, but it is a bit of a pain. He wasn't exactly my ideal gardener, although he just about kept on top of the weeds. Now heaven knows what will happen." Helena was at Wharfeside Nursery buying trays of antirrhinums and nicotianas and sharing her staffing problems with Jock MacGregor. Makepiece, the gnarled old gardener who had stepped in to fill Rob's shoes when full-time education lured him away, had finally decided that it was time to retire. He'd given a week's notice and thrown in the trowel.

"And at bedding-out time, too," groaned Helena. "Mrs Ipplepen says she'll send her Cyril round but I think he's a parsnip-and-potato man. He'll probably want to earth up the petunias in a few weeks' time."

Jock was loading her selected trays of summer bedding plants on to a low, flat-bedded trolley. "Have you said yes to him yet?"

"No. I thought I'd talk to you first, and see if you had any ideas. The trouble is that everyone who's available is old and grumpy and I'd far rather have someone young and lively." Jock looked up at her as he slid another tray on to the trolley.

Helena looked embarrassed. "Oh, sorry. Well, you know what I mean . . ."

Jock chuckled. "I know what you mean. A bit of youth makes a hell of a lot of difference." He surveyed the plants around him.

Helena smiled. "Well, at least I could bend a young gardener to my will a bit more than one who has, shall we say, set ideas about how things should be done. Jumbo and I never liked beetroot and Makepiece grows eight rows of them. Eight rows!"

Jock put down another tray and stood upright, rubbing his back. "You know, it's funny how things turn out sometimes. You can go through life just missing the boat nine times out of ten, but every now and then the timing of things turns out just right."

"In what way?"

"Have you thought about young Wayne?"

"Sorry?"

"Wayne Dibley – my lad. Have you thought about him?"

"I thought he was settled."

"He was. Had a lady on the far side of town that he used to work for on a Sunday but she's just gone into a home. He needs extra pocket money. Heaven knows, I can't afford to pay him more than the basic rate, and I'd have thought he'd be just what you need."

"Do you think he'd be interested?"

"Ask him yourself. He's coming over."

Wayne had just rounded the corner of the greenhouses and was making his way towards them. What became evident as he approached his boss was that he was not happy. He seemed preoccupied. He stopped for a chat with a couple who were selecting a container-grown tree, but there was no sign of the flashing smile and the bright eyes that normally shone from his face. Having answered the shopping couple's question he continued his journey to Jock and Helena.

"You look as if you've lost a shilling and found a sixpence," offered Jock. "What's the matter?"

"Oh, just a bit fed up," answered Wayne, doing his best to offer Helena a smile.

"Well, Lady Sampson has some news that might cheer you up."

Wayne looked at the lady from the big house up at the top end of town.

"I wondered if you might be able to help me, Wayne."

"How's that?" he asked, hopping from one foot to another.

"My old gardener, Mr Makepiece, has just left me and I need someone to take his place. Not full time, just part time . . . with hours to suit. Mr MacGregor thought you might be interested. Would you?"

"Cor! Nor'arf!" Wayne's eyes lit up, the white teeth flashed, and his mood changed. "That would be really great." Then a little hesitation. "But only if you're sure I could do it." He looked at Jock and Helena, and received the confirmation he was looking for.

"I think you know enough to be able to cope," Jock assured him.

Helena was quick to take up his offer. "Wonderful. When can you start? I could do with these bedding plants being put in this weekend."

"Fine. This weekend, then. Great. Wow! That'll really get me out of a spot. Thanks." He was his old self again now.

"So what was the problem?" Jock asked.

"Problem?" asked Wayne.

"You looked miserable. What was wrong?"

"Oh, that. Just me roses. Something's gone wrong."

"Which roses?"

"The ones I was forcing. You know, the ones from Professor Wilberforce."

"I thought you were only forcing one of them?" There was an edge to Jock's voice. He had allowed Wayne to go ahead, on condition that he start off slowly by forcing one of this and one of that. This way, if things went wrong and the shrubs failed to respond or simply curled up their toes and died, Jock's losses would be minimized.

He had been particularly specific about Professor Wilberforce's rose-bushes, asking Wayne to force only one. He'd instructed the lad to leave the other bushes outdoors, fearful that he might lose them all if Wayne's growing skills were not up to scratch.

Wayne detected the disapproval in Jock's tone and began to defend himself. "It's just that I wanted it to work. I really wanted to prove that I could do it but it just seemed to go wrong." The lad began to panic and Jock realized that he had been a touch heavy-handed.

"Never mind, never mind. Did they all curl up and die?"

"No. Not exactly."

"What, then?"

"It's just that something seems to have happened to the flowers. They're a funny colour."

"Well, they shouldn't be. The flower colour will be exactly the same as it would be in the garden. It's only the timing of the flowering that will be different." Jock looked at Helena, who was wondering if this was the right time to make a quick, quiet exit.

"Come and look," suggested Wayne. "I did exactly as you said, gave them plenty of water when they needed it, and ventilation, and I fed them once a week. I just don't know what's up."

Jock followed Wayne back to his greenhouse, with Helena tagging along behind, unable to extricate herself without being ungracious.

Wayne opened the door of the greenhouse, which was now almost empty, the bedding plants having been moved outside over the last couple of weeks. The pots of roses stood on the path at the very end of the house, which Wayne had begun to scrub out in readiness for its next occupants.

"Good grief." Jock looked at the rose-bushes from just inside the door and advanced on them slowly.

"I didn't give them anything I shouldn't have. I did exactly what you said," pleaded Wayne.

Helena followed in Jock's wake. "Oh, goodness me!" Her hand rose to her mouth.

The sounds of the rest of the world were blocked out from Jock's ears as he walked towards the three potted rose-bushes that stood on the old stone path at the end of the greenhouse. Their leaves were dark green and glossy, their stems rigid and strong, and the well-shaped flowers that had opened at their shoot tips were a pure, clear, unadulterated royal blue.

On the blue-painted verandah of the plantation house on the Caribbean island of Grenada, Guy D'Arcy put his feet up on the steamer chair and asked for another rum punch. He looked down across the slope of lush tropical foliage towards the turquoise sea below and reflected that it would take quite a lot of work to transform this patch of undergrowth into a paradise garden. Never mind. He had all the time in the world now. And quite a bit of money, too. Serena Clayton-Hinde, her tanned legs revealed at their full length in the cutaway black swimsuit, leaned over the back of his chair, kissed him full on the mouth and slipped the glass of punch into his hand. She ruffled the hair at the back of his head. "I'm going for a shower. Don't be long." She slinked into the cool interior of the plantation house and disappeared from view.

Ah, well, thought Guy, sipping the sweet, fruity mixture through a straw, life has its compensations.

Rob sat for a while on the riverbank watching a speckled brown trout nosing upstream through the dappled water, and then he lay back among the long stalks of foxtail grass, breathing slowly as their sweet odour drifted on the air. He closed his eyes to the bright gold of the early-evening sun and reflected on the events of the past weeks – the highs and lows, the revelations and the disappointments, the excitement and the underlying hollowness.

At least now his father would not have to worry about staying in business: the plant breeder's rights in 'Wharfeside Blue' would see to that. The royalties payable by nurserymen for propagating the plant and growing it under licence would yield a small fortune. A smile flickered across his freckled face at the name his father had chosen for the rose so generously bequeathed to him by the late professor of genetic engineering.

He'd read in *Scientific Horticulture* that plant breeders were boasting of being able to play around with genes and give scentless plants perfume and unusual colours. Disease resistance was regularly being bred into plants now, and scientists had indicated that it was just a matter of time before the blue rose was reality. It seemed that Professor Wilberforce had pipped everyone else to the post, and decided that his old friend Jock MacGregor was the man who should benefit.

He smiled again as he thought of Bertie Lightfoot, and of the young Paolo who had clearly endowed the old stager with a new lease of life. Then his thoughts turned to Guy D'Arcy and to the fact that, there, but for the fickle finger of fate, would he have gone himself. He shuddered as the first cool breeze of the evening rattled the leaves of the alders overhead.

And now here he was. Alone. He thought of Bex; of her kindness and concern. And her generosity. He liked her. A lot. He remembered what she'd said, just before they parted: "She won't wait for ever."

The scent of the grasses around him grew fainter in the cool air; their fragrance had changed now. It was some other perfume; a reminder of some other place. The scent of home.

He rose to his feet and dusted off his jeans, then strode over the grassy tussocks of the riverbank and up the lane towards the town. Towards Katherine's flat at Wellington Heights. He knew quite clearly now what he wanted to say. He rang the bell. There was no answer. Just the muted sounds of conversation from the bakery below.

He looked up at her window. It was slightly ajar, as it always was, and the curtain billowed gently in the evening breeze, but no sounds of occupancy came from within.

Sluggishly he retraced his steps towards the river. He would walk past his father's nursery and up the valley to End Cottage. There would be time for the half-hour stroll before it got dark. He was barely a hundred yards upstream of the nursery when he saw a small, familiar figure sitting down by the water's edge, gently tossing pebbles into the shallows.

He walked silently up behind her, stooped to pick up a pebble then threw it into the water in front of her. She started, then turned round and saw him, squinting as the sun caught her dark eyes. He stood and looked down at her, the evening light turning his hair to fiery bronze.

"Hello," she said softly.

He lowered himself on to the grassy bank beside her and looked, like her, towards the shimmering water. "I've been looking for you."

"Oh?"

"I couldn't find you."

"I was here."

"Why?"

"It seemed the right place to be."

They sat silently for what seemed, to Rob, an age.

"How are you?" he asked.

"I'm OK. How are you?"

"Better now," he said, looking upwards towards the moor. "I – I can't go on without you, you know. I was wrong to do what I did. So wrong. But I can't – I can't be without you."

She put her arms around her knees and pulled them up to her chest. "I see," she said.

"I've missed you so much." He put his arm around her and slowly, she leaned her head on his shoulder.

"I don't like it when you're not there," she whispered.

"Nor me."

They sat together, watching the water, mesmerized for a while by its music.

"Promise you won't go away again?" he asked.

She pulled away slightly and gazed at him, a hurt look in her eyes. "Only if you won't."

He cupped his hands around her face and kissed her gently, remembering the softness of her lips. Then he moved his head away from her a little and looked into her eyes. "I promise."

"You see, I try very hard to cope without you. I *can* cope without you. But I don't like it."

"I know. I know."

Tears filled her eyes. "When you're here I feel safe, and calm, and, well . . . just right. And when you're not . . ." She hit the rough turf with her hand and turned her head away.

Rob sank his face into the hair at the back of her neck. "Shh . . . Oh, my love, my love." He rocked her gently, and felt himself filling with warmth and love for her.

"How have you been?" she asked, almost whispering.

"Pretty rotten. When you're not here it's like being half a person. I so much miss sharing things with you. When you're not here it's like going through the motions. Nothing really matters. It's like marking time, just waiting to be with you again." He held her gently, and through his tears watched the river gliding by. "You see, I wasn't sure before. I didn't know whether it was just habit – just convenient and nice and cosy. I had to be sure."

"And are you sure . . . now?" Her voice faltered and a single tear coursed down her cheek. He turned back her head with his outstretched hand, intercepted the tear at her chin and licked it off his finger.

"Oh, I'm sure. I'm absolutely sure." He paused. "Can I ask you something?" He held her head against his cheek.

"Yes?"

"Would you mind very much if we sold your flat?"

"No."

"And would you mind very much moving in with me?"

"No."

"And . . . would you mind . . . marrying me?"

She opened her mouth to speak, but could make no words. The battle against her emotions lost, she began to shake with deep, silent sobs, looking first at the sky and then into his pale green eyes.

He whispered to her gently, "I'm here now. I won't go away again."

"Not ever?"

"Not ever." He put both arms around her and held her so tightly she felt the breath being squeezed out of her. It took all her effort, through the tears and the lack of breath, to say the words he had been frightened he would never hear again. "I love you, Mr MacGregor."

"And I love you, Miss Page, with all my heart."

They sat until the sun sank behind the alder tree. Then he helped her to her feet, dusted the grass from her bottom and put his arm around her shoulder. She leaned into him, put both her arms around his waist, and they walked upstream for home.

The Last Lighthouse Keeper

Acknowledgements

I am very grateful to the many folk who have helped me with background information for *The Last Lighthouse Keeper*. Breda Wall of Trinity House arranged for me to visit the Lizard light in Cornwall, and Eddie Matthews the Lizard's principal lighthouse keeper (who was almost the real Last Lighthouse Keeper and remains custodian of the Lizard light) showed me around his domain and provided masses of useful information about a keeper's life. Both were subsequently patience personified on the telephone when I remembered questions that I had forgotten to ask.

Rob Stokes of the Association of Dunkirk Little Ships was helpful in providing details of this club of indomitable enthusiasts, and David Bintley of the Birmingham Royal Ballet patiently advised on dancing injuries and their likely consequences in spite of a manic rehearsal schedule.

Nigel Rickman of Bucklers Hard Boat-builders has answered all manner of boating questions during the course of repairing my own vessel, without once becoming irritated.

I am also grateful to two unnamed members of the Metropolitan Police Force, who were happy to answer questions on the elasticity of police procedure, and the Kent policeman who furnished me, at my request, with the caution! Surrey Police were helpful in other ways. Any irregularities in police procedure at St Petroc police station are down to me!

Several books have been a rich source of inspiration, particularly Christopher Nicholson's *Rock Lighthouses of Great Britain*, Craig Weatherhill's *Cornish Place Names and Language*, Peter Collyer's *Rain Later, Good* and Frank Cowper's *Sailing Tours*.

As ever I'm tremendously grateful to Clare Ledingham and Peta Nightingale, my editors, who know just when to encourage and when to admonish, and to Hazel Orme, my copy editor, who always does more than that.

Luigi Bonomi continues to be unflagging in his encouragement.

The chapter titles throughout the book are names of English lighthouses or lightships under the jurisdiction of Trinity House, every one of them now automated. It is up to the reader to decide why I considered each one appropriate for a particular chapter. Start Point is obvious; St Anthony and Varne might take a little more working out.

This is not a book about lighthouses, just a story about one fictitious lighthouse and its keeper. You will not find Prince Albert Rock on any map, but you may be able to find the part of Cornwall that it occupies in my mind. If the story leaves you with a feeling of admiration for the work of the men of Trinity House I will be well pleased. It is no more than they deserve. Along with a lot of others who go down to the sea in ships, I am sad they have gone.

A.T.

For Bill and Sue
with thanks

The Corporation of Trinity House
TRINITAS IN UNITATE

There are 72 lighthouses and 11 light vessel stations under the
jurisdiction of The Corporation of Trinity House.
Every one of them is now automated.

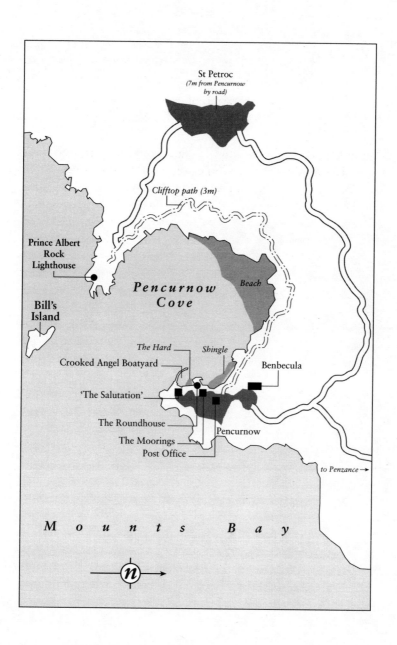

St Petroc
*(7m from Pencurnow
by road)*

Clifftop path (3m)

Prince Albert
Rock
Lighthouse

*Pencurnow
Cove*

Beach

Bill's
Island

The Hard   *Shingle*

Crooked Angel Boatyard

Benbecula

'The Salutation'

The Roundhouse

Pencurnow

The Moorings

Post Office

to Penzance →

M o u n t s   B a y

n

Prologue

"Viking, North Utsira, South Utsira." The varnished oars slipped silently out of the sea. "Dogger, Fisher, German Bight." Salt water dribbled off them, disturbing the glassy ripples. "Sole, Lundy, Fastnet." The oars dipped in again, propelling the little wooden boat towards the shore with practised ease. "Channel Light Vessel Automatic." One oar tumbled clumsily from its metal rowlock, a seagull shrieked in mockery and the oarsman cursed.

The litany of sea areas he recited to himself as he rowed was more familiar to him than the multiplication tables he had learnt at school, but Channel Light Vessel Automatic? It was the thin end of the wedge. A wedge that had now been driven home.

Still, it was too late to grumble about all that. Too late to cherish comfortable dreams of the distant future. The future was here. He suspected that what really rattled him was the prospect of his failure to make those long-held dreams come true.

The bows of the clinker-built skiff met the pebbles of the shore with a sliding crunch. The rower shipped the oars and heaved the boat a yard or two further up the shingle bank. He looked up at the sky – as blue as a heron's egg, with just the occasional wisp of cloud. A perfect April day. A perfect day to begin a different life.

Chapter 1: Start Point

Will Elliott pulled off the thick, grey, hand-knitted fisherman's sweater that had kept out the chill April air on his half-hour passage across an unusually calm Pencurnow Cove. He tied its sleeves around his waist, checked that the skiff was well clear of the tide line and began the climb up the shingle bank.

It was a strange feeling. For the first time in his life there was no grid to his day, no timetable that would tell him where to be and when, just a clear sky and a clean slate. He felt half elated, half terrified at the prospect, glancing back at the lighthouse on the other side of the bay to make sure it was still there, even though it need no longer concern him.

As he crunched up the shore, his welly-booted feet sinking deep into the shingle and slowing his progress, he made a mental checklist of the positive aspects of his future. First, he would stay in Cornwall – for the time being at least: coping with a new set of people and a new place all at once held no appeal. And, anyway, he loved this outpost at the toe of Britain, where the sea and the rugged coastline appealed to his solitary nature. He might have spent just a sixth of his life here, but he felt Cornish now, not Oxonian.

He had to find a boat. If the dream was to become reality he'd better get it soon. Put that sort of thing off and you might just slide into indolence. That scared him more than anything. And he didn't want to live in a house – certainly not one without a view of the sea, and those with sea views in this part of the world were beyond his means.

The logistics of his plans swam around in his head, as did his concerns as to whether or not he had thought this thing through properly. The boat he would buy would probably need attention before he set off: with the amount of money he had to spend he was unlikely to find a vessel in the first flush of youth. While he repaired it in readiness for the Grand Voyage he would have to find some way of earning a living. With any luck he'd be able to sell his little boats – but for how much? He'd started making his scale models of local boats – the clinker-built rowing boats they called Cornish cobles – during his first winter at the lighthouse. Ernie had told him he'd need something to occupy himself on dull, uneventful shifts and Will had found that his steady hand, keen eye and irritating perfectionism had suited him well to a hobby he had previously regarded as the province of sad old men whose idea of excitement would be watching the bacon slicer in the Penzance Co-op.

He would never make a fortune with his models. But, then, he only wanted enough for food and drink, and a book or two. The days of high ambition were long gone, with another life in another place with another person. Now he had to be positive. There were a few thousand pounds in the building society, and the small legacy left to him by his Aunt Alice the previous November should see him all right for the big boat at least. Lucky, and unusually well timed. Thirty thousand would hopefully get him something without too many holes in it. But it was all so iffy.

He reached the top of the bank and struck out for the lane that led to the village. He stopped abruptly. There was no need to rush. His mouth twitched. He turned round, squeezed his hands into the pockets of his jeans and looked back across the bay once more, at the squat white finger pointing upwards into the blue. Prince Albert Rock Lighthouse had been his home, and his refuge, for the last six years. Now he needed to find another. Sadness and irritation, anger, fear, excitement and anticipation vied within him for the upper hand.

He'd had enough warning about the demise of manned lighthouses. He'd come to terms with the fact that his chosen way of life – or the life that had been chosen for him – would come to an end. He was resigned to it, even if he still resented its inevitability. How could a machine replace a man? How could electronics and automation be a substitute for observation and intuition? But there was no point in being obsessed by it. The lighthouse had served him well. If he was honest, it was time he struck out on his own now.

Trinity House had been pleasant enough about his redundancy. The principal lighthouse keeper, Ernie Hallybone, had officially retired a month earlier but would stay on as custodian of the newly automated light, showing visitors around in summer. Will and the other assistant lighthouse keeper, Ted Whistler, could stay in the blockhouse until they found alternative accommodation.

Ted had left already. Couldn't wait to get out, he said. He'd packed his stuff the previous morning, muttering under his breath as he thrust the few possessions he had accrued over the years into an ill-assorted collection of cardboard boxes and carrier-bags. He moved straight into rooms in the Salutation, the rough-and-ready hostelry on the quayside. Ernie remarked that at least he'd be nearer to his daily pint (or three) that way. Ted grunted.

Will cast his keen, practised eye over the short stretch of coastline he now knew so well. Prince Albert Rock Lighthouse sat on its rugged granite promontory a mile to the west of where he stood, and beyond it the hazy blue-grey hump-backed whale that was Bill's Island surfaced from the glinting Atlantic – which today was the colour of blue-black ink, though he'd seen it in every shade from deepest purple to evil brown and menacing battleship grey.

In front of him Pencurnow Cove arched gracefully round to the right, its pepper-coloured sand fresh washed by the retreating spring tide, and beyond it, over the cliffs and crags, the spire of the church at St Petroc came and went in the morning haze. Herring gulls shrieked and wheeled over the bay and the beach, which at this time in the morning and so early in the year, was mercifully quiet and free of tourists. Only the matchstick figure of a local woman in a headscarf was visible in the middle distance, throwing a stick into the waves for a yellow Labrador that clearly had the courage of Hercules and the brain of a pea.

He listened, as the waves lapped on the sand, which curved round towards the short headland nearest the village. This small knob of tussocky ground sheltered the shingle bank on to which he'd pulled *The Gull*, the clinker-built, copper-riveted skiff it had taken him two years to complete. He looked at it and smiled, pleased with his handiwork. The varnish on the pitch-pine timbers glowed in the sun. But it wasn't big enough for what he had in mind.

Above him crouched the village of Pencurnow, and at the end of the promontory to his left, an arc of granite sheltered the three fishing boats that still endeavoured to bring home lobsters, bass and whatever else they could catch.

It was, admittedly, a small world. But it suited him. Correction, *had* suited him. He squinted as the keen rays of the morning sun bounced off the sea, then turned and walked up the lane towards the Post Office.

The bell pinged brightly as he pushed open the battered bottle-green door of Pencurnow Post Office and General Stores. He walked towards the unmanned counter, but before he reached it a strangulated voice from the back room instructed, "Hang on, I'm on my way. I'm just getting these damn papers out." A series of grunts and the popping of plastic webbing came to Will from the rear of the tiny shop, which was piled high with a thousand things that might be useful to somebody, if not to him.

On either side of the metal-grilled post-office cubicle, festooned with exhortations to buy Premium Bonds and Post Early for Christmas (and April, indeed, was early) stood perilously lopsided pyramids of tinned peas and butter beans. A tower of red plastic trays containing the day's supply of fresh bread leaned Pisa-like towards him, backed by shelves stuffed with cigarettes and corn plasters, matches and Mintoes, and an array of cleaning substances that would have impressed the most zealous daily help. The stone floor presented itself as a maze of cartons, pop bottles, garden tools and galvanized buckets. Gold-painted fire guards enveloped coppery companion sets, and the smell that reached his nostrils was compounded of cardboard and paraffin, soap powder and mothballs.

Tucked here and there Will noticed such irresistible temptations as pink shampoo in a poodle-shaped bottle, an implement for taking dents out of car doors (handy in Cornish villages with narrow lanes), and bottles of Mrs Pengelly's Home-made Piccalilli – a villainous-looking yellow decoction that would probably take the skin off the roof of your mouth before you had a chance to swallow it.

Above the bare Formica counter, magazines hung from a washing line, *Practical Boat Owner* alongside *The People's Friend*, *The Lady* sandwiched uncomfortably between *Farmer's Weekly* and *Cosmopolitan*. *Loaded* and *FHM* were under the counter for a local youth who aspired to the fleshpots of Newquay.

Beneath this literary fringe, appeared the Amazonic figure of

Primrose Hankey, her face only half visible above the pile of daily papers, which hit the counter with a thud. She greeted her customer with a warm, toothy grin and boomed, "Morning, Mr Elliott. Come to look at your picture?"

Will looked suitably embarrassed and asked, "What have they said?"

Primrose took a copy of *The Cornishman* from the top of the papers and read out the headline: "'Farewell To Britain's Last Lighthouse Keeper.' Nice photo of you – and Mr Hallybone. Ted Whistler don't look too pleased. But, then, when do he?" She tutted disapprovingly and handed Will the paper.

He took in the front page and its banner headline, the black-and-white picture of the six keepers in their uniforms – his shift of three and the other shift – and of the Elder Brethren of Trinity House who had come down to Cornwall for the momentous occasion. Evan Williams and his team stood to the left of the picture, Ernie Hallybone, Will and Ted Whistler to the right. They made an uneven trio, Ernie short and stocky with white hair and a face seemingly carved from English oak, Ted tall and gaunt with hooded eyes, and Will at the end of the row, not quite six feet, square jaw, high cheekbones and black curly hair under the peaked cap. He looked good in uniform. He felt better out of it.

The sextet of lighthouse keepers stood in a semi-circle, hands clasped neatly in front of them, surrounding the Master of Trinity House – the Duke of Edinburgh.

"What was he like?" enquired Primrose, anxious for gossip to recount for the rest of the week to her avid customers. Not for nothing was Primrose known as 'the human telescope'. Her shop had a panoramic view of the village and none of her windows boasted net curtains. Little passed her by, and there was even less on which she was unable to offer information, thanks to a multitude of sources.

"He was very nice," offered Will.

"But what did he say?" Her beady eyes were bright.

"Oh, he thanked us all and told us we'd done a valuable job very well and that he hoped we'd all remember our days at Trinity House with pleasure."

"Is that all?"

"Well, just about, yes." Will felt a bit of a failure. Nothing there with which Primrose could impress her customers. "Mr Elliott said the

Duke of Edinburgh was very nice." Hardly spicy. "I did notice a bit of shaving foam behind his ear, though."

"Really?" Primrose's eyes lit up and she leaned forward on to her counter. "So he wet-shaves, then?"

"Must do." Will tried to conceal a grin, and held up the paper in front of his face as camouflage, knowing that Primrose would now be a happy woman and could speculate for weeks on whether the Queen's husband used Gillette or Old Spice shaving foam.

"Well I never." Will lifted his eyes over the top of the *Cornishman* and noticed that Primrose's had already glazed over, and that she was playing with the single grey-brown plait that hung over her right shoulder. She chuckled to herself and made chomping noises with her mouth. She tossed the plait behind her with a jerk as Will said, "Hey-ho," and fished out some change.

"I see Spike made it, then!" remarked Primrose.

"Sorry?"

"Into the photo."

Will unfolded the paper again and looked at the picture. There, at the feet of the Master of Trinity House and curling his tail around the highly polished brogues, was Spike, the lighthouse cat, in his own black uniform with a white bib, clearly aware of the gravity of the occasion.

"Cheeky blighter," laughed Will. "Now I know why he was looking so pleased with himself this morning." Spike had turned up on Prince Albert Rock two years ago and had latched himself firmly on to Will. "I only hope he takes to his new home just as well."

Primrose scented another potential snippet of gossip. "Oh? You've found somewhere, then?"

"No, not yet."

"Not much for sale in the village at the moment. Or will you be moving away?" The tentacles were out.

"No. I plan to stay – hopefully – but I don't want a house."

Will was momentarily undecided as to whether or not he should reveal his plans to the human telescope, but decided there was little harm in telling her. It might even result in him finding a boat, although like as not he'd have to move into grotty rooms until something suitable turned up.

"You don't want a house?" Primrose broke in on his thoughts.

"No."

"Well, what, then?" She looked at him quizzically, wondering if he planned to become a cave-dwelling hermit.

"I want a boat."

"A boat?"

"Yes."

Without looking upwards, Primrose reached above her head and yanked at one of the magazines that formed the proscenium arch around her ample frame. She slapped it on the counter in front of him. "There you are. Two pounds sixty."

Will looked down at the glossy cover of *Boats and Planes For Sale*.

He looked at Primrose, and she looked right back, smiling. He fished into his pocket and found three one-pound coins. "Suppose I'll have to start somewhere."

Primrose punched at the buttons on her cash register. It made a few grinding noises then spat out a drawer from which she extracted his change. She pressed the coins into his hand and asked her next question. "What sort of boat do you want?"

"Oh, an old sailing boat."

"Just to live on?"

Will was trapped. Either he became evasive, or he would have to admit to Primrose that the real reason he wanted a boat was to sail around Britain single-handed. Every time he thought about it he felt self-conscious and a bit embarrassed. If he told the postmistress this, the entire village would soon know, and he'd never escape the repeated enquiries: "How's the boat doing?" "When are you going?" and "Haven't you got it sorted out yet?"

He tried not to be rude and fudged his answer. "Oh, I just want to be near the sea, and I can't afford a house with a sea view." Which was quite true.

"You could try the Crooked Angel."

Will looked at her incredulously. "What?"

The small boatyard, adjacent to the cobbled yard where the fishing fleet was pulled up during its off-duty hours, was not an obvious place to start looking. Its proprietor, Len Gryler, was not highly regarded within the community: he had a shady past and a shadier collection of boats at his disposal – the Arthur Daley of the waves.

"You're not serious!" said Will scornfully.

"Oh, I know he's a bit of a rogue, but even rogues have a decent boat every now and then."

"In Gryler's case I wouldn't bet on it," muttered Will, running his hand through his unruly hair.

"Well, I know for a fact he got a new one in a couple of days ago. Told me it came from some old sailor who was devoted to it."

"Oh, I see. One careful lady owner – probably an ex-Wren – only ever pottered around the bay on a Sunday. Kept in a heated boathouse since new?"

"You're teasing me!" Primrose admonished him. "I'm only trying to help. I know Len Gryler isn't the most reliable type . . ."

Will raised his eyebrows.

" . . . but you never know. It might be just what you want." She went back to her newspapers.

"Well, I might have a look on the way down."

"You've nothing to lose, have you?"

"Only thirty thousand quid," he said, under his breath.

She looked up. "Pardon?"

"I said, I'll try an early bid."

Primrose eyed him suspiciously. She'd always thought he was such a nice, quiet young man, but she had now detected an element of spirit she hadn't noticed before. She looked at him sideways. He wasn't going off the rails, was he? Funny lot, lighthouse keepers. Loners most of them. Men with secrets.

She snapped out of her reverie. "If you're going down there, can you give these to young Applebee?" She fished *Loaded* and *FHM* from under the counter, slid them quickly into a brown paper bag snatched from a nail on the shelf behind her and handed them to Will. "I've put them in a bag to save any embarrassment."

Christopher Applebee was Gryler's general dogsbody at the Crooked Angel, and clearly yearned for more excitement than he could find in Pencurnow.

Will slipped the bag between the folds of the *Cornishman*, realizing that he would now have to visit the boatyard whether he liked it or not. He made for the door.

"Oh, and don't forget to look in on the Roundhouse," said Primrose, through a mouthful of crisps.

"Mmm?"

"The old capstan house. It's being done up. Some artist is renting it."

"What for?"

"As a gallery. It'll make a change from all that junk the old woman from St Petroc has been selling in there for the last couple of years. I hope it's a success, for the sake of the village. The Roundhouse has never been the same since they retired it from hauling the fishing boats up the hard, but it's a lovely building. I've always thought of it as the heart of the village. It's time someone brought it back to life."

"Yes." But Will was miles away, his mind on the boatyard. He hardly looked round as he tossed a vague "'Bye" in Primrose's direction. Nor did he notice, in the early-morning light, the shadowy figure through the window of the old capstan house as he walked past it towards the boatyard. But she noticed him.

Chapter 2: Longships

The sign attached to the high granite breakwater certainly had romantic appeal. Its royal blue paint was flaking, but the words 'Crooked Angel Boatyard' were still visible in ornate, once-gilded script, coupled with the additional information, 'Berths and Servicing'. A crudely painted, lopsided figurehead of a seraph, plundered from the wreck of some ancient schooner, was bolted to the wall above the sign, and another piece of wood tacked beneath it proclaimed 'Boats for Sail'.

Will was unsure whether this betrayed an aptitude for puns or ineptitude in orthography. He sighed, took a deep breath, and went through the solid blue gates fastened back against the walls into the boatyard.

It was a modest marina, but then it probably had a lot to be modest about, he reflected, as he looked at the motley collection of vessels that creaked and groaned alongside the half-dozen wooden pontoons.

But in spite of its general air of decay the place was not unappealing. Funny, he thought, that what in a town or city would be looked upon as ramshackle and down-at-heel was regarded on the coast as charmingly rustic. Add water, stand well back and you had allure rather than atrophy. The Crooked Angel Boatyard was undoubtedly picturesque in a tumbledown way, from the robust wooden piles that penetrated deep into the Cornish mud, to the limpets and lime-green seaweed that festooned them.

Even the boats – mostly old and worn – had an air of contentment about them. About a dozen and a half were scattered across the still, dark grey water, straining gently at their mooring warps as the effects of the tide disturbed the water. They came in all shapes and sizes, from small, brightly painted fishing smacks filled with tangled skeins of line and tethered while their owners took breakfast in the Salutation, to larger 'Tupperware' boats of uncertain age. Nothing here to inspire a millionaire intent on finding a gin palace, thought Will.

There were boats with tattered canvas cockpit covers, and boats with punctured white plastic fenders and the occasional car tyre slung over the side to protect once-pristine paintwork from the ancient cobbled jetty. Masts towered above him, their frayed burgees lifting gently in the breeze, with the occasional ting-ting of a halyard as it rattled against hollow alloy.

The boatyard was barely a couple of miles from the lighthouse, as the fish swims, but Will could not recall ever having set foot in it. Most of the locals disapproved of Gryler, and Will had never needed to come here. It was not a public marina, more a nautical builders' yard.

Several small motorboats of relatively recent vintage bobbed alongside larger ones of greater antiquity and ugliness, and one or two of the ancient wooden vessels clearly owed something of their ancestry to Noah. Their names were as varied as their condition. Will walked down one of the pontoons, past *Racy Lady* and *Pinch of Thyme*, *Ultra Vires* and *Sokai* – perhaps the owner had Japanese associations. Beneath his feet, the water made glooping noises as the floating pontoon rose and fell gently, anchored by robust yet rusty fixings to the tall piles that towered eight feet above him on the falling tide.

"Can I help you?"

Will turned at the sound of a youthful voice. Its tone was neither solicitous nor aggressive. Before him stood a tall, scrawny youth of nineteen or twenty, a lopsided mop of sandy hair falling over his eyes. He wore a paint-spattered sweatshirt that had once been navy blue, and a pair of jeans with more holes than a colander, though less symmetry in their layout. There were two rings in his left ear. He looked like a latter-day pirate.

"Oh. You're one of the lighthouse keepers, aren't you?"

"Yes."

"I'm Chris Applebee. I work here."

"In that case I've got something for you." Will pulled out the bag with the magazines from the folds of the *Cornishman* and handed them to the lad. "Primrose sent them."

"Oh, thanks." The youth looked up at Will with a grin. "I bet she's read 'em both!"

"More than likely."

"We've never seen you here before, have we?" asked Christopher Applebee, tucking his magazines under his arm.

"No. I've not got around to it until now."

"Plenty of time now, eh?"

"Yes." Will was unsure whether he detected a note of mockery in the lad's voice, but chose to ignore it anyway. "I hear you've a new boat in for sale."

"Yeah, that's right. But you'd better see the boss, not me. I'll go and fetch him." He turned and walked down the pontoon towards a peeling, blue-painted shed on the jetty.

"Where is it?" Will called after him.

He didn't look back. "Pontoon number three."

Will looked up at the white numbers painted on the piles at the end of each pontoon. He was standing on number one. Number three was in the central part of the small pool, so he retraced his steps and walked back towards the main jetty. He turned left past the shed which he could now see was in the terminal stages of collapse. In this part of the world that probably meant it would last another twenty years.

As he passed the door, a short, round, oily man bounced out of it. "Mornin'," he growled, and offered a fat, greasy hand. "Len Gryler." The oily fist gripped Will's.

Len Gryler looked as if he was of Italian ancestry. He was balding, but the hair that remained on his spherical head was black as pitch and joined to the dusky stubble on his chin with long sideburns. He wore a dark blue one-piece overall, a stranger to the laundry, and carried in his left hand a monkey wrench. "So you're after a boat?" He wiggled the wrench.

"Well, yes. I hear you've got one for sale, but I'm only in the early stages of looking. Nothing's certain yet." Will was anxious to cover himself.

"Oh, don't you worry. You'll love this little beauty." Len Gryler slid effortlessly into his sales patter. He was a born trader. Here was a man who could not only sell ice-cream to Eskimos but a deep freeze to keep it in. He put his hand gently in the middle of Will's back and propelled him in the direction of pontoon number three.

A couple of small day-boats were bobbing at the end nearest the jetty on which they stood, and on the pontoon's starboard side, at the far end, lay an old, green-painted Cornish yawl, perhaps fifty-feet long, with the name *Florence Nightingale* carved into her gunwales. She had a squat wooden cabin amidships, behind the varnished wooden mast, and was littered with an assortment of nautical paraphernalia from an old brass binnacle to lobster pots in the process of repair, voluminous coils of old rope and assorted pieces of timber.

Will took to her immediately. "Very nice."

"No, not that one. That's Aitch's boat. This one."

Gryler pulled Will by the arm so that he faced the port side of the pontoon. There he beheld an altogether different vessel.

It was an ageing motor yacht, rather shorter than the sailing boat, with a row of portholes running from six feet abaft the bows to somewhere amidships. She was clearly a pre-war vessel, with wooden wheelhouse and aft cabin, once-varnished rails and two wooden masts, from which hung rotting ropes. She had once been someone's pride and joy, but those days were long gone.

"Ah," said Will. "She's a motor launch. I wanted a sailing boat. Stick and rag man, I'm afraid." He offered Gryler an apologetic look, but before he could make his escape, the man blocked his path.

"She's got two masts," he countered, defensively. "OK, so they're not what you might call powerful sails but look at the workmanship. Pitch pine on oak. Built in nineteen thirty-one by Staniland and Company in Yorkshire. On the River Ouse. Wonderful lines. Piece of history."

"But the engines—"

"Work of art. Twin diesels, Perkins M30s, recently reconditioned. And I'm going to have a look at them meself." He waggled his monkey wrench again as if to emphasize his skills. Realizing he had more work to do on this particular customer, he moved into second gear. "I dunno. These sailors. Make such a fuss about motorboats, rave on about the joys of 'proper' sailing then spend three-quarters of their time battling against the tide on a windless day with a piddling little engine that just about stops them going backwards. You'll be able to move in this one whether there's wind or not."

Will tried to interrupt, but Gryler was in full flow. And although the villagers considered him a rogue, he sounded as though he knew his boats. "A gentleman's yacht, without a doubt. Length overall thirty-six feet, beam nine foot six, draught two foot six – get you well up any estuary, that will."

"But what about her sea-keeping qualities?"

"What do you want her for? Crossing the Atlantic? All right, so I wouldn't recommend her to Sir Francis Chichester, but for estuaries and inshore waters she'll be fine. Built to last. Very sea-kindly." He slapped at her bulwarks and dried white paint fluttered off like a flock of miniature doves.

Again Will tried to protest.

"I'll tell you what, just look her over. I won't hassle you. I'll go and put the kettle on. The cabin door's open so hop aboard and see what you think. Needs a bit of work, I know, but for someone with time on their hands . . ." He paused to let the point sink home. "She'll repay any work that's put into her. Great live-aboard. For one." He looked up with a twinkle in his eye. "Or two. She's a little cracker, even if she has got a man's name."

Will looked at the bows of the old motor yacht and saw the engraved board fastened to the gunwales: *Boy Jack*, it said.

How can you call *Boy Jack* she? thought Will. He looked at her, or him, frowning, and opened his mouth to decline the offer, but Gryler was already at the end of the pontoon, heading kettlewards.

"Oh, well," he muttered to himself, and stepped up on to the deck. It was the first step in his ensnarement.

The mooring warps chafing against the fairleads caused the boat to let out a sound that was not so much a creak or a groan, more a sigh. "Yes," said Will, half aloud, "I'm not surprised you're sighing. Look at the state of you."

The deck was littered with herring-gull droppings. One of the culprits shrieked from the masthead and took off angrily. Will rubbed his hand along the timber, and remnants of varnish came away in crisp, translucent flakes. But the timber itself seemed sound.

He looked at the decks. Plenty of green algae, especially on the shaded areas. He glanced about to see that the coast was clear, took out his penknife and sank it into the planked decking in a particularly damp spot. Surprisingly it was hard and unyielding.

He leaned over the side to look at the hull. The seams between the planks were cracked. There would be plenty of recaulking needed if she were not to leak like a sieve. He hopped off again to see how the hull lay in the water. Quite evenly. A second surprise.

Will scolded himself for bothering to go through all these checks. He wanted a sailing boat. A Cornish yawl like the one in the next berth would do him nicely. He did not want a pre-war motor yacht. He made scale models of Cornish cobles, not motor boats.

Yet he climbed aboard once more and walked around the deck, past the old anchor winch at the bows and the iron jack-staff atop the stem. Well-balanced lines. He walked astern. She had plenty of deck space and the stanchions seemed well anchored to the topsides. He turned and pushed open the cabin door. It wouldn't budge. Gryler had said it was open. He put his shoulder to it and it yielded with a crack followed by a loud creak as the old brass hinges reluctantly turned on their spindles.

He stepped down into the wheelhouse, where the smell of mildewed carpet and cloth hit him. A thick layer of dust had settled on every surface, except where it had been recently disturbed, clearly in bringing the vessel to its final resting place. Black mould speckled timber and fabric alike. A small galley with a filthy porcelain sink was built into the starboard side. It was unclear whether the metal fixtures and fittings, from taps to knobs, portholes and the cabin-door lock were of brass or base metal, so dark and dull were their surfaces.

He tugged at a curtain to let in more light, and a swatch of rotten brown cloth came off in his hand. He pulled it away until the morning light beamed in diagonally, highlighting the dust motes that hung in the air. Will sneezed, and blew his nose.

The wheel was of the traditional type – wooden spoked and varnished. There were aged instruments on the fascia and a tarnished bell hanging from the bulkhead. Will resisted ringing it in case it summoned the boatyard owner.

Instead he searched for the entry to the engine room. Under assorted lumps of rotting carpet, he discovered a metal ring, and found that the hatch came up quite easily. He removed it and stood it to one side before lowering himself into the bowels of *Boy Jack*.

He had no torch, but the hatchway was large enough to let in sufficient daylight for him to be able to inspect the two Perkins engines. They were not in the first flush of youth, yet were excessively oily, rather than rusty. Will dredged up from the back of his brain the information he'd digested on a marine diesel-engine course a couple of years ago and married it to his knowledge of the generators at the lighthouse. He was relieved that the engines were not petrol-driven:

diesel was far safer, and low-horsepower engines like these, could go on for a long time – if you looked after them.

He spotted a loose wire here, a leaking pipe there, but not the seized-up piles of rusty metal he had expected. He put his hand down into the bilges. About an inch of water. He licked his finger. It was fresh water, not salt. That boded well. Then, again, he chastised himself for going through all this rigmarole, even if she was a boat with character. He heaved himself up from the engine room, and replaced the hatch.

Three steps led down into the aft cabin where he discovered a double berth with a damp, stinking mattress that sported a number of unidentifiable stains, and a wooden-doored cubicle that contained a small marble basin, an antique-looking hip bath, and an old lavatory – a Blake's head of the sort with two hand pumps, one to pump in salt water, the other to let it out. He pumped at the latter and was rewarded with a loud gurgle and a vile stench. He turned on his heel and moved through the wheelhouse to the fore-cabin, lit by several port-holes and a deck hatch.

He fought with the catch and finally succeeded in pushing it upwards and outwards. Light streamed in and he gulped at the fresh air.

The forward cabin was longer than he'd expected, and quite narrow, with one curving berth to port and another to starboard. Lockers filled the space between the hull and the inboard side of each berth and he opened them to take a look at the state of the boat's planking. Some of the caulking was coming away and he could see faint signs of moisture. The timbers were clearly not the originals: the boat had been restored and the hull replanked within, he guessed, the last twenty years. The pitch pine was in good condition, and many of the original mahogany stringers had been replaced with new.

The locker beneath the berth on the starboard side was empty, except for a few 1960s newspapers, old beer cans and some rusty spanners. He opened the locker on the port side to make a similar inspection and found a pile of sacking. He tugged at it and it fell out with a hefty thump. He picked it up and a hessian-wrapped lump dropped on his toe. "Bloody hell!"

He looked down, and saw a clumsily tied parcel, held together with fishing twine. He took out his penknife again and carried the parcel into the wheelhouse. As he cut away the twine and pulled off the rough hessian wrapped around it, the brass plate became clearly visible, as did the legend upon it. It bore a name and a date, and marked the point at which Will Elliott knew that there was no escape from the clutches of *Boy Jack*.

The plaque read simply: 'Dunkirk 1940'.

Chapter 3: Needles

It took exactly eleven days for the surveyor's report to confirm that *Boy Jack*, in spite of her appearance, was seaworthy. Gryler was asking £25,000 for her but Will managed to knock him down to £23,000, to include three months' free berthing at the Crooked Angel – time enough, he hoped, to do the boat up. With any luck the spare £7,000 would be enough to fund repairs sufficient to make her seaworthy. He'd be on his way by midsummer.

With an armful of cardboard boxes, courtesy of Primrose Hankey, he walked up the rough gravel path from the lane that led to Prince Albert Rock, conscious that this was a journey that from now on he would make as a visitor.

The wind had swung round to the north-east and had more bite than of late. Leaden grey clouds ballooned up from landward and the sea looked restless, breaking heavily on the rocks below the clean white tower. It had lost the blueness of mid-April and seemed to hark back to winter in its chill grey tones.

Will walked around the side of the building and pushed open the door into the engine room.

"You all right, then?" It was Ernie Hallybone, broom in hand, sweeping the floor by the old foghorn compressors.

"Fine. Just got some boxes for my stuff. Should be out by lunchtime."

Ernie smiled thoughtfully and carried on with his sweeping. They'd had all their conversations about the rights and wrongs of automation. "Loony," Ernie called it. "You can't get instinct and experience from a computer."

Automation had been on the cards since the sixties and had begun in earnest in the eighties. Few keepers regretted the conversion of rock stations such as Longships and Wolf Rock, Bishop Rock and Eddystone – Ernie had been stuck on Wolf Rock once for three and a half months, thanks to the weather. He'd regaled Will with stories of storms that shook the tower, waves that passed right over the lantern, and boats standing off in violent seas to relieve the keepers of their watch, then having to go away again, the sea too rough to transfer the men.

Will had arrived too late for such a posting: today the rock stations were visited only by helicopter when maintenance was needed. At the time he had longed for such isolation. The suddenness of the tragedy had left him oblivious to anything but his grief. The healing process was slow. Even now it was far from over, and there was still a huge part of him that he dare not explore too deeply. But he had learned to live with that. In time it might change, perhaps not. Whatever the future held, the Cornish coast and the kindliness of his principal lighthouse keeper had done much to ease him back into life.

When he had arrived Ernie had found him difficult to communicate with, but had been wise enough to give him time to come to terms with his future. As a rule, lighthouse keepers were a patient breed, and Will knew that the service had something of the Foreign Legion about it. It was a way of life suited to a few, usually those who needed an escape. Every man joined the service for a different reason. Those who stayed had in common only a unique brand of self-containment, their patience and, often, a love of nature. Few other vocations could satisfy such men, except the monastic life, and that precluded certain activities that many lighthouse keepers would have been reluctant to forgo.

Will climbed the brass-railed stone staircase to his room, opened the door and dumped the boxes on the floor. His packing was almost complete. There were just a few more odds and ends to wrap and box before he could load the whole lot into the back of Ernie's van and transfer them to his new floating home.

He looked out of the small window towards the sea, crashing on to the rocks, its crests blown back by a brisk offshore wind. He knew that stretch of water in every mood and yet really hardly knew it at all. It was totally unpredictable; every day was different.

The half-dozen completed models of Cornish cobles had already been packed. He put the remainder of his wood, his knives and twine, the paint, varnish and assorted bits and pieces together in a box, pushed bubble wrap carefully around it, sealed the box with sticky tape and wrote in neat script on the lid: 'Boat Bits'. To a man, lighthouse keepers were tidy. They had to be, to avoid falling over things in confined spaces, and irritating each other.

As with every other lighthouse in Britain, six men had been assigned to Prince Albert Rock, divided into two sets of three, each three working one month on, one month off, a twenty-eight-day tour. Ernie Hallybone was the principal lighthouse keeper, Ted Whistler and Will Elliott his assistants. The other team, led by Evan Williams, had left the service at the end of their last tour a month ago.

During their month on duty the keepers would live in the lighthouse; some – Will, Ted and Ernie – lived there all the time, others moved inland to their homes during their month off.

The eight hours on and sixteen hours off had been a routine that helped Will rebuild his life. Each watch was different. From 4 a.m. till noon you could see the sun rise over the cliffs, hear the dawn chorus of land and sea birds and feel justifiably virtuous. From noon until 8 p.m. you could take things steadily and in summer enjoy a watch entirely in daylight. From 8 p.m. till 4 a.m. you were up and about while the rest of the world slept. For many it was the unfavoured watch, but for Will it was the ultimate escape, a time to look out to sea and watch the sun go down. Never had he experienced the fabled "green flash" that Ernie boasted of seeing on the horizon twice in his life – when the sun sets over a flat, calm sea and the weather conditions are just right – but he had seen and enjoyed, times without number, the moon glistening on the Western Approaches.

He would miss it. He would miss the ships passing in the night. They were often lit more brightly by the moon than the sun and even when there was no moon, they were clearly visible under the stars in darkness illuminated only by the light from the lantern, one flash every three seconds.

He emptied the chest of drawers, five sweaters and ten shirts, three pairs of jeans, underwear and socks, and packed them into another box, before clearing his bookshelves. A small pile of CDs – Rameau and Philip Glass, Pat Metheney and George Shearing – were tucked alongside the books: the five volumes of Frank Cowper's *Sailing Tours*, Joshua Slocum's *Sailing Alone Around the World* and Libby Purves's

One Summer's Grace. He was relieved that, unlike her, he would not be battling around Britain accompanied by fractious children.

He filled another box with back numbers of *Classic Boat* and the exercise books he had used as diaries since his first day at the lighthouse six years ago. He flipped open the one dated "Apr – May '94" and read a paragraph. "Noon. Better today, I think. Still hard not to think of E all the time, even when trying hard to concentrate on something else. Thought of what she said about the colour of the geraniums down the steps at Oriel. Saw a skiff rounding the headland and remembered that day on the Cherwell in the rowing boat."

He felt a pang in the pit of his stomach, and flipped the pages. "4 p.m. Sea vile. Almost black. Terns trying to stay airborne. Painted wall behind generator. Wish Trinity House knew what it was like using this shitty-coloured paint. Ted being equally shitty to all and sundry. Must be his time of the month. 6.30 p.m. Watched fishing boat PZ 291 picking up lobster pots around Bill's Island. Two men getting a soaking. Seemed to catch quite a few."

Will smiled, closed the book, and stacked it with the rest.

That was almost it, bar the sweeping up. Oh, and the certificate. He walked over to the windowsill and picked up the framed citation that had been presented to him the day before:

This is to Certify that
William Elliott
entered the Service of the
Corporation of Trinity House of
Deptford Strond on
19th April 1993 and left
the service on 7th April 1999

This Certificate is issued as a mark
of the Elder Brethren's appreciation
of many years of faithful service
rendered.

Trinity House   Patrick Rowe
Tower Hill   Deputy Master
London EC3

Not that many years, thought Will, but maybe enough. He slipped the frame on top of the diaries and closed the box.

He had left the most difficult job until last.

"Come on, then. We've got to go."

The cat was asleep at the bottom of the iron-framed bed, curled up on the neatly folded blankets. Or, rather, he was pretending to be asleep, having watched carefully the previous preparations through one half-open eye.

Will walked over to him and prodded him with a finger. "Are you coming or staying behind?" He eased his hand under the animal who remained relaxed until he caught a glimpse of the cat basket, at which point he became rigid and totally uncooperative. It would have been easier for a camel to have passed through the eye of a needle than for Spike to have entered the kingdom of the cat basket. He travelled to his new home on Will's knee, both eyes tight shut.

"Are you sure you want to be moving out now?" Ernie Hallybone was driving towards St Petroc, through which they had to pass to get to Pencurnow Cove.

"Yes. The longer I leave it the harder it will be. I've got to get on."

"I can't believe it's all happening, really. It's been so long coming I suppose I should be ready for it, but I still can't take it in."

"Nor me."

"Forty-three years. It's a lifetime, isn't it? A bloody lifetime."

"At least you'll still be living here. I'm being kicked out into the big wide world."

Ernie looked across at him. "It's a bugger, isn't it?"

"Yes."

They passed through St Petroc and turned west towards Pencurnow village.

"Are you taking all this lot with you?"

"Can I leave a few boxes with you until later?"

"Course you can. May's got plenty of storage space in the spare room. What about the state of the boat?"

"Oh, I can cope with that. I've got rid of all the old carpet and curtains and scrubbed it out. It's clean . . . ish. Bit spartan, though."

"And cold."

"I've got plenty of sweaters, and a good sleeping bag. It's been recommended by an Antarctic explorer."

"Scott?"

"No. Someone who survived."

Ernie was trying to make light of the occasion. He'd grown fond of the lad who'd worked with him for the last six years. He'd miss him. He had more rapport with him than he'd ever had with the dour Ted Whistler. Will had regularly been invited into Ernie's flat at the lighthouse for supper, cooked by his wife May, who had a smallholding in the village. He always ate well at Ernie and May's – fresh eggs and ham and home-grown vegetables. May was the sort of figure Will had always imagined as a farmer's wife – amply proportioned with grey hair dragged back into a bun – one wisp always managing to escape, and rosy cheeks. She had a high-pitched, sing-song voice, almost always wore a brown overall coat and wellies, and looked, Will thought, like Beatrix Potter.

Ernie's face was as weatherbeaten as that of a deep-sea fisherman. He seemed always to be smiling, and he and May, a childless couple, rarely had a cross word. It was, Ernie claimed, because they had always let each other have their own space. Ernie loved nature and bird-watching, May loved her livestock, and the one complemented the other. They were married, said May, "for better, for worse, but not for lunch".

"You'll keep comin' to see us?" asked Ernie with concern.

"Course I will. What's started you worrying that I won't? I'm only round the corner."

"Ten miles. A long way round 'ere, ten miles."

"Yes, but only by road. It's closer across the water and the cliff path. You've got too used to your van." Will turned to look at Ernie, whose eyes had glazed over. His jaw was set firm and he looked straight ahead.

Will hesitated. "There's something I want to ask you."

"Mmm?" Ernie's response was distant.

"The boat. The rowing boat – *The Gull*."

"What of it?"

"I want you to have her."

Ernie began to protest, but Will cut him off: "I'll have a bigger boat, and the *Gull* will be too heavy either to mount on davits or to tow behind. Anyway I want you to have her. No arguments, that's it."

"OK," Ernie said quietly. "Thanks."

"You all right?" Will had not seen him like this before. He'd always been relaxed and sanguine about anything life threw at him. But right now Will detected a note of apprehension in the older man's voice.

"Fine. It's just been a long time, that's all." He brightened unconvincingly. "I'm fine."

Ernie had worked on almost half of Trinity House's seventy-two lighthouses, ending up back on home territory in Cornwall. The only time Will ever saw his feathers ruffled was when Ted Whistler droned on about the inevitability of automation. "We're not coastguards," Ted would moan. "We don't have to look out for anything, just clean things up, that's all." When this happened Ernie would give him chapter and verse on the benefits of manned lighthouses, on how many potential disasters had been averted because of a lighthouse keeper's observations and instincts, and how many lives had been saved because of man rather than machine.

"Look, it might be ten miles by road, but it's only a couple of miles by sea," Will repeated reassuringly. "You can row over when it's calm. And when it isn't I'll get on my bike, when I've got one."

"Course you will. Don't mind me. Just bein' daft."

"Old bugger!" Will mocked him, and nudged his arm.

"Aye, daft old bugger." He laughed and jerked a thumb in the direction of the slumbering Spike. "He don't seem to mind, then?"

"You wouldn't have said that if you'd seen him half an hour ago."

"How are you going to stop 'im comin' back?"

"No idea. He'll do what he wants to do, I suppose – always has."

The cat began to purr.

"May says you 'ave to butter their paws. It makes the smell of their new place stick to them and then they don't try to go back home."

"I can't afford butter. Does it work with marge?"

"Now who's a daft bugger?"

Ernie laughed again. Their journey to the Crooked Angel boatyard continued in silence, except for the hum of the engine and the purring of the cat.

Chapter 4: Portland Bill

Their first night together passed uneventfully. The gentle swaying rocked both man and cat to sleep at around midnight, and Will awoke to the sound of scratching and seagulls at seven in the morning.

One thing he had not done was buy food, so there was no margarine to put on the cat's paws. But he couldn't leave Spike cooped up while he walked up the hill to Primrose's: the boat had an ample sufficiency of aromas already, without adding one of a feline nature. What's more, the ship's timbers were beginning to suffer the effects of Spike's claws.

Will struggled out of the sleeping bag, stretched, pulled on a fisherman's sweater and a pair of shorts, then opened the door and let the cat out.

Spike crept gingerly over the threshold into the bright morning, his whiskers twitching and his tail held vertically aloft. He looked, thought Will, like a little boy who had just been introduced to a fairground. Eyes wide, he padded around the boat, familiarizing himself with his new territory. Then he hopped off and went down the pontoon in the direction of the jetty.

Will considered calling him back, but resisted, thinking that he might wake his boating neighbours. Instead, he watched through the window of the wheelhouse as Spike plodded towards the jetty. Gryler would not be in his office yet. He had told Will he generally started work at around eight. The cat reached the jetty and looked to left and right before disappearing behind a pile of old wooden crates. For fully five minutes he was lost from view and Will was getting ready to go in search of his lost shipmate when Spike emerged from behind the crates with the remains of a fish.

Will's thoughts turned to his own breakfast. Then he gazed at the bare interior of the boat, and wondered yet again if he had done the right thing. But he'd had no option. The boat had spoken to him that day a couple of weeks ago and he'd felt responsible for it somehow. What he had to do now was make it more reliably seaworthy and more comfortably habitable.

He sat back on the hard wooden bunk, acutely aware that his daily timetable had gone. What he did now, and when he did it, was up to him. It was tempting just to stay in bed and brood or, at least, it would be when he'd found a mattress. He could put off the voyage for a year or two if he wanted. It was a hare-brained scheme anyway. Why was he preparing to do it? How long would it take? Cornwall alone had 417 miles of coastline, counting all the twiddly bits. The distance round England, Scotland and Wales amounted, geographically, to 6,872 miles, though the voyage would be nearer 2,000 miles in reality. And what would he find at the end of it? Would he be back where he'd started in more ways than one? He wanted to voyage alone, but part of him wished he didn't have to. If things had gone according to plan . . . But they had not.

He took stock of himself. It was no use thinking like this. He had to be positive, practical. For three years he had promised himself this voyage. It was now or never. He had a year to do it – he could probably eke out his present funds over twelve months but no longer. Then he would have to find another job. He would probably have to go back to making clocks. Unless something else turned up. There. Sorted.

He pulled on a pair of deck shoes then sneaked off the boat. He walked down the pontoon, across the jetty, let himself out through the blue gate and went up the hill in search of provisions.

Primrose could not disguise her surprise at his appearance. She said nothing, but her eyes spoke volumes. It amused Will to think of the gossip she'd be passing on today: "Mr Elliott, the lighthouse keeper, has really let himself go. Used to be so neat and tidy. You wouldn't know him now. Such a pity."

He walked back down the hill towards the boat, loaded with four carrier-bags. The threatening clouds of the day before had blown away, and the sky was clear. There was a faint nip in the air. He looked across at the lighthouse and thought of Ernie, hoping he'd soon settle into his new role. He was sixty-two now; time he slowed down a bit. Anyway, he'd have more time for his bird-watching between showing round visitors, which was pretty much a seasonal job in this part of Cornwall.

As he reached the bottom of the hill he turned the corner and walked past the Roundhouse. Primrose had called it 'the heart of the village' and Will noticed that it had been smartened up since he last set eyes on it a couple of weeks ago. The window-frames were glossy white, and the clapboard exterior was now a soft blue. The slate roof sat on top like a coolie hat, and the double doors were crowned with a sign proclaiming 'Roundhouse Studio', framed by bleached lengths of silvery driftwood.

Will mounted the steps to take a closer look inside. He pressed his nose to the glass of the door and started when he saw a face inside looking directly back at him. He lurched back and one of his carrier-bags gave way, spilling an assortment of produce from wild rice to apples, tinned sardines to biological toilet cleaner.

"Sorry! I didn't mean to make you jump." The voice was a mixture of amusement and concern. Will looked up. Standing in the now open doorway was a woman in her late twenties. She wore jeans, a white T-shirt, and a mass of auburn curls cascaded over her shoulders. Her face was pale and expressive, and the corners of her mouth were doing their best not to allow themselves to turn upwards into a grin.

She knelt down and helped him retrieve his shopping. "I'm sorry. What a mess. Aaah!" She looked at the oozing eggs in their battered box. "I'm so sorry!"

"Don't worry. I shouldn't have been so nosy."

"I'm glad you were. It proves the place looks interesting."

"Are you open yet?" he asked, retrieving a tin of soup from the gutter.

"It's my first day today."

"Well, I hope you do well." He smiled. "The place certainly looks a lot better."

"I've done my best, but it's taken a while. It's a couple of months since I started on the inside. The outside was much easier. I only hope it works."

The shopping was back in the bags now and Will stood up, cradling one in his arms and hoping that the handles of the others would last until he made it back to the boat. "What are you selling?" he asked.

"My paintings." And then, belatedly, "Hi . . . I'm Amy Finn. I'm a painter. Sort of."

"Will Elliott. Lighthouse keeper. Well, until last week." He made to shake her hand, then realized he couldn't so grinned apologetically.

"What will you do now?"

"I'm living on a boat over there," he jerked his head in the direction of the Crooked Angel, "but it needs a lot of work doing."

"Well, you've got the summer to come."

"Yes." He found he was staring at her. She was quite small, with fine features and a dusting of freckles on her pale skin. She wore no jewellery, and there was a freshness about her that took his breath away.

"Do you . . . er . . . would you?" He hesitated.

"Yes?"

"Would you consider exhibiting work from other artists, or will it be all your own work in the gallery?"

"Oh, I'll have to take stuff from other artists. I can't paint fast enough to keep the place full – if my work sells, that is. And, anyway, I think people want to see lots of different styles – they might not like mine." She shrugged.

"How will you decide what to sell?"

"I'll keep my eyes open locally and see what I can find. And other artists will hopefully drop in and offer me stuff."

"Just paintings?"

"No, sculpture. All art forms, really." She looked at him inquisitively. "You sound interested."

"Well, it's just that . . . I make these model boats, you see, not Airfix, wooden models of Cornish cobles. Traditional rowing boats. Do you think you might have a look at one . . . just to see? I have to make a bit of cash somehow and–"

"Love to. Why don't you bring one round?"

"You sure you don't mind?"

"As long as you don't mind me turning you down if it's not the sort of thing I think I could sell."

"No. Not at all."

"Are you free tonight? I'll be closing at five. Why don't you come round then? If you'd like to?"

He felt a brief sense of elation. "Yes. Fine." He nodded nervously, a touch embarrassed, then walked backwards for a few paces down the lane before realizing that he must look silly, at which point he nodded again and turned. He began to whistle. He couldn't remember the last time he'd felt like this. He took a deep breath and headed for the boat and breakfast.

The cup of coffee revived him. Gryler had supplied him with a cylinder of propane and Primrose had sold him a twin burner. He also had a kettle, a saucepan, a single set of cutlery and some plastic plates, bowls and mugs.

The plumbing would have to be his first priority, along with a mattress. He found a pencil and pad in one of his boxes and drew up a list of things to do.

He was at the bottom of page three when he heard a call. "Halloo? Hallooooo?"

A bearded face was peering above the rail of the boat. "Halloo?"

"Yes?" Will got up and ducked through the door of the wheelhouse.

"Permission to come aboard, skipper?"

It was the first time Will had been given the rank and it made him laugh. "Yes. Er . . . do."

His visitor clambered over the rail, a gangly man with long, thin limbs, grubby corduroy trousers that had once been green, and a navy-blue Guernsey threadbare at the elbows. His sandy whiskers matched the hair on his head – an unruly thatch unused to a comb.

"Utterly," said the man, offering his hand. Will looked about apologetically.

"Yes, it is a bit, I'm afraid."

"No!" The man threw back his head and laughed, displaying a mouth full of uneven teeth. "Aitch Utterly – I live in the boat next door." He scratched his head. "Good to have you with us. Not that there are many of us, but we're a jolly bunch."

Will noticed that the man hardly stopped smiling. He had one of those faces that probably smiled when he was asleep.

"You're the lighthouse keeper, aren't you? The last lighthouse keeper. Read all about it in the paper."

Will's heart sank. Suddenly the prospect of living in a community once more – albeit a small boating community – filled him with dread. He'd imagined that on his own boat he could enjoy his own company. He'd not taken into account that he would have neighbours.

"Now, look," Aitch had seen the panic in Will's face, "you've probably come here for a quiet life so don't worry. Everybody on these boats does their own thing. We don't live in each other's pockets but we're good company when you want it. Well, most of us. We stick together. Great community spirit, but most of us know where to draw the line. Sorry to go on a bit. Spend a lot of time on me own. Think it makes you a bit of a chatterbox when you get in company. Sometimes." He chuckled. "Depends whose company it is, of course. One or two folk round here wouldn't give you the time of day. Can't be doing with them. Life's too short. Mmmm. Too short." He became introspective, as if transported to a different time and a different place. Then he was back. "Anyway, there I am, in my boat – *Florence Nightingale*, the yawl." He pointed to the other side of the narrow pontoon. "Bit close, I know, but I think we'll get on. I won't get in your way. Mmmm. No. Leave you in peace now. Let me know if you want anything – tools or whatever – only too pleased to oblige. Till then, cheerio." And he leapt over the side, on to the pontoon then back into his own boat, disappearing through the hatch with a wave.

"Well," said Will, to his cat, "I think we've just met our neighbour." For the second time that morning he felt unusually happy.

Chapter 5: Coquet

Getting clean is not easy when all you have is a bucket. Will arranged a carpet of pages from the now unwanted *Boats and Planes For Sale* in the middle of the wheelhouse, put the bucket in the centre and added a kettleful of boiling water to the chilly contents. He had a bar of Wright's Coal Tar soap and a flannel, a bottle of frequent-use shampoo, a throw-away razor and some shaving gel.

He set to work removing his stubble. He squinted into a small mirror and caught Spike's eye. "I know it's not what you're used to but at least you've got your own bit of blanket." The cat blinked. Will finished shaving, shampooed his hair then set about washing himself in the bucket. The absurdity of the enterprise suddenly struck him. He laughed. "The sooner we get that bath and shower sorted the better," he said to Spike, as he towelled himself dry. "If Gryler wasn't too mean to have a shower block we'd be OK. Thank goodness he's got a loo." Spike ignored him: he was trying to remove the margarine from his paws.

Will dressed as tidily as he could in a clean pair of jeans and a sweatshirt, and brushed dried mud from his deck shoes. Then he went to the boxes at the sharp end of the boat to fetch out one of his models. It was carefully wrapped in tissue paper, and he eased it out of the box. He told Spike he wouldn't be long, then he closed the door behind him and locked it. It was safer than leaving Spike loose on what was only his second night as a sailor.

A meal was being prepared in Aitch's boat as he passed, and he could hear shipboard voices on pontoon number two, accompanied by the gentle lapping of water at the bows of an old speedboat named *The*

Slapper. In the sunset the water of the boatyard glowed a dull orange. The cry of a single gull echoed across the glassy water. It was, he thought, as he walked down the jetty towards the gate, not a bad place to live.

He tapped on the glass of the gallery door. There was a pause, then the sound of feet, and Amy unlocked the door.

"Hi!" She flung back her arm to invite him in. He felt himself blushing. It surprised him. He was thirty-seven, for God's sake. He cleared his throat. "Hi. How was your first day?"

"Oh, a bit slow. Quite a few people came round but I didn't sell much – it's early in the season."

She dropped the latch behind him and pulled down a linen roller blind. "So what do you think?"

He looked around. "Wow!" The Roundhouse consisted of a circular space on two levels, linked by a spiral staircase on the far side. The floor was of ancient oak planks that had been scrubbed clean of the nautical detritus of a century or two. The walls were white and lit with tiny bright spotlights fastened to wires that criss-crossed the room. On the floor, towards the middle of the room, stood half a dozen different artworks made from 'found objects' – lumps of driftwood, rusty old nails and chains. There were a couple of erotic sculptures of abstract figures, but it was the paintings that caught his eye, canvases of Cornish beaches with burning white sand and sky of the most brilliant azure. Each radiated a freshness and energy that amazed him.

"There's hardly anything here yet. There'll be more over the next few weeks, I hope, but I don't want to fill it with too much."

"No." He was gazing at one of the paintings, transfixed.

"Do you like them?"

"Yes." It seemed lame. "Very much." Then he found his breath. "I think they're wonderful."

"Oh, that's a bit strong."

"No, I do. I can take or leave the driftwood but the paintings, wow!"

"Well, that's honest!"

"Whose are the sculptures?"

"Oh, a friend. I want to get more smaller things for a sort of plain wooden counter over there. I'll have to sell little souvenirs, too, but I want them to be good. Anyway, come upstairs and have a drink. I've got a bottle in the fridge." She walked towards the staircase. "It's a bit spartan, I'm afraid."

Amy's spartan was not Will's spartan. The floor was covered in coir matting, the walls were washed pale blue and a vast cream linen curtain was hauled back at one end to separate the sleeping and living areas. Will noticed a large double bed with white pillows, and in the living area two blue and white striped chesterfields faced each other across a low, scrubbed-pine table.

A cello lay on its side on the floor, near a music stand and a pile of music. A few pictures were propped up against the wall.

"The bathroom is through there if you want it."

A single white-painted door was sufficiently ajar for Will to see an ancient iron bath with ball and claw feet and brass taps. "It's better than my plumbing. All I've got at the moment is a bucket." He put the boat on the table between the sofas as she came towards him with a bottle of Chardonnay and two glasses.

"Could you do this? Do you mind? I'll put some music on."

As he peeled off the foil she pressed the buttons of a small stereo, which eventually produced the soft sounds of a Bach string quartet.

The cork came out with a loud plop and he tipped the wine into the glasses as she returned.

"Mmm, that looks good."

"Well . . . here's to you and your gallery."

"Studio, please. Gallery sounds a bit posh. Cheers!"

They sipped and she motioned him to sit on the sofa. She sat opposite, tucking her bare feet under herself. "Now, then, show me the boat." He put down his glass and carefully undid the tissue paper to reveal the Cornish coble.

She slid off the sofa on to the floor, and studied it seriously. He began to believe it was not really her sort of thing. "I don't mind if it's not suitable," he said.

"What?" She was preoccupied.

"I don't mind if you feel it won't really fit in."

"It's beautiful." She spoke quietly. "Absolutely beautiful."

He sat still and quiet, filled with unexpected pride as her eyes ran over the boat's lines.

"I don't usually go much for model boats. They seem phoney,

somehow. But yours has life. How long does it take you? Oh, God! I hate it when people ask me that about my paintings and here I am asking you."

"I've no idea. I've never timed myself. But a long time, I suppose."

"So often models like this are . . . well, numb. But yours isn't. I love it."

"I'm glad." He felt ridiculously pleased with himself.

"Can I exhibit it tomorrow?"

"Fine. Great." He could hardly believe his luck.

She climbed back on the sofa. "What made you start making them?"

"Oh, I had time on my hands and needed to fill it with something."

"But you could have done anything. Why model boats?"

"Because I love the sea and the escape it offers. And I love the idea of escaping on a wooden boat. So a model wooden boat seemed appropriate. I could dream while I made it."

"About what?"

"Sailing away."

"From what?"

"Oh . . . life."

She looked at him and sipped her wine.

"Is that why you became a lighthouse keeper? To sail away from life?" She made light of it, smiling as she spoke.

"Yes."

She noticed his shuttered look. "I'm sorry. I'm too nosy. I didn't mean to pry."

"No. It's OK." Will always felt self-conscious when conversations took this turn, but she looked at him with a combination of gentleness and concern that made him feel secure rather than threatened. He felt under no pressure to speak, but found that he could without the usual burning desire to run away. "It's six years ago now. I know it's stupid but I still find it hard to talk about."

"Sorry. Typical of Finn. Barging in. I'm sorry."

"No, really, it's fine. I should be used to it now."

She sensed the echoes of grief. "It is and it isn't. Some things stay raw and others fade. I know."

He looked at her open face. She didn't seem to be prying.

"I was working in Oxford. I was a clockmaker. I'd been married a year, to Ellie. We met at college – went out for ages." He smiled to himself. "Two days after our first anniversary she was killed. Hit-and-run driver. Just like that. Gone. She was expecting a baby. I lost the two of them in one go."

Amy sat looking at him, shocked, as he continued in a calm, measured voice. "I didn't know what to do. I just knew I wanted to be on my own. I don't mean I don't like company – I'm better at it now – but I still need space and time on my own. I find it difficult to be in a room full of people."

He was sitting on the edge of the sofa, his arms resting on his knees and his pale blue eyes gazing into the middle distance. "I'm so sorry." Amy wanted to put her arms round him and tell him he was a lovely man and that it would be all right. "Did you ever think of seeing anybody about it?" she asked.

"Not for long. Didn't want to admit to anybody that I couldn't cope. I wanted to sort myself out. Share your troubles and they just keep being brought back to you. I didn't want that. Didn't want somebody else getting involved."

"So you shut yourself away?"

"Yes. I thought that way I could get over it in my own time. Cry myself silly. But I still haven't." He smiled. "Funny, isn't it? My world fell apart and I couldn't even cry."

"It's more common than you'd think. "

"I didn't feel I could be a monk." He brightened and she took the joke. "Anyway, Ellie wouldn't have wanted that. And I didn't know what I believed in, which was a bit of a drawback, so I looked for another solo occupation. As a lighthouse keeper I could be remote, solitary, have time to reflect. Then I found I'd be working with two other people, but our watches were solo so that meant I could be alone a lot. And I like Cornwall. It's out on a limb. Like me."

"No family?"

"No. Mum and Dad both died when I was young. I was brought up by my granny and she died ten years ago. Sorry story, isn't it?"

"I'm glad you told me. Pleased you felt you could."

"Thanks for listening. I'm sorry to go on. Talking about myself."

"Don't be silly." She moved across to sit nearer to him. "I did ask you – you didn't volunteer it."

"No, but when you spend so much time thinking about yourself and your own problems you have to be careful not to forget other people."

"It's not the easiest thing to get over, is it? Losing the person you loved most and your unborn child at the same time. It's the most devastating thing imaginable. I think anyone would understand that."

"Like you? I'm not sure they would."

"Oh, I'm not that special."

"Special enough to come here all on your own and open your own place. That's special. It takes courage." He paused, anxious to move the conversation on to a happier subject. "Have you always been a painter?"

"No." She looked up. "Like you, I'm an escapee, except that it was my career that was taken away from me."

"Oh?"

"I was with the Ballet Rambert. Then I moved to Ballet d'Azur. I was doing quite well. Principal dancer. And then my knee went. Lateral meniscus." She rubbed at the offending joint. "That was it."

"God. How awful."

She laughed sardonically. "Yes, it was a bit. Life devoted to my art and wham! Finished overnight."

"Do you miss it?"

"Like hell. It nags away all the time. Like unfinished business. I still do a bit of barre work every day" – she pointed to a rail along part of the wall – "but my career is finished."

"How can you be so sure? Won't it get better?"

"Oh, it is better. But there's always a danger it will go again."

"And you don't want to take the risk?"

"I wish I could. The trouble is, it's not just the knee. It's the nerve. I haven't got the guts to carry on, if I'm honest. I try, but I keep feeling this nagging doubt. Some days I think it'll be fine, and then others I know it's over. To be perfectly honest I'm terrified it'll go again and that I won't even be able to walk."

"So you decided to paint?"

"I'd always dabbled. I needed to find another way of earning a living so I thought I'd give it a go. I managed to sell canvases to friends and the time came when I had to get away from London. So I rented this place and here I am." She got up, picked up the bottle and came back to fill up his glass. She sat closer to him than before. He admired the clearness of her complexion.

"What about the cello?" He gestured towards it.

"Oh, I'm not very good, but it lets me get rid of the pent-up frustrations I have when I do a crap painting."

"I know what you mean. It's like me and boats. Stay off the water too long and I get withdrawal symptoms."

"Is that why you're living afloat?"

"Yes."

"For ever?"

"I wish. But for now anyway. I've always had this nagging idea about sailing around Britain. I kept telling myself it was daft but it's become a sort of personal challenge. I've learnt how to sail. I can navigate. And now I've bought a boat with two engines and no sails because I fell in love with it. Crazy!"

"How did you come to fall in love with it?"

"It turned out to be one of the little ships of Dunkirk, and I'm just a sentimental old fool."

"How old?"

"Thirty-seven."

"It's a dangerous age – fast approaching the big four-oh."

"How old are you?"

"Never you mind." She paused and looked him in the eye. "Oh, all right, then, twenty-nine."

"Not a dangerous age?"

Amy laughed. "What about supper?"

"Oh. No. I couldn't. I'm holding you up."

"You're not holding me up at all. It's nice to have someone to share things with. I've been on my own for a few weeks now."

"Well . . ." He hesitated. "Only if you're sure."

She smiled her relaxed smile. "I'm sure."

Will wondered about her attachments, but told himself it was both too soon and too obvious to enquire.

They talked on. She made supper – simple pasta with olive oil and broccoli – and they drank the rest of the wine.

It was after midnight when he left. They parted at the door of the studio and she kissed his cheek lightly. For a moment he was unsure how to leave.

"Thanks," he said. "I'll see you soon."

"Hope so."

"Thanks for listening," he murmured.

"It was a pleasure." They stared silently at each other, and then he was gone into the night.

Chapter 6: Smalls

"Jump, then! Go on, jump." Will heard the commotion and felt the bump from the engine room of *Boy Jack*. It was an East London accent, male, and more than a little irritated. Friday afternoon and the weekenders had arrived.

"Get it nearer, then! I can't jump that far." A female voice responded to the shouted order.

"Bladdy hell, woman. I'm as near as I can get it! Jump bladdy off." There was a loud bang followed by "Christ! Tie the bladdy thing off, then."

Will swung up from the engine room, arms smudged with black oil, and stuck his head tentatively out of the doorway. The speedboat whose name had intrigued him on his first visit to the boatyard – *Sokai* – was at right angles to his own pontoon, her engine burbling and her bows nudging one of the wooden piles. A long smudge of paint along the transom of *Boy Jack* showed where contact had been made, and a blonde, fluffy-haired woman in a blue-and-white-striped Breton jersey and white pedal-pushers lay spreadeagled on the pontoon, a length of rope in her hand. On the foredeck of the boat, his legs surrounded by jumbled coils, was a man in white jeans and a white Arran sweater, a fat cigar-stub clamped between his lips, his face getting redder by the moment.

"Stupid bladdy woman. Tie it off, we're drifting." The pile of fluff in the pedal-pushers scrambled unwillingly to her feet and tied her end of the rope in an elaborate knot to a cleat on the pontoon.

"Now the other one. *Now the other one*," he bellowed as she tottered along the pontoon in her high heels. He hurled at her a tangled web

313

of rope, which dropped into the water just inches from her reach.

"Jesus wept! Where's the boathook? *Where did you put the boathook?*"

The woman, now on the verge of tears, answered in a quiet but frustrated tone: "You're standing on it."

Her tormentor looked down, swore silently to himself and pulled it from beneath his deck shoe. Then he poked and slashed at the water, as though he were stirring a gigantic pot of stew, and eventually hooked out the rope. This he tossed at the woman. She threw up her arms to catch it and received a faceful of muddy seawater as the rope looped itself around her neck.

Screwing up her face, she picked it off and held it at arm's length.

"Pull it, then!"

The woman's patience snapped. "I am pulling it, Jerry MacDermott, and if you don't think I am you can sodding well pull it yourself." Her voice cracked and a tear rolled down her cheek. "Now look what you've made me do! I've broken a nail and I only had a manicure yesterday. Bugger!"

"Have you done? Is that it? Are we tied off?"

"Yes, we are. Tied off and pissed off. I've had enough." And she teetered away down the pontoon in the direction of the jetty and the village, leaving the man to tidy up after her.

He switched off the engine then leapt unsteadily on to the pontoon and caught Will's eye. "'Allo, squire! Sorry about that. Not much of a sailor, my missus." He laughed, without dislodging the cigar, and continued to fasten a tonneau cover over the cockpit of his boat. "She enjoys a glass or two when we've anchored but she's not so hot on the ropes. Wants a bigger boat where she can entertain 'er friends. She'll 'ave one soon but she gets a bit uptight about 'andling this one."

He looked at the transom of *Boy Jack*. "Sorry about the bump. Not that it shows much. 'Ere, 'ang on a minute."

He disappeared below for a few seconds, then emerged with a bottle of whisky.

"Cop 'old of this. Goodwill gesture." He leapt off the front of *Sokai* and walked towards *Boy Jack*.

"No, really. It's OK. I haven't started painting her yet."

"Take it, take it. Sort of welcome present." He offered his hand. "Jerry MacDermott. Live at the big 'ouse – Benbecula – up on the 'ill.

Come down at weekends. The missus misses London but it does 'er good to 'ave a change of air."

The missus was now sitting in a Mercedes on the lane by the jetty.

"You're new 'ere, aren't you, squire?" Will agreed that he was. "Thought so. 'Aven't been 'ere that long ourselves but we know a few faces in the boatyard and the village. Didn't think we'd seen you before. Stayin' long?"

"For a while," admitted Will.

"Lovely spot, ain't it? Olde-worlde charm. Wouldn't mind livin' 'ere full time but the missus wouldn't wear it. Too much of a townie. Likes 'er social life. Still, we've plenty of room to entertain down 'ere and I like gettin' away from it all."

Will smiled, not knowing quite what to make of the East End wideboy who didn't appear short of a bob or two. He was around the fifty mark, sharp as a razor, with dark brown hair that owed its colouring to something in a bottle. His wife was younger, perhaps by twenty years. Probably married him for his money, Will thought.

"You've got your work cut out."

"Sorry?" Will came back to earth.

"With this thing. Bit of a state, ain't it?"

"Yes." Will's pride in his old boat was momentarily bruised, but he found it difficult to disagree.

"As long as you're not thinking of sailing round the world – heh-heh!"

"No, not quite."

"Plenty of character, though, eh?" Jerry MacDermott eyed the boat up and down, seaching in vain for some redeeming characteristic. "Funny name. *Boy Jack*."

"She came originally from Yorkshire."

"Bloody cold up there. Went to Yorkshire once. Couldn't understand a bladdy word they was sayin'."

"What about yours?"

"Eh?"

"Your boat, *Sokai*. What does it mean?"

"'Aven't you guessed?"

"Something Japanese?"

"Nah. It stands for 'Spending Our Kids' Anticipated Inheritance'." He chuckled. "Not that they're *our* kids. My kids. She's my second wife, is Trudie. Got rid of the first one. Couldn't cope with the success.

Wanted to stay in 'Ackney. I couldn't wait to get out. We just grew apart. Well, you've got to enjoy your success, 'aven't you? Can't 'ang around livin' like you used to when funds 'ave improved. Nah. Enjoy it, that's what I say. That's why we're goin' for a bigger boat. If you've got it, flaunt it. That's my motto." He looked around him at the picturesque decay. "Wouldn't mind gettin' my 'ands on this place. Gold mine if it was run proper. Gryler 'asn't a clue." Will could see that Jerry MacDermott was visualizing a fleet of floating gin palaces tied up in a West Country version of Monte Carlo. "Yes. A bit of imagination and you could transform this place. Not a bad idea."

He cast a glance at the Mercedes and the beckoning arm of the blonde inside it. "Well, better be off. She wants to 'ave a look in that new art gallery. Plenty of walls to fill at the big 'ouse. Be seein' you. Keep at it!" He unscrewed the cigar butt from his mouth, tossed it into the water and lurched off down the pontoon in the direction of the gleaming car.

Will shook his head, then turned back to *Boy Jack* and slapped the side of the wheelhouse. He stepped inside and was about to lower himself into the engine room once more when Aitch's head appeared from a hatch on *Florence Nightingale*. "What was all that about?"

Will turned round. "Hi. Oh, just some husband and wife having a disagreement about how to berth a boat."

Aitch looked in the direction of the speedboat. "Ah. Mr MacDermott and his floating bathtub."

"You know him, then?"

"Well, I wouldn't say I know him, but I've encountered him a few times. Bought Benbecula when Hugo Morgan-Giles moved out. Keeps talking about buying the boatyard and sorting it out. I rather hope he never gets round to it. Made his money in mobile phones apparently. Rolling in it. Ha-ha. Lucky man. Think of all the books you could buy if you had that sort of cash."

Will grinned. He'd hardly encountered Aitch in the previous few days. *Florence Nightingale* had been shut up, the curtains inside her port-holes drawn and no sign of her skipper.

"Books?"

"Yes. Wonderful things, books. Never mind all this technology. Who wants to sit and look at a screen when you can turn pages that were printed centuries ago? Look at this . . ." He dived from view inside his vessel, and returned with a mighty leather-bound volume. "Been shopping. Had a few days in Dartmouth. A bit naughty, I know . . ."

Will jumped down from *Boy Jack* and walked across the pontoon to where Aitch was standing with his prize, his eyes shining with excitement.

He opened the large volume, about the size of a family Bible, reverentially, exposing marbled end-papers. He turned several pages to reveal the title: *The History of Devonshire* by the Reverend Richard Polwhele. "Look at that," he instructed, as though he were guiding a party of tourists around ancient ruins. "Been hunting for a good copy for years. Promised it to myself one day." He closed the book and stroked its spine with a loving hand. "All of Devonshire within my grasp." His eyes had a faraway look.

Will was struck by the look of pure pleasure on his face.

"And," said Aitch, "listen to this." He thumbed through the pages. "I thought of you when I read it." He found the page he was looking for and cleared his throat. "'The storm that marked the twenty-seventh of November, 1703, was attended with awful consequences to the western counties . . . Daily intelligence of shipwrecks arrived, whilst great numbers of dead bodies were washed upon the coasts from Hull to Land's End. But the destruction of the *Eddystone Lighthouse* will long fix the memory of this dreadful night. Its architect, Mr Winstanley, had often wished to contemplate a storm from his lighthouse, imagining that the stability of his fabric was proof against the elements. He had his wish; but the violence of the weather increasing to a wonderful degree, his resolution forsook him and he made signals for help. No boat, however, could venture off the shore: and neither lighthouse nor its architect were any more seen. The morning opened on bare rock!'" Aitch closed the book. "What about that?"

"Quite a story, isn't it?" agreed Will.

"You know about it, then?"

"Yes. They replaced it with a lighthouse built by a man called Rudyerd, but that one burned down in 1755. Then came Smeaton, a Yorkshireman who built his lighthouse on the principle of the trunk of an oak tree. You can still see the stump of it, and the one that's there now was built by James Douglass in 1882 – it's the fifth. Winstanley lost his life in the second one he built."

Aitch scratched his head "Well I never. I should have known you'd know."

Will felt guilty at stealing his neighbour's thunder.

"Wonderful thing, knowledge," Aitch went on. "This book's full of it. Amazing chapters – 'The Air and Weather', 'Indigenous Plants', 'The Religion of Danmonium'."

"The what? As distinct from C of E?"

"Danmonium is what the Romans called this part of the world."

"Oh, I see. Which shows that I don't know as much as you thought I did!"

Aitch laughed. "Coffee? I'm just brewing up."

"I'd love some. All I can taste is oil at the moment. It's filthy down there." He indicated the engine room.

"They're fine when they're working," Aitch said, "but when they're not they're a pain in the nether portions. Come on board." And then, seeing that Will was concerned about his state of cleanliness, "Don't worry about the mess. It's not exactly spotless in here."

Will pushed his head through the hatch of *Florence Nightingale*'s wheelhouse and was startled by what he saw. It was like a shrunken Victorian study. The walls of the wheelhouse were almost totally lined with books. A long seat down one side was covered with a threadbare red plush cushion, on which were tin boxes full of artefacts and hanks of rope crafted into Turk's head knots. Bits of brassware gleamed here and there, and there was hardly room to put a foot down for clutter, most of it ancient nautical gear. On an old mahogany table a tarnished sextant tumbled from a broken wooden case. A couple of telescopes were in the process of being fitted with new lenses from a box filled with circular bits of glass and brass ferrules. A stuffed cormorant in an advanced stage of moult surveyed the scene from its glass case perched on a shelf, and plates of half-finished food sat on top of piles of books and periodicals. This was the domestic equivalent of Primrose Hankey's shop.

"Excuse the stuff. Can't seem to stop picking it up. I should have enough of it by now but, well, when you see it looking forlorn at a boat jumble you can't really leave it there, can you?"

"Er, no." Will looked about in vain for somewhere to stand.

Aitch took the kettle off the hob of the tiny stove and poured it into a jug, releasing the pleasing aroma of coffee. "Tell you what, let's have it out there – more room than in here. I'll clear it up soon and show you round properly."

Will backed out of the doorway and on to *Florence Nightingale*'s rope-strewn deck. Aitch thrust a mug of coffee into his hand and asked, "How's the restoration coming on, eh?"

"Slowly. I've had a plumber in to sort out the water, and I'm just cleaning up the engines. I reckon I can do some of the work myself – I've found an old manual. I'm trying to save as much as I can for the hull repairs."

"Mmm." Aitch cast his eye over *Boy Jack*. "She'll clean up well. Good lines. I probably won't be here by the time you finish, though."

"Oh?"

"No. Got to set off soon. Moving back to Devon. 'S where my family came from. Going to Dartmouth or Salcombe. Spend a while there."

"And then what?"

"No idea. Mr Micawber had the right attitude. Something'll turn up." He sipped reflectively at the coffee, his eyes misty. "Well, I'll let you get on. Chuck the mug back when you've done. I've got a telescope to fix. Early one. Probably used by Nelson!" He winked at Will and disappeared whistling 'Rule Britannia'.

Back on *Boy Jack*, Spike, who had been absent all morning, returned with another fish. "If you keep pinching the fishermen's catch we'll be thrown out of here. Go and eat it where no one can see you." Spike rubbed along Will's legs, then lay down in a coil of rope in the pulpit and began to chew off the head of his prey. "You know, you're really quite disgusting," Will muttered. "How we're going to live together in this old wreck I have no idea."

A mooring warp groaned. "I'm sorry. I didn't mean it. You might be a wreck now but in a few weeks – or months – you'll be fine." The rope groaned again under the wash of the tide. "Honest."

Chapter 7: Lizard

Amy Finn's first week at the studio had been quiet. She'd had a few locals sniffing round, but more to find out what this girl who had rented the old capstan house was really like than to invest in her works of art. Some had politely taken their time, going to the trouble of feigning an interest in her work, others had darted in and out in the space of a couple of minutes. She'd had one or two enquiries about her paintings, a few tuts from village matrons at the erotic sculptures, and a few more from those who thought her sea views were overpriced.

Three hundred, thought Amy, is not a lot. Really it isn't. By Thursday night the cello was singing out the Elgar concerto, and by Friday afternoon she was feeling dispirited.

The arrival of a middle-aged London spiv with his candy-floss-haired floozy in tow did nothing to cheer her, and she busied herself quietly with a spot of framing while they looked around, surprised when the floozy made nice noises about the driftwood sculptures. Trudie persuaded her other half that one of them would look good in the hallway of their house up the hill and Jerry MacDermott pulled out a wad of notes, peeled off three fifties and handed them to Amy with a flourish.

"About the paintings . . ."

"Yes?" Amy was hopeful of a sale.

"A word of advice."

"Yes?" She was less hopeful.

"Get a few in that really look like the sea, eh? Might be interested then. Bit simple, these. Bright. But simple. Still, we'll pop back and see how you're goin' in a week or two. We'll need some pictures and it's nice to patronize local talent. Take care, sunshine. Ta-ta."

Amy stood open-mouthed as they departed, then looked at the notes in her hand and walked over to the cash desk. As she slipped the money into the drawer she admonished herself: "It is not up to you to tell them what they like, Amy, just provide them with what they want." She looked up at one of her paintings. "Get a few that really look like the sea . . ." Then she laughed, a brief, ironic sound, before going back to her frame, expecting to be undisturbed for the next half-hour.

She cleaned a pane of glass, cut a new cardboard mount with a craft knife and was just about to frame a print of Lamorna Cove when the door opened again. She turned round to offer a greeting to her customer, but as soon as she saw his face she found herself lost for words.

He looked at her with a casual smile, exuding a mixture of self-satisfaction and arrogance. "Hallo, Ame!"

The hairs on the back of her neck bristled. She could not find her voice.

"Surprised?" He looked at her with one eyebrow raised.

She tried to answer but could not, then managed, "How did you . . . ?"

"Know you were here? Find you? I asked a few questions. Simple really." He was dressed entirely in black, his chiselled features emphasized by a polo-neck sweater under a black jacket. He leaned casually against the side of the door.

"You shouldn't be here."

"Yes, I should. I wanted to see you. And, anyway, you've got my sculptures." He pointed to the two erotic figures in the centre of the floor.

"I'm selling them. I don't want them any more."

"You can't sell them. They're us." He looked irritated, his pride wounded.

"That's why I don't want them." Having turned pale at the sight of him, the colour now rose in her cheeks and fire leapt into her heart. "How dare you come back? How dare you find me here? You have no right to come barging in . . ." She ran out of words.

"I opened the door. It wasn't locked. I didn't barge, I stepped." The words were heavily overlaid with sarcasm.

"But why?" Her voice cracked. Desperation and sadness were now mixed with the anger: desperation at not being free of the clutches of the man she had tried to wipe from her life, sadness at his continuing interference, and anger at her own feeble response to his persistent harassment.

"What do you mean, why? It's obvious, isn't it?"

Her eyes rose heavenward. "Please go away, Oliver. Please, *please*, go away."

He walked towards her and placed his hands on her upper arms. She turned her head away from him.

"Look at me."

She strained her head even further away.

"Look at me, Ame!" He shook her, pressing his fingers into her flesh, and she turned to him. His nearness made her heart beat faster. His face had a strength and beauty that made her weak.

He spoke softly now. "I want to see you. I need to see you. Come on!" He shook her again. "Why did you run away?" He sighed impatiently. "Your knee will mend, you know. Why won't you believe in yourself? If you really want to we can dance again. You just have to want to. Why won't you?" He lifted a hand and stroked her hair. She turned her cheek and winced.

"We can't . . . I can't find it . . ."

"Why?" Oliver Gallico was even more insistent.

"Because – because I've had enough." He pressed himself closer to her and a wave of fear overwhelmed her. "I don't want this any more. I'm so tired of . . . being tired. Hurt and tired." She let out a sob. All strength seemed to be leaving her. She was trying hard not to resign herself to the usual course of events. The trying to escape and the failure to get far enough away. Her inability to shake him off. His inability to understand that she really did want to escape. She thought that down here, at the edge of the world, she might at last have eluded him but she should have known he would find her, would persuade some young dancer desperate for promotion to wheedle Amy's whereabouts out of her friends.

She felt so hopeless, so fatigued by it all. Perhaps unhappiness and frustration were to be her lot. The prospect shook her. She lifted her arms and flung off his hands. "Just go. It's too late. I'm not here for you any more. You can't keep behaving like this."

He looked at her disbelievingly, and had begun to approach her again when a rattling sound surprised him.

Amy turned and saw Will standing in the doorway. "Can I come in?"

"Yes. This gentleman was just going."

"I'm not," he said defiantly.

"Yes, you are."

He looked hard at her, but Amy stood her ground. Gallico shrugged and walked to the door. "Your loss." At the threshold he turned. "I'll see you later." He glanced expressionlessly at Will, then back at Amy before stepping out into the street and closing the door silently behind him.

Will watched him go, then turned to Amy. Thoughts whirled around in his head. What had happened? Who was the man? What had he done to Amy? He blurted out, "What was all that about? Are you OK?"

"No, I'm not OK." There was anger in her voice, then apology. "I'm sorry. Yes, I'm fine. I think. Funny, I thought I could make a new life here and my old one has just caught up with me." She sniffed, and tried to smile, feeling in her pockets for a tissue. Will handed her a slightly oily one. She thanked him and blew her nose.

"Do you want some tea?" he asked. It was feeble, but it always seemed to work in *The Archers*.

"No, thanks, I couldn't." And then, "Oh, yes. Why not."

"Come on. Upstairs." He motioned her to the staircase then stepped to the door, shot the bolt, turned round the Open sign to read Closed and pulled down the blind before following her to the apartment above.

"You picked a good time to come in." She smiled at him.

"I'm not sure I did." He filled the kettle and switched it on, then gathered together the cups, milk and teabags.

"Oh, you did. I don't know what would have happened if you hadn't."

"So you do know him?"

"Oh, yes. All too well. He's been in my life for eleven years. Eleven years," she repeated, as though she could not believe it herself. "Eleven years of torture, one way or another."

She made the tea, and then, as she carried a mug over to him, she explained, "His name is Oliver Gallico. He's the artistic director of the Ballet d'Azur."

"I should have guessed that. He looks the part."

"And acts it. He'd be funny if he wasn't so serious. He's so up himself it's not true. When I first met him he was with Rambert. A soloist. Brilliant. Drop-dead good looks, an amazing dancer. He took a shine to me. We started dancing together and then we became lovers, off and on – more off than on for me. He was arrogant – *is* arrogant – but I could cope with that. He has such a tremendous talent. I tried not to love him but you know what it's like." She looked at Will, half smiling and almost apologetic. "You can't always love the people you feel you should love."

"No," he said quietly.

"Anyway, it was pretty intense. But he started getting violent. Nothing serious at first, just heavy-handed. He's very strong – beautifully made," she said, ruefully, but Will caught the sparkle in her eyes. "Then it began to get out of hand. He'd really hurt me when we were . . . you know. He never struck me or anything, it was just a sort of rough brutality. I wasn't physically strong enough to stand up to it. I used to hurt for days afterwards."

Will was appalled and saddened by what he was hearing. "The bastard," he said softly, his face suffused with fury.

"Then he'd say things about me that really hurt. God, it sounds so pathetic. He'd tell me about other dancers in the company. About what they had that I hadn't got. It was clear that I wasn't the only woman in his life." She paused and sipped her tea, leaning against the wall.

Will looked at her incredulously. "Why didn't you leave?"

"I was trapped. Mesmerized. Under his spell – whatever you want to call it. I wanted to dance with him – had to dance with him. Then he decided to leave and set up his own company. Couldn't bear to be told what to do by other people. He asked me to go with him. I said no, that I wanted to stay with Rambert. I think I knew by then that I had to get away. Finally I saw my opportunity. But he wore me down. Pitiful, isn't it? Why didn't I just tell him to sod off? I wish I knew."

"So you went with him?"

"Not at first. Only after a few months. I didn't seem to be getting anywhere with Rambert. My dancing had lost its spark. To tell the truth I missed the excitement of his company. We were great together. Some kind of telepathy, two people dancing as one. You can't make that happen, however good a dancer you are. Either it's there or it isn't. The technique can be brilliant, but if there's no chemistry the result is soulless. I've never felt elation – exhilaration – like I felt when we danced together." Her cheeks were colouring, her eyes glowed. Then she talked of her injury, the evaporation of confidence that followed and his unbearable lack of feeling and disdain at her inability to dance with him. His suggestion that her weakness had ruined his career.

"But he's still in your life?"

"He wants to be. He doesn't believe my career is over. Says that a meniscectomy isn't the end. That I could come back if I believed in myself enough to work it through. Other dancers have had the same injury and gone back. I also think he feels I owe him something. He still directs Ballet d'Azur but he rarely dances. He says he doesn't want to dance with anybody else. Instead he sculpts. Those two are his." She pointed to the writhing figures in the centre of the studio. "They're supposed to be him and me. I can't bear to look at them so I thought I'd try and sell them to make some money. But I think I'll just cover them up and stick them in a back room. They don't seem to have brought me much luck."

"Do you think he'll come back?"

"Oh, I know he will."

He put his hands on her shoulders. She noticed the difference in touch between his hands and Oliver's. The strength was there, but the contact was lighter. "You know where I am. If you have any trouble come round whenever you like. You shouldn't have to feel like this."

She looked up at the slight, dark man before her, whose own life had been torn apart by tragedy. There he stood, in a fisherman's sweater several sizes too big for him, his bare feet showing above the deck shoes beneath a worn pair of sailing trousers.

"Thank you. You're very kind." She smiled into his eyes. Yesterday she had almost believed she had finally escaped the past; today she seemed manacled to it.

"I'll go," he said gently. "Thanks for the tea. Just let me know if I can do anything."

"I will. Thanks." She shot him another smile and he felt a surge of protectiveness.

"By the way, what did you come for?" she asked.

"I brought the rest of the boats. There are five." He picked up the bubble-wrapped parcels from just inside the door where he had left them. "I thought they'd be safer here than with me while all the work's going on. Has anyone shown any interest in the other?"

"Not yet, but they will. It's only been a few days, and we've the weekend ahead of us now. Just watch this space."

"I will. And don't forget, you know where I am."

Chapter 8: Mumbles

Saturday lunchtime in the Salutation was not the time for a quiet, contemplative drink. While not exactly heaving this early in the season, it was still thronged with locals aware that soon their time would not be their own. Pencurnow Cove fell short of being a tourist honeypot in summer, but it relied more heavily now on day-trippers than it had in the past, thanks to its dwindling fishing fleet.

Over the past couple of years the number of ships in glass cases inside the pub had grown as the fleet declined outside. The place had seen an influx of decorative glass floats, fishing nets, binnacles and brass telegraphs, but it had still not shed the seediness of a former life. The ashtrays were too full and the lavatories too malodorous for the ladies, which meant that the clientele in the off-season was predominantly male.

Ted Whistler leaned over one end of the bar, ordered his customary pint and lit his Camel cigarette, drawing the rich mixture deep into his perished lungs. The reason for Ted's profound personal sorrow was lost in the mists of time. He'd probably even forgotten himself. He was, and always had been, a miserable sod whose glass was always half empty rather than half full.

A trio of fishermen muttered in desultory fashion at the other end of the bar, while the landlord Alf Penrose attended to the wants of an increasing number of customers, his pint pulling only slightly impeded by the size of his gut, the legacy of a lifetime spent drinking ullage.

By the time Len Gryler arrived he had to shoulder his way to the bar. "Pint of best, landlord," he shouted, over the swelling din. "And a lager for the lad." Christopher Applebee slouched over to the pin-ball machine.

The landlord looked round, nodded to acknowledge the order, while serving a cycling couple who had rashly committed themselves to one of his cholesterol specials, extravagantly described on the menu as Mixed Grill.

Had each of his creations carried an indication of the amount of saturated fat they contained this one would have warranted a public health warning. He pushed a note of the order through the hatch at the back of the bar, from which steam, the noise of an impatient cook and the fragrance of burning oil emanated in rich mixture, then waddled over to the pumps and pulled Gryler his pint.

"How's trade?" he enquired of his maritime regular.

"Not bad, not bad."

"I should think you're quids in, aren't you, after selling that rotting hulk?"

"What do you mean, 'rotting hulk'? That's a seaworthy vessel of historical importance, that is. Rescued hundreds from Dunkirk during the war. Only wish I'd known that at the time. Might have got a bit more for her."

"More? Dream on!" Penrose smiled.

"So how's the ex-lighthouse keeper?" Gryler asked of the hunched figure next to him at the bar.

"No better for you asking," replied Whistler, pulling on his pint.

"Your mate's a damn sight more cheerful than you are."

"Huh. I don't know why. He's got no reason to be."

"Well, at least he's keeping himself busy doing that boat up. Can't let yerself slide." Whatever accusations were levelled at Gryler (and there were a goodly number) indolence was not on the list. A rogue he might be, but he was a busy one. "'Ere! Sunshine! Yer lager's ready!" he roared across the bar. Young Applebee waved acknowledgement without turning round, evidently at some crucial point in his pin-ball wizardry.

"Want to get yourself a job," offered Gryler.

"What, like yours?"

"Why not?"

"Couldn't risk being found out."

"What do you mean?"

"You know what I mean," muttered Ted, into his receding pint. He was well aware of Gryler's reputation as a dealer in all things shady and a purveyor of goods of doubtful provenance.

"Just you be careful what you say in here," whispered Gryler. "Them fishing floats has ears."

"Anyway, I've had a job," countered Ted. "Having a rest now."

"Suit yerself. Elliott obviously doesn't agree with you. Working like a Trojan. Seems to be getting on with Aitch, too. Couple of oddballs together, if you ask me. Nutty as a fruitcake, Aitch. He's been setting off for Devon every week for the past three years, and he's still here. But at least Elliott looks as if he's enjoying himself."

"Just because he's busy it doesn't mean to say he's happy," said Ted. "Everybody has their way of coping – his is to keep busy."

"Is that why he enjoyed lighthouse keeping?" Gryler winked at the landlord. "I thought you only worked for a month and then had a month off. And when you were on duty you were on shift work. More time off than the rest of us put together."

"Aye, well, you keep busy. Well, *he* did."

"What doing?"

"Making his boats. Writing up his diary."

"Not much going on round here to write about."

"Nature diary – birds. Staring out to sea most of the time, then writing up notes of what he saw in the evening."

Christopher Applebee came over and took his lager. "Ta," he said, before going back to his machine.

"Every day?" Gryler sounded interested, but there was also a note of unease in his voice.

"Every day."

"Sounds a bit boring."

"I suppose it does to you, but you notice things when you're a lighthouse keeper."

"What sort of things?" He was fishing, and probably not for the first time that day.

"Anything out of the ordinary. Weird weather. Movements of shipping. Bird migration."

"Sounds bloody boring to me."

"Aye, well, it would. It bored me in the end. Glad to get out of it."

Gryler drained his glass and thumped it back on the bar. "This conversation's depressing me. Give us a couple of pies, Alf, and I'll be off. Might as well sit in me shed and eat 'em." He tossed a couple of pound coins on the bar, then retreated with his lunch, leaving his assistant to play with his balls.

She might have known he wouldn't come back straight away. Oliver had always liked to keep her waiting, to make her nervous. He had succeeded. Since the previous evening she had been on edge, hardly sleeping, making sure the door was properly locked, alternately sweating and shivering.

In the morning she had showered and put on a clean pair of Levi's, some canvas shoes and a pale blue shirt. She tied back her hair and opened the studio at nine thirty, determined to carry on her life and not be threatened by his impending return.

Thankfully, customers had been in and out all morning, taking her mind off the situation a little. Late in the afternoon her spirits had lifted with the arrival of a smartly dressed middle-aged man, who was interested in buying a painting. Hugo Morgan-Giles introduced himself and welcomed her to Pencurnow Cove. "We've had quite a few artists in the past but I'm sure you'll make a go of it. I think your paintings are wonderful. Where did you study? St Martin's?"

"No. No . . . I wish I had. I haven't studied anywhere. I'm self-taught."

"Really? Remarkable!" He looked closely at her work, leaning forward with his arms held behind his back and making appreciative noises.

He was the epitome of the English gentleman, she thought, from his highly polished brogues to his neatly brushed receding fair hair. He was in his early fifties, she guessed, corduroy trousers of good cut, and a bottle-green cashmere sweater with a touch of cravat showing above the checked shirt at his neck. Even the signet ring was in place on the little finger of his left hand.

"Did you paint these down here?" he asked, gazing at one seascape with intense interest.

"No. From memory. But I want to paint from life now that I'm here."

He turned and smiled at her. "I hope it doesn't spoil your technique!"

"Me, too!"

"Look, I rather like this one. Is it for sale?" He pointed to the scene of an azure blue bay, surrounded by a white curve of sand.

"Well . . . yes. Would you like to take it now?"

"Could I come back with my wife to make sure she likes it? I think it will be OK but I really ought to check. Could you put a red spot on it, or whatever it is you do?"

"Yes, of course."

"I'd say yes straight away but I don't want to be told we haven't the space for it. There was always plenty at Benbecula, but since we've been down at the Moorings it's a bit tighter." He looked slightly embarrassed.

"I'm happy to reserve it for a few days."

"Marvellous. Well, I've enjoyed meeting you, Miss . . . er . . ."

"Finn. Amy Finn."

"I'll be back, Miss Finn. And very good luck with your enterprise. I'm sure it will work." He walked to the door, then paused as something caught his eye. "That's nice." He pointed at Will's Cornish coble, then walked over to it. She had stood it on a solid chunk of oak just inside the door. "I haven't seen one so well fashioned for a long time. Did you make it?"

"No. Will Elliott did. The lighthouse keeper that was."

Hugo picked it up and examined it. "This is excellent." He looked closely at the cut of the planking, the intricate copper riveting and the flawless varnish. "I'll have it."

"Goodness."

"Well, you see, I don't have to ask about this. It's for my study and that's my domain!" He looked at the price tag. "Are you sure this is right?"

"Yes. I think so."

He pulled a chequebook from his back pocket. "I'll round it up." He gave her the completed cheque.

"Do tell Mr Elliott that he really ought to price them a little higher or he'll never keep pace with demand. They must take so long to make that he should be well recompensed."

"I'll tell him. I'm sure he'll be pleased."

Amy wrapped the coble in its original tissue paper and a square of bubble wrap then put the cheque in the back compartment of the cash drawer.

"Well, thank you again. And I'll be back at some point with Mouse – sorry, my wife – and I'm sure we'll have the painting, too. Goodbye!"

As the door closed she could not resist a loud "Yessss," and she punched the air. For a few seconds she forgot her troubles and felt a flush of satisfaction, even thrill, at her first sale. She had sold a painting, and that must make her a painter. For the first time in her life she had earned money from something other than dancing, and she glimpsed a chink of light in the gloom that had lately surrounded her.

She looked at her watch. Five to six. She would close the studio, have a long soak in the bath then find Will and give him his money. She would also tell him the good news about her own painting. Nervously she opened the door of the studio and looked out. Behind Bill's Island there were clouds on the horizon – prophetic, she thought – and a gentle breeze was blowing in off the sea. But the lane was empty. There was no sign of the expected dark figure hovering in the shadows. She stepped back inside, flipped the sign to Closed, pulled down the linen blind and locked the door.

Oil was in his hair, underneath his fingernails and his clothing reeked of it. Even the cat had begun to turn up his nose. It was time to have a break from the sordid confines of the engine room and think about supper. He replaced the hatch, cleared up the assorted bits of oil filter and rubber hose then set about washing in the hip-bath. It made a change from the bucket, and he'd perfected a way of using very little water and even less soap in deference to the plumbing on the boat and the marine life in the boatyard.

He was drying himself, concealed from the outside world by a newly purchased shower curtain, sporting seahorses and starfish (the least garish that Primrose Hankey could supply), when he heard Aitch's now familiar "Halloo." He wrapped the towel around himself, clambered up into the wheelhouse and stuck his head out of the door.

"What are you doing for supper tonight?" enquired Aitch.

"Hadn't thought. Too busy with my heaps of metal."

"Right, then. Dinner will be served in one hour. Aperitifs in twenty minutes. Does that suit?"

Will was taken aback at the offer of hospitality, then suddenly realized how hungry he was. "I'd love to."

"Fine. I'll see what I can rustle up from the gastronomic Aladdin's cave that purports to be my larder. Most of it will be unidentifiable, but it should at least be edible." With that he vanished and a clattering of pans and crockery ensued.

When Will emerged from *Boy Jack* twenty minutes later, with the punctuality born of six years' shift work, he was welcomed aboard *Florence Nightingale* with enthusiasm.

"Come in, come in! Ah, yes, and you can come, too."

Will looked round in the direction of Aitch's gaze and saw Spike peering at them. Slowly he sauntered towards *Florence Nightingale*, trod tentatively over the threshold. He pummelled the red plush seat cover with his paws, his whiskers twitching as they took in the rich aroma of cooking. Then he saw the stuffed cormorant. The hair on his back became vertical and he spat wildly at it before leaving the cabin without touching the floor.

"Oops. I don't think he's taken to Draculus."

For the rest of the evening Spike sat and stared at them through the cabin window.

Aitch had gone to great trouble for his guest and it occurred to Will that the invitation had not been quite as spontaneous as it had seemed. For a start there was space to sit among the nautical paraphernalia, and the table was laid with a deep red cloth, cutlery and glasses. Nothing matched – there was one plate of this pattern and one of that – but the effect was welcoming, especially when lit by the glow of paraffin lamps as the sun set.

They were sipping a glass of sherry apiece – Aitch's recommendation – and Aitch was poking and prodding at a clutch of pans on the stove, in a galley lined with bottles of spices and chutneys, when they heard footsteps on the pontoon outside and a polite "Is anybody there?"

Will looked up to see Amy peering into his boat. "Hi!" he called. "I'm over here!"

"Hallo! They told me this one was yours." She pointed at *Boy Jack*.

"She is, but I'm over here for supper."

Aitch put his head out of a hatch. "Company?"

"Aitch, this is Amy Finn. She's running the Roundhouse Gallery – sorry, Studio. She's trying to sell my boats."

"Not trying to sell them. Selling them." She took an envelope from her pocket and waved it in the air.

"Crikey! Have you got rid of it, then?"

"Yup. And a painting – I think."

"Good for you!"

Aitch endeavoured to continue stirring his culinary creation while leaning out of the hatch. "Have you eaten, Miss Finn? Would you like to join the sailors for supper?"

"Oh, I couldn't. I'd love to but I only came to give Will his money." Then she added guiltily, "Minus my ten per cent."

Aitch dropped his spoon and clapped his hands together. "Well, stay, then. There's plenty for three. A spot of female company would be very pleasant. I promise we'll have no salty sea talk!"

"Oh, what a shame! But I'd love to, if you're sure."

"Come aboard, then."

Amy picked her way among the coils of rope, the lowering sunlight glinting on her curls now freed from their daytime ties. Will was relieved by the change in her from the previous day, although she seemed tense at his proximity. He moved along the red plush seat to make room for her. It was a tight squeeze, in spite of Aitch's clearing up, and he found himself closer to her than he had been before. He felt a sudden thrill.

She pushed the envelope of notes into his top pocket, almost afraid to touch him, as Aitch passed her a sherry.

"Cheers."

"Cheers!" she responded, and sipped at the tawny liquid from the dainty engraved glass. 'Trafalgar – 21st October 1805', it read, and there was a depiction of the *Victory* firing its cannon.

"This is lovely!"

"The sherry or the glass?" asked Will.

"The glass."

"Probably used by Nelson," quipped Aitch.

"Along with the telescope," added Will.

"Well, you never know," said Aitch, and winked at him.

They dined more lavishly than Will had anticipated from Aitch's invitation: crab bisque was followed by seafood risotto, then crème brûlée.

They sat and drank and talked as though they were old friends. The dry white wine gave way to a full-bodied red, and the faces of the three, flushed with warmth and wine, became more animated.

"Oh, I've forgotten Auntie Betty!" exclaimed Aitch. He leapt to his feet and out of the hatch. He reappeared rolling up a red ensign on its staff. "Left her out after dusk. Bad form. Sorry, Auntie Betty." He laid the furled flag on the long, narrow shelf that was clearly her nocturnal resting place.

The two onlookers laughed and Will noticed that Amy now seemed happy to be sitting close to him, comfortable and relaxed in his company. Occasionally she would rest her hand on his arm to make a point. He was acutely aware of how good it felt. He wished that the evening would never end.

Aitch was recounting one of the more outrageous episodes of his life at school when Amy complained, "But you still haven't told us what the Aitch stands for."

"Oh, my dear girl, you don't really want to know that."

"I do!" She leaned back against Will.

"Come on!" Will said. "We need to know. We deserve to know! It can't be that bad!" He put his arm around her shoulders and she leaned into him.

"Oh, it is," replied Aitch.

"Well, my full name is Amaryllis," confessed Amy.

"Amaryllis?" Will spluttered.

"Yes." She giggled. "Grim, isn't it?"

"Oh, I don't know. It has a touch of class." He pulled her close again and she giggled.

"Amaryllis is as nought compared with mine," mused Aitch, with just a hint of moroseness.

"Come on, then."

He blustered some more, then eventually drew a large breath. "You need to understand a bit about my background. The Utterly family come from a long line of retailers. Retail. Not wholesale. Tut-tut. Below the salt." He took another sip of the rich red wine. "My father followed his father into the bakery and he hoped that I would do the same, continuing the Utterly tradition of baking loaves for the gentry. That was why he generously bestowed on me a name that he hoped would spur me on my endeavours. But it had the reverse effect. It put me off for life. I was christened in honour of my father's favourite loaf. My name is Hovis Utterly."

Will and Amy wanted to be polite. They tried to be polite. They sat holding one another for at least fifteen seconds before dissolving into fits of laughter.

At first Hovis regarded them dolefully, but eventually joined them in wild hilarity. From then on, he knew they would never call him Aitch again, but for the first time in his life he didn't really mind.

*

It was twenty past twelve when they left. She'd looked nervous suddenly at the prospect of departure and he saw the fear in her eyes. "I'll walk you back."

"It's OK."

"No, I don't want you walking there on your own." The words came naturally and she made no further protest.

They went along the jetty towards the lane, his arm around her shoulders, keeping her close, and her fear subsided. They talked casually, about Aitch and about the meal, then stopped by the railings of the jetty and looked out over the sea, the moon streaking the water with silver, and the clouds shot through with orange and purple.

She caught her breath. "Isn't it beautiful?" she said softly.

"Beautiful," he agreed, but for once his mind was not on the sea. They stood quietly for a while, then she shivered a little and they walked on up the lane.

At the door of the studio she turned to face him. "Thank you for a really lovely evening."

"No. Thank *you*." He looked at her face. Before he knew it she had wrapped her arms around his neck, drawn his face to hers and kissed him with a tenderness he had all but forgotten. They paused briefly and he put his arms around her, held her even closer, stroking the back of her head and kissing her again.

Eventually they drew slightly apart, and she rested her head on his chest. He inhaled the fragrance of the soft skin at the nape of her neck and rocked her for a while. At last she lifted her head and said, "Thank you for being there."

"I'm always here. Just let me know when you need me." He squeezed her to reassure her. "I'd better go. You've the studio to open in the morning and I've a boat-builder to see about my planking."

"How romantic."

He smiled at her, then realized with a profound shock that this had been his first intimacy since Ellie's death. The pleasure of the moment was replaced by a stinging sensation of guilt, which he did his best to mask.

She saw it. "Are you all right?"

"I'm just a bit out of practice."

She pulled him to her again and held him close. "I'll see you soon, I hope."

"Yes. Are you sure you'll be OK?"

"Sure. Go now. And take care."

"*You* take care."

She nodded silently. He turned as she reached the bottom step. "Lock it."

"I will."

He heard the mechanism click home as he walked back down the moonlight-washed lane. For the first time in six years he felt alive. His fingers seemed to be tingling, his head reeling with an intoxication not wholly due to the wine. Yet the guilt deep inside him gnawed at his heart.

He paused by the railings where they had stopped on the way up, and looked out across the moonlit waves. His mind swam with conflicting emotions. Below him the sea toppled on to the loose pebbles, sucking them away then flinging them back. He gripped the cold iron railings as tears filled his eyes, and he shook uncontrollably as his words spilled out over the sea. "I have to go on. I have to live. I can't stay, Ellie. Don't make me stay. Please . . . let . . . me . . . go." For the first time since her death, he looked to the heavens and sobbed.

Chapter 9: Inner Dowsing

The boat-builder had good and bad news. The good news was that the state of *Boy Jack*'s hull was better than Will had feared. The bad news was that for the duration of the work – around two weeks – she would have to come out of the water and would be uninhabitable.

The prospect of having to find a temporary home threw him into confusion. It had not occurred to him that he would have to live elsewhere while the work proceeded, but the builder was adamant. The clearer the decks, so to speak, the faster the work could be done.

The whole scheme had not been without its ups and downs. Gryler, anxious for as much profitable work as possible, had been less than pleased when, out of courtesy, Will had asked if another boat-builder could come to the yard to work on *Boy Jack*.

"Is he accredited?" he asked, officiously. The irony of the remark was not lost on Will, but he felt it best to play along.

"Yes. He advertises in *Classic Boat*, and he's well established as a restorer of wooden craft."

"Only I don't want any old Tom, Dick and 'Arry comin' in 'ere and givin' the yard a bad name."

"No. Quite." It was the best response he could think of under the circumstances.

"I suppose you'll be wanting to use my boat lift?" asked Gryler, waving in the direction of the rusting metal giant alongside the jetty.

"Please."

"It'll cost yer. It's free if I do the work but I have to charge for it when I don't."

"That's fine."

"When do you want to get her out, then?"

"Some time this week – as soon as I can sort out temporary accommodation."

"Aye, well, I suppose that'll be all right. It's irregular, though. Do you know where you're going to put her?"

"Er . . . well, I was hoping . . ."

"Hoping what?" Gryler was doing his best to be tricky. He stood firm in his oil-encrusted boiler-suit, his trademark wrench clasped in his right hand like a sceptre.

"I was hoping that you could help me out by letting me put her over there." Will pointed towards an area of hard standing to one side of the yard.

"What? Just like that?"

"Well . . ."

Gryler was intent on extracting as much from this encounter as he could. "I shall have to charge."

"But you'll have the berth free while I'm out of the water."

"Not the same. I've had no chance to advertise it, and who's going to come and take it at this time of year? Specially on a temporary basis. I suppose you'll be wanting it again when your boat goes back in the water?"

Will remained silent, thoroughly miserable at the thought of having to grovel to Gryler every time he needed anything out of the ordinary.

"How long would you want to be there for?"

"Just a couple of weeks."

"A hundred pounds a week."

"What? But you agreed to three months' free berthing when I bought the boat."

"In the water, not out of it." He slapped the wrench in the palm of his left hand. "Call it a hundred and fifty quid for the fortnight and I'll throw in the use of my lift."

"A hundred."

"Hah!" He laughed derisively. "Oh, go on, then. I'm a fool to meself where boats is concerned. Where's that lad got to? Better get him to grease the nipples." He beamed at Will, confident that he'd come out ahead.

Will watched him head back to the peeling hut and cursed under his breath at the loss of another hundred quid that he could ill afford.

He tramped back to the boat, climbed aboard, and slammed the kettle on the gas burner. He looked around him at the squalor.

"Shit," he muttered, under his breath. He had just a few thousand pounds put away, five model boats to sell, and a voyage ahead of him. How was he going to survive? He looked across at *Florence Nightingale*. Hovis Utterly. Now there was a happy man. How did he make ends meet? He didn't seem to have any income. Perhaps he had a hidden legacy.

The kettle whistled and he made himself a mug of coffee. There was no sign of Spike. It occurred to him that the ship's cat had yet to meet Amy. He'd put her out of his mind during the encounter with Gryler, though she'd been in his thoughts constantly since the night before. But he hardly knew her – had met her just three times. How could she come even close to Ellie?

He'd tried to come to terms with the tragedy, to counsel himself rationally, but six years on he still could not bring himself to admit that Ellie was dead. He could not form the words, even in his thoughts. The reason was plain. Inside him she was still alive. Every hour of every day she was with him. Her face was as clear as day – the short black bob of her hair, the wide almond-shaped eyes, the way her face crinkled when she smiled. He could still see her naked. He could still feel the touch of her skin, her hand in his, hear her teasing him and getting irritated when he was stubborn about something in-consequential. But last night a part of him had been trying to move on.

Amy had come into his life with all the force of an earthquake, rocking him to his foundations. The merest hint of resentment crossed his mind. He had had enough anguish already without falling in love. Yet he saw her face in his mind's eye and the resentment faded. He wondered where she was now, what she was doing and what she was thinking.

He drank his coffee quickly and looked through the port-hole at the morning. It was bright, and a stiff breeze blew from the south-west. He needed a walk. He would take the coastal path to the lighthouse and see how Ernie was getting on. It was time he called in. Ernie would think he had been forgotten.

Will pulled the sailing jacket around him against the force of the breeze as he rounded the corner from the boatyard. He looked across at the Roundhouse and saw that the blind was down on the door and the Closed sign in position. He checked his watch. Five past nine. She must be having a lie-in. He looked for some sign that all was well. He thought about knocking but didn't want to alarm her. Nor did he know where to pick up the threads of the night before. He strode on, up the lane and past the little cottage known as the Moorings, where a middle-aged man in a tweed jacket and corduroys was looking out across the cove with a pair of binoculars.

Will looked in the same direction. The woman with the pea-brained Labrador was at her stick-throwing as usual, and a couple of fishing boats butted their way through the water, which was generously sprinkled with white horses.

"Good morning," Will greeted the man as he passed.

"Morning." The man was startled, then recovered himself. "Lovely day for a walk."

"Hope so. I think I'd rather be on land than out there today."

"Yes. Bit choppy, isn't it?"

Will carried on up the hill.

The top of the lane petered out into a rough footpath that led across the cliffs. Benbecula was the only house that remained above him now. He gazed up at it on its lofty eminence and thought what good views it must have of the bay.

Sitting down on the tussocky grass through which the thrift was pushing its flower spikes, he took out his binoculars and watched as the boats at sea headed off in different directions, one to the east, and the other westwards towards Bill's Island. This, he reflected, was what he would be doing in a couple of months' time. The prospect thrilled and frightened him at the same time.

The boat heading towards Bill's Island looked familiar. He took in the markings on the bows – PZ 291 – it was Gryler's, an old fishing smack he had obviously bought for a song from a redundant fisherman. Christopher Applebee was at the tiller in yellow oilskins and there were lobster pots and fishing lines in the bottom of the boat. A bit of poaching, like as not, thought Will. He put away the binoculars and continued his climb.

The path levelled out on the cliff top and, on the promontory of Prince Albert Rock, he could see the lighthouse. Three sandpipers wheeled overhead, buffeted by the breeze, and as he rounded the cove he noticed a small figure ahead of him, seated and looking out to sea.

As he came closer he saw the easel, and instantly realized it was Amy.

Fearful of startling her he began to whistle.

She turned round, irritated at first by the intrusion then pleased to see him. "Hi!"

"Hi, yourself. You're up early."

"I thought I'd have a breath of fresh air and see if I could get any inspiration." She remained seated, the wind blowing strands of coppery hair across her face. He leaned down and kissed her cheek. She put her arm around his leg as he stood beside her, and he felt a surge of warmth in spite of the breeze.

It was a brief touch, but reassuring. He crouched beside her as she continued to paint.

"How do you stop everything blowing away in this wind?" he asked.

"Clothes-pegs and will-power." She grinned.

He studied the beginnings of the painting. "It looks good."

"Oh, it's only a quick daub. Just a few ideas. I can't stay long – I'll have to open up in half an hour but I thought a breath of fresh air would do me good." She began to pack away her brushes. "Where are you off to?"

He stood up. "I'm on my way to see my old boss. Haven't dropped in on him since I left and I'm feeling a bit guilty."

"Well, don't get blown away."

"I won't. I'll see you later." He was unsure whether or not to kiss her again. He settled for stroking his hand across the top of her head, and felt again the texture of her hair. They both recognized the awkwardness of the moment, neither quite sure how to pick up the threads. Will smiled and walked on across the cliff top, leaving Amy to pick up her bag and her chair and set off towards the lane.

"We thought you'd forgotten us." Ernie Hallybone was only half serious, but Will apologized for his long absence.

"How's the boat coming along?" May asked, as she ferried the kettle from the stove to the table.

"Slowly. I've got to get her out of the water for a couple of weeks while the hull is sorted out and that means I'll have to find somewhere else to live." The moment he had said it he realized it might sound as though he were angling for accommodation.

May jumped in immediately. "Well, you'll be welcome here. Your old flat has been turned into part of the visitor centre but we've a spare room at our end. Your odds and ends are stored there, anyway. Why don't you come here?"

"No, really, that's not why I came. I mean, that's not why I said it."

May laughed her free and easy laugh, and her plump cheeks reddened even more than usual. "I know. But it's up to you. There's always a room here for you if you want. Now, then, are you joining us for breakfast? Eggs from the Marans, bacon and sausage from the pig, and beans from Mr Heinz."

Will did his best to decline, but the sound of the bacon and sausages sizzling on the old stove and the sparkle in May's eyes meant that he hadn't a chance. Ernie brightened at the prospect of company, and Will sat down at the table, as his old boss gave him chapter and verse on the current developments at Prince Albert Rock.

"*The Gull*'s been useful."

"I'm glad."

"Caught a couple of mackerel off the back of her for tea last night. Made a change from pig."

"Don't you go knocking my pork and bacon, Ernie Hallybone. Keeps us alive it does," May scolded from her position by the stove. She stood there, every inch the farmer's wife, errant strands of hair escaping from the bun at the back of her head.

"How's the farm?" asked Will.

"Lambs aren't worth a penny piece but folk still wants bacon and sausages," May replied, "but I do it for us, really, rather than anyone else."

They tucked into a hearty breakfast, catching up on local news. May was still running her smallholding single-handed, though she'd cut it down to five acres now and sold the rest to a local farmer. Ernie was OK, he said, but a bit bored. Still, that would improve when the tourists started coming in a month's time. "You sold any of them boats yet?" he asked Will.

"One of them. Somebody called Morgan-Giles."

"Hugo Morgan-Giles?"

"That's him. Do you know him?"

"Not exactly, but I know of him. With May's relatives being out St Petroc way we tend to know more folk over in that direction than in Pencurnow, but the Morgan-Giles family has been around for years. Used to live in the big house up at the top – Benbecula. Now they lives in the little one lower down. The Moorings."

May brought a pot of coffee over to the table. "Yes. Been there for a few years now. Sad business."

"This Morgan-Giles," said Will, "is he in his fifties, sandy hair, Army type?"

"That's him."

"I think I saw him this morning. I didn't realize it was him. I should have said thank you. What's so sad about him?"

"Well, not so much him," explained May, "more the family situation. He was one of them Names. You know, the ones that lost a lot of money. Something to do with insurance."

"You mean Lloyds?"

"That's it," confirmed Ernie. "Family money. All tied up. Then it all went pear-shaped, didn't it? Lost the lot. Well, almost everything. They'd owned Benbecula for generations and Morgan-Giles had to sell up and move into The Moorings, which they used to let. Bit of a come-down. I don't think his wife was too pleased. Kids at public school an' that."

"And those folk from London now live in Benbecula," added May.

"That's right. Some East End tycoon, by all accounts. Made his money in televisions."

"Mobile phones," corrected Will, and told them about his encounter with the MacDermotts. He did not mention Amy, but filled them in about Hovis, and Gryler's penny-pinching ways.

"You shouldn't be surprised." Ernie mopped up his egg-yolk with home-made wholemeal bread. "You be careful in your dealings with Gryler."

"Oh, I know he's a rogue," admitted Will. "But I think he's a straightforward rogue."

"Just don't cross him," Ernie continued. "There've been funny goings-on at that boatyard over the years."

"What sort of funny goings-on?"

Ernie continued with his mopping. "Rumours of smuggling and the like. Don't you get yourself too involved."

"Smuggling what?"

"Dunno. I choose not to ask. Ted Whistler knows more about it than I do, not that you heard me say."

"Are we talking serious stuff or just the odd bottle of booze?"

Ernie looked at him earnestly. "I wouldn't know."

Will thought back to his walk across the cliff and the fishing smack helmed by Christopher Applebee. He felt a sharp thrill at the prospect of being surrounded by illicit trading, and worried at the implications.

He kissed May and promising Ernie that he would not leave it so long before he visited them again, Will began the return trip along the cliff top path, his mind whirling with the events of the previous few days and the news gleaned over the past couple of hours.

Chapter 10: Anvil Point

The sight of Len Gryler scuttling into his blue hut reminded Will of a rabbit running into its burrow. He wondered what the old rogue was up to now. He took off his sailing jacket as he walked along the jetty and down the pontoon, refreshed after his walk and his mighty breakfast. Halyards pinged in the breeze and the gentle slapping of water against hull reflected the state of the tide. He stepped on to *Boy Jack* and stopped short. The port-side door was slightly ajar. He could have sworn he'd locked it when he left. He felt in his pocket for the key, and there it was, still firmly attached to the lump of cork that would make sure it floated were it ever to fall into the briny.

He slid open the door and stuck his head inside. Nothing seemed amiss. The place was apparently exactly as he had left it. He stepped down into the wheelhouse and walked through into the forward cabin, calling for Spike as he did so. There was no sign of the cat. He turned and walked aft, noticing a long, oily smudge on one of the cabin windows. He stopped and cursed himself. Then he realized that he had not made the smudge. The pathological tidiness that had been instilled in him during his days as a clockmaker, then as a lighthouse keeper, had made it impossible for him to endure what many would consider normal signs of wear and tear. That oil stain was not his. Someone had been on board the boat. Perhaps it had been Hovis, looking for him. But Hovis never had oil on his hands: his engine room was not a venue to which he was especially attached.

The sinking feeling in the pit of his stomach abated at the sight of Hovis walking down the pontoon with a shopping bag on one arm and a baguette under the other. Will ducked through the door of the wheelhouse and hailed him. "Hovis!"

"Ssh, dear boy. Our little secret. Aitch in public, please."

"Sorry. You haven't been on board, have you? On *Boy Jack*, I mean."

"Today?"

"Yes."

"No, I've just been up to see Primrose." He gestured in the direction of his provisions. "Why?"

Will knelt down on the deck, the better to explain without broadcasting to the entire boatyard. "Somebody's been on board. The door was ajar and there's oil on the wheelhouse window."

"Could be Gryler. Oil is his equivalent of aftershave. Did you ask him about letting you have a dry berth while your hull's being done?"

"Yes."

"Maybe he was just eyeing her up."

"From the inside?"

"That's a point. Are you sure?"

"Somebody's been here, I know it. I can feel it."

"Anything missing?" asked Hovis.

"Nothing obvious."

"Mmmm. Odd. Well, perhaps he was just having a nose. I caught him sizing up my binnacle once." He pointed in the direction of the brass compass sitting atop its varnished pillar. "He was looking at it just a bit too covetously for my liking, so I had a go at him a few days later about security here. I thought that might let him know I had my eyes open. He talked about installing video cameras. I knew he wouldn't do anything but at least I'd made my point."

Will looked thoughtful. "Are you here for a bit?"

"Yes."

"Can you keep an eye? I've some phone calls to make so I need to go up to the village."

"All right, dear boy. I'll keep the beadies open. Mmmm."

"Thanks." Will walked back up the pontoon, checking that the piece of paper with the telephone numbers on it was in his pocket, along with a handful of change.

"Give her my love," shouted Hovis.

Will turned to protest, then smiled. "I will."

*

347

He made two phone calls from the box outside the Post Office: one to the boat-builder Harry Gwenver, telling him that *Boy Jack* would be out of the water by the day after tomorrow, and the other to the Association of Dunkirk Little Ships asking for more information about his boat. The voice at the other end asked him for details of *Boy Jack*, explaining that brass plaques bearing the legend 'Dunkirk 1940' were not uncommon on ships that had played no part in the evacuations. Will quoted the information Gryler had given him, along with various keel markings, and was pleased when his inter-locutor confirmed that *Boy Jack* had indeed played her part on the Normandy beaches, though at that time the vessel had been known as *Graceful*. He would be sent a membership application form, and would he like a pennant that could be flown from his jack-staff on entering and leaving port, and when in the company of other Dunkirk Little Ships? Will, rather proudly, said he would. He also enquired about how many of the Little Ships had survived. "There are around a hundred and seventy still in existence and we have a hundred and twenty-four registered with us as members. We'll be glad to add you to the list."

Will put down the phone, feeling better disposed towards *Boy Jack* than he had recently. Perhaps the old girl was worth persevering with, after all.

He walked down the lane again and as he approached the Roundhouse he saw Amy on the doorstep. She saw him, waved and called him over. He worried at first that something was the matter, but then, as he walked into the studio, he saw the man he now knew to be Hugo Morgan-Giles, with a well-dressed woman in a tweed skirt and sweater, whom he assumed to be Mrs Morgan-Giles. Amy effected introductions.

"You really are quite a craftsman, you know," offered Hugo, once the pleasantries were out of the way. "I was telling Miss Finn that I thought you were rather selling yourself short."

"I'm just happy that someone likes them enough to buy them," demurred Will.

"Yes, but you might as well get as much as you can for them in recompense for your effort, eh, Mouse?"

Mrs Morgan-Giles half smiled.

"I've just brought Isobel in to see the painting I fancied. I think we can find room for it, dear, can't we?"

"Well, yes . . . if you think . . ."

"Oh, I'm sure we can afford it. Can't keep economizing all the time. Have to allow ourselves the occasional treat, you know!"

"Well, if you're sure, Hugo. It *is* a lovely picture . . ." She looked wistfully at the blue sea and sky, the white sand, almost as though she were trying to spirit herself into the idyllic landscape.

Will thought she looked deeply sad. He suddenly felt sorry for this couple who had once been the lord and lady of the manor in all but name, and who now had been relegated to the Dower House while some East-End-barrowboy-made-good had taken over their old family home. It must be galling. But with a staunchness imbued in them since childhood the Morgan-Gileses had mucked in and carried on.

"Can we take it with us?" asked Hugo. "I'd love to hang it today."

"Yes, of course." Amy lifted the painting from its hook and took it to the counter.

Their painting was wrapped and handed to them, and the Morgan-Gileses left. Will watched them go.

"It's a shame, isn't it?" Amy broke in on his thoughts.

"Mmm?"

"Such a sweet couple. It's a terrible shame about all their troubles."

"You know, then?"

"Primrose told me."

"Ah, so you've been talking to the human telescope."

"Don't be rude. She's a poppet."

"Just don't tell her any secrets, that's all. She's better than the BBC at spreading the news."

"Well, she did tell me a bit about the Morgan-Gileses."

"How much?"

"Oh, that they lost a lot of money in the Lloyds fiasco, and that they're living in the little house now and not the big one, and struggling to keep their kids at public school. The boy's at Eton and the girl goes to St Mary's, Ascot."

"So how does he earn his living now?"

"A couple of consultancies in the City, according to Primrose. Goes up to London two or three times a month."

"You did get a lot of information!"

"Well, I was curious. And he's the first person to buy one of my paintings so he must have exquisite taste!"

"Just a bit biased I should say!"

"Cheeky!" She came and stood in front of him, looking up at him. "Thank you very much for last night. It was so lovely. I hope you don't think that–"

He butted in, anxious for neither of them to spoil the moment by analysing too much too soon. "It was a pleasure. *Is* a pleasure. I really enjoyed it."

She took his hint, disappointed. "I thought Hovis was sweet. Funny, too. Another lovely man."

"He's turning into a good mate. Haven't known him long but he seems to know when I want company and when I want to be alone."

"You sound like Greta Garbo."

"Oh, you know what I mean."

"I know exactly what you mean." She looked at him hard and struggled for words. "Look . . . I was wondering if perhaps you might like to come to supper?"

"I'd love to." Will had the strangest sensation that she seemed able to see through the outer Will Elliott and the veneers and defences he had spent so long building up. What shocked him was that he didn't mind. It seemed the most natural thing in the world.

He stared at her and felt a deep inner warmth and security that he had almost forgotten existed.

They didn't hear the door of the gallery open, only the words, which struck like a bolt of lightning: "I seem to have lost my sense of timing."

It was Oliver Gallico. He removed his dark glasses, to look Will up and down. "This is getting a bit tedious." He regarded Will with the sort of displeasure that most cat owners reserve for a regurgitated fur ball. "Who is this?"

"This is Will Elliott. Will, Oliver Gallico."

He stood squarely in front of them, arms folded, and nodded carelessly in Will's direction. "When is he going?"

Amy was recovering herself now. "He isn't going."

"Oh, come on, Ame. Let's sort this out. Tell him to piss off."

Amy interrupted, "Look, just leave, will you?"

"You can tell me to leave as many times as you want. But I'll come back. I'll keep coming back. I'm not giving up, you know." He smiled insolently. "You know you'll have to come. Why pretend that you won't? It's only a matter of time. You always come in the end." He tapped his foot repeatedly against the white wall, leaving black marks on the once pristine paintwork.

Amy tried hard not to appear rattled. "I'm not going to leave all this."

"Why not? What are a few paintings compared with what we have? You're prepared to give all that up for this?" He looked around him at the vibrant Cornish seascapes.

"Yes," she said firmly.

He walked towards them but Will stood his ground. "I think you should go now," he said.

Gallico looked him directly in the eye with undisguised contempt. "Piss off."

Will persisted, "It's time you left."

"Or else what?" He sounded cold and threatening.

Will reined in his emotions and spoke steadily. "Just leave."

Gallico moved closer to Will, who could now feel the heat of his breath on his cheeks. "What's it to do with you?" He looked towards Amy. "Tell him about us. Go on, tell him who we are!"

"We're nothing, Oliver. Not any more." Amy looked frightened. "Please, just go. It's too late. It's all over."

"You stupid bitch!" he said. "It'll never be over. Not what we have. You hear? Never!"

He paused, waiting for something else to push against. It did not come.

He turned to Will. "All right, I'll go. But I'm not giving up. I'll be back."

"No, you won't." Will fixed him with a steely gaze. "You'll go now and you'll stay away. Amy's had enough, and you don't belong here."

"I'll–"

"No. You won't. Come on, out."

He took great care not to touch Gallico, but walked round him to the door and held it open. "Goodbye."

The arrogant dancer made to speak, but thought better of it. "Shit!" he sneered at Will, cast a backward look at Amy then strode out.

Will hoped he had also swept out of their lives, but felt it unlikely.

Amy stood perfectly still, the gamut of emotions she had run during the past few minutes robbing her of the power of speech.

As Will walked towards her the door of the gallery burst open again. "Will! Come quickly!"

Will spun round to see Hovis in a state of breathless agitation. "What's the matter?"

"Fire at the lighthouse. Engines on their way. Thought you'd want to know." Hovis leaned against the door frame, doing his best to catch his breath.

Will shot a look at Amy and said, "I'll call you," then bolted out.

She shouted after him, "Take my car!" But he was too far away to hear, running up the lane towards the cliff path as fast as his legs would carry him.

Chapter 11: St Anthony

He could see the smoke billowing from the buildings behind the lighthouse as he ran along the cliff path. Above the sound of the breaking waves he could hear the sirens. His pounding footsteps took him round Pencurnow Cove and along the headland towards the lighthouse, but it was still impossible to see which part of the building had caught fire. It was only when he finally leapt up the steps towards the tower and rounded the corner that he saw flames licking out of a downstairs window adjacent to the rooms occupied by Ernie and May. He could see neither of them in the confusion.

His lungs felt as though they, too, were on fire, and he rested his hands on his knees for a moment, lowering his head and catching his breath. The journey had taken him the best part of twenty minutes, during which the fire had taken hold. Where were Ernie and May?

Then he saw them, on the other side of the veil of grey smoke that was now blowing across the craggy rocks and out to sea. Ernie had his arm around May, who was wringing the corner of her apron in her hands. They were watching as the firemen worked, directing their hoses through the window from which angry flames licked upwards towards the roof.

"Are you all right?"

Ernie was surprised and relieved to see him. "We're fine. I think."

"What happened?"

"Don't know. One minute we were in there minding our own business and the next minute the place was ablaze."

Fifteen minutes later, the flames had died away, to be replaced with a gentle hissing as red-hot timbers cooled under their saturation. The visitors ambled off, the spectacle over and the acrid smell of charred wet timber biting into their nostrils. The firemen rolled up their hoses while Will comforted May.

The two policemen were with Ernie, fixing up a time for him to attend the station in St Petroc to make a statement. They warned him not to touch anything until Forensic had been out to examine the scene. Plastic tape was fastened to slender poles driven into the ground with the intention of keeping out trespassers, not that anyone would have wanted to get near the blackened, sodden mess, thought Will.

"Lucky," commented Ernie, though the expression on his face did not accord with the word.

"What do you mean?" asked Will.

"It's only damaged one room. It could have been much worse."

"What's gone?"

"Just some old furniture. We were using it as a store . . ." He stopped short as he was saying it, and looked at Will, his face etched with regret. "Oh, Will! It was where we'd put your stuff. Your books and things."

The three of them gazed at the blackened window frame. There was little likelihood of anything being salvageable. What the flames had not destroyed, the water would have finished off.

Will gazed at the yawning hole almost in a trance. Why had he not taken all his things with him to the boat? His books, his charts, the few CDs, his old boating magazines all gone. His Trinity House certificate – well, that could easily be replaced – and his diaries. His diaries. His legs weakened and he flopped down on the grass beside Ernie and May. His life was between their covers. The record of his existence since he had lost Ellie. He felt sick. It seemed as though he had lost her for a second time.

Events of the last episode of his life swam in his head, from his arrival on this spot six years ago, to the building of the *Gull* and the maturing friendship with Ernie. He had put down between the covers of the twenty or more exercise books his daily thoughts and observations, his feelings about Ellie and his feelings about himself. Now they were all gone up in smoke.

"I'm sorry. I'm really sorry."

He looked up at Ernie. "No, no." He didn't want to add to their misery. It would be better to appear unconcerned. "It's not your fault. It's not anybody's fault. It's just one of those things." He shrugged and tried to look as though it were no great tragedy.

"We can still put you up if you want somewhere to stay," offered May.

"No. I mean, don't worry."

"Oh, but your things . . ." May looked agitated.

"Just books and stuff. It's all replaceable." He remembered them individually. The pilotage books, the navigation manuals, and the five volumes of Cowper's *Sailing Tours* that he had so looked forward to taking with him on his voyage. Now all gone.

"I expect the insurance will pay up," remarked Ernie.

"Yes. I suppose so." It had taken Will a long while to find each of the five volumes of Cowper. He expected it would take him even longer to replace them. But right now what did it matter? He snapped out of his introspection. "Look, the important thing is that you two are safe. Who cares about a few books? What are you going to do now?"

"Can't really do anything until the police have given us the say-so. It's a good job that the room is a bit out on a limb. The rest of the place should be OK, even if it is a bit smelly. Trinity House will want to come and have a look. I suppose I'll have to leave it up to them as to what happens next. But I'll tell them about your stuff. You'd better give me a list of what you think you've lost."

Will ducked under the streamers of police tape to take a look inside the window. The small room looked like the black hole of Calcutta. It was about twelve feet square. The iron bedstead against one wall was intact, in shape at least, but everything else had coagulated into an amorphous charred mass, dripping with water. The door on the far side had remained shut. Will heaved a sigh of relief that Ernie's assiduousness at closing doors behind him had prevented a small conflagration from turning into a major blaze.

"There's nothing salvageable in there." Will dodged back under the tape to where Ernie and May stood. "Is there anything you want me to do?"

"No, you get off. I'll let you know what happens." Ernie put his arm around May's shoulder. She dabbed at her eye with the corner of her apron and Will saw she was crying.

He stared at the pair of them, standing on the grassy knoll with the gigantic white tower rising up behind them, and thought how small they looked.

Boy Jack looked massive from this angle. Will stood under her bows as she sat on the concrete hard to one side of the boatyard, supported by a flimsy-looking rank of wooden poles, secured with slender wooden wedges. It was the traditional way of propping up a boat when it was out of the water, but he always marvelled that such a Heath Robinson approach could be effective.

A ladder leaned up against her side, fastened with rope at the top, and Will shinned up the rungs to fetch a wire brush and have a go at the barnacles on the propeller while he waited for Harry Gwenver to turn up. He liked this kind of work: his mind could wander while he scrubbed. He'd returned to the Roundhouse after the fire to explain what had happened, but had been called away yet again to supervise the lifting out of *Boy Jack* when Gryler had finally succeeded (probably courtesy of a few smart clouts with his monkey wrench) in getting the boat lift to work. He'd spent the night on board, high above the jetty, with Spike looking puzzled about their sudden elevation.

The day had dawned bright and clear, but the prospect before him was still cloudy. Early in the morning he strode up the hill and fixed up accommodation at Mrs Sparrow's B and B for two weeks, hoping that that would be long enough. He also hoped he could carry on working on the boat during the day, if he didn't get in Harry Gwenver's way.

"You!" The voice startled him. It was old, male and Cornish. Harry Gwenver, sixty-something, in brown overalls, a tweed jacket and a tweed cap stood, with his hands on his hips regarding the boat. He was tall and angular, the opposite of Len Gryler, and he had a quizzical look on his face, which gave way to a broad smile. "You ready for us?"

"Er . . . yes. I think so. But I can't be out of her just yet. I'm still sorting myself out." Will saw the smile on Harry Gwenver's face replaced with a frown. "I'll keep out of your way, though – but I can't promise about him." He gestured in the direction of the furry face surveying the scene from the rail above the transom. It would take more than a refit to get Spike away from a home that provided such a rich supply of fish suppers.

Harry Gwenver laughed. "Oh, we'll cope with him. Is he friendly?"

"Nothing much worries him. Except stuffed cormorants," he added.

"Right," said Harry, "we'll make a start."

He returned to his van, parked at the end of the jetty, to fetch his tools, while Will climbed the ladder to reassure the cat that he wasn't about to be made homeless. The two sat, on the wheelhouse roof, looking out to sea, and Will was engulfed in a wave of self-pity. His books had gone and his diaries were no more.

He felt like a man whose history had been taken away. But they were only diaries. Only a record of things gone. They were not of now and although they had vanished the memories were indelible. Through the sense of loss and desperation came a new feeling: release.

Chapter 12: Casquets

Mrs Sparrow was a decent sort. She let Will have the front bedroom of Myrtle Cottage because it had the sea view, though she did explain that, should he stay longer than anticipated, he might have to move when the holiday season arrived.

Will's biggest problem was breakfast. Persuading Mrs Sparrow not to cook him a full English every morning was no easy matter. She was tiny and bird-like herself and clearly assumed that her guests also ate like birds – seven times their own bodyweight daily. As a result Will found himself wading through egg, bacon, sausage, fried bread and black pudding for the first two mornings of his stay. Finally he managed to convince her that a bowl of what she called 'rabbit food' would do very nicely during the week and he would save his fry-up for weekends.

He breakfasted early – at around seven thirty – and tried to be 'on site' at the boat soon after eight when Harry Gwenver turned up. The old man didn't seem to mind Will pottering around doing his own thing, provided he kept out of his way, and Will was gradually getting used to the peppering of Cornish language that decorated Harry's speech. He now understood that "You!" meant "hello", *durdathawhy* good-day and *benetugana* goodbye, but it had taken him a while to work out that *durdaladawhy* was thank you. He'd asked Harry why he used such expressions, only to be told that someone had to keep the old Cornish language going, and that he didn't see why it had to die with Dolly Pentreath in 1777.

Will watched Harry disappear into the hold of *Boy Jack* and set to work himself removing the old antifouling with a paint scraper and a

358

wire brush. He was surprised when Ernie turned up.

"You all right, then?" enquired Ernie, looking up at the towering hull.

"I'm fine. How about you?"

"A bit shocked."

Will stopped scrubbing and looked at him. "What do you mean?"

"Police think the fire was started deliberately."

"What?" Will was stunned.

"They found traces of a bottle and petrol. Reckon it was lobbed through the window."

"But why?"

"Blowed if I know." Ernie looked troubled.

"Have you told May?"

"No. I thought I wouldn't."

"You'll have a job keeping it from her."

"I suppose so. I just don't want her worrying." Will saw the fear in his friend's eyes. "It can only have been some yobs, can't it, having a bit of mischief? Couldn't be anything else, could it?"

"No. I shouldn't think so." Will hoped Ernie was right. What other reason could anyone have for torching the lighthouse?

"Do you want a look round?" Will tried to cheer him by showing him over the boat, but Ernie was preoccupied. After ten minutes or so he made his excuses and left. "Got to get back to the rock. May's nipping over to her pigs and I can't leave the place unattended."

Will watched as the older man walked round the jetty to his van, got in, started up and drove off. He put down his brush and scraper, walked along the jetty and down the pontoon towards *Florence Nightingale*. Hovis was bending down and attending to his mooring warps. He looked up at the sound of Will's footsteps. "You look a bit fed up," he offered.

"Confused, more like."

"What's the problem?" Hovis stretched.

"Ernie says the police think the fire at the lighthouse was started deliberately. They found glass and petrol. Reckon it was a fire-bomb."

"Good grief. Who'd want to do that?"

"I wish I knew. Local oiks, probably."

"First time ever if it is. I know we've a few tearaways round here but rollerblading down the middle of the road from Primrose's to the jetty is about their limit. They've set fire to a few litter bins in their time but I wouldn't have thought they'd have touched the lighthouse. Too much a part of their lives. And their dads'."

"But who else would have done it?"

"Can't imagine. What does Ernie think?"

"Hasn't a clue. I think he's in shock."

"And Whistler? What about him?"

"I haven't asked him."

Hovis looked at Will. "Don't you think you should?"

"Yes. I suppose so. What time is it?"

Hovis glanced at the marine chronometer through the glass of *Florence Nightingale's* wheelhouse. "Half past nine."

"He's probably still having breakfast at the Salutation. I'll nip over and see if I can catch him."

Ted Whistler was just coming out of the door of the Salutation as Will turned up on his doorstep. "What do you want?" he asked plainly. He had never held the social graces in high regard.

"Just coming to see you."

"Oh? That's a turn-up for the books."

Will ignored the gibe, and asked Ted if he had heard about the fire.

"Where do you think I've been living for the past month? Course I've heard about the fire. The talk in there," he gestured over his shoulder, "has been about nothing else since it happened."

"What do you think caused it?"

"Somebody must have been careless. Fag end or something." That reminded him that he had not lit up his post-breakfast Camel, and he rummaged around in his donkey-jacket.

"It wasn't an accident."

"What?" Ted was looking for matches and asked the question absentmindedly.

"The fire was started with a petrol bomb."

This time Ted Whistler heard. He stopped what he was doing and asked for confirmation. Will explained about the storeroom and his belongings, about what the police had found and the conclusion they had drawn.

"I wondered if you had any idea who could have done it. Or why?"

"Why me?" Ted was defensive.

"Just asking, that's all. Ernie and I can't figure it out."

Ted leaned on the iron rail at the edge of the pavement across from the Salutation, the wind temporarily knocked out of his sails. His hunched but lanky figure with his thinning grey hair swept back from his face, gave him a cadaverous appearance. "Was it only that one room that was damaged? The storeroom where you had your stuff?" he asked.

"Yes."

Ted shrugged. "Funny that."

Will wondered what he was getting at.

"What do you mean?

"Maybe they want to make sure you don't keep any more records."

"Who?"

Ted shrugged again.

Will faced him squarely. "What's going on?"

Ted looked out to sea. "I don't know. I'm sorry you lost your diaries, but it's none of my business."

He turned away from Will and walked back along the sand towards the Salutation, leaving his former colleague determined to get to the bottom of a mystery that seemed to be deepening by the hour.

It had not occurred to Will that the police would want to question him. The statement was taken at St Petroc police station by an apologetic detective sergeant sympathetic to his loss. Providing a list of possessions that had gone up in smoke lowered his spirits again.

"Is that it, sir? You're sure that's all?" The portly sergeant, his Brylcreemed head bent low over the statement sheet, proceeded in his methodical longhand.

"Yes. I think so." Then he remembered the photograph album. He had forgotten about that. A sinking feeling in his stomach. Then a brightening of spirits. He had not put the album into store at Ernie's. He had meant to, but something had made him wrap it in polythene and put it at the bottom of a canvas holdall filled with clothes, which now sat in the bottom of the wardrobe at Mrs Sparrow's. He still had a reminder of Ellie.

"You all right, sir?"

"Mmm? Yes. I just remembered something I didn't lose. That's all."

"I'm afraid I have to ask you where you were, sir, when the fire started."

Will filled in the officer on his movements that morning.

"So you did visit the lighthouse, then?"

"Yes. I had breakfast there."

"And then you left?"

"Yes. I walked back over the cliff-top path to the boatyard. Then I made some telephone calls and then I went to the Roundhouse Studio."

The sergeant asked questions about the phone calls and precise details of timings. He asked if Will thought there was a reason why such a fire had been started. Will said he had no idea. He had already mentioned his missing diaries and what they contained. If the police thought this had some bearing on the case they would no doubt follow it up. It struck him as unwise to mention Ted Whistler's conjecturing and, anyway, he was not sure he believed it. It seemed sufficient to say that he had kept diaries during his time at the lighthouse and that he had made no secret of it.

The policeman beavered away with his Biro. He might be slow and steady, thought Will, but he's thorough. His questioning over, and his painstaking calligraphy completed, the sergeant asked Will to check his list of lost possessions and confirm that it was correct.

"Have you any ideas at all who might have done it?" asked Will, curious to know the detective sergeant's take on the case.

"We have our suspicions, sir," replied the officer, "but as yet there's nothing to go on. We think it might be something to do with your diaries, sir."

Will was surprised that the sergeant was so candid. "Do you?"

"Yes, sir. They could pose a threat to someone who didn't want their movements known. But, then, you'd probably guessed that, sir, hadn't you?"

Will looked suitably abashed. "It just seems so far-fetched."

"Not at all, sir. You'll hear all sorts of rumours about romantic notions of smuggling and the like. But it's not romantic, sir. It's against the law and we have to make sure that those who participate in it are brought to account."

"And you think that . . ."

"I can't really tell you what we think, sir. I would just tell you to be careful. It's unlikely that anything else will happen now, sir. The diaries are gone and that's probably all they were after. I should think you're quite safe now, sir. But it might be a good idea not to keep another diary."

Will smiled weakly. "Yes. I suppose you're right."

Chapter 13: Varne

The next few days Will spent in a daze. Dispossessed of his living quarters, his concern for Ernie and May jostled in his mind with confusion about his feelings for Amy. He had deliberately stayed away from her, though he yearned to see her again, and to add spice to his jumbled brew of emotions there was now the possibility that somebody in the village had it in for him.

Mrs Sparrow cleared away the breakfast dishes from his little table in the front bay window at Myrtle Cottage, flicking the dust off the aspidistra with her tea cloth as she passed. "Dinner at seven thirty then, Mr Elliott."

"Thank you. Yes." Will got up from the table and walked through into the hallway. He grabbed his sailing jacket from the mahogany coat stand, unconsciously straightened one of the flying ducks that was doing a nose-dive towards the skirting board, and left the house to begin another day of restoration.

Harry Gwenver was already lost in the bilges of *Boy Jack* when Will arrived. It seemed a shame to interrupt him. The poor man was getting used to being watched as he worked. Not that he seemed to mind.

Will looked up at the sky – pasty and pale – then down when he felt a familiar rub on his leg. Spike was gazing up at him, silently miaowing.

"Hallo, old lad! Where've you been?" He had neglected his old shipmate for the better part of a week. "Come on. Do you fancy a walk?" Leaving Harry in peace on *Boy Jack*, Will went along the jetty and out towards the cliff path. Spike followed, trotting behind him as obediently as any spaniel. They reached an outcrop above Pencurnow

Cove and Will clambered up it. The cat reached the top in a couple of light bounds.

They sat together looking out to sea and across to the lighthouse, still white as chalk in spite of the fire.

"Oh, Spike! What are we going to do, eh?" The cat rubbed his head along Will's arm, purring. He smiled. Sometimes the silence of animals was their most attractive quality.

"People, Spike. Sometimes I think I don't do people." It dawned on him, now that he was here, how much he had needed to get away from the boatyard, the village and dear old Mrs Sparrow. How much he had missed solitude.

The sea lapped at the sand below them, and whispered across the nearby shingle. A pair of black and white oystercatchers were probing the shore with their scarlet bills, fluttering out of the way when the incoming waves interrupted their scavenging. Among the tussocky grass that surrounded their lump of granite, slender drumsticks were pushing up from the tufts of sea pinks, and a watery sun did its best to cut through the clouds.

A fishing boat bobbed gently on the waves half a mile from the shore, its crew hauling up their lobster pots, emptying them, then tossing them back overboard. Tiny orange floats marked their position, dotted across the surface of the dull green sea like a sparsely beaded necklace.

Man and cat sat and watched as the tide receded, leaving the beach fresh-washed, the colour of fudge, and unsullied by footprints.

As the waves advanced and receded Will remembered the Cornish holiday he and Ellie had enjoyed the year before they married. It was on the north coast, even more rugged than Pencurnow. They had walked, and eaten, slept and made love in the front bedroom of a boarding-house not unlike Mrs Sparrow's.

He felt a rush of sadness. From the blissfully happy days of being together, living for each other, he had returned to being a man happiest in his own company. Until now. He stroked Spike, and remembered the night on Hovis's boat, with Amy sitting close to him, the kiss in the doorway, the looks between them. The tears that had finally come after six years.

Was he wrong to want to start again? To be happy? When he thought of how happy he and Ellie had been together, it seemed impossible to imagine that he could ever feel the same about anyone else. And yet he could not deny his feelings for Amy. That, in its way, would be as wrong as betraying Ellie's memory.

"Oh, Spike!" He leaned forward, resting his hands on his knees and looking out to sea. A freighter edged slowly across the horizon and he remembered, with a sickening feeling, his diaries. "What to do?"

"Come on, then, Spike." He chucked the cat under its chin, caressed the white bib that ran like a starched shirt front across its breast. The cat chirruped. "Let's see how far you can walk. I'll carry you if you get tired." He got up, stretched his legs and set off in the direction of Land's End, striding out and breathing in the salt air. The cat was never more than a couple of paces behind him.

They stopped for lunch at a pub near Logan Rock, where the sight of a man with a black and white cat in tow was greeted with good humour by the laconic landlord. Will got himself the other side of a Cornish pasty and a pint of bitter, while Spike tucked into mackerel pâté and a saucer of milk before they retraced their steps on the return journey.

The cat walked almost every inch of the way, even though Will offered him a lift from time to time. He would sit in Will's arms for a couple of minutes before letting out a brief harrumph, bounding down and off in the direction of home. Spike took the lead all the way back, sometimes running fifty yards ahead, until the Crooked Angel boatyard came into view and he sat on a rock and curled his black tail around his white feet with a smug expression on his face.

Will scooped him up and walked down to the yard. When they reached *Boy Jack* there was no sign of Harry. Will looked at his watch. A quarter past five. Their walk had taken them the best part of the day, and he felt better for it. Spike leapt up the ladder and on to the deck. Will followed, keen to see how Harry had got on in their absence.

He fished in his pocket for the spare key for *Boy Jack*, opened the wheelhouse door, found a torch by the hatch and shone it down into the hold. Harry was making good progress: the once gappy planking now looked uniform and watertight, and part of it was even painted. With any luck he would finish on time and *Boy Jack* would be back in the water where she belonged.

He swung up from the hatch, replaced the torch on its narrow shelf and came out on to the deck. The early evening was still, bathed in a soft light. A movement caught his eye. A distant figure was running down the lane. He watched as it rounded the corner of the jetty and continued towards the boatyard. He could see now that it was Primrose Hankey, clad in a baggy navy blue tracksuit, her long plait bobbing from side to side as she jogged across the yard.

"Mr Ell-ee-ott," she panted, her face the colour of smoked salmon, perspiration running off her chin.

"Primrose! What's the matter?"

She was unable to speak. Instead, she bent forward from the waist (not an easy movement for a woman of such unusual weight distribution) and plunged her head between her knees. Will wondered if she would be able to straighten up again.

"Nothing wrong. Just getting a bit of exercise," she gasped. "Letter arrived for you this morning. Thought I'd drop it off. This the boat?" In the battle of curiosity versus exhaustion, the former now gained the upper hand.

"Yes."

"Mmm. Lot of work."

"Yes."

"Still. I'm sure she'll look nice when she's finished." She held the letter aloft, having checked out the ladder and decided against a precarious ascent. "I didn't know you were old enough to have been at Dunkirk," she quipped, as Will came down the ladder and took the letter from her.

"Not quite." He looked at the postmark and the frank of the Association of Dunkirk Little Ships.

"Is this boat one of them, then?" asked Primrose, her breathing almost back to normal.

"Yes." Will felt guilty at not offering more information after her exertions, but suspected that Primrose already knew more than she was letting on.

"What a week you've had, Mr Elliott. We've all felt very sorry for you."

We? thought Will, wondering just how far round the cove his tale of woe had spread.

"Yes. It's been a bit tricky," he said,

"I can imagine." Her complexion had now returned to normal. "But it's so nice that Miss Finn has been such a good friend."

"Sorry?" He was unnerved at Primrose's conjecture.

"Miss Finn. I gather you've become quite friendly."

Will was staggered at her candour. "Er . . . well, friendly, yes."

"Lovely. Very nice for both of you."

"Yes. Well. Thanks for bringing my letter." He felt irritated at her intrusion and didn't mind if she knew it.

Primrose realized she'd overstepped the mark, and seeing that he was not about to share the contents of the envelope with her she flapped her arms a couple of times and said, "Yes. Well. Must be off, back up the hill. The hard bit now."

Will felt a pricking of conscience. "I didn't know you jogged."

"Oh, yes. Got to keep fit. Once a week. Vary the route. Always out for a good fifteen minutes. Gets the circulation going. Keeps me trim. Back home for supper. 'Bye, then." She lumbered away up the jetty.

Will took out his pocket knife and slit open the envelope. Out fell an assortment of papers. There was a membership form, some general information about the Association and a covering letter explaining that the enclosed document had been sent to them by *Boy Jack's* previous owner in case they were interested in the boat's history. They had retained photocopies but were sending him the original as the new owner of the boat. Will's heart leapt. He unfolded the yellowing piece of paper and read:

To whom it may concern:
'Boy Jack' (originally 'Graceful')
Built 1931 Staniland & Company, Thorne, Yorkshire.
Length: 36ft
Beam: 9ft 6in
Displacement: 8 tons
Draft: 2ft 6in
Engines: 2 × 30 h.p. Perkins M30
Hull: Pitch pine on oak.

The following history is what I have been able to piece together during the thirty years I have owned the boat. She was brought down from Yorkshire by a Thomas Cherry in 1937 and moored on the Thames at Oxford. At that time she was called 'Graceful'. In the middle of May in 1940 she must have been moored further down the Thames as she was used in the evacuation of Dunkirk.

She broke down twice on her first crossing but is credited with saving the lives of 246 men.

Her life immediately after the war is not well documented, but I found her in a poor state of repair on the Thames at Oxford in 1962 and decided to take her on. My wife and I sailed her down to Dartmouth that summer, where she was used very happily for summer holidays and weekend excursions. We lived in Totnes at the time. She became a regular cruiser up and down the river Dart and along the Devon coast.

I endeavoured to keep 'Graceful' in good repair, and to this end the hull was refurbished and new stringers put in place in 1967. I also replaced the deck planking. We then moved to Falmouth so that we could enjoy boating in Cornwall and live by the sea which is what we had both dreamed of. Sadly, in 1969 my beloved wife died while giving birth to our son. The boy himself died a week later.

I planned to sell the boat and move away, but she was the one thing that we had shared and I could not bring myself to part with her. For this reason I renamed her 'Boy Jack', after our son. I have continued to use her ever since, and more restoration work was carried out in the 1980s. Now, in my later years, I do not get out on her as often as I would like and my circumstances make the cost of repairs difficult.

I explain these facts in the hope that the person who next owns 'Boy Jack' will remember her history, and mine, and take good care of her. She saved the lives of many British soldiers during the war and gave me, and my family, many hours of great pleasure. She deserves to be looked after.

Yours sincerely,
Walter Etchingham

Will folded the piece of paper and put it back into the envelope. For the second time in a week he was in tears.

Chapter 14: Hartland Point

Amy looked at the old station clock on the wall of the studio. It was ten past one. The morning had dragged by. A few customers had turned up. One had even shown a passing interest in one of the erotic sculptures and she hoped at last that it might pass out of her life. But no, the customer left with the familiar "I'll have a think about it", which meant that she'd never see him again.

She set up a canvas on her easel in one corner of the studio and made a start on a rich blue sky, spreading the azure acrylic paint with her palette knife, all the while wondering where Will was and what he was doing. Had she been too pushy? Perhaps she had frightened him off. And who could blame him? Here was a man who had not known female company for six years, who had sought the solitude of a lighthouse. What made her think she could snap him out of his introspection in a matter of a few days' acquaintanceship. But it was more than that, wasn't it?

She wiped clean the palette knife on a piece of rag, replaced the cap on the tube of paint and climbed the spiral staircase for her jacket. She came down, threw a purple woollen scarf around her neck, and pulled the blind over the door. She needed a walk. A twenty-minute tramp along the beach would be just the thing

The salt tang in her nostrils filled her with renewed energy. The brisk breeze blew through her hair and made her scalp tingle as she waded down through the tussocky grass alongside the cliff-top path towards the sand. She ambled along the waterline, looking down at the bubbles that erupted from the sand as the white waves retreated, stooping occasionally to pick up a razor shell or a whelk, and looking at the indentations in the sand that were instantly washed away by the next thin sheet of advancing tide.

She thought of him, and tried not to think of him, then threw back her head and breathed in deeply.

"Had enough shop-keeping for one day?"

The voice surprised her and she jumped. Hovis was walking towards her.

"Oh! It's you!"

"You look as though you've just escaped from prison."

"I have. In a way. Just needed some air."

"Me too. What have you got?" He nodded towards Amy's fistful of shells.

"Oh, just some razors and a whelk or two. And one large mussel."

"I think that's what Will needs."

"Sorry?" She tried to look unconcerned.

"Large muscles. His boat looks bigger out of the water than it does in. I think he's a bit daunted by all the work."

She tried a smile. Hovis watched as she turned and looked out to sea. Then he said, gently, "Shall we go and see how he's getting on?"

Amy looked at her watch, half wanting to make an excuse.

Hovis offered her a way out. "Oh, I forgot. You'll be opening up again soon."

Suddenly her way was clear to her. "No. I'm going out. But I've time to see how he's doing. Will you walk with me?"

"Happy to."

They strode back along the beach, where the receding tide had left the sand firm, and Hovis showed her his treasure trove – a rusted metal ring from a boat; a length of silvery driftwood and a dogfish's egg, the black purse equipped with wispy handles at each corner.

They found *Boy Jack* sitting on the concrete hard, propped up like Noah's Ark waiting for the flood, with wooden shores sticking out from the hull like the legs of a gigantic insect.

"I've brought a visitor," Hovis yelled up at the deck, dwarfed by the massive hulk.

Will stuck his head over the side, his face smeared with white paint. "Hi. How are you?"

"I'm fine. Just wondered how you were getting on." She leant on one of the shores.

370

"Don't lean on that! I mean, be careful. I always get nervous when boats are propped up."

"Sorry!" She looked crestfallen.

"So am I. I didn't mean to snap. I just can't believe that these things can ever stay upright when they're out of the water." He climbed down the ladder, grinning, and the uncomfortable moment passed.

"She looks huge."

"I know. Frightening, isn't it?"

Hovis made his excuses. "Must dash. Got to get some stuff from Primrose's. See you later." He executed a slow pirouette and shambled off.

Amy walked around *Boy Jack* and looked up past the propellers at her stern. "She looks like the *Titanic* from here."

"Well, with any luck, when Harry's done his job she won't suffer the same fate."

He took a piece of sandpaper from his pocket and began rubbing at a propeller blade.

"Have you got enough lifeboats?" she teased.

"I'm getting a raft."

"Big enough for all the passengers?"

"It depends how many there are." He looked at her steadily.

"How many are you thinking of taking?"

"Oh, just a couple." He looked upwards past the towering top-sides and a small black and white face peeped back at him over the rail.

"There's him . . ."

"A cat?"

"That's Spike. We've been together a couple of years now."

"Just you and him, then?" She posed the question jokingly.

"Well, it all depends."

"On what?"

"You do ask a lot of questions."

"Only because I'm interested."

He turned to face her. "I'm very glad you're interested." He bent down and kissed her forehead.

She looked at him steadily. "You've got paint on your nose."

"I've got paint everywhere."

"I was just wondering . . . You said you'd come round for supper."

"I will when I'm asked." His eyes danced.

"Well, I'm asking. Tonight, if you like. I'm shutting up shop this afternoon. There's an arts and crafts exhibition in St Ives and I want to see if I can find some new stuff for the studio. I'll be back around six. Come round at about eight?"

"Sounds fine to me. It'll take me that long to get this paint off."

"OK, then. Don't get tangled up in your propeller. Oh, and don't lean on those props. It always makes me nervous." He started, aware that he was, indeed, leaning against one of the shores.

She laughed. "Take care!"

"And you."

He watched her go, the purple scarf trailing behind her like a pennant.

She returned just after six, happy but exhausted, with promises from four artists that they would call in during the week and bring some of their work. As she opened the door of the studio the first things that greeted her eye were Oliver's sculptures in the middle of the floor.

"Enough!" she shouted, then walked to the storeroom at the back of the studio and wheeled out a sack barrow. She wrapped old blankets around each of the sculptures, eased them on to the barrow and trundled them into the store. Now she would not have to stare her past in the face every day.

She took a shower, then pulled on a pair of jeans and a baggy sweatshirt and began to prepare supper.

It was only supper, he told himself. Nothing more. She had asked him for supper. There was no reason to feel so apprehensive.

He walked up the lane towards the studio. The blind was down. He tapped lightly and tried the handle but the door would not yield. He tapped again.

Footsteps approached and the door opened. They looked at one another, he leaning against the wall, a bottle of wine in his hand, she barefoot, her hair, fiery in the studio lights, tumbling over her shoulders.

"It's cold out here, you know."

"I'm sorry." She came out of her daze. "Come in."

They kissed, then Amy led the way up the spiral staircase to the living area.

"I've brought you a bottle. I think it's chilled enough."

She rummaged in the kitchen drawer and eventually found a corkscrew.

"Here, let me." He took it from her, opened the bottle then handed it back to her. She poured the wine into two blue glasses, and handed him one.

"Cheers." It seemed such an innocuous thing to say, devoid of real sentiment. Her eyes told him how she felt.

"Cheers," he replied, and they sipped, all the while staring at one another. Will noticed the flickering muscle in her upper lip and the nervousness in her eyes.

He set his glass down on the table then took Amy's glass and put that beside it. He folded his arms around her and she laid her head on his chest. "I'm so glad you came."

"And me."

"I thought you wouldn't."

"So did I."

She eased away from him and looked up into his eyes.

"But then I knew I had to." He stared at the floor, discomfited by his own admission. "I knew I wanted to."

"Are you hungry?"

"Starving."

"Good. There's masses. I thought a boat-builder might have a good appetite."

They dined by candlelight at the small round table, sharing the day's news. Amy told Will about the artists who would bring their work over the next week – an ex-headmistress who made stunning New England patchworks, a potter who worked in vivid ceramics, another painter, and a Bohemian jeweller who had BO and probably fancied her. Will told her what he'd discovered about *Boy Jack*. Amy's eyes shone, and she held his hand as he recounted the story of the old boat and her owner.

"How sad. But how lovely."

"Why lovely?"

"Because you know now that she was meant for you."

"Do you think so?"

"I know so. He even had the same initials."

"I hadn't noticed," he said in surprise.

They dawdled over lemon mousse, laughing and chattering like old friends. Will could not remember when he had felt so rested and happy. The meal finished, they rose and moved towards the sofa.

"Coffee?"

"I'm fine. It was lovely." They kissed, longingly and tenderly as though they had been waiting for the moment when they could let go. Her tongue darted in and out of his mouth and he felt an intensity of passion that took his breath away. He broke from her momentarily, his heart pounding.

She looked at him anxiously, longingly, searching in his eyes for the love she knew must be there, then took his hand and gently led him towards the bed. He stood quite still, as though time had stopped, then slowly began to undress her. He pulled off her sweatshirt and her amber hair tumbled over freckled shoulders. Her breasts were rounded and firm; he stroked them lightly with the back of his hand. She unbuttoned his shirt, pulled it off and kissed his forearm. He began to kiss her body and she threw her head back with pleasure before they tore away each other's remaining clothing and made love beneath the covers. The tension Will had lived with for so long slipped away, and that night he slept more soundly and peacefully than he had for years, with Amy curled up alongside him, and his arms cradling her. He felt as though he had come home.

A scream awoke him. He sat upright with a jerk. It was a gull. His heart was beating wildly in his chest, but it subsided, and the inner calm returned. He lay back on the pillow and Amy stirred. He watched her surface, beaming from ear to ear, her eyes not yet open. He stroked her hair, breathing in her fragrance.

She laid her head on his shoulder and touched his arm. "You have lovely arms," she murmured. "I'd like to paint them."

He studied the look of contentment on her face with deep pleasure. He wanted to keep this moment going, to stop the clock and let it always be like this.

Amy opened her eyes. "Hallo."

"Hallo."

They said no more for several minutes, then he kissed her and they made love again. Eventually she slipped out from under the covers and made her way to the bathroom. He watched her go, her lithe body almost floating over the floor.

After a few moments he slid out of bed and followed her, into the bathroom where she was turning on the brass taps above the iron tub.

She poured essence into the steaming water, then stepped into it and looked at him with one eyebrow raised. He walked across the room and got in after her.

Later, over breakfast, they said little but smiled a lot. The thing that struck him most was the serenity. Until he remembered the fire, the break-in on his boat, and that it was no longer in the water. Spike would need feeding, his books had been lost and . . . Ellie.

"Hallo?" Amy said.

"Sorry. Just remembering."

"Don't."

"No." He smiled apologetically. "I'd better go. You have to paint. And I have to . . . paint."

She looked at him across her bowl of cornflakes, a droplet of milk balanced on her lower lip. He reached over and wiped it away with his finger, and felt a wave of love envelop him. "See you later, then?" he asked.

"Yes."

He kissed her lightly on the cheek and spiralled down the iron staircase. He could not remember when he had last felt so unassailable, so powerful and so alive. The guilt that had gnawed for so long at his soul seemed to be relaxing its grip.

Chapter 15: Strumble Head

Primrose Hankey was having a high time of it all. On a scale of one to ten in terms of quality gossip, Pencurnow would normally struggle to reach two. But the past few days had yielded rich pickings, which she gleefully retailed along with the paraffin and Pampers. Not that her face betrayed any pleasure in passing on the information: it was all done with an innate sense of duty.

Will had avoided the shop for the best part of a week, but eventually had to call in for provisions. Mrs Sparrow's hospitality did not run to lunch, and a boat-builder, as Amy had discovered, had quite an appetite. His curiosity also encouraged him to acquaint himself with the lie of the land as Primrose saw it.

Will hated himself for falling prey to her desire to inform and be informed, but something inside him told him that she might have some knowledge, however scanty, that would give him a better overview of what was going on. And he felt guilty at not having shown more appreciation of her athletic personal delivery service.

Primrose was up a ladder, which was unfortunate, not only because the view of her from ground level was less than flattering but also because when she set eyes on Will Elliott her excitement was so great that she almost lost her footing. In the event, she descended to the concrete floor with greater speed than was good for her, and a shelf stacked high with tinned goods vibrated dangerously on impact.

"Mr Elliott! How nice to see you. Come for your magazine, have you? Lovely to see your boat. So glad I was able to help!" She reached under the counter for *Classic Boat*, anxious to ingratiate herself after their last meeting.

"Yes." It was as good as Will could manage, and a considerable accomplishment, bearing in mind the short space that Primrose allowed between sentences.

"About Miss Finn . . ."

"Have you any Cornish pasties?" Will waded in to change the subject.

"Over there in the cool cabinet. She seems such a nice person. Very genuine. I'm sorry if you thought I was interfering."

Will delved among the chicken and mushroom slices and sausage rolls, seeking vainly for a pasty and wishing he'd shopped elsewhere.

"Sorry to hear about the fire. It must have been dreadful."

"Yes. Terrible."

"Poor Mr and Mrs Hallybone. Are they both all right?"

"I think so. A bit shocked but I hope they'll get over it. It's just a good thing that the fire was fairly contained."

"I'm sorry you lost your diaries. All those memories gone."

Will had finally located a battered pasty. He closed the cabinet and came over. "No. Not the memories. Just the diaries. But you have to move on, don't you, Primrose?"

Primrose was unsure whether or not this was delivered as a reproof. She paused to consider. Will felt that the best form of defence was attack. He became the inquisitor rather than the one who was being quizzed.

"What do you make of it all, then, Primrose?"

Primrose was an old hand at being pumped. If anything, she enjoyed dispensing information even more than discovering it. What was the point in having theories and bits of intelligence if you didn't spread them around? Every now and again her conscience niggled, but she invariably failed to restrain herself. This made her popular with the ladies of the village, except when the piece of gossip being retailed concerned them personally. Under these circumstances Primrose was regarded as an interfering busybody.

"Very strange." She looked conspiratorially to left and right. "There's something very unpleasant going on, I think. I reckon we've not heard the last of it yet."

Will leaned on the counter and did his best to sound casual. "What sort of something?"

"The sort of something that goes on by the sea. Things coming and going, if you know what I mean."

"What sort of things?"

"Oh, not for me to say, Mr Elliott. Gracious me. I mean, if the lighthouse has been burned down on account of your diaries it would be very silly of me to start saying things, wouldn't it?"

"I'm sorry, I shouldn't have asked. I'm just rather confused about it, that's all." Will was amazed that Primrose had cottoned on to the significance of his diaries.

"I think it's been going on for quite some time, Mr Elliott." She was whispering now. "Ever seen *Whisky Galore?*" she asked.

Will nodded.

"Well, you know what I mean, then. Them folk from the city like to think they have a hold on us down here in Cornwall, when they don't have a hold on us at all. It's a sort of gesture of defiance, if you know what I mean."

Will could not help but show a little surprise, and Primrose read his reaction. "Oh, don't you go thinking that we're all at that game!" She pointed to the bottles on the shelf behind her. "My stocks come from the wholesaler!" She chuckled.

"But you could get some that didn't if you wanted to?"

Perspiration was forming on Primrose's upper lip. She clearly thought she had said more than she should and changed the subject. "Anyway, how's Mr Utterly?"

"Hovis?"

"Sorry?"

"Hovis. Bread. I need a brown loaf. Have you got one?"

"Yes." She looked at him as though he had had a brainstorm.

Will recovered himself with commendable and unusual speed. "Mr Utterly. Yes. He's fine. Says he's leaving in a few weeks, though. Going back to Devon. Salcombe or Dartmouth. I shall be sorry to see him go." The moment he had said it he bit his lip: in covering up his slip about Hovis's name he had revealed different information, which Primrose would now impart to the rest of the village.

"Oh, don't you worry about that. Mr Utterly has been leaving for Dartmouth or Salcombe every month for the past three years to my certain knowledge."

"Sorry?"

"It's a dream he's always had. Going back to his roots. Where his family used to live. But, so far, he's never made it. They do say," she leaned over the papers on the counter to speak more confidentially, "that he hasn't a clue how to sail that boat of his. Wouldn't even know which way to turn out of the harbour to get to Devon."

"Really?"

She nodded. "Nobody likes to push him, though. Lovely man. Very good family. Bakers, by all accounts."

"Really?" Will said again. He fished in his pocket for money and scooped up the carrier-bag into which she had deposited his goods. "Must dash, Primrose."

She called after him, "Not a word now!" But it was too late: he was already on his way down the lane, feeling strangely excited about the prospect before him, and even more warmly disposed towards his whiskered neighbour.

Chapter 16: Breaksea

"Wight, Portland, Plymouth, south-westerly five or six, increasing seven or gale eight. Occasional rain. Good becoming moderate . . ."

The sound from the radio on board Hovis's boat seeped out of the port-holes and Will heard the unfavourable forecast as he approached. "Doesn't sound too good."

"No." Hovis was sweeping his decks and looked up. "Sounds distinctly grim. Batten-down-the-hatches time. I think I shall have to put off my voyage for a bit. No point in setting off if there's a gale threatening."

"No." Will didn't like to say any more. "Have you seen Gryler or his lad?"

"He was around half an hour ago. Probably in the pub by now. The lad's gone off in his boat."

"He spends a lot of time in that boat, doesn't he?"

Hovis stopped sweeping. "You think he's up to something?"

"I don't know." Will looked thoughtful.

"How's *Boy Jack* coming on?"

"Better than I'd hoped. Harry reckons he'll be done by tomorrow. That means I can finish painting and antifouling the hull and have her back in the water some time next week, weather permitting."

"Well, it might not. You heard the forecast."

"How imminent?"

"Pretty imminent. And talking of pretty, how's the lady?"

"She's fine, thanks. Fine."

Hovis chuckled as Will's eyes grew misty. "Well I never."

"Mmmm? Sorry?" Will realized his momentary lapse.

Hovis grinned. "What have you got planned for the afternoon?"

"I want to nip over to the lighthouse and see if Ernie and May are OK. If that weather is as imminent as you say it is, though, I'd better get a move on or I'll get a soaking."

Their conversation was interrupted by the throaty rumble of a powerboat and they turned in unison to see a white gin palace bearing down on them, with Jerry MacDermott at the helm. The boat, almost fifty-foot long, was slewing precariously towards the pontoon, and Will, anxious to avoid a repetition of the MacDermotts' last berthing exercise on a vessel barely a third the size of their new model, dashed along the pontoon to fend it off before it could do any damage. Hovis followed.

"You OK?" Will asked the helmsman, before laying a hand on the boat.

There was a look of panic in Jerry MacDermott's eye, as though he knew that this time he had bitten off more than he could chew. He lobbed his cigar butt into the water, the better to grind his teeth and bite his lip. "Bit tricky, son. Could do with a hand. The missus is on her way down by car. Thought I'd surprise her."

"You on your own up there?"

"Yes. Broker said it could be 'andled by one at a pinch."

Yes, but not this one, thought Will. "Put your rudder amidships then go astern on your port engine," he said.

"Sorry?"

"The left-hand engine. Ease it into reverse. Keep your starboard engine – the right-hand one – in neutral."

"Right." The port engine gave a rich, deep growl, and the water churned at the stern of the boat.

"Not too much. Now go ahead gently on your starboard engine."

The boat did a stately pirouette.

"Put them both into neutral and throw us a rope."

Jerry MacDermott did as he was told and threw ropes to both Hovis and Will.

"Just ease back on both engines now – very gently," instructed Will. "That's it. A little more. Fine. OK. You can switch off." He fastened the new black mooring warp around a rusty cleat on the pontoon and Hovis did the same. The one thing Hovis knew how to do was keep a boat in port, thought Will, watching his companion deftly wind the rope around another corroding cleat.

"You're a gent, squire." MacDermott tossed the compliment with a note of relief in his voice.

Will read the name on the transom of the new boat: *Sokai Again*. Jerry MacDermott had pushed the boat out in more ways than one.

"Like her?" asked her new owner proudly.

"She's . . . er . . . very big," said Will diplomatically.

Hovis stood perfectly still, eyeing her up from stem to stern, scratching his head and wondering just how much money had been spent on the largest piece of Tupperware he had ever set eyes on. He didn't have to wonder for long.

"Two hundred and fifty grand," boasted her owner. "Only a year old. Barely run in."

"How big?" asked Hovis, his eyes like saucers.

"Forty-eight feet," replied MacDermott. "Got everything. Radar, GPS, generator, two TVs, CD player, cocktail bar, twin staterooms – both with *en suite* showers – two fridges, fly-bridge, bathing platform. It's even got a gangplank."

"Passarelle," supplied Will.

"And one of them as well," confirmed MacDermott. "The missus will love her."

"Are you sure you've got enough fenders out?"

"Not blown it up yet."

"No. Not your tender. Your fenders – to stop it scraping."

"There's some in that crate thing at the back."

"I'd tie a few more of them down the pontoon side, I think. And your springs and your head and stern lines will need to be strong. Some high winds are forecast. You'll want her secure." Will hated dishing out orders, but the prospect of that amount of money at the mercy of the impending elements drove him into offering unsolicited advice.

"Are you going to leave her here?" asked Hovis, still in awe of the stately hulk.

"For a bit, squire. Thought she'd give this place a touch of class." MacDermott had recovered and was back to his swaggering ways. He hopped down.

"Are you sure she'll be safe?"

"Oh, I think so. With the likes of you on site I shouldn't have too much to worry about."

"Yes, but it's a lot of money."

"Nah. Bit of fun, really. Take us along to Brighton in a jiffy. Trudie'll like that. Likes Brighton. Good shopping."

"Brighton?" Hovis was musing on how long it would take a Cornish yawl to get from Pencurnow to Brighton, with a favourable wind. Pencurnow to Falmouth. Falmouth to Salcombe. Salcombe to Weymouth. Weymouth to Lymington. Lymington to Brighton. He reckoned on a good five days, allowing for overnighting in port.

"How fast does she go?"

"Thirty-odd knots."

"Good grief. It's not natural."

"No. But it's the business, squire. Anyway, mustn't 'old you up. Old Gryler around?"

"Pub, I think," murmured Hovis.

Will had been watching silently. MacDermott and his boat seemed so out of place in this tiny Cornish boatyard. Perhaps it was a sign of the times. A sign of the way things were going.

"Old bugger. I'll go and tell 'im 'e's got a new charge to keep an eye on. Be seein' you."

"Yes." Hovis stood, entranced. "Two fridges," he muttered. "And a cocktail bar."

"Yes", said Will, "but once he plugs into shore power just think of the size of his electricity bill."

Hovis brightened. "That's a point. There's a lot to be said for a locker below the water-line. Let nature do the cooling. And anyway . . ."

Will looked at him quizzically. "Yes?"

"I've never liked Brighton. Not a patch on Salcombe."

Amy turned the envelope in her hand and ran her fingers over it. She had put off opening it, half afraid of its contents, half annoyed at its encroachment on her life. The handwriting was assured, over-elaborate. At least it meant, hopefully, that Oliver was now some distance away. That much should have been a relief, but it was not.

She walked to the counter and picked up a pair of scissors, sliced neatly through the top of the envelope. She pulled out the single sheet of crisp white paper and unfolded it.

The message was written in black ink.

Ballet d'Azur

Dear Ame,

I didn't mean to upset you, angel. You know I wouldn't do that for anything. [Amy threw her head back and let out a single sharp laugh.]

I just want you back. Need you back. You know what it's like – the not dancing. The not being near you. You must miss it as much as I do. I only get angry when I think we won't be together again. I have so many plans for us. We *can* get back what we had. You know we can. Trust me and it will all work out.

I'm planning to take the company to Nice – the place where we thought up the name. Remember the hotel? The room over the terrace? Five times a day? Again perhaps?"

She winced, half at the painful memory, half at the cloying sentiment shot through with arrogance that Oliver seemed to think would override everything that had happened since.

Don't shut me out. Give me a chance to show you that we can do it again. We have so much together, you know that. We shouldn't waste it.

I'll come and see you again, soon, and this time I won't take no for an answer. You must come. We can make a fresh start. There is nothing else for either of us. Believe me. O

She dropped the letter on the counter. Then she picked it up, tore it into little pieces and threw it into the wastebin.

The walk along the cliff top was not pleasant. His thoughts of Amy warmed him, but the sky was threatening and the wind building in gusts. He wondered what she was doing. He saw the *Gull* pulled up on the patch of shingle to one side of the lighthouse. Ernie was coming out of the door below the tower and hailed him. "Not looking so good."

"In there?" Will was concerned about the lighthouse.

"No. The forecast. Blowing up."

"I know. I thought I'd nip over and see you before it bucketed down."

"Nice of you. They reckon we're OK for a few hours yet."

"How's May?"

"Oh, coming along. Getting over it. She was a bit shocked, you know. Nothing like that's ever happened to her before. Not to either of us."

"I know."

"Still, got to carry on. Look forward, not back. That boat of yours," he pointed at *The Gull*, "good at catching mackerel. Hooked another two this morning. Reckon I'm on to a winner there." He patted Will on the back. "Fancy a cup of tea?"

The two men walked through to Ernie's kitchen and he brewed up.

"Seen much this morning?" asked Will.

"Not much. Quiet, really. *The Scillonian* pushing out to St Mary's. Young Applebee out there with his lobster pots but that's about all."

"Still out, is he?"

"Reckon so. Motored off behind Bill's Island an hour or more ago. Haven't seen him since. Time he was getting back in." Ernie searched for clues in the sky.

"Strange."

Ernie stared at him. "You think he's up to something?"

"Might be. Not sure."

"Best not enquire. Not after . . . you know."

"I know." Will was anxious to avoid worrying Ernie. They chatted for a while, about *Boy Jack*, about May's livestock and the lighthouse, the visitors who would come with the warmer weather. Will was relieved to see Ernie cheerful at the prospect of his new job.

"I'm getting used to the idea. Got all me patter off. Listen to this, see what you think." He stood up and cleared his throat. "Prince Albert Rock Lighthouse was constructed in its present form by William Tregarthen Douglass, the same engineer responsible for the construction of Bishop Rock Lighthouse, which is positioned on rocks beyond the Isles of Scilly. It was completed in 1873 and is now one hundred and twenty-six years old. The lamp is hand made and for almost a hundred years nothing has been replaced except the bulbs. It floats on a bath of mercury and weighs three and a half tons. The beam is 1.2 million candle power and is visible for twenty-six miles."

Will stayed silent, anxious to be as encouraging as possible.

"There are four 'bull's-eyes' in the lamp and one revolution takes twelve seconds, which therefore means that there is one flash every three seconds – the signature of Prince Albert Rock Lighthouse." He paused for a reaction.

"Very clear."

"You've heard it all before, haven't you?" He looked crestfallen.

"But you won't be telling it to me. I think you're doing well."

"It's a real bugger trying to stop it sounding too technical."

"Well, why don't you weave a few stories in?"

"Like what?"

"Oh, you know. The story about the lighthouse keeper on Smalls. The one who died and his mate had to hang him over the side to stop the smell."

"And that's why there are always three keepers not two, so that the third one can provide . . ."

"The alibi," they said in chorus.

"That's it. And the three keepers on Flannan Isles who just disappeared."

"The *Mary Celeste* of the lighthouse world." Ernie's eyes lit up. "That would be a spicy one, wouldn't it? Perk things up a bit."

"You're a good story-teller and you've got all the yarns. Use them."

"So long as Trinity House don't mind."

"Oh, I can't see them bothering. Enjoy yourself."

Ernie looked across the table at him. "You know, I think I just might!"

By the time Will had walked back, the wind had strengthened and banks of ominous-looking purple-grey clouds were building to the south-west. *Boy Jack* sat on her shores. She looked as if she was itching to get back into the water. "It won't be long now, old girl." Will patted her hull and noticed an envelope from Harry Gwenver pinned to the planking. He pulled it off, tore it open and read the note it contained: "Fatlagena whye? Have done my bit. Over to you now. Hope you are pleased. Will send my bill when Mrs Gwenver has worked out the sums. Darzona. Harry Gwenver."

He looked at the note and frowned. *Fatlagena whye* he remembered as meaning 'how are you?' but *Darzona*? He'd not heard that before.

He wandered down towards *Florence Nightingale* and called Hovis, who emerged towelling his beard. "Caught me at my ablutions, young man."

"Sorry. Just wondered how you were at Cornish?"

"Ropy. Very ropy. What sort of Cornish?"

"*Darzona.*"

"Ah. Emphasis on the second syllable to rhyme with gone. *Dar-ZON-a.*"

"Meaning?"

"Very simple: God bless."

Chapter 17: Blacktail

Towards mid-afternoon the wind had built up to force five or six, and Will studied the props supporting *Boy Jack*. They would hold, he convinced himself, protected by the high jetty wall, which offered some shelter from the worst of the south-westerlies.

Halyards in the boatyard rang against the alloy masts with the insistence of unanswered doorbells, and Hovis was at work lashing down anything on his deck that was in danger of moving. Even the water in the boatyard was choppy, and the sea was becoming decidedly lumpy.

Will climbed the wall of the jetty and looked out towards Prince Albert Rock. White crests topped every wave. It would soon be an uncomfortable passage home for anyone not yet in port.

His thoughts turned again to Amy. The previous night seemed so far away now. Would she want to see him tonight?

His introspection was interrupted abruptly by the arrival of Len Gryler. "Your boat-builder finished, is he?"

"Yes. Down to me now."

"When do you want her back in the water, then?"

"Probably by the end of next week, if that's all right."

"Should be. But I'll need a couple of days' notice. Need to make sure the machine's up to it. Busy time coming now. Boats going in and out of the water. New shower block going up." He tossed his head towards a small portable building being craned from the back of a truck alongside his peeling cabin. "That should please the punters." But his entrepreneurial tone lacked its usual relish and he seemed distracted as he looked out to sea. "Bit rough out there. Getting worse,

388

too." He was edgy. Uneasy, thought Will. He wasn't carrying his monkey wrench, and his hands were stuffed into his pockets. He seemed to be clenching and unclenching his fists.

"Is your lad still out there?"

Gryler's gaze raked the waves for a sign of his boat. "Yes."

"In this?"

"He should've been back an hour or more ago. Don't know where he's got to. Must have broken down."

"What are you going to do?"

"Dunno. Wait and see, I suppose. He might have put in further along the coast and be walking back. Can't see him on the water."

"There's not much of a view from here. I'll climb the cliff path and have a look," Will suggested.

"No. He'll be back. He'll have put in further along. Probably waiting for the weather to calm down." Gryler looked at Will with a stubborn glare, then rolled off down the jetty to his shed.

"You sure she'll be safe in this?" Will turned to find Hovis at his shoulder, looking up at *Boy Jack*.

"I hope so. I've checked all the shores and the wall's offering a fair bit of shelter. Nothing else I can do now. How's *Florence?*"

"Oh, she'll be fine. I've stowed everything that might blow away, and what I can't stow I've lashed down so she'll just bob about a bit until it's over."

"You look a bit pasty. Fancy a walk?"

"In this?" Hovis looked at Will as though he were off his head.

"Young Applebee hasn't come back. Gryler reckons he's put in further along the coast. I reckon he's still out there."

"Once a lighthouse keeper always a lighthouse keeper."

"I suppose so."

"I thought it was the coastguard who kept an eye on the movements of shipping?"

"I know, but old habits die hard. Anyway, the lad might be in trouble."

"In more ways than one by the sound of it. You sure you want to get involved?"

"I can't just mess around here if he's out there."

Will remembered his first encounter with Christopher Applebee, giving him the magazines. It was hard to think of the indolent youth as a smuggler. He was more than likely poaching lobsters. Nothing more.

"Well, I'm nipping up there for a look."

"Let me grab my oilskin. It's starting to rain."

While Hovis went back to *Florence Nightingale* for his waterproof, Will nipped up the ladder on to *Boy Jack's* deck, grabbed his sailing jacket and secured the hatches.

They met at the end of the jetty as heavy rainclouds passed overhead. The two men braced themselves against the strengthening wind as they climbed up the sandy cliff path between the tussocks of grass. They could make out a figure with a dog walking towards them as they crested the first knoll. It was Hugo Morgan-Giles.

"Good afternoon. Not going out in this, are you?" He was holding on to his flat tweed cap and reining in the yellow Labrador. "Steady, Elsie."

Hovis began, "We're just—"

"Out for a breath of air," Will interrupted. "Before it gets too bad."

"Bit grim, isn't it? Even mad dogs don't enjoy this," agreed Hugo, trying to remain upright in the face of a stiff breeze and a strong dog. "Don't get blown away." He carried on past them, hauled by the Labrador in the direction of the Moorings.

The rain became heavier, and as the two men breasted the highest point of the cliff the full might of the sea came into view below them. There was a ten-foot swell, and white spume flew in the air to twice that height as the breakers crashed on to the rocks below. The thundering of tide on granite was deafening, and the rain stung their faces. Hovis reached into the pocket of his grubby yellow oilskin, pulled out a matching sou'wester and clamped it on his head, pulling the strap firmly beneath his chin. "You look like the man on the tin of pilchards," teased Will.

"Yes, but at least I'll be dry."

They walked across to the edge of the cliff, planting their feet carefully on the uneven turf, strewn with rabbit droppings, and peered out to sea, scrutinizing the water between the boatyard, Bill's Island and Prince Albert Rock as rain and salt spray blew into their eyes.

On the horizon a container-ship ploughed its course doggedly. "That's about the only thing I'd want to be on in this weather," shouted Will, his hair soaked and clinging to his head like a tangle of black serpents.

"I wouldn't even want to be on that," countered Hovis.

It was fully five minutes before they saw the boat, tossing like a cork on the heaving waves between Bill's Island and the lighthouse.

"Christ!" Will reached into the pocket of his sailing jacket for the binoculars. It was difficult to hold them steady in the near gale-force wind, and impossible to keep them clear due to the lashing onshore rain. He tucked his elbows into his sides, the better to keep the glasses steady, and tried to focus on the small boat between the massive rollers.

"He's still in there! Look!" He handed the binoculars to Hovis who finally located the buffeted fishing smack.

"Good God! His outboard must have packed up." Hovis rubbed the lenses clear of rain again. "He's got no oars, as far as I can see. We'd better call the lifeboat. Where's the nearest phone? Pencurnow or the lighthouse?"

"Pencurnow's nearer. You run there and call them out, I'll get round to the lighthouse."

The two men set off in different directions, Will unsure why he was heading for the lighthouse, but knowing that he needed to be there. He ran as fast as the gusting wind and rain would allow, keeping his eye on the little boat as it pitched and tossed ever nearer the rocks strung out like jagged teeth at the foot of Prince Albert. The nearer he got, the more clearly he could make out the tiny figure spreadeagled in the bottom of the boat, one arm braced against each side, clinging on amid a tangled mess of lobster-pots, fishing-nets and rope.

The rain was torrential now, flung sideways by the wind. Will reached the end of the path and began to pick his way over the rocks at the base of the lighthouse, spray thrown high above his head.

At first he thought he was seeing double and rubbed his eyes to clear them of salt water. Then he knew that his eyes were not playing tricks: there were now two small boats on the water: the fishing boat PZ 291, containing Christopher Applebee, and a smaller rowing boat manned by an oarsman negotiating the waves and travelling in the direction of the stricken craft. It took only a moment for Will to grasp that the second boat was *The Gull* and that the oarsman was Ernie Hallybone.

Rooted to the spot, rain running off his chin, he watched as Ernie, now a hundred yards from the rocks, rowed towards the other craft, which was still fifty yards away. The fishing smack tilted alarmingly from side to side and Christopher Applebee clung to the port side as the boat heaved to starboard. His right leg was entangled in the fishing net, which had been dragged from the boat by the waves. He fought to disengage himself, then lost his grip and slipped rapidly from view. The boat turned turtle and the outboard motor parted from the transom.

Will's heart was pounding and he spotted Christopher Applebee's head bobbing between the waves, then disappearing as he was dragged down by fierce undercurrents.

Ernie pulled rhythmically on his oars in spite of the towering waves, cresting one as though he were on the back of a heaving whale, then hurtling down into the hollows between the watery mountains.

He was barely twenty yards from the youth now, and closing, but all the while the two of them drifted towards the rocks at the foot of the lighthouse. As he watched Ernie battle against the water, Will could barely breathe, praying that he would reach Christopher Applebee in time and that he would be able to stay clear of the rocks until help arrived.

The head above the water seemed nearer to the boat now. Ernie was in with a chance. Without warning *The Gull* twisted in the water, pulled by the current and pushed by the wind, and a rolling breaker caught her beam on, flipping her over and tossing Ernie into the water like a crumb.

Will shouted, "No!" as the oars were flung aloft like matchsticks, only to tumble back into the sea and be swallowed up. *The Gull* righted herself, then caught the crest of a roller and was propelled toward the rocks. Under the thunder of the waves and the scream of the wind, Will heard the cracking and splitting of timber on rock as she was riven into splinters against the jagged granite below the lighthouse.

Fear seized him as he leapt from rock to rock, searching for Ernie amid the spray and spume. He scanned the water for him, hoping with every passing second that his friend would appear, but the only thing visible was the upturned hull of PZ 291, slewing and tumbling ever nearer to the rocks.

He tore off his waterproof and shoes, then breasted his way into the oncoming tide. Where was Ernie?

The waves slammed into Will as he tried to swim, sweeping him towards the rocks. He was powerless to resist their force as he somersaulted headlong into the next wave, which seemed to be coming from a completely different direction. Deafened and gasping for breath as the water swirled around him, he heard it echo thunderously in his ears. His head bobbed up, only to be submerged again by a towering roller.

His arms aching from useless exertion, he pulled even harder towards the spot where it seemed Ernie had been tipped out of the boat, only to be flung with violent disregard against a rock. He felt the sharpness of limpets against the side of his head and saw the redness descending in front of his eyes.

He held on to the image of Ernie, willing him with every fibre of his body to appear from the waves, and praying that the sea would give him up. Again and again Will dived forward. He wanted to let go, but struggled to keep his mind on what he was trying to do. The vision of the craggy face became fuzzy and another took its place: a younger face, framed with amber curls; a smiling, loving face. Another gigantic wave broke over his head, pushing him deeper into the sea. His body was willing to be taken now; Ernie had gone and he could feel the life being pounded out of him, sucked from his feeble grasp. But with Amy's image shining like a beacon in front of him, and with one final burst of energy, he raised his head above the waves and looked for the shore, before another mighty wall of water picked him up, turned him round and scooted him like a surfboard towards the edge of the rocks.

Dragging himself upright in the few seconds between waves, he hauled himself clear of the tide as it sucked back the crushed shells and pebbles with a threatening roar. With the last of his energy he scrambled on to the grass above the granite outcrop.

As the lifeboat rounded the headland Will fell to his knees in desperation, his hands gripping the sodden grass until his knuckles turned white. He prayed pasionately for Ernie's salvation, but above the howling din of the wind and waves his anguished entreaties remained unanswered.

Chapter 18: Sunk

"What on earth's the matter?" She had opened the door and found him standing there, his face ashen, except for the bloody graze on his forehead. "Tell me."

He found it impossible to speak.

"You're soaking. Come in. What's happened?"

"Ernie." He sought for words. "He went after Applebee in *The Gull*. He'd lost his outboard. He just disappeared. Just went. One minute he was there and the next he wasn't. Washed over the side."

She wrapped her arms round him and held him. He shook with fear and cold. "Why did he go after him in a sea like that? In a bloody rowing boat?" He spat the words out angrily. "How could he even think of it?"

"Ssh. Ssh." She rocked him from side to side as he clenched his jaw and fought back the tears.

"It was my boat. My bloody boat."

She kept silent while his body went into spasms of shock. "Have they found him?"

"No."

She tried to hold back her own tears. "And the boy?"

"Yes. Lifeboat picked up his body. They're still looking for Ernie."

For several minutes neither spoke until Amy said softly, "Let's get you out of those wet things."

She led him upstairs and took off his clothes as he stood and shivered. His hair was matted with brine and she towelled him dry, found him a pair of baggy canvas trousers, then slipped a T-shirt and a thick sweater over him.

"I have to get back to May. Her sister's come over from St Petroc but I said I'd go back."

"How is she?"

"Frighteningly calm. She's going to stay with her sister tonight. Doesn't want to be on her own."

"Poor woman."

"Yes. I have to go." Will looked distracted.

"Will you come back?"

"Yes. No. I don't know. I have to go to the police station at St Petroc. I'm not sure when they'll finish with me. I don't know what I'll feel like . . . if I'll want to . . ."

"Whatever," she said, masking her disappointment. "I'm here if you want me."

He looked at her absently. "Thanks. I . . . I'm sorry." He walked to the door, turned back hesitantly, then left her.

"I'm sorry you've had to come in again so soon, sir. And under such circumstances." It was the same detective sergeant who had taken his statement after the fire.

"Yes." Will sat on the hard wooden chair, slumped forward with his elbows on his knees. He could not remember feeling so low since Ellie had died. He seemed to be tumbling into a deep pit of despair, free-falling into misery. Ernie. Friendly, understanding, generous Ernie. The nearest Will had come to having a father. Only yesterday the old man seemed to have come to terms with his new life; now the tourists wouldn't hear his patter. His hand shook and he held on to the edge of the table to steady it.

"Are you able to answer a few questions, sir?"

"Yes."

"Can we start by finding out how you came to be there when the accident happened?"

"I was in the boatyard – the Crooked Angel – talking to Gryler, the owner. He said his lad had been out during the afternoon in his boat, and that he hadn't come back. I was concerned. Decided to go up the cliff path and see if I could spot him."

"Why did you feel a need to do that?"

"Don't know. Just did. I suppose it's what comes of watching boats all the time from the lighthouse. You get used to things not being quite right. Develop a sort of sixth sense. Can't really explain it any more than that."

"Did you know the lad?"

"Not really. I'd met him a couple of times but I wouldn't say I knew him."

"How did you know he was in trouble?"

"I didn't know, I just surmised."

"I see."

The detective sergeant made occasional jottings on an A4 notepad.

"Did you go on your own – on the cliff path, I mean?"

"No. I went with Mr Utterly. He has the boat next to mine in the yard."

"Yes. I've already spoken to him. He called the lifeboat out."

"Yes. I went to the lighthouse."

"Why was that, sir?"

"Again, I don't really know. Sixth sense."

"And what did you see?"

Will filled in the sergeant on the events he had watched with horror earlier that afternoon, of Christopher Applebee clinging to his boat, of Ernie's attempted rescue and of the wave that washed him overboard. He did not mention his own attempt to rescue his friend. The sergeant listened intently as Will told of the Sennen lifeboat's arrival, its combing the sea for the bodies, and the discovery only of Christopher Applebee.

"Popular man, Ernie Hallybone. Sad loss."

"Yes."

The detective sergeant got up from the desk and walked to the window, where the rain was running down the panes.

"Any idea why the lad was out there?"

"None at all. Unless he was after a few lobsters."

The sergeant turned round. "Or something else."

"Sorry?"

"Lobsters might gain him a few bob but I don't think he'd have gone out in this weather for a few bob, do you?"

"I suppose not."

"Seen any sign at your boatyard of booze?"

The sergeant's direct questioning threw Will off-balance. "Booze?"

"Yes. You know – whisky, gin, vodka. Rémy Martin."

He regained his equilibrium. "No. Not at all. None."

"Not in a shed? Or being offloaded from boats? In boxes? They probably wouldn't say Famous Grouse on the side. Bit obvious, that.

But if they'd said Golden Wonder you'd have noticed if they'd looked suspiciously heavy?"

Will was taken aback by the note of irritation in the policeman's voice. "Yes. There's been nothing. It's very quiet down there." Then the implication of the question hit home. "You don't think . . ."

"What, sir?"

"You don't think *I* had anything to do with this, do you?"

"At the moment, sir, I'm keeping an open mind."

Suddenly Will felt the weight of the world upon his shoulders. The sergeant read his reaction and offered a placatory smile. "Using my sixth sense, sir, you're not high on my list of suspects, but I have to ask the questions. I also have to try to get to the bottom of this."

Will tried to smile back, but found it impossible.

When he had given precise details and times, the sergeant was seemingly satisfied, and brought the interview to a close. "I think that's all I need to know for the present, sir. You can go now."

Will thanked him, for the second time in a week, and wondered if this was to become a regular occurrence. Until this week he'd only ever been in a police station once to report his grandmother's lost Jack Russell, and now here he was every few days.

He rose to go, and the sergeant coughed. "Er, sir?"

"Yes?"

"I'd be grateful if you could keep our conversation to yourself for now."

"Yes. Yes, of course."

"Especially as far as Mr Gryler is concerned."

The rain had petered out to a light drizzle, and the wind was no more than a gusty breeze in the dark, wet night. He glanced at his watch. Just after ten. Where had the day gone? The agonizing, dreadful day. He unlocked the door of Ernie's van, slid on to the driver's seat and slammed the door. Ernie's peaked cap, its white top fresh-laundered for his new job, lay on the passenger seat. He picked it up and looked at the marks around the inside of the headband where years of sweat had stained the leather. He studied the badge and its legend, TRINITAS IN UNITATE. Three in one. He couldn't bring himself to smile, but he hoped in his heart that Ernie had gone somewhere where the Trinity House motto would be appropriate.

Amy sat up in case he came. Ten o'clock, then eleven, then midnight.

She hoped he would want to be with her to share his sorrow. At twelve thirty she slid into bed, keeping one small lamp on just in case, and listening to music on the stereo to keep her awake, until finally came the song that touched her soul.

"You may wish that he would tell you all the feelings in his head, and say that life's worth living when you're there."

Tears ran down her cheeks and soaked into the pillow.

"But deep inside your heart you know, when lying in your bed, he can never ever know how much you care."

Chapter 19: Blacknore

He thought he had reached a point in life where sadness could no longer affect him as it once had. He had been so deeply sad for so long, had become so used to battling through it. But Ernie's death was so unfair. It was not just the sorrow of losing a friend and father figure, it was the injustice. First Ernie had lost his job. Then he'd been given another that he hated. But he had soldiered on, determined to make a go of it, seizing the opportunity to forge a future for himself. He had a wife who loved him and to whom he was devoted. He should have been heading for a retirement in which he could have enjoyed his beloved Cornwall. Instead, life had been snatched from him.

Will had taken himself back to *Boy Jack* on the night of Ernie's death; had felt that old black cloak of despair rising up to envelop him once more. Half of him wanted to go to Amy, but the other half was gritting its teeth and battening down the hatches with a vengeance. What was the point in risking yet another attachment? Better to be in control of his own destiny than risk handing it over.

He lay inside the boat, wrapped in his sleeping bag, cold and stiff, the cat curled into him for warmth. He hardly slept, listening to the wind.

The morning dawned, not unusually after a storm, with a sly calm, weak sunshine slanting in through the wheelhouse port-holes. He stirred from shallow sleep and lay still, the events of the previous day replaying in his mind.

Spike lay still, purring in the curve of his body. Will raised his head and looked out at the yard and the sea beyond. He saw, with the bitter taste of irony, a perfect May morning. The first day of May. May's first day alone.

Amy woke to find the bedside light still on. She switched it off and looked up at the skylight and the pale blue sky. She wondered why it was blue when it should be grey; the deep, dark, threatening Paine's grey of a watercolour palette.

She lay still and thought of him, hoping he would call in. She knew she could not seek him out, that she must wait. She gazed up at the deepening blue of the morning and realized for the first time just how much she loved him.

It was nine o'clock before Will could drag himself out of his cocoon and brave the day. He walked up on deck and shivered in the cool, clear morning air, drawing the sleeping bag about his shoulders. Spike looked up at him; then tumbled down the ladder and ran away along the jetty. Will was about to head back inside when he saw a figure walking along the hard standing towards his boat. Hovis raised his hand and walked up to *Boy Jack*. He climbed the ladder. "Need anything?"

"No. Not really."

Hovis cleared his throat. "I'm going to make myself unpopular."

"Mmm?" Will was looking out to sea, his eyes unfocused.

"You're going to go and shower in Gryler's new, if makeshift, facility and then you're coming on to *Florence Nightingale* for breakfast."

"No, really, I'd rather be—"

"I know what you'd rather be, but that's not on."

Will kept looking at the sea.

"It's not your fault, you know."

Will spoke quietly. "It was my boat."

"It was his choice. He chose to go after that lad. You can't blame yourself."

"But I do." He looked at Hovis for the first time, and the despair in his eyes was plain. "Everything I touch turns to dust."

"You mustn't do this." Hovis used none of the bluff brightness that normally characterized his conversation. Instead he spoke calmly, firmly. "You mustn't be so hard on yourself."

"But it's my fault."

"No. It is not your fault." He laid his hand gently on Will's shoulder. "It is a most dreadful thing to happen, but you have to get over this. Do you hear?"

Will looked at him, pleadingly.

"Come on." Hovis eased the sleeping bag from Will's shoulders and stowed it in the wheelhouse, before ushering him down the ladder and propelling him towards the newly positioned shower block beyond Gryler's office. He walked back to *Florence Nightingale* for a towel and flopped it over the top of the cubicle door as the steam rose and the hot water did its best to wash away the troubles of the previous day.

Will returned to *Florence Nightingale* as though in a trance, the towel over his shoulder. The smell of bacon and eggs went unnoticed as he sat down at the table.

Hovis pushed the plate in front of him, along with a large mug of black coffee. He sat down with his own plate at the other side of the table and began to eat, noticing that his fellow diner was letting his breakfast go cold. He tapped his knife on the side of Will's plate. The ringing sound brought him to earth. "Sorry?" He looked at Hovis as though he had missed part of the conversation.

"Eat."

"I don't think I–"

"Eat!"

Hovis tucked in himself and watched as Will began to toy with a scrap of bacon and then his egg. He ate reluctantly at first, then more avidly – he hadn't eaten a meal for almost twenty-four hours. He cleared his plate before Hovis had finished.

"Better?"

"Thanks." He tried to smile but his face still had a distracted, hunted look. He made to leave.

"Where are you going?" Hovis asked.

"Just back."

"Wait for a bit. Don't go yet. More coffee?" Hovis offered the pot.

"No, thanks."

He put it back on the stove. "Can I say something?"

"Mmm?"

"Don't go there."

Will looked at him. "Where?"

"Where you've been before."

"What do you mean?"

"Don't go into yourself. Not now. It's not worth it. A waste of time."

"How do you know?" Will was surprised and a touch irritated by Hovis's plain-speaking.

"Because I've been there." He began to clear the table. "Just try and see ahead, not backwards. That's all."

"It's just that I thought—"

"You thought that at last things were going right for you. You had a glimpse of something special. Something real. Then suddenly you're back where you started." Hovis was filling the sink with water and looking out of the port-hole.

"How do you know?"

"Because I see things. Things that people don't think I see. You see boats coming and going, I see people. People's faces. People's hearts." He turned to face Will, a cup in one hand and a dripping cloth in the other. "Sometimes their souls."

The two men looked at one another for a few moments before Hovis spoke again, very softly. "Some things in your life you have no control over. It is quite pointless worrying over them. They are the way they are, and they will be the way they will be. Call it fate. Then there are the other things, the things that are yours to decide. And one of the strangest and saddest things in life is that some people cannot differentiate between the two. They spend all their time punishing themselves for things that have happened and which they can't change, and while they're busy doing that they fail to see life's opportunities." He smiled. "Don't miss out."

"On what?"

"Oh. I think you know."

The talk in the Salutation at lunchtime was of nothing but the previous day's events. Alf Penrose dispensed his pints with quiet circumspection and listened as the fishermen and other locals chewed the fat. Ted Whistler, perched on a stool at the end of the bar, stared blackly into his glass.

Gryler had been carted off to the police station the night before and had not, as yet, returned. Speculation grew until, at half past twelve, the door swung open and he bowled in, his face like thunder.

"Usual?" Alf Penrose enquired.

"Usual," he growled.

The bar, exuding a low rumble before Gryler's appearance, was hushed as Alf pulled the pump. The beer gushed into the glass and the slooshing sound echoed in the silence.

Gryler looked around. "You needn't look so surprised." The customers studied their feet. "They didn't keep me in."

Alf broke the ice. "What happened then?"

"Asked me about the lad and his boat."

"Oh, aye? So what do they think?"

"The lad was out pulling up his lobster pots. Outboard packed in and he hadn't taken any oars. Storm blew up and he got thrown out. Drownded."

"Didn't he have any flares?" asked one of the three fishermen at the end of the bar.

"No. Daft sod. No flares. No oars. Shouldn't have been out in that weather." Gryler took a sip of his beer. "Bloody lighthouse-keeper, neither. Bloody waste."

Ted Whistler pushed his stool noisily away from the bar, crossed the room and walked out.

"Taken it hard, has he?" asked Gryler, eyes on the disappearing figure.

"Must have done. Hasn't said a word. Hasn't even finished his pint." Alf gestured towards the half-full glass on the bar. "What happens now?"

"Dunno. Nothing, I suppose," said Gryler, taking another pull on his pint. "Misadventure, they'll call it. Misadbloodyventure."

One of the fishermen shot a look at Alf Penrose and Gryler caught his eye. "I'm telling you, it were nothing to do with me. I didn't even service the engine – he did it himself. I might have been his boss but I weren't his keeper. 'Ad a life of his own, you know." He registered the suspicion on the faces of those still at the bar. "Ah, bugger it. I've got work to do. On me own now, too." He slammed his glass down on the bar and stormed out, all eyes on him as he went.

Amy had not expected him so soon. She had steeled herself for a wait of a few days. Instead she looked up from her painting and saw him in the middle of the afternoon. She got up from her easel and walked over to where he stood. "Hi."

He put his arms around her, and kissed the top of her head. "I'm sorry. About yesterday."

She eased away from him and put her finger up to his lips. "Don't. No need."

"But there is–"

"Sssh . . . no." They stood, their arms around each other, gently swaying from side to side.

"I just felt so . . ."

"I didn't expect you. I knew you'd want to be on your own. It's OK, really it is."

"I just . . ."

"Just hold me, will you?"

He bent his head into her shoulder and sighed a long, deep sigh.

The door opened. "Anybody at home?"

The two sprang apart as Jerry MacDermott and his wife burst into the gallery.

"Oh. Sorry, squire. Didn't see you there. Didn't realize you were . . ."

Amy spoke first. "It's fine. Can I help you?"

"Well, me and the missus – don't want to interrupt or anything, but we've just come to look for something for the 'ouse. Sorry to 'ear what 'appened, though." He spoke to Will. "Sorry about the old man. Terrible thing, the sea. Very sad. Knew 'im well, did you?"

"Yes. I used to work with him."

"What would you like to see?" Amy tried to change the subject.

"You 'ad a couple of sculptures. They were 'ere . . ." He gestured to the middle of the floor. "Sold, are they?"

"Er . . . no. I just put them in the back room."

"Could you get them out again? I'd like Trudie to see them. She didn't notice them last time."

The blonde, clad in a bright pink sweatshirt, white leggings and stilettos, had been simpering on Jerry's arm. "Jerry says they're awfully sexy." She giggled.

Amy stood transfixed by the suntanned vision in pink and white. She looked like a slice of Neapolitan ice cream.

"Yes. I'll get them out." She turned to Will. "Can you give me a hand?"

"Sure."

The two writhing figures were brought out and stripped of their blankets so that Trudie and her squire could behold them in all their glory.

"Ooooh!" she half cooed, half giggled. "What do you suppose they're doing?"

"I dunno, love, but they seem to be enjoying it."

Amy looked abashed as Trudie MacDermott continued her eulogy. "Ooh! 'E's big, inne? Looks a bit like, you know, wassisname . . . That one we saw in Florence, Michelangelo's David."

"Well, sweetheart, if that's David, I'd like to see Goliath." Jerry guffawed at his own joke. "What do you think, then?"

"I think they're lovely," responded the blonde. "Can we have them?"

"Course we can," replied her spouse, patting her bottom. And then, to Amy, "Can we take them with us?"

"Yes. Of course. If you're sure you can manage."

"Yes. We can, can't we, love?"

"Let me help." Will came forward and took the sack barrow towards the first of the sculptures. He put the blanket over it, not just for protection, eased it on to the wheeled trolley, and pushed it towards the door.

"Now then," said Jerry. "Five 'undred apiece, wasn't it?"

"Well . . ." She wondered whether she should offer a discount for bulk-buying but Jerry took a large wad of notes from his back pocket and peeled off twenty fifty-pound notes. He pressed them into her hand with rather more pressure than was necessary.

"Thank you. Thank you very much." Amy did her best to sound polite but not too grateful.

Will bumped down the steps of the studio with the trolley, one hand on the first sculpture to prevent it taking a nose-dive down the steps. He repeated the exercise with the second, and the two were loaded on to the back seat of the MacDermott Mercedes then driven off up the lane in the direction of Benbecula.

Amy and Will stood on the steps watching the car climb the hill.

"I really didn't expect that," said Amy.

"Why?"

"I don't know. I'd just given up hope of ever getting them out of my life."

"Well, you have. They've gone."

As the Mercedes purred around the corner and out of sight, she looked up at him, tired and pale against the blue sky. "Time to start again."

He smiled at her and nodded. "Yes." He sighed, gazing out over the calm blue-green water.

Amy only wished that she had not received Oliver's letter.

Chapter 20: Skerries

Mrs Sparrow had done her best to be pleasant about Mr Elliott's departure. As she explained to Primrose Hankey, he had not been home the night before the storm and she had sat up for a while, wondering if something had happened. The following day she would have dropped into the conversation a few pointed remarks about his absence, had it not been for the tragic events that put matters into perspective. She related these facts to Primrose when making her call for groceries, the bits and bobs she had run out of before her monthly shop at Tesco's in Penzance.

Primrose's pique at Mrs Sparrow's shopping habits was put to one side as she listened attentively. Even though Will Elliott had stayed with Mrs Sparrow for two weeks, the information Primrose had gleaned had been minimal. Now, with the death of Ernie Hallybone casting a pall over the entire village, it was a relief to have something more spicy.

But Mrs Sparrow had few details – either that or she was keeping them strictly to herself – and the conversation turned, inevitably, to Ernie's funeral the previous day.

"A good way to go," Mrs Sparrow opined.

"What – drowning?" asked Primrose.

"No. With that sort of funeral. Uniforms and whatnot. Very smart. Gave it a sense of occasion." Mrs Sparrow added a packet of Bourbon biscuits to her pile.

"Mrs Hallybone looked tired," said Primrose.

"Worried, I suppose. What with the body being washed up three days later it must have taken it out of her. All that not knowing for certain. She'll have to find somewhere to live now." Mrs Sparrow sorted through the pickle jars and plumped for a bottle of Mrs Pengelly's lurid brew.

Primrose tried another gambit. "Miss Finn looked nice. She didn't sit with Mr Elliott, though."

"Why should she?"

Primrose decided that she was evidently in possession of more information than Mrs Sparrow. But, then, Mrs Sparrow was not the sort to trade in gossip; she merely handed out opinions. "Nice hymns. 'Eternal Father Strong to Save'. Even if it was a bit late. And 'I Vow to Thee My Country'. Good choice. Important, like."

Primrose put aside her newsmongering and recalled her feelings at the funeral. "I was all right," she said, "until they carried him out – Mr Elliott and the other keepers. That's when it was all too much for me. Seeing their faces. Their caps under their arms. Mr Hallybone's cap on top of his coffin." She put her hand into her tracksuit pocket, pulled out a man's handkerchief and blew hard.

"The lad's funeral was in Penzance, apparently. Family affair. Quiet."

"Well, at least Mr Hallybone had a good turn-out."

"Majestic," said Mrs Sparrow, reflectively. "My Arthur would've liked that, instead of just a service at the crematorium. It's not the same. I think a burial's preferable."

"Yes. Nicer, really. And they've put him in St Petroc churchyard where he can see the sea." She realized what she had said, and blew her nose again.

Mrs Sparrow asked for her goods to be totalled up. Primrose patted each item, her lips moving in time with her mental arithmetic. "Seven pounds seventy-five, please. So Mr Elliott's back living on his boat now, is he?" She delved in the till for change to Mrs Sparrow's ten-pound note.

"There or somewhere else. He left the day after the accident. Didn't say much. Just thank you. A bit quiet. Understandable, I suppose."

"Yes."

"Still, he was no bother. Apart from the one night. And it'll soon be the start of the season. Only a few weeks to the May bank holiday."

"Yes." Primrose was lost in thought as Mrs Sparrow left, the bell on the door pinging behind her.

*

Will watched as *Boy Jack* swung out over the water. He was pleased with his brushwork; the newly painted white hull reflected the ripples below, although it was a dull day.

"All clear?" Gryler's voice asked, from the seat of the boat lift.

"I think so. Go ahead slowly." Will watched as the boat descended, the keel touched the water and the propellers disappeared from view.

Amy and Hovis observed from the safety of the jetty as the Dunkirk veteran took to the water once more, settling evenly as the massive straps of webbing slackened and she found her own equilibrium.

Gryler jumped down, extracted the straps, then drove the lift back along the concrete hard to its usual parking place.

Will watched him go, trying hard to control his feelings. He had no proof that Gryler had had anything to do with Ernie's death, or even Christopher Applebee's. Nobody had. It was all speculation. He tied off the boat alongside the jetty as Hovis and Amy approached.

"Round of applause and a bottle of champagne, I should think," suggested Hovis.

"Thought we'd celebrate on board tonight," said Will. "Time I repaid the compliment. Dinner at eight?"

"Sure?" asked Hovis, sensitive to his neighbour's feelings.

"Sure." Will winked at Amy. "Can you come round at about seven?"

"Love to."

"What about getting this old girl back to the pontoon?" asked Hovis.

"Gryler's going to tow me over with his dinghy. I've a few checks to make on the engines yet, but with any luck we should be able to try her out in a day or two. See how she runs."

"All very exciting," said Amy. "Anyway, it's all right for you two, but I've a studio to open. See you both later." She blew Will a kiss. He watched her walk along the jetty, and found it difficult to turn away.

They had not slept together since Ernie's death. Will had expected her to be hurt, but instead had been heartened by her understanding. Amy, determined to do the right thing, had given him space. They saw one another every day at some point – either Will would call in at the studio for coffee or a meal, or Amy would nip down to the boat.

She surprised herself with her own willingness to wait. Normally she would have given up by now, grown tired of being messed about.

But she knew he was not oblivious to her feelings, that he was trying hard to rebuild his life. Letting him down was not an option. She had never felt this way about anyone. Yes, she had been in love before. And she was in love with Will – she could admit this to herself now, if not to him. But it ran deeper than that. She *cared* about him too. It was unnerving yet comforting. In his company she felt complete. Without him she felt more alone than she could ever remember feeling before. She would wait. And hope.

She had watched him at the funeral. He had looked so desperate. She could not take her eyes off him as he helped carry Ernie's body from the church. At the graveside he had stood beside her and slipped his arm through hers. She looked up at him. He had seemed taller somehow in his uniform, his eyes that piercing pale blue, the muscles in his jaw expanding and contracting as he fought to control himself. His hair had been cut. He looked older, weary.

That night he came back to the studio for supper and told her about the interviews at the police station. He thought it better that she knew, even though she might worry. She felt elated at his willingness to share it with her, but made no fuss, just sat calmly and listened as he told her about the police suspicions of illicit alcohol and Gryler's possible involvement.

They had parted after midnight. He had kissed her lips and held her for a long while, his cap under his arm like a polite serviceman going off to war.

So much had been spoken, but so much remained unsaid. Somehow it didn't seem to matter. She knew that he was mending, that she had to be patient.

At seven o'clock on the dot she left the studio, a cool-bag clutched in her arms.

He heard her approaching footsteps on the pontoon and jumped down from the deck of *Boy Jack* to greet her. "Just a minute. Don't come any further." He held up his hand like a traffic policeman. "It's here somewhere." He located an old wooden beer crate on the foredeck and picked it up. It was heavier than he had expected. Then Spike hopped out of it and stalked off across the deck without a backward glance. Will placed the crate in front of the gangway.

Amy's eyes followed the cat. "I don't think he likes me."

"Jealous, that's all. Never been keen on company." He checked that the crate was stable. "There we are, madam. Ready to be piped aboard!" He took the cool-bag from her and helped her climb on to the deck. She wore white jeans, deck shoes and a T-shirt that almost matched her hair. "You look stunning," he said softly.

"Don't drop that! There's something in it to christen your boat."

He came back to earth. "Sorry! It's just that you're so beautiful."

She stood on tiptoe to kiss him. "I'm glad! Do I get to see round this vessel, then?"

"Lucky timing. The evening tour is about to commence." He held out his arm, directing her into the wheelhouse, and she walked down the two newly varnished steps.

"Wow! I had no idea! So this is what you've been doing!" Amy gazed at the immaculate woodwork. "But you've had less than a month. How did you get it like this?"

"I didn't sleep much."

"I can believe that." She was amazed at the transformation. She'd only seen the outside of the boat before, but the condition of the interior had been obvious from the state of the carpets and curtains she had seen hauled away and dumped. She had feared it would never be fit for human habitation. Now the varnish on the deep mahogany timber gleamed, a new brass bell engraved 'Boy Jack' shone, and the wheelhouse smelt of polish and paint. There were no curtains as yet, but the wooden floor sported an Indian rug and the table-top shone like a mirror.

The propane cylinder and burner had been replaced with a small stove fitted among wooden worktops to one side of the wheelhouse; from the oven came an appetising aroma. A brass oil lamp dangled from the wood-panelled ceiling and another stood on the table. Every catch and knob, every hinge and bracket had been buffed to within an inch of its life.

She turned to look for'ard and saw the mahogany wheel with its brass cap, and the glittering instruments surrounding it. Positioned centrally among them was fixed a brass plate bearing the legend 'Dunkirk 1940'. She turned towards him, her eyes glistening. "You've worked so hard. Walter Etchingham would be proud of you."

"Oh, there's a lot to do yet, but at least now you can see that it'll look good when it's finished. Old Mr Etchingham looked after her well. She's as sound as a bell, really. She must just have been neglected after he died. Most of the work we've done has been cosmetic."

"What's left to do?"

"Oh, there's still a bit of rigging to sort out, the masts to varnish, anchor winch to repair, curtains to find, navigation equipment to put in. I'd like a fixed GPS but I'll have to settle for a cheaper hand-held one. Still, I think I can run to an autopilot."

"I thought it would be you doing the steering."

"Not all the time."

"You mean it can steer itself?"

"On a straight course, yes. And if it's a long passage I won't want to be stuck to the wheel the whole time."

"But if you're not looking where you're going you could hit something."

"Oh, I won't just go to my cabin and forget it. Not unless I decide to cross the Atlantic."

"No." Suddenly she remembered what the boat was for. It was the means by which he would leave her. She felt chilled.

He noticed her change of mood. "What's the matter?"

"Nothing. Just looking at the front bit."

He put a hand on her arm. "What's the matter?"

"I was just thinking."

"About what?"

"About you going away."

He said nothing at first; just turned her round to face him. She avoided his gaze.

"Look at me."

She stared at the floor, then at the wooden panelling to one side.

"Look at me." He said the words softly but insistently. She raised her eyes to meet his. "I'm here now. Don't think too far ahead. Please."

"I can't help it."

"I know. But try not to." He paused and stroked her cheek. "I'm trying not to."

"Are you?" She looked at him questioningly.

"I've got something else to show you." He took her hand and pulled her towards the hatch that led to the aft cabin. He bent down and flicked a switch. Two small brass lanterns, one to port the other to starboard, illuminated the previously dim interior.

"Oh!" She caught her breath.

The cabin, like the wheelhouse, was lined with mahogany, and most of the space was taken up with a large double bed, covered in a deep red quilt with fat pillows propped up against the bulkhead at the aftermost end. In one corner the door of the bathroom stood open, revealing the marble basin and the now pristine hip bath. The old Blake's head had been restored, and while the effect was not quite up to Dorchester standards it had, on a miniature scale, undeniable charm.

He bent down and kissed her, wrapped his arms around her, then let one hand slide down to stroke her bottom. Then he pushed a stray wisp of hair from her cheek. "Shall we cook? We've company coming."

She nodded and he looked at her intently, then grinned and pushed her up the steps into the wheelhouse, trying hard to reconcile within himself the conflicting feelings of love and the anticipation of his impending expedition. What had Hovis said? "Some things in life you have no control over. Other things are yours to decide." He remembered the words that had followed. "And one of the strangest and saddest things in life is that some people cannot differentiate between the two."

They worked together, she topping and tailing beans and scrubbing Jersey Royals, he dressing a crab for starters. His hands worked deftly at the claws and she saw the muscles in his forearms flexing. Feeling her eyes on him, Will looked up. "Glass of wine?"

"Yes, please."

He ran his hands under the tap and dried them on a towel before heading to the aft cabin.

"Where are you going?" she asked.

"For the wine. I keep it in a locker below the water-line. It stays cool that way."

"No need. Have you forgotten?" She gestured towards the cool-bag sitting at one end of the worktop. He came back up, unzipped the top flap, plunged his hand in and withdrew the first of three bottles.

"Oh! What have you done?"

"I don't know what you mean." She began to scrub again at the potatoes.

"Bollinger!"

"I should hope so. This is a class boat – or so you tell me."

He kissed the back of her neck, and pulled three glasses out of a cupboard at one end of the galley.

"Shouldn't we break it over the bows or something? That's what the Queen does."

"Not on my boat she doesn't."

"Spoilsport."

"For a start it would ruin my paintwork, and as it's Bollinger it would be a criminal waste of champagne."

"Well, you'll have to give her a glassful, then." The voice came from outside. It was eight o'clock and Hovis had arrived punctually, which Will lost no time in pointing out to him.

"Not much traffic on the pontoon tonight. No hold ups at all. Normally get stuck among all those commuters on pontoon number two at bank holidays but those delights are a few weeks away yet."

"Don't remind me. How busy *does* it get here on bank holidays?"

"Oh, not terribly. Bit more bustle on the jetty, and the day-boaters turn up to dust off the cobwebs and hose off the gull-shit – oh, sorry, muck." He grinned apologetically at Amy, who laughed.

"You're just in time for a glass, Hovis." She greeted him with a kiss.

"Oh, I say. Things are looking up."

Will handed round tumblers that were more used to plain water than bubbly, popped the cork and let the golden liquid fizz into them. "Ladies and gentlemen," he said, struggling to keep any trace of emotion out of his voice, "I'd like you to drink a toast to two ladies."

"Hear, hear!" said Hovis, then, "Sorry. Jumping the gun." He looked sideways at Amy and raised his eyebrows. She giggled.

"Two ladies who mean a lot to me." Amy blushed. "One is sixty-eight years old, and the other–"

"Steady!" cautioned Amy.

"–isn't. But I wouldn't have survived the past few weeks without either of them." He looked pointedly at Amy and raised his glass. "Neither would I have managed without a certain gentleman, but we'll let his identity pass."

"Best thing," agreed Hovis.

Amy raised her glass. "Here's to *Boy Jack*. God bless her and all who sail in her."

The men repeated the toast and all three sipped their champagne, gasping with pleasure as the bubbles hit the back of their throats.

"Come on, then," urged Hovis. "Let's wet the old girl's bottom."

They climbed the wheelhouse steps to the deck, then stepped down over the beer crate on to the pontoon where Will hurled what remained in his glass over the bows of *Boy Jack*. He stepped back and looked at her, no longer an apologetic hulk but a graceful lady reclining on the rippling water that sent a mosaic of reflections dancing up her clean white hull. Graceful. He saw now that she had deserved her original name. He reached out his hand to grasp Amy's and squeezed. She returned his gesture with a flickering smile.

"God bless all who sail in her," he whispered, so that only she could hear.

The meal was as great a success as the one on Hovis's boat, and the conversation even more relaxed. They knew each other now, had been through things together. Appreciative noises were made over the crab; the duck with orange was cooked to perfection, but Hovis reckoned, with a wink in Amy's direction, that the vegetables were better than anything else.

Chablis followed the Bollinger, and Amy lay back against Will on the long bench seat. Over coffee the conversation became reflective. Nobody intended it to be sad, but Ernie's name could not be avoided. Will was determined not to be morose, and instead regaled them with stories of his early days at the lighthouse, and Ernie's generosity during that tough time so soon after Ellie's death. Then they returned to the present. To the fact that Evan Williams, Prince Albert Rock's second principal lighthouse keeper, had agreed to act as temporary custodian until a permanent replacement could be found. Hovis was reminded of young Applebee: he could not understand the boy's stupidity in being out in the storm.

Will explained what had happened at the police station.

Hovis was astounded. "You reckon Gryler's running a booze racket?"

"I don't know. The police told me not to mention it. Certainly not to Gryler."

"No. Certainly not. Oh, no!"

"I wonder if we'll ever find out any more," mused Amy.

"I don't know," said Will. "Maybe not. The police are on to it now, but I can't help being curious."

"Best to leave things alone," said Hovis sharply.

"That's what Ernie said," replied Will, ruefully.

"They've had Gryler in," added Hovis. "Questioned him all night, apparently."

"Let him go, though."

"Maybe they're watching him."

"Ooh! Makes you shudder," said Amy, nestling closer to Will.

"Anyway. Never mind all that. Who's for a spin around the Cove tomorrow?" offered Will brightly.

"What?" Amy pulled away a little.

"Tomorrow morning. Maiden voyage, I think. Weather looks fair. Tides are right. Engines are raring to go. Won't travel far. Just see how she feels in the water."

"But what about the studio?"

"Close it. We'll only be a couple of hours."

She looked at him squarely. "All right, then, I will. You're on. Hovis, what about you?"

"I think you two should do that on your own." Hovis eased out of his seat. "Make it special."

"Oh, come with us," pleaded Amy. "You've watched all the work being done."

"No. Not this time. This is your treat. I'll wave you off. I'll even dress overall if you want."

"What?" asked Amy.

"Dress overall. Put all me flags out. Look like a regatta."

"Don't you dare," said Will. "I want to slip out quietly, not with a fanfare of trumpets."

"If you insist. But I'll give you a push off and I'll be here to catch your line when you come back."

"That would be helpful."

"That's sorted, then. And now I must be off. I know I got here punctually, so I'll leave punctually. Stroke of eleven. Not bad. Oh, and that reminds me. Hang on a minute." He slid open the door and dived from view, returning half a minute later with a small wooden box. "For you. A boat-warming present. Bit of a cheek, really. It's broken but I thought you wouldn't mind, if you see what I mean."

Will took the brass-bound mahogany box, which was about six inches square. He knew precisely what it contained. "Hovis, I can't take this."

"Of course you can. I told you, it's broken, of no use to me. But I know you'll be able to fix it."

Will pressed the round brass button and lifted the lid to reveal the

416

marine chronometer under its protective pane of glass. "I don't know what to say."

"Well, don't say anything. Just enjoy fixing it." And with a smile Hovis left.

Amy put her arms around Will's waist and looked with him at the clock face. "Charles Shepherd – Makers to the Royal Navy" was engraved in elaborate script across it. On the front of the box was a small ivory panel bearing the number 1205. "It's beautiful."

"Isn't it? What a man." He put the clock on the table and turned to her. "I wondered if you – would you . . ."

"Mmmm?"

"Would you stay the night? Here. On the boat."

She smiled. "I've no toothbrush."

"We carry a spare."

He pulled the wheelhouse hatch closed and picked up the brass oil lamp that had provided them with light to dine. He led her down to the aft cabin where the rosy glow of the mahogany panelling seemed warmer still by the lamplight. He slid the cabin door shut, put down the lamp on the bedside locker and turned to kiss her. She stepped back from him and began to peel off her clothes, looking at him all the while. He watched her entranced: the light caught the soft curves of her body and turned her hair to fire. Naked now she stood in front of him, her arms by her sides, quite still. Then she moved to the bed and slid under the quilt, never taking her eyes off him.

He watched her as she lay there, then undressed, gazing at her, until he, too, stood naked in the lamplight. He could hear the silence ringing in his ears and feel the passion rising deep inside.

"You're so beautiful," she whispered.

He walked to the bed, pulled back the quilt and looked at her for a moment before sliding in beside her and feeling the soft warmth of her body.

Spike was curled up inside the beer crate. Tonight he would sleep outdoors.

417

Chapter 21: Round Island

Amy woke first. She propped herself on one elbow and looked at him lying next to her in the bed. His dark curls shone in the early-morning sun that slanted through the port-hole. She listened to his slow, regular breathing. He was peaceful now, no creases on his brow, no troubled expression. Just a sleeping boy.

She realized how familiar she had become with his body. She knew each blemish, each mole, and the precise position of the darker flecks on the pale blue irises of his eyes.

His right arm rested on top of the quilt. She looked with the eye of an artist at the sculpted, lean biceps, the powerful forearms, the craftsman's hands – a combination of strength and sensitivity. She looked at his right hand; at the veins standing up beneath the weatherbeaten skin, the relaxed fingers. The callouses born of boat repairing could not disguise the delicate touch needed for mending a clock or making a model boat. There were scratches and grazes where the skin had been damaged, and paint ingrained where it had escaped the scrubbing brush and the soap. The short nails were chipped and battered, the cuticles irregular. How she loved his hands.

She reached out to touch his fingers and his eyes slowly opened. He looked at her, then reached up to cup her chin.

"Hallo."

"Hallo, you." She eased her body closer to him.

"I've been thinking," he said.

"No, you haven't, you've been sleeping."

"Yes, but when I was sleeping I was thinking."

She smiled at him. "Go on."

"You've only got a pair of white jeans. You're going to get a bit mucky crewing a boat in those."

"Is that the sort of thought that goes through your mind when you're lying naked next to me?"

"I'm only being considerate."

"I worry about you." She dug him in the ribs with her index finger and he jumped, then put his arms around her and squeezed her, nuzzling into her neck.

"What time is it?"

She looked at her watch on the bedside locker. "Half past seven."

He sat up and looked out of the port-hole. "And it's a lovely day. No wind. Sun on the water. Brilliant. Time we were up if we're to catch the tide."

She frowned at him. "Which tide?"

"We need to leave about an hour before high water if we want to avoid battling against heavy currents. That way we can get in and out without having to fight the tide."

"I see. I'm not sure I'll ever understand it. All those nautical terms and all those bits of rope – sheets and warps and shrouds and stuff."

"Don't worry about it." He bent over to kiss her nose. "The most important thing is still to feel the thrill of the water underneath you. Hang on to the enjoyment. Some sailors are so busy being technically correct in their terminology and their practices, and worrying about what might happen, that they forget to have a good time while they're doing it. Cowper said something like that."

"The poet?"

"No. The sailor. Frank Cowper. Wrote a series of books called *Sailing Tours* in the late nineteenth century. I lost them in the fire. He said, 'A boating book should be written by a man who has bumped ashore and afterwards has found the way to the proper channel. Such a man learns where the dangers lie.'"

"Sounds a bit irresponsible to me."

"He wasn't suggesting foolhardiness, just that instead of taking notice of somebody else's wagging finger you rely on common sense and observation."

"Sums you up, really, doesn't it? Common sense and observation."

"Listen to me going on. Here I am stark naked next to a beautiful woman and talking about boats."

"Well, you could make it up to me."

"We'll miss the tide."

"Oh, bugger the tide. Let's just bump ashore."

"Have you opened the sea cocks?"

"Yes."

"Turned on the batteries?"

"Yes."

"Checked over the engines?"

"Yes."

"Go on, then, start her up." Hovis was standing on the pontoon. Will was at the helm inside the wheelhouse door. Amy crouched down on the foredeck, ready to catch the lines as instructed. She tightened the belt on an old pair of Will's jeans and pulled up the sleeves of the baggy fisherman's jersey beneath her lifejacket.

"Here goes, then." He turned the key of the port engine and the warning buzzer sounded. He pushed the port throttle forwards for about a third of its capacity and pressed the starter. The old Perkins engine turned over a few times then rumbled into life. He waited for the rev-counter to spring up to 500 revs, then repeated the process on the starboard engine. It refused to fire. He glanced at Hovis and tried again. Nothing.

"Once more. She's had a long rest," said Hovis encouragingly.

Will pressed the starter button a third time, giving just a little more throttle, and the engine growled into action, the rev-counter springing up to 700 revs.

Will looked at the dials in front of him. Water temperature low, as yet not warmed up. Oil pressure fine. Batteries fine. Rudder indicator amidships. He pulled the throttle levers to their lowest position, then stepped out of the wheelhouse and on to the deck.

"I think I'll just let her warm up for a minute or two."

"Good idea," said Hovis. "Everything else all right?"

"Seems to be. Have we got water coming out of the back?"

Hovis walked aft and confirmed that the engine-cooling system was working – regular squirts of water were slopping out of the exhaust pipes just above the water line. Will turned to Amy. "You OK?"

"Fine. Noisy, isn't it?"

"Should be better at sea."

"No, I like it. It's sort of comforting. Like a big cat purring."

"Talking of cats, where is he?"

Hovis pointed to a coil of rope on the foredeck of *Florence Nightingale*. Seated in the middle of it was Spike, ears up, eyes wide as he inspected the throbbing vessel that was his home.

"Oh dear. I think we might have upset him." The cat continued to watch their progress with detached interest from the comfort of the neighbouring vessel. Will walked around the deck of *Boy Jack* checking that the fenders were in position and that the mooring warps were secure.

"OK. This is it."

"Haven't you forgotten something?" asked Hovis.

Will frowned. "What?"

"Auntie Betty." Hovis pointed astern. "Bad form."

Will laughed, stepped into the wheelhouse, and returned with the red ensign wrapped around its newly varnished flagstaff. He unrolled it as he walked astern, and slotted it into the brass holder above the transom. Then he walked to the bows and picked up another, smaller flagstaff that had been lying on the deck. He slotted it into the jack-staff holder on the pulpit and unwound the smaller flag of St George, with its central shield – the emblem of the Association of Dunkirk Little Ships.

"Better?"

"Much better!"

"Daft bugger!"

"Well, there are standards to maintain. Mind you, your ensign will be better when it's faded a bit."

"Don't start!" He wagged an admonitory finger at Hovis. "Are we ready, then?"

"I can think of no further reason to detain you."

"OK. Cast off."

Hovis undid the two springs and threw them to Amy. She caught them both, then the head line, and finally the stern line.

"Can you coil them?" Will shouted at her.

"How?"

"Just tidy them up so you don't fall over them."

He moved the two throttles forward, relying on the paddle-wheel effect of the propellers to push him sideways from the pontoon, then eased them off to slow their forward progress to a minimum. Hovis leaned on the hull of *Boy Jack* to reinforce the movement. The boat swung slowly outwards, the bows creeping into the water slightly ahead of the stern.

"Lovely!" said Hovis, encouragingly.

Suddenly Will saw a flash of black and white. He looked up, wondering what had fallen from the mast.

Hovis pointed to the sharp end of the boat. There, seated in front of the Samson post, was Spike, like some feline figurehead.

"It looks as though he's coming, then!" cried Amy.

"I just hope he doesn't fall overboard. I haven't got a lifejacket for a cat."

Will eased the port engine into forward gear, keeping his helm amidships, and as they cleared the pontoon to head towards the entrance of the boatyard he switched between the engines, using them, rather than the wheel, to steer the boat out into the cove.

"*Bon voyage!*" Hovis waved them off, and they cruised slowly past the other boats – Jerry McDermott's *Sokai*, gleaming like a newly scrubbed bathtub in the morning light, a couple of guano-spattered day-boats and Gryler's replacement for PZ 291, another redundant fishing boat.

The sea hove into view as they rounded the corner of the jetty, and they chugged out into the cove at a steady five knots. Now Will realized how it felt to have your own boat. He stood at the wheel, passing it slowly from hand to hand, remembering not to "take great fistfuls of it" as his instructor had taught him three years ago. The butterflies remained in his stomach, but he had a sense of freedom.

Small wavelets broke against the bows as *Boy Jack* slid through the water, and the sound of the engines was indeed, as Amy had suggested, comforting, now that they were clear of the harbour walls. He pointed his boat westwards, towards Bill's Island, the only thing in view on the calm, glittering sea.

"This weather is just unbelievable. It's as if it knew she was going out for the first time today. Sort of welcoming her back," Will said.

He stuck his head through the wheelhouse door and felt the gentle breeze of their forward motion. He pulled at the hatch in the coach-roof and slid it back to let in the fresh air. The boatyard receded into the distance behind them. He looked at the fluttering ensign and the foaming white wash that fanned out behind them. "Do you want a go?" he asked.

"Can I?"

"Just hold her steady and aim for the island." She took the wheel from him and he stepped away to stow the ropes. In the event he didn't have to.

"What have you done?"

"What do you mean?" She sounded troubled.

"With the ropes?"

"You said to coil them so I did."

"But I didn't expect this!" They were neatly wound into flat spirals. "She looks like the *Victory*."

"I should hope so. You forget, I'm a painter. I notice things."

He leaned through the door and pecked her on the cheek. "I'm just going to stow the fenders. Back in a minute."

"No. I'll do it. I'm the crew. Where do you put them?" She motioned him to take back the wheel.

"In the lazarette."

"Sounds like someone out of the Bible. Give me a clue."

"There are two hatches on the afterdeck. If you lift them up you'll find a stowage area under them. It's called the lazarette. The fenders can go in there."

"Aye-aye, sir." She mock-saluted him and went about her duties.

They had been out for about an hour, and Amy had observed how relaxed he was. She had been prepared for him to shout at her, as that was what most men in charge of boats did, but he had simply asked her to do things clearly and firmly.

Will felt a sense of release and vindication: release because of his new-found ability to escape the land, and vindication in that *Boy Jack* handled like a dream. He patted the wheel as if it were a well-behaved dog, and put his arm round Amy as she stood beside him.

"Better be getting back, I suppose."

"Suppose so. Not that *he* seems bothered at all."

Spike had hardly moved since the voyage had begun. He had eased forward a few times and looked over at the bow wave, but decided against leaping down and chasing it. He had ignored his two shipmates, which was not unusual, explained Will.

Will looked ahead as they began to round Bill's Island. It rose up out of the sea like a giant hump-backed whale, its rocks alive with chattering gannets and guillemots, its grassy slopes dotted with sea pinks and yellow vetch. They watched as the sea splashed on its shores, where sandpipers and oystercatchers paddled and prodded for food.

"Who was Bill?" asked Amy.

"He was Prince Albert Rock's lighthouse keeper in the nineteenth century. Did a bit of a Grace Darling. Rescued a family in a storm. Just like Ernie." His voice lowered. "Except that he survived." He felt the keen sense of loss again. How different the sea was today. Like another country. He was brought to earth by a sudden grinding sound. The boat juddered and slowed dramatically. Amy was thrown against the bulkhead and cried out as she bumped her head. Will braced himself against the wheel and pulled the gear levers into neutral.

"Are you OK?" he asked.

"Fine. What happened?"

"I don't know." Will leapt out of the wheelhouse door as the cat scampered in, frightened by the noise and the unexpected jolt.

The boat rocked gently from side to side as the engines continued to tick over. Will walked astern.

"What is it?"

"Something round one of the propellers, I think. Or both of them. I bet it's a bloody lobster pot. Damn. I should have been looking."

"Sorry." She felt guilty at having distracted him.

"Not your fault."

He leaned over the transom and looked down into the water. "Bugger." He could see it now: a lump of rope floating in the water with a dark grey plastic container at the end. The sort of cheap float fishermen used to mark their lobster pots.

"If they used proper fluorescent ones they'd be easier to pick out from a distance. Look at that. Bloody dark grey and half submerged. Nobody's going to spot that until they're on top of it. Shit!"

"Can you untangle it?"

"I'll have a try, but I bet it's bloody cold in there."

"Can't we just fish it out with a boathook?"

"No. It'll be wrapped round the propeller. I've got a diving mask. I'll jump over and hang on to the side and see if I can do it from there."

He stepped into the wheelhouse and turned off the engines. They were both aware of the silence, broken only by the gentle lapping of waves on the hull and the distant cries of seabirds on Bill's Island.

The sky was pale blue streaked with wisps of cloud. Amy suddenly felt the urge to reach for her paints. She watched him slip over the side clad in a pair of shorts and a face mask. He held on to a knotted rope secured to a stanchion and lowered himself over the transom. He came up several times, then at last raised his hand above the surface triumphantly with a coil of battered rope.

He scrambled aboard, tied the rope to a cleat and pulled off the mask, panting for breath. She looked at his body, running with rivulets of seawater and spattered with kelp. His chest heaved as he took in massive gulps of air.

"Not wound round too far – only one propeller . . . The other's OK." He bent double, his head between his knees, and she laid her hand on his back.

He raised his head, flinging water from his black curls, and smiled at her.

She gazed at him, her eyes speaking volumes.

He looked down at her in her oversized jeans, rolled up above her bare feet, at her body encased in the baggy sweater and the lifejacket, and at her hair tied back from her face. He wound his arms round her, dripping water over her clothes.

"I'm getting awfully wet," she said softly.

He eased away from her, grinning. "Shall we see if there's a lobster for our trouble?"

"Are we allowed to?"

"It's damn near taken off our propeller and it isn't properly marked. I think the least it owes us is a decent supper."

He untied the rope from its cleat and between them they hauled up the pot. But it did not contain a lobster. It contained a plastic food container, sealed in a polythene bag.

Chapter 22:
Trinitas In Unitate

"What is it?"

"I don't know. Pass me the knife."

Amy handed him the one that was kept in a sheath by the helm, and he cut away the polythene to expose the plastic food container, which was sealed with waterproof tape. He ran the knife round the seal and lifted the lid to discover several plastic bags filled with white powder.

Amy was the first to speak. "Oh, my God!"

Will looked up at her face, from which the colour had drained.

"Don't ask me how I know this," she said, "but it looks to me like heroin."

Will swore. Then he said, "The lowest drawer in the chest to one side of the helm – there's some waterproof tape in it."

Amy disappeared into the wheelhouse and returned with it. Will resealed the plastic box, shivering as the breeze brought up goosebumps on his wet skin. Then he replaced the container in the lobster pot and lowered it back over the side, allowing the dark grey float to bob away from them on the water.

He stepped into the wheelhouse and returned with a nautical chart, then walked to the foredeck and motioned Amy to follow him He laid the chart on the deck, weighting it at each corner with their shoes, and looked about to get his bearings.

"If I had my GPS . . ."

"Your what?"

"My GPS – a navigation system that uses satellites to fix your position. If I had it I could get a precise bearing on where we are to within fifty metres or so."

"Impressive."

"Yes. But I haven't got one yet so we'll have to guess." He looked at the sun and at his watch, at the position of Bill's Island and at the mainland, then took a pencil and made a cross on the chart. "I reckon we're about here." He looked around him at the sea. "Can you make out any more lobster pots with dark grey floats?"

"They're difficult to see."

"I know. That must have been the idea."

"What do you mean?"

"Fishermen with lobster pots generally lay a string of them. They use individually coloured floats so that they can identify their own pots. That stops them pulling up pots belonging to other fishermen."

She looked at him and the significance of what he was saying became clear.

"So Christopher Applebee used dark grey floats?"

"Exactly."

"Which were difficult to see . . ."

"Unless you knew precisely where to look."

"And other fishermen would leave them alone?"

"That's right. He made them even more difficult to find by part-filling the floats so that they didn't stick out of the water too much."

Amy looked out across the water towards Bill's Island. "Is that one over there? Directly in line with that big rock."

"Probably." He screwed up his eyes and scanned the water. "Yes. And there's another one there – see? Just in line with the end of the island. All his pots are round this side, so nobody could see him from the mainland when he emptied them."

"Clever trick."

"Yes. But simple, really. It's surprising that the police haven't cottoned on to it. But, then, they were looking for booze, not lobsters."

"Or drugs. So what do we do now?" she asked.

"Head back. I'd better go into St Petroc and explain to my friendly sergeant what's happened."

"Are you sure you want to?"

"What do you mean?"

"Do you think he'll believe you? You said he was questioning you as though you might have been involved."

Will paused and looked at her. "Don't sow seeds like that in my head. What's the alternative? That I turn detective and stake out the lobster pots until someone comes and pulls up the booty? No, thanks. I think I'd rather face the music with a detective sergeant than with the West Country Mafia."

"I suppose so."

He felt the chill of the onshore breeze. "Earghhh! I need to get dry. Towel me down?"

"Towel yourself down!" She smiled at him. "We've got to get back. No time for pleasure. I have a studio to open and you have some explaining to do. Wait till Hovis hears about this. He'll wish he'd come along."

The sun rose slowly in the clear, pale sky, glinting on the soft peaks of the ripples that shimmied on the surface of the water. They said little as they motored back but stayed close, Amy with her arm on his shoulder as he steered for the Crooked Angel.

"I know this sounds stupid, bearing in mind what's just happened, but I'm desperate to paint," she said softly, as the jetty grew closer.

"Mmm?"

"I've been doing nothing but shop-keeping – I've been tied to that till for too long. And with the holiday coming I'll need more stock."

"But who'll mind the shop?"

"Primrose has a niece in St Petroc who helps her out sometimes. She said she doesn't need her at the moment, so I thought I'd ask her."

"What if the girl takes after her auntie? Gossip-wise, I mean?"

"Well, I'll have to decide that when I meet her. But I'm just desperate to paint."

He ruffled her hair, amazed that after their startling discovery she could still be thinking of painting. He didn't say anything, but felt a great surge of love for her, and a dawning realization that now he could remember Ellie without feeling guilty.

They rounded the corner of the jetty and the sound of powerful engines met their ears. Jerry MacDermott's boat was on the move and coming directly towards them. Will swung the helm of *Boy Jack* to starboard so that the boats would pass, according to the nautical rules of the road, port to port. But MacDermott was still clearly driving on the left and the two boats began to make a bee-line for each other. Deciding in a split second that a chance of salvation was better than the certainty of being crushed against the harbour wall, Will pushed both throttles forward and spun the wheel anti-clockwise, shooting *Boy Jack* across MacDermott's bows with inches to spare. His heart thumped in his chest as the great white iceberg of a boat rumbled past them, close enough to nudge their fenders, with the MacDermotts waving merrily from the top, unaware of the disaster that had nearly befallen their titanic Tupperware.

Amy looked at him with incredulity etched on her face. He looked back apologetically. "Close."

She gulped. "Very close."

They gently chugged round the boatyard to pontoon number three, to discover that Hovis was already there, waiting to catch their lines. He was shaking his head. "I don't reckon that man has a clue about boats."

"That's the understatement of the year. He's a bloody liability," confirmed Will. "Thank God he doesn't come here often."

"Yes, well, I think that's about to change," remarked Hovis. "How was she, by the way?"

"She was a dream, apart from a little local difficulty. But what do you mean 'that's all about to change'?"

Hovis tied off the four mooring warps of *Boy Jack* and then reached into his back pocket for a white envelope. "There's one of these for you inside *Florence Nightingale*." He waved the envelope aloft.

"What is it?" asked Will, shutting down the engines.

"An invitation." He read: " 'Jerry and Trudie MacDermott will be at home on Sunday 24th May and request the pleasure of your company for lunchtime drinkies, 12 noon till 2 p.m. RSVP Benbecula, Bosullow Lane, Pencurnow Cove, Cornwall'."

"Lunchtime drinkies?"

"That's what it says."

"Lucky you," chirped Amy, mockingly.

"I think you'll probably have one, too," said Hovis.

"Oh, God!"

"Yes," said Will. "And you can't risk upsetting your customers, can you?" He grinned at her.

"I am not going on my own."

"Don't look at me." He raised his hands in front of him in self-defence.

"I don't really have to go, do I?" Amy moaned.

"Well, that all depends if you want to slight one of your patrons. Not really advisable, I'd have said, when you're new to the area. Not with a man who's spent as much as he has at your studio."

"Come with me?" She looked at him beseechingly.

"Can we talk about more urgent things? Like out there just now?" he teased.

"Yes, of course. Sorry." She perked up and looked in Hovis's direction. "We've had a very interesting voyage."

"Er . . . I think we ought to nip inside." Will motioned her and Hovis towards the wheelhouse of *Boy Jack*. "Cup of coffee, Hovis?"

"So what will you do?" asked Hovis, his face displaying the sort of excitement more associated with the children in *Swallows and Amazons* than with grown men.

"Go to the police."

"Best thing, I suppose. Not right to keep that sort of thing to yourself. Be careful, though."

"What do you mean?"

"Don't breathe a word about it to anyone else. Best if it's kept between us three – and the police, of course."

"Well, I wasn't thinking of knocking on the door of Gryler's Portakabin and saying, 'Guess what I've just found.'"

"No. Of course not." He paused. "Clever idea, though. The smuggling thing. I mean, dreadful but clever." He took a gulp of his coffee. "Much safer to bring the stuff over from the continent and pass it on down here in sleepy Cornwall. It's quicker to nip it across the Channel at the shortest point, but that's also the busiest point, isn't it? Kent. Sussex. Coastguard always on the lookout. Customs hot on anything untoward. Makes more sense to get it over here in a little fishing boat, round the back of Bill's Island where a small boat could be relatively inconspicuous."

"Mmm," grunted Will, thoughtfully.

"Except to observant lighthouse keepers, of course," remarked Hovis, pointedly. "Shame about your diaries."

"I'm relieved they're gone, in a way."

"But not in another?" asked Amy, who until now had been listening quietly.

"No. I wish I could go through them and check. But then . . ." He thought of the past life he would have to wade through, and the emotional turmoil of reliving his recovery. "Perhaps it's for the best. Fate." He looked at Hovis. "Pointless worrying about the things I can't change."

Hovis drained his coffee cup. "I'd better get on." He rose and so did Amy. "Me, too."

"Good luck with Primrose," said Will. "I'll catch up with you later." He gave Amy a hug and kissed her, then watched as she walked towards the village. As usual he found it impossible to take his eyes off her until she was out of sight. Then he made sure that the boat was secure and set off to catch the bus for the police station at St Petroc.

"Do you mind if I hang on to this, sir?" The detective sergeant folded up the chart.

"No, not at all."

He blew his nose loudly on a large tartan handkerchief, then stuffed it back in his pocket. "It was just the one lobster pot you hauled up, was it?"

"Yes. The one that caught my propeller."

"Mmm. I see." He looked thoughtful, as though struggling with his conscience. "We carried out a search, you know."

"Sorry?"

"We searched the lad's room in the village. Young Applebee's room."

"I see."

"We found the usual sort of stuff – dirty magazines . . ."

Will found himself wondering if the sergeant meant *Loaded* and *FHM*.

". . . and we also found some bottles and some weedkiller."

For a split second Will mused on the unlikelihood of Christopher Applebee being interested in gardening, then realized what the policeman was getting at.

"According to Forensic, there's no doubt that he was responsible for the fire at the lighthouse."

"Oh." The pieces of the jigsaw fell into place, and the conclusion now seemed obvious.

"Whether or not Gryler knew anything about it we've been unable to discover. But I thought you ought to know. It clears things up. The fire, that is. At least we know who started it. What we don't know is if he was acting off his own bat. Maybe we never will."

"Yes." Will hardly knew what to say. The implications whirred in his mind.

It was Christopher Applebee who had set fire to the lighthouse. It was Christopher Applebee whom Ernie had been trying to save when he lost his life. Where was the justice in that? But Will knew better than to expect fate to mete out justice.

"I know how it must seem, sir," the sergeant spoke compassionately, "but I think it's best to just try to forget it."

"One of life's bitter ironies?" Will said.

"Something like that. The longer I do this job the less I try to understand the things that happen. Life's a funny old thing."

"Yes. Thank you for telling me."

"Oh, and again, sir. Under your hat if you would."

"Yes. Of course."

The sergeant smiled sympathetically as Will plunged his hands deep into his pockets and walked out into the bright, sunny day. If he had known how quickly he would have to return he would not have bothered leaving. He shopped for food in St Petroc then caught the bus home.

The police car intercepted him as he walked along the lane at Pencurnow from the bus stop. A uniformed constable was at the wheel and leaned over to wind down the window.

"Do you think you could get in, sir?"

Will opened the passenger door. "But I've just—"

"I'm afraid the sergeant needs to see you again."

"Why's that?"

"Didn't say, sir. Just asked if I'd pick you up and take you there."

On the way back to St Petroc, Will's mind worked overtime, trying to understand what could be the reason for his return to the police station. It dawned on him as the sergeant walked into the interview room. "It wasn't there, was it?"

"No, sir. No sign. Just empty lobster pots. All six."

"You found six?"

"Yes, sir. All empty."

432

Will felt silly. "Well, it was there this morning, that's all I can say."

"Mmm. Did anyone see you around Bill's Island?"

"No. Not as far as I'm aware – no, I'm sure not."

"And you saw no boats in the vicinity?"

"Mine was the only one."

"Mmm. Bit of a bugger, that. Someone's been there between your visit and mine. But we don't know who."

Will sat at the Formica-topped table feeling like a schoolboy being interviewed by his headmaster. The sergeant did not question Will's honesty, but a hint of incredulity crept into his voice. He came at the problem from a number of angles and, finally realizing that he was not getting any further, agreed that Will could leave. He seemed annoyed, and Will hoped that the cause was the unresolved situation rather than his own involvement.

"Do you think I could have my chart back?" Will asked.

"Yes, of course you can." The policeman led the way from the interview room to the counter at the front of the station, and reached below it to retrieve the chart, now folded up and tucked neatly into a polythene bag. He dangled it in the air and looked at it. "Never understand these. Know where you are with a map, roads and that, but not one of these."

Will looked at him questioningly and the sergeant read his mind. "Oh, don't worry, sir. I wasn't on my own, I was with the coastguard. He can understand them. And so can the person who got to the stuff before we did," he added, under his breath. "Be in touch, sir." And with that he walked into the room behind the counter.

Chapter 23: Beachy Head

"I just don't want to go. They're awful people." Amy snuggled up to him.

"Well, sometimes we all have to do things we don't want to do."

"Beast!" She dug him in the ribs with her elbow and he collapsed with a peal of laughter.

They were lying side by side in her bed at the studio. For the last week they had revelled in each other's company, Amy trying to put Will's voyage to the back of her mind, convincing herself that he might not go after all, and Will busying himself during the day with further work on the boat, and telling himself it would be a good while yet before she was ready.

It was early on a Sunday morning and the MacDermotts' 'drinkies' party was just a few hours away. Will pulled her closer and she curled into him.

"What a way to ruin a Sunday."

Out of the skylight Will could see plump white clouds. "It'll probably rain on them. Anyway, it's only for a couple of hours. We can arrive late and leave early. Say you've got the studio to attend to."

"Which is true. Angela can only stay a couple of hours."

"How's she been?" He stroked her pale back.

"OK. She's very quiet. No danger of her providing Primrose with any useful information."

"I'm relieved to hear it."

"But at least I've managed to paint."

"How many?"

"Three."

"When can I see them?"

"Soon. I've got some finishing off to do and I don't want you to look until they're done."

"I suppose we could get out of going."

"It was you who said we ought to go, not me," Amy reproved him.

"I've changed my mind. I'd rather stay here with you. All day."

"No. You were right the first time. The MacDermotts spent a lot of money at the studio and I could do with more of their business."

"Oh, I see. Getting serious now, are we? Businesswoman of the Year all of a sudden?"

She grinned. "Well, I suppose we don't have to get up just yet, do we?" She slid her hand down underneath the quilt and his stomach muscles contracted.

It was another hour before they emerged.

It was a quarter to one when they walked up the hill towards Benbecula, holding hands, Amy grumbling quietly and Will trying to suppress a smile, though he, too, was hardly looking forward to an hour or more of small-talk with the denizens of Pencurnow Cove. He was, he told himself, only there to provide moral support. He looked out across the deep turquoise sea and at the blue sky, gradually filling with cumulus clouds, then squeezed her hand reassuringly. It was a soft, delicate hand with long, fine-boned fingers, and he loved the feel of the tender skin in his own.

He darted a look at her face, shadowed by a wide-brimmed straw hat. The feeling of complete pleasure in her company grew daily. Often it was simply enough to be in the same room. He felt no need to say anything: he could draw strength and warmth from her presence alone. At other times he wanted to hold her so tightly that her body almost passed through his. And soon there would be his voyage. He put that thought to the back of his mind and held her hand tighter as they crested the brow of the hill and heard voices at the garden party.

Benbecula was a Victorian gentleman's residence built of granite and planted squarely at the top of the lane where it commanded a fine view of the cove. Stone gateposts topped with pineapples supported ornate wrought-iron gates, which opened on to a gravel drive that led, in a sweeping curve, to the white-painted front door set in a generous porch equipped with a shiny brass ship's bell. There were two sets of mullioned bay windows at either side of the door on the ground floor, and four gabled dormer windows protruded from the blue slate roof. Virginia creeper, in its shiny late-May livery, caressed mullion and finial with its rampant tentacles, softening the harsh, chiselled lines of the architecture. It was a solid house, not elegant in the Regency sense but robust Victorian. William Ewart Gladstone rather than Beau Brummel.

The rear of the house overlooked the bay, and handwritten notices pinned to wooden stakes directed guests along the drive and round the side of the house towards the striped lawn. A sprinkling of tables decorated the turf alongside a newly created putting green speckled with scarlet flags. The terrace alongside the house boasted a tall white flagpole, and strings of bunting led from it to the surrounding trees of macrocarpa, bent by years of onshore breezes into crouched wizened shrouds of greenery.

"It looks like the vicarage fête," whispered Will.

"And here comes the vicar," murmured Amy, as Jerry MacDermott strode across the lawn in his pink sweater and white trousers, the ubiquitous cigar clenched between his teeth and a glass in his left hand.

"Glad you could make it," he boomed, patting Amy on the back. Will thought the wide-brimmed hat must have put MacDermott off giving Amy a kiss: the prospect of negotiating access with a glass in one hand and a cigar in the other might have been more than he could manage without one of them coming to grief.

"Squire," MacDermott acknowledged Will. "Come and meet everybody."

Will's heart sank as they were dragged across the lawn, where a Pimm's was thrust into their hands by a local girl dragooned into waitressing.

"Great place, eh? Bloody good views of the cove."

"Wonderful," Will admitted, truthfully. Benbecula might not have been the prettiest house in Pencurnow, but it was certainly the largest and boasted the best panorama of the bay. Beyond the house, the lawns sloped away towards the sea between banks of feathery tamarisk. Bill's Island rose up from the ocean, looking even more like a whale than it did from the shore of the cove, and Prince Albert Rock Lighthouse pointed immaculately skywards from its granite promontory.

"You should come and paint up here," suggested MacDermott – with the merest hint, thought Amy, that the location might improve her technique. She smiled noncommittally.

"Said to the missus when we bought it that it was the best house in the area. No point in settling for anything less, eh? Course, we had to do a fair bit of work on it. Decoration a bit on the dreary side. Still, the missus has a flair for that sort of thing. You're artistic, come and have a look."

Before either of them could demur, Will and Amy found themselves propelled towards the French windows at the back of the house to peer into a room that made the Sistine Chapel seem lacklustre. Gone was the country chintz favoured by the previous owners, and in had come silken curtains, fringed with gold and gathered in great folds and ruches on either side of every window by fat tie-backs that swept up yards of sumptuous fabric. The sofas and chairs were white and richly padded, coffee tables of gilt and onyx held glossy books devoted to racing cars and stylish interiors, and glass shelves on either side of the new marble fireplace displayed a quantity of Lladro and Capo di Monte that could have restocked Lower Regent Street.

The telephone was an ornate pseudo-Victorian confection in amber and gold, and Amy guessed that even the lavatory pan was probably equipped with swags and tails.

The two gazed on the profligate display of newly acquired wealth in silent bewilderment.

"Done well, hasn't she?" said their host, with pride. "Knows just what to put with what. No point asking me – I'm colour blind."

It was at this point that Amy noticed the two sculptures she had sold the MacDermotts. They were standing at either side of the double doors leading from the ornate sitting room into the hall, each placed centrally on a goatskin rug. Her heart sank when she thought that she had provided something that was to the MacDermotts' taste. But then she saw the funny side and wondered what Oliver would have said if he had known where his works of art had ended up. Poetic justice. She shivered, remembering his letter and his promise of a return visit, but her thoughts were interrupted by Jerry MacDermott's voice.

"Who do you know?" he asked, wheeling them away from his Aladdin's cave towards the scattered tables on the lawn.

Unless Will acted quickly they might be saddled with a detailed itinerary involving visits to most of the local population. He waved at a figure a couple of tables away. "Look, there's –" he stopped himself in the nick of time from mentioning Hovis's Christian name – "Aitch. We'll go and say hello."

Hovis hailed them. "Hallo, me dears. How are we?" He was sitting with a couple of old ladies from the village who ran the tea-shop. He rose, doffed his battered Panama and pecked Amy on the cheek. The two ladies beetled off in search of another gin.

Will glanced at the diverse groups of people seated at tables and standing chatting. "A bit like an Agatha Christie whodunit, eh?" Hovis remarked.

"Mmm?" Will was preoccupied.

"All gathered in the garden for the inspector's revelations."

"What do you mean?"

"Well, the likelihood is that someone here knows about the . . . er . . . *catch* you made. All the usual suspects are present." He indicated the far end of the garden by the cliff, where Len Gryler, standing alone in a shirt of unusual whiteness, was swigging from a bottle of Newcastle Brown.

Hovis warmed to his subject. "Then there's the *nouveau-riche* set." Will looked towards the house, where Trudie MacDermott, her blonde hair whipped into an even more spectacular froth than usual, was giggling in the company of an elderly but distinguished man in a navy-blue blazer with gold buttons. She wore a short, tight white miniskirt and a pink T-shirt that left little to the imagination. Her red-faced companion was having trouble in lifting his eyes from her cleavage but she seemed to mind not at all.

"The Admiral's happy, then," observed Hovis.

"The Admiral?" asked Amy.

"Old Scalder. Very keen on the ladies. His wife's the one with the moustache leaning against the drinks table."

Amy sipped her Campari. "That's very wicked of you."

"Perhaps. But it's true."

She watched as the Admiral's bushy eyebrows twitched. He grinned lasciviously at Trudie, the ice-cubes rattling in his gin and tonic.

"Is he really an admiral?"

"No," chipped in Will. "Ernie used to say that he was a petty officer with delusions of grandeur. Sidney Calder, known to his shipmates as Scalder. Always getting into hot water with the ladies. Harmless enough, though."

"Unless you're a lady," added Hovis.

Will chuckled. "Unless you're not a lady!"

Amy looked around. "I didn't realize there were so many people in the cove I didn't know."

"They only come out in summer," said Hovis. "Spend most of the winter tucked away in their cottages making ships in bottles."

"Watch it," said Will, threateningly.

"Ah. Sorry about that. Bit near home, eh?" Hovis sipped his Scotch and water.

"How long do you think we'll have to stay?" asked Will.

"Well, we can't go yet," admonished Amy. "We've only just arrived."

"You don't look the most reluctant people here," remarked Hovis. "I'd say there were two others who will want to stay as short a time as possible." He nodded in the direction of a couple standing alone lower down on the lawn towards the sea.

Will shielded his eyes from the sun and looked in the direction of Hovis's gesture. "It's the Morgan-Gileses. I'm surprised they came."

"Very surprised," agreed Hovis. "It must be upsetting to be a guest at a house you once owned. Especially when the new incumbents are not exactly of the same water."

"Come on," said Amy, "let's go and have a word. They look really uncomfortable."

"But –" Will tried to stop her, but she was already crossing the lawn. He looked exasperatedly towards Hovis, who shrugged. Will sighed, then followed her.

The Morgan-Gileses brightened at Amy's approach. "How nice to see you." Hugo offered her his hand. His wife nodded and smiled distantly.

"We thought you looked a bit out of it," said Amy, as Will caught her up.

"Oh, well, you know . . ." Hugo's good manners prevented him from expressing his real feelings. "It's nice to be able to take in the view again, isn't it, Mouse?"

His wife lowered her eyes before turning them towards the terrace, where Trudie MacDermott was now walking with the Admiral, whose deep laugh echoed across the lawn. The four onlookers watched as she took the blazered old boy by the arm, clattering in her stilettos across the York stone flags that led to the old conservatory.

"Lovely vine, you know," remarked Hugo.

"Sorry?" asked Amy.

"In the conservatory. Wonderful grapes. 'Muscat of Alexandria'. Isobel was a dab hand at thinning, weren't you, dear?"

Mrs Morgan-Giles, her discomfort growing, finished the drop of sherry in the bottom of her glass, then looked at her watch. "I think we ought to be going now. The joint will be ready soon."

Hugo looked embarrassed at his wife's eagerness to leave. "Yes. Yes, I suppose we must. Would you excuse us? It's lamb and we do like it pink." He shook hands again with both of them and held out an arm to shepherd her towards the gate of the garden they had once tended together. Isobel Morgan-Giles barely acknowledged them as she hurried across the turf, her husband following her with his hands clasped behind his back. They looked, thought Will, just like the Queen and the Duke of Edinburgh, making a state visit to a country that had once been part of the Empire but which was now an independent territory. The Morgan-Gileses' Union Flag no longer flew from Benbecula's flagstaff: it had been supplanted by cheap bunting.

Chapter 24:
Royal Sovereign

They left each other at the entrance to the Crooked Angel, Amy to take over from Primrose's niece at the studio, and Will to visit May Hallybone in St Petroc. The sky looked angry: vast grey-bottomed clouds blotted out most of the blue, and a sharp breeze whipped at the waves in the cove. Will grabbed a jacket from *Boy Jack* and unfastened the padlock of his newly acquired bike. Tiring of frequent bus journeys into St Petroc, he had bought the old green Raleigh a few days previously from an advert in Primrose's window. He had chained it to the stanchions on the boat for safety. Already one or two new faces were appearing at the yard – like the surly youth with the day-boat who had turned up on pontoon number one. He looked shifty and seemed obsessed with his ropes. Will became more security-conscious and reminded himself to lock up whenever he left.

He wheeled the bike along the pontoon and on to the jetty, mounting as he approached the new shower block. Len Gryler walked out of his hut as Will cycled past, the white shirt now replaced by the familiar oily overalls and the Newcastle Brown with a pint pot of tea. He nodded silently, and watched as Will pedalled slowly up the lane, past Benbecula and on to the St Petroc road.

It was a steep climb for the first couple of miles, but he enjoyed the physical exertion after the hour of enforced politeness at the MacDermotts'. At the top of the lane the road flattened out. To the right were fields of sheep surrounded by hedgebanks, and to the left,

441

rougher countryside of bracken and foxgloves, vetches and coarse grasses, running down to the sea-pink-studded turf that topped the cliffs.

He hopped off the bike and pushed it through the bracken towards a lump of granite that offered a good view of the cove. He perched there, looking out to sea through the swaying madder-pink spires of foxgloves and inhaling the fresh, crisp air. Shafts of sunlight beamed down between the clouds, highlighting patches of sea with gleaming silver. The glittering water contrasted sharply with the blue-grey clouds, which threatened at any moment to shed their watery load. Perhaps the clouds would blow by today. Certainly, brighter sky seemed to be in the offing.

He looked at the patterns of light on the water, and again the crystal clear image of Ernie disappearing beneath the waves came into his mind. He rubbed his eyes as if to wipe it away, and turned his thoughts to his impending trip. For weeks now it had loomed ever larger in his mind. But so, too, had Amy. She had not brought up the subject since the day she first visited *Boy Jack*, and neither had he. Amy hoped it would go away, and Will wasn't quite sure what he hoped.

How long would it be before he was ready? Two weeks? Three? He could not put off his decision much longer. But was there a decision to make? He was about to sail around the coast of Britain. This is what he had planned all these years. It was why he had bought the boat, spent most of his savings doing it up and equipped himself technically, physically and emotionally for the journey of a lifetime, leaving behind the past and its tragedies – the loss of Ellie then Ernie – and making a new start.

But he had not accounted for Amy, or falling in love. He stared at the sea, hoping that it might yield up some sort of solution but, as ever, it was intent on its own business. It had its own agenda; if he wanted to be a part of it, all he had to do was put out in his boat. If he did not, he must remain as a spectator, watching from a distance, and wondering what it would be like to be involved. He sighed heavily. What had once seemed simple was now fraught with complications.

Below him a boat cut through the waves. A large white boat. A fast white boat, slapping against the crests and roaring on past Bill's Island. He recognized it. It was the MacDermotts'. Having said goodbye to their guests they had clearly decided to go out for a spin. He waited for the boat to come into view again at the other side of the island, but it did not. He looked at his watch. Half past two. It was five to three before the boat reappeared, travelling back in the direction whence it had come. It was returning to Pencurnow, as fast as it had left some twenty-five minutes ago.

Thoughtfully Will picked up the bike and cycled on towards St Petroc.

"Could just have stopped to admire the view." Hovis was sitting in the corner of the bench seat on *Boy Jack*.

"Did you see them go out?" asked Will.

"Yes. Usual fuss and bother with ropes, even though they had old Scalder with them. Mind you, he'd probably had too much gin to be of any help. But he looked the part, standing on the bridge in his blazer and peaked cap."

"What do you think I should do?"

"You've two choices, haven't you? Go to the police to report something you think is suspicious, or keep it to yourself."

"Mmm." Will looked thoughtful. "It's not much to go on, is it?"

Hovis shook his head. "Not really. Odd, though, all the same. Especially as they were out of sight for less than half an hour. Not really long enough to drop the hook, put the kettle on and put your feet up, and too long to be simply turning round."

"Did you see them come back?"

"Yes. By then I think old Scalder was *persona non grata*. Probably tried to touch up MacDermott's missus." He winked.

"Did they have anything with them?"

"What sort of thing?"

"I don't know. Polythene bags or plastic boxes or something."

"Well, they had a couple of holdalls – you know, those things they use to keep bottles of wine chilled, cool-bags. But I expect that was just their picnic."

"Do you fancy a trip out there?"

"Where?"

"Bill's Island."

Hovis looked uneasy. "Oh, I don't think you should go there. Keep out of the way. Best thing."

"But if we go out there now and find that the lobster pots aren't empty any more then the chances are that the MacDermotts put the stuff in them."

"Don't you think the police will have thought of that? They'll be keeping an eye. Bound to be. Don't get involved. And, anyway, the MacDermotts are presumably taking stuff out of the lobster pots rather than putting it in."

"Well, let's just go for a sail and see if anything's going on."

Hovis grew more agitated and made to leave.

"Just a quick trip. That's all. I'll show you how my new GPS works." Will felt driven to push the issue, even though to his own ears he sounded childish. Something inside him was goading him on.

"No. I'd rather not." Hovis walked towards the hatchway, intent on leaving.

Will blocked his way. "Why not? What have we got to lose? We might even see something that will help clear this lot up."

"I can't."

Hovis was panicking. He tried to push past Will. Will wondered what was the cause of this sudden fear. Surely Hovis couldn't be involved. His mind raced as he stood in front of the bearded figure.

"What is it you know that I don't?" asked Will, looking his friend straight in the eye.

Hovis avoided his gaze. "It's nothing."

"If it's nothing, why won't you come?"

"Because . . ."

"What?" Will snapped impatiently. "Because what?"

Hovis rubbed at his beard, then wiped his hand over his forehead where beads of sweat were already forming.

"Because I get seasick." He slumped down on the bench seat, took a red and white spotted handkerchief from the pocket of his grubby corduroys and mopped his brow. He sat limply, the picture of despair. "Nobody knows. Not a soul. Truth is, I even get queasy in the boatyard when the wind blows up. I've tried to get over it, like Nelson. Thought it might subside with age, but it seems to have got worse."

"Dartmouth and Salcombe," Will whispered, half to himself.

"A dream, I'm afraid. I only ever go there by train. Old *Florence Nightingale's* destined to end her days here. Like me."

"But have you tried–"

"Everything. All the cures. Pills. Potions. Those little armbands

with buttons on them. Nothing helps. Ten minutes on the flattest sea
and I'm heaving over the side. Went to the doctor. He said it was
something to do with my inner ear. Balance, that sort of thing." He
looked up at Will with a feeble smile. "It's a bit of a bugger, isn't it?
Always loved the sea, and all I can do is look at it."

"I won't tell anybody. Don't imagine that."

"Thanks."

"Just for a minute there I thought . . ."

"I know. I saw it in your eyes."

"Sorry."

"You weren't to know." Hovis exhaled loudly. "Would you mind
not saying anything to Amy?"

"Of course not."

"Only I don't want . . ."

"I won't breathe a word."

Amy listened avidly to his story of the MacDermotts' boat and found
herself agreeing with Hovis that this was something for the police, not
Will.

"Should I tell them?"

"Supposing the MacDermotts had just broken down?"

"In a new boat?"

"It happens, doesn't it? New cars break down."

"Well, yes, but . . ."

"Just keep it to yourself for a while. You can always mention it later
if you have to."

She was sitting on the sofa at the studio, her feet tucked beneath
her blue and white striped cotton dress. She sipped at a glass of
Chardonnay. In spite of the wide-brimmed hat the sun had caught her
cheeks, and she seemed to glow. A shaft of sunlight darted in through
the skylight, its beam turning the scrubbed wooden floor the colour of
honey. The heavy clouds were all but gone and the evening was still.
Will sat cross-legged on the floor, looking up at her.

"How was May?" she asked.

"I almost forgot." He took a gulp of the clear amber wine. "She was
a bit tearful. But pleased."

"Pleased?"

"They've awarded Ernie the George Medal." He felt his throat
constrict.

Amy's face creased up with delight. "Oh! How lovely. I mean . . ."

"I know." He came and sat beside her, putting his arm around her and his head against hers. "At least his life hasn't gone unrecognized."

"She must be very proud."

"She showed me the letter. Somehow it seemed such a final thing." He put down his glass. "I went to his grave. Put some flowers on it. You know, buttercups and foxgloves. He preferred those to garden flowers. It's a lovely spot. Looks right out over the sea."

They sat quietly for what seemed like an age, and then he said, "About my trip."

She sat perfectly still, her eyes fixed on the floor. She had put it all to the back of her mind; had tried hard not to think about it, imagining that if she were to distance herself from it sufficiently it would disappear. His words surprised her.

"I want you to come with me."

She swung round to look at him.

"I don't want to do it on my own. I want to do it with you." He watched her. Waiting for an answer. When, eventually, it came, he felt the pit of his stomach sink.

"I can't." She spoke gently and looked away.

He had half expected this, but still it came as a shock. "Why not?"

"Because." She found herself unable to meet his eye. "Because of all this. I've just got myself started up. I can't just leave it all."

He thought he must have heard wrongly. Perhaps that was not what she meant.

"But I thought . . . I thought you . . ."

"Wanted to come?"

"Yes."

She turned to face him. "Oh, I do. I really do. But I can't just throw it all in. Just like that."

He stared at her, shaking his head in disbelief. "I don't understand. I mean, do you want to be with me or not?"

"Yes. I do."

"Well, then, come with me." A note of exasperation crept into his voice.

"It's not as easy as that."

"It is. It's perfectly straightforward. I don't want to go without you. I don't want to be on my own any more; I want to be with you. You seemed to want to be with me so I thought you felt the same."

"I do feel the same, but I can't just up and come. I can't."

"But how can you say that?" He almost shouted the words. He was angry now. Angry at letting himself be lulled into what was clearly a false sense of security. She had led him on. Made him think that he was important to her, got him to lower his guard to the point where he had offered her his life to share and she had rejected him. They had talked as he had not talked in a long time; shared their feelings so completely, made love in a way that he had never made love before; become soulmates, and here she was, turning him down simply because his voyage – which she knew about and had always known about – got in the way of her gallery, studio, shop or whatever she wanted to call it.

She interrupted his thundering confusion of thoughts.

"I thought you might have changed your mind about going."

He looked at her with real pain etched on his face. "But I've been planning it for so long. You know that. I've never made a secret of it. It's what I've always wanted to do."

"Until I got in the way?"

"Don't say that."

"But it's true isn't it? You had your life mapped out and then you bumped into me and I messed it all up."

"It's not like that."

"Oh I think it is." She tried to keep her voice steady and level. "You need this trip to clear your mind. Start you off on a new life. Leave the past behind. I know that. You've longed for it. Why should I imagine that you'd give it up?"

"Because I love you."

Amy looked at him hard, biting her lip to rein in her emotions. "But not quite enough." She looked away.

"Please. Don't say that. Don't think that I don't love you enough. I couldn't love you more."

"No. Well; there we are then."

He felt empty. Cold. Why had it all suddenly gone wrong? He wanted her to go with him, to make the trip of a lifetime and she had turned him down. They sat slightly apart on the sofa now, neither of them capable of taking the conversation any further.

Will got up. "I'd better go."

Amy said nothing.

He looked down at her, his feelings numbed. "I'm sorry."

She did not answer. Just carried on looking at the pictures on the wall. The pictures of white beaches and blue sea and clear skies.

The last thing she heard was the gentle closing of the door and the tapping of the 'Closed' sign against the glass.

Chapter 25: Nab

His jaw ached. For two weeks now he had been clenching his teeth, telling himself he was right to press on with his plans. He had offered to take her with him and she had declined. She knew it was his intention to go, always had been. He felt annoyed with himself for having given so much of himself away, betrayed, too, because she wouldn't go with him. How could she say that he didn't love her enough when he had offered to share his life and his dreams with her?

She continued to occupy his every waking hour. As he studied the charts he would need for his voyage her face kept smiling at him from harbours and creeks, compass roses and tide tables.

There were days when he felt low enough to call it all off, and others when his bloody-mindedness saw him ploughing ahead doggedly with his preparations. From time to time he caught Spike looking at him questioningly with his head on one side. And Hovis had been quiet of late, allowing him to get on unhindered. He had told him of Amy's refusal to go with him, and been surprised at his reaction. Hovis had absorbed the information quietly, averting his eyes, as though the subject had nothing to do with him. Which, of course, reflected Will, it had not.

The late May bank holiday came and went. June had arrived and at weekends now the place would be alive with tourists. He would have liked to have been away by now, but there were still engine refinements to make, the anchor winch to be repaired, windscreen wipers to fix – fiddly jobs that seemed to take up large chunks of his day. Two of the port-holes leaked during heavy rain and needed sealing; a small area of deck planking had sprung and needed recaulking, and a cleat had come away from its mounting. Old boats, like old houses, seemed forever in need of attention.

Half of him wanted to cast off, leave and sort out such problems along the way. What did it matter where he was berthed? He could make running repairs in any port. Yet the perfectionist in him wouldn't let him set off until everything was shipshape. Only then would he have the satisfaction of knowing that his voyage was underway and the past left behind.

But where did the past end and the present begin?

He sat on the edge of the bed, weary of thinking. The brass clock on the bulkhead showed a quarter to eleven. He looked out of the port-hole and saw the moon glinting on the rippling water, heard the gentle slapping of the tide against the hull. It was a sound he loved: comforting, promising, exciting. The hairs on the back of his neck stood on end at the prospect of adventure, but a black cloud surrounded him as he slid under the quilt and waited for the soothing motion of the sea to rock him to sleep.

The tapping sound woke him slowly. At first he thought it was something in the water, knocking against the hull – a bottle or a can. He sat up. The tapping had stopped, but he could not settle. He heaved his weary body from the bed and walked up the cabin steps towards the door of the saloon. He pulled back the curtain and looked out. Nothing. Just a silent boatyard with vessels straining at their mooring warps. He turned to go back to bed, but a flash of white caught his eye. He looked down. A piece of paper lay on the cabin floor. He opened it and strained to read the words that were printed in capitals in handwriting he knew. The words were few but the message was clear: "0300 HOURS. OUTSIDE THE SALUTATION. TED."

He looked at the clock. It was half past two. He sat on the bench seat, rubbed his eyes and reread the note. It was like something out of a spy thriller, yet Ted Whistler was not given to flights of fancy. He pulled on his clothes in the dark, slipped on a pair of deck-shoes, slid open the door and padded down the pontoon towards the jetty, his heart thumping in his chest. He must be mad. Ted must be mad. What was going on?

He eased open the hefty gate of the boatyard as silently as he could and squeezed through, closing it behind him before walking along the lane that led to the Salutation. The pub was dark now, its clientele having long departed to their beds. Alf Penrose had never been prosecuted for serving after hours – he was too partial to a good night's sleep.

Will looked around. Nothing. No one. Perhaps it was a joke. Perhaps he'd dreamt it. A hand touched his shoulder and he almost cleared the iron railings in one leap.

"What the – !"

"Ssh." The voice was familiar.

"Bloody hell! What's going on?"

"Sorry," Ted whispered. "Come over here." He led Will to a stretch of railings overshadowed by buildings, where the moonlight failed to provide illumination.

"What's wrong?"

Ted pointed out to sea in the direction of Bill's Island. "Just wait."

The two men had little in common other than a shared background of lighthouse-keeping, but each knew from experience that once the eyes were fully accustomed to the dark they could see almost as well as in daylight – especially on a moonlit night when the shadows were as contrasting as any provided by the sun.

Will's eyes were used to the darkness, but he could see nothing other than the hump of Bill's Island rising out of the water, the glint of the moon on the rippling tide and the wavelets breaking on the island's shoals. The regular flash of the lighthouse added its own intermittent brilliance.

For fully twenty minutes they stood there, and just as Will was about to suggest there were better ways of spending the early hours, his eyes focused on a small inflatable dinghy making its way back from Bill's Island.

"Night fishing?"

"In one of those?"

There was only one alternative. "Smuggling?"

Ted nodded.

"How do you know?" He kept his voice low.

"Been watching regular."

"How long?"

"Three weeks."

"Why?"

"Dunno. Had a feeling, that's all. Pissed off about Ernie."

"You've been out here every night?"

"Mostly."

The two men watched as the dinghy made its way towards the shingle bank – not to the boatyard or the adjacent hard. Ted spoke again softly. "Seems to happen on Thursday nights, about this time. Not always, but twice before. The other night there was too much wind. Sea was too rough."

"Fancy going out in a boat that small. Any kind of sea and it would be over. Must be mad."

"Desperate, more like."

"Why haven't you been to the police? Come to think of it, why haven't the police spotted it?"

Ted ignored the second question and answered the first. "Didn't want to get involved. Anyway, there never seems to be anything in the boat. No fish. Nothing. But they must be up to something."

"Why have you got me out here?"

Ted shrugged.

"What happens now?"

"Watch and you'll see."

As the boat approached the bank of pebbles the rower shipped the oars and stepped out before pulling it clear of the tide. He bent to pick something from the bottom of the dinghy. Will could not make out what it was.

"That's a first," said Ted, a note of surprise in his voice. The oarsman deflated the tiny vessel, folded it and stuffed it into a large holdall. The night was calm and silent, apart from the sucking of the tide on the shingle, but all the while the figure looked about nervously, clearly waiting for something or someone.

Ted nudged Will's arm and nodded in the direction of the cliff path. Will screwed up his eyes and could just make out another figure descending towards the beach. The first figure had also seen the newcomer, but made no move to depart. The newcomer walked down the shingle bank and picked up the object that had been removed from the boat, put it into a bag, then took the handle at one side of the holdall that now contained the dinghy. The figures then set off with their two pieces of baggage towards the cliff path.

For a moment, Will and Ted looked at one another, unsure of their next move. Then Will cocked an eyebrow, Ted nodded, and they walked silently across the narrow lane to climb a small, steep path that would join the one that ran along the top of the cliff. In the space of two minutes they would be able to intercept the oarsman, his companion and their cargo.

The suddenness of it all took them both by surprise. As they breasted the grassy knoll before them, two large figures blocked their path.

Both Will and Ted stopped in their tracks, straining hard to make out the features on the faces that confronted them. With the moonlight behind them it was difficult, but Will thought he recognized one of the men as the policeman who had driven him back to the station in St Petroc. The other looked vaguely familiar but Will could not place him.

"Stop there, please," commanded the second figure, quietly but firmly. Will and Ted did as they were told. His companion, the young policeman, looked back over his shoulder towards the path where the oarsman and his companion must have been climbing. Will could see nothing over the knoll.

The four stood silently for what seemed like an age, until the young policeman said, "That's it. They're in the bag," in his voice a mixture of relief and triumph.

"Right," said his companion. "Down there, please." He pointed to the path they had just climbed, signalling them both to make their way down. Silently they descended, looking neither right nor left, until they reached the lane. A police car purred silently into view and Ted and Will were motioned into the back seat by the second policeman, who then climbed into the front. No siren sounded, and no words were spoken during the short, speedy journey to St Petroc at half past three on a Friday morning.

Will knew what would happen when they arrived at the station. He could hear the voice of the detective sergeant now, could see the expression on his face. Who could blame him for the conclusions he would draw?

On arrival at the police station they were split up and shown into separate interview rooms. Will sat alone for twenty minutes before the sergeant arrived with the young constable in tow, switched on a machine, gave time and date details and uttered the words that previously Will had heard only on television: "You do not have to say anything, but it may harm your defence if you do not mention, when questioned, something which you later rely on in court. Anything you do say may be given in evidence."

Will felt a cold sweat break out on his brow.

"I think you need to explain a few things to me, don't you?"

Will recounted the events of the night – Ted's message, how he had accompanied him to the coast road and watched the boat bringing back its cargo.

The detective sergeant looked grim. He listened attentively, asking questions that showed clearly he had already talked to Ted. For the best part of an hour the interrogation was relentless, the sergeant's manner intimidating. Then he sighed and got up. "You're lucky, aren't you?"

"Sorry?"

"Lucky I believe you. And at least your stories tie up."

Will could think of nothing to say.

"I know you were drawn into this by a series of events, sir, but you'd have helped more if you'd just stood back and left us to get on with it."

"I thought I had."

"Until tonight."

"Yes. I'm sorry."

Will was unsure where the conversation was leading, but relieved that the sergeant was not treating him as a suspect. His curiosity got the better of him.

"Did you get them? The two on the cliff path?"

"Yes, sir. We did. No thanks to you. A couple of minutes more and you'd have blown it. Do you know how long we've been watching them?"

Will shook his head apologetically.

"Four weeks. Every night for four weeks. Along with your friend next door. Well, actually, we've been at it eight days longer than him."

Will looked at the sergeant enquiringly. "Ted?"

"He didn't do anything, only watched, so we thought we'd leave him alone. Just keep an eye, you know."

"He wasn't . . . ?"

"No. He wasn't. From the start we were fairly sure he wasn't, but we didn't want him to do anything that might prejudice the outcome, so we decided to leave him be, provided he didn't overstep the mark. Only this was the first night they actually came away with anything.

You can't arrest people for rowing around in a rubber dinghy late at night. You might want to arrest them for stupidity but we chose not to. Waited until we had something a bit more serious to go on."

"Did they pick it up, then?"

"I can't really say any more, sir."

"No, of course not."

"I'd be grateful if you'd keep tonight's events to yourself. It will be public knowledge soon enough, but I'd like to be in charge of the timings myself, if that's all right with you?"

Will was conscious of the sergeant's sarcasm.

The policeman moved towards the door. "Wait here for a few minutes and I'll arrange for someone to drive you back." He left the room, along with the young constable, and Will stared unseeingly at a poster advising against drink-driving. It was then that he remembered where he had seen the other police constable before, not the one who had just left the room but the one who had stood beside him on the cliff path. He was the surly youth who had arrived on pontoon number one in the battered day-boat. He must have been watching Will, Gryler and the boatyard ever since. Will shuddered, remembering how close he had come to revisiting the lobster pots.

The door reopened and the boating police constable gestured to Will to follow him, his face expressionless. Ted was waiting outside, looking as though he had only just survived an attack by a Rottweiler. As they walked down the corridor together they passed another interview room. The door was in the process of being closed, but as they walked past, Will saw the two figures sitting at a table.

The door slammed shut but the vision of Hugo and Isobel Morgan-Giles remained imprinted in his mind.

The sergeant was careful never to let his personal life spill over into his work. He had endeavoured, over the last few years particularly, to keep the two separate. Whenever they looked as though they might conflict, he made sure that someone else took the reins. His colleagues knew this, and knew, too, that he never let his own experiences colour his judgement.

He questioned Hugo Morgan-Giles calmly and thoroughly, with little display of emotion. "You do know what was in the packages?"

Hugo considered. "I'm not sure."

"Do you know what they were worth?"

"No."

"Around fifty thousand pounds each, street value. That's a quarter of a million pounds."

Isobel Morgan-Giles shot her husband a glance laden with reproach.

Hugo's head jerked up. "I'd no idea!"

"How much were you getting?"

He hesitated. "Five thousand."

"Each?"

Hugo looked crestfallen. He shook his head.

"Where from?"

Hugo turned to his wife, who stared at him with disgust. He realized he was now on his own. "A few years ago, when we were still living at Benbecula, we encountered financial difficulties." He looked almost embarrassed to admit to it. "We lost a lot of money. Lloyds. I was a Name. We found ourselves heavily in debt. We struggled to keep the big house going for a long time but in the end we only just managed to hang on to what we used to call the Dower House – the Moorings – and we moved in there and sold Benbecula to . . . other people." He said it politely, without any hint of recrimination. His wife let out a suppressed but scornful snort.

"I tried to find a couple of consultancies in the City, but I failed, and I realized that very shortly I would have to declare myself bankrupt, which would mean losing everything, even the Moorings. I was desperate to find a way of just hanging on in there, I think you'd call it. The children are both at private schools and that was the one thing I was determined they should continue to have – at any cost. Benbecula had been in the family for three generations. I'd already let them down enough.

"I tried everything I could think of. Went to see old friends, almost begged for work, but nothing was forthcoming. You're not equipped for much when you've been retired from the Army for ten years. Except for being chairman of the village-hall committee. I just didn't know where to look. People were very sympathetic but . . . nothing." He spoke calmly, almost relieved to get it all off his chest.

"So you found an easier way to make money?"

"I'd never done anything illegal in my life. I haven't even had a parking ticket. It wasn't easy. I didn't do it without a lot of soul-searching. But in the end I couldn't afford self-respect. Too much pride for that, I suppose. Too much family pride. If you see what I mean." He didn't wait for an opinion, but continued, "Just over a year ago I caught the two boys up in the attic smoking pot."

The sergeant raised his head. "The two boys? I thought you only had one son."

"He had a friend. A lad from the village. Used to muck around together. I gave them a hell of a tongue-lashing, bawled them out. Told them if I found them at it again I'd give them what for. Tim – my boy – went back to school and I thought that was that. It was about a week later when the lad came to see me at the house. I wanted nothing to do with him. Told him not to come back, and not to see Tim again either. He left, shouting something abusive about money. About how I was wasting an opportunity."

"Who was the lad?" asked the sergeant.

Hugo spoke very quietly. "Christopher Applebee."

"Go on."

"I never thought much about it. Then this man turned up at the house the following week. Said he was from the Inland Revenue. I invited him in, thinking that this would be the end of things, that we'd lose what little we'd managed to save. I took him into my study. He said that I owed more money than their calculations had at first shown, and what was I going to do about it? I thought I'd reached rock bottom. Then he smiled. Said he wasn't really from the tax office but now I knew how I'd feel when they really did come.

"I didn't understand what was going on. I asked him what he was doing, who he was, why he thought he could come into my house and talk to me like this. I asked him to leave. Then he said he was a friend of the lad's and that he'd heard I needed money. I told him I wasn't interested, that I wouldn't do anything underhand or illegal. He said what he was suggesting was quite safe. He explained that I could earn money by joining his import-export business."

The sergeant rested his chin in his hands and sighed.

"Yes. Deep down I knew what was going on, but it was the first offer anyone had made to me."

"And you took it?"

"Not at first. He was very persuasive. Said that he had plenty of people who could collect things for him. What he needed was someone reliable – senior management sort of thing – who could make sure that goods were delivered to a prearranged address at weekly or monthly intervals. That was all. There was no need for me to know what was in the packages. All I had to do was make sure they were delivered. That was all."

"So you said yes." The sergeant's voice was devoid of emotion.

"Eventually," Hugo agreed wearily. "You've probably never been there, but it's amazing what you can make yourself do when there's nowhere else to go. When you've explored every conceivable avenue and found no way out. I even managed to convince myself that the packages contained nothing illegal. Stupid, isn't it?"

Still no reaction.

"And so it started. Christopher would collect the parcels from the lobster pots and bring them to me."

"Always on a Thursday?"

"Yes."

"But not every Thursday?"

"No. We weren't told when they were coming. The man said that's the way it would be."

"Were there always five parcels?"

"No. Sometimes fewer."

"And did you meet the man again?"

"He said there would be no need."

"So where did you take the parcels?"

"To a waste skip behind a hotel near Green Park, in London."

"And where did you get your money?"

"By post. In a padded envelope."

"And Applebee?"

"I don't know."

"And you always got five thousand pounds?"

"Always."

"Not a lot, considering the value of what you were delivering."

"But I didn't know that." Hugo realized as he said it that his claim of ignorance would count for little.

The sergeant persisted with his questioning until he was satisfied that there was little more to be gained by continuing at this hour of the morning.

As the sergeant stood up to go, Hugo said, "I do just want to say one thing. My wife has had nothing to do with this. It was entirely my doing."

The sergeant looked balefully at his interviewee. "Until

Christopher Applebee was drowned trying to pick up the packages and you had to start collecting the stuff yourself. Then, of course, you needed someone to help you carry the dinghy up to the house."

Hugo gazed at the floor.

"The firebomb at the lighthouse?" The sergeant asked the question as though he were asking the time of day. "Your idea or Applebee's?"

Hugo answered, without hesitation, "Mine. Applebee knew that the lighthouse keeper's diaries were there. Heard about them in the pub. Said we ought to steal them. I thought a firebomb would be quicker. Neater."

"And who threw it?"

"I did."

"Noble of you to admit it," the sergeant said flatly, "but the stuff we found in Christopher Applebee's flat tells us otherwise."

The Morgan-Gileses were detained for further questioning. The sergeant returned briefly to his desk before going home to snatch some sleep. He picked up his car keys from the desk drawer, then looked at the framed photo that stood next to an overflowing in-tray. It was a picture of his daughter. She had been only fifteen when the picture was taken. She had died four years ago now, after taking a single Ecstasy tablet at a disco in Penzance.

Chapter 26: Nash

Amy rose early. She had become accustomed to lying awake from around six o'clock and had decided after several days of moping until eight that the only way ahead was to work. The bank holiday weekend had gone well, and she needed more stock. She contacted the jewellery maker, the patchwork stitcher and the rest of her suppliers to make sure she had enough for what she hoped would be a good season ahead.

Her three new paintings were finished, but she was not sure she liked them. They were bright enough, but lacked sparkle. She hung them where they would catch the eye of a prospective purchaser as soon as the studio door opened. She took a shower and sat down to orange juice, bran flakes and slices of banana.

Just occasionally it was impossible not to think of him. Just occasionally, several times a minute. She pushed back her chair and crossed to the sink with the glass, the bowl and the spoon, slamming them into the washing-up bowl with unwise ferocity. The glass broke. "Shit!" She clutched at the rim of the sink and closed her eyes to prevent the tears spilling over. "Oh, shit!" A wave of sorrow engulfed her and her body contracted in wild sobs.

She reached for the kitchen roll, tore off a couple of squares and blew her nose loudly, cursing herself. "Stupid woman! Pull yourself together and get on with it. He's not worth it. They never are."

She mopped up her tears, sniffing all the while, and wiped away the smudges of mascara before they descended from her lower eyelids on to the freckled cheeks.

"Oh, God! What a state! What have you done? Why did you turn him down? So bloody anxious to prove you can go it alone. So keen to be bloody independent. Well, now you are, and where has it got you? On your own again. Huh!"

She sniffed again and binned the kitchen roll, heading for the bathroom to sort out her face before opening the studio. It was, after all, what she had always wanted.

Will sat on a canvas chair at the bows of *Boy Jack* looking out across the cove to the lighthouse. It seemed ages since he had been there, but there was little reason to return now. May Hallybone was staying in St Petroc with her sister. She'd decided to make a home nearer her friends. That's what she'd said when he'd called in the week before. Will had been worried about her, but May had allayed his fears. "Got to get on with life. No use moping about," she'd said. "I just remember all the good times, forget the bad. You can't brood on what might have been."

"Will you stay with your sister?" he'd asked.

"Good Lord, no! We're all right for a while but we'll drive one another mad if we have to spend the rest of our lives together. I'll find a little place on my own. I'll be happy – always comfortable in my own company. And with the animals." Will smiled at the thought of her living out her days with her pigs and chickens, a woman contented with her lot, accepting what life had given her – and taken away.

The sound of a hatch opening came from the boat next door, and the sandy-whiskered head popped out. "Good morning! Looks as though it's going to be a nice day. Suit all those trippers."

"Hallo." Will grinned reluctantly.

Hovis looked at him, sitting in his faded director's chair, surrounded by coils of rope. "Your boat's beginning to look like mine."

Will looked down at his feet where the snaking mooring warps and sundry strings were sprawled like some gigantic cat's cradle, defying his efforts at measuring them and getting them into any order.

"Just trying to make sure that I've got enough of them."

"I should think the answer to that question is almost certainly yes," Hovis remarked.

"Do you want some coffee?" asked Will.

"Not just now. Going shopping."

"I think you might want to put it off for a while when I tell you the news." Will remembered the sergeant's request to keep things to himself, but he considered Hovis to be pretty near to family.

"What do you mean?" Hovis's eyebrows were raised. They rose even higher when Will explained the events of the previous night.

"Well, bless me! Who'd have believed it? Have you told anybody else?"

"No. The sergeant asked me to keep it to myself."

"It'll be out in the open soon enough, though. You can't keep that sort of thing quiet round here. Not with Primrose on the lookout." The prospect of her reaction made Hovis chuckle. "She'll have a field day with this one." But then the sadness struck him. "Poor buggers. I wonder what made them get involved."

"It's not too difficult to see, I suppose," offered Will. "Lost all their money in the Lloyds business – house, everything. Still have two kids at expensive schools. Needed to keep them there. Found a way of doing it."

"Yes, but drugs. I wouldn't have thought that was the Morgan-Gileses' way of getting out of a hole." He shrugged. "Still, that's modern society for you. In the old days it was rum, now it's heroin and cocaine."

He looked reflective. "Just a minute, though. What about the MacDermotts? I thought we had them lined up for it, with their flash boat and their half-hour wait behind Bill's Island."

Will gestured to the other side of the boatyard where Len Gryler's legs stuck out of the engine-room hatch of the MacDermotts' bathtub.

"Engine trouble. Gryler's been up to his elbows in grease and diesel since first thing this morning."

Hovis perched on the side of his boat. "You know, I will have that coffee." He looked up at the sky where just a few wisps of white cloud floated in the increasingly rich blue. "It does make you count your blessings, doesn't it?"

"I suppose so."

For the next half-hour, while they chomped their way through digestive biscuits dipped in coffee Hovis endeavoured to piece together the jigsaw, quizzing Will after the fashion of Dr Watson with Sherlock Holmes. The only difference was that Will was less sure of the answers.

"Christopher Applebee. Presumably he was doing it for the Morgan-Gileses?"

"I guess so."

"But you'd have thought that they'd have called a halt to it after the accident, wouldn't you?"

"Depends how desperate they were for the money. And they didn't know that the drugs had been found, only that Christopher Applebee and Ernie had been drowned. As far as they were concerned, everybody still thought Applebee was catching lobsters."

"Do you think that they were the brains behind it all?"

"Don't know. Either that or just couriers. The stuff would be put in the lobster pots by some foreign fishing boat and the Morgan-Gileses would pick it up and pass it on, getting a cut for their trouble."

Hovis looked back towards Pencurnow. "Just a sleepy little Cornish fishing village and it's caught up in all this. Well, well, well."

Will looked out towards the lighthouse. "I think I'll take a walk. Haven't been over there for ages."

Hovis risked a question. "When do you think you'll set off?"

Will threw the dregs from his coffee cup over the side and they landed with a plop in the water. "Next week, I hope. Get a few more jobs done and then be on my way."

"Which direction will you go?"

"West. Thought I'd go to Scilly first. Put in at New Grimsby on Tresco. Sheltered harbour. Good seafood. Stay there a while. No rush."

Hovis slapped at the bows of *Boy Jack*. "We'll miss you, you know."

Will looked at him, temporarily wrong-footed. Spike padded from the bows and wrapped himself around his master's leg, tail held high. Will looked down then back at Hovis. "We'll miss you, too."

There was a pause, neither knowing how to proceed with the conversation. Hovis broke the silence. "Still going on your own?"

"Yes," replied Will softly. The cat rubbed against his leg again. "Well, not entirely. If he stays." Spike looked up at him, inscrutable as ever, then hopped off the boat and down the pontoon in search of amusement.

"I'm sorry," Hovis said.

"Yes. Me too." Will took the proffered mug from Hovis and put it with his in the saloon before he locked up and headed for Prince Albert Rock. In all probability, it would be the last time he saw it for a long while.

He walked slowly along the coastal path, aware that as the weeks passed, it would become more populated. The smell of the vegetation filled his nostrils – a rich mixture of herb Robert and foxglove, bladder campion and kidney vetch. It seemed as colourful as a herbaceous border. Below, the sea glinted and glimmered, fresh white waves breaking on the Cornish granite and catching the sun in rainbows of spray. It was all tantalizingly beautiful.

He stood and watched as a kittiwake keeled through the air, shrieking its name to anyone who would listen. The granite-sand path beneath his feet crunched as he trod, and he wished now that he'd put on a pair of shorts. The day was turning into a scorcher. He walked faster now, forcing positive thoughts into his head. He would go it alone. No problem. He'd done it before, could do it again. He kicked a shard of granite, which bounced down the cliff to be swallowed up silently by the waves.

The beach beyond sported half a dozen deck-chairs – the early arrivals had landed – but there was no sign of the woman with the Labrador. It struck him in an instant that she must have been Isobel Morgan-Giles. He stopped and wondered if her walks with the dog had been part of the set-up. The same dog that had been towing Hugo when Hovis and he had bumped into him on the cliff. The day that Christopher Applebee went out in his boat for the last time.

He walked on, gradually descending towards the lighthouse as the cliff path curled around Prince Albert Rock. It was hard not to feel a pang of fear, coupled with sorrow at his leaving. The white-painted granite tower had been the place where he had sheltered from life – and death. The physical rock to which he had turned when he most needed comfort. He had found it there, in the company of Ernie and May and, to a lesser extent, Ted Whistler, whose dourness now seemed less forbidding. But that was yesterday. It was time to move on. Impatience bit into him, but not so much that he could not stop to think.

He perched on a rock that was almost on a level with the lantern, and watched the sunlight glinting on its lattice panes. Through the mantle of forced optimism came the echoes of Ernie's voice: "Prince Albert Rock Lighthouse was constructed in its present form by William Tregarthen Douglass, the same engineer responsible for the construction of Bishop Rock Lighthouse." Soon he would see Bishop Rock for himself, when he sailed off in the direction of Scilly. On his own.

He missed her. He who had learned to prefer his own company. What had happened to the loner?

He cursed himself for having let down his guard then cursed himself for losing her because of his single-minded desire to sail away. Here he was, on the verge of his lifetime's ambition, so why didn't he feel more elated? He knew why. He just chose not to admit it to himself.

He looked at the sturdy white tower and forced his emotions to one side. Built all those years ago, when there were no elaborate pieces of lifting gear, no JCBs and no electricity. How many ships had it kept away from the rugged Cornish rocks below? How many had perished there before it was built? And since? The bitter pain stabbed at him. He breathed in deeply and continued down the final stretch of path.

If Evan Williams was in a good mood there might be a bottle of beer for him. After all, they were neither of them on watch any more. All Evan Williams had to do now was take care of the fabric of the place and show around the tourists. A bottle of beer seemed a safe bet.

Recently Amy had managed to keep Oliver Gallico out of her mind. If she had considered the odds she would probably have laid money on his returning when emotionally she was at her lowest ebb. It would have been a safe bet.

The studio was busy. The early tourists, enjoying a lunchtime stroll after their long journey down the A30, were looking at pictures, fondling ethnic jewellery and scrutinizing pieces of sculpture. Amy and Angela – who had fortunately agreed to help out for the rest of the summer – wrapped gifts, popped postcards in envelopes and hoped constantly for a sizeable sale. Angela was getting better at the job. She was more chatty with the customers now, and her course in bookkeeping at the local tech was coming in handy. Primrose had taught her about stock-taking, too, and she did her best, during quieter moments, to explain to Amy what it was all about. Amy did her best not to glaze over.

There was little time for such conversations at lunch-time, though, and that was when Oliver chose to make his entrance.

Angela mistook him for a customer and was not surprised by his arrogance: they saw all types down here. It was only when he said he was a friend of Amy's that she went across the studio to interrupt her employer, who was explaining the firing process of a salt-glazed pot to a couple who had driven all the way from Chalfont St Giles.

Oliver watched her reaction. It was not what he expected. Instead of looking hunted, her normal response, she glanced in his direction then continued dealing with the couple before she even raised her eyes to his. He felt uneasy.

She walked towards him and flashed him a polite but steely smile. "Hi!"

"Are you OK?" Oliver asked, with genuine concern for the first time.

"Fine. And you?"

He didn't like this approach. What was the matter with her? "You seem strange. You sure you're all right?"

"I told you, I'm fine. What are you doing down here again? Looking for talent?"

Oliver found it hard, in such circumstances, to bring his customary conceit to bear. There was nothing to push against. Nothing to respond to. "I've come for you."

Amy raised her eyes heavenward. "Oh, not that old chestnut again, please. I'm busy. I've an army of customers and only one assistant. Today is not the day for all that. It's all done with, Oliver. Go and find a young thing from the English National to go to Nice with you. I've had it." And with that she turned on her heel and went to sell the salt-glazed jar to the couple from Chalfont St Giles.

Oliver looked after her with blank disbelief, then searched for his sculptures. They had vanished, like the Amy he had once known. Even his hopes for a dramatic exit were dashed when a family with buckets and spades, windbreak and cool-bag almost fell over him as he tried to sweep out of the studio.

Amy closed the till and cast a surreptitious eye in his direction as he lurched down the stone steps. She was surprised to find she wasn't shaking. Surprised but somehow saddened.

Will was walking along the other side of the lane when he saw Oliver Gallico leaving the gallery. He looked different from the last time they had met. He was no longer swaggering. Will wondered what had brought about the change in his demeanour. And then he thought he knew. Clearly Amy had a good reason for not leaving the studio and sailing away with him. He watched as Gallico rounded the corner and was lost from view. Yes. It was definitely time he got on with his life.

Chapter 27: Crow Point

All weekend Will stayed on *Boy Jack*, concentrating on his charts and keeping out of the way of the seething mass of humanity. Pencurnow was not in any way Newquay or Padstow, but the influx of even a modest population of tourists turned it from the quiet village where most of the locals knew one another into something approaching a coastal resort between the months of June and September.

Things quietened a little after the half-term week, but he still felt safer on board than in town. He looked from the deck towards the Roundhouse from time to time, allowing himself to wonder what she might be doing, if she were missing him as much as he was missing her.

Spike, like most domestic animals, could sense something new in the offing. Instead of spending the better part of every day looking for free fish, he relied on Will's offerings of tinned catfood and watched the preparations for the voyage with intense curiosity.

Will found himself talking more to Spike, sharing his thoughts, until he realized that he did not even want to share them with himself. He sat up late into the night, poring over pilotage books, making notes and plotting courses, checking tide tables and working out passage plans.

It irritated him that the raw thrill of the voyage had been replaced with a more methodical approach, that the technical, navigational and mechanical aspects had come more to the fore than the romance and escapism. Perhaps that would return once he had finished the basic planning. He hoped so.

By Wednesday he was ready to take the boat out for the day to brush up on his solo handling. He didn't want to involve Hovis in the exercise, which he felt he ought to be able to carry out alone, so he waited until he was out shopping and slipped a note under the cabin door of *Florence Nightingale* explaining that he would be back in the early evening. There were two high tides and he could enjoy a day away from it all, still confident of being able to return with enough water beneath him.

The moment of slipping his moorings made him apprehensive. But the engines pounded reassuringly beneath his feet and he let go first of the springs, then the head and stern lines before using a little throttle to nudge the boat away from the pontoon. Slowly he motored through the boatyard, past the jetty and out into the open sea. Len Gryler watched him go from the doorway of his cabin, raising a hand aloft as he chugged by. It was eight thirty in the morning, bright but overcast, force three, maybe four.

Amy was walking down the hill from Primrose's with her shopping when she saw the boat leaving. She stood quite still, leaning on the sea wall, watching *Boy Jack* butting gently through the low waves. She knew it was him, not just from the shape of the boat but because she could see a black and white cat sitting like a figurehead on the prow. Her heart sank, and she could not remember ever feeling so empty.

The boat sailed well. It pleased him that after a while he did not hear the engines. In the days when he had been convinced he wanted a sailing boat it was the sound of wind on canvas and hull cutting through the water that had given him pleasure. Now it was the foaming white wash that appeared in his wake, the reliability of forward motion that could never be guaranteed under sail, and the feel of the sturdy boat beneath his feet as he took the helm.

Spike had surprised him by finding the whole exercise an adventure. There was no timidity about him when it came to the water. He sat, mesmerized, looking over the side at the bow wave, as if waiting for a fish to leap into his clutches.

Will tried out the autopilot. It maintained the set course and he allowed himself the satisfaction of knowing that his calculations of tidal streams had been correct. He checked his position on the chart with the pocket GPS and discovered that they seemed to agree. None of the gauges – water temperature, oil pressure or battery level – showed anything untoward. It would, hopefully, be an uneventful shake-down trip.

He dropped anchor further along the coast at a smaller, unpopulated cove, and a weak sun glinted though the thinning clouds. He tipped cat biscuits into a saucer for Spike, whose appetite had been sharpened as much as his own by the short voyage, then tucked into a Cornish pasty and an apple.

They bobbed gently on the water, the hook holding well, and Will watched as the head of a grey seal emerged above the water ahead. It blinked, then dived. Spike sat wide-eyed. It was the largest fish he had ever seen.

After an hour at anchor, Will switched on the winch and hauled up the hook before motoring down the coast. They hugged the shoreline pretty well and a germ of what it would be like to sail away from it all finally began to grow inside him. For three hours they cruised on autopilot, before Will changed course, came about and set off back in the direction of Pencurnow. The sky was still grey, but the wind had risen a little and the sea now had a distinct swell. He felt uneasy, unsure how the boat would cope with such conditions, and how Spike would take to the more violent motion.

Both questions were answered quickly. The boat turned not a hair, simply put its head down and pressed on, neatly parting the waves and snaking its way through the swell with a comfortable, predictable motion. Will rode the waves as though standing on the back of a bucking bronco, bending his knees to counter the rolling, and Spike made for the saloon, where he spent the rest of the voyage curled up on a cushion.

It was seven o'clock in the evening by the time they returned to the calmer waters of the cove, and Hovis was waiting for them, beaming from the pontoon as they came alongside. He caught the lines as Will threw them, and tied them to the rusty cleats on the pontoon before hailing the crew and asking how it had all gone.

Will had hosed down the boat to remove all traces of salt, scrubbed the decks, checked the warps, eaten his supper and fed the cat. *Boy Jack* was ready. There was no apparent reason for him to stay here any longer. All he needed now were provisions for the first leg of the journey. He would go to Primrose's in the morning and stock up. The tides would be right for a mid-morning departure. There was no sense in delaying. He might as well be off.

He picked up *The Shell Channel Pilot*. He put it down. He went up on deck. Dusk was falling. There was no sign of Hovis. Spike lay curled up in a coil of rope as if waiting for further instructions.

Will looked up towards the Roundhouse. The lights of the village glinted. A gentle breeze stirred the halyards in the boatyard. He would go for a walk.

He ambled down the pontoon, hands in pockets, feeling the walkway bob under his feet. He strolled out along the jetty and up the lane.

Through the windows of the Salutation he could see the orange glow of lights on glass fishing floats and brass binnacles, and hear the conversation and ribald laughter of tourists through the open door. He walked on, staying on the other side of the lane to the Roundhouse, from which a different sound emerged.

He paused, strained to catch a little more, then crossed the empty lane. Hesitantly he mounted the steps to the studio and heard more clearly what he thought he had caught from a distance. It was the sound of a cello playing Elgar. He felt his heartbeat quicken and found it difficult to swallow. The sound of voices in the Salutation died away and all he could hear now was the music.

Calmly he turned to face the sea, leaning back against the wall of the old building. In the pine and the granite he could feel the notes as they vibrated through timber and stone.

It began to rain, softly at first, then more heavily. He pushed himself away from the wall, walked silently down the studio steps and along the lane towards the beach. He approached the water's edge and paddled through the waves, finally sitting down on the wet sand just beyond their reach. He could feel the damp rising through his clothing, and the sea against his skin. He could still hear the cello.

His breathing was slow and deep, and the rain eased off to a steady soaking drizzle as he sat on the sand and looked out to sea. His head felt clear. A calm acceptance took the place of the self-pity that had gone before, and for a long time he sat motionless in the cool, wet evening, gazing out towards the horizon in the direction of the rest of his life.

Chapter 28: Bishop Rock

The popping of webbing carried from the back room of Pencurnow Post Office and General Stores as it had every morning since heaven knows when. Will waited patiently for the proprietress to appear and finally, after much snipping of plastic and muffled cursing, Primrose Hankey bustled in with the piles of newspapers to dump them on the counter in front of her. Will waited for her to start asking questions, but she did not refer to his domestic life, his travel arrangements, or even to the news that shrieked in banner headline from the front of the local paper: PENCURNOW COUPLE HELD IN DRUGS SWOOP. She spoke quietly and simply: "We'll be sorry to see you go, Mr Elliott. What can I get for you?"

This was not at all what Will had expected. Surely Primrose had never had a better time for gossip, what with the Morgan-Gileses' arrest and his own departure. There was enough material for conjecture here to keep Primrose in inquisition mode for the better part of a year. But she seemed reserved, preoccupied.

Angela came out of the back room, pulling on a jacket and munching a slice of toast. She tossed a cheery goodbye in the direction of her aunt and opened the door with its customary ping. For the first time, Will noticed that it sounded slightly flat.

"I've got a list." Will pushed the sheet of A4 paper across the counter.

"Mmm. Shipping order." And then, realizing her unintended pun, "Oh. Sorry."

He watched as Primrose mumbled to herself as she worked her way through the list, slowly piling his goods upon the counter.

"You setting off straight away?" she enquired.

"As soon as I've said goodbye to Mrs Hallybone."

"I see." Primrose ferried packets of cornflakes, cans of pilchards, bottled water and tins of five-minute rice towards the ever-increasing mountain of groceries.

"You'll never carry all this. I'll ask the postman to drop it off on his way down, if you like. He'll be here in half an hour."

"That's very kind. Thanks."

"Funny to think of the two of you leaving at the same time."

"Sorry?"

"You and Amy Finn. You arrived in the village within a week of one another and now you're leaving in the same week. Strange, really, how things work out."

Will was numbed by the news, even though he had suspected what was about to happen. She had decided to leave the studio after all. She was going away with Oliver Gallico.

"Why has she . . .?"

"Angela's going to look after the gallery for three weeks. They had a good bank holiday weekend, sold quite a lot of stuff, by all accounts. Nice, after all this time, to have a success story in the village. I think Amy just wants a break."

He was half relieved, half disappointed. Relieved that it did not appear she had gone back to Gallico. Disappointed that she seemed to be sorting out her life without him.

As Primrose systematically piled up his provisions, the truth of the situation hit him with the force of a fifty-ton juggernaut. With a clarity of mind that he had not experienced for a long time, he saw clearly what he must do. He could only hope he had not left it too late.

He excused himself and walked smartly out of the door, sprinted down the lane and slowed up only when the Roundhouse came into view. He paused at the foot of the old stone steps, hesitated, then climbed up and pushed open the door.

The studio was empty, apart from the two figures standing on either side of the counter. He stood just inside the door, suddenly self-conscious. Amy looked across at him, paused, then said to Angela, "Could you go and get some milk? And a packet of biscuits or something?"

Angela took in the situation quickly, grabbed her coat from the hook behind the counter and walked out as fast as she could, without breaking into a run. She closed the door quietly behind her. Will and Amy stared at each other.

It was she who spoke first. "I thought you'd gone. I saw you setting off yesterday and I thought you'd gone."

"No. Just seeing how she sailed, that's all."

"I see. When do you go?"

"This morning. I was going to go this morning."

"Going to go?"

"Yes."

"But . . . not any more?"

He sighed and turned towards the door. She thought he was about to leave. Perhaps the tides were wrong or something and she ought to have realized. But he turned the key in the lock, flipped the Open sign to Closed and pulled down the blind.

"I saw Oliver leaving the gallery."

"Yes. I finally got rid of him."

"But I thought . . ."

She looked at him, disappointed.

"And I just wanted to go. To run away from my past and start again. That's what I was doing before you . . ."

She nodded resignedly and looked down. "I know."

"But I got it wrong. It isn't the past any more. It's now. The past has sailed away on its own, without me having to sail away from it. There I was, heading off in my own direction, expecting you to fall in with my plans and thinking that if I offered to take you with me you'd give up everything and come. I thought you must, if you loved me as much as I loved you."

She looked up.

"I'd been so wrapped up in this voyage. It had become so important – all my life was pointing towards it – so the need to do it became . . . a mission, if you like."

"I know."

"But when it came down to it, when I really thought about it, there was no reason to go. Just one big reason why I should stay."

She looked at him, hoping that what she had heard was what he really meant. "But what will you do if you don't go?"

He answered without hesitation. "I'll look after the lighthouse and live with you."

It took her breath away. She gulped. "But you can't. It will drive you mad. You'll hate all those people."

"Not half as much as I'll hate being on my own without you. Evan Williams doesn't want the job full time and they'll be happy to let me do it if I want to."

She stared hard at him, half afraid to let go, then ran into his arms. "You can do the last bit but you don't have to do the first. I can't have you being in charge of a tourist attraction. It's just not you. Build model boats. I've sold out. You'll earn far more doing that. Here."

She opened the drawer of the till and took out an envelope on which was written 'Will – £500'. "They walked out of the studio. Couldn't price them high enough. You'll just have to work faster." She stuffed the envelope into his shirt pocket and grinned at him through her tears.

He wiped them away with his fingers as she looked up at him and said, "You know why I wouldn't come, don't you?"

"I do now. I didn't see it then."

"I'd had my fill of being at the beck and call of men. However much I loved them. I needed to know that someone loved me enough to give up what they had just for me. Until now I've always been the one to give it up, and then it's always seemed to go wrong."

"I know." He threw his arms around her and held her tightly. "I know, I know."

"I'd have given up anything for you – painting, dancing, studio, anything – but I had to be sure you would do the same for me, and it didn't seem as though you would."

"Well, I have, and I'm here, and I will."

"Don't sail away without me," she sobbed.

"I won't, my love, I won't." He stroked the back of her head and the deep love that had eluded him since their parting came flooding back. He was home now.

They stood for a while, until Amy broke the silence. "What about *Boy Jack*?"

He smiled, but sadly. "I'll sell her."

She shook her head. "No, you can't. *Boy Jack* was meant for you, I've always known that." She eased away from him. "Wait a minute." She turned and ran up the spiral staircase, returning with a package wrapped in brown paper.

She held it out to him with both hands. "Here. I didn't have time to wrap them up. I got them a couple of days ago from one of my artists, then when you sailed yesterday I thought it was too late, so they're still in the paper from the shop."

He looked at the package and felt its weight. He knew instantly what it was.

"Hey! Open it!" She watched him with sparkling eyes as the brown paper fell away to reveal the five gilt-decorated volumes of Frank Cowper's *Sailing Tours*. "Only now, Mr Lighthouse Keeper, there is no way you're going on your own."

He gazed at her through his own brimming tears.

"We're not going to do it all in one go, but over the next three weeks you can take me exactly where you want."

"Any preferences?" he asked, his eyes gleaming.

She smiled. "Well, I've asked a friend of mine who owns a Cornish yawl, and he tells me that of all the places around Britain there is one particularly sheltered and secluded harbour in the Isles of Scilly called New Grimsby. Now, it doesn't sound much like the Bahamas, but I expect it will be quite pleasant when we bump ashore."

Animal Instincts

Acknowledgements

As ever, I've been helped enormously by unsuspecting friends and acquaintances when it comes to verifying facts about things of which I am relatively ignorant. Any mistakes remain my own, but I am infinitely grateful to Steven Alais for legal advice, Dr Phil Cunliffe for answering questions of a medical nature and David Aston of Harris Walters for helping me with accounting matters.

David Goldthorpe of Sotheby's provided historical literary information, Mark Andreae kindly allowed me to follow the Hampshire Hunt, and Carol Collins answered all manner of strange questions relating to dogs, foxes and men. Luigi Bonomi offered his welcome lashings of encouragement, along with Clare Ledingham, my patient editor.

Geoffrey Grigson's *The Englishman's Flora* has provided the inspiration for the chapter titles (all but one), and the staff of English Nature have been helpful in other ways.

This is not a book about the rights and wrongs of the countryside, just a bit of a romp through the beautiful conundrum that is country life.

For Clare
with love and thanks

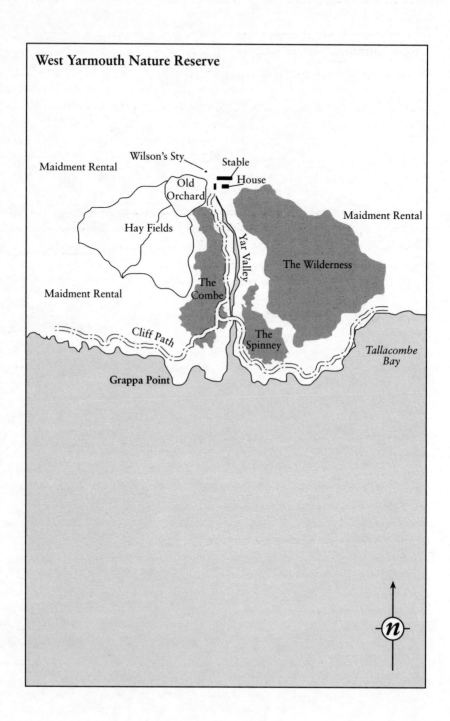

West Yarmouth Nature Reserve

Maidment Rental

Wilson's Sty

Stable

House

Old
Orchard

Hay Fields

Maidment Rental

The Wilderness

Maidment Rental

Yar Valley

The
Combe

Cliff Path

The
Spinney

Tallacombe
Bay

Grappa Point

n

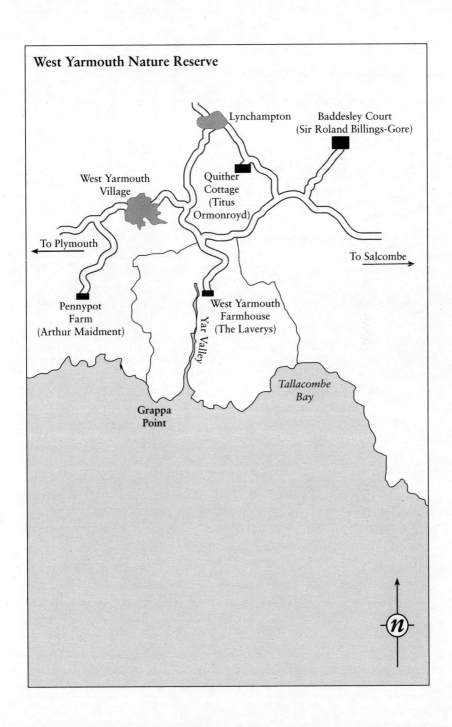

West Yarmouth Nature Reserve

Lynchampton

Baddesley Court
(Sir Roland Billings-Gore)

West Yarmouth
Village

Quither
Cottage
(Titus
Ormonroyd)

To Plymouth

To Salcombe

Pennypot
Farm
(Arthur Maidment)

West Yarmouth
Farmhouse
(The Laverys)

Yar Valley

Grappa
Point

Tallacombe
Bay

𝑛

Chapter 1: Angels

(*Geranium robertianum*)

"Could you fold your table away, sir?"

He was miles away. Half a world away.

"Sir?"

"Mmm? Sorry."

"Can I take your cup?"

"Oh, yes. Sorry." He managed a weak smile

She was quite pretty, her hair tied back in a smooth, shiny dark brown bun, her lipstick the same bright red as the pattern on her uniform. The sort of lipstick his mother used to wear. Strangely old-fashioned now. He folded up the table and secured it with the clip, then leaned sideways to look out of the window.

The landscape was gradually rising up to meet him. It should have been grey – he had been convinced it would be grey, to match his mood and the image of the country he had left behind ten years ago. But it was soft green and dusky purple, pale russet and dark brown. There was no hint of battleship grey anywhere, except on the roads that snaked though the countryside. He sighed, and looked down at the newspaper folded open on the seat next to him in row fourteen. It should have been row thirteen, but they had left out that number, skipping straight from twelve to fourteen. On this occasion the thoughtful adjustment by British Airways seemed futile.

The *Daily Telegraph* was less tactful. On page 13 he read, again, his father's obituary:

Rupert Lavery, who has died aged sixty-two, was best known for his work at the West Yarmouth Nature Reserve in Devon where, over the space of thirty years, he built up a reputation as a conservationist of unusual stance and individual reasoning.

The writer had clearly known his father well.

Not for Lavery the left-wing activist approach. He concentrated, instead, on influence by example. He steadfastly refused to allow hunting on his land, but remained on good terms with the Lynchampton Hunt, whose territory surrounded him. He made sure his own land was farmed organically, but took a broad view of genetically modified crops, refusing to join in with those who condemned them as 'Frankenstein foods'. On one occasion, when interviewed, he suggested that the widespread invasion of ragwort was currently the greatest threat to the British countryside and was being overlooked by both farmers and government alike.

Here, at least, was something upon which they agreed. Ragwort was deadly to horses.

Lavery endeavoured to reintroduce the red squirrel to Devon, with little success, alas, but is credited with contributing to the saving from extinction in Britain of the large blue butterfly.

He looked up, blinking back the tear that had come to his eye. Dear old Dad. A failure with the red squirrel but a winner with the butterfly. What a legacy.

Those who perceived Rupert Lavery as a crank missed the point. A tall man, with a gentle but determined nature, Lavery regarded himself as a responsible custodian of 300 acres of Devonshire. Though never an evangelical animal rights campaigner, he maintained steadfastly that the link between badgers and bovine tuberculosis was largely unproven, and won a following for his dedication to local natural history in South Devon. But for his tragically early death due to a fall, there is no doubt that he would have continued to be one of the country's most influential conservationists.

Rupert Christopher Lavery was born at West Yarmouth, Devon,

on 2 May 1937, and educated at Radley and Trinity College, Cambridge. He attended the Royal Agricultural College, Cirencester, before beginning a career in estate management, finally taking over the family farm from his father in 1970.

He was a Fellow of the Linnaean Society and a member of the Royal Corinthian Yacht Club, but was seldom seen on the water.

Rupert Lavery married, in 1965, Rosalind Bennett, who predeceased him. He is survived by a son.

Kit folded the paper so that he could no longer see the obituary. An insistent *ping* accompanied the illuminated 'Fasten Seat Belts' sign, and the 747 tilted slowly to reveal, through the small oval window, the sprawl of London. Now it *was* grey, with only the muddy ribbon of the Thames to guide the aircraft towards Heathrow.

He would stay just long enough to sort things out. A few weeks. Maybe a month. Perhaps two.

Had he known what lay ahead of him, he would have transferred his baggage to a Qantas flight and headed straight back to Balnunga Valley.

He had completely underestimated the ladies. But, then, he hadn't met any of them yet.

Chapter 2: Earthgall

(*Centaurium minus*)

Kit took a bus to Reading, then a train to Totnes. He gazed out of the windows of the railway carriage, reacquainting himself with the countryside into which he had been reluctantly plunged. Anything less like the landscape of south east Australia would be hard to imagine. The brightly painted clapboard houses of his adopted settlement had been replaced by damp brickwork. The names of the stations – Taunton and Tiverton Parkway, Exeter St David's and Dawlish – were all exquisitely, stultifyingly English. The clean white fences of the stud farm in Balnunga Valley had been replaced by posts and rails of dark brown, and by leafless hedges of increasing height and thickness as the train rattled on through Newton Abbot.

By the time the grubby carriages trundled into Totnes, Kit felt world-weary and bone-achingly tired. Doors thumped and slammed, the vibration fizzing through his head. He heaved the single weighty suitcase from between the seats and shambled off the train and on to the windswept platform. A female passenger passed him, smiling sympathetically at his apparent bewilderment, his tanned face marking him out as a foreigner on unfamiliar ground.

Devon in February. The air nipped at his nostrils, and he pulled the inadequately insulated jacket around him to keep out the sudden rush of cold. A handful of grubby litter swirled in a sudden eddy at his feet and he looked along the platform for the exit.

Elizabeth Punch had offered to pick him up at the station, but he'd said that he would make his own way to the farm: he could not be sure that his flight would arrive on time, and he didn't want her to be hanging about. That had been only half true: the thought of sharing a journey with someone he had never met but who had lived and worked with his father for the last ten years filled him with apprehension.

He'd tried to imagine what she looked like from their brief, crackly telephone conversation across the world. She'd sounded matter-of-fact, and there was little trace of emotion in her voice, which surprised him. He was unsure of the nature of her relationship with his father, knowing only that she had worked with him on the reserve since just after his own departure, and that his father, whenever they had corresponded or spoken on the phone, had never suggested that this was anything more than a working association. Perhaps Rupert had been attempting to spare his son's feelings. Perhaps not.

For a moment Kit wondered where to go. The station, once so familiar, now seemed completely foreign. The exit sign swung squeakily in the breeze, and his head swam – a combination of jet lag and tiredness.

"Come on," he said to himself, and walked purposefully down the platform and out of the station to the taxi rank.

The motley parade of cabs was headed by a battered Japanese model that had seen better days. Originally it had been white; now it was grey and more than slightly foxed. Kit reached for the handle of the rear nearside door. As he did so the electric window by the front passenger seat buzzed downwards.

"Where to, zirr?"

"West Yarmouth, please." And then, realizing that some more particular destination would be needed, "The farmhouse. The nature reserve."

"Very good, zirr. Mr Lavery's place?"

"That's right." Kit eased himself on to the worn brown leatherette bench seat and slammed the door. As he did so the handle came off, and he shot to the far side of the seat.

"Don't worry, zirr. Allus doin' that."

Kit smiled, remembering the silver-grey Porsche Boxster now shrouded in cambric in an Australian garage, then pushed himself upright and filled his lungs with the acrid tang of stale tobacco. He eased down the window a little and the icy air cut through the oppressive fug in the car.

The driver turned the key in the ignition, and they began their lumbering journey southwards. The cabby tried his opening gambit. "Sad about Mr Lavery, ain't it?"

"Yes." Kit hardly knew what to say. He had not had to talk about his father's death to anyone acquainted with him, and realized now that over the next few days he would be doing little else.

"Know him well, did you?"

"I'm his son."

The car jerked as the driver's foot slipped off the pedal. "Oh, I'm sorry to hear that, zirr. I didn't know."

"No, it's fine. No reason for you to know. I've been gone a long time."

"Australia, weren't it, zirr?"

"Yes." Kit wondered how much the cabby knew, wondered if the locals had an opinion about him. Not that it mattered: he would not be here long enough for it to matter.

"Lovely man, your father."

"Yes."

"Well respected in these parts. Well liked too, and the two things don't always go together, if you knows what I mean." He shook his head. "Great shame it was. Great shame. Man of his age falling like that. Could happen to any of us. Makes you think, doesn't it?"

"Sorry?"

"How we're all human. How we don't know when we're going to . . . well, you know. . ." He tailed off.

The journey continued in silence until the cabby's curiosity finally got the better of him. "You be here for long, zirr?"

"No. Just until I've got things sorted out."

"Not staying, then?"

Kit did his best to remain noncommittal. "For as long as it takes."

"Lovely place, West Yarmouth. Especially the reserve. Picturesque."

"Yes."

"Be a shame to see it go."

Kit did not reply, just stared out of the window.

As the late-afternoon light dimmed and the taxi drew nearer to West Yarmouth, nervous apprehension took over from the sense of irritated resignation he had felt for most of the journey. It seemed as though the house lights were fading before an impending theatrical performance, and that the recurring dream, to which actors alluded, of being in a play in which you know neither the moves nor the lines, was now reality.

But as he looked out of the window the scenery was familiar. He recognized the towering oak on the corner of the village green at Lynchampton, the signpost saying 'West Yarmouth 5, Plymouth 18', and the cottages at the side of the road, fronted by a broad verge.

His heart beat faster. He had been away ten years, yet he might as well not have been away at all. He had spent a decade in another culture, another world, and yet here he was, back where he had started, feeling just the same. But not. He found the two Kit Laverys difficult to reconcile. The Venetian Twins. The West Yarmouth Twins. The Man in the Iron Mask. He tried to blame his confused thoughts on jet-lag.

The taxi slowed as it rounded the final bend then turned into the rough lane. The headlights briefly illuminated the sign, 'West Yarmouth Nature Reserve', printed in white on a dark green background.

"Here we are, zirr. A little bit of 'eaven."

Towering hedges to left and right masked any view of the surrounding fields. The hedges had grown – it used to be possible to see over them. He peered between the two seats in front of him, his eyes scouring the track ahead for familiar landmarks, but now the lie of the land seemed strange, not quite as he had remembered it. Smaller. More overgrown.

A distant light, veiled at first by the hedge, grew brighter. The small Queen Anne farmhouse looked even more like a doll's house than he remembered. The rugged iron lamp that had hung over its front door for at least two hundred years was still there, still burning. He felt a pang, and a feeling, had he been able to admit it to himself, of coming home. The taxi ground to a halt with a crunch of tyre on gravel.

"That'll be eighteen pounds fifty, zirr."

"Damn." The Australian dollars he held stared back at him mockingly. He'd forgotten to change enough currency. "Can you hang on a minute? I'll have to get some English money." And then, chancing his arm and smiling at the driver, "I don't suppose you take Australian dollars, do you?"

"Not in Devon, zirr. I'm afraid not. Even though my name is Sydney."

Kit smiled and shrugged, stepped out and left the driver to haul the bag from the boot. He wanted to walk straight up to the door, but instead he stood and looked up at the front of the house, which he had left, exasperated, ten years before. Its countenance was as friendly as he remembered it, the mellow brick warm and welcoming.

Movement at an upstairs window to the right of the heavy, white-painted door caught his eye. He thought he saw a face. Then a heavy bolt slid back inside, and the door opened to reveal a tall, angular woman with a questioning expression.

"Miss Punch?" Kit enquired.

"Yes?" For a moment, she looked wrong-footed, but quickly regained her composure and asked, "Is it Kit?"

"Yes, I'm sorry, but I've come with no English money. Do you think you could give me some for the taxi?"

"Yes, of course. Come in." She tried to smile, but Kit detected fear in her eyes. He moved towards the door as she disappeared into the house, and decided to stay outside for fear of invading what had once been his territory but which was now probably hers.

"Here we are." She returned with her purse. "How much do you need?"

"Eighteen fifty. Well, twenty pounds with a tip."

"Just a minute." He watched as she counted out the money. "There we are. Nineteen pounds. That should do."

He made no argument, and she made no criticism of his intended magnanimity either with voice or expression. She snapped her purse shut and asked, "Just the one bag?"

"Yes."

The taxi driver sighed in disappointment at the lean tip and eased himself back into his car. The engine coughed to life and, with a wink in Kit's direction, he drove off down the lane in search of greater profit.

Kit turned to pick up his bag, but found that it had vanished, along with Elizabeth Punch. He ran his eyes once more over the face of the old house, partially swathed in ivy, and this time saw quite clearly the other face at the upstairs window. It was small, with spiky, orange hair. It stared at him, and he stared back, until it receded into the darkness.

He lowered his eyes to the door and saw, in the flagged hallway, the tall oak dresser under which he used to play. The light from a single brass oil lamp glinted on the serried ranks of willow-pattern plates and spilled soft amber rays on to the smooth, cobbled path. An owl hooted in the distance. He shivered, then stepped over the threshold and closed the door quietly behind him.

Chapter 3: Lady's Fingers

(*Lotus corniculatus*)

"We thought it best that you sleep here." Elizabeth Punch held open the door of the main upstairs bedroom. "It was your father's room so . . ."

Kit looked at her enquiringly.

She read his thoughts. "Jess and I sleep in the barn next door. The top floor's been converted – well, not really converted, just turned into habitable rooms . . ." She stopped abruptly and regarded him with a confused mixture of sympathy and impatience. "Dinner will be in half an hour, if that's all right. We'll see you downstairs then." She struggled to add some comforting epilogue, but managed only a bleak "I'm sorry," before turning on her heel, shutting the door and clumping down the old wooden staircase.

Kit sat down slowly on his father's bed, feeling eerily detached from the goings-on around him. He raised his eyes and looked around the room. It had been the hub of his father's small universe – the room in which he slept, wrote, read and thought. Three of the walls were book-lined – volumes on natural history and farming, wild flowers and poetry; a few were new, most old, some leatherbound. In front of the large window, which stretched almost to the floor, stood a Victorian roll-top desk. The papers on it were neatly categorized into orderly piles, but pigeon-holes were stuffed with a mixture of feathers and luggage labels, a pale blue eggshell on a wad of cotton wool, the stub of a candle in an old brass stick. A pot of pencils stood like a vase of faded flowers to one side of the ink-spattered blotter, on which rested the old Waterman pen that his father had used for as long as Kit could remember.

He felt a stab of sadness, got up and walked towards it. He turned round the chair in front of the desk and lowered himself into it, then leaned forward on the battered leather top and gazed into his father's world, as though looking for guidance. None came.

He swivelled round and took in the rest of the room – the old brown dressing-gown on the back of the faded pine door, the piles of magazines stacked on the threadbare Indian rug that covered the floor – the *Countryman* and *Farmer's Weekly*, the proceedings of the Botanical Society of the British Isles, and obscure publications with strange titles. It reminded him of the visit he and his father had made when he was small, to Churchill's home at Chartwell. There, Churchill's study remained exactly as he had left it, even to the glass of whisky on the desk.

He felt a sudden chill, and the if-onlys began to well up in his mind. If only they had talked more. If only he had known his father was about to die he could have told him . . . what? He hardly knew. Except that this was not how it should have happened.

The knock on the door found him still sitting on the chair, lost in thought.

"Yes?"

The door opened slowly and a head peered round it – the one he had spotted half an hour ago at the upstairs window. It seemed at first as though it might belong to some rare form of wildlife that his father might have wanted to conserve. The hair was foxy-red and sparkles of light reflected from studs, several around the rim of each ear, one in the nose and another in the left eyebrow. The skin was pallid, the lips soft purple. The plumage of this particular species was more drab than would have been expected from its head: a long, khaki-coloured sweater of coarse knit, baggy black leggings and high-laced Dr Martens. A hand did not appear from the sleeve that slid around the door to hold it open, and he read fear in the pale blue eyes. "Dinner's ready," she said.

He looked at her. He was pretty sure it was a 'her', but there were few real clues as to the sexuality of his interlocutor.

"Yes. Fine. Sorry. I'll be down in a minute."

She hesitated, looking at him from under her long black eyelashes. She risked an introduction. "I'm Jess Wetherby. I helped your dad with the reserve." She pulled back the long sleeve and pushed out a hand and walked slowly towards him He was surprised at the firmness of the handshake from such a small woman. Each looked the other in the eye, warily, and Kit managed a smile. She quickly withdrew her hand, which receded, once more, into the long, khaki sleeve.

"Elizabeth says they'll get cold. The roasted vegetables."

"I'll just wash my hands, then I'll be down."

She nodded, then reversed out of the room, never taking her eyes off him until the door closed.

The meal began uncomfortably, the two women avoiding his eyes. Elizabeth Punch served him a generous helping of potatoes and courgettes, red and green peppers, celeriac and turnips, glistening with olive oil and heaped into an earthenware bowl. It was the first time he had had a chance to look at her properly. The three candles that flickered on the scrubbed pine table seemed to highlight her features. Her silver-grey hair was cut into a no-nonsense bob. Her face was clean of makeup, the cheekbones high. Her skin had little colour, except where the heat of the stove had reddened her cheeks. She wore a sleeveless dark green gilet, a sensible russety Shetland sweater and brown corduroy trousers. Her hands were robust and workmanlike, and she wore one chunky ring, set with an amber stone. She was a slender woman, on the surface dour and humourless, but Kit thought he detected a hint of warmth beneath the grim exterior. The atmosphere was not chilly – just quiet and uneasy.

Elizabeth sat at one side of the rectangular table, Jess at the other. The large wheelback chair at the head was his, then. He sat quietly until they had all been served, then picked up his knife and fork to tackle the vegetables. Jess Wetherby coughed gently, and he looked up to see her sitting with her hands on her lap and her eyes cast downwards. Elizabeth's hands were similarly placed, but her eyes looked directly at him.

Slowly he lowered his implements to the table and slid his clasped hands on to his lap as Elizabeth spoke quietly but clearly: "God, grant us the serenity to accept the things we cannot change, courage to change things we can, and wisdom to know the difference."

Kit's eyes flickered upwards as the two women intoned "Amen".

"Amen," he whispered in their wake.

"Water or wine?" Elizabeth asked matter-of-factly.

"Wine, please." He pushed his glass towards the proffered bottle and she poured him some Chilean Cabernet Sauvignon.

"Thank you." He lifted the glass to his lips and gulped a generous mouthful. He felt warmth suffuse his cheeks and glanced across to the old cream-coloured Aga that nestled under the high mantel of the kitchen chimney breast. At least he wouldn't freeze to death in here, having crossed from an Antipodean summer to an English winter.

His thoughts returned to Australia. He could see the lavender blue distant hills below a sky that seemed to go on for ever. He felt the sun on the back of his neck and saw the close-cropped, bristly pastures where the horses grazed. A kookaburra laughed – and a fork clattered on a plate, bringing him back to the Devon kitchen.

Elizabeth picked up the fork, and Jess poured herself a tumbler of water from the stoneware jug, then some wine.

"Please start," said Elizabeth.

Jess was sawing chunks of wholemeal bread from a cob loaf sitting on a board in the centre of the table. She offered him a piece, still fighting shy of eye-contact. He took it and thanked her. The meal continued in silence. Kit struggled for something to say, but talk of the weather seemed inappropriate, and the discussion of more weighty matters premature.

Here he sat, with two women, in his father's house. He knew neither their relationship with his father, nor their expectations now that he had died.

Elizabeth, aware of his discomfort, said, "I think the best thing we can do is leave you to rediscover the place over the next few days. Does that sound all right?"

Kit seized on the lifeline. "Yes. Thanks. It's a long time since I was last here."

"It's probably changed quite a lot. I came here just a few months after you left. Your father couldn't run the place on his own so I've been a sort of manager since old Ted Burdock and his brother retired."

He detected the faintest note of criticism. Neither had the words of the prayer she had used before the meal gone over his head.

"I dealt with the day-to-day running of the estate and Jess just got stuck in. You can't just leave nature to take its course – even on a nature reserve. It needs guiding. The things you want to encourage must be given a chance to thrive, and you have to keep on top of other things – like vermin and ragwort – unless you want to be overrun by them." She realized that she was lecturing him, and stopped to sip her water.

He turned to Jess and asked, "How long have you been here?"

At last she raised her eyes from her plate. "Coming up for two years."

"What made you want to work here? You don't sound local."

"No. Streatham." A pause, a sip of wine. "But I wanted to be in the countryside, not the town. I've always felt . . . well . . . right when I'm in the country. Some people think townies don't know anything that goes on here. Sometimes it's true, but sometimes living in the sticks is like . . . well . . ."

"Instinctive?" he offered.

"Yeh. I wanted to help from the inside, not the outside. Only I didn't really know that until Mr Lavery offered me a job."

Kit tried to imagine how the paths of his father and this girl from the London suburbs might have crossed. He failed.

"How did you meet him?" he asked.

"At the hunt."

"But he didn't hunt."

"No. Well, it wasn't exactly *at* the hunt, it was afterwards."

"You mean *you* hunt?"

"Nah. Sab, wasn't I?" And then, seeing that he was having difficulty in following her, "I was a saboteur."

Elizabeth cut in. "Everybody finished?"

Hastily Kit forked up what remained in the bottom of his bowl. "Yes. Fine. Thank you. It was lovely."

Jess was warming to her subject, the red wine having the same effect on her cheeks as the warmth of the Aga on Elizabeth's. Again Kit noticed the soft blue of her eyes underneath the camouflage of kohl. There was a warmth in them that belied her outward appearance.

"I used to carry placards and stuff. Never did the animals any damage, just got in the way. Went everywhere – Belvoir, Quorn, Eglinton. Then I came to Lynchampton and–"

Elizabeth said, "I think Mr Lavery's probably heard enough for one evening. He's had a long journey. Cup of coffee before bed?"

Kit looked at his watch. A quarter past nine. Suddenly he was aware of a draining tiredness. "No. No thanks. I'm feeling a bit, well . . ."

"I'm not surprised. It's a long way from Australia. You go on up. We'll clear up and see you in the morning. We generally rise at around six thirty, but we'll keep out of your way when you surface."

He felt like saying, "Yes, Miss," but restrained himself. He drained the rest of the wine from his glass, stood up from the table and made to leave.

Elizabeth's voice stopped him as he was about to turn into the hall. "We're very sorry, Mr Lavery, about your father."

He looked at the two of them – Elizabeth standing at the side of the table with a pile of bowls in her hand, and Jess sitting quietly, but now looking nervously in his direction.

"We were very . . . fond of him. He was a good man, a far-sighted man, and we want to carry on doing the work he started. There's still lots to do here and, with your help, we can make this place even more valuable to wildlife than it is now."

He looked at them, like a rabbit mesmerized by a pair of ferrets. They looked back unblinking. He nodded. "See you in the morning," he said, then climbed the stairs to bed.

Chapter 4:
Love Lies Bleeding

(Adonis annua)

At Baddesley Court, three miles from West Yarmouth, Jinty O'Hare screwed up her eyes as she tried to focus on the alarm clock on the bedside table. Seven a.m. "Damn!" She pulled the pillow over her head, smothering her unruly blonde curls, but failing to keep out the ringing. Finally, using one hand to stuff the goose-feather pillow even closer to her ears, she thrust out an arm – long, fair-skinned and slightly freckled – located the button that would bring the throbbing in her head to an end. She found it, pressed it, and then lay sprawled in an untidy heap, unwilling to leave the warmth of the plump white duvet on the four-poster bed.

But rise she must. There were horses to muck out. Couldn't she let them get on without her this morning? She would have liked to stay in bed for another hour, maybe even two. But no. She had sworn to herself when she came to live with her aunt and uncle that she would work her passage, not behave like some spoilt brat as most of her old schoolfriends seemed to.

She lifted her head above the quilt to test the air temperature. It was cold. The central heating at Baddesley came on at seven thirty precisely, as per Sir Roland's instructions. She shrank beneath the feathers again and drew her naked body into the foetal position for added warmth, allowing only the top half of her head – from the nose upwards – to remain above the duvet line.

She wondered about the weather – was it sunny or cloudy? Cold or mild? Raining or foggy? She yawned and ran her fingers through her hair, but failed to banish the thick-headedness she put down to one glass too many of amaretto in the George Hotel at Lynchampton the night before. Then she remembered why she had drunk it.

He was such a bastard. She should have seen it coming. For two years, off and on, she had been seeing Jamie Bickerstaffe. Or not seeing him, thanks to his foreign trips with his blessed property company. He was something to do with investments at Hope, Tonks and Gunn – or Grope, Bonk and Run as she thought of them. He'd be away for days on end, then turn up and whisk her out for the weekend, bonk her senseless, then resume normal service in the City or some far-flung corner of the globe. But last night Jamie had broken it to her that he was seeing someone else.

The events of the previous evening replayed slowly though her tired mind. The candlelit meal in the George. The soft yellow of the walls, the chilled white wine, the fish in the delicate sauce, the orange soufflé and the brush-off. It had come with perfect timing over the coffee and liqueurs. She should have guessed something was up. She was an old hand at this sort of thing. She was thirty, for God's sake, and experienced in the ways of men. Not that it ever got any easier.

She had kept her cool when he had told her, patronizingly laying his hands over hers, gazing at her earnestly with his deep brown eyes from under the broad forehead and swept-back jet-black hair. He explained how much he loved her but was sure she knew that their relationship didn't seem to be going anywhere . . .

Why did he have to be so bloody good-looking and such good company? Why didn't he want to see more of her rather than less? They laughed a lot together and their lovemaking was always good – wasn't it? At least he hadn't offered the excuse that his career had to come first – he had always liked women too much to let that happen, but his work provided the finance for his lifestyle: the BMW Z8, the Patek Philippe watch, the Ozwald Boateng suits. He had finally made his position clear and ordered her another amaretto. She thought of throwing it over him but her Irish blood refused to contemplate such waste so she downed it in one before telling him quietly but firmly exactly what she thought of him and walking out of the hotel.

It was then that she realized she had no transport home. She had been lucky to spot the battered old white cab as it ambled through the village. She hailed it and persuaded the driver to take her the few miles down the road to Baddesley Court. He obliged, and looked happier when she'd thrust a ten-pound note into his hand and told him to keep the change. "Thank the Lord you're not Australian," he'd said, as he pulled away, leaving her under the tall portico of the front door. She hadn't a clue what he meant, but the tears were flowing as she felt in her bag for the key.

Now it was morning and she lay awake with the rest of her bleak life in front of her. Since her arrival here she had been determined that it would not be aimless, though that, now, was exactly what it seemed to be. She had left home in County Donegal six years ago to come and live with her 'aunt and uncle' Sir Roland Billings-Gore and his wife Charlotte. They were not really her aunt and uncle, but good friends of her late parents. When they had died within a year of each other, Uncle Roly had insisted she come to live at Baddesley Court for as long as she wanted.

She had agreed, provided he would let her earn her living in the stables. As Master of the Lynchampton Hunt, Sir Roland's stables boasted three foxhunters, which needed more care and exercise than he was able to give them, and he had been delighted to agree to the arrangement with his favourite 'niece', whose horsemanship he had encouraged since she had first climbed into the saddle at the tender age of three.

But it was not a job she saw as her ultimate goal. What were the options for a girl in her position? A post in London with an upmarket estate agent? A round of parties with It girls? Helping an old schoolfriend run a dress shop in South Molton Street? No. Jinty wanted a real job that utilized all her talents, if only she knew what they were. Or a real man, if only she could meet one. It was time she sorted herself out. Perhaps she should move away and live on her own for a while.

She flung back the duvet and the chilly morning air nipped at her naked body. She slid her feet to the cold oak floor, stood up, stretched, and caught sight of herself in the cheval mirror across from the dressing-table. Slowly she lowered her arms and looked at herself, almost as if sizing up bloodstock at a sale.

"Oh, why can't you get a decent man?" She scrutinized her thighs – was that cellulite or a trick of the light? – then her bottom, which was still not overly round from riding. She worried daily that she'd develop rider's bum, and that her breasts would sag and that there would be no other option open to her than to become a harridan Master of Fox Hounds, who terrified all the men around her and never married.

She ran her hands over her flat stomach, wrapped her arms around her breasts to keep herself warm, then shuddered suddenly and ran to the bathroom for a shower.

As the white bubbles of shampoo ran down the plughole she smoothed back her wet blonde hair and raised her face to the powerful jet of water, vowing never again to let herself be subservient to any man, and never again to feel sorry for herself.

It was nine o'clock before Kit surfaced, his head muzzy. He shaved, showered and changed into a clean if creased set of clothes before looking out of the window at the clear, bright February day. Frost rimed the grass beyond the rough sweep of gravel drive, and he caught his first tantalizing glimpse of the valley below the farmhouse where the West Yarmouth Nature Reserve sloped down to the sea.

He retreated from the window and sat down in his father's chair, looking round him at the relics of a life he must now wrap up. He refused to feel guilty about it. His father had had his life and Kit had his own. It was unfair to expect him to take on the old man's legacy. His life was now in Balnunga Valley with horses, not here fighting a losing battle with a patch of land in Devon. And, anyway, it was bloody cold.

It seemed only hours since he had been walking the paddocks of the stud farm in a T-shirt and a pair of shorts. Now he pushed the wayward fair curls off his face and went in search of a thick sweater in the tall mahogany chest of drawers. He found one – dark brown and ribbed – and pulled it over his head. The smell of his father caught him unawares, a combination of pipe tobacco and grain. He sat down on the edge of the bed. "Oh, Dad," he muttered, under his breath, as though half expecting a reply. Suddenly he realized the size of the task ahead of him. He would have to clear up and dispose of all his father's possessions, then sell off the land before he could head back to Australia. And he would have to explain what he was doing to the women. How long would it take? Weeks? Months? He got up and went downstairs in search of breakfast.

There was no sign of either Elizabeth or Jess, but he found a fresh loaf in the bread bin and made some toast on the Aga. Coffee proved more difficult to locate, but he found a jar of something decaffeinated.

After a few sips, he poured it down the sink, pulled on his father's old duffel coat and walked out of the door.

In spite of the crisp morning air, his head felt clogged: a walk would do him good. He set off in the direction of the old farm buildings. He should at least size up the estate and reacquaint himself with what it comprised.

There was the stable block – a row of eight stalls – and the rooms overhead that Elizabeth had talked about. He would not venture up the stone steps just yet. Beyond them, and at right angles to them, stood old pig-sties in which were stored old bits of machinery, now redundant. A towering yew tree shaded them at one end, its branches spreading sideways like thick green curtains.

Round the corner were a couple of low stone buildings surrounded by chest-high walls. Kit sauntered past them on his way to the upper slopes of the valley, and heard a low, snuffling sound. He stopped, walked towards the wall and looked over it, to be confronted by the broad snout of a black and white pig. He jumped. "Hello! Who are you?"

"Wilson," answered a female voice, which, for a moment, Kit imagined came from the pig.

"Her name's Wilson, and she's a Gloucester Old Spot." He realized now, with just a hint of sadness, that the voice was not coming from the pig but from Jess Wetherby, who was standing behind him holding a pitchfork.

"I didn't know Dad had a pig."

"Had her for years. Said it made him feel calm to look at her. Liked to scratch her back with a stick while he was thinking."

"Lord Emsworth."

"Sorry?"

Kit looked at the pig. "Lord Emsworth. P. G. Wodehouse. He had a pig called the Empress of Blandings. Dad always used to say that if he could have been anyone else it would have been Lord Emsworth so that he could have a pig, lean over the wall of her sty and scratch her back."

"I didn't know about that." She looked thoughtful. "But he was crackers about her. She's been miserable since he's gone. Seems to know. Went off her food for a bit. Not right even now." She put down the pitchfork and gazed at the mountain of muddied, piebald pig.

"Why Wilson?" asked Kit.

"After the Prime Minister."

Kit laughed softly. "Yes, it would be."

"What do you mean?"

"Harold Wilson. He was Prime Minister for years after I was born. Dad used to say that he was the only other person who faced the same sort of economic problems as he did." Kit looked at the pig, who looked balefully back at him.

"Here you are." Jess fished in her pocket and pulled out an apple. "See if you can tempt her. I can't."

Kit took the apple and offered it to the mucus-laden snout that pointed towards him. The pig became perfectly still, then the snout twitched and with the gentlest of motions eased the apple from his hand and quietly crunched it.

The two of them watched in silence as Wilson turned her back and walked away towards the dim interior of her shelter. She paused, and then, with a flick of her stubby tail, disappeared into the gloom.

Jess smiled. "She must like you."

Kit shrugged. "Must have been hungry."

Jess picked up her fork and regarded him quizzically. "You goin' to sell up this place, then?"

Her candour caught him unawares. "Yes. Well, I think so."

"Knew you would. Elizabeth thought you might take it on but I knew you wouldn't."

"What do you mean?" he asked, more to gain time than because he wanted to hear her answer.

"Got your own life. Your dad said so. Said you'd done well in Australia. Proud of you, he was, but I think it's a shame."

He stood and looked at her, unsure of whether to defend himself or to let her carry on. He opted for the latter. She seemed only too willing to get things off her chest.

"He's taken years getting this place into the state it is. Really put West Yarmouth on the map. It was a tired old farm until Rupert poured his life into it and turned it into paradise. We've even got red squirrels here, rare birds and things. Some of them come just because of what we do to the land. Twenty-eight species of butterfly breed here, and rare beetles. It's tremendous what he achieved. How can you see all that go to waste, just because you fell out with him all those years ago?"

Anger flared unexpectedly in Kit. "I didn't fall out with him, and if that's what he told you, he's wrong. Was wrong. I just needed to be my own person. Not to feel that I was in his shadow. We didn't fall out. I just needed space to find myself."

"Couldn't you do that here?"

"Not with my father on my back, no."

"But he was a good man. A kind man." The tears sprang to her eyes and she, too, looked angry.

"That was the problem. Did you have a parent you had to live up to? Who everybody told you from the day you were born was a saint? Have you ever thought what it would be like to live with somebody like that? To be expected to follow in their footsteps?"

"No!" She almost barked the words at him. "I never had the chance."

"Well, I did. And it's hell. If my father had been unkind to me, or unreasonable, or insufferable, I would have had a reason to leave. As it was I had to go because he was too good."

"That's stupid!" Impatiently she wiped away the tears.

"It's not stupid, it's real. And until you've experienced it you don't know how difficult it is."

"But he's gone now." She looked about her despairingly. "Why can't you just forget all about it and take over from him?"

He was exasperated that she could not see what he was getting at. "Because this is Dad's place, Dad's life, not mine."

"But it could be yours now . . . if you wanted it."

He looked at her, a small figure in an oversize waterproof and baggy sweater, her eyes now as red as her spiky hair.

"Look, I'm really sorry." He clenched his jaw to keep a tighter rein on his emotions.

"Is that it, then? Sorry? Sorry to all the wildlife? Sorry to all the birds and the butterflies? Sorry to your dad?"

Her words went straight to the heart and he clenched his fists. "How dare you?" He fought for more words but could not find them. She stared at him, holding the pitchfork in front of her like a sword. He gazed at her, saddened that she should be so venomous, wounded that she should think he would physically harm her.

What he failed to understand was that, for her, the loss of West Yarmouth was only part of her grief: she was also mourning the man who had taken her under his fatherly wing, rescued her from a violent world and had never really known the true depth of her feelings for him. Kit Lavery might have been grieving for his father, but Jess Wetherby was grieving for the only person who had made her life worth living.

Chapter 5:
Knights and Ladies

(Arum maculatum)

Sir Roland Billings-Gore had not had a good day. His favourite hunter, Allardyce, had cast a shoe while out hacking, three of his hens had gone broody, and now, judging by the back pages of the paper, Partick Thistle, a team for which he had always felt a certain empathy, were plunging even further down the Scottish league table. He reasoned with himself that this last disappointment was academic since he had never seen them play, knew the names of none of the players, and boasted Irish rather than Scottish ancestry. But that was not the point. Partick Thistle was a happy sort of name and when the team did well he seemed always to be in good spirits. Today they had lost 4–0 to the feeble-sounding Motherwell, and he felt dispirited.

The grandfather clock in the hall at Baddesley Court struck six. His spirits rose. He put down the newspaper and made for the drinks cupboard. A large measure of Irish whiskey – the Scots had no look-in here – soon revived him, and he sat on the club fender of Baddesley's library fire, gazing into the embers.

Roland Billings-Gore, the eleventh baronet, was a strange contradiction of a man. Born into the aristocracy, he clung steadfastly to his family seat and his position as Master of Fox Hounds, but evinced not a shred of the grandeur and snobbery that many would associate with these roles. He was far happier in the company of his whipper-in and his woodman than with the county set who invited him to this dinner and that ball.

506

He bred a mean Exchequer Leghorn, jumped well over hedges for a man of sixty-two, and only his appearance lived up to his name and standing. He was stocky, with a florid face, a black moustache and iron-grey hair, and frequently shocked those who spoke to him for the first time by barking a greeting rather than speaking what appeared to be English. This elocutionary eccentricity came about as a result of deafness from his days in the Royal Artillery when a young lieutenant had rashly let off his rifle next to Roly's head as a joke. He was often to be found fiddling with the little pieces of pink plastic sunk deep into his hairy ears, before hurling them into the coal scuttle with an oath when they appeared to respond with nothing more than a shrill whistle.

One whistled now as Jinty came into the room, but he silenced it with an unusually well-placed forefinger before rising and stepping forward to give her a peck on the cheek and ask what kind of a day she'd had.

"Oh, OK. Nothing special. Sorry about Allardyce's shoe. We've had the farrier check Seltzer and Boherhue Boy as well and they seem to be all right."

"Mmm." Roly looked thoughtful. "Good thing it happened today, eh?" The Lynchampton Hunt was due to meet the following day. When Roly thought about it, the timing was actually a cause for celebration. "Drink?" He rubbed his hand on Jinty's arm, and she smiled at him, took it, gave it a squeeze and said, "I'll have a Martini."

"Charlotte on her way, mmm?" he asked.

"I think so." She made her way towards the fire and perched on the padded seat of the fender. She was wearing a scarlet polo-neck sweater, and her long legs were encased in black boot-leg trousers.

Her uncle returned with her drink and handed it to her. "You look colourful," he said.

She grinned. "So do you."

"What?"

She pointed at the canary yellow waistcoat and the tweed suit cut from what her aunt would call a 'sudden' check. It was more orange than brown, and of a coarseness that could have removed the most stubborn food from a saucepan, were it cut up to make dishcloths – a course of action his wife had contemplated on more than one occasion.

"Don't know what you mean," barked Roly. "Just comfortable, that's all, mmm?"

The sound of yapping gave them both warning of Lady Billings-Gore's arrival. Two Bichon Frizé dogs bounced into the room, like white pom-poms on elastic, running in circles around Roly and reducing Jinty to helpless laughter.

"What! Charlotte!" He bent down to fend them off. They immediately bounced up and licked his face. He drew himself upright and pulled a red-and-white spotted handkerchief from his breast pocket and wiped away the saliva with a frown.

"Oh, Roly! They can't help it. They're only pleased to see you."

"Huh! Gin?"

"Please."

Charlotte was an unlikely match for her husband. Tall, elegant and immaculately dressed in grey wool that was almost the same colour as her silvery hair, she lowered herself into a chintz-covered chair by the fire. "Come on, boys, lie down." With much snuffling and tumbling, they did as they were told, occasionally nudging each other to see if further play was on the cards.

Roly handed his wife her drink then moved towards the fender, planting himself at the opposite end from Jinty.

"Dinner in about twenty minutes, dear. Mrs Flanders's liver and bacon casserole."

Roly beamed. Liver and bacon. His favourite. He took another mouthful of Irish whiskey and went to replenish his glass, raising his eyebrows in Jinty's direction to enquire if she wanted a refill. She smiled and shook her head, then gazed towards the fire.

"You're very quiet tonight," remarked Charlotte. "Everything all right?"

Jinty kept her eyes on the flaming logs and sighed. "Oh, just man trouble."

"Oh dear. Mr Bickerstaffe?"

She nodded.

"Mmm. Well, I can't say I'm surprised. Not my sort of man, I'm afraid."

"Charlotte!" Roly shot her an admonishing glance.

"Well, he's never here, apart from anything else. I think you deserve rather better."

"Another drink, dear?"

"No, thank you. I've only just started this one." She looked at him reproachfully then turned again to Jinty. "I'm not really interfering. Just concerned, that's all."

"Well, there's no need to be concerned any more. He's buggered off to Bermuda or somewhere. Securing his securities or whatever it is that he does."

Charlotte was about to offer her opinion on the good fortune of Jamie Bickerstaffe's departure, when her husband inadvertently gave her more food for thought.

"I hear young . . . er . . . Kit Lavery's come back."

"Kit Lavery. Now there's a nice young man. Or he was, before he went away."

"Rupert Lavery's son?" Jinty was only mildly curious.

"Yes. Went out to Australia, ooh – eight years ago?" Charlotte said.

"Ten," Roly corrected. "Did well for himself, by all accounts. Good eye for a horse. Got himself a job at some stud farm out there. Bred a few winners. Melbourne Cup. Very successful."

"What will he do with the reserve?" asked Jinty.

"Heaven knows, dear. I suppose he has two options – sell it or run it."

"What's he like? I mean, what was he like when he left?"

"Pleasant boy, as far as I remember. Fair curly hair, tall, pleasant manners. Quite a catch, really."

Jinty perked up. "Sounds a bit of a dish." She sipped her Martini. "Why did he leave?"

"I don't really know. Roly, why did the Lavery boy go to Australia?"

"Mmm? Doing his own thing, I suppose. Shadow of his father and all that."

"There's no doubt that Rupert Lavery was a hard act to follow. Everybody expected Kit to take on the reserve and suddenly he upped and left."

"Suddenly?"

"Yes. One day he was here and the next he'd gone. Rupert said little about it. I think he was disappointed that Kit didn't stay, but he wouldn't hear a word against him. Said that everyone should be allowed to plough their own furrow and that if Kit's furrow was in Australia rather than Devon that's just the way it had to be."

"When's the funeral?"

"There isn't one."

"What?"

"Left his body to science apparently. No body, no funeral."

"What about a memorial service?"

"According to Mrs Flanders, the word in the post office is that he wanted no memorial service either. Happy to slip away unnoticed. Shame, really."

Jinty didn't hear the last remark. She was gazing at the fire wondering what Kit Lavery was like.

The solicitor laid the large buff envelope on Rupert's desk and spoke to Kit in measured tones. "I think you'll find it's all straightforward. The entire estate comes to you. Your father appointed me joint executor with yourself – you being so far away. There are no complications, except for the land leased to Mr Maidment. That was done on a ten-yearly basis but either party can break off the arrangement after five years, provided they give notice. The five years are up at the end of May, which is convenient. You'll need to check that out and drop him a line." He clicked the fastener on his briefcase. "Shall I leave it all with you? You can come in later in the week to sign a few things when you've sorted yourself out. There's no particular rush."

"Yes." Kit was restless. "Can we tie it all up fairly quickly? I need to get back to Australia."

"I'm afraid it will take a little time." The solicitor, a short, dapper man in a grey suit, looked at him reprovingly over the top of wire-rimmed glasses.

Kit felt remorse at his eagerness to rush things through. His father had died barely a week ago and here he was trying to tidy him away as quickly as he could then get on with his own life. "Yes, of course. I'm sorry. I didn't mean to sound . . . well . . ."

"The coroner has released the body. Your father died of a ruptured spleen. There was internal bleeding and head injuries too. The body is still in the mortuary at Totnes. I don't know whether you want to see your father or–"

"No. No thank you," Kit interrupted, and then, lest the solicitor should think him unfeeling, "I think I'd rather remember him as I knew him . . . if that's all right?"

"Yes, of course. You'll find details of the . . . arrangements in there." He pointed at the envelope. "It will be two or three months before everything can be tied up – probate obtained and so on. I'll do my best to speed things up but much of it will be out of my hands. The alternative is for you to return to Australia for the time being and leave me to handle it all."

"No. It's something I ought to do. Want to do."

"I think I should warn you, Mr Lavery, that there is little in the way of liquid assets. Just a few thousand pounds. Inheritance tax, I'm afraid, will take up some of the value of the estate, though the fact that it is agricultural land will reduce the burden a little."

"So I have no option but to sell?"

"It would seem not – unless you have other means."

"Not much. Did my father have any life insurance?"

"Redeemed a few years ago – against my advice, I might add. He ploughed all his money into the reserve. Said it was an insurance policy for nature he was interested in rather than for himself."

"How long could he have kept going?"

"Not very long, I'm afraid. Months. Maybe a year at most, under the present circumstances, unless he had taken out a mortgage on the estate, which he seemed reluctant to do."

"I see."

"From your point of view it makes things neater. There is no lien on the estate. After tax, the proceeds come entirely to you."

"There are no bequests?"

"None, surprisingly." The solicitor took off his spectacles and slipped them into his top pocket. "Your father was a kind man but also, it seems, unsentimental. I asked him, when we were drawing up his will, if he wanted to make any special bequests – bearing in mind his staff and his commitment to conservation and so on – and he was quite emphatic that he did not."

"Really?"

"Yes. He was very firm about that. He said that, aside from the reserve, his only responsibility was to his family. You."

Kit stared at the little grey man in disbelief.

"Well, you have my number. It's on the letterhead. I'll wait for you to get in touch." The solicitor left the room, went down the stairs, got into his car and drove off.

Kit sat on the bed. Guilt surfaced. Guilt at not being there when his father needed help and when he died. Guilt at wanting to sweep away his life's work and escape to the other side of the world.

He blew his nose loud and long, in an attempt to banish the stuffiness that seemed to be turning into a cold.

He walked to the desk, pushed back his hair and picked up the envelope. He slit it open with a brass paperknife, tipped it up and a wad of papers tumbled out – legal documents and plans of the estate. There was also a smaller envelope, addressed simply to 'Kit' in his father's handwriting. He opened it, took out a letter and sat down on the bed to read it. It was dated two years previously.

My dear Kit,
There are a few things I need you to know, and sometimes it's easier to say such things in a letter than it is to say them face to face. I'm afraid it's been one of my failings in life that I've always found it difficult to be open with my feelings when I've thought that such openness would lead to unhappiness in the other person. This lack of honesty, if you like, is sometimes also apparent when you want to praise somebody, but feel that such praise might come over as being patronizing or insincere. Perhaps now I can be more honest on both counts.

Kit felt uneasy about what might be coming. He read on.

I was very sad when you left. You must have known that. But I hope my sadness didn't transmit itself in a way that interfered with your striking out on your own and achieving your own goals. A son should never feel that he has to follow in his father's footsteps, or that he's tied to his father's way of life. A father can hope for such a gift, but he has no right to expect it.

I admit that when you left I felt bitter. Sorry for myself, to be honest. But that sorrow was gradually replaced by admiration. I don't think I ever made it completely clear how proud I am of your achievements. That they were accomplished on the other side of the world, with no help from your friends or family, only adds to your standing. Your mother would have been very proud of you too.

Kit was unable to continue. He stared out of the window as dusk fell. The leaves of the ivy on the wall of the farmhouse rattled in a gust of wind. He picked up the letter once more.

I think I can understand why you needed to go. Sometimes it's not enough for a father to give his son space, or to let him have enough rein. In your case I realize that I must have cast a long shadow, but it gives me no satisfaction to know that.

Throughout my life I've made plenty of mistakes. I've tried to be a good man, but goodness is a funny thing. Some people see it as saintliness – seldom an admired quality except in nuns or prisoners of conscience. Others see it as a naive hope. I suppose, in truth, that it's somewhere between the two.

I've always promised myself that I'd never lecture you, but now that I've gone (funny thing to say when, as yet, I haven't) perhaps I can be allowed just a small homily. Ignore it, if you want, but it makes me feel better to get it off my chest. A last wish, if you like.

It seems to me that the most important thing in life is that you should be guided by your own true feelings. The trouble is that these feelings are sometimes difficult to divine. Experience produces veneers of learning that can mask what we intuitively or instinctively know is right. Your gut reaction is often the one which is most reliable, so never underestimate it.

Don't let the fact that people let you down, or act in ways which are less than honest, make you believe that humankind is bad. It isn't. It's just sometimes misguided, confused and frightened. Neither should you be persuaded that mankind has no place on the planet, except to tiptoe around other forms of life. Mankind is as vital here as other creatures, and in the same way that other creatures must sustain themselves, so must man. The difference is that man is entrusted with a conscious responsibility for other forms of life.

Look further than the obvious when endeavouring to work out what is right. Too many people enter into heated emotional arguments based on envy and distrust.

I'm sorry if this is beginning to sound too much like a sermon. I didn't intend it to. What I really wanted to do was to communicate to you the joy and the pleasure I have had in my life, much of which has come from working this small patch of countryside. As you will discover from my bank balance, it is not financially rewarding, but then financial reward is not what I sought.

It's been my greatest belief in life that a man entrusted with land must hand it on in a better state than it was in when he inherited it. I hope that this is the case with West Yarmouth. When my father farmed here the ground was given over to sheep and turnips. Now butterflies and bats breed, wild flowers thrive, and the red squirrel is beginning, slowly, to recolonize, though few, as yet, are aware of that. Sometimes it's good to be quiet about things.

I have made sure that the areas of the farm still under cultivation are worked responsibly and organically, with an eye to the ground being kept in good heart. Land must be productive – whether it produces wild flowers or wheat – but it must be husbanded, not plundered.

Deciding what to do with the land will be a problem that I cannot solve for you, and I make no apology for presenting you with a difficult decision. I can't pretend that I don't want you to pick up the torch, but I won't force my beliefs and responsibilities on to you, except to ask you to make sure that somehow the reserve continues to thrive. Whether you do this by selling it to someone who will carry on my work, or by taking it on yourself, is up to you. The books might be of help.

Kit raised his eyes to the book-filled shelves that lined the room. It would take more than nightly reading to get to grips with three hundred acres of Devonshire. He turned to the last page of the letter.

Writing this makes me heavy-hearted. I have no wish to alter the course of your life – the course that you must steer for yourself – but I feel a need to explain my actions in the hope that you might at least see why I did what I did.

There are some who achieve their goals in life in a forceful way – particularly in the field of conservation. They have their place in bringing matters to public notice, but I've never been of their number. I chose to work differently but, I hope, just as effectively. I'm firmly of the conviction that more can be achieved in life by proceeding quietly but positively. Too many people concern themselves with the general rather than the particular; I chose the opposite course. All I can leave behind me to prove my point is the reserve.

Again, I'm sorry to land you with what I suspect will be a difficult decision, but then I cannot really apologize for my life. Do what you must, and know that you gave me much satisfaction in the way you led your own life. Your mother and I hoped, above all else, that you would be your own person, and in that we were never disappointed. Please continue to be yourself and know how much we loved you.

To finish on a practical note, I ask that there be no funeral and no memorial service. I have given instructions to Dr Hastings that my body be left to science – if it's any use to them. This will surprise some who will doubtless expect me to be buried on the reserve. My spirit will be there. Plant a tree for me.
With love, always,
Dad

Kit laid the letter on the bed, and for the next hour, until it was quite dark, sat staring silently into space as tears streamed down his cheeks.

Chapter 6:
Devil-in-a-bush

(*Paris quadrifolia*)

The following morning Kit's head felt like lead. He tried to lift it from the pillow, but dizziness and a streaming cold told him he'd be better off staying where he was. The crisp sunny weather of the past few days was replaced by wind and rain that whipped at the old sash windows of the farmhouse.

At nine there was a knock on his door, and he croaked, "Cub id."

Elizabeth Punch put her head around the door, immediately sized up the situation from Kit's general demeanour and gave her instructions. "Stay there. I thought this was coming. The best place for you is bed." She walked towards him, and laid a cold hand on his feverish brow. "Mmm. I'll bring you some honey and lemon. Bit of a stinker you've got. Change of weather, I expect," and she stared blankly out of the window at the swirling rain. "A bit warmer where you've come from?" She looked down at him.

Kit nodded, then regretted it as his head throbbed like a kettle drum.

"Well, you're in the right place. Might as well give in to it." And then, lest her good nature be taken advantage of, "I can't nurse you, mind – too much to do. But I'll keep an eye on you and bring you some broth later. All right?"

Kit managed a weak "Thank you," and she closed the door quietly behind her. He lay back on the pillow, aware of a whispered conversation outside the door, but disinclined to do anything except fall asleep.

For the next two days he coughed and spluttered his way self-pityingly through a heavy cold as only the male of the species can. Sweat poured off him at one moment, and shivers gripped him at the next. Visions of swaying trees and crashing seas came and went, as did the trays of hot lemon and honey, watery consommé and dry toast that Elizabeth brought in from time to time. Through it all came a vision of his father sitting at his desk writing page after page of notes, which were flung to the floor until they merged into a snowy white carpet.

He wanted to reach for the telephone and speak to Australia but his aching limbs and throbbing head dissuaded him. His father's words swirled around in his head like a litany – "Do what you must . . . continue to be yourself . . . know how much we loved you . . ." As soon as he felt better he would start things moving with the sale of West Yarmouth.

Gradually, his temperature returned to normal, and Elizabeth decided that as the weather had changed so, too, should the location of the man in the master bedroom. On the third morning she appeared with a tray of tea and toast. "Breakfast!" Her voice was louder than it had been before, and Kit detected in it a note of impatience. She put down the tray on the desk and went to the window, threw back the curtains and let in what passed for the morning light. The wind and rain had subsided, to be replaced by a watery stillness.

"If you're feeling up to it I thought we might walk the reserve this morning," she said.

"Fine. Yes." Kit dragged himself upright and ran his hand through his matted hair.

She looked at him, half naked in his father's bed, and excused herself. "Right. Well I'll see you downstairs when you're ready. Ten o'clock?"

"Yes. Absolutely." He felt unable to argue.

She nodded and left, closing the door quietly. This time there were no whispers.

She reminded him of a Japanese tourist guide – the sort who marches in front of her charges with a scarlet umbrella held aloft, anxious that none should go astray. This particular tour began in front of the stables. Elizabeth's hands were thrust deep into the pockets of a Drizabone cape. "You know about the stables – general storage space underneath, machinery, mowers and the like, our accommodation above." They walked on, past the pig-sties. "We don't use these as yet, but we were thinking of getting some rare breeds to fill them. Just a thought. Nothing certain."

"I see." Kit felt a fraud – as though he was a prospective purchaser who had already decided that they were not interested in the property in question but would let the vendor carry on so as not to cause offence. He was unsure whether Elizabeth knew that she was wasting her time. Certainly, there was a degree of casualness in her manner that surprised him. Where was the missionary zeal he had expected? Perhaps she knew that, financially, West Yarmouth Nature Reserve had reached the end of the line. If she did, she was certainly keeping her cool.

"You've met Wilson, I understand." She leaned over the low wall to look at the snuffling hulk that lay in the mud.

"Yes."

"She seems to have perked up a bit since you arrived." She turned and walked towards a five-barred gate. "This is the old orchard – it must have been here when you were a child."

"Yes. Trees look a bit older now."

"That's because they are," she said tartly. "We turn Wilson out here in decent weather. They used to say that the spots on the back of a Gloucester Old Spot were the bruises from fallen apples. A load of rubbish, of course, but at least here she can lie under the trees and not get sunburnt."

"Sunburnt?"

"Yes. It's a serious problem with pigs – especially the fair-skinned ones. Wilson is tougher than most but we still have to keep an eye on her."

The prospect of a pig suffering from sunburn made Kit smile. He pictured Wilson on a lilo on a Mediterranean beach, smothered in Ambre Solaire, but his reverie was cut short.

"The two fields over there are the ones we take hay from. Organic, of course. No fertilizer, just muck. Good mixture of grasses and wild flowers. The local horses love it."

Kit looked out across the grassy landscape, which was presently an unpromising shade of light green. "What about the land beyond?" He pointed to the fields where sheep grazed and to others under some sort of cultivation.

"Those are let to Mr Maidment, a local farmer. He grazes sheep and grows a few daffodils. They're managed organically – your father insisted on that."

"How much land is there altogether?"

"About three hundred and fifty acres all told. Maidment rents about two hundred and the reserve occupies the rest. Your father talked about extending it as time went on, but we really have our hands full with what we've got. If we took in more land we'd need more bodies to look after it."

And more funds, thought Kit. He stared out over the fields. "And beyond them?"

"The sea. Nobody owns that."

Kit looked at her. She looked straight back. "Come on." She strode through the orchard towards another five-barred gate which she held open for him. "This is where it all begins. We call this the Combe. It's light woodland running down the side of the valley to the sea. But you must remember it?"

"Very well. I used to play here. Is the bridge still there?"

"Oh, yes. Solid as a rock. We'll go down that way."

The two of them walked purposefully down a snaking path through the woodland, the wide stream that locals called the river Yar tumbling past them in the bottom of the steep-sided valley. Eventually they came to the old stone hump-backed bridge and Kit leaned over it to look into the water, memories of his early years flooding back with the gushing current.

"Has it changed much?" Elizabeth asked.

"No. Not at all. Not this bit – it's just the same." He sounded far away; lost in childhood. His father's voice echoed in his ears. 'Go on, then, throw it!' And they tossed their sticks down into the water and ran to the other side of the bridge to see whose came out first. Pooh Sticks. He had played it with his father every weekend when he was tiny. He was snapped out of his daydreams again by her voice.

"Most of the reserve is on the other side of the river." She walked ahead and he followed.

"How often do you open to the public?" he asked.

"Weekends between April and September. We restrict where they can go to make sure they don't disturb nesting birds and so on. We don't get crowds, just a steady trickle. Your father thought it important that we shared the place with other people."

In front of them the sides of the valley rose steeply, thickly carpeted with undergrowth and sprouting healthy young trees. "These have all been planted over the last ten years." She waved a hand at the branches overhead. "British native broadleaves, but capable of coping with salt spray. Sycamore is quite useful. We've put in lots of pines higher up. Hopefully you'll see why."

They climbed on. She seemed to have boundless energy while Kit, struggling to get over his cold, frequently found himself breathless.

"We call this the Wilderness." She took him into a small clearing near the centre of the wood where a log seat was tucked into a group of bushes. "Sit down," she whispered, "and don't say anything." He looked at her. "Just watch." She pointed to a stand of Scots pine in front of them.

Kit watched. A few small birds twittered from branch to branch. Long-tailed tits and greenfinches. He was pleased that some of what his father had taught him remained. The birds flitted off. For fully five minutes the two of them sat on the bench while a gentle breeze rustled through the lofty pines. Just as Kit was beginning to wonder how long this would continue, he felt Elizabeth nudge him. He turned and she indicated, with a nod, a movement in a pine tree slightly to the right of them. Kit screwed up his eyes to focus them and saw the squirrel, gnawing at a nut held in its paws.

Elizabeth turned to him and smiled. Then she whispered, very quietly, "They said it couldn't be done. That it was all but extinct on the mainland. But Rupert did it. He got the red squirrel re-established here."

Kit looked with wonder at the small fluffy rodent sitting on the branch of the pine tree. Its ears were long and tufted, its colour a reddish grey. It reminded him of *Squirrel Nutkin* – which his father used to read to him at bedtime when he was four or five. He'd always found it rather scary. Now he felt a sudden thrill at seeing a red squirrel in the flesh for the first time.

Elizabeth said nothing. She sat back and watched the animal, which seemed unaware of their presence. Occasionally she glanced at Kit.

The squirrel finished its snack, dropped the nutshell and scampered off into the wood. Elizabeth got to her feet and turned to him. "It's taken us ten years to get this far," she said, and headed downhill. He followed her, half a dozen paces behind, until they came to a smaller, lighter patch of woodland fringed with gorse. A few yellow flowers studded the prickly bushes. "When gorse is in bloom . . ." intoned Elizabeth.

". . . kissing's in season," finished Kit.

"You haven't forgotten, then."

"No."

"Your father left his mark on a lot of people."

"So I'm discovering."

She pushed her way through the spiky undergrowth. "We call this the Spinney." Kit followed, the sharp spikes of the gorse perforating his clothing. Finally the bushes stopped abruptly and they came out on to a close-cropped sward of grass that ran steeply down to the cliff edge. Kit stopped and gazed at the view. From this lofty vantage-point, he could see the morning sun glinting on the crests of the waves. The reserve was behind them now and the sea below a deep navy blue. The sight of it took his breath away. The gentle morning breeze was clearing his head and he looked up into a pale blue cloudless sky.

He looked round for Elizabeth, but she was nowhere to be seen. She had vanished as quickly as the squirrel, and just as silently, leaving him quite alone to face the sea and an uncertain future.

It worried him that he gravitated naturally towards Wilson. As an animal, the pig had hitherto held him in no particular thrall. Horses were different: breeding and bloodstock lines fascinated him. Pigs couldn't compete, when it came to sleekness of coat, conformation or general demeanour, and yet here he was, leaning into the old girl's sty and scratching her mud-encrusted back with a stick.

"What do you make of it all, then? Eh?"

The pig responded with a snort.

"Yes. Exactly. Bit of a bugger, really, isn't it?" He rubbed the stick behind her ear and her eyes closed with pleasure.

"It's all right for you. All you have to do is eat and sleep. I've got to sort all this lot out. I mean, I've got nothing against you – nothing against pigs as a race – but horses are my thing. You might be a prizewinning Gloucester Old Spot for all I know but I can't tell that from your lines or your conformation – if you've got one. But I can with horses." The animal peeped at him, occasionally, from under her floppy ears while she foraged for food.

Kit tried harder to impress. "I've had a few winners – Melbourne Cup. Not mine, of course, my boss's – but the breeding was down to me. I'd like a stud farm of my own, really. Got a bit saved. Not enough, though. You could come with me if you want. As long as you're prepared to travel." The pig showed no interest. "I suppose you'd rather stay here, but I haven't enough money to keep this place going even if I wanted to. Tax to pay, no obvious buyer and . . . a couple of women who are . . ."

He was just about to ask Wilson's advice on the particularly knotty problem of what would become of Elizabeth and Jess when the latter called him from across the yard. She was standing by the barn with a tall man in an old tweed jacket and a flat cap. He stood, hands in his pockets, watching, as Kit walked over to where they stood.

"This is Mr Maidment," said Jess, then walked off in the direction of the orchard.

Kit shook the man's large, horny hand. "Arthur Maidment," the man introduced himself. He was tall and angular with a slight stoop, a ruddy, clean-shaven face and pale blue eyes. He touched his cap before he spoke. "Thought I'd better come and see 'ee."

"Yes." It was the best response Kit could manage.

"I know 'tis early days but I thought y'ought to know that my lease comes up for renewal soon."

"Yes."

"Just wanted to know if you knew, like, what would be 'appenin'."

"Well, not yet, no."

"You goin' to sell up?"

"Almost certainly."

"'Cos if you is then I might be interested in buyin'. At the right price, of course."

"I see." Kit brightened.

"But if you're not sellin' we ought to talk about the land anyway."

"Sorry?"

"This management lark. Can't go on like this. Makin' no money. Can't go on with this organic business. Too much labour and not enough return. Need to think about a different management scheme."

Kit's head was swimming. He had barely come to grips with the extent of the estate, had only just walked around it, and he was being asked to make decisions about its management when all he had really wanted to do was to get rid of it.

Though if Arthur Maidment wanted to buy it where was the problem? Hadn't it just been solved? Or could he sell off part to pay the inheritance tax and keep the rest? But why should he do that? And if Maidment was not happy with organic farming, what would happen to the reserve if he bought it? "Shall we go inside, Mr Maidment?" he asked. "Talk this through over a cup of coffee?"

"If you like."

Kit led the way to the kitchen, found the kettle and a decent jar of coffee then sat his neighbour down at the kitchen table. Maidment took off his cap, revealing a snowy white thatch of hair. He ladled three heaped spoonfuls of sugar into his mug and took up the conversation. "Got a plan for more sheep. More daffs, too. But I needs to use fertilizers to get better crops."

"Can't you use organic fertilizers?"

"Not to get enough early bite – enough nitrogen in there. Need to use more fertilizer to make the land more productive. Herbicides, too."

"So if you bought the reserve what would you do with it?"

Maidment smiled. "Have to farm it. Sell the timber, make the land productive."

"No conservation area?"

"Can't afford it. 'Twould be a few year before 'twere all taken into cultivation, mind. Can't rush into these things. Would offer a fair price, though."

Kit experienced a sinking feeling in the pit of his stomach. Refusing to carry on his father's work himself was one thing; seeing it all go under the plough or the axe was another. "What about the house?" he asked.

"Not interested, unless it were at the right price."

Maidment might look like the archetypal son of the soil, but he was no fool. He had as sharp a business mind as any City slicker, Kit decided. "Right. I'll let you know," he said.

Maidment rose from the table and picked up his cap. "They 'as my number, the ladies. I'll wait to 'ear."

"Thank you."

Maidment nodded, put on his cap and loped out of the kitchen, leaving Kit with a crisis of conscience that he would have given anything to avoid.

Chapter 7:
Forget-me-not
(*Myosotis sylvatica*)

It was not at all what he had expected. He had been ready for hysterical entreaties not to sell West Yarmouth from both Elizabeth and Jess, instead of which, after Jess's initial outburst at the pig-sty, they had kept their peace. It was as though they had made a pact. It was unnerving, but maybe that was what they wanted – to unsettle him. If so, they had succeeded. A temper tantrum from Jess or icy reproach from Elizabeth would have been helpful: it would have cleared the air. As it was, he remained uncomfortably uncertain, both of their thoughts and their *modus operandi*.

Shortly after supper the phone call came as a welcome relief. Elizabeth took it in the hallway and stuck her head round the door into the kitchen. "It's for you," she told Kit. "Someone called Heather?"

His thoughts tumbled from the Devon farm across the water to Australia. He got up quickly and went into the hall, carefully closing the door behind him before picking up the phone and sitting on the stairs. "Hello?"

"Hi! How are you? I thought you'd forgotten me."

The voice sounded as though it was in the next room, not thousands of miles away.

"No, not forgotten. Missing you like hell. Wishing I was still with you. Trying to survive without you. How's it going?" The Australian vernacular came back to him.

"OK." There was a question in her voice, which he did his best to answer.

"Look, I'm sorry I haven't rung. I've been laid up with flu. Well, a bad cold anyway. Could hardly speak. It's bloody cold here."

"Yes. I guess so."

It was good to hear a friendly voice.

"What's happening over there? When do you think you'll be back?" she went on.

"Oh, heaven knows. It's going to take longer than I thought."

"How long?"

"Several weeks. Maybe a couple of months. There's so much to sort out."

"I knew this would happen."

"What?"

"That it would take ages. I told you it wouldn't be easy." She sounded disappointed. "I'm missing you."

"Me, too. I could do with a friendly face around here. Everybody seems to think I'm up to no good."

"Do they know you want to sell up?"

"Yes."

"Are they being difficult?"

"No. That's the trouble. Apart from the odd bit of temperament they're all being fine. I've even had a neighbour round who wants to buy the land."

"Well, that's good, isn't it?"

"It's not quite as easy as that." Kit tried to explain the situation, taking care to keep his voice down.

Heather listened, then said, "You can't worry about what they'll all think. It's your life."

"I know. It's just that . . ."

"What?"

"Oh, I don't know. Seeing all Dad's work go up in smoke doesn't seem fair. I'd rather sell to somebody who would at least keep the reserve going, rather than turning it all over to farmland."

"That could take ages."

"I know." He asked about the stud farm and the horses.

"They're missing you. I'm missing you. Pa's missing you. We're all missing you."

"And I'm missing you. I'd be there tomorrow if I could but– Look,

I'm sorry this is all so complicated, but I'll get back as soon as I can. And I'll ring you. Every week."

"Is that all?"

"What?"

"I thought you might ring every day."

"Sweetheart, it would cost a fortune."

"Oh." She sounded hurt.

"Hey . . . a couple of times a week then."

"Only if you can."

The enthusiasm he had heard in her voice at the start of their conversation had ebbed away. He could picture her at the other end of the line, standing in the doorway of the white-painted clapboard house, looking out across the white-railed fields where sleek horses grazed. Her dark hair would be tied back in a ponytail, she'd be dressed in T-shirt and shorts, her tanned legs crossed as she propped herself against the porch, an ice-cold beer in her hand. What he wouldn't give to be standing there now.

They'd had a great Christmas together, the three of them. Kit had become Heather's father's right-hand man, supervising the breeding programme. Her older brothers worked at the stud, too, but they lived with their own families in other ranch-houses. Kit lived in the main house with her and her father, and he'd almost become a member of the family. Almost. They'd started off as wary acquaintances, but their relationship had built over the years. Boyfriends had come and gone, and Heather and Kit had become closer as he helped her over broken relationships, and they slowly forged one of their own.

He could hear distant shouting. "I'd better be getting back," she said. "Pa's breaking Wackatee's colt. Ring when you can. We're eleven hours ahead of you."

"I'll remember."

"Oh . . ."

"What?"

"Nothing. I just wanted this to be a good phone call, that's all, and it's not."

"I'm sorry."

"Not your fault, I suppose. Just wish you were here, that's all."

"And you."

"Speak soon, then."

"Yes. Soon."

"Love you."

"Love you, too."

"'Bye." There was a click at the other end, and he lowered the handset into the cradle. From thoughts of a sunny Australian day he was plunged back into the chilly gloom of a dark English night. Right now he would rather be in Australia. Right now he would rather be anywhere than here.

Chapter 8: Teasel

(*Dipsacus fullonum*)

At the end of the first week Kit seemed to be no further forward than he had been when he arrived. Jess engaged him in conversation only rarely, and Elizabeth seemed irritable with him. He decided on an olive branch. "Is there anything I can do?" he'd asked over breakfast.

"There is, actually," retorted Elizabeth.

He was surprised at the swiftness of her reply. He'd expected a "No, not really," instead of which he was despatched with a mattock to the Spinney to clear a patch of brambles that were overtaking a grassy bank where Elizabeth wanted to protect the wild thyme and ants' nests – egg-laying sites for the large blue butterfly.

She walked down there with him on the grey, blustery morning. More as a way of making conversation than anything else, Kit asked, "Where did Dad fall?"

"We'll pass it in a moment," she replied.

She said nothing more until they were walking along the steep-sided ravine where the Yar made its way into the sea. Then she stopped. "Just down there." She nodded towards a small apron of sand and shingle. "That's where I found him."

They both stood silently for a while, listening to the waves lapping against the shore.

Kit asked "Did he . . .?"

"Dr Hastings thinks he had a blackout. He was dead by the time I arrived."

"How long . . .?"

"He can't have fallen more than five minutes before I found him. He left the house just before I did. We were coming to look at the state of the Spinney. I saw him lying on the sand."

"I'm sorry."

"It's I who should be apologizing. If we'd left together it might never have happened." There was a crack in her voice.

"You musn't think like that."

She turned on him. "I can and I do. Stupid. It should never have happened. He should be here to see things through. Misadventure, they said at the inquest. Such a pointless word. Childish." She said nothing more for a few moments, then turned to face him. "Don't let us down," she said. Then she walked on with him to the Spinney and instructed him in the indelicate art of grubbing out brambles.

For three hours he flailed away, the blackberry stems lacerating his cheeks and wrists, which were the only parts of his body open to attack, thanks to a thornproof Barbour and thick leather gloves. He stacked the uprooted plants on the edge of the Spinney as per Elizabeth's instructions.

"Why can't I just burn them?" he'd asked.

"Carcinogens. Benzopyrene. Ozone layer. Better not to burn them. Stack them in a heap and they dry out and make a protective thicket for nesting birds."

"Fine." He considered himself told.

The manual labour did him good: it cleared his head and blew away the cobwebs born of his cold and the jet-lag. Colour sprang into his cheeks and he paused from time to time to gaze at the sea and at the gulls wheeling over the cliffs, their normally black heads white in winter plumage. He nearly leaped over the cliff himself when a voice surprised him.

"Hello!" She laughed when he jumped a foot into the air and slapped his hand to his heart.

"You made me jump," he said.

"Obviously." She smiled broadly, looking down at him from her horse.

"You must be Kit."

"Yes."

"They've got you working already, have they?"

"'Fraid so." He looked up at her, in her white Aran sweater and black hard hat, dark brown jodhpurs and brown suede boots. He looked, too, at her horse, a powerful grey gelding of seventeen hands, his ears pricked, mouth champing at the bit.

"He looks a bit of a handful."

"Oh, he is. Keeps me on my toes." And then, realizing she had not introduced herself, "I'm Jinty O'Hare from Baddesley Court. We're neighbours – well, almost." She leaned down to shake his hand, and he noticed how green her eyes were.

"What's his name?"

"Seltzer. Ex-team chaser. Good hunter. More energy than I have." Her accent betrayed her Irish origins. She smiled again, and dimples appeared in her cheeks. "You work with horses yourself, don't you?" she asked.

"Yes. But not here. Out in New South Wales. Not as hands-on as you. More into bloodstock, stud work."

"That sounds pretty hands-on to me."

"Oh, I'm more concerned with who should do what and to whom."

"Mmmm!" She looked at him mischievously. "Fascinating."

So this was Kit Lavery. Jinty eyed him up from her vantage-point atop the muscular grey. He was looking up at her, his chiselled features and pale blue eyes topped with a strangely boyish mop of fair curly hair. There were beads of perspiration on his brow, thanks to his exertions, and he was breathing heavily. She patted the horse's neck to calm him.

"What are you doing here?" he asked.

"Oh, just walking the cliff path. We've been for a gallop on the sand." She patted Seltzer's neck again. "He likes that, don't you, boy?"

Kit gazed at the vision before him: tall and elegant, her cheeks pink from riding, her long legs flexed in the stirrups, the powerful horse straining beneath her. His heart beat faster.

"Back home for lunch now." She kicked the horse into a walk. "You should come and look at the stable sometime, unless you're rushing back Down Under."

"No. I mean, yes. I'm not rushing back."

"Fine. See you sometime, then." And then, over her shoulder, "Good luck with the spiky things. The ones you're cutting, I mean."

Kit watched her go, and Jinty felt slightly ashamed of her own bare-faced cheek, which did not stop her smiling to herself as Seltzer picked his way down the cliff path.

Jess Wetherby, who had watched the encounter from the other side of the valley, let fly with her pickaxe in an attempt to rid the hole she was digging of a hefty stone and her mind of pent-up frustration.

"So what's he like?" Sally, the Billings-Gores' groom, was responding to Jinty's news that she had encountered Kit Lavery on her hack along the coastal path.

"He's a bit of a dish, actually."

Sally, hard at work with the hoof-pick on Allardyce's left foreleg, took Jinty to task. " I bet you only took that route to see if you could bump into him."

"What a dreadful thing to say." Jinty suppressed a giggle. "As if I'd risk incurring the wrath of the two battleaxes just to see if I could spot a bit of talent!"

"Oh, heaven forbid!" Sally's voice was heavy with sarcasm. "So, come on then. Describe him."

Jinty, vigorously brushing Seltzer's flanks, kept her eyes firmly on the horse and the job in hand. "He's about six foot, fair curly hair, good-looking."

"Hunky?"

"You bet." She paused to scrape Seltzer's hair from the dandy-brush with a curry-comb. "Quiet, though." She looked reflective. "Not wet. Gentle . . . you know."

"Strong silent type?"

"God, I hope not. I've had enough of them."

"Oh, so we *are* prospecting, then?"

"No, we are not. I was just being neighbourly."

Sally muttered something under her breath.

"What?"

"Nothing. Bet you're going to see him again, though."

"Nothing to do with me. Up to him." She carried on grooming, while Seltzer tore a mouthful of hay from the net on the stable wall.

"You sowed the seed, then, did you?" Sally finished Allardyce's hoof and stood upright, her plump cheeks rosy from exertion.

"Might have done."

"Oh, come on! What happened?".

"Nothing." Jinty did her best to play down the encounter. "I just said that if he wanted to come and look at the stables he was welcome. That's all."

531

"Fast work!" said Sally. "Very impressive."

Jinty lobbed the brush at her, but she sidestepped and it landed with a splosh in Allardyce's water bucket.

"Cheek!" Jinty grinned, then recalled the figure standing on the cliff top. "Fun, though." She took Seltzer's halter and led him out across the yard, calling over her shoulder, "Great fun . . . I hope."

Sally shook her head and sighed. Only yesterday Jinty O'Hare had sworn that she had lost all interest in men. She had known it wouldn't last.

Kit felt nervous at the prospect but it had to be addressed. He had told Elizabeth that he wanted to go into Totnes to hire a car so that he would be independently mobile. It was only partly true: he also wanted to call in at the estate agent's.

A letter from a firm who sounded as though they ought to know what they were doing had landed on the doormat barely two days before. Clearly they had seen the chance of rich pickings, but if they were keen maybe they could sell the place quickly.

The well-spoken young man in country tweeds and a burgundy-striped shirt greeted him just a little too familiarly, and motioned him to take a seat in front of the large wooden desk.

Kit explained the situation.

"Yes, of course." The fresh-faced agent was more oleaginous than a bottle of extra-virgin olive oil. "I think, though, to be perfectly honest, it will be almost impossible to sell the nature reserve as a reserve. I would have to recommend that it is sold as a country estate with just a mention that part of the land is at present run as a conservation enterprise. That, really, is as much as we can hope to do."

Kit bridled at the prospect of his father's work being undervalued.

"West Yarmouth does have a good reputation as a reserve, locally, though it is still a very difficult market. But as a small agricultural estate, and occupying the position it does – with excellent coastal views – I think you'll have no trouble in selling."

"I'm sorry, but I really do want to sell the reserve as a going concern. It's what my father wanted."

"Well, if you're sure." Then, seeing the look of determination on Kit's face, "We'll certainly have a try, Mr Lavery."

"How much do you think it might fetch?" Kit felt guilty at putting a price on his father's life's work.

"Something in excess of a million pounds. Perhaps a million and a half. More if we can find a determined buyer."

"Wow!" Kit slumped back in the chair, reeling. He tried to make sense of the figure, then remembered Arthur Maidment's offer for the land. "What if the land were to be sold separately from the house?"

"I wouldn't advise that. I think it would be best to attempt to sell the estate as a whole, which should be more profitable, and perhaps split it up only if no offers are forthcoming. We don't get many estates like this coming on to the market, and when they do they often command a high price. You're in a very strong position, Mr Lavery – even given the conservation side of the property. And, of course, the inheritance tax will be reduced because it's an agricultural estate. As you probably know, agricultural land is not subject to the same level of tax as other property."

"Yes, I realize that." Kit had now grasped the nature of his father's legacy. If he sold the land leased to Maidment separately he would be unlikely to get a high price for it – certainly not enough to allow him to continue running the rest of the estate himself and pay off the inheritance tax.

He could sell the entire estate, but only if he could find a buyer who would maintain it as a nature reserve – and he would make sure of that. In spite of the estate agent's misgivings, surely he could check out prospective purchasers to make sure that they intended to carry on his father's work. His choices were clear. His head was anything but.

Pigs do not necessarily go to sleep when it gets dark, which is a good thing. Wilson had to do a good deal of listening that night before she turned in. But she enjoyed the apples.

Chapter 9: Bittersweet

(*Solanum dulcamara*)

Titus Ormonroyd was not what you'd call refined. He called a spade a bloody shovel, rather than a non-mechanical earth-moving facilitator, and thought a gentleman was someone who got out of the bath to have a pee. For twenty years or more he'd been huntsman to the Lynchampton, serving the Master, Sir Roland Billings-Gore, and his late predecessor, Lord Tallacombe. When Kit was a boy he'd spent much of his school holidays with Titus at Quither Cottage, set half-way between West Yarmouth Farmhouse and Baddesley Court. Titus's cottage went with the job. It was here that the Lynchampton hounds were kennelled, and here that the young Kit had helped with feeding and whelping, begging his father, on the arrival of every litter, to let him have a pup. The answer was always the same: 'Sorry, but no.' His contact with horses had begun here, too, kindling an interest that blossomed in later life and turned casual appreciation into skilful breeding.

Surprisingly, Kit's father had always got on with Titus. They were, maintained Rupert, two men approaching the same problem from different angles. He frequently disagreed with Titus – certainly in his opinions about hunting – but he recognized in the straight-talking Yorkshireman another countryman with a sympathetic approach to the countryside. Even if he did kill things.

Kit would have called on Titus sooner, had he not been laid low by the cold and diverted by solicitors and estate agents. As it was, it took him the best part of a week before he got round to paying a visit.

If Titus hadn't changed, he would be just the sort of company Kit needed. He was male, for a start, and male company had been in scant supply lately, he had a sense of humour that the generous would call robust, and the puritanical filthy, and he was a good listener, with a powerful sense of reasoning based on common sense.

The sound of hounds giving tongue led Kit round to the back of Quither Cottage. It was just as he had remembered it. Rows of low, brick-built kennels, fronted by concrete pens surrounded by metal railings. Hounds of all patterns, their sterns wagging furiously, were calling for their food. In the middle of the canine mayhem, Kit recognized the familiar figure. He was grey-haired now, and his hairline had receded a little, but the short, bandy-legged man in wellies and dark blue overalls, with a bucket in each hand, was still the Titus of old. "Gedout y'old bugger! Wait a minute. Gerraway!"

Kit stood and watched from the corner of one of the outbuildings as Titus went about his work. Kit smiled. It was good to hear the northern tones again. It made him feel more at home than he had so far, even though he had been living in his old house. The unfamiliar company of Punch and Wetherby had left him feeling alien.

He waited for the commotion to die down. Titus came out of one of the kennel yards with his empty buckets, slipped the bolt on the gate and began walking down the path towards Kit, a preoccupied expression on his face. Then he saw Kit standing ten yards away and his face lit up. "Well, I'll be buggered. Look who it isn't!" He put down his buckets, marched up to Kit and ruffled his hair. "You're still a big bugger aren't you?" He squeezed Kit's arms with his hands, then stood back and put his hands on his hips.

"Well, I'd heard you were coming back." His expression changed, to one of sorrow. "Reet sorry about your dad. Dreadful thing." He looked at the ground, and Kit reacquainted himself with his old friend's appearance. His cheeks were ruddy, the Roman nose was as hooked as ever, and the glass right eye sparkled like the dew. Titus had lost the original to a cantankerous cow at the age of thirteen. A cow with a horn, as he was wont to explain with a wink.

The appropriate consoling remarks having been made, Titus allowed his joy at the return of the Prodigal Son to resurface. "Ee, it's grand to see yer! Here for long?"

"Looks like it. Something of a can of worms."

"Oh, I can imagine." He raised his eyebrows. "You've met the ladies, then?"

"I have."

"They'll be leadin' you a right dance, I'll bet."

Kit smiled ruefully. "A bit."

"'Ere, come on. Cup of tea. I was just goin' to put kettle on. Fancy one? A cup of tea, I mean. I can't offer anything else."

Kit laughed. "You've not changed. I'd love one."

"Won't be long, Becky," Titus shouted, to the fair-haired kennelmaid, who was mucking out lower down the run. She raised a hand in acknowledgement.

They walked towards the cottage, Titus dropping off the buckets in an outhouse whose smell rekindled old memories in Kit – the sweet aroma of hay and feed, corn and meal. The smell of the countryman, the keeper, the man of the woods.

As Titus opened the kitchen door, a pair of dark brown eyes glinted in the gloom. "'Allo, then, gel," he greeted the liver and white spaniel bitch, as she wiggled her way across the floor to him.

"Who's this, then?" asked Kit.

"This is Nell, and she's a lovely gel, in't she?" he asked as the dog rolled over on to her back. "Look at that. Soft as putty." He stroked the soft hair on her belly.

"You've not lost your touch, then," teased Kit.

"Not bloody likely! And she's goin' to be a little belter, is this one, once she's properly trained."

"Gun dog?"

"No, I don't think so. Just company. Lost me appetite for shootin'. 'Appen yer dad's influence finally paid off."

"What happened to Fly?"

"Ah, poor old bugger. Went blind in the end. Died six month ago. Good age though. Sixteen." Titus carried on tickling. "Now it's just the two on us, in't it?"

"Thought you were a border collie man?"

"Well, I were. But then this little lady landed on me doorstep. Don't know where she came from, but thought I'd better take care of her."

The huntsman, fresh from his no-nonsense marshalling of the hounds outside, was clearly besotted with the spaniel at his feet. Kit looked around him. The kitchen had hardly changed at all. The ancient black range still stood against one wall, with a threadbare armchair to one side, at its foot the dog's basket. An old pine table with green-painted legs occupied the centre of the room, and a couple of spoke-back chairs were pulled up to it.

Titus had lived on his own for the last fifteen years. His wife, a good sort, popular in the village and a stalwart of the WI, had died of cancer when Kit was away at school. Some had thought Titus would never recover – he and Edie had been a devoted pair – and he had taken it hard, but he had pulled through, and never missed a meet. He diverted his sorrows, he said, into being better at his job.

He filled the kettle at the brass tap above the old porcelain sink and put it on the range, then turned to the cupboard to sort out mugs, milk and sugar. He looked over his shoulder as he did so, and threw his favourite question at Kit. "Are you courtin', then?"

"It's taken you seven and a half minutes to ask that. You're losing your touch."

Titus shook his head, and the twinkly brown eyes became a little glazed. "Must be me age."

"I've got a girl in Australia. Heather. Her dad runs the stud where I work."

"Blonde, brunette or redhead?" asked Titus, as though studying racing form.

"Brunette."

"Mmm. You could have children with hair of any colour, then."

"We haven't got that far yet."

"Shame. You can't afford to hang about, you know." The twinkle returned to both eyes. "Has she got nice legs?"

Kit laughed. "Never you mind."

"Just wondered."

Titus's eye for a girl was well known, and he had always liked 'a good pair of legs', but his devotion to Edie had been absolute, and in spite of the frequent anatomical enquiry he had never strayed. He had asked the question even when she was alive, to her annoyance and mock-embarrassment. She blamed it all on the fact that Titus's early days had been spent with the local butcher.

There were those in the village who regarded Titus Ormonroyd as coarse and crude, but he was a man of contradictions: always well-mannered with the ladies, and the life and soul of a party of men. He always had a fresh joke up his sleeve – the dirtier the better – and when a few pints had been downed in the Cockle and Curlew, he would whisper it in conspiratorial tones to the assembled company, his glass eye somersaulting at the juicy bits.

Titus made the tea, then sat with Kit at the table as Nell curled herself around her master's feet. "So how serious is it, this girl in Australia?"

Kit sipped his tea. "Too soon to say."

"That doesn't sound very good."

"Well, yes, it's serious, but I don't know whether I'm ready for that sort of commitment."

"Mmm." Titus looked at him curiously. "But you love her?"

Kit raised his eyes. "Of course I love her."

"Coming over here won't have helped much, then?"

Kit gazed into his mug of coffee. "You can say that again."

"My guess is you really want to sell up 'ere and go back there. Right?"

"Yes. I keep having visions of how it looks in Balnunga Valley. I can smell the bush. Feel the heat. It's only a few days since I was there – perfectly happy, cruising along with a nice girl for company, doing the sort of job I'm good at, reasonably well off, no worries. I just want to sell up everything here and bugger off back. This place is nothing to do with me."

"But you feel guilty about lettin' your dad down?"

"Yes."

"Can't really 'elp there, can I?"

"Nope."

"Give yerself time. You'll work it out in the end. No point in rushin' things. You might just as well settle yourself 'ere for a while until it's clear in yer head. Does yon lass in Australia mind?"

"Well, she's not exactly delirious."

"Good test."

"What do you mean?"

"If she's keen she'll wait."

"And what about me?"

"Maybe it'll help you decide about that commitment thing. How keen do you think you are?"

"What is this? The Spanish Inquisition?"

"Just tryin' to 'elp."

"I know." Kit rubbed his hands over his face, as though wiping away his worries. "What I really need is to forget about the whole thing for a few days. I've been thinking of nothing else."

"What you need is a bit of female company," said Titus, with a twinkle that was especially noticeable in his glass eye.

Kit laughed. "I think I've had enough of that!"

"No, not the two Land Girls. A bit of, you know . . . something to take your mind off things."

Kit looked reflective. "Actually, it's funny you should say that."

Titus looked at him sideways. "Why?"

"Met someone yesterday."

"Who?"

"Jinty O'Hare."

"Ha!" Titus beamed from ear to ear.

"What's she like?"

"Young Jinty? A cracker. Bit of a handful, though. Nice legs. If I were your age . . . well . . ." Titus shook his head. "Where did you meet 'er?"

"She was riding along the coastal path. Big grey."

"Seltzer," Titus said. "She was takin' a risk."

"What do you mean?"

"Well, your dad didn't really approve of her riding along there – not that he could stop her, it's a public right of way, and the two Land Girls never really liked her."

"Why not?"

"Jealousy, amongst other things. Your dad thought she was a bit flighty. Doubt if the Land Girls ever talked to her much, but they don't approve of huntin' and Jinty hunts, so . . ."

"What made her come along there, then, now that Dad's gone?"

"Can't imagine." Titus flashed him a wicked grin.

"Go on . . . you don't think . . . ?"

"Sizin' you up, I suppose. You're not a bad catch."

"Get away! She wouldn't be interested in me. She's far too good-looking." He saw her in his mind's eye, sitting on the grey, and felt the heat rising in his cheeks.

"Well, you're no oil paintin' but you're not exactly ugly as sin either."

"Well, she did say I could go and look at her horses."

"There you are, then. Too good to waste. Get off round there and ogle her 'orseflesh."

"You know," said Kit, draining his mug and leaning on his elbow, "you've not changed a bit in ten years."

"Glad to 'ear it," retorted Titus. "I should bloody well 'ope not."

The prospect of supper with Titus in the Cockle and Curlew rather than vegetarian fare and uneasy company in the kitchen of West Yarmouth Farmhouse left Kit feeling more buoyant than he had since his arrival.

He was about to bath and change when Elizabeth called him to take another phone call. She anticipated his question. "It's not from Australia."

"Oh."

"No. It's Dr Hastings." She gave him the handset, retreated to the kitchen and closed the door. Once more Kit seated himself at the bottom of the stairs in the draughty hall.

"Hello?"

"Mr Lavery?"

"Yes."

"Hastings. Your father's doctor. Look, I'm sorry to bother you, but I wonder if you could pop in and see me sometime in the next day or two? Nothing too serious. It's just about your father's body."

"Oh, yes. He wanted to leave it to science. I think he told you, didn't he? That's what he said in the letter he left for me."

"Yes. Exactly. It's just that there are slight complications. I'd rather not discuss it on the phone, but if you could pop in we should be able to clear things up fairly easily. Tomorrow morning, perhaps? Or this evening, if you prefer. I'll have finished surgery in about an hour. Come in then, if you like. We're in Farthing Lane."

"Yes. I remember."

An hour later, he was sitting opposite the large, untidy Dr Hastings in the large, untidy consulting room of the West Yarmouth practice.

Dr Hastings came straight to the point. "I'm afraid that we're not going to be able to comply with your father's wishes to leave his body to science."

"Oh?"

"No. The Department of Anatomy, er . . . no, Human Morphology, they call it now, at the local medical school won't take a body that has been the subject of a post-mortem. This means that your father will have to be either buried or cremated."

"I see."

The doctor hesitated, then looked down at the papers in front of him. "There's also another, more important reason why the body can't be used by the medical school."

Kit sat perfectly still, aware of a note of concern in Dr Hastings's voice.

"This isn't something that anyone except your father and I were aware of but as his doctor I had to share the facts with the coroner and, consequently, the medical school."

Kit looked questioningly at him.

"When did you last speak to your father?"

"At Christmas, I think."

"A long conversation?"

"No. Not really. He had to go – I forget why. I said I'd ring him again in the New Year and then . . ."

"When had you last spoken to him before that?"

Kit thought back, wondering why this was so important. "September or October."

"I see."

"Why does this matter?"

The doctor folded the file in front of him and looked up again. "Mr Lavery, under normal circumstances I would be careful about sharing such information with my patient, but in your father's case . . . well, he was a man who felt quite determined to face life and all its eventualities." He paused, then went on, clearly with a degree of reluctance, "Your father was suffering from Alzheimer's disease. The medical school can't accept a body when any form of dementia has been present – fears of CJD, the human form of mad cow disease." Dr Hastings saw the horror on Kit's face. "That most certainly was not what your father was suffering from. It's just that teaching hospitals prefer not to take any risks when dissecting cadavers so your father's body . . ."

Kit nodded. "The phone calls?"

"I wanted to know if you had detected any absentmindedness in recent conversations with your father. The disease had only lately begun to manifest itself."

"I didn't notice anything unusual."

"I'm sorry to have to tell you all this, but I felt you should know."

"Yes, of course."

"It can strike quite out of the blue," said the doctor, endeavouring to offer some consolation, "and it's no respecter of intellect. Your father was a fine man and a good friend. I'm so sorry."

"Thank you." Kit tried to appear grateful for the doctor's concern. "Did my father know that . . ."

"He knew he had the disease. He did not know that under such circumstances his body would not be useful to science. To be honest, neither did I until I made enquiries after his death."

"I see."

"I'll explain to the mortuary that you will be making arrangements. Is that all right?"

"Of course." Kit rose from the chair, juggling with his confused thoughts and the prospect of a funeral, which his father had tried so hard to circumvent. Rupert, who had thought of everything else, had failed to consider that the mind that had led him through life might let him down in death.

If only he had been here, perhaps he would have been able to help. The idea of his father ending his days in lonely isolation distressed him more than he could bear. If only.

He dined with Titus at the pub, and shrugged off his friend's concern that something might be wrong. The two men said goodbye at the door of the pub, each departing for his own bed. Titus knew better than to probe too deeply, but he understood that something had happened between the mug of tea at Quither Cottage and the steak and kidney pudding in the Cockle and Curlew.

Kit lay awake for hours, watching dove-grey clouds glide past the moon, sometimes hiding it altogether. The cold white glow came and went as he tried to come to terms with the fact that his father – the brightest, sharpest man he had ever known – had fallen victim to the cruellest of diseases.

The hands of the clock at his bedside were illuminated in the darkness as the clouds cleared once more. Ten past one – lunchtime in Australia. He slid out of bed, slipped on his father's dressing-gown, walked to the telephone and dialled the number.

Heather answered quite quickly. "Balnunga Valley Stud, hello?"

"It's me."

"Hello, me, how are you?"

"I'm OK."

"No, you're not. What's the matter?"

"Oh, just a bit down."

"What is it?"

"Just been to see Dad's doctor. Apparently he was suffering from Alzheimer's. Had been for a few months."

"Oh. Gosh, I'm sorry."

"I hadn't rung him for so long. I might have noticed if I had."

"You can't blame yourself. There's nothing you could have done."

"But there might have been."

"Don't be silly. How could you tell?"

She sounded impatient and he wanted reassurance, which she was giving in her brisk, no-nonsense fashion, but not in the way he needed it.

"I just wanted to tell you, that's all."

"Well, you musn't worry about it. Really, you mustn't. Anyway it's too late now."

"Yes." He was perched on the edge of the desk, looking at the pattern on the rug beneath his feet. "Too late."

"Promise me you won't worry."

"Yes. OK. Look, I'd better go. It's the middle of the night. I need some sleep." And then, as an afterthought, "What are you doing?"

"Just going out to a barbie at the Johnsons'. Nothing special."

"OK. Well, you take care."

"And you. Speak soon. 'Bye."

"'Bye. Love you . . ." But she had already hung up, and all he could hear was a continuous dialling tone in his ear.

Chapter 10:
Deadmen's Thimbles
(Digitalis purpurea)

There was no way Kit could keep it from Elizabeth and Jess. For a start there was a body to deal with. But he did not feel obliged to acquaint them with the main reason for the medical school's refusal to participate; the post mortem rejection would be enough. He brought up the matter over morning coffee. It came as a shock to both women.

"It's not right," protested Elizabeth. "Those were his wishes."

"Yes, but I can't make them take him."

Jess said nothing. Kit had become used to her moody silences now. He tried to be practical. "We have two choices – burial or cremation."

"Your father didn't want either," snapped Elizabeth.

Kit asked calmly, "You have an alternative?"

Elizabeth looked away and shook her head, though Kit had half expected her to suggest burial at sea.

Jess spoke for the first time. "I think we should bury him on the reserve. Quietly. He didn't want a funeral, or a fuss. We could – you know – lay him to rest on the edge of the Spinney. If we're allowed to."

Kit nodded. "Yes, I think I'd rather have him at home." The moment he had spoken he realized the implications of what he had said, and could have bitten off his tongue. Selling the reserve was difficult enough; selling it with his father's body interred within it was unthinkable. "But maybe it would be better . . ."

Elizabeth spotted her chance. "No, I think you're right. This is the best place for him, not some impersonal crematorium where he'd be just a name in a book."

"What about the churchyard?" asked Kit, in a last attempt to stave off what now looked inevitable.

"Full. They haven't buried anyone there for six years. It would have to be Lynchampton Cemetery."

Kit saw that any further discussion would be futile, and felt an uneasy mixture of emotions: relief that his father would be laid to rest on home ground, and despair at the added complications this would now present.

He could have sworn he caught Elizabeth smiling, but chastised himself for being heartless. His father would be buried in the ground he had tended, and that would be an end to it. He hoped.

They buried Rupert Lavery on a clear blue morning in the first week of March. The Spinney dripped with sulphur yellow catkins, and the first primroses, defying the chilly onshore breeze, pushed up through the tussocks of needle-like turf. The coffin was of oak, there were just three people at the graveside, and the two local gravediggers went about their task with quiet efficiency.

Kit watched silently as the coffin was lowered into the grave. He had thought he was coming to terms with his father's death, but the ceremony revived the feelings he had struggled with over the last week, and he gritted his teeth to keep control.

Jess suffered from no such restraint. As Rupert's body was lowered into the earth she sobbed into a handful of soggy tissue. Elizabeth stood in a long black coat with her eyes closed, her expression giving little away, but her knuckles white as she dug her nails into her palms.

As the coffin came to rest in the bottom of the grave, Elizabeth opened her eyes and took from her coat pocket a small notebook. She opened it and began to read:

> "He leaves no mark, the man on earth,
> To cause rejoicing at his birth,
> Unless that mark be growing still
> When he is laid 'neath yonder hill.
> If at his death they cannot see
> The branches of a sky-bound tree,

Whose roots he laid in leafy soil
When but a sapling, then his toil
Will count for nought in hill and dale
And vivid memory fade to pale.
But were that life to nature giv'n
Then man on earth createth heav'n
And heaven liveth evermore
Upon the tide-washed leafy shore."

Kit looked up as the final words fell upon the chilly air, and saw Jess's face screwed up in pain. He put his arm around her shoulder and she leaned into him and wept.

Elizabeth, her own eyes brimming, slipped the book back into her pocket and impatiently blew her nose. As the gravediggers shovelled the stony cliff-top loam into the hole, the three mourners walked back to the farmhouse in silence, with the sound of stones falling on oak ringing in their ears. The sun slipped behind a grey cloud, and an hour later it was raining hard.

Kit watched the rivulets of water shimmying down the pane of his father's study window. Tomorrow he would plant a tree at the head of the grave, and see about a memorial stone. Just a small one. His father would not have wanted anything ostentatious, and neither did he, but he had to make sure that anyone who came after would know just where Rupert Lavery was buried.

What do you do after a funeral? Sit quietly for the rest of the afternoon reflecting on a life well lived? Partake of a 'lovely ham tea' and gossip about the dear departed in northern tradition, or try to get on with your life? Kit opted for the latter. He took Titus's advice, and went to call on Jinty O'Hare, hoping that neither Jess nor Elizabeth would get wind of it.

When he arrived at the stables at Baddesley Court she was not to be found. The rain had stopped now, and weak sunshine caught the cobbles outside the stables, making them glisten as though they had been lacquered.

"Can I help you?" The voice was female, but robust.

"I'm looking for Jinty. Is she out?"

"Due back any time. Out with Allardyce. Hang around if you want." Sally's face broke into a smile. Kit looked at her – a stout dumpling of a girl with leg-of-mutton thighs encased in grubby fawn jodhpurs, and topped by a black and white Fair Isle sweater. Her plump cheeks were the colour of Victoria plums, her hair short and dark brown. She carried a bucket and a shovel. "I'm just clearing up. Have a look round. She won't be long."

"Thanks." Kit felt uneasy, but walked along the row of neat boxes looking at the inmates. He recognized the grey leaning out of his stable, and the horse recognized him. Seltzer whickered as he came close, and threw up his head in greeting. "Hello, boy." He patted the horse's neck and rubbed his nose. A handsome gelding, perhaps six years old. Some Arab blood in him, about a quarter, he guessed. Spirited, but not too much of a lunatic.

His thoughts were interrupted by the sound of hooves clip-clopping into the yard. He looked round to see Jinty on a statuesque chestnut gelding, her cheeks flushed, her hair neatly netted beneath the black velvet hard hat.

She dismounted at the corner of the stable block, brought the reins over the horse's head and led it towards him. She stretched out a gloved hand in greeting and smiled a smile that took his breath away.

"Hi! Glad you could make it. Phew! Bit out of breath. He's a handful, this one."

"I can see that. Irish?"

"Me or the horse?"

Kit laughed.

"Yes to both. Boherhue Boy's Irish, too," she pointed to the stable at the far end where he could see the head of a bay, "but not Seltzer."

"Bit of Arab in him?"

"Yes. Very good!" She looked impressed, and curious.

"About a quarter?"

"Exactly a quarter."

"Age?" enquired Kit.

"You tell me."

"Six?"

"Seven. Not bad."

"I do my best."

Jinty looked to right and left. "Have you seen Sally?"

"End stable."

Sally stuck her head out. "You looking for me?" She was trying to suppress a grin – not very successfully.

"Can you unsaddle him and sort him out? I'll show Kit round."

"Yes, ma'am!" Sally tugged at an imaginary forelock, and Jinty shot her a mock frown.

"Just three?" asked Kit, pointing to the horses.

"Hunters, yes, but there's an old cob – Patsy – at the end there by the barn and Norman's a Connemara pony. I rode him when I was little."

"The Irish are out in force here, then?"

"Got to stick together, especially this side of the water." She took off her hat, tugged at the hairnet, and her fair curls bobbed free. She shook her head to let the fresh air reach her scalp, and when she looked up at him Kit felt again the scrutiny of the pale sea-green eyes.

"So, how are you doing? Getting used to the ladies?"

"Slowly. So do you . . . er . . . spend all your time looking after this lot?"

"They're a demanding bunch."

He noticed the gentle lilt in her voice, the white teeth and the clear complexion, made rosy by her afternoon's exertions. She was quite tall, her long legs encased in jodhpurs, but the white Aran sweater she was wearing, as she had been the first time he saw her, hid her upper contours. She was, quite simply, the most devastatingly good-looking woman he had ever met.

"Tea?"

"Mmm?" He was lost in his thoughts.

"Cup of tea? I'm gasping. Come along to the tack room."

Its walls were hung with framed photographs of horses and hounds, its roof timbers decorated with rosettes. Gleaming bridles and harnesses hung from hooks, shining saddles sat on stands as regimented as in an army barracks, and all around was the general clutter of everyday stable life – boot jacks, New Zealand rugs and numnahs – and the air was rich with a mixed aroma of saddle soap, horse liniment and pony nuts.

Jinty walked to the sink in the corner, filled the electric kettle and set about making tea. Kit asked how long she had lived at Baddesley Court, and she told him what had happened to her parents, about her adopted uncle and aunt, and the horses she looked after. They sat beside each other on the slatted bench that ran down one side of the tack room, and he listened as she told him the story of her life.

Suddenly she turned to him and brightened. "Enough! What about you? Have you decided what to do with the reserve?"

"I haven't got much option but to sell. But I really do want it to be sold as a nature reserve – in fairness to Dad. Trouble is, that's not going to be easy, according to the estate agent. Arthur Maidment's interested in the land, but he doesn't want to farm it organically. Also, the estate is worth more if I sell house and land together. I've just got to find a buyer for the whole lot but I don't know if anyone will be interested."

"Oh, someone's bound to be interested, but I'm surprised you don't want to give it a go yourself."

He was surprised at her suggestion. "What do you mean?"

"It's a lovely bit of countryside. People would die for it. Why do you want to sell it?"

"I can't afford to keep it and, anyway, I have my own life to lead somewhere else."

"Well, you did have. But that could always change. Why be so set in your ways?"

Suddenly he was on the defensive, and from a different angle. He'd got used to thinking that he was doing his own thing, breaking away from tradition, and now this woman was suggesting that he was in a rut.

"But supposing it's not what I want?"

"How do you know what you want?" Her eyes sparkled as she teased him. "Why don't you take a bit of time to make up your mind? No sense in rushing."

He looked her straight in the eye. "You're the second person who's said that to me in two days."

"Must be some sense in it, then."

She unnerved him. Not only was she devastatingly attractive, she also had a way of looking at him that completely disarmed him. Suddenly he was laughing. "What is this – a tack room or a psychiatrist's consulting room?"

"We aim to satisfy all requirements." She peeped at him from under her long lashes, her mouth turning up at the corners, and he felt a frisson of excitement.

"Come out to dinner?" he asked.

"When?"

"Tonight." He could hardly believe he'd said it, but something inside goaded him on.

"Yes," she replied positively.

"Well, that's sorted out, then." He was conscious of trying to sound cool, when his mind was anything but. "I'll pick you up at about eight, but you're not to nag me any more."

"Nag? Me? I'm simply clarifying the range of alternatives open to you instead of allowing you to go your own blinkered way." And then, as an afterthought, "Though why I'm suggesting you do exactly what those two dreadful ladies would want you to do I have no idea."

"They're not dreadful," he admonished her. "They're just . . . single minded."

"Mmm. I'll give you – and them – the benefit of the doubt. Anyway, I'd better help Sally with the boys, otherwise I'll have a mutiny on my hands."

"You don't look a bit like Captain Bligh."

"No, but I'm just as demanding!" She winked, and disappeared, leaving Kit feeling like the champion of the world. But at the back of his mind something gnawed at his conscience.

Chapter 11: Kit Willow

(Salix triandra)

"Well?"
        "Don't ask."
"Dishy?"
"Unbelievably."
"And?"
"Dinner . . . tonight."
"You fast little–"
"He asked, not me." Jinty could not stop smiling.
"Some people have all the luck."
"Not all the time." Jinty was stuffing hay into a net. She looked across to where Sally was brushing Allardyce's flanks. "After last time, I think I deserve a bit of a break."
"Wonder what he's like in bed?"
"You have a one-track mind."
"Mmm. Lovely, isn't it?"
Jinty hung up the hay-net. "You OK, then? I'd better go and get myself sorted out."
"It's only four o'clock!"
"I know, but I want to take a bit of trouble. 'Bye!" She waved ostentatiously, and left Sally to carry on grooming Allardyce, muttering under her breath balefully.

When Kit got back to West Yarmouth Farmhouse the two women were waiting for him in the kitchen. It was clearly a deputation.

551

"We'd like a word," explained Elizabeth, motioning him to a chair. "Sorry about this, but we thought it best to clear the air."

Kit decided to come clean. "Look. I'm sorry, but it's just that–"

Elizabeth interrupted, "Please don't say anything. Jess and I have had a chat and we've decided that we must apologize for not being . . . as understanding as perhaps we should have been."

Kit wondered if he was hearing things. "I'm sorry?"

"We realize that you must be given time to get over what's happened. As you know, Jess and I are totally committed to the reserve and it's sometimes difficult to understand why other people don't feel quite the same as we do. Naturally, we hope you'll eventually see it that way," she did her best to smile, "but we know that the loss of your father must have been a great shock and we want to say that we're sorry if we've appeared less than welcoming. It's just that . . . well . . . it was a great shock to us too. And a great loss."

Kit looked at the two of them, unsure what to say. Jess sat at the table. As his eyes caught hers she offered him the glimmer of a smile, before looking down in her customary fashion.

"Yes. Yes, of course. Look, I don't quite know how to say this." He tried to marshall his thoughts, having been given no time to get his act together or work out what he needed to communicate to them.

"I have to admit that selling the estate is what I plan to do. I have some savings of my own, which would help to pay the inheritance tax, but I would still have to sell part of the estate simply to keep our heads above water if I decided to stay here – and I don't know if that would yield enough to keep the place going. I know how much the reserve means to you, and I don't want you to feel that you're no longer a part of it. If it is sold, there is no reason why you both shouldn't carry on working here – so long as whoever buys the estate wants it that way." He paused, looking at the two women, both of whom were doing their best to meet his eye but finding it difficult. "But it will be a couple of months, maybe more, before probate comes through, and I can't do anything until that happens, so please don't think I'm not concerned about you or the reserve."

Elizabeth made to protest but Kit raised his hand.

"I've arranged for you to be paid, too," he said. "You can't work for nothing for ever. It's not much but it might help."

Jess's mouth opened, but no words came out.

"I have great feelings for West Yarmouth. It's where I was brought

552

up. It was as much a part of my life – *is* as much a part of my life – as it is of yours and I won't see it torn to pieces. But I have to decide what I want to do and where I want to be. You've both chosen to be here. I haven't. You both work here because that's what you want in life. I envy you both. I've yet to find out what I want in my life, but it has to be something that satisfies me as well as being true to the memory of my father, because if it wasn't then I'd be living a lie. However noble that is, it's a waste of a life. Is that fair?"

Both the women were looking at him now. Jess's eyes were brighter than he had seen them before. She nodded, and for the first time since they had met she kept looking at him.

Elizabeth spoke first. "Yes. You're quite right." The words were measured, not warm but compassionate. He felt that at last he had transmitted to them something of the quandary in which he found himself. He also hoped that they realized his motives were no longer entirely selfish; that in spite of wanting to make his own way in the world, he was not prepared to sacrifice their lives or his father's work on the altar of personal progress.

He had finished his speech – his policy statement – and now he felt a fraud, as though he'd made excuses for his behaviour. What made it worse was that he was about to go out to supper with the niece of the local Master of Fox Hounds. He felt that Jess and Elizabeth had probably had enough for one day. He said quietly, "So there we are. I'll let you know the moment anything happens, and I won't do anything without discussing it with you, I promise."

Elizabeth was almost embarrassed. "Well . . . that's . . . very kind."

"Thanks," Jess said gratefully.

"Er, I'm out to supper tonight."

"Of course." Elizabeth nodded.

"So . . . I'll see you later." He smiled at them, left the kitchen, climbed the stairs and went to his room. There, he heaved a sigh of relief.

All manner of thoughts ran through Kit's mind on the short drive to Baddesley Court. What had he been thinking of? What about Heather? It was just a bit of fun, that was all – entertaining company. Heaven knows, he was ready for that. He arrived at Baddesley Court at five to eight. He'd booked a table at the George and hoped she'd approve.

He rang the bell at the imposing front door, which was opened by a harassed-looking woman in a flour-dusted blue gingham apron, her salt-and-pepper hair doing its best to escape from the bun into which it had been crafted.

"Hello, Mrs Flanders."

"Good heavens above! Kit Lavery! How are you! Come in. I'll tell the master you're here."

"I'm not here to see the master. I'm here to collect Jinty."

"Oh, I see. Goodness! Well, come in."

Kit tried not to look embarrassed. Mrs Flanders had been cook-housekeeper for the Billings-Gores ever since he could remember. She was a kindly soul and a good cook, but always seemed to be chasing her tail. She closed the door, then stood and looked at him, her hands on her hips and her tea-towel over her shoulder.

A gruff voice from a room across the hall interrupted her inspection. "What is it, Peggy? Mmmmm?"

Sir Roland came out of the library to see the cause of the commotion. "Good Lord! Well I never! What?" He strode up to Kit and pumped his hand. "Good to see you. Looking well, eh? Mmm? Very well."

"Good to see you, sir."

"Drink before you set off, eh?"

"No, thanks, I'd better not. Hire car. Better ration myself."

"Yes. Yes, of course."

A distant scuffling down the hall betrayed the arrival of two yapping balls of fluff followed by Charlotte Billings-Gore clad in lavender wool.

"Kit! How lovely to see you." She offered a cheek and pecked the air on either side of Kit's head while the canine delinquents played tag at his feet.

Kit heard footsteps descending the stairs, and turned to see Jinty dressed entirely in black – narrow trousers and a tight woollen jumper. His mouth fell open.

"You all right?" asked Jinty.

He gulped. "Yes. Fine. You look . . . so . . . different."

"I should hope so. I scrub up well, you know." She flashed him a smile.

Her hair was fresh-washed and bouncy. Her eyes shone under long dark lashes. Her lips glowed. She looked stunning.

Roly and Charlotte stood side by side, and a wry smile crossed Charlotte's lips. "You both look rather lovely," she remarked.

Kit, who had little to choose from in the way of a wardrobe, had found a pale blue shirt and moderately smart navy crew-necked sweater in his father's chest of drawers. The navy blue R. M. Williams trousers and black boots he'd brought with him hopefully didn't look too bad.

Jinty eyed him. "Shall we go?"

He felt himself colouring. "Ready when you are."

Jinty kissed her uncle's cheek, waved at her aunt and led the way across the hall to the door. "Your car or mine?"

"Oh, I'll drive, provided you don't mind a hire car."

"What've you got?"

"A yellow Fiat Punto."

Jinty raised her eyebrows.

"It's the best they could do at short notice. I can have a bigger one next week, if I want."

"Well, there's an offer you can't refuse." She closed the front door and they walked to the car.

"Where are we going?"

"The George. OK?"

"Ah!"

"Sorry?"

"Oh, it's just that that's where my last man gave me the Spanish fiddler."

"The what?"

"El Bow – the brush-off. Haven't been back since."

Kit felt awkward. "Would you rather go somewhere else? I can cancel. They only just squeezed us in anyway."

"No. I'll have to get over it and the sooner the better. It doesn't matter, really it doesn't." She put her hand on his arm and squeezed it. The tang of her perfume caught his nostrils.

The George Hotel in Lynchampton was a deceptive building. From the outside it was well proportioned with Georgian casement windows and stone quoins to the corners of the brickwork, but the paintwork was battered and peeling, the swinging sign faded and creaking on its hinges. The inside, however, was all casual, if studied, elegance. Kit and Jinty were seated in the corner of the packed restaurant. Eyes followed them as they snaked their way between the tables, though neither of them noticed.

They ordered crispy duck and salad leaves as a starter, until Jinty said that it was boring if they both had the same and plumped for scallops. They decided on plaice and monkfish as their main courses, and a bottle of Pouilly Fumé.

They talked about everything and nothing. Kit could hardly bear to take his eyes off her. He watched her as she talked, noticed how she used her hands, with their long, slender fingers, to make a point.

She saw how his brow knitted when he addressed a problem, how his eyes smiled even when his lips did not.

They shared a crème brûlée, with one spoon, and then came the coffee.

"This is where I was ditched last time I was here. Oh! I forgot the amaretto."

"Do you want one?"

"*No!*"

Kit looked directly at her. "Thanks for coming. I've really enjoyed it."

She looked back. "Me too. It was fun."

"And thanks. For not nagging. For not asking me what I'm going to do. And for not telling me what I *should* do."

"I wouldn't dream of it."

He reached across and stroked her cheek. She smiled. "Take me home?"

She invited him in. He accepted, not wanting to leave her until he had to, not wanting the evening to end. She took his hand and led him across the hall to the library, where the room was lit only by the last flickering embers of the log fire.

"The olds have turned in. Nightcap?"

"Small one. Scotch."

She smiled at him. "Irish."

He laughed. "All right, then."

She motioned him to sit on the overstuffed sofa in front of the fire, went over to the drinks cupboard and poured two Irish whiskeys into large glasses, then returned and handed one to him before slipping off her shoes and curling up at the other end of the sofa with her glass.

For several minutes they said nothing, just sipped their drinks and gazed at the burning logs. Kit looked across at her, then rose, took her glass from her and put it with his on the floor. He sat down next to her and put his arm around her shoulders.

Jinty looked into his eyes, silently, expectantly. He leaned forward and kissed her. Her lips were soft as down, her hand stroked the back of his head and her tongue crept into his mouth. They lost themselves in each other and their breathing became more intense.

She pulled away from him slightly. "I don't do this with everybody, you know."

"I should hope not," he whispered.

"I don't want you to think I'm some kind of floozy." She pushed his hair away from his eyes.

Kit bent to kiss her again and felt a powerful longing to make love to her in front of the fire. His hands caressed her back, her arms and her neck, and her teeth nipped gently at his lower lip. His arm was around her waist now, and her fingers ran through his hair. Finally he eased away from her. Jinty looked up at him expectantly and lay back on the sofa.

"I'd better go before I do something we'd regret in the morning," Kit said.

"Or, worse, not regret."

He pulled away and looked at her. "My father warned me about women like you."

She looked crestfallen. "But you wouldn't listen."

"No. Not always."

They kissed on the doorstep, and she watched him drive off into the night in the bright yellow Punto, unaware of the jumble of thoughts whirring in his head. As its rear lights disappeared from view she sighed, and smiled. Next time he would not get away so easily.

Chapter 12:
Love and Tangle
(*Trifolium campestre*)

What made him feel so guilty was that he did not feel guilty. He knew that he should, that he had let Heather down, but how could he regret or be sorry for what had happened last night? He could think of nothing but Jinty. Even the complications and convolutions of the estate were pushed aside in his mind as he replayed the image of her walking down the stairs at Baddesley Court or forking fish into her perfect mouth. And when they had kissed . . . He had experienced nothing like it in his life before. He half laughed to himself, not believing that he could feel like this – so overpowered by another human being. It was unreal. Overnight he had changed from a determined, single-minded yet rational man into a heap of tangled emotions. Single-minded but in another direction.

He closed the front door and walked across the stableyard to the pig-sty. Wilson was putting away a trough of mixed vegetable scraps that had once been Elizabeth and Jess's supper. She snorted and chomped her way though it, but raised her head at the sound of his voice.

"What do you make of it all, then, Wilson? Bloody complicated, eh?"

Wilson grunted, as if in agreement, and flicked around the rim of her mouth a long and particularly unappetizing potato peeling.

"It's all right for you. All you do is wait to be fed and watered. I tell you, when I come back I'm coming back as a pig."

"Me, too."

Kit nearly leaped over the wall of the pig-sty, and spun round to see Jess walking towards him with another bucket of scraps.

"You made me jump."

"Sorry. Just bringing Wilson's afters."

"Hasn't she had enough?"

"Nah. Got to keep her weight up, haven't we, old girl?" Jess tipped the contents of the bucket into the trough, and Wilson grunted in gratitude.

"What you doing today?" she asked, more brightly than he had heard her speak before.

He was caught unawares. His mind was so addled that getting up, getting dressed and getting out of the house had been about as much as he could cope with so far. He thought quickly. "Well, I need to sort out Dad's headstone – just a lump of granite to mark the spot – have a good look round the house, which I haven't done yet, and then I thought I'd walk the reserve on my own, just so that I can get the feel of it." It sounded pathetic but it was the best he could do.

"Could you help me with some electric fencing round by the orchard first? Only it's easier if there's two, and Elizabeth's down at the Wilderness putting up nest-boxes."

"Sure. What do you need electric fencing for?"

"We want to make a decent-sized vegetable garden. Elizabeth's fed up with buying stuff in the winter, so we thought we'd grow more of our own."

The sulky, tragic figure of the past few days had been replaced with a more buoyant one. The spiky orange hair seemed to have softened to an auburn shade. Her eyes darted here and there as she spotted a bird, or a patch of primroses. In spite of her appearance, she was clearly a child of nature who had found her true place in life. For the first time he could see why his father had taken her on.

"I still don't see why you need electric fencing."

"I want to turn Wilson out during the day. She'll clean the land up better than any spade, and then, when she's grubbed out all the weeds, I can fork it over in a few weeks' time and get sowing and planting."

"You doing it on your own?"

"Yeh. I told Elizabeth I wanted to. Never grown veg before. Fancied having a go. Got all the books. Think I can do it."

"Good for you."

He went with her to the stables where she loaded up a wheelbarrow with a roll of bright orange electric fencing, yellow, plastic-covered posts, and a power unit on a spike. She thrust a hefty car battery into his arms, flashed him a grin, and then said, "Follow me."

It took them the best part of two hours to rig up the fencing, by which time Kit had discovered more about Jess's early life. How her mother had run out on her father, who had beaten her regularly when he'd had a skinful. How she'd taken the two younger children with her, but left behind Jess, who was already too much of a handful. By the age of fourteen Jess had been up in court twice for shoplifting, been put into care and done soft drugs. She'd survived all this and finally fallen in with a group of dropouts who ran a commune in Wiltshire, but left when she found her life going nowhere. Her encounter with Rupert Lavery at the Lynchampton Hunt meeting had changed her life.

"I still don't understand how you met Dad at the hunt."

"He was talking to the huntsman."

"Titus?"

"Yeh. I was listening. Heard him speaking about the reserve. Went up and asked if I could have a look round. He was a bit wary at first. I mean, it's not surprising, is it?" She pointed at her hair and the studs in her ears and nose. "Don't look serious about conservation and that, do I? I'm everybody's idea of a hunt saboteur. Townie who knows nothing about the country, just going out for some fun and a bit of bother."

"And were you?"

"Suppose I was, really. Then I thought it was about time I got to know what it was about. I'd had enough with the lot in the commune. Too pissed out of their heads most of the time to know what was going on. I was with Dave, the leader, but he got a bit – you know – possessive. I saw things going the way they had with my mum and dad. So after your dad had shown me round I asked him for a job."

"And he said yes?" Kit asked incredulously.

"Not at first. Said he had no money to pay for more staff. I kept pestering him – nicely, of course – and said I'd work for nothing. In the end he agreed. Said I could live over the stables next door to Elizabeth."

"How did she take to all this?"

"She didn't. She had rows with him. Not that your dad ever argued.

I just thought I'd better keep me head down and do a good job and that in the end she'd come round."

"What happened?"

"She came round." She chuckled. "I learned it from your dad – stay calm, be single-minded, go about your business quietly, and there's every chance you'll succeed in what you want to do. Make a fuss and a noise and you get noticed, but it doesn't mean you'll achieve what you want to achieve."

Kit stopped hammering in the stake for the fencing. "You really believe that?"

"I know it. Just look at me."

The estate agent in Totnes had been insistent that Kit call in as soon as possible, so he appeared at the office that afternoon. The fresh-faced young man who was too eager to please, explained, "I wouldn't normally be so precipitate."

Kit thought what a pompous word it was. Why didn't he just say 'quick'?

"Only we have had interest expressed from a certain quarter."

There he goes again, thought Kit. Why does he have to be so mysterious?

"The party concerned . . ."

This is getting ridiculous . . .

". . . has expressed a wish to make an offer for the entire estate."

Kit was taken aback. "But we haven't put it on the market yet. You haven't even seen it."

The estate agent motored on. "This party is willing to wait, provided that they have an assurance that their offer will be accepted."

"What sort of offer?"

"I'm not in a position to say exactly, but it is likely that it would be in the region of one and a half million pounds."

Kit was stunned. That was around three million Australian dollars. After inheritance tax it would be more than enough to set up his own stud farm. Myriad thoughts flashed through his mind. He saw Jinty riding his string of horses. He saw a square stable block with a gilded clock on a cupola above the tackroom, neatly fenced paddocks and a sand-filled manège. The options seemed limitless. Here was a chance to go it alone, to achieve what he had always wanted to achieve: to run a stud founded on the best bloodstock available. To make a mark.

Then the cold hand of reason gripped him, and he asked, "What does the buyer intend to do with the land?"

"He is happy to keep it as it is." The estate agent smiled.

"The woodland – everything?"

"Yes. The surrounding land would still be farmed, and the woodland would probably be increased."

"Wow. It's just that I didn't expect–"

"Well, I did think it might be possible to sell it as a whole, and it only took a few enquiries to confirm my suspicions."

Kit stood up. "I shall need to think about this. I can't give you a decision now. And I shall need guarantees that the reserve will continue to be managed on existing lines."

"Yes, of course. I'll be in touch, but I just thought you ought to know this as soon as possible."

"Yes. Thank you." Kit left the agent's office in a daze. Finding the car in the car park took him a good fifteen minutes, in spite of the fact that it was bright yellow.

The estate agent was well pleased, as was the prospective purchaser when he phoned and gave him the news that the vendor had seemed agreeable.

"He has asked to be given time to make his decision, but I think we can safely say that your offer will have priority, Mr Bickerstaffe."

It did not take the agent long to work out the extent of his commission on such a deal. And there would be no need to print out so much as a brief description of the property.

Buoyant. The market was definitely buoyant.

The drive back to West Yarmouth passed in a blur as he mused on the likely outcome of events and the options ahead of him. He could sell up and go back to Australia. But what about Jinty? Would she come with him? His imagination went into overdrive as he steered the car down country lanes, the tall Devon hedges blinkering his view even more than usual until, on the outskirts of Lynchampton, he saw two horses in front of him. He recognized them immediately, and their riders – Jinty and Sally.

He overtook slowly, then pulled up some yards further on and got out of the car. Eventually the horses drew alongside, Jinty in a tweed hacking jacket, and Sally in her uniform of black and white Fair Isle.

"Hi!" he greeted them.

"Hi! Still in bright yellow, then?" teased Jinty, pointing at the car with her riding crop.

"'Fraid so." He nodded at Sally.

The two riders fought to control their powerful mounts.

"Could have changed it today, only in all the excitement I forgot," Kit went on.

"What sort of excitement?"

"Might have found a buyer."

"For the reserve?"

"Yup."

Sally looked across at Jinty, who was reining in an impatient Allardyce.

Kit saw the look she gave Sally. "Confidential, though. Not a word, please."

"Course not."

"You fancy celebrating? Tell you all about it."

"Love to." She flashed him a smile that had a hint of unease about it – was this the beginning of the end? "Come round at about eight?"

"OK."

"I'll cook you some supper."

At this point Allardyce had had enough and started turning in his own circle, pulling at the bit and unnerving Seltzer.

"Steady, steady!" Jinty kicked him back into line.

Kit grasped the situation. "I'll get out of your way. See you later."

He ran ahead of them to the car, jumped in and took off down the lane.

At the turning into the field, Jinty and Sally let the impatient animals have their heads and galloped off. At the top of the hill the pace slowed, as the riders had known it would. They pulled up by a clump of beeches.

Fighting for breath, Sally looked across at Jinty and grinned. "Almost as good as sex!"

It took Jinty a few moments to catch her breath. "Almost!" she agreed.

Roly and Charlotte were out for the night – staying with Roly's brother in Dorset. Jinty greeted Kit at the door, clad in her red cashmere sweater and black trousers. Again, the sight of her made his heart beat faster. He could see the contours of her body clearly through the soft wool of the sweater and the tailored cut of the trousers.

She cooked supper in the kitchen while they chatted and drank a bottle of chilled Frascati. Then she loaded trays and they took the lemon chicken and stir-fried vegetables into the library. Kit filled her in on the estate agent's offer.

"So will you accept it?"

"It'll be hard not to."

She picked up her wine. "I hope you don't."

He looked surprised and stopped eating. "Why?"

"What happens if you sell? What will you do?"

"I'll have enough money to start my own stud."

"Where?"

"I don't know. It all depends."

She gazed at him and said, quite calmly, "On what?"

"On what happens."

She put down her glass and took his tray, bending down to place it on the floor. Then she sat up and fixed him with her gaze. "So what do you want to happen?"

He looked at her for what seemed like an age. It was as if every sense in his body was heightened, as though he was looking at life though a magnifying-glass. He reached out with both hands and pulled her towards him, firmly but gently. She wrapped her arms around him and they kissed with a passion he had neither known nor felt before.

The closeness of her was overwhelming him with a longing to be a part of her. She rolled on top of him and kissed his cheek, his neck, his forehead. Then she eased away, looking intently at him with her sea-green eyes, before bending down to him once more and slipping her soft, sweet tongue into his mouth. He felt himself stir as they fell from the sofa to the floor. He stroked her hair, kissing her brow, her temple, her chin, then moved his hand down over her shoulder to her breast. She sighed.

She moved her own hands from his back to his waist, then reached down and stroked him between his legs. He let out a brief moan and arched his back before pulling away from her slightly and staring at her as though on the brink of a precipice. For several seconds they lay transfixed by each other's proximity, their breathing deep and rapid, their eyes searching for some mutual signal, until they fell upon each other once more. He pulled the scarlet sweater over her head to reveal full, pale breasts restrained by white lace, and she struggled with his belt.

Never had he felt so overcome with longing. He kissed her breasts, then her soft, flat stomach while she stroked him and arched her back with pleasure, moaning softly.

He reached down for her and she let out the smallest of screams, writhing and murmuring with ecstasy.

Time after time they came to the edge of delirium, until finally in an unstoppable torrent of passion they gave themselves to each other completely. Kit felt as though all life and breath had been squeezed from him. In one massive surge of emotion he threw back his head and cried out, only to turn back to her and see the look of pure pleasure on her face. He held her as the firelight played on their entwined bodies, until their pounding heartbeats subsided and the burning logs were no more than ruby ashes.

Chapter 13: Bread and Cheese and Cider

(Anemone nemorosa)

Jinty woke first, to find herself entangled with Kit. She lay quite still, looking at his head, half submerged in the soft, white pillow. The sun, slanting through a chink in the curtains, caught his fair curls and turned them to gold. The same colour as her own hair. She lay gazing at him, listening to his slow, regular breathing.

He stirred. His eyes flickered open and for a moment he looked confused. Then his mouth curled into a gentle smile and he lifted his hand and stroked her cheek. For fully ten minutes they lay there, breathing softly, in perfect harmony.

Then she slipped out of bed and walked over to the window, pulled back the curtains and let the brilliant sunlight flood the room. The rays of early-morning light dazzled him and shone around her tall, curvaceous figure. She stretched her arms upwards and the bright, white shafts of sunshine gleamed and danced around her.

He watched, transfixed, as she turned towards him. Then he got up, went to her, and took her in his arms.

It was another hour before he left Baddesley Court and made his way back to West Yarmouth. His feet did not once touch the ground.

By the time Roly and Charlotte returned from their awayday, Jinty was mucking out the horses, and Kit was away with the fairies.

The weather matched his mood. March is not noted for its clemency, but as he sat on a fallen tree on the edge of the Wilderness and gazed

566

out over Tallacombe Bay he might have been on the Côte d'Azur. The sunlight glinted on the crests of wavelets far below, and a pair of oyster-catchers wheeled over his head, their plaintive 'kleep-kleep' echoing over the water.

He watched them, buffeted by the wind, until they alighted on the smooth, biscuit-coloured shore and began prodding the sand with their rosy bills. How different it all was from the dry, grassy plains of Balnunga Valley. How green the fields. How cold and fresh the sea. How . . . homelike. The feeling caught him unawares. He turned his head abruptly to the left, and the beauty of the landscape struck him like a hammer-blow.

Behind him, the purple twigs of the Wilderness, relieved by the snow-white blossom of blackthorn and the pale lemon of hazel catkins, rose like a plump cushion on the cliff top. The dense, fine grasses that made up the sward beneath his feet were now speckled with primroses. The scent of an early spring drifted up the Spinney, and the tumbling waters of the tiny Yar whispered through the Combe far below.

Suddenly he ran forward and began to climb down the cliff path towards the beach, the sound of waves crashing on to the shore growing louder as he descended. As the path zigzagged down, the wind dropped and the tang of salt spray caught his nostrils and made the hairs on the back of his neck stand on end. On reaching the soft, honey-coloured sand he began to walk towards the water, but stopped suddenly at the sight of a figure emerging from behind the sea-washed rocks ahead of him. They jutted up from the sand like some massive shark's fin, gnarled and black, and hung with glistening bladderwrack.

It was Jess. She had her back to him and was naked, her clothes tossed over the rocks. She walked towards the waves, slowly at first, then began to run. Kit, torn between leaving her to her morning swim and embarrassing her by being seen, slipped into a tall but narrow fissure at the foot of the cliff. He watched, aware of the voyeuristic conclusions that could be drawn from his actions, and yet powerless to come up with an alternative solution.

Jess dived into the first breaker that tumbled on to the shore. Kit watched as her shapely legs disappeared into the foaming water. It seemed an age before her head emerged from the surf and she shook it to clear the salt water from her eyes. He pulled back into the safety of his hiding place as much as the narrow aperture would allow, and felt guilty at being a party to her private bathing. She did not see him.

For several minutes her head bobbed on the water as she floated among the waves. He could see the rapt expression on her face, the pure pleasure of relaxation among the elements, in spite of the icy chill of the sea. Eventually she neared the shore. He wanted to look away, but could not. He watched, mesmerized, as she walked out of the sea – first her strong shoulders, then the small, rounded breasts, smooth stomach and slender legs. She looked completely at home as droplets of water trickled down her. He watched as she towelled herself dry, pulled on her clothes, then began to walk across the sand towards the cliff path. Finally, certain that she had gone and ashamed of his curiosity, he walked back up the slope towards the farmhouse and thought about where his future might lie. With Heather or with Jinty? The vision of Jess punctuated his thoughts. Did he want to be in England or Australia? He saw her rising from the waves again and felt a tightening of his stomach muscles. He fought, consciously, to get the image out of his mind, but it was too powerful to erase and, he had to admit, too enjoyable. For the first time since his arrival, the place of his birth seemed to be exerting a pull – sentiment? Or a true sense of belonging? And Jinty – infatuation or the real thing?

The path that had once seemed so obvious was now as obscure as the view through the thicket of gorse that caught at his jacket and filled his head with the scent of coconut.

Maybe soon the way through the woods would become clearer.

The farrier was satisfied that both Allardyce and Seltzer were fine in the hoof department, and the vet, dropping in for coffee on his way to another patient, had complimented the Master of Fox Hounds on the overall health of his beasts. It was a state of affairs that left Roly Billings-Gore in good heart. In two days' time the meet would set off from Baddesley Court and he'd have two fit and healthy mounts. He patted Allardyce's neck, thrust a Polo mint into his mouth on a flattened hand, and went off to do the same for Seltzer.

"Uncle Roly!" He turned to see Jinty walking towards him with a numnah and a saddle over her arm. She looked troubled. "Are you riding today?"

"Ah. No. Into town. Man to see about the lead on the roof."

"Oh."

He looked at her questioningly. Roly might have been everyone's idea of an unworldly country colonel, but his observational powers were as sharp as a surgeon's scalpel. "Everything all right?" he asked.

"Mmm?" Jinty had opened the door of Seltzer's stable and was beginning to tack him up.

"You look . . . er, preoccupied."

Jinty looked around and smiled at him. "Sorry. Just a lot to think about that's all."

"Nothing else?"

"No. Nothing else." She fastened the girth around Seltzer's belly, checked the length of the stirrup leathers and led the horse out of the stable into the yard before mounting "I'll take Seltzer out now, then come back for Allardyce. Sally's taking Boherhue Boy out this afternoon."

"Jolly good. He's looking fighting fit."

"Yes, he's a fine boy, aren't you, Seltzer?" She leaned down and patted the horse's neck. "See you later. Have fun with the lead man."

Roly watched her go. He could not put his finger on it, but there was something strange about the girl. She didn't seem herself at all. Not unhappy, quite the reverse, but certainly distracted. He strolled across the yard and offered the remains of the Polos to Norman and Patsy before reluctantly shambling off towards the house.

Jinty walked the horse down the drive of Baddesley Court and turned left for a few hundred yards along the Salcombe Road before leaving the thoroughfare and turning down a lane. Flecks of green were beginning to speckle the plum-purple twigs of hawthorn. She urged Seltzer into a trot and felt the fresh morning air biting into her lungs. Images from the night before swam in her head. She could see him standing in front of her, feel his breath again, smell his skin. She had enjoyed making love to other men, but last night. . . . And yet he was talking about selling up and leaving. How could he even think about that when they were so good together?

Seltzer blew loudly and flared his nostrils, then tossed his head.

"All right, you can have a run in a minute. Hang on." The pair trotted on down the lane in the direction of the sea towards a field with a wide track where she knew she could let him have his head.

Kit had left her feeling alive with passion.

"Ohhh!" she cried. "What to do?" The horse shook his head again
and his tack jingled. "It's all right for you," she exclaimed, through her
deepening breaths. "You're cut out to be a bachelor. Simple for you.
You can look all you like but you can't touch." Then she thought
about what she had said, and remembered, again, the closeness of the
night before. "Sorry, old boy. Not fair, is it? Just not fair."

At the end of the lane the road petered out under an old oak tree,
and a gap in the fence led on to a farm track alongside a field of winter
barley, whose green shoots perforated the damp brown earth. She
turned Seltzer on to the track, squeezed with her legs, pushed her heels
down and let him go.

Seltzer needed no encouragement. She slackened the reins and let
him fly. As he got into his stride, she felt the adrenaline rising within
her, felt the air rushing past her ears and the thrill of the gallop. The
ground began to slope upwards but the horse powered on. She felt the
sinew and muscle beneath her, could hear the rhythmic pounding of
hoofs on firm ground, and as always felt elated.

Carefully she steered him around obstacles – a fallen branch, a
pothole in the track – taking firm but gentle action with her knees
and her hands. Seltzer, for all his speed and power, seemed to listen to
her unspoken instructions while he careered on at full tilt.

The ground began to even out now and Seltzer slowed to a canter,
blowing hard. Jinty was panting too: the horse might have done the
bulk of the work, but she had expended a great deal of energy in
staying aloft and guiding him across the uneven ground. By a hedge at
the top of the field she pulled him up and patted his neck. Her cheeks
were flushed with the exertion of the ride. She laughed and ruffled
Seltzer's mane, as a thought came to her. "You're almost as good as he
is, but not quite," she assured him.

Kit's sense of purpose was no better defined than Jinty's. He spent the
morning walking the reserve, reacquainting himself with the lie of the
land, and looking over the fields that were let to Arthur Maidment.
They were well tended, but Rupert Lavery would not have left his land
in the charge of a slack farmer. Much of the land was given over to
pasture, on which grazed flocks of Devon Closewool sheep. Kit
watched as the lambs nudged and fought for their mothers' milk, their
tails shaking like catkins in the breeze.

Other fields grew turnips, but there was one, in a sheltered hollow, in which rows of women were bent double. Kit walked along the wire stock fence that led towards this sheltered patch of land, and saw that they were cutting daffodils. Among the glaucous blue-grey spears of foliage, the acid yellow buds sat plump and firm in their papery sheaths. The women worked deftly, slicing through each stalk with a knife, bundling the flowers together with elastic bands and dropping them into trays, which were carried to a trailer in the far corner of the field. Devon daffodils. Kit wondered what the field would look like if they had been allowed to flower where they stood, and turn the blue-green sea of foliage into a cloth of gold.

His reverie was broken by the voice of Arthur Maidment. He had come up behind Kit, having walked along the other side of the fence.

"Nice sight, eh?"

Kit started. "What? Oh, yes – sorry. You made me jump."

Maidment carried on. "Want to grow more of 'em next year. Thinkin' of turnin' that field over to 'em as well."

"I see."

"You any nearer decidin' what to do?" Arthur Maidment was not a likely candidate for Diplomat of the Year. Having spent a lifetime refining his brusque approach, he now had it honed to perfection in the manner of a well-sharpened machete. "I shall need to know soon."

"Yes." Kit was unwilling to share his knowledge with Maidment until the time came when he had to. To tell him now that he was unlikely to be able to buy the land might be burning his boats prematurely. He would play his cards close to his chest. Neither did he want Maidment informing the rest of the village as to what was about to happen. "You'll know as soon as I do, but there's a lot to sort out yet, I'm afraid."

"Lease is up soon, you know."

"Yes, you said when we last met."

Under Kit's direct gaze, Maidment shuffled off, grumbling gently under his breath.

Kit climbed the hill towards the farmhouse and reflected on the size of his inheritance-tax bill. If he managed to sell the farm and nature reserve for the sum intimated by the estate agent, he would have enough for his stud. But somehow his heart wasn't in it any more.

He used a wheelbarrow to take the headstone to the grave, which somehow seemed fitting. It was not a large piece of granite – barely two and a half feet by eighteen inches. Perhaps its size and the brevity of the inscription were the reason why it had been completed so quickly by the monumental mason in Lynchampton. Or perhaps the man had got on well with Rupert and didn't want to keep him waiting.

Kit did not tell Jess and Elizabeth that it had arrived. He wanted to perform this particular ceremony on his own. He pushed the unevenly balanced barrow down towards the Spinney; the two women were cutting down hazel coppice in the Wilderness and would not see him.

As he neared the grave he lowered the front of the barrow gently, and let the granite slab slide on to the soft grass, along with the spade. The patchwork of turf that covered the low burial mound would soon knit together, dampened by spring rain. He dug out a narrow trench at the head of the grave, then walked the stone towards it, slid in the base and heaved it upright. He eyed it to make sure it looked reasonably level, then pushed the stony earth back around the base with his foot and firmed it with his heel. With his hands he scrabbled around in the soil, levelling it and removing any large stones until, finally satisfied with his work, he stood up and looked at the stone and the legend it bore:

RUPERT LAVERY
1938–2000
WHO MADE
HEAVEN ON EARTH

He had not intended to have anything except his father's name and dates carved on the stone, but Elizabeth's words, read so quietly at the graveside, seemed almost to have written themselves into it.

He stood for several minutes, then turned and looked in the direction the stone faced. The sun was needling its way in one narrow shaft of brilliance through a dense welter of cloud to highlight the crinkled waves below.

Even the weather seemed to behave appropriately for his father. He turned back to the stone, which was no longer bare and grey. It was decorated at one corner with a splash of bright yellow. The first brimstone butterfly, woken from its winter hibernation by the warm Devon air, had settled to bask in the sunshine.

Kit watched as it batted its fragile sulphur wings to and fro, before fluttering off over the turf and away towards the Spinney. His father was no longer the master of all he surveyed; he was now just part of the scenery. Kit smiled to himself. Rupert would have liked that.

Chapter 14: Devil's Bit

(*Succisa pratensis*)

"Come 'ere, you daft bugger!" Titus Ormonroyd was out walking with Nell, while his horses, Mabel and Floss, and the hounds were left in the care of Becky, the kennelmaid. Titus was glad of a break. His tattered Barbour flapped in the breeze as he breasted the top of the cliff, and he held tight to his greasy tweed cap with one hand and his shepherd's crook with the other as Nell bounded ahead of him in search of rabbits.

He whistled, a short, piercing blast, and the dog turned at the cliff edge and came bounding back to him.

"You come over 'ere, come on. Stay away from that edge."

The dog, her bright pink tongue hanging from the side of her mouth, jumped up at his leg in response, but Titus met her nose with the flat of his hand and a stern "No!" Nell, now wearing a crestfallen expression, put her tail between her legs and looked up at him with sorrowful eyes.

"Aw, don't look at me like that. You're not to jump up, right?"

Nell, sensing a breakthrough in the sympathy stakes, wagged her tail slowly and put her head down at his feet. Titus bent to stroke her and she rolled over on her back, her legs in the air and her paws folded in submission.

"You little tart – I should've called you Fanny, not Nell." He tickled the dog under the chin. "Come on!" The dog rolled over and on to her feet, then shot on ahead of him. It would be a few months yet before she was well trained enough to stay to heel and would not need to be put on the lead at any sign of a distraction.

Titus looked at his watch and at the darkening sky. A quarter to four. It would probably be raining by six. Time he turned back.

Jinty was tired. Having given Seltzer a good run for his money in the morning, she had gone out on Allardyce in the middle of the afternoon. Most days she could manage the two of them quite happily, but the activities of the night before had left her lacking her usual energy. As she walked the horse along the firm sand of the beach, her thoughts turned to Kit. Would he call her tonight? Should she call him? They had left each other without making any arrangements. It had not seemed necessary. But now she wondered what would happen. Where did they go from here?

Allardyce showed his impatience with the dull ride and yanked at the reins. Jinty read his thoughts. "Just a short one today, old lad."

Allardyce strolled on, nodding, seemingly picking up the vibes from his rider.

"Go on, then. We'll have a quick burst." The horse sensed the instruction through her body, and she hardly needed to move her limbs to have him bounding forward across the long, firm arc of sand that stretched around the bay. The tide was out, having left in its wake a wide crescent of fudge-coloured racetrack that Allardyce was only too happy to make use of.

As the beach buzzed by, Jinty relaxed her legs and allowed Allardyce to slow to a steady canter, then into a walk as she turned him up on to the narrow, sandy track that led through the lower dunes to the cliff top.

She did not see the dog running towards them – it was lost in the clumps of marram grass on the dunes – but Allardyce, normally well used to hounds, was startled by the sudden yapping at his hoofs. He whinnied and reared. Jinty fought hard to keep her balance and stayed in the saddle, only to have Allardyce turn in a half-circle and shoot off towards the steep cliff path ahead.

She struggled to hold him back, pulling alternately at the left and right rein, but Allardyce was having none of it: with the wind up his tail he bounded up the path like a mountain goat, trying to plant his hoofs among the rocks that speckled its flinty surface.

Titus, whose head had risen above the long grass, took in the scene at once and yelled at his dog. Nell, panicked by the fleeing horse, was only too willing to return to her master, skittering across the loose sand in the direction of his voice.

Jinty fought for control, trying to pacify Allardyce with her voice, which would only come out in stertorous bursts. "Steady, *steady!*" she gasped, as the horse clambered higher and higher. The beach had receded below them now, but the horse showed no sign of slowing down.

Titus stood among the dunes below and stared anxiously as horse and rider scaled the cliff path. His heart thundered in his chest as he watched Jinty endeavour to control her mount.

Gradually, the steep path began to flatten out, and the horse slowed a little. "Yes . . . yes . . . there's a good boy . . . Gently, gently . . ." Allardyce's pace was finally slackening and Jinty was succeeding in reining him in – until the horses's right foreleg struck a rabbit hole.

His head went down, his shoulder followed and Jinty was over his head, bouncing down the cliff like a rag doll.

On his return to the farmhouse a postcard was waiting for Kit. It was propped up on his father's desk against the pot of pencils. He bent down to look at the picture. It was the rear view of a couple of naked men standing on a stretch of white, sandy beach. 'Australian Beach Bums' was the caption. He smiled and turned over the card.

> Just a line to remind you of home. Bloody hot here but not complaining. Wackatee's colt is coming on well. It's taken us ages to name him but we've called him Sundance because that's what he seems to do. Went to the Johnsons' for supper. Great fun. Marcus is a good laugh and cheering me up. Wish you were coming back soon. Missing you and looking forward to hearing from you. Lots of love, Heath X

He turned the card over again and looked at the picture. Marcus Johnson was obviously doing his bit. He felt a pricking of jealousy, then chastised himself for his own misdemeanors. And anyway, Marcus had always had a soft spot for Heather, but she'd made it plain that he was not her type. So far, at least. He slipped the card into one of the pigeon-holes in the desk and did his best to forget about it before he showered and went downstairs to make himself some supper.

He sat at the kitchen table with a plate of cheese on toast and a mug of tea, wondering whether he should call Jinty, or whether he should leave it for a day.

Perhaps if he appeared too keen he would frighten her off. But, then, she had seemed as carried away as he had the previous evening. Surely she would be waiting for him to call.

He rang Baddesley Court, but there was no answer. Odd. Usually Mrs Flanders was there even if everyone else was out. He shrugged and hung up.

An hour later he left the house to go and call on her. He couldn't believe she wouldn't want to see him and wondered why the telephone remained unanswered. As he drove up the drive of Baddesley Court he saw the Billings-Gores' car draw to a halt outside the front door. Roly got out and glanced at the approaching vehicle. It was then that Kit realized something was wrong. Roly's face was drained of all colour and his expression was one of profound despair. Charlotte remained in the front seat, her head in her hands.

Kit stood at the foot of the hospital bed, trying to equate the prone, battered figure with the beautiful girl he had held in his arms. All feeling seemed to have left him, except for one of overriding concern for her life.

He walked round the bed and lowered himself slowly into the blue plastic chair beside her head, without taking his eyes off her. He looked at her arm lying still by her side, and at the pure white gauze that fastened the transparent tube to the back of her wrist. Only a short while ago she had been laughing and loving, now she lay still, her breathing slow and shallow.

He was afraid to touch her, afraid to speak. He just sat and looked at her, taking in the grazed face, the strapped and splinted arm raised up by a series of pulleys. He looked at her body, covered with the pale blue blanket, and wondered how badly it had been injured.

He gazed at her face, willing her to open her eyes and tell him that she was fine, that she couldn't wait to go home, that she would cook for him tomorrow. But she did not open her eyes. She had not opened her eyes for three days now. Perhaps tomorrow. He would wait. He would wait for as long as it took. He would tell her that he would stay for as long as she wanted.

The nurse was kind but firm. He really would have to go now. He asked to be allowed to stay a while longer. The nurse gave in and suggested just another half-hour, after which she thought he should get some rest.

An hour later she ushered him from the room. "Come back tomorrow. We'll take good care of her."

He looked at the woman in the dark blue uniform and white pinafore.

"What do you think?"

"We're still waiting to see."

"Could she still be all right?"

"We hope so. We'll do our best."

Kit turned and walked down the corridor. The nurse went back into the room where Jinty lay, and eased her fingers under the wrist of the still body. She checked the steady beat of the pulse against her watch, which said it was three o'clock in the morning.

She pushed a stray strand of hair back into the clip behind the girl's ear. Bald patches dotted her scalp, but the blonde curls would grow back, God willing, if all was well. The eyes of the patient flickered, then closed again, and the nurse made a note on the chart.

She looked out of the door at the retreating figure of the man who came to sit beside the girl's bed every day, and prayed that she would soon have good news for him.

"Perhaps tomorrow, my love," she murmured, and stroked the back of Jinty's wrist with her forefinger. "Perhaps tomorrow."

Chapter 15: Gracie Day

(*Narcissus pseudonarcissus*)

Roly could not settle to anything. He'd tried to busy himself on the estate but, like others around him, his mind was on nothing but Jinty. The house seemed quiet and cold; even when there was a roaring fire in the library and he and Charlotte came together for supper, a pall of sadness hung like a dark shroud over the evening. Jinty's smile and chatter were missing.

He poured himself a large whiskey. Charlotte came in and perched on the arm of the sofa, her face drawn and tired, her elegance overlaid by a despondency that robbed her of her usual sparkle. Roly turned round, startled to see her. He had failed to hear her come in and poked at his hearing-aid. It let out a piercing whistle, and he winced, poked again, then enquired as to the whereabouts of the dogs.

"In the kitchen. Didn't feel like falling over them tonight." She smiled wanly and took the proffered gin and tonic. "Oh dear."

"Yes." Roly nodded. "Oh dear." He took a large gulp of whiskey and rolled it around his mouth before swallowing and exhaling loudly. "Still no news, then?"

"Nothing."

"What's the verdict?"

"The longer it goes on the more difficult things become."

"Mmm." Roly gazed at the flames licking around the logs. A spark spat out on to the rug and he trod on it, then bent down and threw a tiny splinter of charred wood back on to the fire. "A spark. That's what we need. A spark."

Charlotte said nothing, but the tears welling in her eyes spilled into the small lace handkerchief she pulled from her sleeve. Her husband walked over and cradled her head in his arm. "Oh, now, now," he whispered. "Where's all this come from? Mmm?" He rocked her gently as she sniffed back the tears then blew her nose.

"Been holding it all in, I suppose. Sorry."

"Ssh . . ." He stroked the top of her head.

"Oh, Roly. What a to-do."

"Mmmm. Yes. A real to-do."

"If only . . ."

"No, no. No if-onlys. Come on. Got to hold up. Be positive. Think positive."

"I know, but it's been three days now . . ."

"Yes . . . Any news of the lad?"

Charlotte brightened. "Goes in every day. Stays far too long. The nurses are worried about him. Doesn't say much."

"Mmm. Understandable." He sipped at his drink.

"Apparently the two women at West Yarmouth were a bit surprised. Didn't even know he knew Jinty. Not sure they approve. But they seem to be doing their bit – making sure he eats when he does go home. Well, trying to."

Roly looked again at the fire and sighed. He drained his glass and tapped his wife gently on the shoulder. "We should eat, too."

She looked up at him. "Do you feel like anything?"

He shook his head.

"Nor me." She blew her nose once more, and the two of them sat in silence, while in the kitchen Mrs Flanders put the freshly made casserole to cool before transferring it to the freezer, which was now bursting with ready-prepared meals. She left out a jug of home-made soup, hoping that perhaps hunger might get the better of them before they turned in for the night. Then she switched off the kitchen light and slipped quietly out of the back door. She hadn't eaten much herself over the last three days.

Gradually Roly came to. The ringing in his ear caused him to reach for the hearing-aid once more, but it was not there. He had removed it when he went to bed. It must be the alarm clock. He stretched out for the bedside light and switched it on; the clock said a quarter to two. His alarm was set for seven. Why was it ringing now? At last he identified the sound as coming from the telephone. He lifted the handset and put it to his ear. He could just make out the muffled voice at the other end of the line.

"Hello. It's Kit. She's woken up. *She's woken up!*" Then the line went dead, and Roly Billings-Gore was up and dressed faster than he had ever been since his days in the army. Within five minutes he and Charlotte were in the car and speeding towards Plymouth, hardly daring to think what they would find on their arrival at the hospital, but praying that the brevity of the message meant that the news was good.

"Please, God," muttered Charlotte, under her breath, "let her be all right."

They found him sitting in the chair at her bedside holding her hand. Her pale green eyes were as clear as ever, but her face bore a faraway expression. Charlotte found it difficult to speak, but smiled through her tears, while Roly, leaning over the bed, stroked her shoulder and said, "Hello, old girl."

Jinty smiled weakly. "Sorry."

"Nothing to be sorry about. Mmm? How are you feeling?"

"Bruised," she said softly. "A bit battered." She had difficulty forming the words, and, for the first time, Roly felt a pricking at the back of his eyes. He cleared his throat. "Er, Nurse – where's the nurse?"

"Sir Roland?" The nurse put her head around the door and raised her eyebrows, indicating that he should follow her. She took him to a desk opposite the room in which Jinty lay.

"She came round about an hour ago. Her eyes had been flickering during the night so we were hopeful of some progress. She was on a ventilator at first but now she's holding her own."

"And is she . . . er . . ."

"We're very hopeful. Pity she hadn't fastened the strap on her hard hat – it gave her some protection until it came off. Fortunately the brain scan is clear, but we'll need to keep her under observation for a while. Run a few tests. But the fact that she's come out of the coma and seems to be reasonably lucid is a good sign."

"Thank the Lord for that." Roly ran his fingers through his iron-grey hair.

"I really think the best thing you can all do is go home and get some sleep now. We'll keep a close eye on her. We're not through the woods yet, but things are looking much better. We'll know a little more after the doctor's rounds in the morning. Perhaps if you came in the afternoon?"

"Yes. Mmm. Of course. Thank you. Thank you very much." He shook her hand, then walked across the corridor to the room opposite to collect Kit and Charlotte.

Jinty was looking at him when he walked in – she had turned her head slightly in the direction of the door – a head with shaved patches among the blonde tresses. Roly could hardly bear to meet her eye, but he did so, firmly and fixedly. "You rest now," he instructed. "We'll be back tomorrow. Mmm?"

Jinty closed her eyes then opened them – the nearest thing she could manage for a nod.

Roly took Kit by the elbow and raised him from the chair. "Come on, let's get you home for some rest."

Jinty moved her lips again, and Roly leaned forward to catch the arduously enunciated words. "Take care of him. Very precious . . ."

Roly nodded. Then he kissed his forefinger and placed it gently on her cheek before shepherding Charlotte and Kit back to Baddesley Court.

In the morning it was a few moments before Kit realized where he was. It was nine o'clock and as the events of the last few days crystallized in his mind he woke properly with a start.

A tap on the door followed – the first must have woken him up. He pulled up the bedclothes to cover himself and called, "Come in."

Charlotte entered with a tray bearing a silver teapot and milk jug, toast and marmalade. She wore a long, pale blue dressing-gown of shimmering satin, and looked, thought Kit, like a gracefully ageing Greta Garbo.

"Breakfast." It was an instruction, as much as a description of the contents of the tray.

Kit looked up at the tall, elegant figure, wondering how she had managed to keep her hair perfectly in place even after a night's sleep. (In fact, Charlotte had removed the net that had safeguarded it during the night. It was not something that should be seen by anyone other than Roly who, by now, had ceased to notice it.)

She put down the tray at one end of a large ottoman at the bottom of the bed, and perched on the other end.

"How are you feeling?"

"Knackered . . . er, tired."

"No. I think knackered is probably more accurate." Charlotte smiled at him. "You've been very kind."

"No. I . . ."

"Well, whatever. I'm just so relieved that she's come round." She did not want to enquire, put him on the spot. She knew now that there was some bond between them, but she was old enough and wise enough to wait to be told.

Kit sat up in the bed and leaned back on the pillows. Charlotte looked at the tanned torso, beginning to fade to a shade of pale honey. He was a good-looking boy. They were a perfect couple. She chastised herself inwardly for matchmaking and asked, "Will you stay for lunch?"

"I think I should go back to the hospital."

"No. They've asked us not to go until this afternoon. Give the surgeon time to do his rounds."

"Then I'd better get back to the farmhouse."

Charlotte smiled. "I've spoken to Miss Punch and told her that you were here. Just in case she was worried."

Kit looked at her, questioningly.

"It's all right. You won't be struck off for consorting with the hunt fraternity. She was a bit surprised at first, but I think she understood. I told her that I'd ask you to stay for lunch. Said that you were worn out and that it would do you good to have a rest. She'll expect you when she sees you – I said I'd make sure you got back there before dark."

He looked startled, then realized her intended humour and grinned. "Thank you for looking after me."

"It's a pleasure." Charlotte rose from the ottoman and walked to the bedroom door. "The bathroom is at the end of the landing. There are towels in there for you. Roly's down at the stables, trying to repair his relationship with Allardyce."

In his concern for Jinty he had barely thought about the horse. He now felt guilty. "Is he all right?"

"Absolutely fine. Bruised foreleg, but that's all. It took him a while to calm down afterwards. Titus brought him back. Poor man – feels it's all his fault. That little dog of his has been locked up at the kennels ever since. Just a silly thing, really. It could have happened to anybody."

"Poor Titus."

"Yes. Poor Titus. He's a good man. Wonderful with animals. I just hope he isn't too hard on the spaniel. She's only young." Charlotte looked reflective, then came back down to earth. "Anyway, I'll see you later. I'm off to the hairdresser's. Back by lunchtime. Mrs Flanders says if we don't eat a casserole soon we'll have to buy another freezer." She closed the door quietly behind her, and Kit found himself wondering what improvements the hairdresser could possibly make to Charlotte's already immaculately crafted coiffure.

He found Titus looking balefully through the iron bars of one of the kennels at the dejected animal on the other side. Nell lay flat on the concrete floor, her head on her paws, the whites of her eyes pleading for forgiveness.

"Oh dear."

Titus turned round, startled. When he saw Kit he shook his head. "Bugger. Absolute bugger. Any news?" he asked, his face haggard from worry.

"She's come round."

"Thank God!" Titus slapped his hand to his forehead in relief. "And?"

"We're waiting to see. Going round this afternoon. After the doctor's rounds."

"I don't know what to say. It were just so bloody stupid. Only t'orse came out of nowhere. We were down in the dunes. I didn't think anyone would be down there. Stupid."

"Hey, come on. You can't blame yourself."

"Well, I do."

"Not going to get us anywhere, though, is it?"

"Don't know how I'll face Sir Roly. He cancelled the hunt, you know, and Major Watson's standing in as Master for the rest of the season."

"Well, he's not blaming you, if that's what you think."

"I don't know why not. It were my fault."

"It was just one of those things. Come on, it could have been anybody's dog."

"Aye, but it were mine." He looked through the bars at the doleful Nell, who looked back at him with bewilderment.

"You can't leave her in there for ever." ·

"No, I know. I just need to – well, you know. At least now that she's woken up there's a chance she'll be all right." He looked at Kit, whose face bore a distracted look.

"Yes. I hope so. I do hope so."

Roly, Charlotte and Kit tucked into lunch at Baddesley Court as though they had not eaten for days. But then they hadn't.

"Good casserole," muttered Roly, as he spooned up the last of his gravy.

Kit ate ravenously, but declined all offers of a drink. He wanted to keep a clear head for the afternoon – wanted to make sure he understood perfectly the state of Jinty's health.

They motored to the hospital in Plymouth at three o'clock. No one spoke much, although Roly peppered the journey with good-natured but disparaging comments on the inept performance of other road-users. He handled the estate car as though it was a Chieftain tank.

When they walked into the ward the nurse was ready for them. She stood up and greeted them with a smile. Kit allowed himself to hope that it meant the news was good.

"Doctor's very pleased with her. Surprised, but very pleased."

"Why surprised?" asked Kit.

"Because normally someone who's taken a tumble like the one Jinty had is lucky to come out of it alive, let alone with just a broken arm."

"Is that all? A broken arm?" Charlotte was amazed.

"She's had quite severe concussion, and some external head injuries, which is why we had to cut off some of her hair. A few stitches here and there, and her face is badly grazed but there won't be any need for plastic surgery."

The three of them mumbled grateful thanks to their Maker, almost in unison.

"So . . . er, when can she come home?" asked Roly.

"In a couple of days. We'd just like to keep an eye on her for a little while longer, but she's much perkier today. Her speech has improved a lot, which is good. Go and see for yourself."

Kit looked at Charlotte and Roly. They looked at each other and Roly nodded in the direction of Jinty's room. "Go on." Kit smiled, walked across to the door, tapped and went in, closing the door behind him.

She was sitting up. Her arm was still held aloft by the pulleys, but she looked altogether more of this world than she had the day before. Her partly shaven head gleamed in places with golden down, and she tilted it to one side and looked at him with her soft green eyes.

"Hello, you," she said, clearly.

He went over to the bed, bent down to kiss her and felt a huge sense of relief at her return to the land of the living.

She nodded in the direction of the elevated arm, and the other with its drip attached. "Bit of a bugger, eh?"

"Bit of a bugger indeed. Just relieved you're OK."

"Oh, I'm OK. But look at my head! What a sight! I look like a punk. Think I'd better buy a pair of Doc Martens."

"It'll grow."

"Yes, but when?"

"Tomorrow."

She grinned. "I've been thinking. . ."

"Well, that's a relief."

"It's funny."

"Not the word I would have chosen."

"No. I mean us."

"What about us?"

"Well, I've only known you a couple of weeks."

He nodded. "I know."

"But it feels like ages."

He bent and kissed her gently on the cheek. "I've missed you."

"I haven't been anywhere."

"Not physically, no. Can you remember anything?"

"Not really. I remember riding out, that's all. Can't remember how I got here. They tell me I fell down a cliff. Exciting. Wish I could remember . . ."

"Perhaps it's as well that you can't. Anyway, I've had enough of people falling down cliffs."

She looked at him quizzically.

A gentle tapping interrupted them. Charlotte and Roly poked their heads round the door. Jinty gave them a warm smile, and the custodians of Kit's lover approached their honorary niece and fussed over her as though she had come back from the dead.

Which, as the nurse confessed to Kit later that afternoon, she almost had.

Chapter 16: Pig's Ears

(Sedum acre)

Kit wasn't absolutely sure but he suspected Elizabeth was rattled. When he came home from the hospital, having been absent for most of the last four days, his reception had been polite but frosty. He thought it best to keep a low profile, but at the same time offer to help with whatever task needed doing.

The following morning she sent him off to clean out Wilson's sty. He got the message, but the company of the pig would not be a hardship, since Jess, too, had been tight-lipped and uncommunicative.

"Like the bloody Montagues and Capulets," he informed the Gloucester Old Spot, while shepherding her out to the fenced-off land by the orchard where she was already making her mark. The journey was slow as the pig truffled her way among the undergrowth at either side of the path through the long grass. Kit prodded her on gently with a stick, diverting her snout in the direction he wanted her to travel.

"What's happening to me, do you think?" he asked her. "I've hardly been here five minutes and I'm up to my ears in the place. *And* the people. What do you reckon I should do, old girl? Run away? Fancy coming with me?"

The pig was not the most stimulating conversationalist, but then she seldom argued, except with the suggested direction of travel. He eyed the freshly churned soil that would soon be Jess's vegetable garden, and ushered Wilson into the electric-fenced enclosure before fastening the netting together and turning on the current. She began to nose her way through the damp, uncultivated loam.

"If you think you're in a mess," he muttered, "just look at me. I've a girlfriend across the other side of the world who wonders what the hell I'm up to, and another over here I'm crazy about. Neither knows about the other, and I don't know who to tell first. Any suggestions?"

The pig had none.

"Ever been in love, Wilson?" The pig grunted. "Very wise. You lay yourself open to all sorts of feelings when you are. Can't stop yourself, though. Just happens. Suddenly find yourself doing things you've never done before." He spoke softly now, almost under his breath. "Feeling things you didn't know you could feel." He poked at the ground with the stick, thinking thoughts that he would not even share with the pig. Inarticulate thoughts; incoherent emotions and sensitivities. He sighed deeply and kicked at a clump of grass.

Was he *really* in love with Jinty? Did Heather *really* want him back or was she happy to see what developed between her and Marcus Johnson? Marcus Johnson – how ridiculous. Or was it?

"Then there's this place." He looked about him at the old trees of the orchard, whose downy buds were fattening, and among whose branches a pair of bullfinches were prospecting for lunch. "It'll be blossom time before we know where we are and I still haven't sorted out what I'm doing. Why not? I'm a decisive guy who knows what he wants."

Wilson looked up at him with a blank stare.

"Don't look at me like that. I'm trying to sort it, but until this probate lark comes through I can't."

She grunted.

"Yes. I know it's a convenient excuse." He watched as Wilson grubbed up a fat root. "OK. What do I do? I sell up West Yarmouth to this guy who wants to buy the place for one and a half million and who'll keep on our two lady-friends. Heather tells me she's found another guy and I'm history. Result? She doesn't get hurt and I get out of the hole I've dug for myself. I pocket the cash and go out to Balnunga Valley with Jinty and buy a stud farm. I breed horses, she rides 'em. We live happily ever after. OK? Simple."

The pig regarded him with a laconic stare as she chewed the root like an indolent teenager with a mouthful of gum.

"It's not going to work, is it? The buyer will pull out. Heather won't find another man. Jinty won't come to Balnunga Valley and yours truly will end up stuck here for the rest of his life with two harridans and a few red squirrels. There you are. Simple, really. The thing is, the prospect of staying here isn't nearly as terrifying as it was a couple of weeks ago, and that's a fact. Must be spring."

He tossed the stick into a pile of brambles and headed for the pig-sty. Shovelling muck might lack glamour, but it was also intellectually undemanding and this morning that was something he would happily settle for.

He had no inkling, at this stage, that one of his idle dreams would come true, and that a second dream, which had yet not manifested itself, would shortly begin to evolve.

Jess leaned on the handle of the spade and looked out across Tallacombe Bay at the small boat butting its way through the waves. For a moment or two she allowed her imagination to drift with it, but her reverie did not last long. She laid down the spade, took up a hammer and began fastening together the planks that would make a stile to cross the fence between the Wilderness and the Spinney.

With every hammer blow she thought of him, and the feelings of betrayal built inside her. He had seemed sympathetic to her, and to what she was trying to achieve on his father's land. It even seemed as though he was about to play his part in saving the place, but now, out of nowhere, he had sprung on her the one thing that she least wanted to believe. Why did it have to be Jinty O'Hare?

She drove the four-inch nail home viciously and the plank split. "Bugger!" She flung the hammer into the soft turf and felt the anger rising within her.

She sat down on the partially completed stile and cradled her head in her hands, rubbing her face in her grubby palms. She felt the metal of the rings in her eyebrow, and the stud in her nose. Systematically, she removed them, then drew back her hand to throw them over the cliff, but stopped short. She looked down at the collection of semi-precious ornamentation in her hand, slipped it into a wad of tissue and pushed it into the pocket of her jeans. Then she got up and walked through the Spinney, down towards the Yar.

There, she crouched on a broad rock on the bank and leaned forward, cupped her hands and dipped them into the water. She splashed it again and again over her cheeks and her tightly closed eyes until they were numb. Mascara ran down her face and she wiped it away until the last traces had been removed and her face felt purified, alive. She wiped her hands on her jeans, stood up and climbed the path that led back to the stile.

She picked up the hammer, knocked out the split plank and replaced it with another, working more carefully this time. When the job was done, she picked up the saw, the spade, the hammer and the nails, climbed over her newly built bridge as if to christen it, and walked back towards West Yarmouth Farmhouse with a faraway look in her eye and a complexion of burnished rose.

The smell of pig muck remained in his nostrils, however hard he scrubbed, and he held up his face to the shower jet in an effort to banish it. Then he got out, towelled himself down and went into the bedroom. He stopped at the desk and looked, as he had so many times over the past few days, at the contents of the pigeon-holes – a life neatly displayed as if in a museum. Then he scanned the bookshelves. He would have to start sorting their contents soon. Clear the place to make a fresh start. Put his father to bed.

There was a brief knock at the door and he spun round, clutching at the towel. The door opened and Jess stood there, staring at him, embarrassed by her own intrusion and unsure of what to say. She wanted to close the door and retreat, yet she could not. She stood rooted to the spot, gazing at him, looking him up and down.

"I – I'm sorry," she managed to blurt out, but still made no move to leave.

Kit, at first startled but then amused, stood still, the towel held in front of him to preserve what little dignity he could salvage. Then he said, almost brightly, "That's OK. I should have locked the door." The two remained quite still for what seemed like an age, Jess gazing at him, Kit looking apologetically at her, until Jess's mouth curled into a smile, the colour rose to her cheeks and she said, without taking her eyes off him, "Dinner in ten minutes." Then she closed the door and padded down the stairs.

Kit remained immobile, the towel clasped to his body with one hand. There was something strange about her. She looked . . . different. Her face was more open, her eyes clearer, less wary. In fact, she seemed like a different person altogether. He wondered why.

Half-way through supper he realized why she looked different. Her face was devoid of studs and the heavy eyeliner had gone, revealing a clear complexion and eyes of purest forget-me-not blue. The red hair, which had become less lurid with the passing days, was no longer drawn up into gelled spikes. Without all the warpaint, she was refreshingly pretty. But he said nothing.

As Elizabeth chomped her way methodically through the vegetable pie, he explained that he would be going to the hospital after supper but would return later.

"How is she?" Elizabeth asked. It was the first time she had mentioned Jinty, even though she had chosen to use the pronoun.

"Better, I think."

"She's been very lucky."

There was an uneasy silence. Kit was unwilling to offer more information, and Elizabeth was unwilling to ask for it.

Jess was not sure what she wanted, except for one thing.

Chapter 17:
Touch-and-Heal

(Melittis melissophyllum)

"You and she courtin', then?" As ever, Titus's questioning was
nothing if not direct.

"Never you mind."

"Go on. Y'are, aren't yer?" He was filling the hounds' water trough
to the accompaniment of an unruly cacophony of yelps and barks.

"I'm not sure I know what 'courtin'' means."

Titus stood up straight. His one good eye looked directly at Kit,
while the other seemed to dart between the kennel gate and a distant
tree. "Goin' out. Knockin' off. Gettin' yer leg over."

"What are you like?" Kit asked, in disbelief.

"Just curious. Just askin'." Titus grinned a wicked grin, and bent
down to stroke a contrite-looking Nell, who followed him like a
shadow.

"I don't know what we are," Kit admitted.

"And what about yon girl in Australia?"

Kit looked pained.

"Nice girl, Jinty. Nice girl." Titus nodded to himself as he closed the
metal-barred kennel gate. "We miss her at the hunt. Always gev it a
bit o' sparkle."

"Mmm." Kit was somewhere else.

"You want ter come and watch."

"What?"

"We've a meet on Wednesday. Why don't you come and follow?"

"Me? I'd be struck off." He jerked his head in the direction of West Yarmouth.

"Oh, you don't want to worry about them. They'll never know. Too busy puttin' up their nest-boxes to bother about us."

"Don't be unkind."

Titus put down his bucket. "Nah. I'm not bein' unkind. I just wish that sometimes they could see t'other point of view."

"Not much chance of that, I'm afraid."

"Funny, in't it? I can see theirs, but they can't see mine."

"You reckon?"

"I know so. I mean it's obvious that a nature reserve is a good thing, in't it? Stands to reason – conserves wildlife."

"And hunting doesn't."

"Ah, well, it does, you see."

"Rubbish. You just kill foxes – the unspeakable in pursuit of the uneatable."

Titus regarded Kit with his head on one side. "You don't really believe that?"

"I know some people who do."

"That's because they can't see further than their noses."

Kit raised an eyebrow.

"Oh, I know we kill foxes, and in some folk's eyes that's unforgivable. I can understand that. But what I can't understand is why they think that bannin' it will be good for the countryside."

"Sermon coming," Kit teased.

"No. Not a sermon. Just common sense. Your dad realized what could happen if it were banned. He knew that man had to work hand in hand with the countryside in all sorts of ways – not just the ways he chose himself."

"But if foxhunting is banned, the countryside is hardly going to go to rack and ruin."

"No. But once it's gone the antis will turn their attention to shootin'. People who pay to shoot grouse and pheasant pay for woodland to be managed – trees to be planted, coverts to be maintained to shelter birdlife. No shooting equals no woodland management. No one's going to look after a wood for the fun of it."

"Dad did."

"Your dad were an exception. When shootin's sorted, they'll start on fishin'. And when fishin's banned the rivers will silt up because no one cuts weed any more, and then one day a silted-up river will flood a village and everyone will be up in arms because global warming is finally bringin' about Armageddon."

"When really it was the banning of the hunt that caused it all?"

"Somethin' like that."

"And what about cruelty? Doesn't that count for anything? And pleasure? Why is it that people who hunt and shoot and fish can rant on for ages about how they are helping to conserve the countryside but forget that the main reason they kill things is for fun?"

"You're beginnin' to sound like your dad." Titus bent down to caress Nell again, and asked Kit if he'd like a coffee.

"Can't I'm afraid. Nipping over to Baddesley Court. Jinty came out of hospital this morning and I want to see how she is."

"That'll perk her up," said Titus. "Or give her a relapse." He chuckled to himself.

"On yer bike, Ormonroyd," Kit tossed over his shoulder as he left. "On yer bloody bike."

She was looking out of the bedroom window at the front of Baddesley Court when he drove up, still at the wheel of the yellow Punto. With her good arm she raised the sash and leaned out to greet him as he stepped on to the gravel drive.

"What happened to the BMW?"

"Too tied up with other things to worry about cars."

"Even little yellow ones?"

"Even little yellow ones." He looked up at where she sat in a window seat, her left arm in a sling, and the sun catching her hair and making it sparkle.

He held up his arms, and made a rectangular frame with the index finger and thumb of each hand. "Don't move. I want always to remember you like this."

She grinned back at him. "Bastard!"

"Deny thy father and refuse thy name."

"That's my line."

"So what's mine?"

"But soft . . ."

". . . what light through yonder window breaks? It is the east, and Juliet is the sun! Arise, fair sun, and kill the envious moon, who is already sick and pale with grief."

"I thought I was looking a bit better."

He smiled up at her. "You look great. Can I come in, or shall I carry on down here?"

"Come in, silly boy."

She welcomed him into her room with one open arm, the other resting against her side under the covering of the white bath-robe. He embraced her carefully and closed his eyes, rocking her gently from side to side. Then he drew away a little and looked at her, pushing a stray curl out of her eyes. Her hair, tousled but gleaming, framed a pale face that sported a russet graze from left temple to chin. The eyes sparkled with a deep lustre.

"Are you still in there?"

"Just."

"You're not fit to be let out."

"I know."

"What a week."

"Tell me what's been happening."

"Not a lot. I've been a bit tied up with this friend of mine who's been in hospital."

She looked at him and he noticed a doubtful look in her eye. "Just a friend?"

"I don't know." He hesitated. "I hope not."

She stepped forward and kissed him tenderly but briefly on the lips. "Me too."

They sat down side by side on the edge of the bed and she stroked his arm. Neither spoke until Kit murmured, "I don't really know what's happened."

"No. Nor me."

"Funny, isn't it?"

"No. Not really. Just nice."

He could hear her breathing, a blackbird singing through the open window, the gentle swish of a muslin curtain caught by the breeze. For several minutes they sat quite still, glad of each other's company in the calm of her room after the anxieties and tensions of the past few days, the clamour of the hospital and the all-pervading tang of disinfectant and laundered linen.

Finally she raised her head. "I need a bath. I'm filthy."

He kissed the top of her head. "I'll go."

"No, stay. Please?" She reached for his hand. "Help me?"

He looked at her.

"Charlotte's out. Uncle Roly's down at the stables. I can't get out of this on my own."

Kit nodded. "I'll run the bath." He walked to a door that led off the bedroom, opened it and regarded the ancient tub on ball-and-claw feet, the network of brass pipes and taps to one side. He pushed a lever or two and turned on the taps. A large bottle of Badedas stood on a shelf at one end; he removed the cap, tipped out a cupful and the gushing water turned to foam.

"Steady! It costs a fortune!" she admonished him from the doorway.

He turned. "Just wanted you to smell nice."

Jinty smiled gratefully and walked forward, pulling at the belt of the white towelling robe and trying to ease it from her shoulder. Kit stepped forward and lifted it off. She was naked beneath the soft white fabric, her once pale skin now brindled with black and yellow bruising. "Oh, my love . . ." he murmured, when he saw the extent of her injuries.

Jinty grimaced. "Not a pretty sight, am I?"

He put his arm around her gently and walked her to the bath. She stepped gingerly over the rim, and lowered herself into the water. "Wash my back?"

He reached for the large sponge on the shelf, dunked it in the water and began to smooth it over her battered neck and shoulders. Then she lay back and he continued over her good arm, her breasts and her stomach, her legs and her feet.

Then he washed her hair, working up the shampoo into a lather, and rinsing off her patchy scalp with a gush of clear water from the shower nozzle.

She closed her eyes as he worked, finally opening them when he dropped the sponge into the water with a soft plop.

She stood up, looking like Botticelli's *Birth of Venus*, he thought, and he draped a white bath sheet around her as she stepped out, and cradled her in his arms, patting her dry.

"That's nice." Her eyes were closed.

"Careful. It might be habit-forming."

"Oh, I hope so."

He ruffled her hair. "What about this?"

"It'll dry on its own. Just pass me the brush."

596

She made four deft strokes with her good arm. Her hair sleeked back, looked different; streamlined.

"You're so beautiful."

"So are you. Thank you for helping me."

"The pleasure was all mine." He kissed her gently and she responded, manoeuvring her injured arm out of the way. Gently he slipped his hand inside the robe and stroked her still damp breast. She caught her breath and drew away from him slightly, sighing with pleasure. For several minutes they held each other quietly until Kit broke the silence.

"I'll have to go. I need to get things moving with Dad's solicitor. Need to find out where I am at the moment."

Jinty nodded. She would have given anything to know where he was at the moment. She knew where his body was, but she could not be certain about his mind. Perhaps she could discover that, too, in time.

Chapter 18:
String of Sovereigns

(Lysimachia nummularia)

Kit wondered how the solicitor managed to find anything in the overcrowded cell that was his office. Thick buff files were piled upon thick pink files, bundles of pink-ribboned documents slithered in disorderly cascades between them, and fat, gilt-titled books teetered in precarious towers against the grimy cream-painted wall. The solicitor sat, like a grey Buddha, in the centre of the paper jungle, a ginger nut and a mug of coffee at his elbow, his glasses on the tip of his nose. He gazed at Kit over the rims as he did his best to answer the question.

"As far as goods and chattels are concerned, Mr Lavery, I think you can now dispose of whatever you wish without any problem."

"And the house . . . the reserve?"

"Well, I've had no problems, and probate should be through within a few weeks now, so you could certainly begin negotiations. Start things moving. It's only the final sale that will have to wait until everything is tied up."

"So I could see the estate agent and get things going?"

"I should think so, yes."

"And you'll let me know the moment you hear anything?"

The little man nodded. "Of course. Ah. There is one thing." He rummaged through the heap of papers on his desk. "This arrived for you a couple of days ago." He handed Kit a large transparent packet upon which the name of a London auction house was stamped in black letters in the top left hand corner.

"For me?"

"Yes. It looks like a catalogue."

"Are you sure it wasn't meant for my father?"

"The label is addressed to Mr Christopher Lavery, not to Mr Rupert Lavery. It's also been directed here rather than to the farmhouse."

"Odd." Kit pulled at the polythene and removed the fat booklet. "It's a sale of natural-history books. Next month. Can't be for me. It must have been intended for Dad." He thumbed through the pages. "Mind you, I can't see Dad paying this sort of money for books. Perhaps they got the name wrong."

The solicitor shrugged. "Perhaps."

Kit tucked the catalogue under his arm and left the solicitor to his coffee and gingernut.

A million thoughts ran through his head on the drive back to West Yarmouth, including the fact that he was still at the wheel of the yellow Fiat Punto. Funny that Jinty was so scathing about it; he'd become quite used to it. Changing it for a more expensive BMW or Mercedes seemed an unnecessary expense. He turned down the lane to the reserve and had to pull in sharply to allow a Volvo estate that he didn't recognize to pass. At the front of the house he discovered Elizabeth looking about her nervously, like a child who had been caught stealing sweets.

Kit parked by the barn, got out of the car and walked towards her. "Who was that?"

"Oh . . . callers." She was agitated, not herself at all.

"What sort of callers? Do they think we're open?"

"No."

"What, then?"

"They were invited."

"By who?"

"Me."

Kit regarded her with curiosity. He had never seen her looking so apprehensive, so guilty.

"I think we'd better go inside," she suggested. He followed her silently, and once in the kitchen she turned round, leaned against the old pine table and said, "I've been worried." She waited for a reaction. It did not come. Kit stood perfectly still, waiting for her to continue.

"Worried that the work we've all put in – your father particularly – would be wasted if the place was sold."

"But I've explained that I want to see the reserve carry on, even if I'm not a part of it."

"Yes. I know. And I wanted to be sure that would happen."

Kit was hurt, as though she felt him untrustworthy. He said, "And?"

"I knew that, because of what we'd already accomplished here, the place was very special – the red squirrels, the large blue butterfly."

"Yes?"

"Your father was always quiet about what he'd achieved. We had visitors, and they enjoyed walking round and looking at the views, but he always kept a lot of his successes to himself. Never boasted about the red squirrels, for instance. Said that what was important was that they were established. People did not necessarily need to know they were here – that if it *were* known they might become threatened. What mattered was that the squirrel thrived, nothing else. But now that everything is up in the air, I didn't feel we could risk losing everything."

"What do you mean?"

"Oh, I know you're doing your best to sort it all out, and I do understand why you want to do your own thing, but I'm afraid we can't endanger the reserve."

"We?"

"Jess and myself. We have to make sure that the work goes on and that what's already been done is protected."

Kit was thrown off-balance. "But that's my job. That's what I'm trying to do."

"But there are safeguards that can be made, and we thought it best to make sure that they were put in place."

"What sort of safeguards?"

"Declaring the reserve a Site of Special Scientific Interest."

Kit looked at her blankly. "What?"

"The man in the car was from English Nature. They have the power to declare a piece of countryside an SSSI. They can prevent it from being built on or its use from changing. It makes sure that your father's work continues here as it did before he died."

Kit was angry now. "And you did this without consulting me?"

Elizabeth looked him straight in the eye. "I didn't feel we had any

600

option. You seem so unsure of what is going to happen to the estate . . ."

He made to speak but Elizabeth raised her hand to stop him and carried on. "We could have just sat around and waited, but we felt that this was something positive we could do. It doesn't interfere with your future plans. You can still dispose of the estate in the best way you think fit. But it does mean that the reserve is protected and that's the most important thing."

He exploded, "What do you mean it doesn't interfere with my future plans? You've no idea about my future plans!"

"But you said that you would be selling it as a reserve."

"Yes, I did. But you obviously don't believe that, so, without taking the trouble to ask me, you go straight to English Nature and tell them – as though I were some sort of villain intending to do the dirty on you."

"I didn't think you would be so upset."

"You didn't care, more like. Ever since I've come back here you've done your best to make me feel like an interloper. I understand how hard you've both worked on the estate, and what it means to you, but you've single-mindedly shut me out and carried on as though the place were yours and I were some kind of tyrannical landlord."

Elizabeth stared at him, shocked by his outburst.

"How can I sort all this out? Have you paused to think about that? I've levelled with you about my own future. I've explained my feelings and made myself quite clear. But you don't care, do you? As long as the reserve goes on and you can live your own narrow little life you just don't mind what happens to anybody else. I've recently spent three days sitting by a hospital bed waiting to see if someone was going to live, and while I was there you were making plans behind my back."

Elizabeth blurted out, "But you've only –"

"Yes, I've only known her for a few weeks. The same length of time I've known you. And she hunts foxes. But she's shown me what life's really about. It's not about money, or possessions, or hatred or fear, it's about people, and that's where you've got me all wrong. The only thing you care about is the reserve. Nothing else is of any importance to you."

Elizabeth tried to butt in, but Kit brushed her interruption aside. "People are just as important as animals and birds. By having people on your side you can achieve far more for your wildlife than if you put their backs up."

Almost without his knowing it, Kit's thoughts had clarified. "This place has been part of my life since I was born. I tried to escape it, and to escape my father, because I didn't want to believe that where I was was necessarily where I had to stay. Everything told me to leave. I'd grown up with a man of nature – a man who believed in the survival of the fittest, in striking out on your own, in fleeing the nest. He pushed me out into the big wide world and made me get on with my own life. He probably didn't even know he was doing it. It was instinctive. I went, and then another part of him felt I'd let him down – the human part, if you like, the overlay of human society that expects its children to stay and follow in its footsteps. We're the only members of the animal kingdom who react like that."

Elizabeth stared at him.

"But when I came back the place started pulling at me again. Then you pulled at me. The life I'd left behind in Australia pulled at me. I was tugged in so many directions I couldn't see clearly where I was going. This place means a lot to me. Over the last few days I've started to feel at home here – remembered feelings I used to have about West Yarmouth. It may be the place, it may be the people – I'm not sure. But I already have a life somewhere else, and the way things have turned out I can't afford to live here so I'll have to sell. The most I can do is make sure it goes to the right person who'll carry on my father's work. I have no intention of making a fast buck then hightailing it out of here."

An oppressive, echoing silence hung over the kitchen. Elizabeth spoke quietly. "I'm sorry. I'm very sorry. I didn't mean . . ."

"Oh, please . . . just try to understand . . ." Kit's voice was soft. Placatory. He had had his say, given voice to feelings of which he had, until now, been unsure. Maybe soon the way to his destination would become clearer, wherever that destination might be.

Elizabeth left the room quietly. Even she did not notice Jess standing in the shadows of the hallway, having listened in silence to the raised voices on the other side of the door. She stayed there for some moments, before slipping out of the front door and down to the sea.

Chapter 19:
Clouded Yellow

(*Colias croceus*)

"I know I shouldn't have done it. It just all came out – like a dam bursting." Wilson was her usual laconic self, intent only on filling her capacious belly with tender rooty morsels. Kit leaned on a post at one corner of the patch of ground that would soon be clean enough for Jess to dig over and fill with vegetables, thanks to the pig's foraging.

"I'm not going back, am I? Suppose you've always suspected as much. Listen to me! What do I mean I'm not going back?" He shook his head. "Do you think anger helps, Wilson? No, I suppose not. Your experiences of it are probably few and far between." The pig approached, hopeful of a tasty titbit. Kit picked up a stick and scratched her back.

"Trouble is, there are other things to sort out now." His thoughts turned to Heather. Life had seemed so settled until his father's death. He'd been content to live on the other side of the world in the company of horses and with a girl he liked – no, loved, and then, bombshell had followed bombshell.

"Do you believe in love at first sight? Well, not exactly first sight but quickly. I never did. Not sure that I do now." The pig looked up. "That's Jinty and me. Don't get excited." The pig looked anything but.

"Am I boring you?"

No response.

"I thought so. But, oh, God, how do I tell Heather?" He felt wretched at the prospect of letting down the girl he had left behind. He could see her now, tanned and smiling, a real Aussie girl, open and pleasant, sparky and quick-spirited. Always ready for a laugh . . . with Marcus Johnson. He lobbed the stick into the bushes.

Was he kidding himself about Jinty? Was this a classic mad, passionate fling? The grass being greener on the other side of the world? Novelty winning out over familiarity? He hoped not. And yet he and Jinty hardly knew each other, so how could he be so certain of his feelings?

The question remained unanswered. He could only hope that the mist, which seemed slowly to be lifting from him and allowing him a clearer view of his future, would continue to rise and that the prospect before him would materialize. Eventually.

He sat at his father's desk, looking at the telephone. He put out his hand towards it, then withdrew it again. He checked the clock. Four p.m. No point in ringing her now. It would be three o'clock in the morning. Damn. He had been psyching himself up for hours. The time difference was an obvious thing to consider, yet he had forgotten it.

When should he ring? Morning or evening? When was the best time to break such news? There was no best time. An unseen hand tightened on his stomach and beads of sweat leaped to his brow.

The auction catalogue sat in front of him. Idly he flipped through the pages, then saw the phone number of the auction house. He would ring them and explain the mistake. Kensington time was the same as West Yarmouth time – no problem there.

"Hello? Can I speak to someone about an auction catalogue, please?"

"Just a moment." The voice was cut-glass. A pause, and then a terse reply from a more matter-of-fact voice.

"Catalogues."

"Hello, I'm ringing about a catalogue I've been sent." Kit explained the situation and suggested that the envelope had been wrongly addressed and that as his father was dead the sending of further catalogues would be unnecessary.

He could hear the buttons on a computer keyboard clicking. "No mistake, sir. The subscription was certainly taken out by a Mr Rupert Lavery, but the instruction was that the catalogues should be addressed to Mr Christopher Lavery care of his solicitor's office. You should receive two more catalogues on that subscription, one for our May sale and one for the sale in September."

Kit was baffled. "I see. Can you tell me when the subscription was taken out?"

"Just give me a moment, sir. Yes, here we are. November."

"I see. Right. Thank you very much." He put down the telephone and looked again at the catalogue and the intricate watercolour of butterflies that decorated the cover. They looked as though they had been caught in flight – lifelike and living, rather than flat as the paper they were printed on.

On the shelf by the desk was a single butterfly in a small glass case, its thorax pinned to a square of cork, and underneath it a label printed with the Latin name *Colias crocea*. Its wings were pale orange, tipped with charcoal grey, a single smudge of grey on the upper part. He looked at it closely and then at the cover of the auction catalogue. The butterflies on the printed page seemed to have more life in them than this poor soul impaled behind the glass. And yet, when the light from the desk lamp caught its wing scales, the butterfly seemed to sparkle.

He took a hand lens from the desk drawer and looked more closely at it, the dark hairiness of its body and the intricacy of its fragile antennae. He remembered his father showing him drawers full of butterflies when he was young, and of learning the names of small tortoiseshells and commas, holly blues and chequered fritillaries.

Now the collection was long gone. Little of great beauty remained in the study, except for the jay's feather in the desk pigeon hole, and the pale blue eggshell, yet in these his father had been able to find enough beauty to sustain him.

He would begin, soon, to clear out the house. He would keep some things, just a few, as reminders of his childhood, but the rest would go to jumble sales and charity shops in the main – there was little here of real value. The furniture would go to the local saleroom where, hopefully, it would raise a few pounds.

And then? It was time to make a decision. He had dithered long enough. What was it he really wanted? Answer: To be with Jinty. Here or in Australia? Answer: Here, or somewhere close. It all sounded so grown-up, but it was time he grew up. He wished now that he had been more assiduous in saving, but there was no way he could ever have saved enough to cover the inheritance tax. He was not the first person to find himself in this situation, and he could not complain: there would be enough left over from the sale to buy some land not too far away and a smaller house. Then he could start his stud farm. Was he dreaming? Not any more. It was time to turn the dream into reality. He felt nervous. Was he rushing things, taking too much for granted? Jinty, for instance. This would all come as news to her.

He tossed the auction catalogue into the wastepaper basket beneath the desk, and went off for a breath of fresh air.

He headed for the cliff top, where the sharp breeze of the afternoon would pump some air into his lungs. He was scrambling down the bank when he saw her climbing up the path along the side of the Yar with a small cage in her hand. Kit approached her with curiosity. She seemed startled to see him, and blushed when he hailed her. "What are you doing?"

"Just sorting out this little feller."

Kit looked into the cage Jess carried in her right hand. It contained a grey squirrel, darting wildly from one side to the other.

"How are you sorting him out?"

"Taking him somewhere where he can't do any harm. Grey squirrels compete with red squirrels and they always win."

"Why?"

It struck her that his questioning was like that of a small child, so she answered him patiently. "No one really knows."

"How did Dad manage to get the red squirrel going here?"

"He started with captive-bred animals and encouraged them to breed."

"By keeping out the grey squirrels?"

"That helped – and a good mixture of trees, broadleaves and conifers."

"But don't the greys just come back in?"

Jess was warming to her subject and he could see the passion in her eyes. "The reserve is like an island. If you look at all the fields around it there's not much cover, so once we'd got rid of all the greys in the Wilderness and the Spinney we could just trap any others that found their way in. Like this one." She held up the cage and looked at the bushy-tailed rodent it contained.

"What will you do with him?"

"I've got a mate who lives in Kent. Just bung him in a travelling-box and send him there on a train and she'll release him in her local wood."

"Why not just . . . despatch him?" He realized the folly of his question the moment it had left his lips. "Sorry. Didn't think. But isn't it a bit irresponsible adding to your mate's problems?"

"One or two more won't make a difference in her part of the world. Greys have been in this country since 1876 – hardly likely to make much difference now."

"Are there red squirrels anywhere else?"

"Not around here. A few on islands in Poole Harbour, and on the Isle of Wight, but nowhere else in the south. It's only in Wales and further north that they're still hanging on. And now here."

"How many do you reckon?"

She thought for a moment. "Maybe a couple of dozen. Maybe more."

He looked at her and marvelled anew at how she had changed in appearance over the past few weeks. And the shy girl who had peered at him from behind the curtain of the farmhouse window when he had first arrived, had opened up. She also seemed to be speaking to him again after the recent silence due, most probably, to his liaison with a member of the foxhunting fraternity. He had no idea what had brought about such changes in her.

Jess shot him a quick smile. "Got to get on. Send this one on his holidays. See you at supper."

"Er . . . not tonight. I'm out."

She didn't turn round, but kept climbing up the bank towards the farmhouse.

As the light faded and the lumbering grey clouds ambled in from the sea Kit walked on towards the Wilderness. Large spots of rain started to fall, hitting his waterproof with distinct splats. His hair began to flatten against his head, and he felt the water trickling down his face. He walked on, turning back only when dusk fell and he was saturated yet freshened by the shower.

Jinty lay on her bed, watching the shadows merge into darkness as the sun set. All afternoon she had dozed on and off, while visions of Kit, Allardyce and Seltzer had pranced about her head. It was a relief to hear household sounds, rather than those of a hospital ward and, in spite of her frustration at not being up and about, she had been relaxed enough to stay in bed and let natural recovery take its course. Soon she would be better. Soon Kit would be taking her out again and she could feel again the thrill of the chase.

She propped herself up on a couple of pillows, anticipating Kit's later arrival. She thought about their night of love-making with warm pleasure, and wondered when she would feel up to it again. Looking down at her wounded limbs she sighed and shook her head, then closed her eyes and dreamed again of the man who had turned her life upside down. If only she had not had to put her body through the same sort of somersault. But it was worth it, she hoped.

She eased her bruised hip so that her weight no longer rested on it, and drifted again into the half-way house between waking and sleeping, wondering how long it would be before he opened the door and smiled his smile.

Mrs Flanders worked away in the kitchen, relieved that once more the household was eating. As she trimmed away the pastry around the apple pie, she mused on the developing relationship between Jinty and young Kit Lavery. How long would this one last, she wondered. She popped the pie into the top oven of the Aga. Here we go again, she thought. Miss Jinty had seemed to have an unfailing knack for choosing the wrong man, but perhaps this time things would be different.

Chapter 20: Blind Eyes

(*Papaver rhoeas*)

"The one thing I can't understand is why your father didn't make over everything to you several years ago." Charlotte was picking delicately at a piece of Stilton and a Bath Oliver while Roly dispensed the port. The four of them – Roly, Charlotte, Jinty and Kit – sat around the gleaming mahogany dining-table in the library at Baddesley Court, putting away the last of Mrs Flanders's huge supper. "That way all this bother over inheritance tax could have been avoided."

"That would have been too simple," Kit replied. "Dad felt that everyone should make their own way in the world. If he'd left me featherbedded he wouldn't have made sure that I got out there and got stuck in."

Charlotte warmed to her subject. "But didn't his father leave him the farm?"

"Yes, but under exactly the same circumstances."

"Well, I think it's surprisingly ill thought-out."

Roly grunted. "Mmm. Not really." He put down his glass of port.

"Sorry, dear?"

"Offers a child a sort of freedom, what?"

"Hardly freedom being stuck with all this to sort out," offered Charlotte.

"No. Roly's right. If Dad had left the place to me in trust, I'd have been honour-bound to carry it on."

"And isn't that what he wanted?"

"Oh, yes, but he wouldn't force his own convictions on to me."

Charlotte looked at him as though he'd lost his marbles. "Sometimes I wonder about your father . . ."

Jinty said quietly, "I think I see what you mean. By not making West Yarmouth over to you in trust, he gave you the choice of staying or not staying. He left you free to lead your own life."

"That's right."

"Who'll buy?" enquired Charlotte, taking a sip of her port.

"Well, I think I've found someone. Or, rather, the estate agent has."

She leaned forward. "Really? Who?"

"I don't know. Some guy who works abroad a lot. Keen to buy the place without even setting eyes on it. At least he'll have to keep it as a nature reserve now that Elizabeth has stuck her oar in."

"Mmm? What?" Roly raised an eyebrow.

"Had a visit from English Nature. She wants them to declare the place a Site of Special Scientific Interest."

"Ah. Mmm. Could affect the price."

"I don't much mind that. I'm all for Dad's work being recognized, and if the reserve were declared an SSSI that would do the trick. I just wish she hadn't gone over my head."

"And is your buyer, ah, keen?"

"I don't know. The estate agent says he wants to keep it as a reserve–"

"He'll have to now," interrupted Roly.

"– but more information than that I don't have."

Jinty's eyes sparkled. "What a mystery!"

Kit looked at her, sitting at the table with a thick knitted sweater draped over her shoulders, her patchy hair held back with clips. His heart missed a beat.

"'Mystery Man Buys Devon Nature Reserve' – I can see the headlines now. Probably going to turn it into a theme park when nobody's looking."

"Not if it's an SSSI," said Roly seriously.

Charlotte looked across to Jinty. "I think you're beginning to feel better."

The commotion outside the door distracted them, and they turned to see Mrs Flanders entering with a tray of coffee and two yapping dogs.

"Lancelot! Bedivere! Come here!" Charlotte patted her leg and the two balls of fluff bundled over in a yapping scrummage to tug at the leather tassels on her shoes. "Stop it! Come on, now, lie down."

Kit looked across at Jinty, who fought bravely to suppress her laughter. Charlotte caught her eye. "You're not to laugh. They have to be disciplined."

Roly coughed and looked at her sternly.

"Yes, dear, I know. But I do try, and they're such lovely boys – aren't you?" She bent down as the two dogs rolled on to their backs in a paroxysm of pleasure. "They just like their mummy to tickle their tummies, don't they?"

Jinty's eyes rolled heavenward, and at the same time she rose from the table and walked over to the fire, nodding at Kit to join her. Roly and Charlotte remained at the table – Roly to finish his cheese and Charlotte to dispense motherly love.

"How are you feeling?" he asked.

"A bit better. Must be Mrs Flanders's cooking. I think I'm actually beginning to wake up. Feel a bit bruised, though – aches and pains."

"I'm not surprised."

"I might go out tomorrow."

"Isn't that a bit soon?"

"Oh, I could do with some fresh air."

"Where will you go?"

"Follow the hunt."

Kit looked stunned. "You're mad!"

Jinty grinned. "Don't worry. I'll only go to the meet. I won't follow them for more than a couple of hundred yards. I'd just like to see a horse or two, that's all."

"Well, you be careful – one bash on that arm and you'll be back where you started."

"Yes, Nurse!"

Kit frowned at her.

"I was wondering . . ." she said ". . . would you come with me?"

"To the hunt?"

She nodded.

"I'd rather not." He hesitated. "Would you mind?"

Jinty looked crestfallen. "And I thought you'd do anything for me."

"I would. I will. But it's just that . . ." There was a frightened look on his face that surprised her. Then he brightened and spoke with mock gravitas: "Do you realize it's more than my life's worth even to associate with you? If I go to the meet I'll probably be excommunicated. I mean, you're talking to the owner of a nature reserve here."

"And a potential Site of Special Scientific Interest."

"Don't remind me." Kit sipped at his coffee.

"Do you think I'm a Site of Special Scientific Interest?" whispered Jinty.

Kit spluttered into his cup and, as Charlotte and Roly looked up, he cleared his throat and replied, softly, "It's not the Scientific bit that interests me."

"You sure you wouldn't like to come upstairs for a quick site inspection?"

Kit's eyes gleamed. "You really are feeling better, aren't you."

"Maybe another day. Still a bit battered for that. But I just wanted to see if the interest was still there."

He looked at her fresh-scrubbed face. "Oh, it's still there."

"So what about tomorrow, then?"

"Mmmm?" He was lost in thought now.

"The hunt. Will you come?"

The troubled look again.

"Of course, if you're not that bothered about being with me . . ." Jinty added.

"Yes. Of course I'll come."

She smiled triumphantly.

"Just promise me you won't tell Mesdames Punch and Wetherby," Kit begged.

She looked him in the eye with all the sternness of a schoolmistress. "There's about as much chance of me telling them that their lord and master went to the meet as there is of Charlotte leaving all her money to the Cats' Protection League."

He kissed her forehead lightly and whispered, "I'm having such a problem with you."

She looked at him steadily. "Good."

That night he lay awake for more than an hour before drifting off to sleep. His head swam with problems and pleasures. Who was the mystery man, Bickerstaffe? He would make enquiries. It was time he knew a bit more about him.

Chapter 21:
Fox and Hounds

(Linaria vulgaris)

Kit rose early – earlier even than Elizabeth – and opened his curtains to discover a clear, dry day. At least they'd not get a soaking. The sun was nudging up behind a distant clump of oak trees; a robin busied itself ferrying nest material into the cloak of ivy on the wall beneath his window, and a blackbird sped off in the direction of a thick hedge, its alarm call cutting through the still morning air like a cleaver.

Kit went to the bathroom to shower and shave, and then came back and stood in front of his father's wardrobe looking for something suitable to wear for the hunt. The prospect filled him with fear and made him feel guilty – even guilty at wearing his father's clothes. What did one wear to hounds? Tweed plus-fours and a check jacket, he supposed. But there was no way he was leaving the house in that sort of get-up. He caught sight of himself, naked, in the full-length mirror of the wardrobe door. His body was still lean and fit, but the tan was fading fast – soon he would be the same pasty colour as his new countrymen. He turned away and took from the chest of drawers a new pair of Levi's 501s and a chunky knitted sweater he had bought in Totnes. Then he studied himself again in the mirror – not exactly the landed country gent, but comfortable at least. He closed the door of the tall oak wardrobe, and tiptoed down to the kitchen in his stockinged feet.

He sawed a thick slice off a loaf of bread, buttered it generously and spread it with marmalade, then made himself a cup of coffee, being careful to take the kettle off the stove before it whistled. Perched on the kitchen table, he ate his makeshift breakfast.

At six thirty he pulled on his father's old Barbour and wellies, and slipped out of the back door and across the orchard.

Jess watched him go from her bedroom window, the bed covers pulled up around her ears. When he was out of sight she rose and got dressed, ready to begin another day.

The meet was scheduled for noon at Lynchampton House, home of Major Watson who had taken on the role of Master for the rest of the season.

Kit had arranged to meet Jinty at Baddesley Court at ten, but until then he'd have to kill time. He was cheered by the prospect of a walk along the cliffs – a three-hour tramp to shake off the torpor induced by lack of regular exercise and lack of purpose.

He took the westward cliff path, striding out across the dense, tufted grass, peppered with rabbit droppings, until he came to the rugged finger of rock called Grappa Point. The wind freshened and he looked down the sheer cliff face to the tooth-like rocks below, watching as rolling breakers smashed into a million droplets of spray, before draping the granite with a veil of rainbow mist.

He inhaled deeply, drawing in the salty air as though it were an opiate. Gulls wheeled around the rock, bickering with one another, erupting into a cacophony of sharp cackles, then gliding off once more on the back of the sea breeze.

Nesting gannets occupied the perilous cavities of Grappa Point's towering pinnacles, clinging determinedly to their footholds and seeing off all attackers who tried to invade their territory. The noise of the colony was deafening as, time and again, marauding rivals were repulsed with sword-like bills and fearsome battle cries.

Kit walked on for more than an hour, passing Mr Maidment's Pennypot Farm, an untidy cluster of buildings nestling in a shallow dip in the land, and eventually striking inland towards the village of Lynchampton, the spire of its church pushing up in a slender pyramid from the rolling acres of green that surrounded it. He could hardly believe he had been away for ten years, so familiar were his surroundings, and so easily did his sense of direction guide him along the way. High Devon banks loomed up on either side of the lane he crossed, already flushed with green as hawthorn shoots burst out of their brown winter scales to open fragile lime green leaves in the early spring air.

On a high knoll between church and sea he stopped and looked about him, more acutely aware than ever before of the difference between his two lives: the one in the southern hemisphere and the other in the north. The south offered warmth and relaxation, a lotus-eating way of life, a life with well-defined priorities. Work, yes, but an emphasis on play. At four o'clock in Sydney Harbour you could hardly move for boats, men going out for the evening with their crates of beer, restaurants thronging with folk intent on enjoying themselves. Wasn't that better than the work ethic here? The Maidment work ethic: living to work rather than working to live. He came up with no definite answers, but only knew that he no longer seemed to have a choice.

He looked at his watch. Half past nine. Time he set off for Baddesley Court to meet Jinty. His heart lifted – and lifted more than it ever had in that land of sun and sea, where warm valleys produced fine wines and fine horses, where the locals boasted that they had 'no worries', and where Heather would be waiting for him to return. Or would she, by now, have made other arrangements? It was time they spoke again, he reminded himself.

The landscape ahead was cool and green, with no vineyards or stud farms, only daffodils and sheep, countryside he had once called home, would soon call home again. He pushed his hands deep into the pockets of the Barbour and set off on a brisk walk to Baddesley Court.

"You look the part!" She greeted him with a peck on the cheek.

"It was the best I could do without looking like a refugee or a hooray Henry."

"Well, it's a reasonable compromise."

"Not as reasonable as yours."

Instead of the cream jodhpurs and navy blue jacket she would have worn to ride, Jinty was decked out in jeans and green wellingtons, her white Aran sweater covering her injured arm, and a Barbour over her shoulders. Her hair was held back under a silk scarf.

"Mmm. I'm not sure about the headgear," she confessed. "Makes me look like something out of *Country Life*. All I need is the string of pearls. But at least it covers up my bald patches."

"They're growing now."

"Not fast enough." She linked her good arm through his. "Do you want to walk or do you fancy a lift? Charlotte's coming with the boys."

Kit raised his eyebrows.

"All right, we'll walk."

"Aren't we a bit early?"

"No, there's a hunt breakfast before they set off. By the time we get there they should be well stuck in. Hope they leave us some."

"Has Roly gone?"

"Yes. Just been down to the stables to see him off. He's taken Allardyce and Seltzer. He'll change horses around half past one. God, I wish I was riding!"

He looked at her pallid complexion. "Look, why don't we go with Charlotte? Never mind the dogs. You ought to take it easy."

"Stop fussing," she said sharply, and he was surprised at her sudden burst of irritation. "I've been taking it easy for more than a week. I need to get back into the swing of things."

"But–"

"Oh, come on." She pulled at his arm and led the way to the track that crossed the fields to Lynchampton House. He hesitated.

"What is it?" she asked.

He opened his mouth to speak, but noticed that her thoughts were elsewhere. She was leading him determinedly in the direction of the hunt. Her mind was on that.

The scene outside Lynchampton House reminded Kit of a table-mat. He had not seen so much horseflesh since he had left Australia. On the curved gravel drive, and spilling out across rough grass that could no longer be called a lawn, were more horses than he had ever seen at one time, their riders jacketed in black and dark green, navy blue and hunting pink.

"Why so many?" he asked Jinty.

"It's a joint meet. The green jackets are from the Beaufort."

Kit looked at the riders and their different liveries. Most were women, exquisitely turned out, their hair in nets beneath black velvet riding hats, their jackets black or navy blue, their jodhpurs a soft shade of yellow – the colour of crème caramel. One turned round in her saddle and flashed him a smile. He thought he recognized the rider, almost called out a greeting, then realized his mistake and gave a half-smile in reply. He watched as the woman walked her horse past the row of boxes, and shivered suddenly at the reawakening of a distant memory.

The men, some in brilliant scarlet hunting pink, some in black with silk top hats, and the Duke of Beaufort's team in dark green, were exchanging pleasantries, as long as their horses would allow them to stay in one place.

Jinty led the way to the back of the house, a large stately pile in red brick with pale stone crenellations and finials about its upper edges. Rooks cawed noisily from the treetops as they walked around a large pond edged with primroses towards a wide, barn-like stable where trestle tables and folding chairs had been vacated at the end of the hunt breakfast.

Down one side of the floor space, several aproned farmers' wives stood behind a long table upon which an assortment of frying-pans were being cleared of the remains of a breakfast.

"Coo-ee! Miss Jinty!"

They turned to see Mrs Flanders staggering towards them with a pile of dirty plates.

"Fancy a bacon sandwich? With an egg? Think we can probably find you one."

Jinty shook her head and turned to Kit. "How about you?"

"Love one, Mrs Flanders – and you should have one too," he told Jinty. "Fuel you up for your walk."

"Not my sort of food. Too fattening."

He squeezed her gently around the waist. "I think you've room for an inch or two after your little local difficulty."

"Cheeky thing. I'll watch you eat yours and even that will probably put pounds on me."

Mrs Flanders pointed them in the direction of one of the frying-pans, and a plump old lady with round-framed glasses beamed at them and cracked an egg into bubbling fat. "Sir Roland's Leghorns. Fresh this morning. Been keeping 'em back just in case. Nice to see you up and about, Miss Jinty. We was a bit worried about you."

Jinty smiled ruefully. "Thank you, Mrs Maidment. It's very kind of you."

Mrs Maidment concentrated on frying, checking the rashers of bacon in the adjacent pan through her misty, fat-spattered lenses. "Crisp or soggy?"

"Crisp, please." Kit looked sheepishly at Jinty, now feeling guilty at the prospect of his tasty sandwich.

As they walked out into the open air, Kit could barely remember an egg and bacon roll tasting so good. He was mopping his chin with a hanky when another hunt follower came round with a tray of plastic glasses, each containing a deep red fluid.

"Stirrup cup?" she offered.

"That's more like it," remarked Jinty.

They took the ruby port from the beaming dumpling of a lady, and sipped at it, standing among the horses, Kit anxious for her arm, and Jinty rather impatiently fielding solicitous enquiries as to her health.

Elderly ladies in quilted green jackets with black Labradors at their heels came and spoke to her; hunky young men on horseback bent to offer her a kiss, and the sun rose steadily in the sky over the girl whose pale green eyes danced like moonbeams on the sea as she flirted.

Kit looked around him at the assorted population – landed gentry and men of the soil in equal measure. There were a few chinless wonders, and women with hearty voices whose ruddy cheeks looked like a relief map of the Volga delta. Patrician tones, male and female, boomed out over the grass, but so too did the earthy voices of farmers and labourers.

"Reckon he's down in yonder copse," said one old man. "Missus saw 'im this mornin'."

"Long gone by now, then," opined another.

Clusters of elderly men in flat caps, with binoculars slung round their necks, and women in waterproof jackets, their bottoms resting on shooting sticks, pointed at this horse, then that one, remarking on the finer points of a hock or criticizing an ugly conformation. Children in jeans and wellies leaned idly on the low wall at the front of the house, and from beyond them all came the discordant music of hounds giving tongue.

The sound grew louder, until the canine army spilled round the corner with the huntsman at their centre. Perched high upon a chestnut mare, Titus Ormonroyd was no longer a glass-eyed, bow-legged man in dirty overalls. In his blood-red jacket and faded black velvet cap he looked like a king or like Jove in his Chair, surveying his kingdom from on high.

Beside him was the Master of the Beaufort, in green jacket, calling to his hounds like a headmaster endeavouring to keep control of a class of rowdy adolescents. "Come on . . . hold up together!" he bellowed.

Titus, seeing Kit and Jinty, winked and raised his cap, before the Master shouted once more at a recalcitrant hound who had scented egg and bacon rolls and was off on a chase of his own.

"Paleface – go on," yelled the Master, and a couple of followers did their best to repel the hungry member of the pack who preferred the taste of pig to that of fox.

"Aren't these Titus's hounds, then?" asked Kit.

"No. The Beaufort bring their own."

"So he's not in charge today?"

"Oh, he's still the huntsman. He'll still tell the Master where he thinks the fox will be."

"I see."

At this point a higher-pitched yapping joined the contralto tones of the hounds, and Charlotte approached them with her two pompoms on leads. Jinty saw her coming. "I think Uncle Roly's waiting until these two are out of the way before he makes an appearance."

Charlotte passed them at speed. "I'm just putting these two in the car. Bit high-spirited today," she offered, as she was swept along almost horizontally behind the delinquent dogs.

"Make sure you leave a window open," Jinty shouted after her. "Sun's up." She turned back to Kit. "Which means there won't be much of a scent. Not a good day for hunting."

"I thought it was a lovely day," he said, looking up at the pale blue sky with just the occasional wisp of linen-white cloud.

"Better scent when it's cold and wet. Sad but true," and she dug her good elbow into his side. "Here comes the boss."

Sir Roland Billings-Gore came round the corner of Lynchampton House with Major Watson. The Major was mounted on a grey and Roly on Allardyce, whose flanks shone in the noonday sun. He walked the horse over to where they stood and raised his cap to Jinty. "All right . . . what? Feelin' all right?"

"Fine thanks. He looks good."

Roly leaned down and slapped Allardyce's neck. "Fine feller. Seltzer's . . . er . . . in the trailer. Later on. Mmm. Not much scent, though, eh?"

"Probably not. Still, you never know," offered Jinty.

"Where's Titus?"

Kit pointed to the other side of the lawn, where Titus and the Master of the Beaufort were engaged in conversation.

"Ah ... yes. Well, good huntin'?" He beamed and prompted Allardyce to walk in the direction of his huntsman.

"Do they kill many?" asked Kit.

"About fifty brace a year," replied Jinty.

Kit whistled. "That's a lot."

"We've got a lot of foxes."

"How many hounds?"

"Sixteen and a half couple – the Beaufort have more, I think."

"What sort of language is that? Why can't you just say thirty-three?"

"Because we don't."

"And why a half?"

"Need one to catch the fox. Come on."

Kit knew the complicated logic of foxhunting but continued to tease as they walked towards the twin brick pillars that sat at either side of the drive. Jinty motioned him to sit on the low wall. Before them now, displayed like some cinematic panorama, was the vista of a Devon valley – clumps of trees and copses scattered at intervals over the greening hills and valleys.

"Wow!"

"Good view, isn't it?"

"Amazing. I've never been to this house before."

"It's why I wanted to come. We shouldn't need to walk very far. We can watch for a while from here – they'll probably be led off down there." She pointed to a distant patch of woodland. "Titus reckons they might be in luck." She turned her head to the right to look down the lane that approached the drive of Lynchampton House. "But I'm not sure that we are."

Kit looked in the direction of her gaze, to see a small group of people approaching. They were clad in combat jackets and balaclavas. They carried placards and sticks, and they were not in pursuit of a creature with four legs.

Chapter 22: Woundwort

(*Stachys arvensis*)

"Do they always come?" asked Kit.

"No. Never seen them before. It's usually the local RSPCA ladies in their old Range Rover. Placards and stuff – FOXES BEING MURDERED IN YOUR AREA TODAY. That sort of thing. We have a good relationship with them."

"Well, I don't like the look of this lot."

"Nor me. Come on, let's go back inside the grounds."

Kit and Jinty made to move off, but the gang of around fifteen individuals had already spotted them and began to shout, "Fox killers! Murdering bastards!"

As though on cue, the hunt rounded the front of the house, the hounds spilling out ahead of the horses as the shrill *ta-roo, ta-roo* of the horn goaded them on. Titus and the Master of the Beaufort led the field, clattering out of the drive amid the sea of hounds.

Jinty and Kit flattened themselves against a pillar to one side of the entrance as the horses came through at the trot, at which point the saboteurs, now maybe twenty yards away, held up their placards and began spraying the road with aerosols.

"Away, away!" shouted Titus, as he rode through a side gate and into a field to avoid the gang and their attempt to put the hounds off the scent.

Seeing their quarry take avoidance tactics, the gang ran forward, but as the number of riders and mounts increased, they slowed, positioning themselves to one side of the turning phalanx of horses.

Two of the gang rushed forward, pushed their placards up into the

621

faces of a pair of riders – a young boy, whose horse shied, then galloped off ahead of the field, and a robust middle-aged woman who struck out with her riding crop, dislodging the cardboard, which read, 'HOMICIDAL FOX KILLERS'.

Other members of the gang surged into the fray as the last of the riders rounded the corner and turned into the sloping field. Most of the horses were cantering away on the lower slopes now, and only the laggards remained. Sticks were raised and with angry cries the balaclava army ran at the last few, waving their weapons high in the air.

One of the horses began to turn in its own circle. The rider, a girl of twelve or thirteen, did her best to rein it in – a fourteen-hand piebald cob – but was clearly having difficulty. She called in vain at her horse: 'Bessie, no! Come on! *Bessie!*" Jinty, unable to restrain herself, started to run at the saboteurs to shield the girl, but Kit saw what she intended and cut her off, interposing himself between the saboteur and the young girl's mount.

The stick came down on his head with a resounding crack, and stars flashed in front of him as his knees buckled and a red curtain descended over his right eye. His head throbbed and buzzed as Jinty cried, "Get off!" Through his one good eye, Kit saw her run at the saboteur who had hit him.

He lunged forward to protect her and came face to face with a smaller saboteur, whose eyes and a wisp of fair hair were the only things visible under the camouflage of the thick balaclava. "No!" yelled the small figure, and the one with the stick raised above Jinty's head backed away and ran off down the lane with the rest of the tiny army in its wake.

Kit squinted at the hazy figure who had shouted, but within moments it, too, had fled. The only people who remained in the lane were the foot-followers who had not yet made their way down the field.

Jinty rushed to his side, pulling a handful of tissues from her jacket pocket to staunch the blood that was flowing from a cut in his eyebrow.

"Are you all right?" she asked, panic in her voice.

"I think so." Kit slumped on to the low wall. "Ow! It bloody hurts."

"Just keep still. Put your head up, if you can, and hold this tissue to it. Press hard."

Three more hunt-followers ran up, one carrying a first-aid case. Within a few minutes Kit's face was cleaned of blood and a large plaster with a wad of cotton wool beneath it was stuck above his eye.

"I think you'd better come with me," said the voice of the older man who was now repacking the first-aid case. Kit looked at him. It was Dr Hastings.

"I think you'll need a couple of stitches. I can do them at the surgery."

"Can't I just–"

"I think it would be a good idea. It's a deep cut."

Kit looked at Jinty. "I'll come with you," she said, concern etched into her face.

They were interrupted by a shriek. The small group turned in the direction from which it had come to see Charlotte running up the lane from where the cars were parked on the wide grass verge. "I don't know what they've done! I don't know what they've done!"

"What on earth . . ." began Jinty.

"My boys! They've hurt my boys!" Charlotte's voice cut through the air in a heartrending wail, as she turned and raced back down the lane with the party of hunt-followers hard on her heels. When they reached her car, they saw her two dogs on the back seat, their eyes streaming with mucus, their breath coming in short gasps. No longer the yapping bundles of fluff they had been but half an hour ago, the only sound that came from them now was a pathetic whine.

"What shall we do?"

Dr Hastings was swift to give his opinion. "Get them to the vet – now! I'll drive. Get in." With Charlotte in the front seat beside him, and Kit and Jinty in the back with the two wheezing dogs, Frank Hastings put his foot down and burnt rubber all the way to the veterinary practice in Lynchampton. By the time they arrived, Lancelot and Bedivere were no longer breathing.

Chapter 23:
Mourning Widow

(Geranium phaeum)

Roly gazed into the fire, a glass clenched in his right hand. "Just can't understand it. Never any bother before. RSPCA ladies very well behaved. But this . . ." He took a gulp of his whiskey.

Kit was seated in the armchair opposite, the large plaster replaced with neat sutures. He took a sip from his own glass and felt the amber liquid burn down his throat. "Hasn't it happened before?"

"Maybe once in the last five years. Never this bad. So much huntin' down here. Competition too stiff for 'em."

"Why now?"

"Lord knows."

Kit rubbed his head. "I just can't see how they can justify harming other animals when they're trying to protect the fox."

"Mmm. No use looking for sense in it. There isn't any. Can understand peaceful protests, yes. But not this. Fox at least has a chance, unless he's from the town."

Kit looked puzzled. "What do you mean?"

"They bring 'em here, town foxes. Catch 'em in town, bring 'em down here and release 'em."

"Why?"

"Think they have more of a chance in the country."

"And do they?"

"No chance at all. Dead within the year – starved to death or set upon." Roly shook his head. "No sense in it."

The door of the library opened, and a weary Jinty came to join them.

"How is she?" asked Roly.

"Sleeping now. Dr Hastings gave her a sedative. Poor thing. Completely beside herself."

"What have they done with . . . er?" asked Kit.

"Left them at the vet's. We can collect them when we're ready. Charlotte wants them buried at home."

The three stared silently into the burning embers, while Charlotte drifted in and out of sleep in the room above. The house, as it had on the evening after Jinty's fall, seemed strangely quiet.

Roly would have given anything to have tripped over a yapping dog.

Kit's return to West Yarmouth had been greeted with concern by Elizabeth, who asked how on earth he had come to be in such a state. An argument with a car door was the best excuse he could think up at short notice, and after a brief but incredulous stare, she appeared to accept it as the truth.

Jess looked at him curiously as he endeavoured to explain. She said nothing and her face betrayed no expression.

For the next few days Kit busied himself with house clearance, doing his best to see through one good eye and one that was half closed.

The spare rooms presented no problem – old beds, ancient mattresses and ring-stained dressing tables he could dispose of with no compunction. The local removal firm took them to the sale rooms in Lynchampton where, in a week or two's time, they would come under the hammer and be dispatched to the spare bedrooms of other local households in a rural recycling scheme that had gone on for centuries. He delayed making decisions about his father's room, the main drawing room and the kitchen, all of which he would use until he decided what he was going to do and where he was going to live. Like a hang-glider, he hovered over the void of his future, waiting to see which way the wind would carry him. In spite of the estate agent's promises of a speedy reply, he had still not heard anything about the offer.

Jinty's recovery had been faster than her doctor had anticipated, but there were still days when she was enveloped in tiredness that weighed her down like a coat of chain-mail.

They had had little time alone together. Kit understood Jinty's need to rest, but each day he called in to see if she was all right, trying not to outstay his welcome, yet longing to stay each time he had to leave.

Their conversation was relatively superficial, both of them anxious not to push the other too far too soon. What he had pledged to do was sort out the Heather situation, and at ten o'clock one morning, knowing that it would be nine o'clock in the evening in Australia, he dialled her number and waited as the phone rang on the other side of the world.

A man's voice answered: "Balnunga Stud, hallo?"

"Stan? It's Kit. Hiya!"

"Hiya, yourself. How ya doin'?"

"Oh, you know."

"Wish we did, sunshine. Wondering what had happened to you."

"It's a bit tangled, that's all. How's everything there?"

"Ripper. No worries. Two new foals since you left – looking good. Wackatee's colt's coming on fine."

"Sundance?"

"Yeah. That's right. Could do with you here to sort a few things out, though. When are you looking to come back?"

"Difficult to say, really."

"Well, we could do with you as soon as you can."

Tentacles of guilt slid around Kit's conscience. "Is Heather there?"

"'Fraid not. Gone off to Sydney for a couple of weeks."

"Oh." Kit was surprised. And disappointed.

"Think she's a bit fed up, if you really want to know." There was a note of reproach in Stan's voice. "Keeps waiting for you to ring and you don't. You know what women are like." He meant it as a softener, but Kit detected a note of fatherly protection beneath the throwaway line.

"Has she left a number?"

"Nah. Gone with a couple of friends. The Johnson boys. Moving around."

"I see."

Kit changed the subject – talked about the horses, the farm staff, and anything that would take his mind off the fact that Heather had taken a holiday with Marcus Johnson without letting him know. She had his number, after all.

When he put down the phone, with promises to call back in a couple of weeks, he felt a mixture of regret and irritation. Regret that he had still not told Heather of his feelings, and irritation at her departure. He knew he could hardly blame her for going off rather than being glued to the other end of a phone just in case he chose to call, but why had she gone with Marcus Johnson? She must have known how he would feel. He did his best to rationalize the situation, but could not stop himself feeling angry and, if he were honest, a bit jealous. The anger, he knew, was at his own weaknesses – his failure to voice the decision he had already made, and his inability to confess to Stan that it was unlikely he would return. Having built himself up to take a grip of the situation, his resolve had slipped through his fingers. The jealousy he could not explain.

He rose from the desk, swore and stomped out of the house.

When Kit arrived, Titus was cleaning out the kennels. "Thought you had a girl to do that," he remarked.

"So did I. Little bugger's buggered off, so bugger 'er. Wish I'd seen it comin'."

"Kill anything yesterday?"

"Nah. Bugger got away."

"Lot of buggers getting away lately, aren't there?"

Titus straightened up and grinned. "Coffee?"

"Yes. I need one."

Titus closed the metal gate behind him. "At least I won't have to do it for long. One of Maidment's lasses is comin' over this afternoon. Thinks she might like the job. Bloody relief."

"So why did Becky . . . bugger off?"

"Conscience. I thought she was OK about it. Never came out huntin', just looked after the 'ounds. Beats me, you know. They'd rather see a fox live for ever, or at least until its teeth fall out with old age. That way it could 'ave a natural death – you know the sort of thing, starvation, disease, agony, misery, the sort of pleasant death an old fox deserves. Shame to kill it before it has the opportunity of a quiet retirement, isn't it?"

"Cynical sod."

"Not cynical at all. 'Untin' keeps down numbers and it keeps the fox population healthy – survival of the fittest and fastest."

"And sport for you?"

"And work and pleasure for the community."

"You could get that from drag-hunting. Why don't you do that?"

"Because it's like kissin' your sister."

"Old one."

"Good, though."

Kit looked thoughtful. Titus made the coffee and the pair sat side by side on an old bench by the kennel wall. Further down the path, Titus's two horses, Mabel and Floss, were nodding over the doors of their stable, Mabel as dark as night, Floss a pale chestnut with a hogged mane. They tugged at hay-nets, hung on the outside wall.

"So 'ow do you stand on 'untin'?" asked Titus, "If yesterday's experience 'asn't coloured your judgement."

Kit rubbed his head. "I think it stinks."

Titus looked surprised. "Well, that's honest."

"Oh, I can understand why you do it, but I think you're wrong. If you really want to keep down foxes you could shoot them. It's quick, it's clean, and it's fairer on the fox."

"But foxes hunt."

"Yes, but foxes don't have any option. They have to hunt to live. We don't."

"But if hunting is banned, hundreds of people will be out of work."

"Tough. That's like saying if burglary was banned then hundreds of burglars would be out of work. Just because people have been doing it for years doesn't mean it's right."

"Have you told Jinty O'Hare about this?"

"Don't be daft."

"I'm surprised you can look 'er in the eye." Titus studied Kit's shiner. "Sorry about that. 'Ow's it feelin'?"

"A bit sore."

"Don't know where that lot came from. There's so much 'untin' around 'ere that we don't tend to see many of their sort. Bastards. 'Ow's Lady Billings-Gore?"

"Coming round – slowly. Poor thing's devastated. Can't understand why people who want to protect one animal can kill another."

"Beats me. Most of 'em don't, to be fair, but every now and again you gets one of these minority groups – I think they just go out for a bit of trouble. Don't really care about foxes at all, just want to join in the class war."

Kit looked thoughtful. "Mm."

"Did you get a good look at 'em – before they 'it you?"

"Not really. Had balaclavas on. Saw the eyes of one of them but–"

Kit stopped abruptly. The hazy image of a diminutive hunt saboteur swam into his mind. He saw the thick woollen covering framing the eyes, saw the wisp of fair hair peeping out from beneath it, and the pale eyes looking straight into his.

"You OK?" asked Titus.

Kit was staring into the middle distance, then rose sharply to his feet. "Yes. Fine. I must go." He left the coffee half drunk and walked briskly back to West Yarmouth Farmhouse. Titus watched him go, wondering if he himself was the only person in this neck of the woods who was not on another planet.

The post was late. He wished it had arrived before he had left that morning. Then, perhaps, he would not have had time to think about the events at the meet and would not have put two and two together. But now he could not dismiss the encounter from his mind. The eyes of the saboteur kept boring into his head. Eyes that he knew had looked into his before.

He opened the letter from the estate agent distractedly and absorbed the information it contained: "Mr Jamie Bickerstaffe, £1.25 million, early completion, no chain." He put the letter down and thought of the implications.

The amount was smaller than the estate agent had previously intimated. Should he ask for more? Was a bidder in the hand worth two out in the bush?

Enough. It was time he acted. He hardly cared now whether he was offered £1.25 million or £2 million. He would ring the estate agent and accept the offer.

The second letter was from the solicitor, informing Kit that the notice period for the rental arrangement with Arthur Maidment had expired, and had he written and informed Maidment that this was so?

Not much point now, thought Kit, and pushed the letter into a pigeon-hole at the back of the desk.

He laid the estate agent's letter by the telephone then went downstairs and out into the yard to look for Jess. She was nowhere to be found.

All afternoon he roamed the estate looking for her. Finally he asked

Elizabeth where she was, only to be told that she had gone into Totnes to see friends. He wished he had asked earlier and saved himself the trouble of combing the estate. But at least the walk had calmed him down.

"I'm afraid you'll have to fend for yourself tonight," warned Elizabeth. "If you're in." Her dig was not lost on Kit. "I'm on the beach at Tallacombe with the naturalists."

Just for a second Kit thought she had said 'naturists', and the prospect of Elizabeth Punch naked on the wind-blown West Country beach, with parchment-coloured flesh clinging in goose-pimpled swags to her protruding bones, made him shudder. "Oh," was all he could say.

Elizabeth made what she hoped would be a friendly remark: "Bivalves of the south-western coast."

"Really." Suddenly Kit realized that his replies were churlish and tried to do better. "Shells?"

"Oysters, mussels, scallops, that sort of thing."

"Very tasty." Again he scolded himself silently for his incivility.

Elizabeth appeared not to notice, and went about her business with a detached air. "Supper afterwards in Lynchampton."

Kit mused on the evening ahead, then brightened. He would invite Jinty round for supper and cook for her, if she felt up to it. He would tell her about the offer and they could celebrate together before the other two West Yarmouth inmates returned.

He checked his wallet then drove into Lynchampton for the makings of a supper he hoped Jinty would never forget.

Chapter 24:
Stinging Nettle
(*Urtica dioica*)

The honey-coloured stone of Baddesley Court gleamed in the soft evening sunshine. He got out of the car, mounted the wide front steps and pulled on the old bell, which responded somewhere deep in the house. Mrs Flanders, her hair in its usual aerobatic mode, opened the door and greeted him warmly.

"Hello, Mrs Flanders. I've come to pick up Jinty."

The old woman smiled indulgently. "She's in the stables, Kit. The master and mistress are out and she's just checking the hay-nets." Flushed from the heat of the kitchen and wiping her hands on her checked pinafore, Mrs Flanders returned to the inner sanctum of the house, leaving Kit to make his way to the stable block.

There was no sign of her at first. The tops of the stable doors were all open, and he saw that both Allardyce and Seltzer were munching mouthfuls of hay.

"Hello?" he called across the yard. No reply. He walked on, past the Connemara pony, until he came to a tall open door, held back with a length of rope. He stuck his head inside. "Anybody there?"

"Only me."

He looked up in the direction of the voice to see Jinty sitting on a pile of bales with a net in one hand. The evening sun shone through the dust-rimed windows on to the cobwebs around her, turning them to silvery gossamer and giving her the appearance of some ethereal beauty wafted in from a fairytale kingdom.

Kit grinned up at her. "You look like the Queen of the Fairies."

"Rather me than you!"

"What are you doing?"

"Silly question. Filling hay-nets, of course – well, the last one."

"Thought you were coming to supper."

"I am. You don't think I normally dress like this for work, do you?"

He looked at her. She wore a sleeveless white cotton dress and her feet were bare. Her long legs were dusted with freckles and her eyes glowed. The shafts of sunlight caught her hair and turned it to molten gold.

"Do you want a hand?"

"Here!" She tossed the hay-net down to him and he caught it and put it on the floor.

"How are you going to get down?"

"Over there." She pointed to a rough staircase made of bales and he watched as she made her way over to it. She was not wearing her sling, and used both arms to balance herself as she teetered across the uneven surface.

"Take care," he warned.

"Don't *worry!*"

"No, but I do." As he spoke the words she lost her footing and slid feet first down a chute of hay. He rushed forward to grab her but his intervention was unnecessary and she came to rest with her dress around her waist in a nest of corn-coloured straw, laughing uncontrollably.

"Why do you do this to me?" he scolded.

She looked up at him, her laughter subsiding. "I don't really know."

They gazed at one another for several seconds. "Pull me up?" she asked, offering her good arm.

He reached for it but she unbalanced him and pulled him down alongside her. For a few moments neither of them moved. Kit breathed in the sweet scent of hay and freshly washed hair, and within seconds his mouth was on hers and his hands were exploring her body. He felt the damp warmth of her lips on his. He stroked her arm, then lowered his hand to her long, slender legs. She moaned softly as he caressed her, running his hand down her thigh to her knee and then back up towards her waist.

"Oh, yes," she whispered. "Let's do it here."

He continued to smother her neck and shoulders with kisses, barely breaking off to murmur, "But what about . . ."

"There's nobody around," she whispered. "Only the horses." She began to unbutton his shirt and to run her hand over his chest.

He knelt up in the hay and took off his shirt, never for a moment looking anywhere except into her eyes. She watched mesmerized as he removed the rest of his clothing until he stood before her in the hay, quite naked.

She looked at the broad chest, strong legs and muscular arms, at the late sunlight glinting on his fair curls. "You're so beautiful," she whispered. He held out his hand to help her up, his heart thundering, and lifted off the thin white cotton dress, easing it over her injured arm with care until she stood before him wearing only the briefest triangle of lace. Her arms were at her sides and her eyes shone. Slowly, he removed the last item of her clothing and they faced each other on the plump mattress of sweet-smelling hay.

For a minute neither of them moved, then Kit raised his hands and held them an inch from either side of her face. His whole body pulsated now, but he could not bring himself to touch her. Instead, he traced the contours of her body with his hands. Although he made no contact with her skin she seemed to feel some electric current passing between them. Finally she could bear it no longer, reached out her own arms, took him by the waist and drew him to her, feeling his hardness against her and smothering his shoulders with kisses.

The deep, rich scent of hay filled his nostrils as they toppled and rolled together in it, their hands exploring each other with an eagerness born of physical longing, their skin slippery with perspiration. He wanted to feel his entire body in contact with hers, to leave no part of her unexplored, unexperienced. He wrapped his legs around her, curved his arm about her waist, and traced the length of her neck with his tongue in a frenzy of passion. Time and again he felt he would explode, teetering on the brink of ecstasy until finally they came together in a shuddering climax of passion.

For half an hour they lay there, naked except for a thin eiderdown of dried grass, until Jinty raised herself on one elbow: "What was that you said about supper?"

Kit heard the question only as some distant echo. He turned to meet her eyes, and to Jinty's surprise, it seemed as though he had been expecting to see someone quite different.

*

"Nice smell."

"Who me?"

"Yes. And the supper."

"You all right with Dover sole?"

"Oh, very classy. Good job I brought white." They clinked glasses and drank.

She eased herself in front of him while he stirred the sauce in the small pan on the stove, so that he had to embrace her as he cooked.

"That's nice." He pecked the back of her head. "Hair's growing. Soon be back to its former glory."

"Wish I could say the same for my arm."

"You'll mend. Be patient."

She sipped her wine and they stood silently for a few minutes.

"So, to what do I owe the pleasure?" she asked.

"Oh, the ladies are out and I thought I'd like to return the compliment."

"Lucky me."

They feasted on the fish as though it were the food of the gods, sitting as close to each other as possible at the kitchen table.

"Why does wine always taste better when I drink it with you?" she asked.

"Because I'm fascinating company."

"Oh, I see." She grinned and took another sip.

"Anyway, it should taste good tonight."

"Why?"

"I've got some news."

"I hope it's good news. I've had enough of the other sort for a while." She reached out and stroked his eyebrow. He reached up his hand to take hers and brushed it against his cheek, before kissing it lightly and lowering it to the table.

"I've had a firm offer on this place."

She stared at him but did not speak.

"A good one. One and a quarter million."

"Wow!" she whispered, all the while looking at him expectantly for some further piece of information that would make her feel better. He was here with her now, attentive and loving, so why did she feel uneasy?

"Will you accept it?" she asked.

"Stupid not to."

"So what happens now?"

"Presumably this guy will want a look round – he's bought it unseen but I suppose he'll put in an appearance once I accept his offer."

"Who is he?"

"Works abroad a lot. Firm of financial consultants or something."

At the precise moment he said the name, Jinty felt the same word spilling from her own mouth. She had no idea why she knew, and at the sound of it she felt a sudden cold rush of fear.

"Bickerstaffe."

Kit looked at her incredulously. "How did you know?"

"You can't."

"What do you mean?"

"You can't sell it to him."

"Why not? How did you know? I don't understand." He looked genuinely bewildered.

Jinty turned away and spoke softly, almost to herself. "Why does he want it?"

"Because he wants to own a nature reserve, and presumably he wants to own this one."

Jinty's eyes flashed as she turned back to face him. "He doesn't want a nature reserve. He's never been interested in anything that moves unless it wears a skirt."

Kit was stunned. He had never seen this side of her before. Her eyes burned into him with a mixture of anger and confusion.

"Hang on a minute . . ."

"You can't sell this place to him –" Tears were flowing and she wiped them away angrily with her hand.

"But I don't understand."

Jinty took a deep breath and picked up her glass, then put it back on the table without tasting its contents.

"Jamie Bickerstaffe." For a split second she wondered if it might not be her Bickerstaffe but somebody else's. "It is Jamie, isn't it?" Kit nodded, and Jinty felt herself tumble into a pool of despair. "There's no way he wants this estate because of plants and animals. He's a money-man. Why would he suddenly become interested in a piece of countryside unless it was for financial reasons?"

"But how do you know him?"

Jinty was reluctant to tell him, but she knew she must if Kit were to understand fully. "Because I used to go out with him. Until he decided he didn't want me any more."

In a sudden flash of comprehension Kit understood the reasons for Jinty's reaction. "Oh, I see."

"No, you don't."

"I think I do. You don't want me to sell this place to an old flame."

Jinty could not believe his coldness. "No. It's not just that –"

"Because he dumped you, you want me to turn him down?"

Her eyes burned. "Yes, I do."

"But I can't – I have to sell this place and he's happy to keep the reserve going, which is what I want."

"Oh, bugger the reserve. I don't care about the sodding reserve. I just don't want Jamie Bickerstaffe muscling in round here."

Kit was hurt. "But what about you and me? Isn't that more important than him?"

"You don't understand, do you?"

"To tell you the truth, no, I don't."

"So will you sell to him?"

"Yes. If he wants to buy and everything else works out."

"What sort of everything?"

"Searches and that sort of thing."

"Nothing else will stop you?"

"No." Kit tried hard to sound reasonable, but in the face of such irrational behaviour from Jinty, how could he hope to make her understand?

"I see." She sounded almost broken. She sat at the table, quite still for a few moments, then got up. "I'd better go."

Kit pushed back his chair and made to get up.

"No. Please." She backed away. "I thought you might understand."

He looked hard at her, trying to divine her true feelings. "And I thought you cared about what I cared about."

She shook her head. Then she turned and slowly closed the door behind her, and Kit found himself standing alone in a kitchen that smelt of overcooked fish.

The walk home to Baddesley Court seemed interminable. The cool breeze sawed at Jinty's bones and she shivered beneath the thick sweater. She had allowed herself to believe that Kit Lavery was different. In the short time she had known him she had convinced herself that he was special, yet he had turned out to be just like the rest. As soon as she had asked him to do something for her he had backed away.

When the chips were down, his own future and his own convenience were what mattered to him. Why had he never asked her what she thought? Why had she even assumed it would cross his mind? At least Jamie Bickerstaffe was up front about everything.

She began to shiver. Stupid! Why had she not asked him to drive her home? Or to call a cab? Instead she had walked out on him in her anger, and now found herself chilled to the marrow in the cold evening air. She turned up a narrow path to cross the side of a wheatfield, anxious to shorten the journey as much as possible.

Kit had left the kitchen hard on her heels, but she had turned left, not right, outside the house. If she had kept to the lane she would have seen the bright yellow Fiat Punto coming in search of her. As it was, the driver missed her by only a few seconds, and returned home at midnight in deep despair.

At the same time, Jinty climbed the stairs of Baddesley Court, her teeth chattering. She removed her clothes and clambered clumsily into bed. It was half an hour before she stopped shaking, and a further half-hour before she fell asleep.

Chapter 25:
Swords and Spears

(*Plantago lanceolata*)

Life was a bugger, that was all there was to it. He tossed a bucket of scraps to the pig and didn't even wait for conversation. It was three days since the row with Jinty. Three days since he had spoken to her. Time and again he felt he should go round and explain, but each time he convinced himself that there was little point. He wanted to sell to Bickerstaffe; she didn't want him to. She cared nothing for the reserve, and until now he had not known just how much he cared for it himself. There was no room for manoeuvre.

He tried to think of other things, but what else was there to think about? Everything seemed to revolve around their relationship, or be tied up with it. Whichever way he moved, whatever he tried to achieve, he always came back to Jinty. He had thought that she was the reason he was doing all this, but she seemed unwilling or unable to understand that.

And Bickerstaffe: had she really finished with him, or was she still seeing him? Jealousy surfaced.

Elizabeth watched him going about the place with a distracted air but, as always, kept herself to herself until he buttonholed her outside the barn.

"No Jess?"

"No." Elizabeth was unsure where the conversation was leading. "I think she must have decided to stay longer than she first thought. She should be back by the weekend, though."

"Does she often go away?"

"No. I don't think it's happened before. I didn't think you'd mind. She works very hard."

Kit was aware that Elizabeth was leaping to Jess's defence. "I wasn't complaining. Just wondering."

There was an uneasy silence. Kit broke it. "Can I ask you something?"

Elizabeth looked apprehensive. "Of course."

"You know Jess was a hunt saboteur?"

Elizabeth nodded.

"Does she still . . . do it?"

Elizabeth regarded him curiously. "No. Why do you ask?"

"I just wondered."

"She stopped when she came here. Your father convinced her that her energies would be better spent doing this sort of work rather than making a nuisance of herself."

Kit looked thoughtful. "And she wouldn't go back to it?"

Elizabeth's reply was emphatic. "Certainly not." She stared at him, unsure of his meaning. Then he asked another question.

"Do you know a man called Bickerstaffe?"

Elizabeth thought for a moment. "No, I don't think so. Why?"

"He's interested in buying the estate. Well, more than interested. He's made an offer."

"I see." Her face remained impassive.

"But I want to make sure he'll keep the reserve going."

She regarded him thoughtfully, then said, "There's an easy way to do that."

Kit raised his eyebrows.

"Explain to him about the SSSI. Tell him it's likely that English Nature will declare West Yarmouth a Site of Special Scientific Interest."

"The ultimate test."

"Yes. A bit of a test for you, too, isn't it?"

Kit looked directly at her. "What do you mean?"

"To find out whether you really do want the reserve to continue or whether you just want to take the money and hope for the best."

He was surprised at her bluntness. He made to answer, but Elizabeth spoke first. "I know what it's like. The battle between money and conscience. I watched your father struggle with it. His conscience won. But only just."

639

"But Dad was passionate about this place."

"Oh, there was an offer a few years ago when your father hit a bad patch. We had gales and the place was in a bit of a state. The red squirrels didn't seem to be increasing, the weather was foul. He wavered. Almost sold up."

"What happened?"

"He got through it. Found his feet. Somehow found enough motivation to keep going."

"Simple as that?" Kit was disappointed at the straightforwardness of her reply.

Elizabeth sounded irritated. "Not simple at all. Took a lot of soul-searching."

"But Dad won through in the end. Just like he always did."

"You do him an injustice, you know."

"Oh, no. I know how good he was."

"That's not what I mean. His life wasn't as straightforward as you think."

Kit leaned on the wall of the barn and folded his arms. "In what way?"

Elizabeth hesitated. Kit wondered if she had been a party to his father's illness. Had he confided in her? Surely Dr Hastings would not have told her.

Elizabeth's reply startled him. "You mustn't hold yourself in such low regard compared with your father."

"Why?"

"Because he was not without his weaknesses."

Kit stared at her, mystified by her unexpected candour.

"Your father was a good man – a great man – but he was a man and, like any other man, he wasn't perfect."

"I don't think I . . ."

"I'm not saying this for any reason other than to make you understand that your father was human, and that you are more like him than you may realize. I know you found it hard to follow in his footsteps and thought you could never be as good as he was, but you are probably being too hard on yourself."

"Why are you telling me this?"

"Because if I don't tell you you may do the wrong things for the wrong reasons. You should be in full possession of the facts before you act on anything. It's only fair."

Kit pressed back against the wall of the barn to steady himself for the expected onslaught.

"Your father was a committed conservationist with his own way of doing things. He loved this place and desperately believed in his work here. He wanted nothing to get in the way of it. But he was also . . . an ordinary man. Look . . . perhaps this is the wrong time."

"No, please, carry on."

"Shall we go inside?"

"No. It's fine." He felt safer outdoors. More able to cope with what might be coming if he had air and space. He could not imagine what she was trying to say.

"I don't want you to think that I am saying this for any selfish motive. I simply want to help you realize your own worth." She leaned against the wall a few feet away from him and looked out over the valley in the same direction as his gaze.

"Your father and I were lovers."

The words echoed out across the landscape as though amplified by some unseen microphone. Kit neither moved nor spoke.

"Your mother was dead, of course, but my husband was still alive."

"But I thought . . ."

"Miss Punch. Yes. Classic spinster. Man-hater." She smiled a painful smile. "I reverted to my maiden name – didn't really want to carry my husband's name for longer than I had to. A difficult man. Not very good at . . . well, relationships."

Kit could not believe what he was hearing.

"Your father and I just had a sort of . . . rapport, that was all. Unspoken, mostly."

Kit tried to disguise his surprise. "Did Jess know?"

"I don't think so. By the time she came along it had all but petered out – the physical side, that is. We were never overly demonstrative anyway. She may have thought there was something between us, but she never said anything and we were always very careful."

"And my father and Jess?"

"She worshipped the ground he walked on."

"And he?"

"Loved her like a daughter. I used to watch him looking at her sometimes. I'd never seen such love in a man's eyes – protective love."

She smiled ruefully to herself. "I used to find it difficult. Easy to feel left out. Stupid old woman."

"Jealous?"

"Deeply."

"But you didn't tell him?"

"No," Elizabeth said softly.

"Why not?" he asked gently.

"No right to."

Kit turned to look at her and saw that her eyes were filled with tears. "I wanted his attention to be concentrated here, not on someone who would distract him."

"I see."

"But towards the end of his life I think I could see into him more clearly. There was something more relaxed about his manner. We seemed, if anything, to be coming closer together. We'd have conversations over supper – when he'd had a few glasses of wine. He asked if I'd take care of things if anything happened to him. I thought at the time that it was odd. He'd never been morose before. And then he fell down the gully and that was it. All over," Elizabeth said softly. "So just remember, you don't have a monopoly on doing things for the wrong reasons. We all mess up from time to time. I'd just like you to get it right, that's all."

She pushed herself up from the wall, picked up the empty swill bucket and walked briskly off towards the barn.

Jinty watched with a trained eye as Sally trotted Seltzer round the manège at Baddesley Court. "Seems all right now."

"Well, at least he's putting his weight on it. It was a bit tender yesterday. Funny old boy." She patted his flank, and Jinty watched as she changed direction and trotted the horse round the other way. Her mind began to wander. She looked out across the rolling fields, fresh green in their spring livery, beyond the budding oaks in which rooks cawed, in the direction of West Yarmouth and the sea.

She could not remember feeling so low since her parents had died. She was Irish, had a way of rising above the worst of her troubles, but the combination of Charlotte's grief at the loss of the 'boys', Roly's quietness in the face of his wife's misery, and the loss of someone she had thought might change her life, left her with a hollowness she found hard to bear.

Sally reined in Seltzer and jumped down by her side. "You OK?"

Jinty came back to earth with a bump. "Yes. Fine." She managed a distracted smile.

"You'll get over him, you know."

"No."

"What?" Sally grinned, disbelievingly.

"I won't get over him. I don't want to get over him."

"Not like you." She slipped the horse's reins over his head and made to lead him off, then stopped. "I didn't know it was so serious."

Jinty winced. "Neither did Jamie." Then she turned and walked back to the house, leaving Sally and Seltzer alone in the sandy arena.

The surgery waiting room was small and almost empty. A woman with a small boy whose fascination for the contents of his left nostril bordered on the unhealthy were finally called in and Dr Hastings's elderly receptionist stuck her head through the hatchway from the adjacent office. "Doctor won't be long now, Mr Lavery."

"Thank you." Kit riffled though the regulation copies of *Country Life* and *House Beautiful*, *Woman's Weekly* and *OK*, all at least a year out of date, then scoured the walls of the small room for anything that might take his mind off his current situation.

Nothing did. He had replayed in his mind again and again the events of the fateful evening, but still could not work out how better he could have handled it. His circular thought processes were interrupted by the departure of the woman and the boy, who now seemed to be scratching at his bottom with unwise vigour.

The head appeared at the hatch once more. "Doctor will see you now, Mr Lavery."

Kit got up, walked along the short corridor and tapped on the cream-painted door at the end. "Come in." The voice was friendly and positive. Dr Hastings was drying his hands on a length of paper towel. Kit wondered which of the young boy's orifices the doctor had been called upon to explore, gratefully noting the assiduousness of his personal hygiene before turning his thoughts to his own state of health and the stitches above his right eye.

"Right. Let's have a look at you." The doctor examined the eyebrow, then lifted the eyelid and shone a magnifying torch into the pupil. "Mmm. Well, that seems to be fine. Coming along nicely. I think we might have these chaps out now." With his half-moon spectacles on the end of his nose, he snipped away at the stitches, carefully drawing them out until Kit's eye was clear of needlework. The he leaned back in his chair and dropped the implements into a steel dish. "There we are. Almost as good as new. Shouldn't take long to heal and the swelling has gone down, as I'd expect."

"Thanks." Kit ran his fingers lightly over the wound.

Dr Hastings was scribbling notes on a small file and Kit saw that it was his own childhood medical notes. "I didn't think you'd still have those."

"Oh, yes. Amazing filing system here." Frank Hastings raised an eyebrow and smiled. "No one escapes until . . . well . . . the final escape." He realized the indelicacy of his remark and cleared his throat before continuing with his spidery writing.

Dr Hastings had arrived in West Yarmouth shortly after Kit's departure for Australia, but had slipped into the mantle of his predecessor, Dr Strange, quite comfortably. A small West Country practice suited him, and his calmness and probity suited his patients.

Kit waited until the doctor came to the end of his writing and looked up. "Well, that's it. You can go now. Just try not to get it bashed again too soon."

"Yes. Right. Thanks. Er . . . could I ask a question?"

The doctor looked at Kit over his half-moons. "Of course."

"My father."

"Yes?"

"Was he a happy man?"

Chapter 26: Knotweed

(*Centaurea cyanus*)

The doctor looked hard at Kit. "What makes you ask?"

"I've been talking to Elizabeth Punch."

"Does she think he was happy?"

"I don't know. Did he confide in you about anything?"

"This and that."

"Were you close friends?"

"Reasonably close. I used to take your father fishing in my boat."

"But I thought he didn't like killing things?"

"No, but he liked eating fish."

Kit looked confused. Frank Hastings read his expression. "I mend people, but I kill fish. The Duke of Edinburgh is patron of the World Wide Fund for Nature but he shoots grouse. Your father encouraged wildlife and saved species from extinction, but he loved fresh mackerel. We're all a mixed bag of convictions and contradictions, you know. We all battle our way through life trying to listen to our consciences and avoid following our instincts, but sometimes they're just too powerful to resist. I've sat with your father and drunk a bottle of Pouilly Fumé and eaten smoked mackerel and the expression on his face has been one of pure pleasure. Is that a bad thing? No."

"Did you see a lot of him?"

"Now and then. We'd go for months without seeing each other then one or other of us would call and we'd meet up for a meal or go fishing. We got along pretty well."

"Did he ever talk about personal things?"

"He talked about you. How proud he was of you. How he felt bad

645

that you had had to go away to have enough room to grow. I think he missed your company, if you want to know the truth."

Kit sat perfectly still, gazing into the middle distance.

"He didn't hold it against you. Quite the reverse. Said he'd have probably done the same under the circumstances." He watched Kit's expression change from sorrow to bewilderment. "Don't expect to be able to cope with too much too soon. Speaking as a doctor, you've a lot on your plate at the moment – emotionally. And speaking as a friend of your father's, he understood what you were going through." He paused. "He missed your mother a lot, too."

Kit looked at him. "Did he talk about her?"

Hastings nodded his head slowly. "Occasionally. He loved her very much." He looked thoughtful. "Can I ask you something?"

"Of course."

"How did your mother die?"

Kit lowered his head then raised it. He spoke quite calmly. "She was killed in a riding accident when I was very small. In Sussex. Foxhunting. It's the one thing on which they disagreed."

"Oh. I see."

"Yes. Funny how life works out, isn't it? How history can repeat itself. No one around here knows. At least, I don't think they do. Dad never spoke of it, not even to me, and I could see it was too painful for him so I never brought it up. I think they were quite different from one another. Mum's family were quite well-to-do, cut her off when she married Dad, a farmer's son, even though they had enough money to send Dad to a good school. I can't remember much about her – except her dresses, and her laugh, and her red lipstick. I know she loved life. She was a bit what I suppose they'd have called flighty in those days. But I know Dad was besotted by her." Kit looked thoughtful. "Was there ever anyone else?"

"No. Not in the same way. He had one or two ladies he'd take out to supper. I didn't know them. None of my business. But as far as he gave me to understand, there was nothing ... physical in his relationships. He never mentioned any of them by name. Too wrapped up in his work, really."

"What about Elizabeth?"

"Elizabeth is a bit of a mystery. I think your father had a bit of a soft spot for her. They might have had a brief fling. That's all. And it's not the sort of thing I should be telling you – except as a friend of your pa's."

"And Jess?"

"Ah, yes. Jess." Hastings smiled. "There's a story."

"What sort of story?"

"A human-interest story I suppose the papers would call it. A latter-day *Pygmalion*."

"That sounds a bit sinister."

"No. Not sinister, heartening. She was a lost soul, a raging voice in a confused world, and your father gave her a sense of purpose. Diverted her energies from spraying aerosols at hounds to caring for nature in a hands-on way."

The anxiety in Kit's voice was noticeable. "Did she really spray aerosols?"

"I don't know. Just a figure of speech. But she turned from an angry young woman into a girl with a great sense of practical purpose."

"He must have been very fond of her."

"If you really want me to be honest, and I've no idea why I'm telling you all this, I think she may have been a bit of a replacement for you – in your father's eyes. As far as she was concerned, the sun shone out of him. It was plain for anyone to see. She changed over the months from an introspective, troubled girl to someone at ease with herself. She changed physically, too."

"In what way?"

"When she arrived she had red spiky hair and a face full of metal. By the time your father died she had banished the studs and her hair was soft and fair."

"But when I arrived she had spiky red hair and studs in her face."

"The armour went back on after your father died."

"But she's fair again now and the studs have gone."

"Is that so?" the doctor said softly. "In which case one would be forced to conclude that she must feel secure again. Either that . . . or she's in love."

The questions that Kit had hoped would be answered by Dr Hastings had given rise to even more questions. But it was Jess who occupied most of his thoughts on the journey back to West Yarmouth.

He wanted desperately to keep an open mind on Jamie Bickerstaffe, and tried to smother the jealousy he felt for a rival.

Jamie looked at Kit in a rather detached way, his thick black hair swept back, his suit fashionably creased. Kit looked at him with curiosity, wondering, as one always did with one's partner's exes, what they had seen in each other. He found this question easy to answer: Bickerstaffe had a relaxed, confident air and looks that could easily have secured him a job in films. He was accompanied by the striped-shirt smoothie from the estate agent's in Totnes. They arrived, as promised, at three o'clock in the afternoon for a look round the place. Kit tried to be positive. Perhaps the light would shine at the end of the tunnel, even though the sky looked threatening and lumpen clouds were bowling up over the iron-grey sea to the south-west.

Bickerstaffe seemed impressed with the house, but then only a Philistine could have failed to be charmed by the delicate if diminutive Queen Anne façade, the warm orange brick and the perfect proportions. "Great. Lovely." He murmured suitably plati-tudinous compliments at the required intervals as they toured the rooms. Outside they approached the stables and Kit explained with some trepidation about the two female residents. "No probs," had been the response. Kit was surprised that Bickerstaffe should be such a pushover on this front, and relieved that neither of the ladies was present, just in case appearances should put off the prospective purchaser. Jess had still not returned from Totnes, and Elizabeth, having been told of the impending visit, had found an excuse to disappear for the afternoon. This had surprised Kit, who had expected her to want to stick around and grill the prospective purchaser.

They walked past Wilson's sty to the accompaniment of grunting. Bickerstaffe approached the enclosure and leaned on the wall, smiling benignly at the robust incumbent. The effect this had on the pig's demeanour was dramatic. Slowly, and with great ceremony, she turned her back on the visitor and expelled a torrent of ordure that even the most dedicated countryman would have found over-whelming. She then trotted off as lightly as her considerable bulk would allow to the back of her sty. From here she regarded her visitors through half-closed eyes, but only for the few seconds it took them to escape the putrid atmosphere that hung like a threatening cloud over her enclosure.

Kit suppressed a laugh and hurriedly apologized to the two men, whose noses were buried in handkerchiefs. "Must be out of sorts," he offered.

"Hope so," muttered Bickerstaffe, whose cheeks seemed paler than they had previously.

Kit felt strangely defensive and could not prevent himself from remarking, "That's the country for you. Unpredictable and smelly." Then he wished he hadn't.

"Mmm." Bickerstaffe seemed unimpressed.

They walked on past the orchard and Jess's newly dug vegetable patch, where a bed of strawberries and a row of raspberry canes had appeared since Kit had last taken notice. "Kitchen garden," he offered, waving a hand at the newly turned earth, hoping it would redeem him in the eyes of the purchaser, who had now put away the square of crisp white linen and was trying to fill his nostrils with cleaner air.

Bickerstaffe nodded, and Kit felt a pang of sadness that Jess's planting and Wilson's soil cultivation had not been appreciated.

They walked on, down through the Combe and towards the fields that had been cultivated until recently by Arthur Maidment. Kit pointed out the extent of the farmland, and then they retraced their steps, crossed the tumbling waters of the Yar, and made their way through the Wilderness and then the Spinney, finally pausing a few yards from Rupert Lavery's grave. Neither of the two men noticed it, and Kit, anxious to move on before they asked questions about it, endeavoured to guide them back up the valley. But they remained rooted to the spot, looking back at the Wilderness and nodding at one another before turning their heads to gaze out to sea.

"Great position," offered Bickerstaffe – his most positive comment so far.

"Well, there we are. That's it," said Kit. "The West Yarmouth estate." He felt an unaccountable lump in his throat and put it down to the presence of his father just a few yards away.

The estate agent cleared his throat. "Right. Everybody happy?"

Bickerstaffe stifled a yawn. "Yep. I think so."

"Mr Lavery?"

Kit looked concerned. "And you're quite happy to continue with the nature reserve? Only it's important, you see, that it carries on." His eyes caught the granite headstone behind them. "My father worked hard here . . . to make it what it is."

Bickerstaffe nodded. Kit noticed that his shoes were covered in mud. City shoes.

He remembered Elizabeth's recommendation and decided to bite the bullet. "There's probably going to be an SSSI put on the place, which makes it even more valuable as a conservation area."

The silence could have been cut with a knife and the estate agent's face bore a look that might have split a plank.

Bickerstaffe pushed his hands deep into his pockets. "Sorry? An SS what?"

"SSSI. Site of Special Scientific Interest," explained Kit. "It'll probably take about a year to come through but it's English Nature's way of designating areas of importance as far as nature is concerned."

"And what does that mean *exactly?*" asked Bickerstaffe.

"It means, Mr Bickerstaffe," said the estate agent, in steely tones, "that the place will have to remain a conservation area by law."

Bickerstaffe's whole demeanour changed, as though he had swallowed something that had violently disagreed with him. He stood perfectly still and drew several deep breaths. Then, speaking slowly and deliberately, said, in the direction of the estate agent, "I think we're a little too late, Stephen."

The estate agent paled visibly, then looked sourly in Kit's direction and said, "I'm afraid an SSSI reduces the value of the property, Mr Lavery. It also reduces my client's interest."

"Removes," said Bickerstaffe icily, before looking down and endeavouring to wipe the mud from his hand-made shoes on to the soft grass of the cliff top.

Kit hardly knew what to say. He stood alone in front of the two men, who looked at one another but said nothing. Bickerstaffe tilted his head in the direction of the climb, then nodded curtly at Kit before beginning the walk back to his car. The estate agent spoke softly to Kit through clenched teeth. "I think it would have been better to have told me about this, Mr Lavery. We could have saved a lot of time and money."

"But you said that he was happy with the arrangement. I explained about the reserve and everything."

"Yes, Mr Lavery, you did. But in addition to the saying '*caveat emptor*' – let the buyer beware – there is another saying we use in estate agency, and it is couched in more colloquial terms. 'Once you've sold it, it's no longer yours.' If you understand my meaning." He strode off up the cliff in the direction of his client and his lost commission.

Kit stood rooted to the spot, feeling profoundly stupid. He stared after them until they disappeared from view, then walked over to his father's grave. A small bunch of primroses had been laid on the bright green turf, and he read again the legend on the simple stone:

RUPERT LAVERY

1938 – 2000

WHO MADE

HEAVEN ON EARTH

For a moment it seemed to him that he had only just escaped turning that heaven into hell. He sucked in the tang of sea air. Jinty had been right all along.

He sat down on the turf at his father's graveside as a lone gull shrieked above him and the tide flung itself on to the beach below, with a thunderous, hungry roar. He lifted his arm and leaned against the rough-hewn granite, then stroked its rugged contours while looking out to sea. He said, very softly, "Sorry, Dad."

Chapter 27: Eyebright

(*Viola tricolor*)

The following morning Jess reappeared. She made no announcement of her return but Kit came across her in the Combe with a strange contraption on her back – a sort of tank, fitted with a length of flexible tubing and a lance that seemed to have an old tin can on the end of it. She was pumping at a handle connected to the side of the tank and occasionally releasing a trigger on the lance so that some kind of spray was deposited on the sprouting weed growth around a plantation of young saplings.

Kit's surprise at her return was put to one side as he enquired about the purpose of the equipment.

"It's a knapsack sprayer – with adaptations."

"The tin can?"

"Old baked-bean tin. Stops the spray drifting on to the trees. It's weed-killer. To give them a decent start – without competition."

"I thought you were organic?"

"We are, as far as possible, but we can't keep control of weeds out here in any other way."

"Convictions and contradictions," muttered Kit, under his breath.

"I'm sorry."

Kit changed the subject. "Good to have you back."

Jess coloured slightly and looked down at her work. "Sorry, I had to go. It just took me longer than I thought."

Kit felt unable to ask directly about her absence. "All sorted?" he managed.

"Hope so."

He watched her concentrating on the spraying.

"Shouldn't you be wearing protective clothing for that, goggles and stuff – stop it getting in your eyes?"

"I'd rather just take care. There's no wind. It's a still day and, anyway, you can't see very well through goggles."

The conversation stumbled along until, finally, the sprayer ran out of liquid and Jess slipped it from her shoulders and on to the ground. She turned to face him. "You think it was me, don't you?"

Kit was startled at the suddenness of her question. "Think what was you?"

"Who sprayed the dogs in the car."

They were facing each other, barely three feet apart. Kit tried to marshal his thoughts and his words. "I didn't want to believe it was you."

"But you couldn't think of anybody else."

"It's not that –"

"Once a hunt sab always a hunt sab." There was sadness in her voice as well as anger, disappointment that he should have drawn the obvious conclusion.

"No. It's just that I saw your face – I mean, a face, part of a face – and it looked so like you."

"She does."

"What?"

"She looks a lot like me. In a balaclava anyway."

"Who does? I'm sorry, I'm not with this."

"I can't tell you. I would, but I can't. Don't want to get her into trouble. She thought she was doing the right thing, just like I used to, but she's been led on, again, like I was."

"Who? Tell me who."

Jess looked defiant. "No. It's enough for you to know it wasn't me. Don't ask me any more."

"But you know what happened to the dogs. Do you want it to happen again?"

"It won't happen again."

"How can you be so sure?"

"Because I've made sure. And, anyway, the hunting season's finished now."

"Is that where you were – sorting things out?"

Jess nodded.

Kit felt sorry for her. Here she stood, a small, frail girl with the willpower of a giant. A girl in a world that she seemed by turns to find frightening and fulfilling, standing with him on the cliffs above the foaming sea with her sprayer at her feet.

He moved towards her and rested his hand on her shoulder. "I'm sorry."

"How could you think it was me?"

A sudden gentle breeze took the fair silky hair from the front of her head and lifted it away from her face. He noticed the smoothness of her skin, the rosiness of her cheeks in the chill sea air and the clear, soft blue of her eyes. All at once he could see, with his father's eyes, just what had captivated him. Without saying a word he opened wide his arms as if to embrace her, and she rushed at him with flailing arms, landing blow after blow on his chest.

Repeatedly the punches rained on to his ribcage, thump after thump, reverberating deep into his bones, as she bellowed and sobbed, "Why did he have to go? Why?"

She battered away at him with a desperate rage and he stood, rooted to the spot, like a human punchbag, taking the assault silently and bracing himself against her attack.

"It's not fair! It's not fucking fair!" she howled. "Why? *Why?*"

The blows became weaker until eventually the small frame, spent of its force, crumpled against him sobbing. "I'm sorry – I'm so sorry," she cried. "I . . . just miss him . . . so much."

He cradled her in his arms and rocked her from side to side as tears trickled down his own cheeks. "I know, I know."

"When you came back, I could see him again," she muttered. "And I thought that . . . maybe you . . ." She fought back more tears.

He eased away from her and took her hands, moving them away from her face. She looked up into his eyes and he felt for the first time a kind of warmth, a deep longing that he could not identify. Slowly he lowered his face to hers and kissed her gently on the lips. It seemed the most natural thing to do.

The breeze picked up. Neither of them spoke or moved for several minutes. Only when her tears had subsided did he release her before picking up the empty sprayer and walking silently with her back towards the farm. His arm was around her shoulders. Slowly she lifted her hand and laid it on his.

*

Jinty looked at the new clothes laid out on the bed – two summer tops, some frilly underwear and a pair of black knee-high boots. They had seemed fine in the shops, but now she couldn't understand what had made her buy them. The tops were too skimpy – she'd look like mutton dressed as lamb – and what had been the point of buying boots in spring – even if they were in the sale? She dropped them into the large carrier bag and put them in the bottom of the wardrobe. She'd hoped that a spot of retail therapy might help raise her spirits. It had not.

She looked at herself in the full-length mirror, naked and bruised. What a sorry picture. Hair all over the place, face pale and puffy from crying and her thighs, she was certain, were not as trim as they had been and orange peel seemed to be forming on them – certainly when she squeezed the skin together it was there as plain as day, the texture of a plump Jaffa. What a bloody mess her life was. She reached for the phone and with her good hand tapped in the number.

"It's Jinty O'Hare. I was just wondering, would it be possible for Guy to squeeze me in this afternoon? No? Whenever he can, then. Yes, that's fine. Tell him I want it all cut off. Yes. Yes, I know he'll make a fuss but my mind's made up. Thanks. 'Bye."

She put down the phone, breathed in deeply and went to take a shower. If Jamie Bickerstaffe was around she was damned if he was going to see her looking like this.

Bearing in mind the sort of day he had had, Kit should have guessed who was on the other end of the phone when he picked it up that evening. His heart sank as he remembered shirked responsibilities and errors of omission.

The voice with the soft Australian accent spoke gently. "It's me." He could see her as clearly as though she were in the room with him and his heart leaped before plunging into the Slough of Despond.

"I tried to ring you." He was aware of the defensive tone in his voice.

"I know. Dad said."

"Where've you been?"

Heather paused. "I was going to ask you the same."

They had always got on so well, spoken so freely, but there was a stickiness about the conversation that had never been there before.

"Oh, it's just been mad. I've had so much to do, so much to sort out.

I even had a buyer lined up but he dropped out. It's just . . . impossible."

"I see." There was a note in her voice that worried him.

"How about you?" he asked.

She spoke very calmly. "I've come away for a couple of weeks. Needed to think."

Silence.

"With Marcus Johnson?"

"Yes."

"Why?"

"Why not?"

"Because of me."

"But you weren't there. You didn't ring. What was I supposed to do, supposed to think?"

"But I did ring."

"Not very often. And you didn't say much. Didn't tell me things. It's as if you've become someone else. I just can't get through to you."

There was a long silence before she spoke again. "It's not very good, is it?"

"No."

"There's someone else, isn't there?"

"Yes."

"Serious?"

"I thought so."

"What does that mean?"

"It means I'm in a bit of a mess."

"You're not coming back, are you?"

He was surprised by her understanding, and even more surprised to hear his own reply. "No." It echoed down the line.

"I see."

"What about you and Marcus?" he asked.

"It's good. It's fun."

He could hardly believe she'd said it so lightly. Just like that. Fun. He listened for further explanation, but it did not come. He hoped that she might persuade him, or argue with him, or show some kind of emotion. But there was no anger, no tears. Instead she calmly said, "I'll go now, then. Take care of yourself."

"And you. I . . . I'm sorry."

"Me too. 'Bye."

"'Bye."

And that was it. A relationship built over several years, a friendship, too, ended with one brief phone call. He felt a pall of regret fall over him. He sat back in the chair at his father's desk and stroked the jay's feather across the film of dust that had settled on the once polished oak.

What would happen now? For the first time it seemed quite clear. His life would continue at West Yarmouth. There was no other option. He did not know why, but somehow the responsibility that had settled on him like a heavy yoke since his father's death seemed lighter now, the prospect brighter. He felt an unreal sense of calm resignation, with which half of his brain could not come to terms, but which the other half accepted without demur.

Maybe he was going mad. Yes, that was it. He was unhinged. He looked up at the dusty bookshelves surrounding the desk. Time for a clear-out. Time to put his own stamp on this place.

His thoughts turned to Jinty and his heart sank. Maybe now that Bickerstaffe had gone away it would all be all right. Maybe not. Had he gone away, or would he be moving in once more on Jinty? Or, more to the point, would she be moving in on him? Surely not. She had tried to tell him that there was no way Bickerstaffe would want to run a nature reserve and he had not believed her. He would sort out the farm and the reserve and tell her she was right after all. If she would listen. But, then, as far as she was concerned the reserve did not count for much. "Bugger the reserve," she had said. He felt sick in the pit of his stomach. It was a sort of betrayal that he did not want to accept, did not want to believe.

But there was another fly in this particular ointment, a financial fly. He gazed out of the window at the distant green fields, and the prospect of a phone call to Arthur Maidment brought him down to earth. He looked up the number in his father's address book and found it alongside another entry: Marchbanks Bookshop (Nat. Hist.) and a Totnes number. He might as well start *that* ball rolling, too. Now he was staying here, there was clearing out to be done. He might as well begin with his father's books. He dialled the number and arranged for the effeminate-voiced man on the other end of the telephone to visit the house the following week and advise on the disposal of the dusty volumes. Then he rang Arthur Maidment and arranged to see him the following morning.

*

"Good Lord! Well, ah, yes. Mmm." It was the sort of comment that Jinty had expected from Roly, so it came as no surprise.

"You don't like it."

"No . . . ah . . . yes . . . ah . . . well, I . . ."

"I know, it's too short for you."

Roly stood with his back to the library fire, looking at her quietly, and ordered his words before he spoke.

"Very short but very . . . attractive. Boyish, what?"

Jinty's brow furrowed. "I'm not sure I want to look boyish."

"Only in a . . . ah . . . feminine sort of way. Peter Pan. Puckish. You know."

Roly was doing his best, but the sight of his niece with hair almost as short as his own had come as a shock. He was used to her blonde curls and preferred girls to look like, well, girls.

The library door opened and they turned, still half expecting the two dogs to tumble in. Instead, Charlotte poked her head around its oaken panels and smiled before she had taken in the sight of Jinty and her shorn locks. "Oh. Goodness."

"Not you too." Jinty went across and put her good arm around Charlotte, resting her head on the older woman's shoulder.

Charlotte put up her hand and stroked the back of Jinty's hair. "It looks rather elfin, actually."

Jinty scowled. "That's it, then. I've obviously become a fairy. I've had Peter Pan, Puck and an elf all in the space of five minutes." Then she forgot her own vanity and asked after Charlotte's health.

"Oh, I'm improving. I still can't believe what happened. I still miss my boys, but life goes on, doesn't it?" She glanced at Roly, raising her hand to show that it lacked a glass.

"Ah. Yes. Gin?"

"Yes, please. But what about you?" Charlotte looked at Jinty with concern in her face.

"I'm mending."

"No, I'm not talking about that. I mean you and Kit."

"Ahem." Roly cleared his throat noisily. "Tonic?"

"Of course." There was irritation in Charlotte's voice at Roly's reprimand. "I'm not being nosy, just concerned."

A knock at the library door heralded the appearance of Mrs Flanders.

"Telephone, ma'am. Lady Millington."

"Oh, not again. What does she want at this time of night? If it's trouble with her daily help again I shall scream. I'm not a domestic agency, really I'm not, but she seems to think I'm the only person who has any grasp of staff management."

Charlotte collected her gin from Roly before raising her eyes heavenward and closing the library door behind her.

"She seems to be pulling round," Jinty observed.

"Mmm. Slowly. Getting better," Roly agreed.

Jinty turned to look at the fire, and Roly planted his squat body in the chair opposite.

"Things not too good?" he asked.

Jinty remained gazing at the flames. "Not really, no."

Roly took a sip of his whiskey. "Lovers' tiff?"

"Not sure. Might be more than that." She came and sat at his feet, leaning back on the rough tweed of his trousers.

"Want to talk?" He rubbed his finger lightly across her shoulder.

"Don't know, really. Think maybe I've been a bit selfish."

"Mmm?"

"Jamie Bickerstaffe wants to buy West Yarmouth."

"Ah. I see."

"I said Kit couldn't possibly sell to him. Kit said he had to – he desperately needs the money – and I threw a wobbly."

Roly listened attentively.

"I thought I was doing it for the right reasons. Jamie's not into nature reserves but I couldn't make Kit see that, so I upped and left. Truth is, I don't think I'm over Jamie as much as I thought I was. Do you think I've been stupid?"

"No. Just human."

"But wrong?"

"Hasty."

She turned to face him. "But supposing Jamie actually buys West Yarmouth? What then?"

"Won't happen."

"How do you know?" She turned round to face him.

"SSSI."

"Site of Special Scientific Interest. I know. Kit told me – about Elizabeth Punch's plan."

"Mmm. Not strictly."

"What? What do you mean?"

"Not, ah, strictly Elizabeth's idea. The SSSI."

"But she contacted English Nature. Kit told me."

"Yes, but she had advice."

"Who from?"

"Ah . . . me."

Jinty thought at first that she was hearing things. She laid her hand on Roly's knee and looked up at him. "You advised Elizabeth Punch to contact English Nature?"

Roly took a sip of his whiskey.

"But why? I don't understand. She hates you. Hates hunting."

Roly shook his head and smiled. "'Swhat they call détente, I think."

Jinty gazed at him bewildered.

"Coalition."

"I don't understand."

"When Rupert died there was . . . ah . . . concern that the son might not feel so well disposed towards the estate as the father. Three hundred acres. Rather . . . er . . . important. All sorts of possibilities. Housing. Prairie farming. Shame to let it all go."

"And you wanted to do something about it?"

"Not just me. One or two of us."

"When did all this happen?"

"Soon after Rupert Lavery died."

"But that's meddling."

"Yes. Best interests of the countryside."

"How could you be so sure?"

"Heard rumblings. Seen how fast estates sell down here nowadays. Diversification. That sort of thing. And knew there were lots of . . . ah . . . Jamie Bickerstaffes about."

"But you didn't know about Jamie in particular."

"Ah, yes. Well, not at first. Came across a few things. Year or so ago."

Jinty rose to her feet. "What sort of things?"

"His . . . ah . . . business."

"But you never told me."

"No."

"Why?"

"Didn't want to meddle in that. Your life. Nothing to do with me. Not my place."

She glowered in exasperation. "You never interfere with my life, do you?"

Roly smiled gently.

"So did you know that Jamie Bickerstaffe wanted to buy?"

"Suspected he might."

"But why Jamie? Why would he want to buy West Yarmouth when he's abroad so much? All his dealings seem to be in foreign countries so why has he suddenly taken an interest in Devon?"

"Nature of his business."

"Foreign securities?"

"Foreign development."

"What sort of development?"

"Golf courses."

Jinty looked at him, open-mouthed. "But he never told me."

"Not in his interests. You might have queered his pitch."

Jinty muttered, "Bastard." Then, more clearly, "And the estate agent?"

"Part of the . . . ah . . . system. Probably gets more commission on this sort of deal."

"But if West Yarmouth has an SSSI slapped on it . . ."

"Bickerstaffe won't buy."

"But somebody else might."

"Only if they respect its status. It'll take a year or so to come into force, but English Nature can act faster if they need to."

Jinty came and knelt at his feet. "Sometimes, Uncle Roly, you really surprise me."

"Only sometimes?" Roly ruffled her short fair hair then drained his glass.

Jinty turned her gaze once more to the fire, her mind a jumble, and through the flickering flames she thought she saw Kit's face – the wayward curls, the puzzled look. But deep down in the embers, the image of Jamie Bickerstaffe refused to grow dim.

Chapter 28: Pissimire

(*Taraxacum officinale*)

Arthur Maidment was late. Kit had arranged to meet him where the daffodil field joined the Combe at Grappa Point. That was where Maidment had said he would be working. Although his lease was up, Maidment was not relinquishing his hold on the land that still carried his bulbs. He'd been quite pleasant on the phone when Kit had expected a rather more cantankerous reaction – he had made his approach rather late.

A quarter past ten. Fifteen minutes late. At least the weather was fair. The sea, calm and glittering, shone below him like a field of diamonds and the tussocky grass on the sloping cliff top was freshly carpeted with dew. He perched on a lump of rock and looked out to sea, then turned and surveyed the nature reserve behind him. How had his situation changed so quickly? He had been so convinced that he wanted a life on the other side of the world, but the irresistible pull of home had been too much for him. And it was not all because of Jinty. He'd thought he had grown out of it, grown away from it, but he must have been fooling himself. Something so deeply buried within him told him that this was where he was meant to be. Melodramatic, maybe, but it was not as if he seemed to have any choice in the matter. A calm acceptance was taking over and it worried him a little that he had given into it so easily, especially since the financial side was unresolved.

But his main worry was Jinty. He had never believed in love at first sight, even less in overwhelming passion. There was lust and there was love: one was rapid, all-consuming and irrational, and the other was slow-burning, sure, steady and logical. So what was this? Love or lust? Whenever she was near him he felt an overwhelming thrill and a desire for physical contact. His stomach churned whenever he saw her. When she had lain in the hospital bed hovering between life and death, and he had prayed with all his might that she would pull through, there was no thought of sex then, just a deep anxiety that she would survive to be with him.

But when it came to his feelings about West Yarmouth she seemed not to understand the pull of the place. She loved hunting and he did not, but that could easily be got over if they loved one another. Something was stopping him from going the course. What was it?

Was there a middle ground between these two extremes? Was there a state of mind and heart where friendship and passion melded into one and became true love, deep love, where spirituality and physicality assumed equal importance and combined to make something bigger, more powerful than either? Or was that the wishful thinking of an incurable romantic? He had never thought of himself as a romantic, just someone looking for something he had never been sure existed.

His reverie was interrupted by a shout. Arthur Maidment had arrived. Kit got up from the rock and walked across the rough turf to the fence.

"Grand mornin'," offered the farmer.

"Yes. Grand."

"Rain later, though."

"Really?"

"Always." Maidment winked.

Kit thought he had better get down to business.

"About the land."

"Aye?"

"Are you still interested in it?"

"Depends."

"On what?"

"The arrangement."

"Yes. You said. It's just that I'm in a difficult sort of position."

"No sale, then?"

Kit was stopped in his tracks. "I'm sorry?"

"No sale to yon golfer."

"I don't understand."

"Never mind."

Kit scratched his head then carried on. "I've decided to stay. But I might be prepared to sell the land at the right price if you're still interested."

"Ah, yes, well, change in circumstances. Daughter marryin'. Missus not keen." He looked embarrassed at having to explain.

Kit's heart sank. His one possibility of gaining some revenue had evaporated as quickly as sea-fret.

"But you'd still be willing to rent?"

"Only if the terms are right."

He had not expected Maidment to be so perverse. He had expected a hard bargain to be driven but this was confusing. Perhaps Maidment's cock-eyed politeness was a softener before he dug in his heels about the organic farming and insisted on the terms Kit knew were coming: a return to chemical fertilizers and the use of herbicides.

"I've thought long and hard about it, Mr Maidment, and I simply can't go against Dad's wishes."

"I see." Maidment's tone was noncommittal.

"He worked all his life to leave this land in good condition and I simply can't let all that go just to make more money. I'd like to, but I can't."

"Good for you."

"I'm sorry?"

"I think your dad would've bin proud."

By now Maidment must have been able to read the confusion on Kit's face.

Kit continued, because he felt it safer to do that than to begin trying to understand Maidment's logic. "So if you'd like a renewal under the same organic terms as before I'd be happy to agree to it."

"Fine."

This was the last straw. "But before you seemed adamant that you couldn't go on farming like that. That you couldn't make a profit."

"That's right."

"So why are you happy to do it now when you weren't then?"

"Because of the lease."

Kit looked puzzled. "I don't understand."

"The lease. Have you read it?"

"Well, not in detail, no."

"Did yon solicitor tell you to?"

"Well, he pointed out to me that it was coming to an end, which is why I spoke to you."

"Did he not tell you to read it?"

"Well, he might have done, I can't remember, with everything else that's been going on."

"Ah. I see."

"Well, I don't. What do you mean?"

"There's a clause in yon lease. If you hasn't given me three months' notice to quit by the time the lease is up, then I has a right to carry on for another five years at the same rent. 'Tis a ten-year tenancy with a breaking clause after five years."

"But nobody told me . . ."

"Well, it's there in black and white. Of course, if you didn't know that and you wants to contest it?" Arthur Maidment looked at Kit in his quizzical way. Kit met his eye and saw the potential can of worms opening.

"The same rent?"

"That's right."

"But I thought you said you couldn't afford to carry on under this arrangement."

"Nor could I, if there were a rent increase."

"And if there isn't?"

Maidment shrugged. "I might just manage . . . somehow."

Kit tried to find words, but failed. He sighed. "OK. Same terms. Five years."

The farmer spat on his hand and held it out. Before he had time to think what he was doing, Kit had grasped it. The farmer released his vice-like grip, raised his cap and turned on his heel. "Good to do business with you, Mr Lavery. Be seein' you." And he strode back over his field whistling and knocking off daffodil seedheads with his walking-stick.

Kit rubbed his damp palm down the leg of his jeans and stared after Maidment. Five minutes ago he had stood a chance of selling his land and maybe struggling to make ends meet. Two minutes ago he might at least have been able to negotiate a rent increase to help fund the bankruptcy into which he was surely heading. Now he was back to square one. If this was how he was going to fare as a businessman in Devon, things did not bode well.

*

It was late afternoon when Titus turned up unexpectedly. Kit was in the old orchard, rounding up Wilson and heading her in the direction of her sty. With a stick in one hand and his other arm flailing, he ducked under the gnarled branches of Bramleys and Worcester Pearmains, whose fat, downy buds were just beginning to break. Blossom-time could not be far away, and he looked forward to seeing the reserve in all its glory, with the waterfalls of may blossom he remembered from his childhood, and the fresh green of spring foliage being buffeted by sea breezes.

The freshness of the air, the scent of new growth gave him a thrill he had not experienced for years. It was different in Australia – the whirring noises of the bush, the acrid perfume of eucalyptus and the feathery flowers of wattle. Here the foliage was softer, more delicate, subtly perfumed. There was nothing quite like an English spring.

"There y'are. Been lookin' for yer." Titus ducked under a low branch, encouraging Nell to follow him with a gentle tug at her lead.

As he came up, Kit could see the worried look on his face. "You OK?" he asked.

"I think so. Bit of a shock, though. Got five minutes?"

"More if you like, once I've got this old lady home."

Titus helped with the directional control of the pig, Nell warily keeping her distance, until Wilson was safely tucking into a trough of vegetables in her enclosure.

"What's the matter?"

"Can we walk down there?" Titus tossed his head in the direction of the Yar valley. "Quieter, like."

Kit was puzzled. There was little activity around the pig-sty, but Titus wanted to be further away from the house. They walked in silence down towards the tumbling waters of the slender river, across the bridge and up the other side of the little valley. Only when they had reached the grassy, thrift-studded knoll of Grappa Point did Titus begin to unburden himself.

"Just 'ad a bit of a shock."

"What sort of shock?"

"Well, you know when the dogs were attacked – Lady Billings-Gore's dogs?"

"Yes."

"I found out who it was."

Kit felt a nervous twist of his stomach. "Who?"

666

"Becky. My kennel lass."

"What?"

"She weren't on her own, though. Got into bad company – them as 'ad done it before."

Kit looked Titus straight in the eye. "Not Jess?"

Titus stared back at him with his one good eye. "Noo."

"Thank God."

"Not Jess. Her sister."

"You're not serious?"

"I am. What the 'eck made Becky join 'em I just don't know. Well, I do, because she told me, but I still can't believe it."

"She told you?"

"Aye. Came back this afternoon in tears. Cryin' 'er eyes out, in a right old state. Took me 'alf an hour to calm 'er down before I could get out of 'er what it was."

"And?"

They perched on a low, flat boulder with Nell lying at their feet and Titus explained, his brow creased with a mixture of anxiety and disbelief. "You know 'ow she packed up wi' me – said she couldn't stand to work for the 'unt any more, cruelty an' all that?"

"Yes."

"Well, she gets in wi' a group over in Totnes – back-to-nature lot, hippies or whatever they call 'em now. Gets involved with some lad called Dave who's into hunt saboteuring. Falls in love with 'im. Crackers about 'im. Only she isn't the only one. Some lass called Philippa Wetherby's mad on 'im, too." Titus groaned. "What do women see in men like that? Anyway, 'e tells 'er that she 'as to prove 'erself. Show 'im 'ow serious she is about 'im. So 'e sets 'er this task. She 'as to go with 'em on one of their days out and join in. She thinks she's just goin' to be wavin' a placard and shoutin'. Maybe sprayin' stuff around to put t'ounds off the scent. Then 'e tells 'er she 'as to spray Lady Billings-Gore's dogs. Doesn't tell 'er what's in the can, so she thinks it's Antimate or summat. Tells 'er to spray it in their faces."

"So she did?"

"She refused. So Jess's sister grabs the can off 'er and sprays their faces 'erself."

"Do you believe her?"

Titus nodded slowly. "Yes, I do. Becky might be easily influenced, a bit daft, but I know she's not cruel. Even if she is in love." He corrected himself. "Was in love."

"She's seen sense, then?"

"Aye."

"And you don't know why?"

"Shock, I suppose. When she realized what she'd done."

"I think she had a helping hand."

Titus looked at Kit, clearly baffled. "Did you know about this, then?"

"Not entirely. Only I've just put two and two together."

He explained Jess's week-long absence and the conversation the two of them had had – that Jess knew who was responsible but wasn't saying.

"Honour among thieves, then?"

"That's a bit unkind."

"Sorry. Just a bit shocked, that's all."

"I think Jess was brave to do what she did. It must have taken her the best part of a week to track them down. They move about a bit, I suppose?"

"Apparently."

"This Dave. What's he like?"

"Good-lookin' but a bit of a bad 'un, Becky said. 'E was fine for a while, then when he'd 'ad a few drinks, and a few other things besides, 'e started knockin' 'er about a bit. Frightened 'er, I reckon."

"He did the same to Jess."

"What?" Titus looked surprised.

"He's the guy she used to be with – when she was a saboteur."

"Well, I'll be buggered."

"I didn't know about her sister, though. She didn't tell me that." Kit looked thoughtful. "Anyway, she reckons that she's sent him on his way, and her sister presumably. And, anyway, now that the season's finished there shouldn't be any more trouble."

"I bloody well 'ope not."

"So what's happening to Becky?"

"Wants to know if I'll take 'er back."

"And will you?"

"I don't know if I can. Nobody knows except me and you. I don't know whether I want that sort of secret 'angin' over me."

"I see what you mean."

"'Ow could I look Sir Roly in the face? And Lady Billings-Gore? Knowin' that I knew who'd done for 'er dogs and that she were still working for me."

"Not easy. But look at Jess. Look at what she's made of herself."

"I know. Grand lass." Titus gazed out to sea. "There are some things I just can't fathom you know. I don't think I'll ever understand folk."

Kit smiled ruefully. "You and me both."

Chapter 29:
Maid in the Mist
(*Umbilicus rupestris*)

"I don' t really know if I can."

The voice at the other end of the the telephone was insistent. "Oh, go on. It's only for a couple of days. Do you good."

Jinty hesitated. "But there's so much to do here and . . ."

"With a broken arm? You could do with a break. Oops, sorry! No pun intended."

Thoughts swam around Jinty's head. What if Kit called and she was not there? Why could she not shake off Jamie Bickerstaffe? Why did he seem to follow her everwhere? It had been days now since she and Kit had spoken. She had come so near to ringing him, or even calling in on the off-chance, but had put it off. It was his place to apologize, not hers. He must see that. And yet the gnawing feeling that she had been unreasonable, selfish even, would not go away.

But supposing she offered an olive branch and he refused it? What then?

Sarah Wakely called her about twice a year. They had been at school together in Ireland and both were besotted by horses. Sarah had married a racehorse trainer and lived at Lambourn, surrounded by beautiful horses and equally beautiful downland.

"I won't keep you away long. Just come for the weekend – a couple of nights. Then you can get back to sunny Devon. We're both dying to see you. Especially Johnny. Says he's missing you. Dirty old man."

Jinty laughed. Johnny Wakely was a roguish sort, devoted to his wife but a great flirt. He always made Jinty laugh. She could do with a laugh right now. And it was only for a couple of days. "Oh, all right, then."

"Marvellous. Look, get somebody to put you on the train at your end and ring me on your mobile to let me know when you want picking up here. I'll have a car full of kids but – Jamie, put that down!"

The name made her start. Then she remembered Sarah's youngest child.

"Little buggers," muttered Sarah. "I'll have them under control by the time you arrive. Huh. Says she hopefully."

Jinty thanked her friend and looked at her watch. "I'll probably be there around eight, then."

"Perfect. Just in time for supper. Hopefully these little mites will be in their jim-jams by then, though there'll be no chance of getting them to bed once they've heard you're coming. I'll give strict instructions that they're to mind your arm. And if you don't stop pulling Jemima's pants down, Jamie, you'll be straight to bed *now*!"

Jinty winced and bit her lip. "Glad I'm coming later."

"I bet you are. See you about eight, then – and don't forget to ring."

"'Bye."

She put down the phone and leaned back in the chair. A feeling of unease swept through her, but the break would do her good, take her out of herself. She walked quietly up the curving staircase of Baddesley Court to pack her overnight bag.

By late afternoon he had made up his mind to go and see her, to apologize for being wrong about Jamie Bickerstaffe and to ask her out to supper. He also wanted to set his mind at rest: to convince himself that she hadn't meant it when she said she cared little for the reserve. Surely she understood, really. Charlotte met him at the door of Baddesley Court.

"You've missed her by about . . ." Charlotte looked at her watch ". . . an hour. Gone to stay with a friend in Lambourn."

"Did she say when she'd be back?" He tried not to sound too disappointed.

"No. Mrs Flanders told me she'd gone. I wasn't here. I expect she'll ring and tell us later."

"Right. Oh, well, if you could tell her I called."

"Yes, I will." Charlotte was desperate to be more helpful but found herself so short of information that it was impossible to sound anything other than vague.

He got back into the yellow Fiat and drove slowly down the drive, looking to left and right as if for some sign of her, as though he would suddenly see her walking through the parkland among the long grass under the spreading oaks, coming towards him and apologizing for the misunderstanding. And yet something told him he was never going to hear those words.

He arrived back at West Yarmouth, downcast, and was met by Elizabeth walking round the house from the stables. "Out again?" he asked, like a disapproving father.

Elizabeth regarded him curiously. "Yes. Naturalists' Society," she said steadily.

"Sorry. Wasn't thinking." He was apologetic now. "What is it this week?"

"Psocids."

"I'm sorry?"

"Booklice."

He tried to sound interested, "Fascinating," but failed.

"They feed on mould in books and on wallpaper. They eat dried insect collections, too, which is rather funny."

"Hilarious." Stop it. He must stop being like this whenever Elizabeth talked seriously about her passion for natural history. Squirrels and butterflies he could understand, but bivalves and psocids were just a bit too esoteric to engender in him the uncontrollable passion evinced by Elizabeth. Still, they kept her occupied and that was all that mattered. Maybe she'd start conserving the books in his father's study as Sites of Special Scientific Interest for psocids.

He called goodbye as Elizabeth mounted her old black bike and cycled off down the lane. He felt in his pocket for the key to the front door. Damn! He must have left it on the hall table. He turned round to shout after her but it was too late, she was now but a matchstick figure, her head bent over the wicker basket on her handlebars as she sped off in the direction of the entomology of Lynchampton.

Kit went to the back of the house to see if Jess was around. The clouds of the afternoon were clearing from the sky, slipping over the eastern horizon. A westering sun caught them on the underside – a mixture of smoky grey and pale orange. The wind had dropped and the evening air seemed warmer than the afternoon. He heard the faint sound of a Mozart string quartet and looked up at the barn to where the sash window of Jess's room was propped open with a book. She caught sight of him and stuck her head out.

"Hello!" Her voice echoed around the barnyard on the quiet evening air.

"Hi. I've locked myself out."

"Who's a silly boy, then? Do you want my key?"

"Please."

"I'll come down." She smiled at him. She had a lovely smile, but he had rarely seen it.

He waited on the cobbles that made an apron in front of the barn, which was stuffed with an assortment of implements and the bales of straw that made up Wilson's bedding. It was a friendly sort of place. He normally just walked past it. Now, while he waited for her to come down, he had a chance to take it all in – the lengths of orange baler twine hung from six-inch nails hammered into the old timbers, the spades, forks and hoes stacked neatly against the old brick walls, the space for Elizabeth's bike, and Jess's mountain bike – far from new and caked with mud from repeated use. It was their workshop, a meeting-place for barrows and carts, and the day-to-day gubbins of country life. A place for everything and everything in its place.

Jess emerged from the door and climbed down the wooden steps that linked the upper storey with the cobbled courtyard. She was dressed in a pale blue T-shirt and cotton trousers, her face shiny and fresh-scrubbed, her hair still damp from the shower. She came up to him and stretched out her hand, dangling a key-ring on her finger. "Lucky I was in."

"Yes. Thanks." He took the key. "I didn't really fancy breaking in."

"Well, there's a crowbar in the corner of the barn if you ever need to."

He looked hard at her.

"Only joking."

He made for the house, then turned back. "Are you in tonight?"

"And every night."

"It's just that . . . would you like a drink? And a bite to eat?"

She shrugged, then nodded.

"Give me half an hour to clean up and then come over. OK?"

"Fine."

He went round to the front of the house and let himself in. He did not notice that Jess stayed rooted to the spot for a full minute before she turned and climbed the stairs to her room.

Why he had asked her for supper he was not quite sure. On his arrival they had all dined together, but since then they had tended to do their own thing. The farmhouse kitchen was communal and used by all three of them from time to time – it was the one part of the house that was open to all – but of late Elizabeth and Jess had used the smaller kitchen above the stable. He had not asked them to, they had simply gravitated towards it once the house had started being emptied of Rupert's possessions. It was as if they were retreating to the safety of familar surroundings, holding on to their own West Yarmouth fortress in the face of a possible invasion.

The tap on the kitchen door alerted him to her arrival.

"Hi!" He greeted her warmly, and she gave him a nervous smile in return.

"It's a bit lean, I'm afraid, but there's a couple of trout. I can whack them in the Aga with some butter and lemon juice. And there are a few French beans and some wholemeal bread. OK?"

"Fine. I'm not picky."

He grinned at her. "Good."

"I brought this." She held up a bottle of Australian Chardonnay. "I thought it might remind you of home." There was a momentary silence. "Sorry. That was a silly thing to say."

"No. Not silly. Just unexpected."

"Well, I like it, really. It's just that I suddenly thought when I was walking over that this is probably the muck they export to the Poms."

She needed reassurance, and Kit said, "It's fine. Really it is. Where's the opener?"

She reached into a drawer, pulled out a corkscrew and handed it to him. He drew the cork from the condensation-covered bottle and poured the straw-coloured wine into two glasses.

"Cheers."

"Cheers." Jess sipped. "Mmm. Ready for that."

He had never seen her so relaxed and at ease. Usually she was scurrying somewhere or other, busying herself in her job, seldom asking Elizabeth what she should do, but always occupied as though she knew, almost by telepathy, what she should be doing today and where on the estate she would be needed.

Kit busied himself with the trout while Jess leaned against the kitchen worktop. The conversation, previously such hard work, seemed easy, until Kit confronted her.

"I spoke to Titus Ormonroyd today."

Jess said nothing.

"He told me about Becky . . . and Philippa."

She stood perfectly still, meeting his eye but silent.

"Thanks for what you did. I think you were really brave."

She lowered her eyes and took another sip. "Yes, well . . ." was the best she could do.

"Drop more?" he asked.

She looked up, saw that he was smiling at her and held out her glass.

"There's something you ought to know," he said.

Jess looked at him steadily. He topped up his own glass and turned to face her. "I'm not selling West Yarmouth. I'm staying." He paused for a reaction, then thought better of it and went on, "I don't know how long I'll be able to keep it going – what with inheritance tax and everything. We'll probably be bankrupt in a year or two, but I want to give it a try and I could really do with your help."

At first she neither moved nor spoke. Then her face broke into a broad grin and her eyes filled with tears as she walked up and flung her arms around him and squeezed.

"Hey! Watch your wine!"

Jess released him and wiped an arm across her eyes. She backed away towards the worktop. "Thank you," was all she said, but she said it with more feeling than he could ever remember hearing before.

They sat at the kitchen table to eat their simple meal. A couple of candles burned in the brass sticks and the first bottle of wine was joined by another of similar vintage plucked from the door of the fridge.

Jess spoke freely of her early life in the London suburbs, of a childhood short on affection and long on troubles. She spoke with a candour that surprised him and an understanding of her situation that seemed breathtakingly detached. She talked about Philippa, explaining that there was only nine months between them and that her younger sibling had seemed always to follow in her wake – for better or worse.

Kit felt brave enough to ask about the hair and the studs. For the first time that evening she blushed. "It's my shield. I put it on to repel boarders."

He laughed. "And I was a boarder?"

"Too right you were. Stupid, really, isn't it? I suppose it's my equivalent of woad. Going into battle and all that."

"You look much better without it."

She blushed again. "Just watch it with the compliments. I'm not used to them."

He watched her eat. "You really like it here, don't you?" he asked.

"Don't like it, love it. It's the only place."

"And you liked Dad, too."

She paused, her knife and fork hovering over the plate. "More than that." Her pale blue eyes gazed into the middle distance. She laid down her cutlery and sat back in her chair, her eyes glazed.

"He taught me so much. Changed my life." She was speaking quietly, respectfully. "And now he's gone. But I'll never forget him . . . what he did for me."

"Nor me."

She looked up at him. "Glad you said that." She brightened. "But what are you going to do with this place?"

"Carry on Dad's work."

"Is that all?"

"What do you mean?"

"Well, I think it's great but I don't know that it will keep you happy."

He looked at her with his head on one side.

"You're not a conservationist."

He made to interrupt but she cut across him. "I mean, I know you want to keep the reserve going, but what about your dreams? I thought you wanted your own stud."

Kit looked surprised. "How do you know that?"

"I talk to pigs." For a moment she looked deadly serious, then her face broke into a wide grin and her eyes sparkled.

Kit's jaw dropped. "You've been eavesdropping."

She lowered her eyes. "Only once, and not for long . . . honest. And there's no reason why you shouldn't do it here, you know. The stud. Plenty of spare land."

"But it's leased to Maidment and, anyway, I haven't got the money."

"Just a thought." Then she sipped her wine before asking, "Have you looked at the books?"

"What books?"

"The books upstairs in your father's study."

"Well, I've seen them, but I can't say I've looked at them."

She stood up and picked up her glass. "Come on, I'll show you. It's what we used to do after supper. I haven't done it since . . . Come on."

There was a spark in her eye. He rose and followed her up the staircase and into his father's – now his – room. Jess put down her glass on the edge of the desk and walked across to the shelves. "These are the best. Can't read them, but the pictures are wonderful."

She took down a large volume and laid it on the desk. "How do you say that – '*Oiseaux remarquables du Brésil*'?"

"Remarkable Birds of Brazil," translated Kit.

Jess stared at him. "I think I'd worked that out." Then she opened the front cover of the large book and began to turn the pages. "Aren't they wonderful? Look at the feathers – the way they're painted. Stunning. I don't know who Mr Descourtilz was but he certainly knew his birds."

"In Brazil."

"We've got plants as well." She took down another volume. "Besler's *Hortus Eystettensis*. Oh, and these are really lovely – humming birds – a man called Gould."

Kit turned the pages with amazement. "I didn't know Dad had these. He didn't when I left. Where did he get them from?"

"Somebody left them to him apparently. Someone who used to visit the reserve and liked what he did. There aren't many, a dozen or so, but they're all beautiful. I like the roses as well. I'd like a rose garden one day, especially with old roses in."

She pulled another book from the shelf and laid it on the bed. "*Les Roses*. No translation, please." She raised her finger in mock warning, then turned back to the large, leather-bound volume and its title page. "P. J. Redouté." She said the word so that it sounded like 'redoubt', but he did not correct her, just gazed in awe at the illustrations that lay before him on the bed.

"Well, I'll be . . ." He said no more, but stood entranced, lost with Jess among the roses.

At half past midnight Jess looked at her watch and said that she'd better be going. He walked her down the stairs to the front door and thanked her for coming. There was a moment of unease.

"It was fun," she said. "I really enjoyed it." She hopped from one foot to the other, unaware how to leave, then leaned forward and kissed his cheek. He half laughed, lifted his hands in an indecisive gesture and kissed her back, feeling the softness of her fine hair, and detecting the perfume of orange blossom on her skin. It was a fragrance he had not encountered since he had left Balnunga Valley. A sudden and evocative scent of the past seemed to propel him forward to the future. The hairs on the back of his neck stood on end as he closed the door behind her.

Chapter 30: Bindweed

(*Callistegia sepium*)

"So, is he the one for you?" asked Sarah, cutting a piece of buttered toast into soldiers, pouring warm milk on to a bowl of Ready-Brek, and lifting a whistling kettle off the gas hob in a segue of movement that came as second nature to a mother of three small children.

Jinty sat at the table of the farmhouse kitchen, placing her bandaged arm on a dry patch between the small pools of milk that made its surface look like a map of the Lake District.

"I don't know."

Sarah pushed a boiled egg and soldiers in front of her youngest daughter, who was doing her best to empty the contents of her mug into the tray of her high chair – a slow process thanks to the small holes in the mouthpiece of the beaker. "Past tense?"

"I hope not. But it all seems to have gone pear-shaped."

"You're giving in a bit easily, aren't you?" Sarah swooped down on the child with a damp J-cloth and wiped up the milk. She confiscated the mug, poked a finger of toast into the gaping mouth, which was preparing to utter a wail, pushed a bowl of cereal in front of the budding delinquent Jamie, and sent another small child off in the direction of the bathroom. "Where's your staying power?"

"Evaporated, I think."

Sarah sat down with a mug of coffee and placed another in front of Jinty.

"This isn't like you," she said.

"I know. What with all this trouble over Jamie, and the accident, I seem to have lost my drive."

"Either that or it really was just a flash in the pan."

Jinty looked up at her, cradling the coffee mug in her hands. "Do you think so?"

"Don't ask me. Only you know that. It's just that I would have expected you to be a bit more positive about him."

"But I am. I just can't help thinking that I've been here before. Not in the same way. I really think he's special but I need him to prove that he thinks I'm special, too."

"Oh, I see."

"And the trouble is . . ."

"Mmmm?"

"I still can't get Jamie out of my mind."

"And I thought you said the sex with Kit was like nothing you've experienced before?"

"Did I?"

"Last night. You'd had a few." She wiped up more crescent moons of milk with a J-cloth.

"I just want someone who won't let me down. Someone who'll do things for me instead of being self-centred."

Sarah raised her eyebrows.

Jinty didn't notice. "Oh, why are men so bloody hard to read? Why do they say one thing when they mean another and then go off and do something completely different anyway?"

"Is that what he's done?"

"No, but Jamie did."

Sarah took a sip of her coffee. "This Jamie thing has really bitten deep, hasn't it?"

"I'd like to think not."

"Do you still love him?"

"He's a bastard."

"I asked if you loved him, not if you'd give him a character reference."

Jinty looked up, paused and heaved a sigh. "I don't know."

Sarah tutted. "Oh, you poor love." The toaster pinged and she got up. As she busied herself with butter and honey she spoke over her shoulder above the din of breakfasting children. "I think you should take your time. Don't rush things. Just make sure you see him again soon and smooth things out, then take it from there."

"Which him?"

"That's rather up to you, isn't it?" She lowered a plate of buttery honeyed toast on to the table in front of Jinty and watched as her friend's eyes glazed over.

Sarah smiled as she took in the domestic carnage surrounding her, glad for just a moment that her own problems, though many and varied and mainly of a juvenile nature, were not quite as mentally taxing as those of her friend.

Jinty nibbled at a piece of toast. Jamie. How could she possibly still be interested in Jamie?

As Sunday mornings go, it was nothing special. The sky was a soft shade of grey, bright enough to cast pale shadows, but nothing to write home about. Kit raised his head from the pillow and felt the muzziness bequeathed by the wine of the night before. He ran his fingers through his tangled hair, felt the stubble on his chin and slid out of bed.

The parted curtains revealed the pallid morning and he threw up the sash window. He breathed in the cool air, which smelt of spring, but his head refused to clear. He knelt down, rested his chin on the sill and looked out over the rolling farmland. "One day, my son," he murmured to himself, "all this will be yours." Then he realized, fully and for the first time, that it was, indeed, all his, along with its pleasures, its pains and its responsibilities.

He thought of Jess the night before. How different she had seemed, how full of enthusiasm, how relaxed. He found himself smiling at the memory of her company, recalled her childlike joy as they turned the pages of the books in his father's study, felt strangely proud that she had agreed to work with him at keeping the reserve going, even though, since the day of his arrival, both she and Elizabeth had made it obvious that this was what they wanted more than anything else. But what really surprised him was how easily she seemed to read him.

It was time he started to make something of it all. He felt different. Responsible. Critical of past actions. Determined.

He went to the bathroom, showered, shaved, then pulled on a pair of jeans and a sweatshirt. He must do something about his limited wardrobe. Apart from a couple of sweatshirts, one sweater, three T-shirts and two pairs of jeans bought in Totnes, he had nothing in the way of clothes, and there was a limit to the number of garments he could utilize from his father's chest of drawers.

He made a mental note to have his hair cut some time during the coming week, and went downstairs. The kitchen carried all the hallmarks of a late supper. He cleared away the pots and pans as the kettle boiled, noticing the crust on Jess's plate. He could see her there now, sipping her wine, her eyes keen and flashing. Eyes so full of life, so full of love. He was surprised by the thought.

He looked out across the gravelled yard towards the stable. There was no sign of activity. He looked at his watch. A quarter past nine. Jess and Elizabeth would probably be out and about by now, even though it was Sunday. They seemed ungoverned by the days of the week, both happy to be on the land at all times and in most weathers. April was not far away. Soon the reserve would be opened up to those who wanted to look round it and the two of them would be getting things ready.

He wondered what Jinty was doing in Lambourn, but found that hard: he could not picture her face clearly. It puzzled him.

The kettle whistled and brought him back to earth. He made the coffee, drank it, then felt moved to get out into the fresh air. He pulled on a sleeveless jerkin of his father's and went out of the kitchen door and across the farmyard, glancing up towards Jess and Elizabeth's accommodation as he did so. The door at the top of the steps stood ajar. Odd. He climbed the steps to close it, and heard a whimpering noise from within.

"Hello?" He waited for a reply to tell him that all was well. It did not come. His stomach tensed. He called again. "Anyone there?" No sound.

He pushed open the door, slowly, until it rested against the wall, wide open. The narrow hallway stretched ahead of him with the doors to the rooms down its left-hand side standing open, all except the third one, which led into Jess's room. He stepped forward gingerly, looking into the first room, the kitchen, and the second, the bathroom, both of which were empty. He walked on, then tapped on Jess's door. He thought he heard a sound, then nothing.

He turned the handle and pushed. The door refused to move. "Jess? Are you there?"

No reply. Then the sound of something being knocked over – a chair? "Jess? Is that you?"

A sharp cry, then silence once more. Kit tried the handle again and still the door remained immovable. "Are you all right, Jess?" He heard a muffled, indistinct sound from within that told him something was wrong. He stood back from the door then ran at it with his shoulder. The solid timber refused to yield and his body crumpled against the slatted panel, an agonizing numbness driving into him. He clenched his teeth at the pain, put his other arm up to ease the throbbing joint and at the same time shot out his foot in the direction of the lock. The door refused to budge. Again and again he landed blows upon it, now using both arms to brace himself against the wall opposite. At the fourth or fifth attempt he heard a crack, and as the shooting pains ran up his thigh he continued to pound at the door until the panel next to the lock began to splinter.

With one final kick the door flew open and he lurched forward into the room. As he did so, someone sprang at him. He saw the blurred features of a tall, bearded man before he toppled backwards under the force of the oncoming figure. As the wind left his body he arched forward to catch his breath and hung on to the man, who was now trying to push past him. The figure, black clad and unkempt, turned and landed a punch over his eye – the one that only recently had been relieved of its stitches. Needling pain stabbed into his skull, but he clenched his hands around the rough woollen sweater and hung on tenaciously as his opponent made a bid for the door. Drawing on reserves of strength he had not known existed, he pulled his assailant to the floor and did his best to dodge the punches that were now being rained down on him.

As one of them, misplaced and mistimed, landed on the plain wooden boards, he levered himself around and clambered on the back of the now sprawling body, noticing, out of the corner of his eye, the cowering figure of Jess in the corner.

A fist landed on one side of Kit's jaw and he let out a cry, then retaliated with a punch that connected with his assailant's right ear. Desperate now, he grabbed at the man's matted black curls and tried, with all his remaining strength, to turn the head away and prevent its owner from lining up yet more accurate blows. As he did so the man shot out an elbow that landed on Kit's chin. He felt his teeth slice into his bottom lip and tasted blood. He reached out to grab the man's arm, but he was tiring and missed. His assailant spun round, landed a final punch in Kit's stomach and bolted.

Kit tried to leap up and go after him, but he fell to his knees, gasping for air through the mixture of blood and saliva that filled his mouth. He turned to where Jess sat huddled in the corner, and saw that her shirt was torn and her jeans were unbuttoned. Her reddened eyes showed that she had been crying, but now she was silent and shaking, her breath coming in short, irregular bursts. He watched, gasping for breath, as she pulled the remains of her ripped shirt over her breasts. A rising tide of rage filled him with renewed strength.

"He didn't . . . ?" They were the only words he could form through gritted teeth.

Jess shook her head, then wrapped her arms around herself and sobbed.

Kit watched as she shuddered with fear and relief. He pushed himself up from the floor and went across to where she sat. With one hand he wiped the blood from his chin, and with the other stroked the back of her head.

For several minutes the two of them sat there, saying nothing, as they fought for breath and the strength to move. Kit got up first, then held out his hand to Jess. She took it, clutching her ripped shirt together with her other hand, and looked at him, half terrified, half embarrassed.

Kit did not know whether to stay or leave. "Are you . . . ?"

"I'll survive. Thank you." Jess tried to smile through the tears, and Kit thought how unfair it was that the girl who had last night been happy for the first time since he had arrived had been, within a few hours, reduced to a quivering wreck.

"Was that him?"

"Dave. Come to get his own back. Give me my comeuppance."

Kit was unsure what to ask or how deep to probe.

Jess looked at the floor. "He started out by saying he missed me. Asked me why I'd gone back to see him if I wasn't interested any more. Told me that Philippa wasn't a patch on me. I told him that I only went to see him to stop him from operating round here, to get him to leave Philippa alone. Then he came on heavy. Tried it on. When I wouldn't have any of it he got physical – like he always did. Seems to think that women go for that sort of thing." She looked at Kit and he saw panic in her face. "You do believe me, don't you?"

Kit held on to the now splintered door. "Of course."

She leaned back against the wall and sighed deeply. "Oh, God!

Why is my life so messed up?" She spoke with angry resignation. "Why am I in such a bloody awful mess?"

Kit looked at her steadily. "Not your fault."

"Who else's, then?"

"Life? Fate?"

"No. Can't blame them. Must be me. Huh!" She smiled a melancholy smile.

Kit's breathing assumed its normal rate. He sized her up. "You are amazing."

"Me?"

"Yes."

"I don't feel amazing."

"You don't look it at the moment, but you are."

Jess grinned at him, not sure if he was making fun of her. "What do you mean?"

"You just seem to be so sorted. Not like me."

"Oh, I think you will be focussed. You're just a bit confused."

"You can say that again. I feel so bloody stupid."

"Why?"

"Made a fool of myself. Let my heart rule my head."

"Was it your heart?"

"I thought it was."

Jess smiled understandingly. "Do you think it might have been your pants?"

He looked across at her and found himself smiling back, feeling not the slightest bit annoyed. "Was it that obvious?"

"Not for me to say."

Kit looked away. "It was pretty powerful."

"It can be."

He looked back. "How do you know?"

"Me and Dave – at first. Not now. Not for years. Past tense. Then the light dawned."

"But he . . ."

"Beat me up? Yes. But it wasn't just that. You gradually realize that something's missing. A sense of purpose. Of wanting to do things together as well as wanting to *be* together. Of feeling the same way about things. When you find it's not there, what you have left doesn't seem to be as big as it was."

"Or as important?"

685

"No."

"Perhaps I'm just a typical man. Ruled by my pants."

She raised her hand and ran her finger lightly over his lip. He flinched, then looked down at her, her shirt gaping, showing the contours of her body. He raised his hands and lightly folded the shirt to cover her, then saw the pale blue of her eyes and, without thinking, put his arms around her and kissed her, feeling her relax into him. It seemed the most natural thing in the world.

As they eased apart he lowered his hands and a worried look flickered across his face. "I'm sorry. Too soon."

"Not for me. What took you so long?"

"Distractions."

"All gone?"

"All gone." Suddenly Jess no longer looked like a frightened creature that needed his protection. It was he who needed and wanted her. It took him a few moments to find the words. "This might sound stupid."

"Risk it."

"It's you that I want to do it for. And it's you that I want to do it with." A weight was lifted from his shoulders as the admission of his true feelings drifted out on to the air.

"I'm glad." She rested her head on his chest and put her arms around his waist.

It was as if a heavy cloud had drifted by and he had walked out into sunshine.

Late in the afternoon Elizabeth returned from her work down at the Spinney and found no trace of either of them. They kept out of her way, not yet ready to explain the events of the morning. She set about making her own supper in the small kitchen in the barn and noticed, as she carried the meal to her room, the state of the door to Jess's room. She set down her tray, took a closer look at the splintered timbers, then went down the stairs and out into the farmyard, glancing up at the window of Kit's room. He was standing to one side of his window, talking to a small, fair-haired figure standing opposite him.

Elizabeth stopped, paused briefly, then quietly retraced her steps. She ate her meal, then wrote some letters before retiring for the night at a quarter to nine.

That night, Jinty lay awake in her room at Lambourn, listening to a tawny owl hooting in the tree outside her window and hoping that soon it would decide to give the vocals a rest. In the shadowlands between wakefulness and sleep, she saw Kit's face smiling at her. The smile never faded, but the face became smaller and smaller until finally it was no more than a speck in the distance. She sat bolt upright in bed, suddenly wide awake, and realized, with complete certainty, that it was over.

Chapter 31:
Lover's Knots

(Galium aparine)

Malcolm Percy, from Marchbanks Books in Totnes, prided himself on his punctuality. He had never arrived anywhere later than five minutes early, and today would be no exception. He checked the time and the address of the appointment in his diary for the umpteenth time over a coffee in the George at Lynchampton, and when he was confident that the fifteen remaining minutes would allow him to reach West Yarmouth in ample time, he paid his bill and returned to his gleaming dark blue car, grinding to a halt on the gravel outside the farmhouse at 9.55 a.m. precisely.

He was surprised by the nature of the property. He had expected a crumbling old farmhouse of iron-grey pebbledash or dreary stone, not a Queen Anne vision in mellow brick. Perhaps the prospective quarry of book-club volumes and cheap thrillers he had resigned himself to encountering might be boosted by a set of the Waverley Novels or G. A. Henty. Not much to get excited about, but a cache of Mills and Boon was unlikely judging by outward appearances. He was still examining the elegant elevation when Kit opened the front door and enquired whether he could be of assistance.

But Mr Percy was overwhelmed by the beauty of the house. "Wonderful proportions," he said, without looking down from the line of the roof or the upstairs windows.

Kit assumed he had been sent round by the estate agent, anxious to salvage at least some of his potential commission.

"Ah. I'm afraid it's no longer for sale."

"Oh, I wish, I wish. Way out of my league but simply lovely." Mr Percy clapped his hands together, lowered his eyes to meet those of his interlocutor and, masking any shock he might have felt at the battered face of the householder, introduced himself. "Malcolm Percy from Marchbanks Books in Totnes."

Kit remembered the appointment he had, not surprisingly, forgotten. "Yes, of course. I'm sorry. Come in."

Mr Percy, in his suede loafers, pink cotton trousers and navy-blue sweater, shook hands with his potential customer and tried not to stare at the swollen lower lip as he walked into the flagged hallway of the old farmhouse.

"It's this way." Kit motioned his visitor to climb the stairs, and the bookseller, his eyes darting around for literary prey, followed. They entered the untidy book-lined study that Kit now thought of as his own.

"What a lovely room." Mr Percy pushed the silver-grey hair out of his eyes and adjusted the silk handkerchief at his neck.

Kit frowned. The room was far from lovely: it was stuffed with the impedimenta of a lifetime's interest in natural history and garnished with a generous supply of dust.

"Which books, exactly, are you thinking of selling?"

"Well, all of them, really." And then, feeling slightly awkward at clearing out his father lock, stock and barrel, "I might keep a few – on wild flowers, estate management and stuff, but most of them can go."

"I see." The bookseller scanned the shelves. "What we'll have to do is go through them together, working out what you want to keep and what you want to sell. I didn't realize there were quite as many, I'm afraid. It looks as though I'll have to come back with the van."

"Fine."

Mr Percy moved closer to the shelves and ran his eyes along them. "I'm afraid these might be difficult to shift." He tapped the spines of the paper-bound transactions of assorted natural-history societies carelessly. "No one really has space for them nowadays. I mean, we can take them off your hands but I can't really offer what they're worth simply because of storage."

Kit had expected as much. The verbal appraisal continued. "Plenty of dust-wrappers, which is good – too many people lose them or tear them. Don't realize that a book is more valuable with them than without." His face lit up at the sight of a large volume. "What's this?" Kit watched as the other man prised the book from the lower shelf and took it over to the desk. "May I?"

"Oh, yes." He cleared a space among the papers and paraphernalia, and the bookseller laid down the volume and opened the front cover. "Goodness me. Well I never." He stared at the title page with his hands planted on his hips. "*Oiseaux remarquable du Brésil*. Is this the sort of thing you'll be selling?"

"I guess so. I really need to raise some money to cover inheritance tax."

"There are more, then?"

Kit went to the places he had remembered Jess going to for the books she had shown him, and pulled them out one after another.

Malcolm Percy became progressively paler as they piled up on the desk. "Could I sit down, please?" he asked.

Kit looked worried. "Of course. Are you all right?"

The bookseller did not speak for a moment. Then he asked, "Can I use the phone?"

"Go ahead." Kit pointed to the back of the desk. The bookseller picked up the handset, dialled a familiar number, sat back and waited. "Stephen? Do you have that auction realization list handy? The one from Sotheby's. Natural history. Yes. Can you get it for me? Thanks."

He looked up at Kit and smiled weakly. Kit, still baffled, stood quietly by the desk.

"Yes? Right. Can you read out the figures for each of these?" He looked up again at Kit and mimed for pencil and paper, which Kit pulled from a drawer and laid in front of him on the small patch of desk to one side of the pile of books.

Mr Percy proceeded to go through the titles in front of him – the Descourtilz and the Besler, the Goulds and the Redoutés; books about wild flowers and humming-birds, roses and lilacs. As he named each one he wrote down the information relayed to him over the phone in a spidery hand that was too far away from Kit for him to see. Finally he laid down the pen, thanked Stephen for his efforts, replaced the handset and sat back in the chair. He reached in his pocket for a handkerchief and wiped his forehead.

"Oh dear."

Kit could no longer retain his curiosity. "What's the verdict?"

"Well, Mr Lavery, I'm afraid we really can't buy these books from you."

"I see." Kit was disappointed. He had hoped that the ones with the fine illustrations might be worth a few thousand at least and go some way towards defraying the costs of the inheritance tax.

"I think you'd better sit down."

Kit perched on the end of the bed.

"We couldn't possibly afford them."

"I'm sorry?

"I'll be happy to take most of the others from you," he waved an arm airily in the direction of the shelves, "but these," he tapped his hand respectfully on the top of the pile, "will have to go to auction."

Kit sat perfectly still as Mr Percy recited the list of books and their values. "Descourtilz' *Oiseaux remarquables du Brésil*, when last sold at auction, fetched £270,000. Besler's *Hortus Eystettensis* fetched £130,000 five years ago. The Redoutés are worth around £250,000 each and the Gould humming-birds approximately £75,000 apiece. You also have a copy of Seba's *Locupletissimi rerum naturalium thesauri accurata descriptio* from the middle of the eighteenth century." Mr Percy paused so that the significance of the last find sank in. "Three years ago a copy fetched £300,000. The total value of this little pile here is around the million and a half mark." He looked wistfully at the tower of leatherbound books in front of him. "There are times, Mr Lavery, when I wish I were dishonest. But thank you, anyway, for letting me see them."

Kit did not hear the last words. He was deep in shock.

Jinty arrived back at Baddesley Court at lunchtime on Monday, to find the house deserted except for Mrs Flanders, who was busily engaged in cleaning a pair of silver candlesticks, her wisps of grey candy-floss hair swirling around her ruddy cheeks like the tendrils of a creeper on a country house. She seemed almost too breathless to hold a conversation, so Jinty climbed the stairs to her room and dumped her overnight bag on the bed.

The three-day escape, which should have done her good, had left her feeling uneasy and alone.

She walked to the window and sat in the chair beside it, looking out over Baddesley's lightly wooded pasture and parkland, brindled with the shadows of elderly oak trees cast by a soaring spring sun. The

— *Alan Titchmarsh* —

Devon countryside was beginning to wake up; buds were breaking, grass was greening, there were sturdy young lambs now where only a few weeks ago lumbering fat-bellied ewes were awaiting the arrival of their families.

She felt a mixture of independence and anger, irritation and eagerness to get on. She must take charge of her own destiny. She was tired of waiting for men to influence her life, tired of marking time, hoping and waiting.

With a sharp intake of breath she got up from the chair, struggled into a pair of jeans, threw a fleece around her shoulders, went down the stairs and out of the front door of the house. It took several minutes to persuade Sally to tack up Seltzer, but Sally knew of old that when Jinty's mind was set on something she generally had her way. She gave her employer's niece a leg up into the saddle and watched as Jinty walked the horse out of the stableyard and down the long gravel drive.

Where she thought she was going in that state and on that horse was clearly not something that Sally was to be told. She just hoped to God that, for the sake of her friend and her job, Jinty would not come to grief riding a horse like Seltzer with just one hand.

Kit caught up with Jess between the Wilderness and the Spinney, overlooking Tallacombe Bay. He was out of breath by the time he found her – guided by the noise – and surprised to discover her wielding a chain-saw and clad in boots, protective dungarees and an orange helmet with a visor and earmuffs.

She switched off the machine, took off the helmet and greeted him with a flicker of a smile.

Kit looked about him. "Some scene of destruction."

"Not for long. Just a bit of thinning. I'll stack the logs for the beetles."

"Is there no form of wildlife that we don't look after here?"

"Nope. All catered for."

"I've just had the bookseller over from Totnes."

She looked at him with her head on one side. "Oh?"

"I hoped that some of Dad's books might help fund the inheritance tax."

"And?"

"I think you'd better sit down."

692

"Among all this lot?" She looked at the devastation around her.

"Yes. Well. The thing is, I think those books we looked at the other night are going to have to go."

"Of course they are."

Kit looked at her quizzically. This was not the reply he'd expected. "You're not upset?"

"How could I be?"

"But I thought you loved them."

"I do, but you also showed me your father's letter."

"What's that got to do with it?"

"He said you'd have to sell them."

Kit frowned. "Hang on. How do you make that out? I've read that letter several times and nowhere does he tell me to sell the books."

Jess shook her head. "You're so obvious, aren't you?"

"What do you mean?" He looked crestfallen.

"He said, 'The books might be of help'."

"Yes, but he didn't say they were worth one and a half million pounds."

Jess whistled and sat down on the pile of logs.

Kit's face bore the signs of sudden enlightenment. "Good God . . . the auction catalogue!"

"Sorry?"

"An auction catalogue of books arrived, addressed to me. I thought it was a mistake, that it should have been for Dad, but he clearly wanted it sent to me. I didn't see it for what it was. I thought that the note in his letter meant that I might need to read them, to get the advice I'd need to keep this place going, not that I'd have to sell them."

" 'There is no truth, only points of view'."

"What?"

"Edith Sitwell. It was one of your dad's favourite sayings. He used to quote it at me whenever I got too bolshy about the likes of Titus Ormonroyd and the Billings-Gores. Made sure I could always see someone else's angle." She hesitated, then asked, "Are you really sure you want to be here?"

For a moment he remained silent, then, looking at her quite coolly, he said, "More than anything."

"Do you know why?"

"Yes." And then, quite clearly and calmly, "Because I love you."

Jess looked startled.

"Sorry."

"Don't be. I'm glad."

"You look like an Amazon."

"Thank you very much."

He walked slowly towards her, took the chain-saw from her hand and lowered it to the ground. Then he wrapped both arms around her and held her close to him. Neither of them said a word, but she felt his hand cradling the back of her head and she could hear his heart beating through the thickness of his sweater. They stood like this for some minutes, Jess convinced that her feet were no longer touching the ground, and then he eased away from her, stroked her cheek with his finger and said, "I'll leave you to your destruction." And then, almost as a second thought, "Have you seen Elizabeth? I haven't told her yet, and I want to let her know she's stuck with me."

"She wasn't in her room when I left this morning. I think she must have beaten me to it. She was working in the Copse yesterday. Probably over there now."

"You're quite independent, you two, aren't you?"

Jess frowned. "Mmm. We get on better at a distance. She means well, though. Good egg."

"Funny thing to say. You got that from . . ."

She nodded. "Your dad. Very public school. Shouldn't use it, really."

"It suits you."

She replaced her helmet and visor, started up the chain-saw and laid into another stump. For the rest of the afternoon she could not stop smiling.

Kit walked across the cliff towards the Copse but paused to turn back and watch her flaying the undergrowth. It slowly dawned on him why he had come to love Jess Wetherby so much. Right from the start of her life she had been given little love, few chances and no encouragement, but she had picked up her metaphorical chain-saw and carved her way through the woods. She was a survivor. And a good egg. And he wanted more than anything to spend the rest of his life with her.

Chapter 32:
Wish-me-well

(*Veronica chamaedrys*)

For a moment it seemed like *déjà vu*. He was walking along the cliff top, with the sea below him and the woods to his right, and a grey horse was coming towards him. He stood still, waiting for horse and rider to approach, wondering what to say if they did, but instead they took a lower path down to the beach. Had she seen him and avoided him?

He watched as they picked their way down the cliff path and on to the flat, fresh-washed sand, then caught his breath as the rider, with one arm in a sling, kicked the horse into a gallop. The pair flew across the sand, following the curve of the tide-line, the girl holding the reins with one hand, while the other rested across her chest. He could hear the distant thump of hoofs, see the divots of damp sand flung up into the air to land and shatter on the shore. He watched as the receding figure, fair hair close-cropped, disappeared out of sight.

He sat on the soft turf of the cliff top and looked out to sea as the wistful feelings of regret were washed away by the tide. But there came, also, a feeling that soon he must see Jinty and explain.

The truth of the matter was that Jinty had not seen him. Her confusion and the dullness of his sweater had offered perfect camouflage. She slowed Seltzer to a walk as the strip of sand narrowed, and picked her way up the lower cliff path with extra care, remembering her last outing on Allardyce.

As always, the exhilaration of the ride had cleared her head. She would return to Baddesley and sort herself out. Get this life of hers on the move again.

When she arrived in the stableyard, Sally helped her down from the saddle with relief. "Thanks. And I'm sorry if I made you worry," Jinty said.

Sally shook her head.

"I know. But it helped."

Roly greeted her at the door, on his way out to a meeting in town. "You look . . . ah . . . refreshed."

"I feel it." She pecked him on the cheek.

"See you at supper?"

"Not sure. Think I'm going out. Speak later."

He turned to watch her climb the stairs, then frowned. Something about her had changed. He didn't know what, but it made him uneasy. With furrowed brow he climbed into the car and drove off in the direction of his meeting. By the time he returned, perhaps Jinty would be back to normal.

There was no sign of Elizabeth at the Copse, so Kit walked on to the farmhouse. She was not there either. Puzzled, he walked round to the barn and climbed the stairs. The outer door was locked. He fished underneath the old milk churn for the key that was kept there, unlocked the door and entered, calling 'Hello' as he did so. No reply.

Remembering his last visit, he walked gingerly down the corridor and tapped on Elizabeth's door. Still no reply. He tried the handle. It turned and the door opened. The room was empty. The bed was made but there was little sign of occupation. He had not visited Elizabeth's room before, and was surprised at the bareness of the shelves and surfaces. He walked to the wardrobe and opened the doors. Empty. No clothes, nothing. It was as if no one had ever lived there. He was baffled. He retraced his steps, locked the outer door and returned the key to its hiding place. At the top of the steps he noticed a bucket of scraps for the pig. He picked them up, and ambled over to Wilson's sty. He tipped the vegetable mixture into the old sow's trough and watched as she devoured the multicoloured mixture of carrots and cabbage, potatoes and cauliflower.

"What do you make of it all, then?" he asked.

"Kit?"

He spun round on his heels. Elizabeth was standing to one side of the pig-sty.

"Sorry. I didn't mean to make you jump."

"No. It's fine. It's just that every time I speak to Wilson she seems to answer in a different voice."

Elizabeth ignored the joke. "I've come to say goodbye."

Kit thought he had misheard her. "I'm sorry?"

"I'm leaving West Yarmouth."

"What? Why? I mean, I thought that you were . . ."

"I've written you a letter." She pulled an envelope from the pocket of her dark green gilet. "I'm afraid I need to go. The letter will explain everything."

Suddenly Kit felt angry. "But you can't go. It was you who persuaded me to stay – you and Jess. How can you go now?"

He remembered that he had not told Elizabeth of his plans. "I'm not selling up. I've decided to stay, make a go of it."

"I know."

He stared at her.

"Arthur Maidment told me."

"Oh, look, I'm sorry. I didn't want you to hear it from somebody else but until I'd talked with Maidment I really didn't know what I wanted to do myself . . . and since then I've just not seen you to –"

"Kit, I'm not angry with you for that. It's something quite different. The letter will explain it."

"But can't you tell me yourself?"

"No."

"Why not?"

"Because I lack the courage." She smiled at him – a worried, haunted smile.

"But I don't understand. Surely nothing could stop you wanting to work here after all the years you've been a part of it? And Dad . . ."

Elizabeth looked down. "No. But there we are." She looked up again and said, briskly, "I must go. Taxi waiting."

Kit could hardly believe what he was hearing. "But –"

"Don't think too badly of me. I thought it was all for the best. And please take care of everything. Both of you." And with that she walked around the back of the pig-sty and disappeared.

Kit stood rooted to the spot, hardly able to believe what had happened over the past few minutes. He looked at the letter in his hand, addressed simply to 'Kit', then pushed his finger along the sealed edge and tore open the envelope. He pulled out the neatly folded writing-paper, leaned on the wall of the sty and read:

Dear Kit,

I'm so sorry to have to do this, but I must regretfully leave West Yarmouth. I know that I have been responsible, more than most, for persuading you to stay here and continue your father's work, so it may seem perverse that now you have decided to do so I should 'throw in the towel', as it were, and leave.

My reason for going has nothing to do with a fit of pique or unhappiness at your arrival and impending management of the reserve. I have watched you grow since you arrived and have every confidence that you will be every bit as successful as your father with this wonderful piece of countryside. I hope that does not sound too patronizing. I certainly do not intend it to.

I am leaving because, in all conscience, I can no longer face you, knowing the events of the past few months.

Kit felt a rising sense of fear.

We spoke, once or twice, about your father, and about the events surrounding his death. I explained to you, as best I could, the events of that dreadful day, but I am afraid that I found it impossible to be perfectly frank with you and for that I have had a very troubled conscience.

The time has come when I am no longer able to live with this burden, certainly not working alongside both you and Jess on the reserve. Some people are able to close off parts of their mind and pretend that certain things have not happened. I am unable to do this. I have always tried to live my life honestly and straightforwardly, and it is to this end that I write this letter.

I am not aware of how much Dr Hastings has confided in you, so please forgive me if I tell you things that you do not know, which perhaps would have been better coming from him. He was a good friend of your father's and thought a lot of him, which would explain his reticence.

You father was diagnosed last year as suffering from Alzheimer's disease. One evening at supper he became rather more frank than usual and confided in me as to the nature of his medical problem.

This is the most difficult thing to have to relate, and I do so apologize for not doing it face to face. Your father confessed to me that, if the future could offer only a life in some institution where he would steadily go more ga-ga, he would prefer to take things into his own hands. My horror at the prospect, and my explanation that I would be quite prepared to see that he never left West Yarmouth, did nothing to change his mind and he reiterated his belief in voluntary euthanasia as being part of the 'survival of the fittest' and 'natural selection'.

However, he never brought up the subject again, and I thought that perhaps he had had a change of heart and that the relatively slow onset of the disease might alter his thoughts on the matter.

Then came the accident. I found your father at the foot of the cliff, as I explained. What I did not admit to you, and indeed have not been able to admit to anyone else, is that when I found him he was still alive. He was unconscious but still breathing.

I am so sorry to have to tell you, Kit, that I sat with your father for over an hour until he stopped breathing and was clearly dead. Only then did I call the ambulance. I did this quite simply to avoid the suffering that your father so feared. I was hopeful that when I found him he was in no pain, and although I would have given anything not to lose him I found that, when the moment came, I had to go along with his desire to die.

Whether he fell or jumped off the cliff I cannot say, but since that moment I have found it hard to live with myself, and even harder to face both you and Jess on a daily basis, knowing what I know. It is for this reason that I must go away.

I do hope that you will find it in your heart to forgive me, though I realize that this is a request I have no right to make. You may even feel that what I did was a criminal act and that I must be punished. If that is the case I will respect your wishes. I shall be staying with my brother for a few weeks at the address below, and then I shall see what I need to do to pick up the pieces of my life.

You are a good man – in that respect very much like your father – and Jess is a brave and courageous girl for whom I have the greatest admiration. I think I can ask you to take care of her without you thinking me an interfering old woman.

You are in charge of a piece of countryside for which I shall always feel the greatest love, and I know I can leave it in hands that will take care of it. I am only sorry I shall not be able to see you all grow.

With my love,
Elizabeth.

Kit leaned on the wall of the pig-sty trying to take it all in. He could feel only an overwhelming sympathy for Elizabeth, in spite of the unwanted revelation. She had clearly loved his father so much that she found herself unable to prolong his suffering, at the same time knowing that her actions would deprive her of the man she loved. For the first time since he had met her, he acknowledged some kind of bond with the woman who had remained loyal to his father until the bitter end.

Carefully, and with a great sense of purpose, he folded up the letter and slipped it back into the envelope, then screwed up both envelope and contents and let them fall slowly through his fingers and into the pig's trough. Within seconds they had become a part of Wilson's meal, and Kit walked slowly back to the farmhouse for a stiff drink, safe in the knowledge that no one else would ever know Elizabeth's secret.

Roly found himself equally devastated at a sudden departure. He sat in his usual chair, by his usual fire, with his usual glass in his hand as Charlotte consoled him as if he were a small child. "She obviously thinks she needs a change. We always knew she didn't see the stables here as her life."

"Yes. I know. But, ah, she's just gone to another stables. Why not stay here?"

"I think you know that. She needs to sort herself out. Away from familiar surroundings. She won't stay at Lambourn for ever, but she's had a tough time of it recently. I think she needs to do a lot of thinking."

"Mmm. But what about me? Mmm? I'll miss her."

Charlotte perched on the arm of his chair and stroked the iron-grey hair at the back of his head as she gazed into the fire. "We'll all miss her. I hate this house when it's quiet. I'm just relieved at the new company. And thank you for being such a darling." She kissed the top of his head and looked across at the basket by the fire and the two sleeping bundles of white fur that had returned with Roly from his 'meeting'. Arthur and Galahad, aged ten weeks, dozed in the warmth of the blaze. It would be only a few minutes before they woke again and made Roly's life a misery. He patted Charlotte's thigh and rose to fill his glass, wishing with all his heart that there were still three of them for supper.

Chapter 33: Rosy Morn

(*Lotus corniculatus*)

What to tell Jess? It was clear that he could not tell her the truth, although part of him wanted to. But to betray Elizabeth's confidence, even to Jess, seemed wrong. He thought about how she must have tortured herself and replayed the events in her mind time and again until finally she could no longer escape the consequences.

But how could he reproach her for taking the course of action she had? What would he have done himself in the same circumstances? He would never know.

But he was only too aware of the strange workings of the human mind. He had been at the mercy of his own over the past few weeks, and only now could he see why he and Jinty could not have remained together. The grand passion needed to be underpinned with a common ground. He had thought at first that it didn't matter. She hunted, he didn't. No problem there – his parents had lived happily in such circumstances. But the gentle niggles that had eaten away at the relationship, couldn't they have been ironed out, talked through? Only if both parties wanted to achieve the same ends. It seemed that they did not.

It was while he was sitting at Rupert's desk, rereading, yet again, the letter his father had written him, that the phone rang.

"Kit?"

"Yes?"

"It's Charlotte Billings-Gore."

"Hello."

"Hello. Look, I'm sorry to ring, and Roly will be furious if he knows

702

I have, but I didn't want to interfere so much as to explain."

Kit wondered what Charlotte was getting at.

"It's just that Jinty's decided to go and live in Lambourn for a while."

The words seemed to echo down the line to him. Guilt mingled with sadness seeped into his mind.

"I see."

"I know things had gone a bit awry, but I just thought you would want to know."

"Yes. Thanks. And she's OK?"

Charlotte sighed. "Just a bit confused, I think. She's had a bit of a time, one way and another. I just hope that more time will act as a healer, if you know what I mean."

"Has she – has she gone already?"

"Yes." Charlotte paused. "She's dropping some things off for Roly at Quither Cottage, Titus's place, and going on to the station by taxi."

"I see." The information sank in. "Thank you."

"Please come and see us sometime. We'd enjoy your company."

"Yes. Yes, of course. Well, thanks for telling me. And . . ." He paused.

"Yes?"

"I hope she's OK."

In the best traditions of the country landowner's wife, Charlotte clung to her dignity. "So do I. Goodbye." She put down the phone gently.

She was bound to have gone by now. Quither Cottage was not far from West Yarmouth, but her stay would have been brief. 'Dropping something off' was how Charlotte had put it. Seconds probably, not even minutes. He drew up in the lane outside the cottage, convinced that he was wasting his time. And then he saw the taxi waiting. He got out, closed the door quietly and walked round to the row of kennels. She was leaning forward, stroking Nell's nose through the iron railings and whispering to her. There was no sign of Titus.

He stood watching her, perhaps twenty yards away, then she glanced up and saw him but did not move. He was shocked by the short hair. She looked, if anything, even more beautiful, but strangely distant. For what seemed like an age they stared at one another, neither wanting to make the first move. Then he walked slowly up the rough little path towards her and stopped alongside Nell's kennel.

"I just came to make my peace with Nell," she said.

Kit looked down at the spaniel, whose tail was wagging slowly and whose eyes seemed to be begging forgiveness. "I don't think she meant you any harm."

"I'm sure she didn't." She stroked the dog's head, and he watched her long fingers as they ran through the brown and white hair.

"Why are you going?" he asked.

She continued stroking the dog. "It's for the best."

"It's all my fault. I'm sorry I was so determined . . . wrapped up in it all."

"It wasn't just you." She turned to face him. "I think I was looking for something that wasn't there."

He nodded. "I think we both were."

"Passion isn't really enough for you, is it?"

He was shocked to hear her say it.

"You have other important things in your life, and other people. I just couldn't bear the thought of sharing you. Call me selfish, if you like, but I wanted all of you all of the time."

"But –"

Jinty shook her head. "It's not just you. It's me, too. I thought I was over him but . . . well, it takes time."

He wondered if she meant it, or whether she was giving him an easy way out. Easy! How could the ending of a relationship like this be easy?

"It's never logical, is it?" she asked.

"What do you mean?"

"Think what we were like together. How could either of us end something like that? I've never felt like that with anybody else – so wrapped up in them, so physically in tune."

"And here we are, saying goodbye. Because you can't get him out of your head?"

She stared at him. "And because you'd rather be with somebody else."

"How do you know?"

"I don't know . . . I just feel it. You're probably not even sure yourself."

He met her gaze. "Oh, I think I am."

"I see. Lucky girl." She stared at him, and he looked into the pale green eyes that had once promised so much, but which now looked so far away.

"Promise me you'll take care of yourself," he said.

"I will. And you." She slipped her hand into his, squeezed it briefly, then walked towards the cab. He leaned against the cold, hard railings as he listened to the wheels of the taxi rumble down the lane.

Peeping through his kitchen window, Titus watched as Kit stood alone by the kennels, his hands thrust deep into his pockets. He reached for the kettle and, with a gnarled, horny hand, wiped away the moisture from both his good eye and the glass one.

It was early evening before Jess came back from the Wilderness. Kit had stayed out of her way, partly because he had wanted time to think about Elizabeth's letter, and partly because he wanted a chance to work out his feelings in the light of Jinty's departure.

He did not encounter Jess until she tapped on the kitchen door and came in carrying a letter. "I found this on my bed."

Kit gazed at the envelope. It was identical to the one that Elizabeth had given him. He saw that it had been opened. "From Elizabeth?"

"Yes. Did you know about this?"

"She told me this afternoon." How could he pacify her?

"Why didn't you come and find me – tell me about it? Why did you let her go?"

"Because I couldn't stop her. I thought it was all for the best."

"But how could you say that?" Jess looked wounded.

"What do you think I should have done?" He waited for Jess to let rip about Rupert, and Elizabeth's failure to help him.

"Oh, I don't know. Just told her that she could have stayed."

Kit was confused. He held out his hand. "Can I see?"

She handed him the envelope. He pulled out the single sheet of paper and unfolded it. Jess came and stood by him as he read, her hand resting on his arm.

My dear Jess,

I've decided after all these years that it's time to move on. I wanted to stay until I was confident that Kit would be able to manage the reserve (or would even want to) and now that he has decided to do so I don't want to be a burden on him. With you to help he'll be in good hands and I rather think it's time I found a new challenge.

705

I'm sorry this is so abrupt, but I can't be doing with long goodbyes. I do hope you'll understand. I have so enjoyed working with you. Please go on being yourself – in spite of everything.
With love,
Elizabeth.

Kit folded the letter, slipped it back into the envelope and handed it to Jess. "Well," he said, "I suppose that's that, then."

"Just you and me, then?" Jess asked.

"And a pig."

"Yes. And a pig."

Kit put a hand on each of her shoulders and turned her to face him. "But there's something you need to know."

She looked up into his eyes, calm, patient, and as serene as he could ever remember seeing her.

"I wasn't going to tell you. I'm still not sure that I should tell you, but I just don't want any secrets between us. I want things to be open." He hesitated. "It's about Dad. And Elizabeth. You see, when he fell . . ."

"He didn't fall. He just stepped over the cliff."

"Do you know that for certain?"

"Yes. I saw him."

Kit felt relief at the lifting of the uncertainty, saddened by the reality, and surprised at Jess's calm retelling of events. She had known all along. She, who had loved his father as much as Kit had, had known of Elizabeth's actions and understood.

"I watched her sitting with him. I knew how much she loved him. I could tell. She just sat there and stroked his head, talking to him all the time. We never spoke about it. We both knew it was what he wanted."

"And you knew about . . ."

"The Alzheimer's? Yes. She did what she – we – thought best." Her eyes glistened with tears. "We all miss him, don't we?"

Kit nodded.

"But he's happy now. We have to believe that." She lifted her hand and stroked his cheek. "And what about you?"

"I'm not sure what I am. Confused. Surprised. A bit bewildered. I'm not sure that I'll ever understand women."

"Don't try too hard."

He turned to face her again. "Jinty's gone."

Jess said nothing, just held his gaze.

"I saw her this afternoon."

She looked fearful.

"She knows it's you I want to be with, that it's you I love."

"Are you sure?"

"Yes. I worried that it was just a need to protect you at first. Then I saw you on the beach one day, having a swim."

She smiled. "I know."

"What?" That sinking feeling was back in the pit of his stomach. "But it was an accident – I didn't want to –"

She laughed. "I know. I could see what had happened."

"But you just carried on . . ."

"I know. Wicked of me, wasn't it?"

He looked at her, bewildered.

Jess looked down. "I fancied you like mad. I wanted you to fancy me, too, not just feel sorry for me."

"But it's more than that."

"I know. Soulmates."

He smiled. "Soulmates."

She looked up at him, her face glowing with love, her fair hair still damp from the shower and her skin scented faintly with orange blossom. The little perforations from the now discarded studs betrayed her days of anger and confusion, but now her face was lit up with a wide smile.

He wrapped his arms around her and kissed her with a tenderness that took her breath away.

In the pig-sty some yards away from the house, her evening repast completed, Wilson snored contentedly. Kit would be forever grateful for the arrival of Jess in his life, and for the robust digestive system and patient counsel of a Gloucester Old Spot sow.